The Twelve Tribes

by Hale Mednick

Julie Sidel

The Twelve Tribes

Hale Mednick

Published by Dream Tides Press
PO BOX 7940
Santa Cruz, Ca 95061
www.12-tribes.com

Cover art and design by Gabe Leonard.

Printed on recycled paper.

Although parts of this book are inspired by historical records and historical figures, this is a work of fiction and all characters are creations of the author. Any similarity to any person alive or dead is coincidental and not intended by the author.

Library of Congress Control Number 2005910812

Astrology of the Twelve Tribes

Traditional Elements		Twelve Tribes Totems
Fire	(Yang)	Flying Hunter
Air	(Yang)	Flying Gatherer
Water	(Yin)	Walking Hunter
Earth	(Yin)	Walking Gatherer

Traditional Qualities	Twelve Tribes Qualities
Cardinal	Aggressive, Fast, Bold, Assertive
Fixed	Determined, Steadfast, Stable, Slow
Mutable	Adaptable, Subtle, Fluid, changeable

Traditional Totems	Twelve Tribes Totems	Qualities and Totems
Aries	Hawk	Aggressive Flying Hunter
Taurus	Beaver	Determined Walking Gatherer
Gemini	Jay	Adaptable Flying Gatherer
Cancer	Bear	Aggressive Walking Hunter
Leo	Eagle	Determined Flying Hunter
Virgo	Raccoon	Adaptable Walking Gatherer
Libra	Swan	Aggressive Flying Gatherer
Scorpio	Wolf	Determined Walking Hunter
Sagittarius	Owl	Adaptable Flying Hunter
Capricorn	Elk	Aggressive Walking Gatherer
Aquarius	Raven	Determined Flying Gatherer
Pisces	Cougar	Adaptable Walking Hunter

A more detailed description of the astrology of the Twelve Tribes is in the appendix in the back of the book.

Map of the Twelve Tribes territories

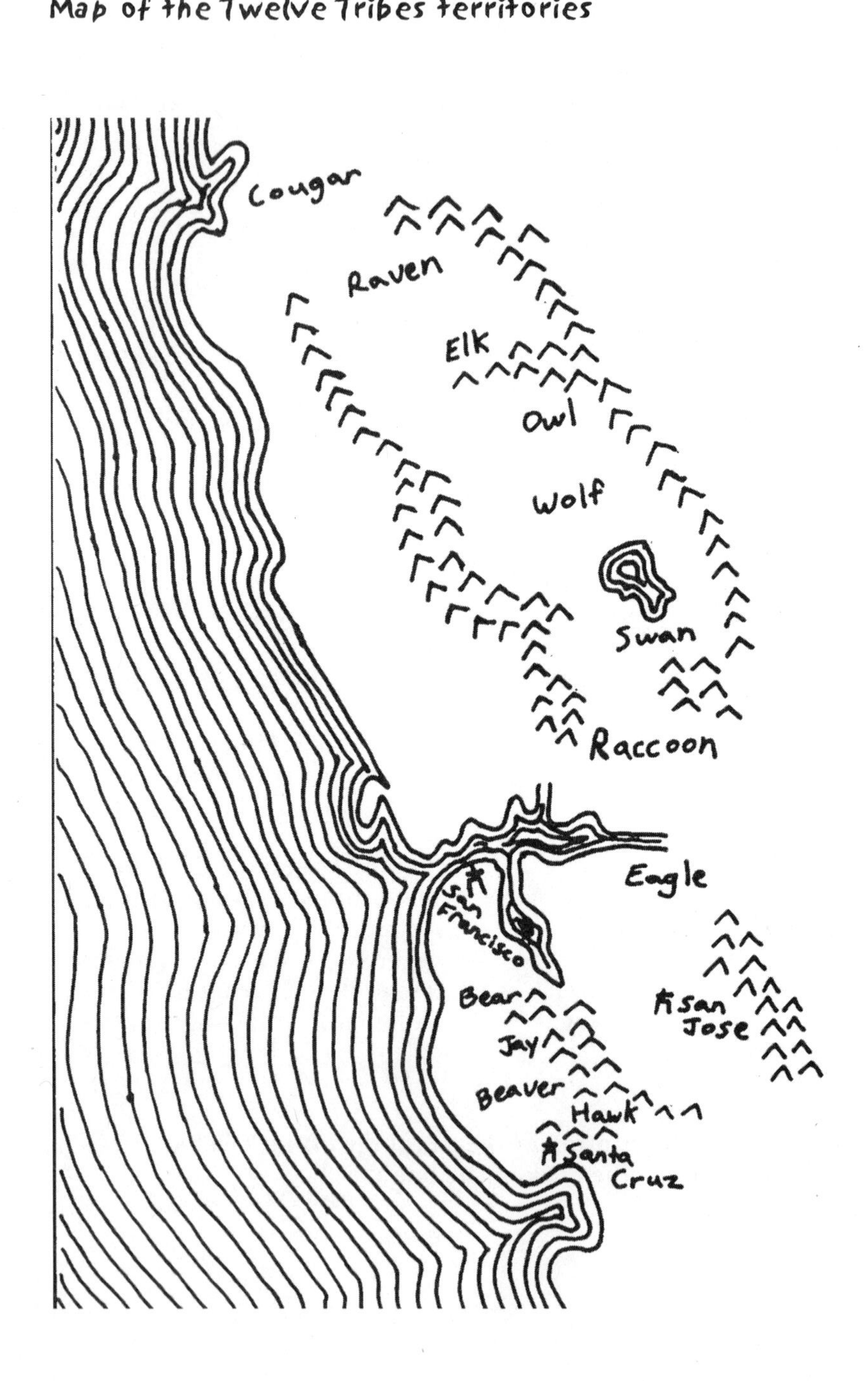

Chapters

The Mission

This tale begins with a little girl, born to a tribe somewhere along the central coast of California late in the eighteenth century. She can remember little of her happy years with her tribe, all of it lost somewhere in her brain as young memories are. She cannot remember how she got there, but she remembers waking up as if from a dream and finding herself surrounded by strange men in a strange place. A man in brown robes says some words to her in a solemn voice, and pours water over her head. Then she is left shivering on the riverbank, soaking wet in a heavy wind, while the men all congratulate each other on their first conversion. She looks around in fear at all of the men and their impossible clothes. She stares at the great swamp that stretches down to the blue sea, and the house that the men are building on top of a hill. A group of Indians gather around her and inform her in several languages that she is the very first person to be baptized in the brand new Mission de Exultacion de Santa Cruz, and that she is a very lucky girl.

She doesn't feel lucky. She wonders where her parents are and how she got here and when they will let her go home. But nobody ever speaks of her parents. They only tell her that this is her new home, and soon it will be much nicer when the church is built and the mission is completed. She is placed in the hands of a group of Indians, who take her to a little tule hut and show her that this is where she will live.

Mission records claim that the first girl converted by the Santa Cruz mission fathers was a young girl from a distant Ohlone tribe, but the details of her arrival at the mission are very vague. Corporal Peralta is her 'sponsor', and whatever else he knows about her is never revealed.

She is soon joined by many other children, most of them without parents. It is the practice of the priests and soldiers of Spain to kidnap children from their tribes and baptize them into the church. After that, the priests and soldiers just sit back and wait for the parents to come forward and ask for baptism, so they can be with their children again. However, mission records show that most of those parents never join their children. Three quarters of those baptized in the beginnings of the mission founding were orphaned children.

The little girl's parents don't come for her either. In a deep state of shock, she is conscious of very little for the next two years. She says not one word to anybody and lives inside a shell of confusion and fear. She has a tule house that she shares with another girl, with whom she is unable to speak. It is big enough for the two of them to stretch out and sleep. An old woman watches out for her and makes sure that she is safe and healthy. But the rest of the people look strangely at her and keep to themselves. They sense that she is different, as she does not speak to them in their varying languages. The priests can do nothing with her. Finally, they just give up and let her wander where she will, being too busy with mission construction to deal with a mute child.

She spends her days wandering up and down a little secluded stretch of beach. All day long she picks up shells, watches the waves, makes sand castles, and talks to imaginary friends. Her best friend is an imaginary little boy with magical powers named Nani. To him alone she will speak. She sings to him sometimes, making up songs to entertain him. Then she does little dances for his amusement. She leaves the mission in the morning and doesn't come home except for meals. Everyone is busy building the mission and the church, planting crops, and tending animals, and they rarely notice her absence as long as she is present for meals and church services. She dreams that someday she will have a house on this beach with nobody to bother her. There she will live with her imaginary friends, catching fish for her supper and dreaming her life away. This is her idea of heaven. She makes plans for the day when she will move out of the tule house and build a house out of driftwood. She even begins to build it, just as an experiment. But she cannot get the pieces to stay up.

One day, out of the blue, she speaks. Father Lopez has been trying to teach her to pray on her knees with her hands clasped a certain way. She isn't paying attention and he is getting frustrated with her. He is just about to send her away when she looks up at him and starts speaking Spanish.

"I have a driftwood house. I can't get it to stay up. Do you know how to get it to stay up? I made a little bed out of shells. Nani lives there too."

While she is babbling away, Lopez turns pale, wondering how this poor Indian girl who has not spoken to a single soul in two years picked up such an excellent command of the Spanish language. He drops to his knees, sure that he is witnessing a miracle. He hugs the child and his eyes mist with tears.

"Thank you, Lord," he whispers, and then looks upon the little girl and smiles.

"Come with me, child. We must visit Father Salazar, and show him this...this miracle."

"Is he good at building houses?"

She walks with him, barefoot on the hard dirt floor that is swept everyday. They stand outside the room of Salazar and knock until he opens his door.

"What is it, Balmodero?"

"The girl...the mute girl speaks. Say something to him, young one."

"I built a house on the beach," she says innocently. "That is where I want to live. May I live there? I will still come to church on Sundays. I promise."

Salazar opens his eyes wide in surprise, and drops to his knees beside her.

"What is your name?" he says softly.

"Esther."

Salazar stares at Lopez for a long time in mutual shock.

"Did you give her this name?" he asks in amazement.

"No."

"Did you just make this name up, child?"

"No. It has always been my name," she says innocently.

"This is no Indian name," he says, his eyes misting with tears. "It is a biblical name."

"She is a living miracle," whispers Lopez, his eyes also tearing up. "God has given her this name. Our very first conversion is reborn a Christian."

"The mission is blessed," adds Salazar, making the sign of the cross.

Soon the church, built of stone and adobe, is completed, and the entire mission square also. From then on, Esther's life drastically changes. She is moved into a room in the mission called the 'nunnery', where unmarried girls are kept. She sleeps with thirty girls in a single room, where she is strictly watched to be sure that she has no contact with any man or boy in a sexual manner. There she will stay until she is married and can move into a hut in the nearby village with her husband. Every moment of her day is supervised, from the time she gets up until the time she goes to bed. Soldiers and priests put her into line with the other Indians and take her to church, to meals, and to work when the bells toll. After evening mass, she is shut up in the nunnery so she will not be corrupted by men. Esther gets no more time to roam at the beach or to play as she likes. She spends hours in the mission church and under a roof with the fathers, and her head becomes filled with the glory of Christ, prayers in Latin and the histories of the saints. She learns to be subservient and humble and do whatever she is told. She is apprenticed to a weaver and learns to make clothes. Only when she walks between work, church and the nunnery does she get to stand under the sun. So she dawdles as long as possible on her way to church, taking deep breathes of the air and enjoying the sunlight while she can.

The food at the mission is bland and always the same - at least the food given to the Indians. Breakfast is unseasoned barley mush. Lunch is gruel, consisting of corn, barley, peas, and beans. Dinner is more barley or corn gruel. The mission keeps vast herds of cattle, but the neophytes do not eat their meat. According to an early rule handed down by the San Francisco presidio, the Indians are not permitted to taste beef, for fear of the evil consequences that might result. Despite the bountiful ocean around them and the abundance of game, roots, and seeds, they eat only what they grow themselves. Occasionally the grain runs out, and they are allowed to hunt and gather berries and anything else they can find. They are often happier when the grain runs out than when there is an abundance of it.

Now that the mission is running strong and the number of neophytes is in the hundreds, the padres and the soldiers become more stern and forceful. There are now about 523 Indians, as well as a small group of soldiers to feed, clothe, and house. Plus, there is always a fresh bounty brought back from the hunting raids on Indian villages. A steady stream of captured children that must be baptized, fed, housed, clothed, cared for, and taught a whole new way of life. There are huge fields of grain and vast herds of cattle, sheep, and horses to be tended to. And there is always work to be done on the buildings themselves. Crude mud and straw bricks are not a good material for a rainy place. The buildings are always dissolving and collapsing when the river floods, and must be rebuilt.

The padres often complain about the endless pressures of mission life and ask to go back to their comfortable world of books and prayers. Father Lopez is the first to be replaced, because he is a hypochondriac. And then Esther meets Padre Manuel Fernandez for the first time. Padre Fernandez was not at all prepared for the hard life of a missionary, and he went mad during his stay in Mission Santa Clara. He was said to have a violent temper and was extremely harsh in his punishments. The other fathers couldn't stand him and he was eventually sent to Mission Santa Cruz, because there was no one else to send. Esther thought that Lopez was a grouch, but she never met anyone like Fernandez before.

She receives a whipping a few days after he arrives, because she wears dirty clothes in church and forgets a prayer too! A couple of high ranking neophytes take her to a secret place to be whipped, so the general populace of Indians will not feel their hearts torn in two at the sight of little girls being whipped and become inspired to revolt. A ten-year old girl is brought along with her, for her refusal to learn Spanish. The neophytes take off their dresses and set them facing the wall, as a soldier comes with a rawhide whip. And then Esther feels the sting of the whip on her buttocks and back. She cries out in pain and looks back in horror, unable to believe that they are actually whipping her. The brave girl next to her bites her lip silently and doesn't even cry, as her buttocks and back are flayed raw. Esther is inspired by the young girl's bravery, and she follows her example and bears it as silently as she can. But she cannot help a loud squeal each time the lash falls on her progressively rawer skin. Each girl receives twenty-five lashes, which is considered lenient for Fernandez. Then she is free to stumble off, her back and buttocks on fire so she can barely walk at first. She looks at the little girl, wondering how she feels. The girl is proud and bites her lip to keep from crying. Only the brimming tears in her eyes show what she is feeling. She walks slowly and gingerly away, sucking on a finger like a pacifier. Esther follows her silently, and tries to be as brave and proud as the young girl whom she admires.

Father Fernandez, who ordered the beating, once met the famous Father Junipero Serra, the founder of the California mission system. In order to maintain the extremely strict life of a Franciscan monk, Serra whipped himself, burnt his skin with torches, and fasted for days. He allowed himself few pleasures and he expected everyone else to be the same way. The mission system was deeply infused with his masochistic style of piety. Fernandez learned at his feet when he was young, and it is his secret goal to be as great a man as Serra was. But Fernandez is more the sadist. He inflicts his tortures on the neophytes as often as he inflicts them on himself.

Soon Father Salazar is replaced by Father Espi, and Fernandez takes over as head of the mission. During Esther's first Sunday church service run by Father Fernandez, the mood is dark and foreboding. It starts out as it usually does. Men and women are seated separately and made to kneel on the floor. Soldiers with large bayonets guard the aisles and doors. Esther watches the Indians singing the opening hymns with their usual blank faces, because they do not know what it is they are singing. They sing because they are told to. She looks at Fernandez, who watches the Indians sing and shakes his head, as if he knows that they do not really mean it. He scowls at them and the veins in his neck bulge. After the opening hymns have been sung, Fernandez begins to give a sermon. Few understand him, but a translator speaks in a common Indian trade dialect that is more widely spoken.

“I felt nothing from your singing. It sounded to me like ducks quacking. That is because you have learned nothing in the time that I have been here. Rise up from the dirt in which you continue to wallow as mere beasts. Give yourselves up to God. Then your singing will mean something!”

He looks about him and he can see that he is getting nowhere. He suddenly grabs a torch that is burning in a stand and holds it aloft, waving it until the flames die down and it is only red embers. Then he rips open his robe and brands the torch into his chest. The neophytes cringe with fear and shout out in horror. Fernandez falls to his knees as burning ash falls around him, and grits his teeth so he will not cry out in pain. Finally Fernandez stands up, gasping for breath. His chest is bright red and blistered where the torch burned the skin.

"Your body no longer belongs to you. My body does not belong to me. It belongs to God now, and if he asks that I burn it, then I must. Just as Abraham was asked to kill his own son, so must I burn my own flesh!”

Father Espi seems shocked by Fernandez's behavior, but he does not move to stop him. The neophytes stare at their feet. Some are shamed that they drove him to such an act and some are just avoiding the priest's wild eyes.

"We are here to serve Jesus. We are here to serve the Lord. That is why I burn myself - to show God that I love Him more than I love my own body. Will any of you come up here and submit to the same test? Your reward shall be salvation in heaven. Show him your love!"

Caught up in the excitement, one man stands up and strides forward bravely. A woman cries out to him, but he ignores her. He takes the torch from Fernandez and plunges it into his own chest.

"I am sinner!" he screams in broken Spanish.

The odor of burning flesh makes Esther sick. She wants to leave, fearing that she will throw up, but a little Indian woman grabs her hand and pulls her back down into a crouch. She points to the soldiers standing near the church doors and shakes her head. Esther fights down the revulsion and manages to stay where she is.

Fernandez does not allow bathroom breaks, as the other Padres used to do. Eventually, Esther has to go to the bathroom badly, but no neophyte is allowed to leave until the end. The old woman notices her squirming and indicates that she should just pee on the floor. Esther notices that the old woman has wet legs herself. So Esther pees all over herself. By the end of the service, the church smells badly of urine. Esther hears a couple of soldiers commenting about it.

“These heathens are so stupid, they pee all over themselves. The Padre is a saint, to try to teach such beasts.”

Esther notices that the soldiers have left twice to go to the bathroom and she glares at them. One of them glares back at her and she looks down at her feet with fear. She doesn't want another whipping!

Life is now very hard for the neophytes, but for Esther it is better than most. She is considered to be a civilized Indian, because she speaks excellent Spanish and is a quick learner. She cannot remember her native language or anything about her past, so she doesn't fall into old habits that are grounds for a beating. She is singled out for her intelligence, fine speech and grace, and thus she is spared some of the indignities of her fellow neophytes.

“If only all of these stupid heathens had your intelligence,” sighs Fernandez one day, making a rare effort to speak directly to her and not simply barking orders. “Then I might teach them something. But they are as stupid as cows and I can teach the poor beasts nothing. But you, however, have at least a brain in your head and decent manners. You learn quickly. And you are more fair and comely than the rest. I could swear that there is some European blood in you, my girl."

He gives her a pat on the head and a piece of fruit and walks away quickly, as if embarrassed by his sudden show of affection. Esther stares at the fruit amazed. It is a pear from the tree in the garden. None of the other neophytes have ever been allowed to eat a pear from that tree.

Inspired to be a better neophyte by the Fernandez's rare display of kindness, as well as out of fear of his temper, she tries harder to learn all the prayers and hymns by heart. Padre Espi is pleased by Esther's singing voice and gives her a place among the choir. She loves standing among the men and women of the choir, singing beautiful hymns in church. It makes her proud to be a part of something so beautiful. The music enters her body and brings her to a peaceful place that she has not known in years. The fathers are impressed by her dedication, and they give her solo parts to sing and place her at the front of the choir. After that, she doesn't have to work as hard as most of the other neophytes, and she is rarely punished. Instead, she is forced to spend many hours learning more songs and prayers and listening to the priests read stories from the bible. They try to make her into an example of a perfect neophyte and Esther tries hard to be one.

It is important to the fathers to have successful, well-adjusted neophytes like Esther, because it makes them feel as if they are not merely wasting their time and getting nowhere. Most of the neophytes are a sad, miserable bunch. They walk around with their heads always down, never looking anyone in the eye. They never joke or laugh. Their only variations in mood are from stoic to gloomy to melancholy. They take no joy in their work and make the least possible effort out of spite. Many refuse to learn Spanish or their prayers. This indifference only makes the padres beat them harder and devise more cruel tortures for them. They have prisons and stocks for runaways and other rule breakers. Many men spend a good deal of time with shackles around their legs. A man could spend two weeks in the stocks as punishment for not doing what he is told, and he will only try even harder to do as little as possible and shrink even further into himself. And the cycle of failure goes on.

One day, Esther sees a little girl, barely six years old, being whipped for refusing to learn Spanish. Esther becomes enraged and starts screaming at the soldier to stop. The soldier orders a neophyte to grab Esther and drag her to see Fernandez. As Esther is led away, she sees the soldier continue to punish the poor girl, who is screaming in pain.

She is led into the church, where Fernandez sits sternly, a hood covering up his eyes. All Esther can see is a stern slit of a mouth twitching slightly, as Fernandez stares at her. Finally he indicates that she should go to her knees. Esther does so hesitatingly.

"Never question my authority!" he intones. "The girl must be trained. Her *soul* is at stake. You are too stupid to understand that, but you must trust those who know better."

"She is just a little girl," Esther says nervously, wishing she could see his eyes. "I felt sorry for her."

"You have always been a good neophyte. I have tried to spare you the lash and I have given you more favor than most. But I have been too soft with you."

Fernandez struggles with the words, but then suddenly falls silent, struck by her beauty and grace. In alarm, he realizes that he wants her. Esther is now in her teenage years and she has blossomed. Despite her rough treatment, she has become quite a pretty young woman. Her hair is long and dark, her eyes large and liquid, and her skin smooth and creamy tan. She has exotic features, which adds to the mystery of her origin. She doesn't look like any Indian he has ever seen before. There is something different about her.

He has kept her from marriage so far, believing that few neophytes are good enough for her. He suddenly understands that his reasons for keeping her single were more selfish than he suspected. He wants her for himself. Finally, he can stand it no longer, and he grabs her and kisses her. His sour breath disgusts her and she draws back. She trembles, frightened by his sudden boldness. He tells her in quiet tones that God has given his approval to this union. He talks to her in forceful and threatening tones and grabs her again in an iron grip. He kisses her again. This time, she is so afraid that she doesn't pull away.

Fernandez does as he likes with her. He has sex with her, forgetting his lifelong vow of celibacy. He does it guiltily and violently, as his nature dictates. And then he holds her for a time, savoring this dirty pleasure for as long as he can stand it. But finally the voices in his head drive him mad.

Lust is in my heart. Forgive me Jesus. How I want her. Oh, forgive me. Oh Fray Serra, my holy benefactor, how I long for the comforting sting of the whip on my back. Only in pain will I be forgiven, as you have taught me. I am no equal to you, Father, who instructed me that lust in the heart is as bad as lust in the flesh. Oh, how far I have to go!

Fernandez grabs the whip from the wall and Esther cringes. But Fernandez does not whip her. Instead he brings the whip down viciously on himself. The snap is like a gunshot.

"I have failed you! Forgive me!"

Esther watches him with undisguised disgust in her eyes.

"You - go! Leave me!" he shouts to her, not liking the look on her face.

She grabs her dress, clutches it tightly to her chest, and starts to walk quickly out of his room.

"Put your clothes on first," he snaps. "Have you no pride in your appearance?"

She stops and puts on her dress with trembling fingers.

"And why are you not married?" he asks furiously.

Esther's eyes open wide, but she has no answer.

"We must soon change that. We must find you a man. It is time for you to be married."

Once dressed, she quickly walks out of the room. When she is gone, the padre shuts the door. He is thankful to be alone, away from the temptation of the young beauty. He imagines her naked, with an Indian man, her body writhing on the bed as she makes love to him. This vision makes him snap the whip more sharply upon himself. The sting drives the fantasy from his mind. He takes off all of his clothes angrily. As he begins to lash at his tortured body, he feels all of it fading away - his sins washing away in a torrent of pain. The sight of his own blood dripping onto the floor makes him sigh with relief. Then, the blood dripping down his back suddenly reminds him of the wet juices of a woman, and this makes him whip himself harder in shame.

After a few hours, when he sits morosely in a pool of his own blood and his back screams in pain, he is sure that God has forgiven him.

Fernandez never finds her a man. Every so often, he orders her into his private chambers for some "private bible study". After that, he whips himself and begs Jesus for forgiveness. It all blends together - the dirty pleasure of his orgasm and the pain of the whip to sanctify the guilt and make him pure again. Occasionally, he takes other neophytes into his bed. It is a release from the guilt and shame that drives every day of his life.

Esther's only release from this torment is to leave her body. She soon learns to float away when he does these things to her, so it will only be her body that endures him. One day, she goes really far out. She hurtles through space, until she comes upon strange colored lights swirling in the blackness. She feels a wonderful feeling of peace and tranquility there. But then she gets scared and rushes back to her body. After it is all over, she thinks that she has just been to heaven. She is happy to know that there is something out there that is better than this endless nightmare. She is not so miserable from then on, because she knows that someday she'll return there and be happy forever.

Meanwhile, the mission is falling apart. The neophyte population is disappearing rapidly and very few babies are born to increase their ranks. This is because one very common practice of the neophyte women is to induce abortions. They do not want to bring babies into the world, to be treated as they themselves are. So when they can, they get a medicine man to make a herbal drink to induce abortion. If that fails, they ask the husband to kick them repeatedly in the uterus area until the fetus is killed. If that also fails, they will kill the baby when it is born. There are many babies born whose fathers are Spanish, and many of these are killed as soon as they take their first breath. The priests try hard to discourage such practices, but they are unsuccessful.

Disease spreads like wildfire. European diseases like small pox, measles, mumps, and even chicken pox bring down many of the neophytes. So many die at once that there is not time to bury them all. They are loaded into mass graves and burned. A strange case of syphilis also spreads - introduced by the Spanish soldiers. The dispirited and unhealthy neophytes no longer care about their health, food production drops and they all start dropping like flies.

The remaining neophytes finally come to their senses and flee the mission. In a bitterly worded letter, Fernandez reports that nearly half the remaining population has fled the mission, and there are few left to do the work. Esther longs to escape also, but she has nowhere to go. And she has seen what happens to runaways who are caught! So she just does as she is told and waits for one of the fatal diseases to take her too.

The mission of Santa Cruz then breaks one of the major standards of the mission system, which is never to force an adult Indian to convert against his will. They send soldiers deep into the central valley, attacking a Yurok village and bringing back a large group of Yurok captives. The Yuroks are treated to a shotgun baptism and then an interpreter explains to them what is happening.

"You are now baptized Christians," he explains. "How lucky you are! Only a Christian may enter the kingdom of heaven. You have all been saved."

Esther has been forced to attend the baptism with the few remaining old timers. She stares sadly at the brand new neophytes, feeling sorry for them. They are confused, angry, and scared by the sudden change in their lives. The men all wear chains so they will not run away. Somehow, they all seem to sense that their lives will never be the same. Fernandez seems like a dark and evil spirit, walking around in his robes with a hood obscuring his heavily lined face in shadow. Over the next several days, he tries his best to scare them into obedience. He makes long speeches, tells them of hell in low, frightening tones, and warns them that they are all headed there if they don't listen. He shows them pictures of sinners in burning agony, and then he drives his point home with shackles and lashings. And he makes them recite Latin prayers, dark and gloomy songs in a strange language. They are forced into a regimented schedule, getting up at the crack of dawn, working all day and learning to be a Christian until late in the night. They long to return to their homes and their old lives, not knowing that other tribes have already moved into their hunting grounds and taken over their lands. Many of the neophytes start to whisper to each other that this is the hell that the padres warn them about.

Besides a shotgun baptism, everyone receives a shotgun marriage too. They are lined up in rows of men and women and forced to choose a partner to marry from the opposite row. Many choose their current partner, but those who have none are forced to pick someone they will marry and have children with. They are given about a minute to choose their lifelong mate. There is one funny moment, which breaks up the gloom of the Yuroks with some mirth. A young man who is the last to choose is stuck with an old wrinkled woman nearly twice his age. He laughs, thinking that the padres would never force him to marry a woman that old. But then the exasperated Padre Fernandez joins his hand with the old woman's and indicates that they must be married. The look on the young man's face is so shocked and crestfallen, that it makes everyone else from his tribe laugh out loud.

Esther wonders when she will be given a husband and what he will look like. Nobody has suggested a man for her yet and she is anxiously waiting. Esther doesn't know that Father Espi had plans for Esther to marry a smart young neophyte that was an accomplished musician, but the boy died of small pox before it was arranged. And Fernandez has no plans to marry Esther off at all. He tells Espi that she is too good for most of these neophytes and she must wait for the right man.

Finally Espi leaves the mission. He has requested numerous times to be sent away from Santa Cruz, because he cannot stand Father Fernandez. His wish is finally granted. A short time later, Fernandez is also replaced. His superiors are fed up with him and he is forcibly retired. Father Carranza and Father Gonzales become the new heads of the mission.

Life immediately improves for Esther. Surprised that she is not yet married, the new fathers immediately choose a husband for her. She is very disappointed when she finds out who it is. It is a boy a few years younger than her named Eunio. Eunio is a boy from the choir, who sings solos in a high, sweet voice. He is a terrible suck up to the new fathers, bending over backwards to please them. The fathers all love him and praise his quick conversion and willingness to please, and they think that she should be honored to marry a good Christian boy like him. But she finds him horribly irritating, and it is about the worst choice she could think of for a husband. But as disappointed as she is, she is relieved that she can move out of the dormitory at last. So she marries him in a simple service in the church and then they go back to the tule hut he has built for them to start life as husband and wife.

She avoids Eunio as much as possible and enjoys married life without him. She gets more time to spend outside now, washing clothes, making food and other chores. She manages to spend less time in church and blends in to village life as much as possible. It is not easy to blend in, because few of the other neophytes speak Spanish as she does. Plus, she and Eunio are known as a 'model neophyte couple', and are often pointed out as an example of how to behave. So of course they have no friends among the other neophytes, who lump her in with Eunio as a suck up. Esther can't stand Eunio and she begins to hate being a 'good neophyte'.

One day, several men and a few women from Mexico show up with a governor's order to start a town right next to the mission. Some are Mexican criminals who were given a choice of prison or becoming a 'Californio'. Others are former soldiers who have served their duty and are now granted leave to start a family. They are sent up to Santa Cruz with a few horses and cows and almost nothing else. Arriving empty handed, they demand materials and neophytes to build their town for them. The fathers are angry, because they know that they cannot control these men, and they will be a bad influence. But they do as their superiors ask and help them anyway. They loan the men and their families several Indians to build them homes and bring them food from the mission's gardens.

The men of Branciforte, as the new town is to be called, sit around and get drunk on wine from the priests' larders, while the Indians build their homes for them. In return, they abuse the neophytes terribly, beating them, laughing at them, or cursing them as the mood takes them. They steal from the mission daily, as they have no food of their own. And they take great delight in getting the Indians drunk and teaching them to gamble, because they know that it enrages the priests.

One summer day, Esther has been weaving all morning long, when her loom suddenly breaks. While it is being fixed, she is released from weaving and allowed to spend an afternoon doing whatever chores she thinks best. She eagerly runs out into the summer heat. The feeling of the hot sun is like heaven. She rolls around in the grass and sighs with pleasure. It is the greatest day she can remember in a long time. She resolves to sneak off and go for a long hike by herself. She'll pick tules on the way, so if anyone catches her, she'll claim she went to gather tules to fix their house.

Suddenly she sees a man standing over her. She has never seen this man before.

"Hello, bonita, my name is Miguel," he whispers. "What a pretty young thing you are."

Miguel is a short, squat man, with thick black hair that flings up in tufts from his head. He is rather ugly, with a nose too big for his face, bad teeth, and deep scars, but his eyes have a pleasant twinkle. He does his best to charm her, makes faces to amuse her, and tells her jokes. She giggles and laughs, finding him funny. She has never met anyone like him before.

With a wink, Miguel offers to show her around Branciforte. She agrees gladly, being very curious about the pueblo. But she points to the soldier standing a short distance away and says that she is not permitted to go there. Miguel winks again and disappears for a bit. Suddenly, gunshots ring out, and Esther hears somebody shouting about bears. The soldier takes off after the noise, and she is unguarded for a moment. Miguel reappears with a satisfied smile and leads Esther by the hand to his home.

They wander around the little wood and adobe houses of Branciforte, and he tells her much of his town. She finds him much different than any man she has ever known. He is wild and carefree, does what he wants, and answers to nobody. She is very attracted to him, and feels a guilty sort of pleasure to be doing something so utterly frowned upon with somebody so inappropriate.

He takes her into his little home and sits her down on a stool. He makes jokes to keep her at ease, while he offers her a swig of wine from his flask. She has never tasted wine before. As the hot liquid burns down her throat, she feels lightheaded and giddy. He insists that she drink more. She drinks until she becomes dizzy.

Suddenly, Miguel leans over and kisses her, his breath stinking of stale liquor. After a moment's hesitation, she kisses him back sloppily. Before she knows it, he has stripped her naked, and is tearing off his own dirty clothes. Bathing does not really seem to be important to him, but she ignores his unpleasant odor. And then they are rolling around on the floor, in a tangle of arms and legs. He maneuvers her over to his blankets, lying in a pile on the dirt floor. And there she learns the thrill of breaking all of the rules she has lived by her entire life and doing something utterly forbidden.

After a short, but wild bout of lovemaking, he finishes, and they lie there in a daze. The world spins in circles and she realizes that she is drunk for the first time in her life. She begins to wonder if she can get back to the mission without being caught, and if they will know what she has been up to. How can she hide being drunk? It will be a severe whipping if she is caught. And she does not think she will be able to hide it.

"I wish I didn't have to go back there," she complains.

"You may visit me anytime, bonita," he says with a smile.

"I'll come back to visit," she says, after a long silence, "if I can ever get away again."

"I will show you a way to get back without being seen," he says graciously.

With his help, she sneaks back to her tule house. Now that she is no longer living in the dormitory, under the watchful eyes of a matron and guards in the nunnery, it is quite easy to get home without being seen.

"Where have you been?" Eunio says, when she returns.

"I was gathering tules."

"Why do you smell of wine?"

"A man from the new town gave me some," she says, after a long pause. "He and his friends were drinking on the beach. Promise me you won't tell."

He nods sullenly. He seems to believe her, which only makes her hate him more. He is so stupid. But at least he is easy to control, which means she can do whatever she wants. Later that night, he tries to make love to her, but she pushes him away.

"The wine has given me a headache. Go to sleep."

The turn of the century rolls around and finds Esther living a dual life. By day she is a good neophyte, doing as she is told and pretending that she only wants to be a good Christian and a good wife. But at least a few nights a week, she goes to Branciforte to sin and have some fun. Miguel is always happy to see her, as there is a shortage of women, and she is quite pretty also. He teaches her to smoke tobacco, drink and gamble. When she is drunk enough, they have sex. She doesn't really like him all that much, once she gets to know him better, but she likes his lifestyle and indulging in all of his excesses. Miguel is supposed to be a farmer, but she has never seen him actually sow anything. The only thing he does is gamble and make wine from barley or whatever else he can get his hands on. He boasts proudly that he was in jail for a time, and that he was only released on the condition that he would go to Branciforte and help build a town.

Eunio is so deeply in love with her, that he accepts all of her harebrained excuses at face value. She cannot imagine why he loves her, because by her reckoning she has made love more often to Miguel, in the short time she has know him, than she ever has to Eunio. And she is mean to him and tells him so many lies, that she can barely keep track of them all. But he continues to worship her and tries harder than ever to be a good husband to her.

She gets pregnant once, but she is not sure whom the father is. There are no more medicine men left to help, so she gets one of the local men to kick her in the uterus to induce an abortion. It is a painful procedure, so she gets very drunk before she tries it. It hurts to walk for a few weeks afterwards, but she considers it worth it. She does not want to give birth to a child ever in her whole life. Especially if either one of the men in her life are the father. Eventually, she learns ways to avoid getting pregnant, like not having sex during her fertile periods. She never gets pregnant again, and she wonders if she has rendered herself sterile through her violent abortion. She mostly hopes so, although a small part of her is very sorry about it.

One day, she goes to see Miguel, and finds him in a foul mood.

"I lost everything in cards," he complains. "All my liquor is gone. Most of my money, too. I have been dry for two days. It is terrible."

"That's not good," she says grumpily. "I really need a drink."

"I have something that will take your mind off of it. Come here and give me a kiss."

She finds the idea of kissing him while she is sober distasteful, and she backs away.

"I want a drink. Who did you say you lost your wine to?"

"Fermin."

"I will go ask him for some. I'll come back with whatever I can get."

"Yes, of course," he says uncertainly. "Come back soon. I'll be waiting for you."

Esther goes to see Fermin, who is hosting a game of cards. She is surprised at her desperation to have a drink today. He seems equally surprised to see her at his door.

"May I have a drink, Fermin?"

"Did Miguel send you? You tell him he is an ass, and it is not my fault that he is a lousy gambler. Tell him this."

"He did not send me. It is not for him. It is for me."

She boldly slides her hand down his arm and smiles at him. His eyes fly open in surprise, and he takes her meaning clear enough. He pours her a glass of wine, she takes it gratefully and has a satisfying drink. Then she sits behind Fermin and watches him continue his streak of good luck. Meanwhile, he continues to give her wine, until she is nice and drunk. He looks over at her suddenly and sees that she is beginning to nod her head.

"Everybody, I am tired," he announces suddenly. "You must go now."

They all complain, but he insists, and soon he is alone with Esther. She allows him to fondle her and kiss her. He tries to undress her, but she stops him.

"I don't know you that well, yet."

"I have given you much wine," he says. "I only ask for a little thing in return."

She finds the remark distasteful, but she smiles, realizing that she is in control of the situation.

"Soon," she says. "You must be patient. I am not that easy."

"That is not what I hear."

She begins to avoid Miguel and spends more time with Fermin, who is both cleaner and kinder. He gives her wine and money to gamble with and lets her keep the winnings. She has a string of good luck, and one night she wins a nice white, woolen nightgown belonging to some careless man's wife. Eventually, Miguel finds out about her affair with Fermin. He has not been to the games in a few weeks, so it takes him some time to discover where she has been.

"You are a filthy whore," he says, spitting on the ground.

He slaps her with the back of his hand.

"Stupid Indian! You are my woman. I will not allow you to act like a filthy whore."

She doesn't say anything. She only glares at him.

"Stay away from Fermin or I will tell the Padres you come here, and they will whip you."

"Then I will not be able to come here again," she says, glad that she is drunk enough to say these things without faltering. "And the priests will punish you also for corrupting the neophytes. They will not help you anymore. They will not give you barley to make wine."

He slaps her again for good measure.

"You are my woman, do you hear me? Stay away from Fermin!"

Miguel eventually has a new batch of homemade wine and he and Esther resolve their differences. They both binge that night and have a wild party, and she passes out in his bed. She wakes up with the sun shining in her face and realizes that she is in serious trouble. She will have to go back home in the daylight. She tries her best to sneak back undetected, but a neophyte who is loyal to the priests sees her and rats her out. Esther is brought before the priests for punishment.

She receives a severe whipping of forty lashes. Then she has to endure several sermons, warning her about the dangers of alcohol and gambling. Luckily they don't know that she has also committed adultery. Iron shackles are attached to her legs, which are humiliating and uncomfortable, and she has to do the 'shuffle' walk for a few weeks. Eunio is scolded because he lets his wife act like a 'harlot', and he is mortally embarrassed and very angry with her. She lies next to him that night and listens to him lecture her about obeying Jesus' teachings. She ignores him and buries her head in her hands. Her back is so raw and painful that she must lie on her side. The iron bites into her legs all night. It is at least a week before she can lie on her back again.

She needs a drink more than ever. But she is closely watched these days and it is harder to get away. It is several weeks before she feels comfortable going to Branciforte again. Several unhappy sober weeks. Finally, she gets desperate and goes to see Miguel late at night, while Eunio is asleep. Miguel gives her a hard time for being away for so long and then they get drunk like old times. They come up with a new plan. She will only come late at night and then she'll sneak back before Eunio wakes up. For a while this new pattern works, although she suffers from lack of sleep.

Then things take a turn for the worse in the mission. Father Quintana replaces Father Gonzales, who was a reasonably kind man. Quintana is another inflexible, rule-crazy dictator and sadist in the style of Fernandez. He imposes many new, harsh restrictions that haven't been seen in the years since Fernandez left. Whippings become a daily custom again. New rules are made to keep the neophytes in line. Strict curfews are imposed. It is harder than ever to escape to Branciforte for a little fun. Half the neophytes are busted for various infractions, and they are forced to walk around in shackles or with a log of wood wedged between their legs with chains.

One bitterly cold, rainy winter's day, Quintana gathers all of the people together to stand in the rain just to hear his new rules and regulations. Then he shows off his new whip. Although he is acting very serious, everyone can see that he is secretly proud of it. He has fashioned it with iron barbs at the end that cut deeply into the flesh with each snap. He punishes two young men and a boy that day, and the screams of the boy as the iron cut into the flesh of his back bring chills to the hearts of even the most numb neophyte who no longer cares about anything. Two girls also feel the sting of that whip on this day, although they are whipped in a secret place. One of them is a girl that Esther is friendly with, who is caught having sex with one of the young men whom she likes - one of those young 'fornicators' who got the public whipping today. That afternoon, she shows Esther the deep gashes in her back, with eyes filled with tears. She curses the shackles on her feet. As a medicine man applies a poultice to the wounds, she screams the whole time.

Quintana scolds Esther that evening for bringing a dirty blanket into mass. Esther is afraid that she will receive a whipping, but he lets her off with a warning. But it really scares her to think that someday she will feel the sting of that metal tipped whip on her own back. A metal tipped whip leaves deep scars, which can last for a lifetime.

Father Quintana works steadily on his instruments of torture for many years. On a day when he plans to demonstrate a particularly sadistic horse whip tipped with steel barbs, Indians take matters into their own hands. They cut off one of his testicles and strangle him until they believe him dead. Somehow he revives later that night, so they crush his other testicle with a rock and he dies in bed. Out of some modesty, the nature of his death is hid for years. Quintana is hailed as a hero and a martyr by the Spanish church.

Late that night, Esther has a fight with Eunio. Every day that goes by, she hates him more and more. And tonight, sleeping next to him is a torture. So needing a stiff drink, she gets up in the middle of the night and goes out into the pouring rain. It is a miserable night to be out, but she doesn't care. She trudges through the rain wearing only her woolen nightgown, which is her favorite piece of clothing. She can only wear it away from the mission, because they will take it away from her if they find it. She goes to visit Miguel and she drinks as much as he can spare. Luckily, he passes out drunk before she has to endure him. And then she wanders back in the pouring rain, stumbling drunkenly through puddles and marshy pools.

Suddenly a hand grabs her. She screams and turns to face a Spanish soldier, his grinning face obscured by rivulets of water. He holds on tight to her as she struggles to escape his grip.

"Well, look at this," he says with a sadistic grin. "A young neophyte doing what she is not supposed to. Won't Quintana be upset to see his orders being broken?"

Esther's face fills with horror, as she pictures the back of her friend covered with ugly welts. And she has done something much worse!

"Yes, you saw Padre Quintana's new whip, didn't you? You know what will happen to you, girl?"

Esther slumps and her face registers defeat.

"I'll tell you what I'll do for you, because I am such a decent fellow. A friend to all animals and beasts. I'll tell you what I will do for you. If you will give me the pleasure of your company for an hour or so, then perhaps I will forget that I saw you out here on such a night as this."

"Any-anything you say," Esther stammers, her teeth chattering from the cold.

"I have built a little shelter over here to keep me dry on my watch. Follow me."

He has a little tarp set up underneath a tree, with a torch for light. He pulls a bottle of wine - Branciforte wine - out of the folds of a blanket and takes a deep drink. Then he lays the blanket out to form a makeshift bed.

"May I have some?" Esther stammers.

"Aren't you drunk enough already?" he asks, and he laughs. "You know that neophytes are not allowed to drink. It corrupts the spirit."

Esther feels the bile rise in her throat, and a white-hot rage fueled by too much wine combined with too much misery. She is suddenly sick of all of it, and for the first time in her life she feels that she is capable of anything.

"I'll do whatever you want," she hisses. "Anything you desire."

"Ah, well, I like the sound of that. Of course, you have no idea what it is you suggest. But I accept your offer. Anything I want? In that case you shall surely need a drink. And then you will get something that you will not soon forget."

He rewards her with a huge smile and graciously hands her the bottle. She takes a deep drink, and then she smashes the bottle onto his head. The glass shatters with a satisfying explosion and the soldier screams and falls to his knees.

"You dirty whore! You dirty beast! I'll kill you! I'll whip you by my own hand, I will, until you pass out from the pain!"

He reaches for her, but he is half blind from the blood in his eyes, and he is dazed from the blow to the head. She easily avoids his grasping hands and backs away. He gropes for his rifle, but she grabs it first. She swings it above her head and brings it down onto his back. He crashes down to the ground and moans with pain. She hits him again for good measure. In a blind rage, she begins kicking him and screaming at him, all of the pent up anger of her years of being abused by Spanish soldiers coming out in her drunken frenzy.

"Don't kick me, my love. I have glass in my eye," he implores feebly, changing his tone. "It hurts so badly. Go fetch help, please! I fear I may go blind. Help me! I won't whip you. I promise. I'll say it was...somebody else. Just get help."

He is no longer angry, but desperate and in pain, and her anger quickly fades. She stands there a moment, not knowing what to do. The urge to run is strong. She knows that this man will make sure that she is beaten within an inch of her life tomorrow – unless he truly goes blind and cannot see her face. And then she hears shouting voices come from out of the rain and she panics. She throws the rifle down and runs off into the rainy night. Moments later, she hears the wounded soldier screaming for his men, and somebody screaming back. They have found him.

Then she hears shouting voices coming after her. They are hunting for her. It seems that she has only one direction where she can lose them. Up into the hills she will go, deep inside the redwood forest. The night is so dark and rainy, she just might disappear into the trees. She begins to run as hard as she can, pure blind terror pushing her harder and harder. She trips and falls many times and soon she is covered in mud and bruises. But still she keeps moving. She sloshes through mud and wet grass and through fields that are turning to swamps. She does not dare to stop until she enters the darkness of the forest. Only then, does she stop to catch her breath and think things through. A wave of nausea passes over her and she falls to her knees and vomits repeatedly. Finally she rises, feeling a little more sober.

The rain falls harder than before, and she realizes she is soaked to the bone and shivering. She stands under a large redwood tree, trying futilely to escape the rain and considering what to do.

She considers returning to the mission and facing her accuser and telling the fathers what he tried to do to her and why she hit him. But then she thinks of a dream that she has been having lately. A dream about a man whom she knows only as Him. He is the man of Esther's nightmares, an elusive devil who haunts her dreams and lurks in the dark spaces of her mind. She does not know who this devil is, but He has told her clues. He said that He controls men. He controls Quintana and tells him to make instruments of torture. It was He who made Fernandez into a monster. And Miguel is under His thumb, as well as the soldier she hit tonight. She thinks that perhaps He might be a servant of the devil. Or maybe He is the devil. She is suddenly certain that He will continue to make her miserable if she returns to the mission. She can never go back there.

She knows suddenly what she must do. She must run far, far away from this place, where He has so much power. There is nothing left for her here. She begins to move again, at an easy pace this time. The rain pours down her hair and into her eyes, but she ignores it and keeps moving. The fear she feels tonight is very, very strong, and she shakes and tremors from it whenever she stops moving. So she continues to move, despite her cold and weariness. She constantly stops to scan the night and listen for sounds, sure that the soldiers are right behind her. She becomes convinced that He will lead them right to her if she does not keep moving. She must find safety, although she doesn't know what safety looks like.

It is a long night of dark fear, disturbing visions, shivering cold and bone chilling wet. But finally, her exhaustion overcomes her fear. She stops running and falls to the ground underneath a tree. It is near dawn now. She has walked for hours and she is completely beat. She cannot move another inch, were He to appear right in front of her eyes and snarl and bare his fangs.

She falls into a dark and troubled sleep.

She awakens at dawn. She is absolutely chilled to the bone and wet through and through. Her whole body aches with cold and exhaustion. The rain has finally stopped, and little gaps in the dark clouds show glimpses of blue sky. She prays that the sun will soon come out, as she stands up on shaky legs and examines her surroundings.

She finds herself only a few hundred yards from the San Lorenzo river. All around her looms a great forest. The river rushes rapidly downhill toward the sea. Esther takes a drink of cold water and shivers as the icy river water fills her belly. After drinking her fill, she sits down on a log to think. She is stiff, numb and extremely uncomfortable, which makes thinking that much more difficult. But the question before her is simple. Where to go?

In the end, it doesn't matter, as long as she never returns to Santa Cruz. If she goes back there, she will find only misery. Out here, she is free. There is no one to tell her what to do, scold her, or do things to her. He cannot find her here, nor will the soldiers be able to track her in this dense wilderness.

She decides to wander deep inside this great forest and disappear forever.

She follows the river north, so she can keep track of where she is going. As she walks, she takes in her new surroundings. The smells are different here. The familiar smell of the ocean - one that she has lived near all of her life - is gone. This place smells of moss, mold, fungus, wet leaves and rotting wood all mixed together. It is a comforting smell and a very fresh smell. The forest is a very beautiful place. She is glad that she has come here. Trees tower over her head and birds sing like she has never heard them before. She can happily spend her last days here.

Esther has no illusions. She is sure that this is the last place that she will ever see. She will not live long out here in the wild with no food and dangerous animals about. But at least she will die a free woman in this beautiful place. She walks naked, as her nightgown is soaked through and through. There is nobody to see her, so she feels no embarrassment. She is relatively dry, although she still craves a good bake in the sun to completely dry everything.

Eventually, the sun does peek through a hole in the clouds. It is a miracle that may save her life. She can dry her wet clothes in preparation for the nighttime. She finds a sunny patch and hangs her nightgown from a tree branch in the weak sunlight. Then she sits down, curled in a ball, and tries to stay warm. Now that she doesn't walk, she cools off quickly, because the sun is not very warm.

She awakens a few hours later. Did she really fall asleep? The clouds have rolled back in and the sun is low on the horizon. She feels her nightgown and it is a little drier, with only a slight dampness. She gratefully puts it on. Walking down to the river, she drinks her fill. It is then that she realizes how hungry she is. She is so ravenously hungry that she will eat just about anything. Unfortunately, there is nothing to eat and little hope of finding food. She is powerless to appease her growling stomach.

She watches a fish swimming in the river. If only she could catch it. But she cannot risk getting wet again and she would probably fail anyway. Better to walk on and find shelter, because it will probably rain again. After a long hike along the river, past endless trees, she finds a hollow trunk that will do the trick. The soil inside is dry and it is large enough for her whole body. She curls up into a ball inside the hollow, brushing away cobwebs. Night quickly comes upon the forest and soon she cannot see a thing. The darkness here is thick and total. Sure enough, it begins to rain again. But she is dry inside her little womb. Not warm…but dry. She listens to the patter of rain until she falls into an uneasy sleep.

She has a horrible dream that night. A hideous demon, black and foul, with pimply skin and bugging, bloodshot eyes comes for her. The demon chases her through the forest for a long time. She trips over a log and the monster catches her. The monster belches a smelly, disgusting burp and then he gives her a kiss with leathery lips. She gags and struggles not to vomit, as she tastes his vile breath. He pulls off her nightgown and rips it into shreds. She screams, sure that he is going to rape her.

"You are Him!" she shouts. "I recognize you! What do you want from me?"

She wakes with a start, her heart racing. Slowly, she takes deep breaths and tries to convince herself that it was just a dream. It is still pitch black, although the rain has stopped. She is very cold and stiff inside her cramped quarters, and she has to pee. But she is terrified of the dark. The dream has totally unnerved her. Finally she creeps out and squats by the tree, then races back to her little hole.

She begins to cry. She sobs for the fear that she has held deep inside for her entire life, for the demon who haunts her and for the cruel turn of events that has left her underneath a tree in pitch black night and pouring rain. She is so cold and so hungry and so thin inside her nightgown. Her bare feet and hands are numb. The misery of her whole life seems to be reflected in this one moment and it overwhelms her so that she can hardly stand it. She wants to die! She is a cursed woman and the world will not be any worse for her passing. She prays for a quick death and an end to pain.

Finally she stops crying. She has made a decision tonight. She will continue to walk on into the forest until she is dead. Another few days of this and she will be too weak to walk. And then she shall lie underneath a tree until something eats her or she just passes away. Feeling much better, she falls back asleep.

In the morning, she awakens, feeling better about her fate. She knows no more fear now. Death awaits her in this forest and she is glad for it. She feels very weak, but she has also found a second wind - a new burst of energy. She is ready to go on. And her stomach no longer bothers her incessantly with its cry for food. Even her stomach seems to have accepted her fate. Her only problem is the cold weather and the rain. She wishes that her last days could be warm ones.

All day she follows the river, as it races through valleys and mountains. She marvels at the trees which go on and on without end. She sings along with the twittering birds and their soothing songs. She spies many animals today, including a large family of grazing deer. She watches them for a long time, wishing she could graze like them. They watch her nervously and then run off, preferring to be alone.

The sun breaks through for a few hours in the afternoon and Esther lies lazily in a sunny patch. She dozes contentedly in its warmth. It is the first warmth that Esther has felt since she left home. Home? She is home. Already she has forgotten Santa Cruz and all its bad memories. She feels like she has been gone for a long time, although it has only been two nights and two days.

She finds another hollow tree just as the rain makes another appearance. This one is much larger and she can stretch out a bit and get really comfortable. It feels like a small room and she feels protected and safe in its belly. The soil inside is soft and fits her body perfectly, and no wind can get through. She sleeps easily and peacefully all the night through, with not a single bad dream.

The next days bring more adventure. Up the mountain she goes, until she feels that she may reach the top of the world. She must stop to rest more and more often, as she weakens. So she takes it easy, stopping to admire a slug or a strangely shaped tree or anything that grabs her attention. Sometimes she just sits by the river, meditating on its gracefulness. She feels so light and airy that she might float away at any moment. It rains often, and she spends much time crouched in hollows, trying to stay dry. To become wet now means certain death. She hasn't the energy to keep warm any more.

How many days has she been walking? She cannot remember. She is getting so thin now. She feels like a walking skeleton wrapped in skin. She caught her reflection in the water today and it frightened her. Her face is so drawn and haggard, it looks almost like a skull with skin. She avoids her reflection now, as she watches the slow current go by. She tries to count the days since she has eaten. Five? Six? Could it be seven? No...not quite that many. She thinks about the Indians from the mission who used to live in the forest. What did they eat? They probably fished and hunted and knew which plants to eat. She doesn't have any idea what to eat. She wishes she had bothered to ask them about it. The Spaniards cared nothing for local foods, other than animal meat. They grew all their own food and had a huge population of cows. Esther never had to worry about being fed, so she never asked about the wonders of the great cupboards of the forest. She tries nibbling on some plants as an experiment, but they taste horrible and she cannot stomach them.

At least the forest grows more beautiful every day she spends inside of it. She is entranced by every nook and hollow. She sits for a several hours by the flowing river, enjoying a peace and tranquility she has never known. Only a herd of deer interrupts her as they go crashing past. Noticing her, they stop and warily make a wide circle around her. After they are gone, a straggler comes, trying to keep up. It wanders slowly past, staring at her nervously. It seems to be wounded. As they lock eyes, its gaze is filled with understanding. It seems to say, "We're both wounded and soon to be dead. We are the same."

She wonders how it would taste if she killed it. Could she eat it raw? She is hungry enough to try. She tries to imagine herself bashing it on the head with a rock. It seems to sense something in her gaze that is unpleasant, for it turns and walks off.

"Don't go," she says sadly. "I won't eat you."

It starts at the sound of her voice and then moves quickly away.

"You are so beautiful," she whispers. "Better that I die than you."

How long has she been in this spot? It is getting dark already. She has spent the entire day sitting in one place. She is so high from fasting, that she can spend an entire day in one spot without realizing it. It has been a wonderful day actually! She laughs to herself as she realizes that once she accepted her death, this has become the happiest week of her life. Every moment is precious, because it could be her last.

Wolves howl mournfully in the distance. Their song seems to speak to her and soothes her. Wolves understand. She howls back at them. Life is so beautiful out here in the wild. If only she had learned to hunt and fish and gather food in all her wasted years in Santa Cruz. Then she could live out here forever, a wild creature of the forest.

What use was learning all the prayers and Latin and hymns? It all suddenly seems a waste of time. None of that is any use out here. She is surrounded by food and she is wasting away. Her body is breaking itself down for nourishment and the cold and wet are quickening the process. She doesn't have much time left. She can feel it.

She awakens with a start. It is late afternoon, and she is soaked through and through. It must have rained and she didn't even wake up. She remembers sitting by the river and it was dry. Now she's in danger. She will surely catch pneumonia. Why didn't she wake up?

She frantically searches for shelter, but she cannot find anything good. She wanders up and down the bank of the river, but nothing seems dry here. Every inch seems to be soaked. Finally she gives up, and just wanders along the river in the rain. It doesn't matter, she tells herself. I'll just die a few days sooner.

Sure enough, she soon catches a cold. Or is it pneumonia? She sneezes badly and coughs. It has stopped raining for the moment, but the sky is dark and gloomy. She finds a tree hollow and crawls inside it to get some sleep. But she is soaked and extremely uncomfortable. She takes off her cold, wet nightgown and tries to bury her naked body deep into whatever dry soil and leaves she can find. She manages to become reasonably dry and warm, covered in dirt and leaves. Exhausted and relieved, she falls into a troubled sleep.

She dreams of Him again. He chases her through the dark woods and she runs terrified before him. His hot breath is like the sulfurous fumes of hell and it drives her mad with terror. He wears a bag on his head, so she cannot see his face.

"Get away from me!" she screams.

He slowly gains on her and she is too weak to run much further. He will catch her and have his way, just like he has so many other times. In her panic, she trips and falls face down on the ground, and he is upon her instantly. His hot breath gags her and she struggles against him as he rips open her nightgown.

"What do you want from me? Why are you following me?" she gasps.

He grabs her by the feet and starts to drag her away. She claws at the ground with her fingers, trying to get free.

"Leave me alone!" she screams. "Leave me alone!"

He only grunts and pulls harder.

"Who are you? What do you want?"

He stops suddenly and he lifts the bag from his head. He has no face. His head swirls with all the colors of the rainbow. Colored lights, swirling together with no form.

She screams as loud as she has ever screamed, and awakens trembling. It is darker than she has ever known darkness. Pitch black with absolutely no light. It is the new moon tonight and the forest lets in no starlight. She writhed during her dream until her dirt blanket was removed, and now she is trembling violently from the cold, coughing and sneezing. She begins to cry miserably, wishing it would all be over.

Some evil presence is following her, driving her to her death. Maybe He is the devil and she will go to hell, because she doesn't deserve heaven. She doesn't know. She begins to cry miserably, wishing it would all be over. She makes a desperate plea to God and

Jesus to save her from hell. To let her die and go to heaven, so she can be with Nani forever and be happy.

A song begins to take form in her mind. It weaves itself in and out of her sobs and her tears. It is a song of lament for her existence. Esther's lament for her misery and her pain and her death. For she will die tonight. She can feel it. She has no more desire to live, and her body is too weak and sick to go on.

Wolves howl suddenly from out of the blackness. A full pack of wolves sing their lonesome song. And their song touches her deeply, for she knows why they sing. And she must sing back to them. She begins to sing in a feeble whisper. But her song grows as their howls fade. And then a dam bursts in her heart. A sudden downpour of feeling overwhelms her and the song bursts in her mind. She begins to wail at the top of her voice, and every ounce of feeling within her is released at once. She screams and moans like a madwoman, releasing every ounce of her soul into this song. It is no longer just a song now, but a tale of her entire life.

The whole forest stops to listen. The wind, rain, bugs, trees and moss all seem to stop breathing to hear her song. The wolves stop howling and they huddle together in silent understanding. She stands up in the utter darkness and begins to spin in a trance, as she howls her lament to the very stars in the sky. Every ounce of feeling leaves her body through her song and pours out into the whole world. She lifts her arms up and spins in the great void. She is going to enter that void. Once every drop of feeling is released in her, then she will be empty at last. And then she will die. She can feel herself reaching a fever pitch, as the song consumes her utterly. Just when she thinks she can sing no longer, she finds a hidden reserve of energy deep inside of her and she releases it. At any moment, she will collapse, utterly spent. It is a wonderful, tingly feeling of release. The song reaches its peak of madness and the whole earth stops for one split second. Then, she crumples to the ground.

She dreams of angels that sing beautiful songs to her in the sky. She floats among them, lost in the clouds where it is always warm and serene. She sings along with the glowing, white angels who sing in great, glad choruses of music - songs from her youth when she sang with the choir. She is so happy up here. There is no hunger. No fear. Nothing but peace and joy forever.

And Nani is here. He floats to her. She has never laid eyes on him before - not so clear as this - but here he is in front of her. He is a beautiful fool, so wonderfully rumpled and messy in a wholly unselfconscious way. Nani has a thick head of brown tousled hair, a loopy grin and great shining eyes. He is small and somewhat puckish, and he dances and leaps about with consummate skill. He clashes with the angels in their white finery, but they accept him without judgment or derision. All are equals up here. Grabbing her hands, he twirls her around, laughing exuberantly. She laughs like she has not laughed in so very long and she spins with him.

"Nani, it is so good to see you!" she exclaims. How wonderful you look. I never dreamed you were so handsome."

"And you are beautiful," he laughs. "Come dance with me."

"I am so happy to be here. Now I can fly with you forever, and sing and laugh and play like the old days."

"No, my precious," he says, gently stroking her hair. "It is not your time yet. Soon, you must go back down."

"No, Nani. Don't say that. Don't make me go back there. I want to stay here with you."

He laughs easily. "It is not so bad as all that, is it? There is so much to see. So much to learn."

" I hate it down there. I want to stay with you. Don't leave me."

"Someday we will be together forever. I will wait for you. But not now. Now you will go back, for you have much to do."

Her great childish grin fades, replaced by a pout. He holds her hand patiently, and waits for her to accept her fate.

"Am I not dead?"

"No."

"But I will be soon?"

"I cannot know when you will die. But I do know that you are not dead now, for I can see a thin thread of light extending down to your body. Your body lives and you are still connected to it. And you must go back. You see, already it is drawing you down."

He is right. She is slowly sinking back down. She reaches out for him desperately, but he is out of reach.

"Nani!"

"I am always with you, and I will always protect you. Don't forget that I love you."

"Nani!"

She falls faster and faster and soon it is all just a blur of lights and color. Suddenly, she wakes up, with the sun shining in her face. Blinking her eyes, she stands up and looks around in amazement. The clouds are all gone and the sky is blue. She is warm and dry, and she doesn't feel hungry any longer. And the strangest part of all is that she stands in a clearing, staring up at an unobstructed sky for the first time in days, in a very different part of the forest than she was before.

Hawk Tribe

Hawk 0' **

Hawk moon

Esther spends all day sunbathing and the sunshine restores her spirits tremendously. She tries to figure out what happened to her, but she cannot figure how she got here. She doesn't know what happened to her from the time she collapsed from faintness in the rain and dreamed that she was in heaven with Nani, until she woke up here. But she knows that she was underneath a roof of trees in a downpour, and now she is in open ground and there is not a cloud in the sky. She was near the river, and now the river is nowhere in sight.

After going over it several times without success, she decides that it doesn't matter. Wherever she is, it is a real place. Bugs bite her, and she is hungry and thirsty again. Finally, she makes a decision to find the river, a beacon of hope in her hopeless wanderings. Rivers make her feel safe within this great jungle. They offer endless water and the remote possibility of finding food. At the very least, having a destination beats just wandering aimlessly or staying here until she is just a skeleton of bleached bones in the sun.

The forest is still except for a lone bird cawing. She watches the big trees, hoping for wisdom, but the trees are silent. Then the leaves rustle in the wind and a drop of water falls from a wet leaf. It lands on Esther's forehead and trickles down her nose.

Her head shoots up to the offending tree. "Did you just do that?"

The tree is silent.

"Do you know where the river is?"

Getting no further response, she confronts the tree threateningly. "I am looking for the closest river. Please, tell me where it is."

The tree doesn't answer. But the lone bird that had been cawing over her head flies out of the tree and heads out over the treetops toward some destination.

"Thank you," she calls out to the bird, although she is not sure if that was a sign or not.

She begins to walk in the direction the bird showed her. She walks until it grows dark, and then she makes herself a bed of redwood needles and falls into a sound sleep. Before she falls asleep, she has a sudden realization that she no longer feels hunted and cursed. Wherever she is now, the demon she knows as Him did not follow.

***Hawk 0' is a calendar entry. Hawk moon means the moon is in the constellation of the Hawk. (See appendix)*

Hawk 1'

Beaver moon

The ground is steep here, and Esther clambers over dead trees covered in moss and around large stumps and blockades of every variety in her climb upwards. By the time she reaches the top of the hill, she is tired again and wants to rest. But she cannot see anything that means anything, just thousands of trees in every direction. After a short rest, she climbs down the opposite slope. More climbing than walking now, as every few feet seems to offer some kind of barricade or another. The moss that grows on the fallen trees is wet, and she is soon soaked. The hours pass, and she feels like she is getting nowhere. She moves slowly, like a snail, weak and tired again. She has caught some sort of cold and she constantly stops to sneeze and to wipe her nose and feel sorry for herself. But finally, she hears the sound of water, and she comes upon the bank of a real river at last. She gives a happy shriek as she makes her way down to the bank.

The river tumbles quickly down a steep hill, jumps over large rocks and fallen trees, and shoves aside anything caught in its path as if it is in a great rush to get to the bottom and nothing will stand it its way. It tumbles into a pool where a beaver house stands proudly, made up of many, many branches of various sizes all piled in a heap. Esther makes her way down to the pool. The ground here is stony, but it is clear of trees. If only the clouds would part, she would be able to bask in the waning sunlight. But the clouds are uncooperative as usual, so she takes a deep drink of water and sits down by the bank to rest.

As she watches the river swirl past, she notices fish in the water. This part of the river seems to be filled with small fish of some unknown variety. She begins to think that she might catch one of them. How hard could it be to catch one fish? She has seen men spearfish in the San Lorenzo before, so surely she could do it.

After a long search, she finds a decent branch. It is broken off at one end into a sharp point. She laughs to herself that she could have done this instead of starving anytime she wanted - if only she had thought of it.

Determined, she walks down to the river and strips off her clothes. She feels the weight of the stick in her hand and makes a few practice stabs. She can do this! She steps into the river and then she steps right back out again. The water is freezing. She could catch a dread cold if she goes in there.

She stands on the bank for a while, waiting for a fish to come close enough to kill it from where she stands. But they stay close to the center. She will have to step into the water if she wants to eat. She takes several deep breaths and steps into the icy water again. Before she can change her mind, she wades up to her waist. Holding her spear above her head, she shivers and her teeth chatter as she stands there waiting for a fish. She prays for a quick kill.

Here comes a small one, about half a meter from her. She moves forward gently, not wanting to scare it away. She raises the spear high in the air and stabs down forcefully. But her body shakes so much from the cold that her aim is off, and she stabs down so hard that her foot slips on a small rock and she loses her balance.

Splash! An icy, gloved hand grabs her by the spinal cord and paralyzes her. She cannot move or breathe for what seems like an eternity, although it is only a few seconds. Then the hand releases her and she manages to take a breath.

It is so cold that she can barely swim. The current has gotten hold of her and is dragging her away. Desperate, she grabs a hold of the beaver's house. Coughing and spluttering, she attempts to climb onto the house, but she only manages to upset the mound of sticks, which collapses in her hands. Esther gasps and tries to grab hold of anything steady. But it is no use. She falls back into the water.

She screams in frustration and terror. She is totally numb and her muscles just won't work right. The current is already dragging her away from the beaver house and down the river. She is sure that she is going to smash into the rocks below and die. She is so panicked, that she doesn't notice the man until he is right in front of her. He stands on the bank just past the beaver dam, clambering over rocks to get to her. As she floats past him, gasping for air and trying desperately to get to the bank, he jumps into the water and grabs her. She lets out a little scream of terror at his unexpected touch. Groaning, he picks her up and carries her out of the water and onto the bank.

He sets her down roughly on the ground. She is in too much shock to do or say anything. She can only stare back at him with wild eyes filled with terror. After a moment, he hands her a blanket and indicates for her to dry herself. He considers her a moment longer, before putting his attention to his wet leggings and shoes. He takes them off and goes down to the river to wring them out.

Feeling numb all over, Esther shivers, shakes, and trembles violently, as she takes deep, panicked breaths and tries to calm down. Wrapping the blanket around her body, she wrings her long hair and whips it around and around until it no longer drips down her back. Finally she takes her nightgown and puts it on, and then wraps the wet blanket tightly around her again.

She watches the man warily as he finishes wringing out his shoes. He is younger than he first appeared, perhaps in his late teens. He has long brown hair, dyed with streaks of red, and a ruddy, flushed face. He is shirtless, showing off strong, well-trained arms bulging with veins and ropes of muscle. A tattoo on his left arm shows a symbol like a hawk in flight.

"What were you doing swimming in the river if you can't swim?" he suddenly shouts, loudly and brashly.

He examines her closely for a long moment. She looks away, not liking his forceful tone or gaze. She is quite surprised to hear him speak Spanish, as she assumed he was an Indian up until now.

"I was trying to catch a fish," she says lamely.

"A fish?" He grins slyly. "If you want to catch a fish, think like a fish. Is that it?"

"I fell in. And I *can* swim."

"I don't know what you do worse," he says, laughing. "Swimming or fishing."

"I'm very hungry," she says. "I haven't eaten in days. Have you any food?"

He walks away, leaving her alone by the river. She wonders if he is leaving. But he returns with a large carrying basket and a thick heavy branch a few moments later. He places the basket down by his wet shoes and leggings and takes a few moments to shape the point of the branch with his knife. Then he reaches into the basket and pulls out a fishing net. He places the net at the end of the sharpened branch and ties it down. He now has a fishing net with a four-foot reach.

Thus equipped, he wades into the water - quite bravely it seems to Esther because he doesn't even flinch - and stands up to his waist in the same spot that she did. He stands still as stone for several minutes, watching the water intensely.

"This isn't the best time for fishing. There isn't much in the water but squimms."

Squimms are small, inferior fish that aren't worth more than a few bites.

Esther marvels how he can stand the icy water for so long, but he seems not to notice it at all. Then he suddenly stabs down by his legs and whips the net through the water forcefully and comes up with a struggling fish. In an instant, his hand is on it so that it cannot escape and he carries it onto dry land. Then he grabs it by the tail and bashes it into a large rock. The fish soon quits struggling and lies still, and the young man dramatically throws the fish down at Esther's feet.

"You can clean a fish, can't you?"

Esther has only cleaned a fish twice in her life, but she assumes she can do it a third time. Except it occurs to her that she has no knife.

"Do you have a knife?"

"After you caught your fish, what were you going to clean it with? A stick?"

He grins again and goes into his burden basket to search for his knife. It is a wicked looking steel blade, well crafted with a handle of polished bone.

Determined to prove her skills in some area, Esther does as good a job cleaning the fish as she possibly can. Her rescuer seems pleased that she can do something right, and that makes her feel good. After the fish is cleaned, she cuts the fish into strips. She is very surprised when he takes a slice of fish from her greasy hands, pops the raw fish in his mouth, and begins to chew. She only looks at the fish flesh lying limp in her hand, and wishes it were cooked. She has never liked raw meat.

"What's the matter?"

"Is there any way to cook it?" she asks timidly.

"Cook it? Do you see any dry wood here? How would you suggest we cook it? Do I look like a Beaver trader who carries around his house on his back? Besides...I thought you were hungry."

She certainly is hungry, and she realizes she wouldn't want to wait until it is cooked anyway. She bites down savagely on the raw flesh and chews. It isn't bad. It has an interesting texture - a bit rubbery, but it breaks down easily enough. It is not as salty as sea fish, but strangely flavorful.

"It's healthier raw. Go ask the seals or the dolphins if you don't believe me."

She instantly feels stronger, so she picks up another big piece of fish and wolfs it down. He laughs and helps himself to another piece. Soon the fish is nothing but bones and skin. He eats some of the skin, and she does the same. She feels a rush of energy fill her tired body. There is something energizing about raw flesh, which is much lighter than cooked meat.

"Who are you?" she finally gets up the nerve to ask.

He shows her his arm and she thinks that he is flexing his muscles for her. But then she realizes that he is showing off his tattoo of a hawk.

"What does that mean?"

"What tribe are you from? Everyone knows this symbol."

"I'm not from any tribe."

"Who are you then? What are you doing way out here?"

"I'm-"

She considers what to say without saying too much.

"I'm from the Spanish mission. I got lost."

"Spanish? We don't take kindly to any Spanish nosing around our land."

"I'm not with them - I mean - I'm not one of them."

"I hope not."

"Aren't you Spanish? I mean...you speak it."
"I speak Alano."
"It sounds like Spanish."
"Trust me, it's different," he snaps, and the matter is dropped.

Before it gets dark, the boy catches more fish for them to eat. When they are both satisfied, he lies down in a little section of sand, with not even a blanket for warmth. He puts on an extra, dry pair of leggings and a thick, warm elkskin shirt, and he is content.

"I am Dohr of the Hawk tribe," he says in a sleepy voice, before he passes out. "Tomorrow I will take you with me to our village."

She sighs and settles herself down in a sandy place with few rocks. She wraps herself tightly in his small blanket and tries to fall asleep. But she is still chilled from her dip in the river, and it is cold because the stars are out and there are no more clouds to trap the heat in. She lies for a long time, watching the stars through holes in the foliage overhead, feeling the chill in her bones. Finally she falls asleep.

Hawk 2'

She awakens when a rough hand shakes her. She groans and rolls over, but the hand is insistent. When the hand grabs her right breast, it is more than she can take, and she sits up angrily. Dohr laughs at her annoyed expression and it is all she can do not to yell at him.

"Good morning," he says with a smile.

She yawns and stretches her stiff muscles. He finishes taking apart several traps that he set yesterday, which he gathered early this morning. He has a basket full of various dead animals he caught in them, and she notices with surprise that a dead beaver sits on top of the bunch. She looks back at the beaver house on the river, wondering if it is now empty.

"Shall we begin our journey?" he asks, when she has risen to her feet and his traps are all packed away in the basket.

"Where?"

"To my home. I told you that already."

His expression makes her suspicious, because he stares at her a little too hard. She begins to wonder if he wants something from her.

"What is there?" she asks.

"More than is here. That is what is there." He notices the way she stares at him, and he suddenly understands. "You are welcome to go back to that Spanish village you came from. Just follow the river that way."

"I will go with you," she says quickly.

"Well then, light a fire under your rear and let us get moving."

Dohr walks at a very fast pace and Esther must keep a light trot going to keep up with him. She tires quickly, and it is soon a struggle to stay near him. She often lags behind, until he disappears in the distance. Then she gets frightened that he will disappear altogether and she shouts out for him until he stops reluctantly to wait for her.

"Can't you slow down a bit? I'm not feeling so well and I haven't eaten in days."

"You ate yesterday."

She ignores him and keeps walking. They soon come upon a particularly beautiful waterfall, cascading over several falling logs and rocks, creating a lush rainbow of mist. She has to stop and marvel at it and takes this opportunity to sit down and rest her feet. Then she feels his hot breath on her back again.

"What now?" he inquires.

"Can we rest for five minutes? My feet hurt and I have no shoes like you have."

He waits impatiently for her, ruining her peace, until she finally gives up and follows him again.

They do not reach any sign of civilization until dusk. By this time, Esther's feet and calves are sore, and she is almost ready to cast herself down and refuse to go any further. She has not ever had to walk this far in one day and at such a fast pace. She feels faint from hunger and dizzy from weariness. But then they pass a little shack, a rickety, hastily constructed thing made up of branches that have been roped together to form crude walls and a ceiling. A rotting bark roof serves to deflect the rain. Hope lends her a little more strength. They have reached his village at last.

Soon they come to a crossroads, with well worn paths leading in four different directions. They take the path that cuts sharply to the right, which leads directly to the river. At the river is a rope bridge - if you could call two ropes suspended over the river a bridge. Dohr jumps upon the bottom rope nimbly and prances across, using the top rope for his hands. Esther has a little difficulty following his lead, but eventually she does manage to climb upon the rope and scramble after him. The rope is slippery and moldy and she inches across slowly. He fidgets impatiently and starts to shout at her to hurry, but then he just throws his hands up in the air and sits down on a log to wait for her.

After that, they continue down a narrow path. The forest here is thinned out, and they pass many burned out stumps and a couple of rotten canoes. Soon they pass houses made out of split boards, with lights in the windows and smoke pouring out of holes in the roofs. It is hard to see in the gloom, but the houses seem to be in poor condition.

"We're going to miss dinner," he complains irritably. "There'll be nothing left."

She sticks close to Dohr, who keeps a brisk pace. She can hardly see anything at this point, except for his body crashing past trees and over branches lying in the path. Then she stumbles and falls into a hole, bruising her ankle. When she crawls back to her feet, she takes some time to test her tender ankle before walking again. After that, he takes her hand roughly and guides her as if she were a blind woman.

Finally they reach his house, which is a dark, shadowy bulk with lights flickering in the windows and good smells to tease Esther's nose. She begins to get excited at the prospect of a hot meal and her nervousness at being surrounded by strangers takes a back seat to her hunger. Famished himself, Dohr throws open the door and pulls her inside.

The house consists of one room. A big fire pit lies in the center, where a fierce fire crackles and pops wildly, making a bright flickering glow. There is a simple kitchen with a few iron pots, steel knives, wooden plates and bowls. On the floor to the left are two large bedrolls made out of bear and other furs. All the walls are old and beginning to rot. Only the roof looks new, as it was recently repaired. There is a big hole in the roof, right above the fire, which acts as a chimney to release the smoke. On the right side of the house is a crude table where three people are seated, a feast set down before them.

"There you are," shouts a woman's voice as the door opens.

Everyone stares at Esther, rather surprised to see her. Esther stands by the door, not knowing what to do or say. Dohr doesn't bother to make an introduction, but merely joins his family at the table. Esther stands by the door shyly, wishing that someone would say something. Finally Dohr looks at her and waves her over to the table to join them.

"Who's the new one?" asks Dohr's father, watching Esther walk slowly toward the table.

"I fished out of the river. I hooked a big one this time."

"I always knew you'd be a great fisherman someday," the man says with a smile.

Meekly, Esther goes to the table and sits on the bench. She is sandwiched in between Dohr's father and brother, a very uncomfortable place for her. She takes a quick peek at all of them, without looking anyone in the eye. Dohr's father seems the kindest of the three. There is a rough outline of strength about him, although he is fat and soft, like a soldier past his prime. He wears a sleeveless shirt of deerskin that goes to the waist and nothing else. Esther is shocked to see that he wears no pants and she tries her best not to become uncomfortable.

"I am Orym," he says, introducing himself.

Dohr's mother sits slumped over her plate. Although not fat, she is a little too fleshy for her frame. She wears a shirt much like her husband and a skirt made from strips of animal skin. She seems like a woman who will not brook any nonsense from anybody, a strong woman with a stern face, and not one to mess with.

"And I am Luce," she says, with a quick, disapproving glance at Esther.

Dohr's brother is young, perhaps twelve years of age. He looks more like his father than Dohr does.

"I am Kahne." *(Kah-nee)*

Esther introduces herself in a meek, quiet voice.

"What were you doing in the river?" asks Orym.

"She's a suicide, I think," Dohr blurts out.

The whole family, including Esther, stares at Dohr with shocked expressions. Then they stare at her. There is dead silence at the table, until Luce finally breaks the silence.

"A suicide? Why did you bring a suicide to my house?"

"Suicide? Must be from the Bear Tribe...." muses Orym.

He laughs, but Luce looks serious.

"Take her back where you found her and throw her in the river. I won't have any suicide in my house." She eyes Dohr suspiciously. "Or with my son."

Esther is mortified and blushing scarlet red. She wishes it were daylight so that she could run out of the house and escape.

"She may not be a suicide," Dohr says quickly. "I don't know. She's strange."

"Let us ask her instead of jumping to conclusions." Orym says, motioning to Esther. "Are you a suicide?"

Esther doesn't want to answer this question, but there doesn't seem to be any way around it.

"No."

"Tell us how you ended up in the river then," orders Luce sternly.

"I slipped on a rock while I was fishing and fell in."

"See," says Dohr quickly, trying to change the subject. "Now let's drop it and eat."

"Agreed." Orym says, looking at his wife. "The girl says she slipped. Let's give her the benefit of the doubt."

Luce acquiesces with a nod of the head and returns to her food. But Esther has a feeling that it isn't quite settled in her mind. Something is bothering Luce. She doesn't look at Esther all through the rest of dinner.

Esther tries to concentrate on the food and not look at anybody. Her stomach is in knots, and she is a little angry that they have managed to spoil this meal, which she has been looking forward to in her dreams for so long. On the table is a feast of roasted deer meat, dried salmon, and a soup of acorn mush. Esther fills her plate and eats. After the first bite, she doesn't care what they all think anymore. She has never had such a good meal in her life. Although the food is bland, her hunger adds all the spice that she needs. She eats until her stomach threatens to burst and then she eats a little more for good measure. There is silence at the table, except for the smacking of lips and chewing noises. After the bulk of the meal has been consumed and everyone picks at the remnants on their plates in a half-hearted way, the attention of the family turns back to Esther.

"What's your name? What tribe are you with?" Orym asks, fixing his eyes upon her.

"Esther."

He stares at her like she is quite dense, waiting for more.

"She's not from any tribe," Dohr explains. "She's from that Spanish town on the coast."

"You're kidding?" says Orym with wide eyes.

"You shouldn't have brought her here," Luce says sternly. "We don't want the Spanish to know the location of our winter homes. They will come and steal from us when we're not here."

"Who cares?" retorts Dohr. "They know of the villages of the Beaver tribe and the Bear tribe, and they leave them alone. They think that they are Mexicans. The Spanish are stupid."

"They are dangerously stupid," agrees Luce. "But the Beaver tribe never leaves home. We are gone most of the year. Our village is more vulnerable than theirs."

"I'm not really Spanish," Esther explains. "I hate them. I was a native girl whom they captured."

They all look at her with much different eyes now. Orym nods slowly and pats her gently on the back.

"We're sorry we doubted you," he says kindly. "No doubt you were treated badly. They have no honor, those people."

"They're weak," snorts Dohr. "Their only means of survival are their guns."

"The gun," snorts Orym in return. "A weapon that requires not a bit of skill or talent. Any fool can use a gun."

Esther sees a way to win them over, as they seem to hate the Spanish almost as much as she does.

"I escaped from them," she says, hoping they will be impressed. "Wandered through the forest for many days without food. That's how I ended up in the river. I was starving."

"What's your tribe sign?" pipes in Kahne.

"What's a tribe sign?"

Luce begins to laugh suddenly. Esther doesn't like the sound of her laughter. It is hostile and unfriendly. She shakes her head, as if Esther were a simpleton who wouldn't understand even if it were explained to her. Obviously, Luce dislikes her for some reason. Luckily, the men in the family seem to like her, relieving the pressure.

"Well, you are pretty," Orym states. "She is quite an attractive girl, if nothing else. Too thin, but it sounds like you have a good reason for it."

"Better to be safe," says Luce, looking her over. "Take off your clothes, girl. Let's have a better look at you."

Esther stares at her in horror. Luce indicates that she should take off her nightgown. But Esther just sits there, not knowing what to do. She is certainly not going to undress in front of these people.

"Luce, she's shy," says Orym supportively. "She's from that Spanish village, remember? You know how they are."

"We just want to make sure you don't have any diseases," Luce admonishes. "Those Spanish are dirty. Carry all sorts of diseases."

Esther is paralyzed with fear, imagining the worst.

Luce sighs, exasperated. She motions for Esther to get on with it. Esther stares at Dohr, her eyes begging for reprieve. Luce picks up on her fear, and she stands up with a loud sigh and strips off her own clothes. Nobody in the family gives her a second look, as if it is perfectly normal for a mother to undress in front of her sons.

"See how easy it is? Come on, you can do it."

Luce's tone is softer now. She grabs Esther's hand and leads her to the center of the room, where she proceeds to undress her. Esther is still frightened, but Luce's actions have calmed her fears to a degree. Soon Esther stands naked, as Luce goes over her body, looking for defects. She spends a lot of time examining her sex, looking for anything out of the ordinary.

Orym whistles appreciatively, eliciting laughter from his sons.

"*Shook,*" Luce hisses.

Finally the examination is through and both women dress. Esther is aware of the intense gazes of the men staring at her.

"Healthy," Luce proclaims. "Very thin though -"

"She's been starving," Dohr reminds her.

"Well, we will fatten her up then," Orym says, and the matter seems settled for the moment.

After dinner, the family all gathers around the fire, which they stoke up to a large blaze. It becomes quite smoky in the room, until Kahne climbs upon Dohr's shoulders and opens a second hatch in the roof, which sucks all of the smoke out in a rush. Esther joins them by the fire, but her full stomach has made her dead tired and she begins to yawn almost immediately. Finally, Luce notices her exhaustion, and she gives her a bearskin to lie upon and an extra blanket that is rough but comfortable. Esther retires into a dark corner, wraps herself in the blanket, and falls into a dead sleep. There she lies undisturbed until morning.

Hawk 4'

Jay moon

Late in the morning, Esther awakens groggily to Dohr's insistent nudging. She has slept for nearly thirty-six hours straight, only waking up twice for meals. As tired as she was, she mostly slept all day yesterday because she was trying to avoid talking to Dohr's family. Now Dohr continues to shake her until she abandons her comforting dreams and opens her eyes. She groans and rolls over, irritated by his rude manner.

"Lazy girl. Wake up. How much can you sleep?"

He just won't leave her alone. Finally, she sits up and blinks her eyes, wanting him to realize how tired she is. She sees Luce and Kahne sit at the table, drinking a pale green liquid. Everyone is dressed and awake already. Once she is sitting up, Dohr leaves her alone. He pours himself some of the green tea, and drinks it down in huge gulps.

"I want to go to the commons," he says after drinking two bowls of the tea. "Why don't you come with me?"

Esther doesn't want to get up, but she is afraid that he will leave her alone with Luce and Kahne, so she slowly nods affirmative.

"Bay nut tea?" asks Luce.

"No thank you," she says, looking doubtfully at the strange liquid.

She accepts a piece of thick, dry bread made from corn flour and drinks a lot of water. While she eats, Dohr goes outside, leaving her alone with Luce and Kahne. Esther stiffens, but Luce ignores her and goes about cleaning up. Finally Dohr returns to get her and she follows him out the door. Esther breathes a sigh of relief, now that they are out of the house. She goes into the trees to pee and then they begin to walk. Dohr maintains his usual fast pace, while Esther struggles to catch up.

They head toward Hawk commons, where all business and town activity takes place. Whether you want to trade or buy supplies, get news and gossip, or just be with people, this is the place to go. It is a mad place, full of shouting voices, pushy traders, busy people and the smell of rich foods in the air. It is located in a big open clearing with a few permanent buildings decaying slowly, along with numerous stalls and tiny huts selling a variety of things.

"I've got some business to attend to. I'll find you later," Dohr tells her, and without another word he runs off.

Esther is frightened of being alone in this strange place and she wants to follow him, but he doesn't seem to want her to. She stands there stupidly for a while, not sure what to do. Finally, her curiosity gets the better of her and she decides to look around. She begins to wander around, hoping that nobody will notice her.

She hears the singing of many women and she is drawn to it like a child goes to a soothing mother when danger is near. Underneath a great overhang, women sing as they grind flour. They lift huge stone pestles and smash them down on stone bowls filled with acorn kernels, grinding them down to powder. The song they sing is repetitive and slow, like their work. But it seems to drive them to lift the pestles over and over. Esther settles down near them and listens to the singing for a long time.

When she begins to feel a little braver, she goes to look at the little trading huts. The huts are filled with baskets of many different things for sale. Some sell furs of bear, beaver, wolf, deer, and any number of strange hides. Some sell sizzling meats, cooking in their juices right in front of you to tempt you. A fisherman sells many types of fish products - whale blubber, dried salmon, clams, mussels, and red and black paint made from salmon eggs. Another man sells dead ducks stuffed with tule grass, to be used as decoys in catching more ducks.

Esther goes to examine a wooden table displaying many hunting items and weapons, including expertly crafted bows and arrows, spears, shields made from tanned hides, and even a few steel swords and daggers that are available at a higher price. The steel swords and knives are Chinese style blades, as they are all imported from China. Behind the table, a blacksmith sharpens dull blades. He stands at a great stone wheel that spins when he turns a large crank and holds a slim dagger to the stone until the edge turns deadly sharp.

"That's a fine dagger right there," he says, casting a glance at Esther, who is examining a blade. "Cut out a human heart or clean a fish. Your choice."

She touches the dagger edge and nods approval, but she is more interested in the long, thick swords and the shields. They fill her with visions of knights, castles and duels, like in the book that Father Salazar used to read to the neophyte children when she was very young. That book told tales of sword fighters and crusaders doing battle for the Lord's glory. This place definitely reminds Esther of those tales, but these people remind her not of the knights and maidens in those stories, but of the barbarian hordes that they fought. Dressed in animal furs to protect against the cold weather, with swords and knives at their sides, they seem primitive, fierce and very wild.

For the first time, it really sinks in that she is immersed in a completely different culture. But where did these people come from?

Who are they? They do not seem like any Indian tribe she has ever met. And they are definitely not Spaniards. Although they speak Spanish, their speech is not typical of mission Spanish but peppered with many strange words and phrases. Their writing is different too. She has never heard of these people before...yet there is something familiar about them. She thinks that she might have known of them once, perhaps when she was a little girl.

She is interrupted from her thoughts by a wandering trader, who pesters her to look at an ugly necklace made of interlocking bones and feathers. He makes her try it on and then he asks her for a tupa. She shrugs and hands him back the ugly necklace and quickly moves on.

A tupa is a small, polished shell used for money. Tupas are only used among the Twelve Tribes. In the greater California area, dentalium shells are the main currency.

Next she walks past a food trader with baskets loaded with corn, roots and potatoes, and a clothes and fur trader with baskets full of moccasins and thick blankets woven from rabbit furs. This group of merchants seems different than the other people around here. They are fat, with warm, ruddy faces that speak of sitting by the fire and eating rich foods. They wear beautiful, warm cloaks lined with beaver and bear fur on the inside and sturdy hemp cloth on the outside. She walks up to one of these merchants who sells the elegant cloaks from his cart.

"May I try one on?"

"Please do."

She puts it on and sighs with pleasure. It is the most comfortable thing she has ever worn. With this on, she would never, ever be cold again, even in the dead of winter. She wishes she had money to buy it.

"Only 20 tupas," he says, as if it is nothing for such a great cloak.

"I have no...tupas."

"Well, I shall only be here till tomorrow and then I must return home. Perhaps you could scrounge up the price. Or I take trade if you have any nice pelts I could make use of."

"I cannot," says Esther, embarrassed by her poverty. She is suddenly and painfully aware that she still walks around in a woolen nightgown that is permanently dirty and full of rips and tears. She eyes the man's selection of clothing jealously. She just wishes that she could afford something - anything - to get her out of this nightgown that makes her look like a little pauper child.

She suddenly hears a high-pitched scream. Startled, she looks around to find the source. A fight has broken out between two little girls of about five years. They scream, kick, bite and scratch each other viciously. The amazing thing is that everyone is watching these two little girls fight and nobody steps in to stop it. Even their mothers watch without interference and they actually seem excited that their daughters might win.

The fight lasts only about a minute, but it is a nasty fight. It ends when the smaller girl pulls the bigger one's hair and then smacks her in the face. The bigger girl starts to cry. This seems to be the cue to end the fight. The mothers step in and gently pull the little girls apart. The hurt girl - or is she just upset - cries loudly, burying her face in her hands. The other girl stands proud and triumphant, head held high, as she receives praise from her mother for being such a brave fighter. She looks on with scorn at the crying girl who is being scolded by her mother for her cowardly tears. The mother shakes the loser until she finally stops crying and falls silent. The interested crowd disperses, satisfied for the moment.

"Why don't they just give them swords and let them fight to the death," Esther says quietly.

"What?" asks Dohr, who was standing right behind her watching the fight.

She turns around surprised and he laughs at her expression.

"Did you say I should give them my sword?"

He shows her his sword, which hangs at his belt.

"I had my sword sharpened and shined."

"It looks good on you," she says.

"Thank you," he beams. "Yes, I look good with cold steel at my side. It's true. I will be a Red Hawk warrior someday."

"Is that like a knight?"

"A knight?"

"Yes. A...um...sword fighter. They wear armor."

"I have armor."

"Can I see it?" she asks, imagining that she is in a fairy tale.

"Sure, later," he says, looking around suddenly. "I'll show you later."

He suddenly walks away, as if he just thought of something more important to do than talking to her. Esther stands around aimlessly again, watching everything happen around her, until a little boy suddenly walks up to her. The boy is about six years old, and he carries a little pointed stick upon which he has speared a mouse.

"Do you want to buy my mousy?" he asks innocently.

Esther stares at the dead mouse, wondering why she would want it.

"What do I do with it?" she asks curiously.

"Eat it."

She makes a disgusted face, thinking about eating a mouse.

"Do you eat mice?" she asks. "Mousys?"

"Yes. I killed this mousy."

"What else do you kill?"

"Grasshoppers," he says in the same innocent voice. "And gof-fers."

"And you eat them all? Grasshoppers too?"

"Yes."

It sounds disgusting to Esther, but she doesn't want to say anything for fear of offending the boy.

"How do you kill gophers?" she asks, thinking he is too small to hunt.

"Do you want me to show you?"

"Sure."

He walks away and Esther follows him. The boy walks for a long time down a small path. Esther thinks of turning back, until she realizes that the boy is walking all this way just to show her something. Soon they come to a part of the woods that is less thick and the boy stops walking. Esther sees burrows in the hillside and assumes that gophers live here. The boy pulls the dead mouse off the stick and starts poking the stick hard into each hole. He pokes his stick into every hole he sees, until finally a little writhing gopher comes out with it. He shows her proudly.

"See. A gof-fer."

"Very nice."

In truth, Esther is embarrassed. This little boy is a better hunter that she is. Esther would never have known how to catch a gopher. Now she feels stupid for starving in the woods, when she passed hundreds of holes that might have held any number of animals to eat. Although eating this little rat-like creature still sounds unpleasant, it is obviously better than starving.

"Do you want to buy my gof-fer?"

"I'm afraid I can't. It looks like a good gopher, but I haven't any of those money shells."

"Goodbye," the boy says a moment later, gathering up his dead mouse and gopher and putting them back on the stick.

"Where are you going?" she asks, wondering how to get back.

"Home."

He seems to live somewhere out here, and the boy walks off into the woods and disappears from view. After calling out to him fruitlessly to show her the way back, she is forced to walk back alone. Her fears come true, and she gets lost and ends up wandering around in a daze. She has no idea where she is, because everything looks the same to her. She finally comes across an old woman who is gathering mushrooms. The old woman points Esther in an entirely different direction from the way she was walking, gives her a strange glance, and continues on her mushroom search. With a shock, Esther suddenly realizes that if she had not found that woman, she might have gotten so lost that she would never have found her way back. And then she would be starving and lost again - no, not starving -

lost and dining off gophers and rats. It seems that Esther has moved up in the world.

By the time Esther finds her way back to the commons, most of the shops are closing up and Dohr has long since disappeared. Only the women grinding the grain are still working, so Esther takes a seat near them and listens to their song some more. She closes her eyes and relaxes. Before she knows it, they too are packing up their flour in baskets and putting away their tools. One of them stumbles over her as she carries her heavy basket home.

"Excuse me," mumbles the woman.

Esther glares at her and rubs her stepped-on leg.

"Don't get in the way of women working," states the woman flatly and then she walks off with head held high.

Red faced, Esther rises and reluctantly heads back to Dohr's house. She doesn't really want to go back there, but she has nowhere else to go. And her stomach is growling and urging her to go where the food is. So she walks back to Dohr's house, dreading every step.

She finds the house just before darkness settles over the forest. She is proud that she found it without help, although it did take a while. She stands at the window of the house for several minutes before getting up the courage to enter. Just another few minutes of peace, before walking into that chaos. She can hear voices coming from inside and she walks right up to the window to listen.

"You're just thinking with your shaft," Luce's muffled voice shouts in exasperated tones. "Once you have stuck it into her, you will soon get bored.

"Just let her stay for a little while-" Dohr complains.

"She's strange, Dohr. She never talks and she doesn't ever smile. She makes me uncomfortable."

"I noticed that," adds Orym. "What's wrong with her?"

"All those Zesti from that Spanish place are very strange," Dohr says conspiratorially. "I don't know why."

The word Zesti refers to any native American that is not of the Twelve Tribes.

"She's an outsider. She doesn't belong here. And she certainly doesn't belong with you. Take her back where you found her and throw her in the river."

"Ah Luce, go easy on the girl. She's not so bad. We can spare a little food," Orym says soothingly.

"I'm not cruel. I don't mind feeding her. But this is a small house, and if Dohr wants to keep a woman, then he must build her a house of his own. That is the way of things. But I hope you have sense enough to see that this girl will make no good wife to you."

Dohr snorts.

"I didn't say that I wanted her for a wife. She's pretty enough, but she's crazy. I just feel sorry for her, because she has nowhere else to go."

"I hope so. The girl is a suicide. You can't marry a girl like that. She can't make strong children."

"I know that."

"Can I have her if you don't want her?" asks Kahne.

"You're not up for that challenge yet," retorts Dohr.

"Yes, I am."

"Where is she anyway?" Orym asks.

"I don't know. She disappeared this afternoon. Maybe I should look for her."

"Forget it," says Luce. "It's dark now. You'll never find her. She's probably gone away anyway."

"I'll find her in the morning. I guess she's just used to wandering alone through the woods."

"Can we eat now?" Kahne shouts. "I'm hungry."

Esther now dreads going into the house even more, but the smell of food calls to her in no uncertain terms. She risks a peek through the window and sees Luce setting dinner upon the table. Esther hates Luce more than ever now, but her hunger is stronger than her pride and she takes a deep breath and enters the house. All heads turn to look at her, surprised. Dohr seems noticeably relieved.

"There you are!" Dohr exclaims. "We were just talking about sending out a search party."

She tries to smile, but it is a bitter grimace that crosses her face.

"Well, sit down," orders Luce. "We're eating now."

Esther takes a seat next to Dohr and sighs. She accepts a bowl of acorn mush and a piece of deer meat and dried salmon. Dinner is pretty much the same here every night and often poorly cooked, but she doesn't mind. She is becoming stronger and her trials in the forest seem just a distant memory.

Hawk 8'

Eagle moon

"Get up lazy. We're going to the battleground," Dohr shouts this morning, waking Esther up in the usual manner.

After a simple breakfast of stale acorn loaf and water, she is given some old clothes of Luce's to wear. Yesterday, she washed her dirty nightgown and it is still wet. Then they walk outside into the gloomy morning.

The battleground is a large open space that used to be a river bed, and has now been converted into a sort of gladiator stadium with large rings of sand surrounded by wooden benches. The soft sand makes it perfect for combat of all types, for it prevents contestants from killing each other through repeated falls. Several roofed areas contain equipment for training and there is also a raised platform from which the contests are organized and judged. It is to this one that Esther and Dohr first go. Dohr inquires about the day's competition from a man standing on the raised platform and frowns when he sees whom he is fighting.

"He's going to be tough," he mumbles to himself.

He goes to talk to a tall man sitting on the platform, and Esther takes the opportunity to watch the battle currently taking place. In the larger circle, two men fight with long, broad wooden swords, each trying to score points on the other by hitting them in sensitive areas. One wears green and one brown. Both men wear wooden helms on their heads. To make it more difficult, a third man throws small spears with blunt wooden tips at both of them. One of the spears hits its mark and the green man is momentarily stunned with the pain. Although not sharp, the spears are heavy and they can hurt. This gives the brown man the opportunity to swipe a blow at his head. The green man is knocked off balance and he falls to the ground. The brown man cheers and waves his sword in the air, just as a spear nails him right in the head, knocking him off balance. He also falls to the ground.

"The battle was over!" he shouts angrily and in obvious pain, picking himself up. "That was not a legal throw!"

An older man, who acts as referee, comes into the circle to talk to them both.

"I declare it a legal throw," the referee says. You were foolish to rejoice in your victory so soon. In a real battle, you would be dead. The match is a tie. Rematch in five minutes."

Cursing, the brown man leaves the ring. The green man laughs loudly. There are cheers from the assembled crowd, who have come to watch the battles.

"Why are they doing this?" Esther asks Dohr when he returns.

"We live in a dangerous land. Especially these days...it is good to be prepared."

"Wouldn't guns be more effective in a battle?"

"My people prefer the use of sword and arrow, except in dire need."

"Why?"

"Guns are not pleasing to the land. They are noisy, destructive, and the animals run away at the noise. And there is no honor in their use. I hunt with bow and arrow, the ancient way."

"What if you are in a fight with people with guns?"

"Our bows are the best in the land and our arrows can travel nearly as far as guns can, and more accurately. But if it is necessary to win a fight with guns, we will take them from the bodies of the soldiers that we have killed."

Now a second battle begins in the smaller ring. This battle is between two unarmed men, one wearing red and one wearing green.

They advance on each other, circling warily. Suddenly one man charges and tries to flip the other over onto his back. He gives a battle cry- He? No, Esther is mistaken. These are two women. Their hair has been pinned back for the fight and they are lean, slim and muscular, but they are definitely women. That was a woman's scream.

"Are those girls fighting?"

"Sure. Girls should learn to fight too. You never know when they might need it."

Esther thinks of the little girls fighting and has to agree with Dohr.

"They mostly stick to wrestling. Less pain. And all girls learn how to shove a knife into somebody who is causing them trouble."

Soon they are both on the ground in a tangle of arms and legs. Esther is about to move closer to the ring to investigate, when she is distracted by two boys, walking directly toward them. They both stare at her as they approach and they pretend not to see Dohr until they have slammed into him at full walking speed.

"Oh, excuse me," they say, laughing. "We did not see you."

"Because you are blind as a bat," he says, pushing them away.

They both appraise Esther again from a closer distance.

"This is my new friend," he says, in response to their glances.

"Where'd you get her?" a tall boy named Mika asks.

"I found her."

"Who is she?" asks a shorter, stockier boy named Karle.

"Stop staring at her. She's more woman than you could ever manage," Dohr shouts.

This insult causes Karle to attack Dohr playfully. Dohr easily deflects Karle's blows and puts him into a tight wrist lock. He forces Karle to the ground and shoves his head into the soil.

"Ji," shouts Karle, grimacing in pain.

Dohr releases him. Then they both bump their foreheads together lightly in the Hawk style of 'give me five'.

"You're going to sweep Hawk wrestling," Karle says, rubbing his arm and grimacing.

Two girls of similar age strut toward them. One of them is wearing the red shirt that symbolizes a contestant in the ring, and she is red-faced and sweaty. Esther realizes that she was one of the women competing just a few moments ago. As the girls swagger up to them, Esther is amazed at how tough and aggressive they seem. She has never seen women like these before. She wishes she could be like them.

"Did you see me destroy Wisa?" asks the red girl, whose name is Sua. "Wisa is regretting she ever called me a weakling now. I've advanced to the finals. Me and Jada."

"Jada is going to destroy you," Dohr says with a grin.

"I know."

"Hi Mika," the other girl, Loa, says coyly. "Give me a kiss."

Mika leans forward and plants one on her. She pulls away laughing.

"No tongue. I don't like you that much."

"That's not what you said during the Wolf moon," Mika retorts hotly.

"You're so stupid, Mika." Sua hits him playfully. "You can't hold her to that if it's said during the Wolf moon. Everyone knows that."

He shrugs and grins.

"Give me a kiss, Dohr," Sua says, lightly stroking his chest. "For good luck."

Dohr plants one on her. Like the other girl, she draws away as soon as he gets excited.

Sua suddenly notices Esther and gives her an appraising look.

"Who's the new girl, Dohr? If Jada catches you, you'll be in trouble."

"Jada had her chance. I don't care about her any more."

"You're the one who showed up at her door, drunk and begging on your knees." Sua laughs. "He was crying, 'I love you, Jada. I love you!'"

"I lost my mind momentarily. It was a Cougar moon. Kahn da kari."

Loosely translated, 'kahn da kari' means 'I'm over it'.

He seems to get sad for a moment, thinking of that day. But then he quickly recovers his focus.

"No time for stupid talk. I have to train."

"When do you fight?" asks Karle.

"I'm in the main circle as soon as the horse battles are over. I hate going after the horse battles, cause you have to roll around in whatever plop they fail to pick up."

The boys laugh.

"Well, I've got to train too," Mika says, and he swaggers off.

They go over to the ropes course, where several ropes are strung up all around the trees. Dohr goes up and down a few times just to warm up. Then he indicates for Esther to try it. She makes an attempt, but she is too weak in her upper arms to even begin.

"You're not even trying," he clucks.

The sky is dark and gloomy and it looks like it is going to rain again. Esther is in no mood to stand out in the rain and get wet. She has had enough of that to last for a lifetime. She is certainly not in the mood to climb about on ropes. So she just shrugs moodily and sits down on a log.

"I hope it doesn't rain till tonight," Dohr complains grumpily, staring at the sky. "I hate competing in the mud.

"Won't they cancel it?" she asks hopefully.

"They wouldn't cancel it if there was a lightning storm and the whole area was being peppered by lightning blasts. They would just say, "In real battle, you never know what to expect. It's just another obstacle to deal with."

Dohr goes up again and this time he stands upon a tall branch, ties a rope around his waist, and attaches it to a rope strung horizontally between several trees. Then he begins to climb hand over hand across the horizontal rope. Esther marvels at his strength, as he zips across the rope using only his hands. He does it until he is tired, and then he lets go and falls a few feet. Esther gasps, but the rope around his waist catches him. He dangles there a while, resting his arms. Then he clambers back up and makes his way back the way he came. Undoing the rope, he slides down.

"That looks hard," Esther says.

"That was just a warm up," he says with a shrug. "I don't want to tire out before I compete."

He motions for her to follow him to the main circle, and walks away in a puff of lingering body odor. After a short rest, he joins a few boys and men in his weight class who are lining up to begin Hawk wrestling. While they wait for the contest to begin, it begins raining. Not a light drizzle this time, but a solid rainfall.

After a few moments of complaining, the first two contestants enter the ring. At the invitation of the referee, they begin to pummel each other with body throws, punches, kicks, and violent wrestling moves. Meanwhile, Dohr moves around nervously, trying to keep himself in a state of excitement and adrenaline. Everyone becomes soaked, but nobody here seems to care. They ignore it as if it weren't raining at all.

After the first match is over, it is Dohr's turn to compete. He steps into the ring with a tall, muscular man a few years older than him. Dohr wears red and the other man green. It all happens quickly. The referee yells "fight!" and they circle each other warily. Dohr lunges - but it's a feint. The green man feints. Then suddenly they are locked in each other's iron grip, and they do a dance, trying to trip the other with a well-placed foot. Dohr goes in for a throw, but the green man does a counter, and Dohr is slammed to the ground. Quickly, he grabs Dohr's arm and uses his entire body to trap him in a painful arm lock. Dohr groans in pain, but he doesn't submit. He fights to escape. But pressure is steadily applied....

"Ji!" Dohr screams.

The green man gets up and struts off. Outside the circle, he butts heads with his friends. Dohr walks away, gloom and doom written all over his face. He walks to a solitary place and sits underneath a tree to sulk. He pulls out his throwing knife and angrily plunges it into the ground repeatedly.

"I couldn't get a grip on his body. I shouldn't have tried to do that kind of a move in the rain."

He throws the knife at a dead stump as hard as he can, but he is so agitated that he misses, and the knife disappears into a bush. This only makes him angrier.

Cursing, he rises to find the knife before he loses it. He spends a long time looking, but the knife is nowhere to be found. It must be buried in the earth somewhere. This sends Dohr into another rage. That was his best throwing knife, with which he has successfully hunted many small animals. That knife has power. He kicks up all the earth in a fury. But the earth has swallowed his knife. It is a telling sign.

"I will never be chosen as a Red Hawk candidate," he curses.

As he searches, he wonders what else he can do to make something of himself. He tries to resign himself to not ever becoming a Red Hawk. He will probably never attend the weekly council, where many important matters are discussed. He will not be famous for his deeds, as Red Hawks so often are.

Dohr thinks of his father. His father was passed over for training as a Red Hawk when he was a boy. His brother was chosen instead, and Luce told him that his father was very jealous of him. And his brother didn't even want to be a Red Hawk and quit after a few months of training! Orym finally made peace with it and became a master fisherman instead. The tribe was happy with him. Dohr will have to face the fact that he takes after his father. He will become a master hunter and the tribe will be happy with him too. Orym says that the people speak well of his ability to hunt deer. They say he has deer in his blood.

He wouldn't care so much if it were not for Jada. Despite what he said earlier, he is still in love with her. His plan was to rekindle their romance after he became a Red Hawk. But if he is not a Red Hawk, Jada will not want him. He had a dream about her last night, and now she is constantly on his mind. He won't admit that he loves her to anybody else, but he has to admit it to himself.

Last year, he and Jada had a brief but intense romance. They spent nearly every day together and they had wild, amazing sex nearly every night. He was deeply in love with her and it was the best three months of his life. They talked about marriage and she told him that she wanted to have his baby.

And then it was over. He can still picture that day clearly. They were in the commons, buying food from the visiting Beaver tribe on a very busy day during the harvest month. He was haggling with a woman over the price of corn, when suddenly the woman leaned over and asked him a question.

"Who is that beautiful woman over there? She is so beautiful, I can hardly stand to look at her."

Dohr looked over, and saw that she was talking about Jada.

"She's my girlfriend," he said proudly.

"You think she is *yours*?" the woman responded, with a little smile.

Dohr looked at Jada again, who was having a conversation with Camo, the Red Hawk. She kept touching him on the arm and laughing at whatever he said.

"Yes," Dohr said arrogantly. "She is."

The woman shrugged, as if to say that Dohr can believe anything he wants but that doesn't make it true.

Irritated, Dohr walked away to barter with another corn seller instead. But he could not stop staring at Camo and Jada. They were standing very intimately and she kept touching him. Suddenly, she kissed him on the cheek. He whispered something in her ear. She laughed and looked him deeply in the eyes. Dohr walked over to break up the conversation and her smile dropped upon seeing him. That moment he knew it was over. He could see it in her eyes. They had a big argument later that night and she told him that she liked Camo. Dohr was devastated. He moped for weeks. Life lost all fun. The entire fall season passed him by.

She was involved with Camo for a while and then she was involved with another Red Hawk after that. And that was when Dohr realized that Jada likes Red Hawks. She has been with many men and the only one who was not a Red Hawk was Dohr.

Because we had a special connection. If I were a Red Hawk, she would marry me.

The thought pops into his head and it makes him depressed again. Would she take him back if he was a Red Hawk? How will he ever find out? Certainly not after his terrible performance in the tournament today.

"Kahn da kari," he mutters, and walks back to the battlegrounds.

Esther follows Dohr back to his house, keeping several steps behind him. He is depressed and moody and she tries to stay out of his way. She feels like he doesn't want her around right now and that scares her. He is her protector. Were it not for his good graces, she would be pitched out of the house, and then she would have nowhere to go. The idea scares her, and she realizes that little has changed. She convinced herself that she was safe, because she found a place to stay and a friendly family to take care of her. But now she realizes that she is still in great danger. She is still an ignorant girl alone in a big, wide world.

She watches Dohr walk ahead of her and notices how attractive he is. She imagines him as her knight, who rescued her from the river. In the old tales she has heard, he is supposed to fall in love with her after rescuing her. If he falls in love with her, then he would build her a house like Luce said.

But she cannot forget that Dohr said she was 'crazy'. He told his mother that he didn't like her. As they reach the house, Esther makes a decision. She'll have to stop being 'crazy'. She'll have to be a normal girl. She'll have to please his mother too, so she will speak good of her. And then they won't pitch her out into the forest to fend for herself, when they eventually grow tired of her. If she becomes normal, perhaps Dohr will even want her to marry her.

Hawk 12'

**Swan moon*

There is a celebration tonight at the commons and the house is in great excitement. Everyone dresses in their finest furs and adorns themselves with necklaces of hawk talons and feathers. Esther sits by the fire in her stained nightgown, waiting for them to get ready and wishing she had something else to wear. She is painfully aware that her dirty, shapeless nightgown is not flattering on her and makes people stare at her strangely.

"Not only is it the full moon, but Mars entered the Hawk sign yesterday," Dohr explains to Esther excitedly, as they sit around the table nibbling on some bread. "That means the great Hawk will be very powerful and we will become powerful through him. Having the sun, Mercury, and Mars in the Hawk sign gives great strength to our tribe."

"What is the Hawk sign?" she asks. "Is it a spirit?"

He stares at her for a second, and then keeps on talking as if he realizes that she was only joking.

"I only have two planets in Hawk, but I have five in fire."

He grabs his little brother and puts him into a playful wrestling hold.

"My little brother has a Bear moon. He's a little crybaby, isn't he? Wah, wah Kahney. Want your blankee? He always did like to cry."

Kahne squiggles around so he can look at Esther.

"Dohr was playing with his shaft yesterday and dreaming of you."

For his sass, Kahne gets a whack to the head that sends him sprawling. Orym laughs as Kahne lands in a heap on the floor.

"Shouldn't antagonize your brother until you're big enough to fight him," Luce admonishes.

Kahne just shrugs it off.

"Kahn da kari."

There is silence for a while. Orym gets up and throws more wood on the fire and Luce hangs another pot of tea above it. And then they just sit there, staring at the fire. Orym pulls out a knife and starts whittling a piece of wood. Kahne sees his father doing that and he pulls out a little knife and does the same.

"Have you heard anything about..." Dohr asks, breaking the silence.

"Mmmm?" says Orym.

"The new candidates for the Red Hawk training."

Orym looks away and stares at the fire. But his eyes betray him. He knows something.

"I'm not going to be chosen, am I?"

"Not this year."

"I don't understand," Dohr says in a quiet voice. "Why do they keep passing me up?"

Orym shrugs, but his eyes are slits.

"Tell him, Orym," urges Luce. "He should know the truth."

"You have not won enough battle tournaments to be considered as a Red Hawk. It is said that you started training too late. It was Thoff himself who told me this. He told me last year."

There is a painful silence.

"But nothing is certain," mumbles Orym.

"In that case, I must accept that I will never be chosen. I am sixteen years old this month. It is too late for me."

"What is wrong with being a hunter?" asks Orym. "A hunter is a noble profession." Orym puts down his whittling for a moment and looks Dohr in the eyes. "Dohr, there is more to life than fighting and Red Hawks are not the only important people in our tribe. It only seems that way, because our chief is a Red Hawk and he has made the Red Hawks more influential than before."

Dohr stands up and walks out of the house. Orym and Luce look at each other with pained expressions.

"I remember the day he told us he wanted to be a Red Hawk," Luce says quietly. "I wanted to talk him out of it, but you insisted that he could do it and you told him that you would train him yourself. I knew that was a big mistake and I should have said something, but I didn't want to hurt your feelings."

Orym startles, as if stung by a bee, and then glares at his wife.

"You are a good father, Orym, but you are stubborn. What did you know about training him to become a Red Hawk? All you accomplished was to get him excited about it, when you knew all along there was little chance. He's just not big enough or fierce enough."

"Size does not matter," Orym insists. "And the boy has a great spirit. He should have been chosen. The problem is there was nobody to speak of him to the council. There are no Red Hawks in the family and it is all decided by influence these days."

"But he has never done the right things to catch the eyes of the Red Hawk Council," Luce goes on relentlessly. "In his life, he has never won a major tournament in the battle grounds. Never killed a bear all by himself. These victories are more important than words."

They stop arguing when Dohr suddenly steps into the room.

"Kahn da kari!" he shouts loudly. "Let us speak no more of it."

"Are you good?" asks Luce.

"I have made a decision. If I am not chosen on this new moon, then I will give up my foolish dreams and settle down to an occupation within my reach."

"Smart lad," says Orym, pounding him on the back.

As the sun sets, Esther follows the family down the path toward the commons. By the time they arrive, dinner is almost ready. Several spits have been set up and many different meats are slowly roasting, competing to see which can smell the best. A barrel of a strong wine has been opened and all hands are fighting to fill their wooden cups.

Dohr brings Esther a hard fought glass. Esther stares at the wine greedily. It seems like an age since she had a glass of wine. She grabs it, toasts him, and then takes a deep, deep drink. As the wine burns down her throat, she sighs with relief, as that pleasant tipsy feeling comes.

Dohr stares at her, surprised, as she drains her glass.

"The girl can drink. Impressive. You want another?"

"Yes," she says, happy that she has found something that impresses him.

He grabs her glass and runs off. It takes him some time to get the glass full again. By the time he returns, dinner is ready. Soon their plates are filled with deer, duck, quail meat, cormorant eggs, and roasted wild mushrooms, and they eat and drink until they're quite stuffed.

After dinner, the cooking fires are allowed to die, and the main fire is stoked up until it is a bonfire. The Hawk tribe loves huge bonfires - really big ones that soar sky high and spit sparks all over the place and cast bright light over everything. All the men get involved with gathering wood and soon a glorious blaze is going. Esther is afraid that they will burn down the forest, but everything is so wet here that it is probably not a real danger.

The tribe all gathers around the fire reverently and glories in its violent beauty. The flames seem to shoot all the way to the sky and the whole commons is bathed in an unearthly bright glow. Sparks fly everywhere, and when they come toward Esther, she fears that she will get burnt and covers her face protectively. For a long time nobody says a word. The only noise is the loud crackling of the burning logs, as everyone falls into a trance.

After a long wait, the fire finally dies down into a huge circle of bright coals. Men with long redwood poles begin to smooth out the surface of the great burning pit, creating an even field of bright red coals. Esther thinks it looks like the road to hell, paved with red hot stones that cast an eerie glow over everything.

A man stands up to address the crowd.

"That's our chief," Dohr whispers to Esther. "Jath, the Red Hawk."

Esther can not make him out too well, as he stands in the shadow. But she can hear him fine.

"My people, we are gathered here to pay tribute to the Great Hawk," he shouts out. "He came to the people in the form of a great red hawk, born of fire, heat and light. And he spoke to the ancient ones, telling them many things. He led them to great victories in battle and taught them wisdom. He speaks of justice, strength and mastery. Mastery! What is mastery? It is purity of will. What is strength but to be gentle, even in war? What is justice but to have honor?"

He raises his hands in the air.

"We will cleanse our spirits in this great fire, to demonstrate our purity of spirit. If we are pure of heart when we cross, then we will not get burned. If we falter on the way, our feet will blister and we will feel it the next day."

And then the chief steps forward. He stands before the bright red road and breathes deeply and slowly. Someone begins to pound a hand drum slowly. For a long time the chief stands like that, not moving. He is stripped down completely naked, from the head to the feet. Then he takes a deep, deep breath and begins to walk. He walks quickly, but he does not run. Halfway across a cry escapes his lips, a cry that grows in volume until it is a piercing yell that send chills to all hearts. And then he stands on the other side, his legs shaking. Everyone cheers loudly. He is congratulated in the typical style of the Hawk tribe. He bashes his chest violently into his friend, and then throws his arms around him, turning it into a manly hug.

Many more line up to cross the fire. Bravely, with maximum machismo, is the way of these people. Each journey has its own drama. Some yell a piercing battle cry as they cross. Some cross slowly, to endure maximum pain, breathing as calmly as they can to prove their bravery. Nobody runs across - like a scared one. Everyone gets a chest-bashing hug at the end, from the person who last crossed.

Of course, Dohr tries to get Esther to do it, but she refuses. Eventually the burning coals slowly lose their bright red glow and become orange, and he tries again.

"Now," Dohr urges. "It isn't as hot as before."

She stares at him and suddenly realizes that this is the kind of thing that she needs to do if she wants him to like her. With her heart hammering in her chest, she nods assent slowly. He grins and leads her to the edge of the coals. Everyone cheers, recognizing that this is her first time. She stares around at the encouraging faces. She feels something welling up inside her, some kind of pride, and before she knows it she is walking across the burning hot coals.

The whole world comes down to her feet. Her feet are so hot, they are one with the fire, but she feels no burning pain. The journey seems to last forever, but in moments she is across. A woman pulls Esther into her arms and whispers her congratulations. Esther feels high and excited. She walked across fire! She looks back at Dohr, who is grinning at her. She smiles back at him and feels prouder than she has ever felt in her life.

The party soon moves to the assembly house, where there will be drumming and dancing. Those who are young and have lots of energy go there, while the older ones go home. Esther stands by the fire, wondering where Dohr went. She last saw him talking to a girl and showing off for her. But now she doesn't see him anywhere. She is too shy to go to the assembly house by herself, so she just hangs by the small fires that are still blazing and savors the dregs of the night's excitement.

Eventually, she borrows a torch and makes her way back to the house by herself. Orym and Luce have already come home, and she can see them sitting by the fire, wrapped in each other's arms. She waits outside for a while, giving them their space. She has a feeling that they don't get much privacy and she doesn't want to be considered a nuisance. Later, she peaks through the window and sees them having sex by the fire. Embarrassed, she returns to her dark vigil under the trees. Finally, they walk outside and go into their own sleeping hut, and Esther gratefully walks inside. She curls up in her little corner, hidden by shadows, and falls asleep.

Hawk 13'

The next day, Dohr wakes her with his usual charm.

"Get up lazy."

Esther rises without complaint. After a quick breakfast, he leads her out the door and moves her along at his rapid pace. He carries a large sack with him, but will not say what is inside. Today they go to visit two small roundhouses that are completely covered in earth. Smoke issues from the ceiling.

"The women say that you may enter their sweat lodge."

"What is it?"

"You do not know what a sweat lodge is? How could you not know that?"

"I have heard the name before."

"Just take off your clothes and go inside. You'll find out soon enough."

He walks away, but then suddenly turns around and walks back.

"It is customary to gather wood when you enter to keep the fire going," he explains. "It's raining a bit, so you have to find wet wood and put it into that little hut over there to dry. Then you can take dry wood from there."

She watches him do just that. Then he takes off his own clothes and crawls through a tunnel into the men's sweat lodge, pushing his pile of dry wood in front of him. Esther does the same and then crawls fully clothed into the woman's sweat lodge and peeks her head inside. The sweat lodge is built inside a large pit that is dug three feet below the earth. A large fire burns in the center of the room and smoke rises through a small hole in the roof. It is so smoky that she cannot see anything at first, but she can smell the smoke and the strong odor of stale perspiration. When her eyes adjust, she sees several naked women sitting on wooden benches, rubbing the sweat off their bodies with some sort of bone.

Esther crawls back out and quickly takes off her clothes. She hungers for that heat with every pore of her body. Then she reenters with her pile of dry wood and throws it onto the fire. Now that she is completely inside, a blast of heat engulfs her, and her entire body goes "Ahhhhhhhhh". As soon as she sits down on a bench, she feels her tight and sore muscles slowly relax and unwind. The heat works itself into every pore of her body and every fiber of her being.

At first, the sweat is very pleasant. Esther guesses that she has never perspired this much in her entire life. Her eyes sting from the salt and she wipes at them constantly. She is dripping wet and her head spins like a top. But soon the heat becomes overpowering, and she is afraid that she is going to pass out. There is a lack of oxygen inside this smoky cave and she has to keep her head down low to breathe at all. Finally she can stand it no longer. She stumbles across sweaty legs and feet until she gets to the crawl space and then she crawls out into the cool afternoon. Taking deep breaths, she fights the dizziness that threatens to drop her to the ground. After it subsides to a slight nausea, she sinks to a sitting position in the grass. There she sits for some time. She notices that nobody else has come outside, although they have been in there much longer than she.

Esther goes back inside, until she can again stand it no longer. By that time her body feels light and refreshed and her muscles are loose and supple. She is ready to take a nap. But first she must bathe in the river like all of the other women are doing or else she will stink.

She walks toward the river, feeling immune to the cold although she walks naked. It is raining slightly, but she cannot feel it. She stands before the river a long time, trying to get up the courage to jump in. Finally, she jumps feet first into the chilly water. Then she quickly climbs out and jumps up and down until she is warm again.

Dohr lies on his side, rubbing his body with a bone. Six men across from him take turns fanning the fire toward him and five other men on his team. They are trying to drive his team outside by making it too hot for them to stand. They have ten minutes to drive someone on Dohr's team outside and then his team gets ten minutes to send the heat in the opposite direction and drive them out. The winner is the last team to go outside. Dohr is good at this game. He can stand a lot of heat. But then all of these men are good also. During the winter, they spend almost every day of their lives inside the sweathouse. It is second nature to them.

Dohr has a special need for the sweat today. He is going hunting this afternoon. The sweat lodge serves many uses for the hunter. Most importantly, it cleanses the body of human scent. The bone scrapes off all the sweat and then the hunter jumps into the river to wash off. Then he goes back inside to sweat out more odor until he is entirely cleansed. When the hunter throws sage and green fir branches onto the fire, it adds the scent of the forest to the hunter. If he is downwind, no animal will be able to sense him by scent. The sweat lodge is also considered good for gathering spiritual power. Dohr will spend all morning inside, eating nothing, so by this afternoon he will be calm, relaxed and ready to kill something.

Esther finds Dohr an hour later, preparing his bow and arrows. His bow is a sturdy yew branch wrapped tightly with animal sinew. The sinew is attached with glue made from sturgeon bladders and Dohr touches up a few loose strands with some freshly made glue. He uses arrows with obsidian points usually, although a few of his arrows are merely wooden shafts that have been sharpened. Hawk feathers are set on the tail of all of his arrows and he touches them up with the glue, making sure they stay on tight.

"Are you going hunting?"

"Yes," he says, not looking up from his work.

"Can I come and watch?"

Now he looks up, and his expression is not friendly.

"Absolutely not."

"I'll do whatever you say."

"It would be bad luck to take you along. Besides, you move too slow."

Esther watches him work a few more minutes and then she leaves him alone.

Hawk 14'

Wolf moon

"Dohr," says Luce from out of the blue, "when is that girl going to leave?"

Dohr and Luce are working in the smokehouse, cleaning the deer that he killed yesterday, washing all the organs and separating the meat. The table is covered in blood and bits and pieces of organs, flesh and hair. The head of the deer lies on the table, staring mindlessly up at the ceiling from cloudy, sightless eyes. As Dohr stokes up the fire so he can start making jerky, he looks up from his work and stares at his mother.

"Why does she have to leave?"

"She cannot stay in our house forever. There isn't enough space." She glares at him, trying to decide what his intentions are. "Haven't you had your fun yet? I hope you are not in love with her. You've always had a soft spot for hard luck girls."

"Just like my father," Dohr thinks, although he says nothing.

"How long do you expect us to take care of her?"

Dohr sighs, exasperated that he has to explain things to his mother that she should understand very well.

"She is an escaped slave, with no knowledge of the real world. You cannot just cast her out. She cannot take care of herself. She'll die."

"She won't die. She'll be fine."

As they talk, Luce begins to wash the intestines of the deer in a wooden bucket of water. She will use them to make sausages and sell them in the market.

"She'll die," he insists.

"If she cannot take care of herself, there is nothing you can do for her. She's not your responsibility. What will you do, care for her like a pet for the rest of your life?"

"Let her stay till the new moon," he insists. "I'll teach her to survive. Then at least she'll be able to take care of herself until she finds something permanent."

Luce sighs. It is her turn to be exasperated with her son. But deep in her heart, she knows that he is right.

"Until the new moon then. But that's it."

That night at dinner, there is an ugly fight between Orym and Luce. It seems that Orym was paying a little too much attention to a beautiful woman almost half his age and Luce caught him giving her a little kiss at the commons.

"Ach! One kiss! So what?"

"You slept with that little slut, didn't you?"

"No!"

"Don't you lie to me! I know you better than that. You can't keep your hands to yourself."

"It was just a little kiss. She was flirting with me all morning as I was trying to sell my fish oil and finally she kissed *me*!"

"Liar!" she hisses.

And she suddenly throws the entire wooden plate of greasy fish and potatoes at him. The plate smacks him in the head. He stands up angrily and there are fish pieces in his hair and beard. He stares at her fiercely, chest heaving. A piece of fish hangs from his hair, right in front of his eyes, and then falls to the table with a little splat.

He grabs his chair and smashes it into the wall, his chest heaving with anger. Then he dumps the table over, spilling everyone's dinner all over the floor. For a moment, Luce seems a bit frightened, but then she recovers her nerve and stares him down bravely.

"Go on, hit me, you cheating fool! Hit me!"

There is a long moment of silence. Esther looks at Dohr nervously, but he seems unfazed by the outburst, as if he is used to such things. Kahne only stares down at his feet, trying to suppress a smile. Orym finally leaves the house, cursing loudly to himself. A moment later, Luce goes out the door herself, leaving the house in shambles.

As soon as they are gone, Dohr and Kahne start laughing uproariously. They slap each other on the back and try to speak, but no words come. Dohr keeps trying to point out all the funny moments that just passed, but he is laughing so hard that he cannot finish a single thought.

"Did you see Father with the fish in his hair?" roars Kahne, when he is finally able to talk.

The laughter relieves the tension in the room. Esther takes a deep breath and tries to laugh along.

"Well, dinner's ruined. Guess I'll just go along to the commons," Dohr says, tearing off a piece of bread that is not covered in dirt and mopping up some spilled fish grease sticking to a plate. "Be careful. Wolf moon is here."

He goes out the door, leaving the two of them sitting amid the ruins of what was once a good dinner.

Hawk 17'

Owl moon

"Wake up lazy," Dohr says, tickling Esther's nose with a feather until she grabs it out of his hand. "We're going to the battlegrounds."

Esther rises dutifully and has some tea and hard bread, before following Dohr outside. It is drizzling once again and the sky is steel grey. She shivers and buries her cold hands into the folds of her nightgown. She begins to dream about the sweat lodge, and decides to sneak off as soon as possible and go there.

"Why do you always go to the battlegrounds on rainy days?" she asks.

"The moon is on fire," he responds. "There are always battle tournaments when the moon is on fire. It has nothing to do with rain." He stares up at the sky. "And besides, this is no rain. This is just a few drops. I bet the sun comes out by the afternoon."

Dohr goes immediately to the board, to see when he is competing. His face falls when he sees that he is not scheduled to compete. It seems a bad omen. It seems to suggest that they have forgotten about him already, because he is not under consideration any longer for the Red Hawk. He goes to talk to one of the organizers, who apologizes and places him into a tournament. He writes Dohr's name in red chalk on a piece of wood with a nail in it and then sticks it to the board underneath the banner of Feather Wrestling.

Dohr sighs. The Feather Wrestling tournament is mainly for the older men and women who are not warriors. No arm bars, chokes or anything useful in a real fight are allowed. It is considered good exercise and good spiritual practice, but not training for battle. Nobody ever watches Feather Wrestling. But Dohr doesn't say anything. To complain would show that he is desperate, which he does not want to seem. He'll just have to do what he was given.

The Red Hawks are training in the battlegrounds today and Dohr brings Esther over to watch. A crowd has gathered around them to watch a practice called Steel Flesh. One person stands completely still, while his partner beats him with a sword. He will hit him with the flat part five times at full strength and then he will hit him with the sharp edge just a little more softly five times. It is designed to make the body so hard, that an enemies weapon will just bounce off harmlessly. Esther watches in amazement. She is sure that just one hit from the sharp edge of a sword would slice a deep wound into her, yet these boys remain unbloodied. After the sword flogging, they are still not finished. Next they stab each other with arrows. Esther watches a man sit there stone faced, while his partner tries to stick an arrow into his skin. Each poke leaves a tiny red dot, but none pierces his skin.

Dohr watches Toyi, a boy he used to terrorize when they were younger, get hit with a sword over and over. He never flinches nor cries out. How different he looks now! No longer a skinny boy with a stupid expression of fear, he is now extremely strong, tall and focused. Dohr wonders if Toyi plans to get revenge on him some day for his childish pranks. He wonders if Toyi could take him now.

Toyi never was much of a fighter. Dohr wonders jealously why Toyi was chosen to be a Red Hawk and not himself. Probably because Toyi's father was a Red Hawk.

"They're so brave," Esther exclaims in amazement.

"They are well trained."

"Look at that one," she marvels, pointing at Toyi. "He's just a boy."

Dohr grunts but says nothing. Then Toyi finishes taking his own beating and starts to beat on his partner.

"How do they do that?"

"It takes years of practice to do Steel Flesh," Dohr explains. "You toughen the flesh up a little bit at a time, until it is as strong as steel. They do all sorts of things. They roll around in rough sand. Beat themselves with rocks. Do belly flops into the water. And they have secrets too. There are special ways of breathing to make themselves stronger. A few of the great ones can take an arrow shot from a bow and not get wounded. I've seen it myself."

"Can they take a bullet?"

"Nobody has ever tried."

Esther nods and continues to stare at them with stars in her eyes. Dohr shakes his head and walks away. Girls always have a thing for Red Hawks. They are so predictable. He tries to fight down the jealousy and scorn that fills his heart. He goes to the ropes course and climbs up and down ropes until he is too exhausted to feel much of anything.

Hawk 19'

Elk moon

Dohr takes Esther upriver this morning. They walk many miles, over rocks and fallen trees, and through endless groves of redwoods. Esther marvels at Dohr's surefooted skill. He never seems to trip over logs or holes like she does, but dances over the rocks like a deer. Esther lags behind, and he has to keep stopping to wait for her. But he is more patient than usual, because he is doing this for her.

"Where are we going?" she asks several times.

"To teach you to survive," is all he says.

He carries nothing with him but a knife and a little hemp sack. He will show her how to survive with as little as possible. Along the way, he points out edible plants that she can eat and roots that she can dig out of the ground. Each plant has its own story to tell. The cattail roots can be eaten once they reach a certain size and density, but they are ruined once the first flowers bloom. The nettles can be eaten when small, but not when they are big. And they must be chewed a certain way or they will sting the mouth. Milk thistle must be eaten a certain way to avoid the sharp thorns. Wild mustard must be eaten when it is young and tender. Wild carrot, radish, and parsnip cannot be eaten till they are older and can be easily identified, or they might turn out to be the poisonous wild hemlock. There is a dizzying amount of information for her to absorb. She tries her best, but it all looks the same to her. She cannot tell the difference between the edible mushrooms and the poisonous mushrooms. She cannot remember which root is medicinal and which is food. Or which cannot be eaten at all. Soon Dohr has a sack full of plants, roots and mushrooms, and Esther cannot tell them apart.

"Of course, this is all rabbit food. You can live on this stuff, but it isn't very tasty and not very filling. In order to live well, you must learn to hunt and fish."

Dohr picks up a long branch and shows her how to whittle it to a fine point. He gives her the knife and shows her how to whittle, so she can do it by herself.

"Why are you showing me this?" she asks him.

"Because you need to learn to survive...because you cannot stay at my house forever."

Esther is very quiet for a long time.

"I understand," she finally says in a meek voice.

"Come now, don't be such a mouse," he retorts. "You need to be strong to survive in this world. This is not the mission any longer. Nobody will make decisions for you now."

"Easy for you to say. You have a family and a home and a tribe. I have nobody."

"Yes, but that just means that you must try harder. Whining will not help you. Nobody is going to hand you a new life in a bowl just because you whine about how you have nobody. You must fight for it. We must all fight for what we want."

Dohr trails off, thinking of his own situation. That advice also applies to him. Because he never got any breaks in his attempts to become a Red Hawk, that just means that he must fight harder to make a name for himself. He is quiet until he finishes the spear.

Dohr shows Esther how to hold the spear and stand as still a tree in the water. He shows her how to stab quickly and definitely, and he describes the angle and force that she should use.

"We sometimes use this to stun the fish," Dohr says, showing her some crushed root. "This will poison the fish and then you can kill them easily."

"Won't that make the fish poisonous to eat?"

"If that were true, do you think I'd use it?"

Dohr wades out into the water with the spear.

"Come on. Follow me in. This is a good place to catch one. It is a shallow pool, with very little water flow and many fish in it. The poison will work well here."

Esther hikes up her nightgown and ties it into a knot, and then she steps into the water. The water is icy cold and she quickly steps out again.

"Come now. Suck it up. Get in here," he orders.

Esther takes a deep breath and braves the cold water. She shivers involuntarily as she stands next to Dohr. Dohr hands her the spear and Esther tries not to shake from the cold as she holds it.

"Don't expect anything too interesting this time of year," he says. "But there are a few squimms swimming about."

He throws some fish poison into the river and they wait. They stand there awhile, waiting for the poison to work. Suddenly Dohr takes the spear from her and stabs it forcefully into the water. When he pulls it out of the water, a little fish wiggles upon it. Smiling, he throws the fish onto the bank. He hands the spear back to Esther, but her feet are numb and she has to step out of the river to warm them.

"You need to toughen up."

"I know. I know. I am a mouse," she says grumpily. "So what?"

"We're not leaving till you catch something," Dohr says with a smile.

It takes her several attempts until she finally catches a little squimm. She catches it because the poison finally works. A stunned fish floats to the surface and she is able to scoop it up with her hand. Dohr isn't looking, so she spears the fish onto the stick, and pretends that she speared it. Dohr is proud of her and he congratulates her. She cleans the fish and they roast it over a small fire along with three squimms that Dohr catches. Her own fish is the best she has ever eaten.

Hawk 24'

Cougar moon

Dohr continues his survival instruction today. Today's lesson is in hunting small animals. He shows her how to find gopher holes and spear them with a sharp stick. Esther laughs, thinking that she can now hunt as well as the little boy who first showed her this trick.

"You can catch many small animals in these holes. If you are lucky, you will get a fat rabbit. But they usually go too deep to be speared with a stick. Mice and rodents are possible."

Esther tentatively thrusts the stick into the hole and pulls it out. Dohr shakes his head and takes it from her. He shows her how to thrust it hard and quickly. She tries again, but her thrust is still too light.

"You won't kill it if you don't thrust hard. You'll just push it deeper into its hole."

She nods and tries again.

"There, look at that hawk," he says, pointing at the sky.

They watch a hawk soar gracefully above the trees. It seems to soar without a care in the world. Suddenly, the hawk plummets to the earth at top speed and disappears into the trees.

"A perfect example of what I am saying. The hawk flies along, thinking of nothing, until it sees prey. Then it strikes without hesitation. It hits hard with its whole body and spirit focused on the prey and the strike. That is the way of the Red Hawk. It is the only way to hunt."

A few minutes later, a brown bird flies right past them at top speed, coming close enough to Esther to make her jump. Right on its tail is a large hawk. The bird tries to evade the hawk, but the hawk does lightning fast swoops and rolls and stays on its tail. They fly into the brush together and there is a furious tussle. Then the hawk emerges triumphant, something in his mouth, and flies away.

"That will teach you to steal a hawk's food," Dohr says, laughing at the poor brown bird. "Did you see that? Hawks don't like to share."

He sets Esther to work spearing holes again. Esther spears her first gopher in a small hole near the river. The small animal appears on her stick, wiggling and bleeding. She is shocked by the little taste of death and she just stares at it.

"Why don't you kill it already? Bash it against a rock."

Esther throws the stick against a tree, but she misses and the poor little gopher ends up on the ground. So Esther takes a stick and hits it upon the head until it is dead. She feels cruel for beating the little thing to death, but she is glad that she knows how to do this. Better it than her! After it is dead, Dohr catches one more. Then he shows her how to cook them.

"It's too small to skin or de-bone. So you just spear it on a stick and cook it whole. And then you can scrape off the fur and eat it right off the stick."

He shows Esther how to make a fire, using a thick piece of cedar, some kindling, and a wooden stick. She spins the stick rapidly back and forth in a depression in the cedar, but she cannot get even a small spark. Dohr eventually has to do it himself and he just tells her to keep practicing until she can do it. Then they cook the little gophers over the small fire and eat them off the stick. They are good to eat after all, although one gopher is a meager meal.

"In two days you must leave," Dohr tells her as they walk back home. "I'm sorry. Luce says that there is not enough room."

Esther just looks down at her feet. She has to accept the fact that Dohr doesn't want her. He is not going to marry her and build her a house.

"Where will you go?" he asks.

She shrugs. She doesn't know.

"Where do you want to go?"

"I want to stay here."

"You cannot stay at my house."

"I could build my own house and you could teach me how to take care of myself."

He sighs. This is not easy. The poor girl has nobody and she doesn't understand the way things are.

"Soon the people will leave here for the Spring Camp, where we will live outdoors in huts until the end of summer. I will be too busy to care for you then. I plan to go on a long hunting trip many miles away. Because you are not one of the Twelve Tribes, you cannot come and live with us unless you are adopted by the tribe. And that will not happen unless you marry a boy in the tribe or you have skills that we need."

Esther fixes her matted hair, smoothes out her dirty nightgown and tries to look as attractive as possible.

"I could be a good wife," she tells him. "With a little practice."

He stops walking and stares at her, surprised. She gives her most charming smile, touches his arm and stares at him with hopeful eyes. He just stares at her, feeling more sorry for her than ever.

"I'm...in love with another," he says quietly. "It is not possible. Sorry."

He walks on in silence, feeling very sorry for her. This woman is pretty enough, but she is not at all his type. Dohr likes girls like Jada and Wisa. The kind of girl he could wrestle with in bed before he slips her the shaft. The kind of girl that could handle a twenty mile hike over difficult terrain without complaining, and then have enough energy left over for some wild sex. This one is thin and weak, and he is not sure how sane she is.

He doubts that she would have a chance of being adopted by his tribe for the same reason. She has been among the Spanish too long and there is an odor of 'slave' about her. Dohr is pretty sure that none of the people in his village would respect her and therefore she would be turned down. He has only to look at Luce's attitude toward her for proof of that.

"I'm sorry," he says again, and there is nothing left to say.

"And that is how it is," Esther says quietly to herself, as they walk home in silence. "I'll catch gophers and live in the woods by myself."

Dohr cannot stop thinking about Jada. He saw her this evening in the commons, and ever since then, he has felt a pain in his chest that won't go away. He can feel his last chance slipping away to become a Red Hawk, and with it goes his last chance to get the girl of his dreams. He curses the Cougar moon for giving him these weak, sentimental thoughts, but they just won't go away. Finally, he rises from his seat by the fire. He cannot just sit around and do nothing.

"Where are you going?" Luce asks, as he opens the door. "Dinner is ready."

"I am going to talk to Thoff."

"Thoff?" asks Orym incredulously.

"Yes," Dohr shouts, already out the door.

A short time later, Dohr knocks at the door of Thoff's fine house. Thoff is a prominent and wealthy member of the Hawk tribe. He is a Red Hawk, a member of the Hawk council of elders, and a very rich man. If anyone can help him, Thoff can. The problem is that Dohr can think of no reason why Thoff would want to help him. But desperation knows no shame and Dohr stands before his door anyway.

His eldest son, Moi, opens the door and stares at Dohr, surprised. Dohr knows Moi well. He beat him in the wrestling match a few days ago and then Moi accused him of cheating. The referee ruled in Dohr's favor, and Moi was absolutely furious. Now the two foes exchange cool glances as they stare at each other.

"I am here to see Thoff."

"Why?"

"There is a quick matter I wish to discuss with him."

"Thoff is busy," he says frostily, and begins to close the door.

"This is important. My father sent me."

Dohr regrets the lie, but it is the first thing that comes to mind, and it makes Moi hesitate. His father would be very angry if Moi refused a caller with important business. As much as he would like to slam the door in Dohr's face, caution prevails. He waves peevishly for Dohr to enter, and goes to tell his father about the visitor.

Thoff sits by the fireplace after dinner, sipping a glass of wine and smoking a pipe. At this time of the year, a personal stash of wine is a very expensive luxury. It shows a man with money to burn and exclusive trading rights. Here is a perfect example of the power and influence of a Red Hawk. Dohr's father couldn't get a glass of wine this time of the year if he saved up for months. The best he can do right now is a cup of vapors at the public house.

Vapors is a homemade vodka, which is rubbed upon the chest and inhaled as vapors. It is mainly used as medicine. However, it often serves the man who needs a drink when the wine runs out.

Thoff looks up, surprised to see Orym's son standing before him. He is aware that Moi is angry that Dohr beat him and tried to make him out to be a cheater. Could this be the purpose of his visit?

"Hello Dohr."

"Hello Thoff. I am sorry for the late night intrusion."

Thoff waves it away, as if it is of no import.

"I assume it is warranted. Speak."

Dohr glances at Moi, who stares at him sourly.

"Can we speak in private?"

Thoff nods.

"Moi, will you give us a few minutes?"

Moi gives Dohr a venomous glance as he leaves the room. Thoff waves haphazardly in his direction, telling Dohr to ignore his son. Then Thoff fixes his gaze on Dohr and waits for him to speak.

"I came because you are a member of the Red Hawk council," Dohr says nervously. "I am turning sixteen years old this year and I have not been considered as a candidate for the Red Hawks. Yet I have a good tournament record and have studied the disciplines diligently. I would like to know if there is anything I can do to...to become a Red Hawk."

Thoff turns back to the fire. This is an annoying request. What does Dohr expect him to do? Ask the council to add him to the list just because Dohr begs him to? The boy knows that he is not considered, and he is too old to begin training. Thoff is about to ask him to leave, but he stops himself. Thoff bears some love for his father, Orym, who was a good friend in the days of their boyhood. Although they are not too close now, he wants to do well by his son. He knows that Orym did not - would not - send the rash boy here, but he would appreciate Thoff giving the boy some advice anyway.

"My advice to you is to forget it. If you are not chosen, it is for a good reason. That reason is not mine to discuss, but it is there."

Dohr nods slowly and turns to leave the room, holding his disappointment inside for later. But then Thoff beckons him closer.

"My son is listening through the door and I don't want him to hear this. He might try it himself and embarrass me terribly. But there is a way, if you are stubborn enough and stupid enough to try it."

"What is it?"

"There is an old rule," whispers Thoff. "If a man can beat a battle master in a round of battle frenzy, then he may become a Red Hawk if he wishes. It is an automatic admission."

Dohr opens his mouth in surprise. He is not surprised that there is a way, but that it is such an impossible way as to be utterly beyond his reach.

"There it is. An option. That is the only way to become a Red Hawk other than being chosen by the council. And we both know that you are now too old to be considered by the council."

"Thank you, Thoff."

"If I give you something for your father, do you promise to deliver it untouched?"

"Yes."

Thoff goes to a large wooden cup carved in the likeness of a hawk's head, and pours a measure of wine into a smaller cup.

"Give him this, with my greetings."

Dohr smiles.

"I'm sure he will appreciate this. He is tired of vapors."

Dohr stands in front of Jada's house, behind a large tree. He can see her beautiful naked body through her window. She is stretching, clasping her ankles with her hands, breathing slowly as she pulls herself into a deeper stretch. Then she stands up and stretches her back. Dohr is struck stupid by the sight, and his heart pounds, as he realizes this is the only girl for him. He would do anything for her, including getting pummeled in tomorrow's tournament.

Dohr takes a desperate gulp of his father's wine. The wine burns down his throat and makes him feel better. But now the cup is only half full. Dohr figures he can't give his father a half a cup of wine, so he drinks off the rest. He'll catch hell from Orym if he ever finds out, but Dohr needs it more than Orym does right now.

Hawk 26'

Hawk moon

Dohr doesn't bother to wake Esther up this morning, so she sleeps very late. When she finally wakes, Orym tells her that Dohr went to the battlegrounds. She has a little congealed acorn mush from the night before and then she goes to find him.

He is training with a couple of boys, practicing fighting moves. He waves distractedly at her and then gets right back to it. Esther wanders around for a while, and then settles down to watch a couple of girls train for a competition this afternoon. They roll around in a tangle of arms and legs, caked from head to toe with mud and bits of twigs and leaves. Esther marvels at their bravery. She would never have the courage to fight like that. Maybe because she was raised to feel that fighting was wrong. It was 'unspiritual' in the eyes of the Padres, who always broke up fights, and then had both parties whipped for it. She always found that a little hypocritical, because they would never stop the Spanish soldiers from fighting. They were allowed to fight as much as they wanted, as long as they fought Indians.

"Who are you?" asks a voice behind her.

The girl is short and big boned, and although she is not fat, she is heavier than the average girl of this tribe. She has a pretty face, although it is a masculine one, and her hair is coarse and looks like it hasn't been brushed in days.

"I am Esther," she replies, not liking the look in her eyes.

"You're Dohr's friend," the girl says, appraising her with a sweep of the eyes. "The one that's been following him around."

Esther looks away and doesn't respond.

"You like him, don't you?" she adds. "I've been watching you."

Esther shrugs and looks down at her feet.

"Is he your boyfriend?" she asks relentlessly.

"No."

"No, I suppose not. I know his taste. He likes a girl that can handle herself. You don't look like you could handle yourself in much of anything."

Esther senses that she is being taunted, and she looks up at the girl in alarm, wondering what she wants.

"Who are you?" she asks.

"I'm Wisa. Dohr and I are...friends. I know what he likes. I can tell you how to get him."

Wisa raises her eyebrows dramatically and smiles. Suddenly curious, Esther lets down her guard and nods for her to continue.

"Dohr likes girls that can handle themselves. Girls that can fight. Tell him to sign you up for the Women's Warrior competition, and I'll make sure that we fight each other. The man running the competitions today is my father, so that will be easy to fix. We'll get in the ring together and I'll let you win. Dohr will like you for sure after seeing you beat me."

Esther stares at her, not sure what to say or do. It seems like a good idea, yet there is something about this girl that Esther doesn't trust. She watches her suspiciously, trying to decide if her smile is genuine. The problem is that these people are all so different than the people she has known, that she doesn't know what is sincere behavior and what isn't. Finally, she decides to give it a try. At worst, she'll get knocked down a couple of times.

Dohr is still practicing fighting moves. She waits until he has separated from his opponent, and then she tells him that she wants to fight in the Women's Warrior competition.

"Women's Warrior?" Dohr asks, laughing. "Are you crazy?"

"No. I want to find out what it's like."

"You'll find out, all right. Are you sure? It's pretty brutal."

"Yes."

"Let's sign you up then," he says, with a big smile. "I can't wait to see this."

Esther watches the beginning of the Women's Warrior competition with horror. Two girls battle it out, pulling each other's hair and kicking each other as hard as they can. One girl throws another to the ground and slaps her face repeatedly until she shouts "Ji". Dohr explains the rules to a thoroughly frightened Esther as they watch.

"Kicks, punches, and hair pulling is allowed. But no punches to the face - you can slap the face, but not punch it. And no scratching or bending body parts in unusual positions. When you've had enough, yell 'Ji'."

Esther begins to wonder if she has lost her mind. But Dohr seems impressed with her, just like Wisa promised.

"I am very proud of you, Esther," he says, putting his arm around her and leaning in with a big smile. "You're finally showing some fire."

Soon enough, Esther is handed a rough, brown shirt, which she is told to put on. A few moments later, her name is called. She walks slowly into the sandy ring, feeling many eyes upon her. There she comes face to face with Wisa, who winks at her, leans in close, and whispers in her ear.

"You're a stupid one, aren't you?"

Esther's eyes open wide in surprise. Wisa laughs at her, while Esther just stands there, stunned with horror. Then the referee calls out for the battle to begin, and Wisa immediately grabs Esther and head butts her as hard as she can. Esther's head feels as if it is ringing like the bells in the mission church. But she doesn't fall. Wisa seems surprised that she is still standing and then she grabs Esther and prepares to slam her down to the ground.

"Ji!" Esther shouts.

"Mastery!" the referee exclaims.

Wisa glares at her angrily, wanting to inflict a little more pain before the match is over. Esther glares back at her, happy to deprive her of this pleasure.

"Dohr, who is this girl? She's got no fire. She's like a puddle of water," exclaims Wisa, sauntering out of the ring.

Dohr laughs and shakes his head.

"It was her idea."

Wisa gives Dohr a quick, playful kiss on the cheek and then she saunters off.

Esther sits down heavily next to Dohr, glaring at Wisa as she struts off. Esther isn't hurt, but she is exceedingly angry, and she feels stupid for having fallen into such an obvious trap. Wisa got an easy victory and made herself look good, while making Esther look bad. It occurs to her suddenly that Wisa likes Dohr herself, and merely wanted revenge against Esther for being with him. She must have assumed that she and Dohr were sleeping together.

"There's blood on your forehead," says Dohr, wiping at it with a rag.

"There is?"

"I told you not to do it," he says, laughing and shaking his head. "You're no fighter."

"I just wanted to try," she says lamely, not wanting to admit the truth, which would only make her look worse.

"Did you like it?"

"Not really."

"Well, don't feel too bad-"

"I feel good," she says, interrupting him.

"Really?"

"I feel good that it is over," she says, standing up. "I'm going to the sweat lodge."

That night, there is dinner and music in the commons, to welcome the coming of the new moon. Several people dance in a small, tight circle to the beat of hand drums and the chanting of four women. Esther sits down by the fire, near a couple of Dohr's friends, and talks to them for a while. One of them tries to get her to dance, but she refuses politely. She tells him that he has to ask Dohr for permission first, and the boy shrugs and goes to dance by himself instead. Watching him go, she suddenly has a strange revelation. She is not frightened to death of all these strange people anymore, like she has been ever since she first got here. She is not afraid to look anybody in the eyes either and she has a confidence that wasn't there before.

She is suddenly thankful to Wisa for smacking her in the head. The blow seems to have jogged her brains loose, and now they are working properly for once. She feels the little scab on her forehead with her finger and contemplates the possibility that a blow to the head might be a good thing. Then she sees Wisa herself, standing moodily by the musicians, slumped over with a sour puss on her face. Esther suddenly wonders who really won the fight in the commons today. She has a strong feeling that it was actually herself that won. It sounds crazy, but she thinks that Wisa gave her a bit of her own courage when they bumped heads.

Hawk 27'

"Wake up lazy. It's the new moon. The whole tribe is at the battlegrounds already, so let's go."

Esther rises dutifully, and sees that there is no breakfast today and the rest of the family has already gone. Dohr slept late this morning, which is surprising because he never sleeps in. She gets ready quickly, sensing that he is impatient, and follows him out the door. The sky is patchy this morning and the clouds cling thickly to the trees, as if holding on for dear life. They tromp silently through the forest, both of them lost in their own thoughts. Suddenly, Dohr trips on a stump and falls onto his face. He stands up, brushes himself off, and keeps walking. This behavior seems particularly strange, because Dohr never trips, and if he did, he would certainly be very vocal about it afterwards.

Esther is surprised to see the battlegrounds packed with people, as she usually just sees the same faces everytime she comes here. Fires are sprinkled haphazardly around the area and the smell of roasting corn is in the air. Dohr goes off by himself without a word, and Esther follows her nose and helps herself to a couple of hard corn tortillas. After that, she joins the crowd that mills about the main platform, standing on her tiptoes to see what they are looking at. They seem to be waiting for something. Dohr appears a few moments later and stands next to Esther, but he is still unnaturally quiet.

The chief, Jath the Red Hawk, stands on the platform along with several others, dressed in full ceremonial costume. He wears a headdress of hawk feathers on his head and a necklace of hawk talons around his neck. He is dressed in a shirt and pants made from deerskin, dyed to resemble a hawk's colors. He scans the crowd several times and then finally blows a whistle for silence. But before he can speak, a man runs across the length of the battlegrounds, screaming with joy. He leaps upon the platform and roars an announcement to all.

"My wife, Jessa, has given birth to a baby boy!"

A great cheer erupts throughout the crowd.

"He will be an asset to our tribe!" says the chief proudly, putting his arm around the man. "Congratulations, this is a good day."

Several men butt chests with him in the manly hug that is the local custom. Jath waits for everyone to finish celebrating the news before blowing the whistle again.

"The new moon is here and there is much to do!" shouts Jath. First, we will announce the new Red Hawks."

Esther feels Dohr stiffen next to her. His eyes become glazed.

"Yohu, step forward," intones Jath.

There are great cheers as a tall, strong boy with a heavily tattooed chest steps forward. He stands before Jath, as Jath places a necklace of hawk talons around his neck. Then the chief hugs him in the usual manner.

"Isu, step forward."

Isu is younger than Yohu, not more than fourteen years old, but he is huge for his age and walks tall and proud like a man. He steps up to the platform to receive his necklace and basks in the cheers and adoration of his people.

"Now we commence with the battle frenzy tournament," shouts Jath, after another boy have been called up and adorned in the same way. "It will be an exciting tournament this year. I have seen that our Red Hawks are well trained and ready. Mastery!"

"What is Battle Frenzy?" Esther asks Dohr.

"You'll see," he mumbles.

A couple of Red Hawks get into the ring and they begin to show off their skills. One man does cartwheels without using his hands - he uses his head instead. The other does flips in the air. One man does a back flip and the other does a one handed handstand.

They spend about five minutes showing off for the crowd and then they begin to show off their fighting moves. They throw kicks and punches at a rapid pace, while demonstrating lightening fast footwork, and circle each other, closer and closer.

One of the men throws a kick in the other's direction and catches him in the side. The crowd roars, as the man turns to face his attacker. The battle is begun. Once begun, it quickly turns deadly serious. The two men begin to pummel each other using every trick at their disposal. Esther has seen many fights since she has been here, but never anything this incredible. She thinks about the practice of Steel Flesh and now she understands why these men do it. They are showing exactly how much punishment a man can take and still keep on fighting.

The fight goes on for several minutes, until finally one of the men is caught in a painful hold. Esther hears someone shouting that he is in a 'bear trap'. Pressure is applied, until the man in the trap shrieks 'Ji', and he is released. The two men do the chest-bashing hug, and then walk out of the ring. Both are bloody and scraped up, and one hobbles a bit, but they both seem happy.

"That was horrible," Esther gasps, looking at Dohr.

"It's very spiritual," he mumbles.

Several intense and bloody battles later, the bloodlust of the crowd is at a fever pitch. When blood from a wounded man splatters his opponent, they cheer gleefully. The more brutal the fight, the happier they are. Esther suddenly has an idea why the Spanish have never tried to convert this tribe.

Finally, the tournament comes down to two finalists, and it is quickly resolved. In the end, one man stands, bloody but unbowed, and he receives the glory that is his due. The crowd screams, their blood boiling from all the violence. It has been a great contest. Kau, the winner, is given a special headdress made from Hawk's feathers, and Jath makes a speech praising his skill and bravery.

"And now, I have a special battle to announce," Jath announces. "There is an old code among the Red Hawk that has been brought to my attention - a code I had forgotten until yesterday. Anyone who can defeat a battle master in a contest of Battle Frenzy may be initiated into the Red Hawk order as a novice. Immediately…without a vote! This is to prevent unfavorable biases or unfair hatreds that may prevent a worthy warrior from being chosen. It is also to keep us on our toes!"

"It has been a long time since I have seen anyone attempt initiation in this way. In fact, I cannot remember the last time anyone who is not a Red Hawk has competed in battle frenzy at all. And for good reason! But we have a young warrior who wants to try. He approached me yesterday with this request. I tried to council him against it, but he was fixed. So I will let him try, as is his right. That young man is none other than Dohr, who is a brave young man, although I will not call him wise at this time. So let Dohr come forward and attempt to defeat our new battle master, Kau, in the most deadly of all our warrior contests. Battle Frenzy!"

The crowd goes crazy. Some cheer for Dohr's bravery. Some shout protests that Dohr will be killed. After today's contest, it is painfully obvious that Kau is nobody to be messed with. Shocked, Esther looks at Dohr, who stands quietly, with a little smile on his face. Finally, everyone is talking about him. But Esther can also see fear in his eyes. He is about to enter a very difficult battle.

Dohr immediately walks to the main circle, to show that he is ready to fight any time. Esther watches him nervously, sure that he is going to get pummeled. Then she sees Kahne, who jumps up and down in excitement as he watches Dohr.

"Aren't you worried about your brother?" Esther asks him.

"No. But I think my mother is."

He points to Luce, who is standing with her head in her hands. Orym talks to her, but she doesn't appear to be listening. Kahne runs over to see what they are saying and Esther follows curiously. She stops a respectful distance away, just close enough so she can hear what they are saying.

"My son is going to be killed," Luce shouts.

"He can always call 'Ji'," insists Orym. "The boy knows what he is doing."

"Kau is a killer. He could kill Dohr before he has a chance to shout out-"

"He won't kill him. Kau is no monster. He's a good man."

"You have to stop him," Luce begs, grabbing Orym's arm. "Dohr won't listen to me, but he might listen to you."

"I'll not do that."

"Then I will!"

"Woman, you will not!" Orym shouts very loudly. "Our son has made this choice and we must let him do as he wishes. To back out now would be an embarrassment that he would never live down."

Luce wilts and nods her head slowly. Orym is right. He grabs her hand tightly and leads her toward the main circle. Everyone parts respectfully, to allow them to the front of the circle, so they can have a ringside seat for their son's mauling.

As if in a dream, Dohr stands in the main circle. It doesn't seem real that he is about to do battle with Kau. What was he thinking? As Kau enters the circle, Dohr feels his knees buckle for a moment. Kau is tall and fierce and every inch of his body is rippled with muscle. Scars cover his face and body and greasy hair runs down his back in a tight ponytail. He is heavily tattooed from head to toe with the symbols of the Red Hawk, meaning he is a very accomplished warrior. He is an ugly man, but somehow that only makes him more fearsome. He stands quietly and confidently, knowing that he will win.

Dohr cannot take his eyes off of Kau. He knows that Kau will not hesitate to pummel him into pulp. That is the object of battle frenzy, and why only well trained Red Hawks are allowed to do it. Men have been accidentally killed in an overzealous round of battle frenzy. Dohr has never participated in a no-holds barred fight before, and that is why he is so frightened now.

Then he thinks of Jath's words yesterday. He spoke these words to Dohr before they parted.

"A salmon keeps swimming until it reaches its destination. Any obstacle in its path it leaps over, and it does not stop, no matter how exhausted or tired it is. Death is not a worry. Only success matters. This is the way of the Red Hawk."

Good words. But no words can help him now. It all happens too fast. The referee raises his hands in the air and brings them down with a sharp whistle. The battle is on.

Kau wastes no time with tricks or showing off moves, as he has already done that several times today. He advances on Dohr, quietly and calmly, but with mastery in his eyes. Instead of preparing himself for an attack, Dohr begins to wonder if he is insane to do this. He fights this feeling, which he knows comes from fear. And then Kau is upon him, and Dohr automatically enters the correct battle posture and just barely deflects a kick. But the kick is only a feint, so Kau can get inside Dohr's defenses.

Kau charges him, thrusts his hip under Dohr's hip, grabs Dohr by the neck, and throws him. Dohr tries to shift his weight, but Kau adjusts his throw in a split second, and Dohr is thrown hard to the ground. As he lies there dazed, Kau punches him once in the face and applies a choke to his neck.

The word 'Ji' bubbles to his brain, but Dohr refuses to say it. Instead, Dohr twists his body around and manages to escape the choke. He rolls backwards and Kau allows him to get away and gives him time to stand on his feet. Kau is a gracious fighter - vicious and deadly - but gracious.

They circle each other warily. Now it is a real fight to Dohr and he is ready to fight. He feigns a few kicks, trying to catch Kau off guard. In response, Kau unleashes an expert flying kick - a very difficult maneuver - that catches Dohr on the shoulder. Dohr is knocked off balance and then he is hit with another kick to the face. Vaguely aware of the crowd roaring approval, Dohr tastes blood in his mouth where he was struck.

With rage, he screams and charges headlong into Kau. Kau goes with the momentum of Dohr's charge, and then he twists his body and sends Dohr sprawling to the ground. He jumps upon him and applies a painful arm lock to Dohr's left arm before Dohr can stand up. He slowly applies pressure, making Dohr scream with pain.

"Yell Ji," Kau hisses. "Or I will break it."

Dohr wants to yell Ji. He wants this all to be over. But he cannot mouth the words, which stick in his throat. He is in the master's tournament today. The people are watching and they will always remember this contest. He must put up a good fight.

"No," he gasps.

Kau's hot breath is in his face now as he leans closer, keeping the pressure on.

"Do you like pain?"

Dohr doesn't answer, because he feels that he is about to faint. Grinding his teeth in agony, he twists, trying to get away. The pain is excruciating. Just before he is forced to concede, Kau suddenly releases him. He felt the arm giving, and did not want to break it. He wants to go easy on this poor young man, who is no match for a Red Hawk. He slaps Dohr instead, and steps back. It is a move intended to embarrass Dohr more than anything. To show him that he is a fool. The crowd gasps at the insult.

Esther feels a tightening in her stomach as she watches the battle. She is afraid for Dohr, yet she is exhilarated at the same time. She feels a little guilty for being so excited, but when she looks around at all the rapt faces, she can tell that everyone is feeling the same thing. They are enjoying every minute of this. Only Dohr's parents are not happy. They watch stoically, holding hands tightly.

Dohr breathes heavily, listening to the sound of the crowd egging him on. Kau let him off the hook and insulted him. As if he is no threat at all! His face flush with embarrassment, Dohr tests his arm and finds it working properly. The crowd howls for Dohr to go get him, but it sounds mocking. Dohr feels his will harden. He will not become a laughing stock. He would rather die.

"There is no shame in knowing when to quit!" hisses Kau under his breath. "He that knows that lives to fight another day."

Dohr stands there, tasting blood in his mouth and feeling stinging sweat in his eyes. He is filled with a stubborn rage as he listens to the crowd mocking him. Pride swells his courage and he feels his will harden. He will not give up, only to be laughed at for the rest of his life. It occurs to him that unless he does something to impress the village, they will never let him live this down.

He stands there, pretending to be dazed, as Kau dances toward him. Kau is showing off for the crowd, which always was his weakness. When he gets within range, he unleashes an extremely difficult kick that was never meant to be used in an actual battle. Dohr ducks easily and then lashes out with his best move, a sweeping foot throw that sends Kau tumbling to the ground. As soon as Kau hits the dirt, Dohr runs forward and manages to slam him in the face before he can get back up. He tries to pin the great fighter down, but it is like pinning a bear. Dohr can hear the crowd roaring for him now, and he feels a momentary elation.

Kau somersaults to his feet and charges Dohr. Now he is angry and his eyes are filled with steely determination. He deflects Dohr's next kick and gives him a brutal hit to the solar plexus. The pain is excruciating, and Dohr falls to the ground, gasping for air. Kau gives him a strike to the ribs and then another to the back. Dohr lies on the ground, gasping for breath.

"Say Ji!" Kau hisses under his breath. "Fool!"

Dohr rises slowly and woozily to his feet. Just as soon as he is standing, Kau lets loose with a perfectly executed roundhouse kick to the chest that will be remembered for a long time. The crowd gasps in awe as Dohr is sent flying onto his back. He sees stars, and he knows that the end of this fight is near.

It takes a great effort to get to his feet this time. He stumbles toward Kau, falls to his knees, and gets up again. He tries to take a swing at Kau, but it is such a wild swing and without strength that it is almost funny. Kau responds with a blow to the chest that sends Dohr crashing back to the ground.

It takes Dohr almost a full minute to rise up on shaky feet that refuse to respond normally. He stumbles forward, carried on willpower alone. He knows that he hasn't the strength left to hurt Kau, but he is pleased with himself that he has lasted this long. Nobody in the tribe has ever taken a beating like this and continued to fight. Nobody will laugh at him now. He stands in front of Kau and smiles with satisfaction, because he has accomplished that at least. Blood drips from his mouth, down his chin, and onto the ground.

Kau is suddenly afraid, staring at this wrecked young man with the bloody smile. Is he supposed to murder him? Why is he smiling? The crowd is deathly silent now. Dohr is in a bad way and it doesn't seem that he can take another hit. Kau comes toward him, and lowers him gently to the ground. He looks at the referee with wonder in his eyes. The referee merely shakes his head, indicating that the fight is not yet over. Frowning, Kau puts his hand around Dohr's neck and slowly squeezes.

"This will knock you unconscious, and I will win by default. It's your choice," he whispers, gently this time. He applies more pressure and Dohr's face turns red. Then it turns white. Dohr is just on the edge of unconsciousness when Kau releases the pressure.

"Your color is bad, and you are not breathing properly. I am afraid I may kill you. Just concede! You have nothing to feel sorry for. You have done well for someone untrained in the arts of the Red Hawk."

Dohr stares at him with wild eyes. His mouth opens to speak but no sounds come out. He cannot explain it, but he just knows that he will not speak the word 'Ji'. He has already come this far. Why back down now?

Kau stares at him, amazed. Nobody has ever voluntarily withstood such punishment before, but Dohr refuses to give up. So Kau is faced with the choice of risking killing him or just walking away. If he walks away, then Dohr will win. If Dohr wins, he will become a Red Hawk. That is what is at stake! Kau's opponent desperately wants to be a Red Hawk. He wants it enough to die for it. Kau stares hard at him, and wonders what kind of a Red Hawk he would make. As he wonders, a hawk flies directly overhead, come to check out the source of the smell of blood. It soars overhead, seeming more like a man with wings than a bird. It hovers, graceful and very still, as if movement of the wings were beneath it. Kau stares at it, humbled by its beauty. It is a good omen.

"Ji!" Kau shouts, making his choice at last.

He stands up and walks off silently, knowing that he has chosen well.

The crowd is deathly silent for a long time. Nobody can believe what just happened. Then all at once, everything explodes. The crowd begins screaming for Dohr. They begin to chant his name over and over again, while clapping their hands and stomping their feet. Meanwhile, Luce and Orym run forward to make sure he is still alive. The healers run forward to look at him. There is pandemonium in the battlegrounds for some time. Finally Jath raises his hands and signals that he would like to speak. It takes a great deal of time to get everybody quiet.

"A man has taught us an important lesson today. I'd say that man deserves to be a Red Hawk!"

The crowd is a mad beast, screaming in exultation. Everyone cheers the bravery and determination of Dohr, who barely manages a weak smile, as the people all gather around him. Dohr is helped to his feet and he hobbles up to the platform. He leans on his father - who is so proud he might burst. Dohr's face is a mess of bruises and as he walks he is sure that one of his ribs is cracked. But despite all this, he is in good spirits. The roar of the crowd is better than the greatest drug he has ever taken and helps to numb the pains that he will surely feel later.

"It seems I had forgotten what it truly means to be a Red Hawk," shouts Jath, beaming at Dohr. "A contest of strength? Ferocity in battle? Is that all mastery is? What about strength of spirit? Indomitable will? Passion? Yes, I did not know that I had grown blind. That is why I thank Dohr for opening my eyes." Jath puts his arm tenderly around Dohr's shoulders. "You were not the strongest or the most ferocious and we overlooked you. But you wanted to be a tribal warrior so badly, that you risked your life for it. You took a beating that none of us will ever forget. For this, I am proud to make you a Red Hawk."

He places a necklace of Hawk talons over Dohr's head. Dohr smiles weakly and waves to everyone, and then his father leads him away. He and Orym slowly make their way to the healer's house, where he will stay for many days. On the way, Thoff comes up to him with a glass of wine to dull the pain. Dohr gulps the wine down, and he is not sure if he is drinking wine or his own salty blood. It tastes the same.

After the tournament is over, it is time for lunch. Everyone descends on the commons, where a feast has been set upon three large tables. Great fires burn, cooking a large deer and several ducks that have been caught for the feast of the new moon. A wine cask is opened and everyone receives a large glass. Esther doesn't know where to begin. She tries a little bit of everything - oysters, clams, pieces of acorn bread dipped in whale blubber, dried salmon. Some of the food tastes strange and some of it is delicious. Soon she is quite full and feeling high from the wine. She sits down underneath a tree to watch everything that is going on.

There is still much to do. Jath presides over two weddings in the lover's glen, and then there is a gathering in the commons to discuss tribe business and plans for the spring migration. Esther does not bother to attend either one. She sits by the fire all alone, watching the deer carcass cooking. She is in no mood for a wedding. A wedding is a new beginning, and today is an ending for Esther. Tomorrow she will leave the home where she has just begun to feel comfortable and wander out into the world alone again. She is afraid of what she will find out there.

That night, the deer and the ducks are consumed, along with a lot of wine. Esther eats by herself, feeling like a stranger, unwanted and unimportant. She wishes that she knew where her own people were. She thinks again of her childhood, trying to raise a picture of her parent's faces and the village where she lived. But she cannot. It is buried down in her mind much too deeply for her to find it.

After dinner, several musicians begin to play music and everyone dances. But Esther cannot stay awake for very long. The heavy food and the wine have made her tired. She craves warmth and sleep more than music, so she rises on stiff legs and stumbles back to Dohr's house to go to sleep.

Hawk 28'

Beaver moon

Esther prepares for her journey in the dim morning light of a cloudy day. She is alone in the house, which is good, because she plans to borrow a few things without asking. Desperation knows no shame. She is going to take the blanket they loaned her and a small knife from the kitchen that she thinks they will not miss. She took a good quantity of meat last night from the celebration, and she finds a little bag made from some animal skin to put it in so she will have a few days worth of food.

She has come up with a plan that seems good to her. She will hide out in the woods while the people get ready to go on the spring migration. She can come to the commons at night to scrounge and sit by the coals of burned out fires. She will haunt this village like a ghost. When they all leave, she will return and hide out in this very house all spring and summer long. She has heard that the village is deserted, except for a few old people who act as caretakers.

She spends a few minutes sitting by the fire, enjoying the warmth as if it will be the last time she feels warm. Just as she is getting ready to go, she hears a noise outside. She tenses, feeling like the rabbit who has stumbled into a wolf pack, as Luce and Orym stride into the room.

"Thank you for everything," Esther says quickly, standing up. "I am leaving today...." She fades out, feeling stupid for saying it when it is so obvious.

"Goodbye," says Luce simply, and she gives Esther a quick smile and gets to work cleaning up the house.

"You take care of yourself," Orym says, giving her a friendly hand on the shoulder. "Got a place to go?"

"Yes," she says. She looks at the rolled up blanket and realizes that she must now ask permission. "Do you think I may keep this blanket for awhile? It will be a long journey."

"Yes, of course," he says, waving it aside as if it is no matter. "May the sun shine brightly on your journey. Stop by for a visit if you are in our village again."

Suddenly thinking of it, Luce hands her a large piece of some kind of hard bread, wrapped in a giant leaf. She gives her warmest smile, as if to tell Esther that there are no hard feelings just because she is throwing her out of the house.

"Thank you," Esther says, letting go of a little of the resentment she has been harboring for Luce. "Thank you for everything."

"Dohr is doing much better," Orym says proudly. "We just saw him. You should visit him before you leave. He's at the home of the healer, which lies right near the commons. There is a statue of a sick man in front. You can't miss it."

It is a warm day, and she feels almost optimistic as she walks to the healer's house. The kindness of Orym and Luce has helped her to find a little hope. The healer is in front of the house chopping wood, and he invites her inside to see his popular patient. Dohr lies on a bed near a roaring fire. He waves at her weakly and beckons her over. When she gets closer, she sees that Dohr's face is covered with bruises, his arm is in a sling and there are strips of hemp cloth wrapped around his chest.

"Hello," he says weakly.

"How are you feeling?"

"I've been better," he admits.

"Does it hurt bad?"

"Yes. You must be laughing at me now because I called *you* a suicide."

"I thought you were very brave," Esther says, not finding that funny at all.

"It seemed brave at the time. But I have sprained my arm and broken a rib. And the healer thinks I might have some internal injuries to my organs. He tells me I may have problems for the rest of my life. I will not be able to start training as a Red Hawk until at least six months."

"I'm sorry, Dohr. That's awful."

"The funny part is that I don't really want to be a Red Hawk anymore. I've had enough of fighting now to last me the rest of my life." He laughs. "I'll probably do it anyway. I might as well after going through all this. Everyone in the tribe already thinks I'm crazy, but if I don't become a Red Hawk now, they'll think I'm totally insane."

He stares at the rolled up blanket she carries in her hands and he looks confused.

"Are you going somewhere?"

"You told me I had to leave today."

"Oh yes...but where are you going?"

She shrugs tiredly, as if annoyed by the same constant question that she has no answer to.

"There is a path leading northwest from the commons. Right near the blacksmith's hut. I suggest you take it."

"Where does it go?"

"An unbearably dull place. It leads to the Beaver tribe. But I think you will like it there."

"Would they mind if I go there?"

"No, not at all. They are a very generous people. And they never leave, so you could stay there for a long time if you wanted."

"How far is it?"

"For you? A few days travel. I can make it in a day."

Esther nods slowly. Perhaps that is a better idea than her plans to be a ghost in the woods. She smiles, suddenly grateful for all of his help.

"Thank you for teaching me all that information about surviving in the wild. I will use it."

"Yeah," Dohr says, hesitating momentarily, "but I think you would do better with the Beaver tribe than going it alone. "You haven't quite learned enough to do it for more than a day or two."

She nods in full agreement. Just then, a tall, very beautiful woman enters the room, ushered in by the healer. It is none other than Jada, who stops walking when she sees Esther. She stands there a moment, checking Esther out, as if deciding whether she and Dohr are involved. Apparently she decides they are not, for she gives Esther a warm smile as a reward, and walks over to talk to them. Esther looks at Dohr's eyes shining with excitement and the big smile on his face and she understands.

"Well, I will let you two talk," Esther says quickly. "I have to go now."

"Good luck to you," Dohr says seriously. "I hope you make it. Come back for a visit someday."

"Goodbye," she says, grabbing her little bundle and heading out the door.

At the commons, Esther heads northwest just like Dohr suggests. She walks uphill quite a ways and all the time her brain spins with thoughts. At first she passes little houses and signs of civilization. But eventually, there are no more, and she is walking through uninhabited forest again. The trees seem to rise higher and thicker than ever and Esther soon feels like a little animal lost in a great wilderness. The little path makes her feel safe, and she does not stray from it one inch as she makes her way northwest through vast trees that appear to have no end.

Beaver Tribe

Hawk 29'

Beaver moon

Esther wakes early with a strong hunger. The hard bread is gone, but she has deer meat left. She finds some milk thistle leaves too and gingerly picks apart the thorns, making as good a breakfast as she can. Then she drinks from the stream and continues walking down the path. The trail begins to head westwards now, down the mountain and toward the ocean.

She walks all day long. She carries a sharp stick, and whenever she passes a hole, she tries to spear herself a gopher or rabbit. After several hours of thrusting her weapon into holes of all types, she finally catches herself a gopher on a stick. Excited, she smashes it into a tree and then pulls out her knife to skin it. But she makes a mess of the poor creature and splashes blood all over her nightgown. Her face has an expression of revulsion as she gingerly tries to peel the skin off the body. Then she remembers that she was supposed to roast a gopher with the skin on, for just this reason. That is when it occurs to her that she has no means to start a fire. Cursing, she throws the mangled carcass against a tree and storms off. She leaves her hunting stick lying next to the dead carcass, which is soon picked off by scavengers.

Late in the afternoon, she hears the sound of a horse coming her way. She turns, surprised and afraid that Spanish soldiers have finally found her, and quickly dives for the cover of the woods. But there is no soldier upon this horse. Instead, she sees a stocky man with wild, frizzy hair sticking out in tufts from an otherwise bald head. As he rides, he smokes intently upon a pipe in his mouth. He seems friendly enough, so she steps out into the road to greet him. He is so surprised at the sight of her, that he drops his pipe into his lap. He jumps up and down on the horse, trying to brush the burning coals off his lap. She picks the pipe up, which has fallen to the ground, and hands it back to him.

"You surprised the pipe right out of my mouth," he says, grinning sheepishly.

She is so happy to see somebody friendly, that she giggles at his crude joke.

"Greetings to you and what are you doing all the way out here?" he asks.

"I'm going to see the Beaver tribe."

"Look at you. Poor defenseless girl, alone in the woods. Easy target for a wolf or a bear. You could get mauled. Why don't you hop on and I'll give you a ride, as I'm a man of that tribe and going that way myself."

"Thank you so much."

"I'm Tork," he says, "of the Beaver tribe."

"I am Esther."

Giving silent thanks for her good fortune, Esther grabs his hand and struggles upon the horse. Esther has obviously never ridden a horse before, so Tork gives her a quick explanation.

"Grip with your knees, tightly," he explains. "That's the trick. Sit up straight and a little forward, and don't lean back. I'll be holding onto the reins, but you can grip onto me as tightly as you want."

At first it is fun, but it soon turns out to be a most uncomfortable experience. There is only an elk pelt for a saddle and her rear hurts after a good hour of bouncing on the horse's hard back. She nearly falls off several times, and she has to hold tightly onto Tork in order to stay up, which nearly brings him down with her.

Just as it begins to get dark, they enter a wide clearing where the grass grows high and you can see far in either direction. They are out of the redwoods at last. Tork stops the horse immediately and they dismount. He ties the horse to a long rope and lets it graze upon the tall grasses.

"I don't like to travel at night," he says. "Even though we're almost there, I think it is best if we continue in the morning."

He is soon snoring softly. Esther lies down on her blankets and stares up at the sky. It feels strange to be out from under the green roof she has been living beneath for over a month. Marveling at the stars and constellations as if seeing them for the first time, she watches the glowing sky for a long time before falling asleep.

Beaver 0'

Jay moon

At the crack of dawn, Tork wakes her up and they continue on. A pink and blue sunrise lights their way as they travel down a steep hill. They soon enter trees again, but now they are riding through oak forest. The path is wider and better kept and they make good time. They come within sight of the ocean and Esther is happy to see its endless blue again.

Before she knows it, they are traveling down a well-worn road in a quaint little village. Pretty little houses, made of expertly carved planks, stand proudly in large clearings. Next to them stand crude barns, filled with tools and carts. Fences surround large gardens and pastures with grazing cows and horses. The village actually reminds her of the mission, but without the dark undercurrents.

Cows were brought to this land by the Spanish in the late seventeen hundreds, and several were stolen by the Hawk tribe and given to the Beaver tribe as trade. Thus began the recent craze of raising farm animals – a craze unique to the Beaver tribe. However, the Beavers have been farming crops like hemp, corn, squash and beans for over a hundred years, well before the arrival of the Spanish.

They pass a cart drawn by a snow white horse. It carries a heavy load of cut firewood, upon which sits a merry fat man, who wears a ridiculous hat and shouts out "Good Day!" as they pass.

"Good day yourself!" Tork shouts back at him.

Soon Tork turns the horse down a small path to a house that sits at the base of a large hill. The house is small by the standards of this town, but solidly built with smooth boards and a solid roof. It is not like the hastily constructed cabins of the Hawk tribe, but a well built, carefully constructed house with neat, clean lines. They pull into a small barn, filled with hay, tools, and junk of every kind. Broken wagon wheels, wrecked tools, old pots, broken baskets, and wooden planks sit in a trash pile that will someday become fire. They jump off the horse and Tork immediately begins to unload his bags. Esther yawns as he stretches her stiff legs and back. The horse is released from duty with an affectionate pat on the rump and immediately goes outside to graze.

Before going into the house, Tork unloads all the unsold corn and potatoes and throws them into a big basket that is already full and falling apart. The basket crumbles under the strain, and potatoes roll everywhere. Tork and Esther run around picking them up and putting them back in so they will not fall out again.

They go to the main house. Esther is amazed at all the junk stacked neatly around the property, all of it growing moldy and waiting to be used for something. For what? They must never get rid of anything here. Tork walks into the house, waving for Esther to follow him. Just before she enters, she gasps and stops dead. Through the window, she can see a wolf sitting inside the house. The wolf wakes as her shadow blocks out its sun and begins to bark at her. She backs fearfully away. A moment later, Tork comes back out.

"Please come in," he says. "We're just in time for breakfast."

"There is a wolf in your house," Esther says uneasily.

"Beggar? He's just a dog. He's no threat. Don't worry about him."

"What's a dog?"

"Nothing for you to worry about. Now come inside before the food gets cold."

Esther's heart soars at the idea of a hot breakfast in this beautiful house. She follows Tork in, uneasily keeping her distance from the wolf. It does her no good. It attacks her with tongue and hot breath and jumps all over her. Then it barks once or twice for good measure.

"Help," Esther squeaks.

"Did Beggar sneak in here?" a voice yells from another room. "Put that dog outside!"

"Sorry Beggar," mumbles Tork. He shoves the dog unceremoniously outside and closes the door in its face.

Dogs are not the domesticated animals in this place and time that they are today. Instead, "dogs" were wolves who were separated from the pack as children. They learned to grow up around humans, although they retained many wolf characteristics and were not quite house pets. Beggar is the product of two such animals, so you might call him a first generation 'dog'. Farmers are particularly interested in having dogs around, as they are good pest control and keep the deer away.

Esther looks around the large family room in amazement. It is cluttered, but very cozy. They have a read wood-burning stove too, instead of just a fire pit. It burns hot, sending out warmth to all parts of the house, while it cooks an iron pan of some delicious smelling food. The room is not smoky, like Orym and Luce's house, and the ceiling is not stained black. Near the wood stove are two chairs for the grownups and a giant bear skin rug for the children to sit upon. In one corner of the room stands a large table, set for breakfast, and two long benches. There are two doors leading out of the family room. Esther can hear children's laughter from one door and a chopping sound coming from the other.

"Hello!" Tork shouts.

One of the doors pops open and two children run in to greet him.

"Hello my children," shouts Tork affectionately, as they give him a big hug.

"Hello Papa," they shout.

"Esther, this is Anri," he says, pointing to a little boy with short, tousled hair. "And this is Sare," he says, pointing to a chubby little girl of eight years with long black hair and an altogether pleasant face.

They hover around their father as he takes off his coat and muddy boots and hangs them on a rack. Esther looks at her own shoes guiltily and then she takes them off and tries to wipe away the mud stains she left on the floor.

A plump, middle-aged woman, covered with flour, suddenly appears from the other door. She has the same chipmunk face as Sare, with big cheeks and a large smile. She is short and stout, and Tork has to lean down to give her a little kiss. She looks at Esther and smiles, waiting for an introduction.

"We did well this last trip," Tork says, forgetting to introduce her. "Sold most of the corn and a few potatoes. And I got a good price for 'em." He pulls out a handful of tupas for proof. "I was hoping for a good trade, but that can't be helped. Tupas will do."

Tara looks at Esther again, and Tork remembers his manners at last.

"Yes, of course, I found something else too. Tara, this is Esther. I found her on the road from the Hawk tribe."

"Poor dear," Tara says, showing genuine sympathy. "You look half starved. Sit down and we'll get some good food into you."

"I thought she might stay a few days," Tork says with a wink. "And she can help around the house."

"Of course," says Tara, noticing her husband's meaningful glance.

"Bela! Bora!" Tork yells out. "Breakfast!"

They all sit down at the table. An older girl appears, bearing a large wooden bowl filled with a dense bread. The girl is about fifteen years old, with her father's wide, puffy face and her mother's pretty oval eyes. She has her mother's short, sturdy body and sunny expression too. She peers at Esther over her bowl and smiles at her.

"Bela, this is Esther," says Tork. "She'll be our guest for a few days."

"Hello, I'm Bela," she says lightly, as she places the bread on the table.

"Mmmm, I want some of that tea," says Tork.

Bela pours a cup of tea for the whole family, except for Sare who doesn't like it. Esther stares at the cup of black liquid and sniffs it experimentally. When she sips it, she finds it extremely strong and bitter. It smells better than it tastes.

"First time?" asks Tork.

Esther nods.

"It's bitter without milk," says Tara. "Let me help you."

She fixes her tea with some milk and gives it back to her. Esther now likes it very much. It goes well with milk. Esther also gets two strips of a strange pink meat and a big piece of bread. The meat smells good, although she has no idea what it is. She takes a bite and finds it delicious. A satisfied moan escapes her lips.

"Good, hmm," says Tara with a smile.

"Yes, what is it?"

"Smoked pig. The neighbors killed a pig recently."

Esther has no idea what a "pig" is, having never seen one. But she likes the taste of it very much. It is greasy and fatty, yet it has this strange sweetness. Esther tries to imagine what a "pig" looks like, but she cannot.

"We got our first pig just two years ago," beams Tork. "One of our ships brought these cute little pink things over from China. Now the tribe is breeding them."

A boy comes out from the other room. He is about fourteen and stocky like his father, with short, black curly hair and a funny pug nose. He sits down at the table and digs into the food without a word.

"Bora, this is Esther," says Tork, introducing her.

"Hello, Esther," Bora says. "What tribe are you from?"

"I'm not from any tribe. I'm a stranger here."

"Where are you from?" asks Tork. "You haven't said."

Esther doesn't want to tell the truth, because she remembers the way everyone in Dohr's family treated her, after she told them she was from the mission. But they are all looking at her, waiting for an answer.

"Branciforte," she says at last. "The Spanish village near the mission."

"Isn't that interesting," Tork exclaims. "You must tell us about it."

And there is silence at the table, but for the slurping of liquids and the chewing of food. Relieved that they don't question her further, Esther finishes her cup of dark black tea. The salted meat and bread has made her very thirsty so she requests another cup, which Tara pours for her. Esther gulps that down also. Suddenly, she feels dizzy and lightheaded. She takes several deep breaths, trying to stay centered.

"What is wrong?" asks Tara. "You don't look well."

"I feel sick," she says, wanting to go outside and throw up.

"Well look at you on your second cup of coffee bean tea already," laughs Tork. "Novices shouldn't drink more than one cup. It is very strong."

"Eat some more food, dear," says Tara with a note of concern in her voice. "You'll feel better."

"What is coffee bean tea?" asks Esther, taking a deep breath.

"It is imported from South America," says Tork proudly. "We do some trading with the Spanish. They are very expensive."

"And very strong," adds Tara. "No more for you."

"Esther, today is the first day of the month of Beaver," Tork says, when breakfast is eaten and everyone relaxes around the table. "We have lost our farm hand to a neighboring farm that pays more than we can. So I must find strays from other lands and bring them home in order to keep up with our richer neighbors. I confess, when I saw you, I thought, 'Well, here is somebody desperate enough to work for me'."

"Tork!" scolds Tara. "You don't have to say it like that."

"Well, it's true. We can offer you a place to stay, some good meals and a few tupas on the side when we can afford it. What do you say?"

Esther is speechless. Such an opportunity as this seems so far removed from reality. To find a family who actually wants her to stay with them seems a miracle.

"We are not the richest among our tribe and we struggle more than others. That's just the truth of it. But we live as the Beaver lives and that is good living indeed," he says proudly. "As you can see."

"Well, what do you think?" asks Tara.

"You'll like it here," adds Bela.

"If you really want me, I would be very happy to stay here and work," says Esther.

The family claps their hands and congratulates her. Esther is not so sure that she is qualified to do whatever they want her to do, but she is not going to say anything.

"And you must come with us to the celebration today," Tork shouts. "Right Tara?"

"Yes, she must do that," says Tara, with a big grin.

Esther thinks that she is dreaming, so perfect is this moment.

After breakfast, the family all goes outside to do chores and various jobs, leaving Esther alone in the house with the missive "Make yourself comfortable." But she is too nervous and jumpy from the coffee and the new environment, so she takes a walk outside. After a little tour, she returns to the house to find Tork sitting outside, smoking a pipe in his best clothes. His best clothes are a pair of dyed black leather trousers and a shirt made from deer skin with a brown and black pattern. Tork waves to her and she walks over to join him.

"What a beautiful day for a party," he muses.

Sare and Anri come running out of the house and pile upon their father, competing for hugs. He sits them on his lap and lets each one smoke his pipe, chuckling to himself as they cough and make faces.

"Don't tell your mother," he warns them, as he takes his pipe back.

Every now and again, a horse draws a cart down the path, loaded with mysterious bundles. The families perched on the cart are dressed in all sorts of gay colors and they smile and wave as they pass.

"What a great idea," Tork muses. "Let's hitch Boo up to the cart and ride there in style."

By early afternoon, everybody is dressed and ready to go. Tara wears a deerskin dress that is dyed red and adorned with many pretty shells. Bela's dress is almost identical, but with different patterns of shells.

"Mother," Bela whispers. "We cannot let Esther go dressed like that. Everyone would stare."

"No, we must give her something else. Why don't you go and get her a dress of yours, Bela?"

Esther is given a dark brown dress made from deerskin and strips of hemp cloth, a little large for her frame but serviceable.

Although the dress is a little scratchy, she feels extremely happy to have it. She feels like part of the family as walks out into the bright sunlight and loads herself into the cart.

"Boo!" yells Tork. "Tch! Tch!"

Boo, the horse, plods lazily forward, but a few swift hits from Tork's long branch motivates him to move more quickly.

"Poor Boo," Esther thinks. "They don't need to hit you like that."

After a short journey down a road towered by oak and buckeye trees, they reach the center of the village. On the way, Esther beholds a magnificent building, tall and awe inspiring, built with dark brown redwood logs and a great sloping roof. Parts of the building are done with little stones, creating a cobblestone effect. A large, well-tended garden exhibits many flowers, which fill the air with a sweet scent. It is the biggest house she has ever seen and her mouth hangs open. Tork stops the cart so she can get a better look. At his urging, she jumps out of the cart and walks in a daze into the garden, where the smell of roses and jasmine is overpowering.

"This is the Beaver House," says Tork, getting out of the cart to show her around. "It is our assembly hall, where all gatherings happen."

He takes her around the house, so she can see it from another angle. It is equally amazing from all angles. A giant cross sits upon the steep roof.

"Is this where you go to church?"

"Church?"

Esther points to the cross.

"Oh, yes," Tork laughs. "The soldiers from that Spanish village called Santa Cruz - the one next to your town - discovered us several years ago, and men in brown robes came to visit us soon afterwards. They kept bothering us, until we promised to try out their strange religion. They gave us a book to read and that thing there. What's it called?"

"It's a cross."

"Yes. We thought it was a nice touch and we put it up like they told us to. Then Huli spent a few days with them, learning a bit about their religion. He didn't care for it and tried to leave, but they gave him a hard time and insisted that he had to learn it or else we would all suffer some horrible fate. He told them to go jump in some quicksand." Tork laughs at the memory. "They were upset, but a few of the Red Hawks paid them a visit and they left us alone after that."

Esther bursts out laughing until her sides hurt. She can completely picture that scene in her head. She only wishes she had seen it with her own eyes.

"Huli wanted to take that thing down, but everyone else liked it, so we just kept it on the roof."

Tork suddenly turns at the sound of barking. Sare and Anri have jumped off the cart to play with a fierce dog across the street.

"Sare! Anri!" Tara shouts. "Don't antagonize that dog. I know you want to play, but we will be at the party soon enough."

"Dad! Let's go!" Bora shouts.

"Yes, let us continue on," Tork says. He leads her back to the cart, and Boo is interrupted from his feeding and told with a sharp slap of the stick to continue onwards.

Soon Esther is bombarded by a symphony of noise, colors, hustle and bustle, as they arrive at the Beaver commons. Beaver commons is huge, with many permanent structures and several little huts with simple thatched roofs perched on poles. The place is teeming with people and activity. An impossible banquet table is piled with more food than Esther has ever seen in her life, and it grows and grows as people arrive and dump food on top of it. Esther wonders how on earth anyone could ever eat all that food. Tara sets up a blanket on the edge of the commons and the family sets their things down.

"Everyone is free to do as they like," Tara announces. "This will be our home base. But Sare and Anri, don't run off too far."

"Yes mother," they scream as they disappear into the crowd.

"I'm going to find Kirth," Bela announces. "Come on Esther, I want you to meet him."

Esther follows Bela dutifully. The crowds make her a bit nervous, but the bright colors and the delicious smells excite her. They find Kirth standing with his cousin and his cousin's wife. Kirth is a tall, slender young man with a pleasant expression. Bela goes over to him and kicks him in the rear. He turns around, surprised.

"Ah, there you are."

"Hello, my Kirth." She gives him a wet, sloppy kiss. "This is Esther, our new farmhand."

He takes her hand in his and says, "Kirth, of the Raccoon tribe."

They stare at each other for many moments, seeing something interesting in each other's gaze.

"I missed you," says Bela, just a tiny bit irritably, not liking his attention moving so completely to Esther.

"And I you," he says, breaking his gaze with Esther and pinning it on Bela.

She gives him a long, deep kiss, as if to claim him for her own.

"You're mine," she says, upon breaking away.

"And you're mine," he says, upon catching his breath.

This is the traditional Beaver declaration of love. They kiss again and Esther decides to go look around instead of watching them kiss. Leaving them locked in an embrace, she wanders around the party for a good hour. She compares these people to the Hawk tribe and finds them as different as night and day. Then a band begins to play and she walks over to watch. They are a lively band from the Bear tribe, playing a style of music that is light and spry, which makes everyone get up to dance. Some dance gracefully, but others dance like silly children with no rhythm and big grins plastered onto their faces.

A few hours later, the band stops playing and lunch officially begins. Esther gets a plate and fills it up with food. She cannot comprehend the sight of so much food laid out for one feast, and she fills her plate with more than she can possibly eat. She is soon glued to the blanket, her stomach bursting. But still she must eat more, because it tastes so good. And she hasn't even gotten to the desserts yet. Tork and Tara feast next to her, and they can pack away much more food than Esther can.

"They're out of moon pies," Tork complains suddenly. "I love moon pie." He stands up. "I must find out if they have any for sale."

"Aren't you stuffed enough?" Tara asks, through a mouthful of food.

"I'll have it tomorrow," he says with a grin.

After dinner, he goes off on a search for the fabled moon pie. He is not gone long.

"Three tupas a pie," he complains, sitting back down. "They've raised the price for the celebration. I'm not paying three tupas."

"I'll make you one at home."

"Nobody makes moon pies like the Bear tribe," he says sadly.

Evening approaches, but there is no sign of the party letting up. The band continues to play and new games are organized for the children. Sare and Anri run off, but Esther feels wonderfully lazy from the huge meal, and she naps with Tork on the blanket. They are awakened when the music stops and Chief Mai stands upon a stool to speak to the assembled crowd. Esther is surprised that a woman is the chief of this tribe. Mai is lovely to look at, with a pleasant face ringed by long, flowing wavy gray hair that is thick and luxurious. She has a thick, solid body with curves and weight around the hips. Esther thinks of the Hawk women, who are often tomboys, and sees how different this tribe's values are from theirs.

"Friends, we have a big month ahead of us," Mai says in a deep, rich voice. The sun enters the month of the Beaver today. The Great Beaver, our guiding spirit, will be with us during this time of hard work. This is the time to plant our crops to yield a bountiful harvest and to begin new projects that will be blessed by her. There will be children born. Decisions made. I want to remind you of the words of the Ulili Butterfly, who travels from the north, beyond the land of the Cougar tribe, all the way down to the land of jungles far, far south. Legend has it that Ulili Butterfly once said that a long journey begins with a single flap of the wings. These are good words."

Today, the Ulili Butterfly is known as the Monarch Butterfly.

She stops a moment and looks out over the crowd.

"I was thinking today about how different this village was when I was a child. There were no horses or cows. Food was still gathered more often than grown. Iron and steel were relatively rare and things were still done in the old ways. We have embraced all the new things that have come to our land and we are grateful for them. But let us not forget the value of the old ways. Let us not throw away the past in unused corners of barns where they will slowly rot away. Keep the past close to you, my tribe. Pass on the old ways to your children, that they will not die completely."

Mai steps off the stool and there is a long, respectful silence before everyone starts talking again.

The evening program is a concert by the Bear singer Gia. Everyone gathers on their blankets, with a plate full of leftovers for dinner and a glass of wine. Children gather around their parent's legs and cuddle into laps. The entire commons falls into a hushed silence, waiting for the music to begin.

Gia is a heavy, middle-aged woman, with a loud and very stirring set of pipes. Her voice echoes through the darkness, accompanied by musicians on flute and drum. She sings songs that are well known by all the Beaver tribe and everyone hums along with her. Esther lies down and stares at the stars, as the beautiful songs seem to rise to the heavens themselves. Gia has a very dramatic flair and she sobs along with the sad songs and laughs along with the joyful ones. She sings for a full hour and all are rapt and motionless - except for the occasional getting up to refill wine glasses.

But all things must come to an end, and when Gia steps off the stage to loud applause, the celebration is over. Families gather their things in the torchlight and load their carts for the journey home. Boo is roused from his slumbering and Tork loads the family onto the cart. Sare and Anri, half asleep already, curl up in the back and fall into dreamland almost instantly.

"Dad, don't forget to get some leftovers for Boink and Beggar. And I want to get some for myself."

"Good idea," Tork says, and he leads the cart over to the food table. They are not alone in this idea, as several families are loading up leftovers and slop for animals into baskets. After filling their own baskets, they get on the road toward home.

They ride quietly, still filled with the magic of the night. Everyone hums his or her favorite tune of the evening. The horse walks slowly home, thumping over the bumpy, muddy road. It is a quiet symphony that sums up the night perfectly.

"Are you tired, Esther?" Bela asks, as the parents put the kids to bed.

"Yes."

"Follow me. You'll be sleeping in the barn, I suppose. Farmhands generally sleep in the barn."

Bela takes Esther outside and walks her to the barn, a candle in her hand. Esther's hopes are dashed, realizing she won't be sleeping in the toasty house. She'll be housed in the cold barn. The barn is pitch black, except for the small light of Bela's candle. Esther stubs her toe twice walking through it. In the back of the barn, away from all the junk, Bela lights a few stumpy candles that are near extinction. The dim light shows a little "guest room" where the farmhands sleep. A crude bed is formed from a large heap of unbound tules, with a few thick, dusty blankets and a fire pit surrounded by stones. Bela makes a pile of wood and kindling and then goes to the house to get a burning branch to light it with. Meanwhile, Esther beats the blankets to get out all the dust.

"There's the wood for the fire," Bela counsels, pointing at a small pile. "Every time you wake up, you should throw a log on. If it goes out, it gets really cold in here."

Esther nods and brushes away the dust that got all over her party dress.

"Well, goodnight," Bela says with a yawn, and she leaves Esther alone.

Once the fire gets going, Esther gets warm enough to be comfortable. She puts on her nightgown and climbs into bed. Coughing from the dust, she promises herself that she will wash their blankets in the river tomorrow morning. Then she falls asleep.

Beaver 1'

Esther wakes to the sound of somebody banging things in the barn. It is dawn, and a pale light shines through the window. The fire is long dead and it is freezing outside, so Esther curls up into a ball underneath her blanket and falls back asleep. A warm, little ball hiding from the cold, wet morning.

"Esther...Esther..."

A hand shakes her a few moments later. She groans, hoping it's just a dream. But it isn't and she finally peeks her head out. Bela stands over her, stifling a yawn. The light is still pale, as it is still very early in the morning.

"Wake up. Mother wants your help with breakfast."

Esther's mind, still asleep, tries to concentrate on what Bela is saying, but she is having difficulty.

"It's cold in here," Bela says with a shiver, as she disappears out the door she came in.

Esther groans and hides under the covers. She only means to stay there a moment, but she falls back asleep.

The next time, Bela is not so nice. She pulls Esther's blankets off. Esther wakes with a start, finding herself suddenly unprotected from the morning cold.

"Tara's waiting on you," she says grumpily.

Bela leaves the blankets curled up at the foot of the bed and leaves the room. This time, Esther gets up and hurries to the warm house in her nightgown. She is suddenly afraid she will lose her job. At the other end of the barn, she passes Tork, looking for his tools. He mumbles good morning as she passes him. Outside, she sees Bela off on some errand with little Sare in tow. Even Sare is up and working before Esther.

Inside the house, a blast of heat greets her. The smell of coffee and frying corn tortillas is overpowering. Tara stands over the wood stove, looking every inch the pleasant, plump country wife. A glorious sheen of sweat on her face shows off all her hard work over the hot stove.

"There you are. Can you go get a bowl of milk from Tork?" Tara says, giving the tortilla an expert flip.

Esther goes on her mission, but the milk isn't ready yet, so she stands there patiently and waits. She becomes caught up in watching Tork pull on the little teat of the cow, sending forth a tiny stream of milk. It is a long time before she makes her way back to Tara with a full bowl. By this time, Tara has finished the corn tortillas and is frying strips of pig meat.

"What took you so long?"

"The milk wasn't ready."

"Next time just come right back here," Tara says. "Help yourself to some coffee bean tea and then you can start cutting potatoes."

Esther has a cup of warm coffee with milk. She is careful not to drink too much, remembering the other day.

"Ahhhh," she sighs.

Tara laughs. She hands Esther a crude apron and shows her how to tie it Beaver fashion. Then she gives Esther a knife and leads her outside the back door into the kitchen. The kitchen consists of a couple of cutting tables made from thick redwood and an assortment of baskets, bowls, and kitchen tools. There is a huge cask of water, a giant dish bowl, and a compost bowl also. Esther is deposited in front of a bowl of small, hard potatoes caked with mud. Tara leaves her alone and returns a short time later to check on her. Esther has washed the mud off and is now cutting them into slices.

"No, no...too thick and uneven. These are for frying in fat, so you want them thin. Like this."

Tara shows her how to do it with a few quick, expert slices. Esther attempts to duplicate her slices. She takes slow, careful cuts.

"Can you go faster?" Tara asks, watching her struggling with the knife.

She tries, and she nicks her finger with the blade of the knife. Cursing, she puts her finger into her mouth. Then she takes an old pair of pants that has been relegated to dish drying status and applies pressure to the deep cut. Tara glances back at Esther's progress and sees the deep stain of red spreading over the pants.

"Why don't you go sit down till your finger stops bleeding. I'll finish cutting the potatoes."

Esther goes into the living room and sits by the fire. "I'm so useless," she tells herself over and over. "I'm stupid and useless." She is repeating the mantra that she learned at the mission.

When her finger stops bleeding, she trudges guiltily into the kitchen, and Tara sets her to work frying potatoes. Tara shows her how to smear fat into the iron pot and heat it over the fire, and then put the potatoes into the bubbling grease. Esther concentrates as hard as she can, not wanting to make another mistake.

"Tara, how's breakfast doing?" Tork yells into the kitchen a while later.

"It'll be a while yet. I'm behind this morning. Getting Esther acquainted with the operation and all."

"I'll just go help Bora with the firewood," he grumbles and Esther hears the door slam.

Beggar suddenly pokes his head into the door. Tara gives him some scraps and sends him outside.

"I think it's a crime how Tork always lets that dog in the house," says Tara, shaking her head. "Beggar scratches up everything and begs at the table. We're the only family around here that allows a dog in the house. It's that husband of mine. He always did have a soft spot for that dog. Spoils him rotten."

After breakfast, Esther is taken out to the fields. She feels sleepy from the heavy food with all the fried fat. She just wants to crawl into bed and go back to sleep, but Tork puts a small, crude spade into her hand and gives her a bowl of corn seeds. Then he shows her how to plant the corn. She has to dig a long narrow trench with the spade, place corn seeds into it, and then cover them up with loose soil. Afterwards, she has to pour a disgusting slurry on top of the trench that smells like decomposing fish.

At first, the work isn't too bad. Bela and Bora join her and they all chat amiably while they move down the rows. But they soon leave her far behind and she is left with no one to talk to. By midmorning, she begins to tire and dreams of falling asleep in the warm sun, and this makes her go even slower.

Lunch comes just in time to save her. She never dreamed that food could taste so delicious. Lunch is a simple meal of leftover meat pie from yesterday and freshly caught sand dabs, which are small, flat fish from the ocean. She doesn't stuff herself this time, remembering how sleepy she was after breakfast.

The afternoon's work is planting more corn. The whole family joins after lunch, except for Tara. As before, she is soon left far behind as everyone else moves faster than she does. Even little Sare is beating her, scrabbling around on all fours and shoving her spade into the dirt with all her might. She can hear Sare and Anri giggling far ahead of her and she wonders if they are laughing at how slow she is.

Soon her knees begin to ache from crawling and then her back begins to ache. Her hands begin to bleed from being scraped by rocks and twigs in the thick soil and she gets blisters and splinters from the spade handle. Will this nightmare ever end? She tries to speed up, but she cannot seem to gain any ground. In fact, she is going even slower now, due to the pain and exhaustion. She finds herself daydreaming at times, mostly of bed and siestas in the forest, and she has to remind herself to keep planting.

Finally the work is done for the day, and Bela comes over and helps Esther to her feet. She rises, and stretches her aching back.

"Go rest up before dinner," Bela says sympathetically.

Esther gratefully trudges off to her bed, which she has been dreaming of all day. She is sure that she has never worked so hard in her entire life – not even in the mission. How can anybody work so hard? She feels sorry for them, realizing that they must work like this all the time.

Bela enters the room just as Esther falls asleep. She drops a pile of tools on the floor, which makes a huge clatter, and wakes Esther up.

"Don't fall asleep yet." Bela chides. "If you fall asleep, you'll be gone to the world till morning. Come into the main house and join us for tea while mom finishes dinner."

Esther walks sleepily into the house and sits down by the fire. Bela hands her a cup of a mild black tea, which she calls China tea. Esther sips it slowly and revels in the warmth and coziness of the main house. This is a feeling totally alien to her - this feeling of home and family. She is afraid for a moment that it isn't real, like her dreams of Nani in heaven.

Tara walks in with the first course and takes a hard look at Esther's dirty nightgown caked with mud from the day's work.

"Esther, could you change your clothes for dinner? I don't like to have dirty work clothes in the house."

Tork rolls his eyes in a mocking fashion, making Esther smile.

"Tork, don't make fun of me. I'm the one who has to clean up around here."

"I don't have any other clothes," says Esther, feeling ashamed of her grimy appearance and poverty. Her nightgown must look a wreck. To think what it's been through. And when was the last time she washed it?

"Of course..." Tara muses. "How thoughtless of me." She appears genuinely sorry and smiles to show Esther that there is no harm done. "Bela, could you get Esther something to wear. Give her some of your work clothes so we can soak that pretty little dress of hers."

"Pretty?" Esther says aloud.

She follows Bela into the bedroom to change clothes. The bedroom is large, because this is where the entire family sleeps. Several beds are set around the room and there are several baskets to hold everybody's clothes and personal items. The room is cluttered, especially the kids section where little straw dolls and toys are scattered everywhere. Bela starts rooting around in one of her baskets and comes up with an old brown dress, which she hands to Esther.

"Ah, how pretty you look!" exclaims Tara, as Esther returns, wearing her new dress. "Perfect."

Esther smiles and sits down. Bela comes to the table ten minutes after that, wearing a clean dress with a piece of silk tying back her hair, but she gets no such compliments from her mother.

"Going somewhere tonight?" Tara asks suspiciously.

"To see Kirth."

"It is your turn to clean up tonight."

"I'll do it tomorrow morning."

"Mind your mother," says Tork. "You can see him tomorrow."

"I'll stay up late then. I'll do the dishes when I get home."

"Do them first."

"He'll go to sleep."

"Well, he's a smart boy then," says Tara in a firm voice.

Bela sighs and stands up again. She tromps to the bedroom door and disappears inside.

"Don't you want dinner?" Tork shouts after her.

The family is having rabbit stew and corn bread tonight. It is completely delicious, as usual, and Esther eats until she is stuffed. After dinner, she finds that she can barely keep her eyes open. The rest of the family sits down by the wood stove and falls into a dull torpor, but Esther doesn't even have the energy for that. She shuffles to her little room and gets underneath the blankets. She does not even bother to light a fire or complain that her blankets are still dusty and make her sneeze. She falls instantly asleep and it is the sleep of the dead.

Beaver 2'

Bear moon

At dawn, Esther hears Tork crashing around in the barn, preparing to milk the cow. She groans and makes a silent plea to be allowed to sleep in. She doesn't think she could get up now even if she wanted to. The Bela appears and shakes her awake.

"Tara wants you in the kitchen. She said that I'm not to leave your side till you're dressed." Bela shivers. "And it's cold in here, so get moving."

"Don't we ever get to sleep in?" asks Esther, sitting up in a daze.

"Nobody sleeps past sunrise in Beaver village. Sleeping late is for the Jay tribe."

Bela sits down on her bed and waits for Esther to get up and get her new work clothes on. Soon, Esther staggers behind her toward the house. She is stiff and sore from head to toe this morning, and she can barely walk for all her aches and pains.

"Right on time," Tara beams at her, as she appears in the kitchen. "Have some coffee bean tea."

Esther drinks the cup slowly, never wanting it to be finished. But eventually, she has to drain it. Once pleasantly fortified with the warm, lightheaded feeling she gets after a cup of coffee, she begins to cook.

"Have you ever made yogurt before, Esther?" Tara asks.

"No. What is it?"

"You take milk and put it on top of the fireplace for a few days to ferment. Then you scrape the scum off the top, sweeten it with berry paste, and eat it. Perhaps you can begin by sweetening that bowl, and we'll have some for breakfast with potatoes and corn cakes."

Esther takes a bowl filled with curdling milk off the fireplace, unable to believe that they are going to eat it. It looks disgusting. She scrapes the yellowish substance off the top and it looks a little less disgusting, but not much. Tara hands her a pot in which are found a few handfuls of dried berries and she is told to boil it down into a thin paste. When it is cooked down, the berry paste is delicious, and it seems a shame to Esther to waste in curdled milk. She has a few fingers of berry paste for herself and then does as she is told.

Tara tries it and pronounces it good. Esther dips a finger in and takes a tiny taste of the yogurt. It is very sour and there is not enough berry paste to make it taste good.

"Yogurt is quite nutritious. It is said to have curative properties for the digestion," Tara informs her, noticing that her face is not pleased by the taste.

After breakfast, Esther is put back on her knees again planting corn. It drizzles all day long, but Tork will permit nobody to quit. He is pleased that it is raining, because now he will not have to water the plants himself, and he wants as much done while it is raining as possible. But Esther curses the rain, which turns the hard ground into muddy sludge, making everything that much harder. She crawls around in the mud, soaked and miserable, planting corn seeds and cursing her fate.

Finally, a thoroughly soaked and muddy Esther trudges off to clean herself up for lunch. She is permitted to work out of the rain for the remainder of the afternoon. Tara puts her to work shelling acorns. She stands outside at the cutting table, which is well sheltered by a roof, and crushes acorn shells with a smooth rock. The white meats are put into one basket and the shells into another. In a few hours, she has filled an entire large basket.

Next Tara shows her how to make flour. She gives her a small, flat basket and a thick wooden bowl. She crushes the meats of the acorns until they are thick flour, which goes onto a flat basket to be sifted. The finest flour sticks to the basket and the remainder is poured back into a bowl to be re-crushed even finer. The finished flour must be leeched before it can be cooked. Tara leeches it with boiling water in a pot over the fire, which is faster than leeching it in the stream.

After dinner, Esther and Bela do the dishes, Tara gets to play with the children, and Tork and Bora relax outside and smoke a pipe. When the dishes are clean, a thoroughly exhausted Esther joins the family outside, and sits down with her back against the wall. She has a pipe of Tork's tobacco, and the smooth, heady mixture tops off the evening perfectly. She watches the sun set and puffs until she is dizzy.

As darkness descends, the family gathers in the main room. The wood stove is stoked hot to prepare against the chill of the night. Tork smokes another pipe and Tara sips tea. Bora pulls out a flute and a little drum and he and Bela prepare to play a tune.

"We're not much good at music," confides Tork. "Not like the Bear tribe -"

"Dad," Bela complains. "Can't you ever just let things be?"

"I was going to say that we have fun and that's the important thing," Tork says indignantly, ending the argument.

Bora pounds out a simple beat and Bela alternately sings and plays the flute. Tork was right. They aren't much good on their instruments. Bela is very theatrical and tries to put on a show for everybody, but the family is quite used to her little shows and it falls on tired and dull ears. Tork and Tara sit in a daze and stare at the fire, barely paying attention. Esther tries to look interested, but the truth is that she doesn't find the music that compelling. She would prefer a comforting silence instead. The little children are more interested in a little game with wooden pieces and they interrupt their sister and brother in the middle of a song to ask if everyone wants to play with them. Their parents hush them quiet, so they play by themselves. Later, Sare tries to explain the game to Esther, but Esther's eyes are sleepy slits and she cannot focus. Sare plows on anyway and explains the game in finest detail, and Esther nods her head tiredly and lets her ramble on.

When Tara begins to nod off, she opens her sleepy eyes and summons up a last little bit of strength.

"Bedtime!"

"One more," yells Sare.

"I'm sorry, Sare, but it's late," Tara says gently.

Tork picks her up roughly and carries her into the bedroom, while Sare shrieks with delight. Anri walks after them dutifully. He is the mellowest child Esther has ever met. Esther mumbles goodnight herself and goes off to her cold little bed with a candle in her hand. She wonders if they will ever let her sleep in the main room in front of the wood stove, as she beats clean the pile of dust and tules she calls her bed. She would give anything to sleep in front of that stove, but she is too shy to ask. She snuggles into a ball inside several blankets, bunches up some clothes for her head, and falls dead asleep.

Beaver 5'

Eagle moon

"Good morning, Esther."

Esther groans and burrows deeper into the blankets.

"When are you going to get up on your own?"

Esther doesn't reply, so Bela pulls her usual trick of pulling off the blankets so Esther will freeze. But Esther is ready this time and she burrows deep into the pile of tules. Bela laughs and begins searching for Esther to drag her out, but Esther keeps on burrowing away from her until it becomes a game. Finally Bela grabs her foot and pulls her out, and they erupt into furious giggling. They are so loud that Tork comes over to see what the fuss is all about. Neither will tell him, so he just shrugs and returns to his morning chores.

Esther enters the kitchen with a bowl of milk already in her hand.

"That's using your head," laughs Tara. "Although I know you only remembered because you like milk in your tea."

Esther grins and helps herself to a cup of tea. Unfortunately, there are no more coffee beans, so she'll have to do with the weaker Chinese black tea from now on. Then it's time for working. Esther finds that she is quickly adjusting to the hectic schedule that the family keeps. She jumps into a batch of corn dough and begins making corn tortillas. Tara comments favorably on her work and praises her ability to learn quickly. Esther smiles and does not mention that she has made many corn tortillas in her time at the mission.

After breakfast, she spends the whole day weeding and seeding hemp plants. It is exhausting as usual, yet she is not totally dead to the world by the end of the day. She even manages to be wide awake after dinner, and she is rewarded with the latest fight between Bela and Tara. They are outside in the kitchen, hands immersed in the dirty hot water of the dish tub, while fighting loudly so the whole family can hear.

"I'll do it tomorrow," shouts Bela.

"I need you to do it tonight," Tara replies firmly.

"But I want to see Kirth tonight. Can't Esther do it?"

"No."

"You just don't want me to see my husband."

"He's not your husband yet," corrects Tara. "And when you are married, you will see him every single night for the rest of your life. You will see him until you are sick of him. So what's the hurry?"

"That's you. Not me," Bela snaps. "I'll never get sick of my husband."

There is a tense moment of quiet and then Tara continues undaunted.

"Bela, don't do this to me. I really need your help. I'm tired and overworked and I have clothes to mend tonight. Please help your family out."

Bela heads inside the house, her hands still wet from the dishes. She is tense and angry, but she reluctantly gives in to her mother's wishes. She mumbles angrily to nobody at all, as if carrying out an imaginary argument with herself as she heads out to the front yard to do whatever chores Tara asked her to do.

Esther peeks her head through the kitchen door, to see Tara scrubbing in a bucket of water filled with little pieces of food.

"Do you need any help, Tara?"

Tara is still very flustered, but pleased by Esther's offer. "You could finish the dishes, if you're not too tired."

Esther jumps into the bucket of warm, dirty water, happy to prove that she can work as hard as any of them. She recalls the days of hard work in the mission, and for the first time she appreciates the value of it. Back then, she never did. She and the other neophytes would work as slowly as possible, as a sort of revenge for their captivity. But now that the work is not forced upon her by threat of the whip, she finds that it can be very satisfying.

Later, Esther sits by the fire with the family, once again reveling in domesticity. Sare and Anri play a game in the corner. Tara mends clothes. Tork smokes his pipe and listens to Bora play the flute absentmindedly. Only Bela is absent, and Esther can feel the hole that it causes in the tight knit family. Finally, Bela breezes through the door, finished with her evening chores at last. Everyone looks up and beckons her to join them. Sare and Anri jump up and try to get her to play with them, but she refuses each in turn by swirling them around in the air and setting them back down by their game.

"Come with me," she whispers in Esther's ear mysteriously, and she disappears out the kitchen door.

“Bela -” says Tara quietly, but she is ignored.

Esther follows Bela outside into the dark night. Bela lights a lantern so they can see, which illuminates the trees behind their house, casting shadows everywhere. Then Bela pulls out a long wooden pipe and a box, and opens the box to show off a thick, spongy little plant. Tara tears off a piece of the aromatic plant and stuffs it into the wooden pipe.

“What is that?” Esther asks.

"Haven’t you ever smoked jimm before?"

Jimm is marijuana.

"No, I haven't." Esther sniffs the plant curiously, which has a strong smell.

“It’s like tobacco, only stronger.”

Bela lights the pipe and smokes deeply and Esther finds the smell enticing. When it’s her turn, she puts the pipe to her mouth and sucks on it. The smoke is hot and burns her mouth, and she quickly breathes it out.

"No, no. You have to hold it in longer," chides Bela.

Esther tries again and manages to hold it in her lungs a bit longer. Then she begins to cough heavily.

"That's better," says Bela.

She smokes some more and then Esther smokes some more.

"Ahhhh," Bela sighs with contentment. "That's nice.” She taps out the pipe. "Most of the people around here don't smoke jimm, except for holidays. Beavers are too worried about becoming lazy.”

She fills the pipe again and each girl takes another puff.

"I’m moving to Kirth’s village in a few weeks. He’s built a house for us. I guess Mother doesn't want me to leave home. She thinks I am growing up too fast. But I'm turning fifteen years old this month, and it’s time for me to leave home. I don’t know why she is taking it so hard. She is jealous, maybe.”

“Why are you moving? Why not stay here?”

“When a girl marries a boy from a compatible village, then she goes to live in his village. That is the way it is done. I don’t really want to move away, but there are no good boys of compatible lineage in my village worth marrying, so I must move away."

Every family in a tribe is assigned a lineage and they may not marry within that lineage. This avoids the dangers of inbreeding. There are also compatible villages that they are encouraged to marry into, and the Raccoon tribe is considered compatible to the Beaver tribe.

She rambles on and on about a great many things. Esther has never heard her talk so much. And it is strange talk. It must be the smoke, although Esther doesn't feel any different. And then Bela goes into the house and returns several minutes later with two cups of tea.

"My mouth is dry. Is yours?"

Esther nods. Her mouth feels like she has eaten dirt. She drinks the tea and it is very soothing. In fact, Esther has never realized how much she likes tea. So much better than drinking water.

"Are you married?" Bela asks.

"No."

"Were you ever?"

Bela's voice seems to be coming from very far away.

"Esther? Esther?"

"Yes," she murmurs. Her voice sounds very far away too.

"You didn't answer my question. Were you ever married? Did you have a man?"

"I was married briefly," Esther says, suddenly finding it difficult to form words. "And there was another man...but we weren't married."

She tries to continue with her explanation, but she cannot form sentences any more. The words are getting all jumbled up in her head.

"I'm just trying to get to know you," Bela says. "You are very mysterious. You appear suddenly, from nowhere. You have no home, no past. Who are you?"

Esther tries to answer, but it feels like she is speaking in tongues. She tries again, concentrating harder, but a different language seems to emerge from her mouth. She becomes scared. What if Bela finds out that she used to be crazy? Maybe she still is crazy! The thought comes to her suddenly and she starts to panic.

"Are you alright?" Bela asks, looking worried. And then her face begins to warp. She becomes much older and more exaggerated, until she is a haggard old woman with sunken eyes and deep facial lines. She seems very angry and Esther becomes terrified and shrinks away.

"What's the matter, Esther?"

"Don't be angry."

"I'm not angry." But as she says this, she becomes angrier. "What are you talking about?"

Esther does not remember anything else Bela says. At some point, Bela goes back in the house. Esther is suddenly alone and frightened. What if Bela tells the family that there is something wrong with Esther? After a long agonizing time, she goes back into the house, but she cannot make it past the doorway. Everything in the house scares her. The wood stove seems like a frightening metal monster. The people in the room, whom she has known only a week, are strangers. She cannot face them like this - half mad and speaking nonsense - she'll scare them and they'll tell her to go away. So she goes back outside.

Grabbing the lantern, she makes her way around the back of the house to the barn. She is so afraid right now, because she sees how warped she is. Had she grown up here, with this family, she would have been a happy, well-adjusted girl. She would probably be married by now. But everything went wrong in her life, starting from the day she was baptized by the mission and became a neophyte.

"Who am I?" she asks herself. "Who am I really?"

She cannot handle the barn right now. She wanders down to the pasture, where the horse and cow quietly graze. They will be good company on a night like this. As she passes the trough where the horse and cow drink water, she catches her reflection by lantern light. There is a frightened, angry, and bitter girl staring at her; a wraith with deep, sunken eyes and lines of fear on her face. Terrified, she puts out the lantern quickly and huddles against the fence in absolute terror.

She hears a long, low screech like a bird. That noise is followed by a strange throaty growl, not like a bird. Like something that just ate the bird. And there is a shadow on the ground moving slowly toward her. She jumps up and runs, bumping into peacefully grazing cow as she flees. Taking this opportunity, she hides behind the cow. She can smell its strong odor and it is comforting. She touches it, and its touch brings her back from terror. Then she puts her arms around it. It is so calm and peaceful that it gives her a sense of security. It makes her think of her new family and how they are like the cow in this respect.

The cow ambles away slowly, not liking to be hugged. Then the horse wanders over and she embraces it too. At first, Boo is receptive and even puts his head on her shoulder. Then he neighs and rears his head up, almost lifting her off the ground, and she lets go.

Esther desperately wants this nightmare to be over. But she has never smoked jimm before, and she does not know how long these intense feelings will last. What if they never go away? What has she done to herself? She must ask Bela for help. Bela can tell her what to do.

As she approaches the house, the dog jumps all over her. She pets it over and over but it never gets enough. She hugs it and it breathes in her ear with hot, sour breath. But it seems to understand her. It is as if this dog is the animal equivalent of Esther, outside in the cold most of the time, eating scraps. Occasionally allowed in the house and given something good to eat. Then back out into its solitary misery.

"I understand," she tells the dog. "I'm a dog, too."

She finally gets to the window. The house is dark and everybody is asleep. There is nothing to do but to go to bed herself. The dog follows her and she allows it to come into the barn with her. She crawls gratefully into bed and curls up underneath her dusty covers. She stares at the cobwebs, illuminated in the moonlight that seeps through holes in the roof. She tries to sleep, but the nightmare introspections continue unrelenting. It is like some other self, unremorseful and cruel, is ripping apart all her false assumptions and securities. All the mistakes she has made spin madly in her head. All the bad things that have happened to her parade endlessly before her.

"I just want to sleep," she whines miserably. "Like they sleep next door. Peaceful and secure in their world, with their family all around them."

The bed is scratchy and uncomfortable, and the room is musty and suffocating. Beggar's hot breath and strong odor make her crazy. She can take this room no longer. She hates it. Standing up, she wanders back out into the cold night air again. The dog trails behind her, occasionally licking her and nipping at her and making a nuisance of itself. She brings her blanket with her to spread out on the ground somewhere. Out here, her thoughts are much smaller. The overwhelming sky, stars and the great world around her make her problems seem tiny and unimportant.

As she walks, she hears a rustling, and then she sees a white thing in a little enclosed area, surrounded by large pieces of bark. That must be where the pig lives. She has never seen the pig, except on the dinner table, and she wanders over to have a look. It is a bald, fat pale mass, with a tiny, curly tail, sleeping in the dirt. It almost reminds her of Miguel, with it's fat, pink body lying around in a dirty bed. Now she understands why the other women in the town always called him a "pig". But she knows it is nothing like Miguel really. Its eyes seem sweet and kind, even in the darkness. She curses herself for even thinking it was like Miguel.

She suddenly feels sorry for it. It always stays in here, with nobody to touch or have any contact with, except for feeding time. Esther has never been to see it once. She resolves to come visit it sometimes. She talks to it a bit, telling it something of her life. She pets it and promises to return in the daytime.

She goes onward to the pasture - Beggar still at her heels. Curling up in the grass with her blanket, she is swallowed up by the stars and the night goes on and on and on.

Beaver 6'

A little pink ribbon of daylight lights up the cloudy sky when Esther opens her eyes. She rises and stretches, momentarily confused. What is she doing out here, in the cow pasture with the dog? Then she recalls the terrifying night clearly. What a relief that it is over! Thankfully, her racing thoughts are gone, replaced by a spacey numbness. She is going to be all right. She isn't permanently insane. Breathing a major sigh of relief, she wanders into the barn to put away her blanket. Then she goes inside the house, lights a fire from last night's coals, and puts up a pot of water upon the wood stove to make tea. When the tea is done, it tastes so good and comforting - even without the milk - that she wants to cry from happiness.

Soon Tork awakens. He is surprised to see her already up, but pleased by the smell of tea. He usually has to make it himself, for Tara doesn't wake up until breakfast time. He has a cup and then joins her by the fire for a moment of quiet companionship. Then off to work he goes.

When Tara wakes, she is even more surprised than he.

"Look Bela," she beams. "Our Esther is becoming a true Beaver. Up before me and you, and she has started the fire and made tea."

Bela gives Esther a strange look. She doesn't know what to make of her after last night. But Esther seems back to normal, so she just shrugs it off and goes about her business. After her tea, Esther does her morning chores and goes out to the kitchen to help Tara with breakfast. She gives thanks to this family for keeping her sane.

Beaver 8'

Raccoon moon

The next few days are filled with work, work, and more work. Esther has never known people to work so hard in all her life. Tara, 'the rock', cooks three meals a day, does laundry for everyone, helps around the farm, watches the little ones, and sews. Tork milks the cows, tends the horses and pig, sows crops, waters, composts, weeds, plows, builds things, fixes things and takes care of business. The children pick up all the loose ends, especially Bora, who has a particularly large round of chores to do, including heavy wood chopping duty. Even the little ones have a round of chores to do, and they help out with the planting and harvesting. Bela is supposed to be a major part of the family operation, but she has been slacking off lately, dreaming of her own family and the new house which Kirth built and she has never seen.

Esther struggles to maintain her energy in the face of such an unrelenting schedule. But the hard work is offset by the comfort she takes from the security that this family offers her. It is a great comfort to no longer have to worry about survival, and to eat as much as she wants three times a day.

In the afternoon, Esther helps with the watering. There is a river running just south of the property, which is used to irrigate all of the crops. Due to the heavy rains, wet earth, and constant mists in the area, heavy watering isn't always required, but new seeds always require a good soaking. So he hitches Boo to the cart, loads up some heavy barrels, and off they go.

At the river, Esther, Tork, Bora, and Gunn - a neighbor - fill barrels and heave them on top of the cart. While the men swap farming stories, Esther discovers a beaver dam and walks over to watch the little brown creature work endlessly on his house. The cute, little brown bundle of energy chews contentedly on a stick and then places it gingerly into his dam.

"Our totem animal," Tork says proudly, coming over to look at the beaver. It's fitting, don't you think?"

Esther admits that the busy little animal could fit in quite well in this village.

"Yes, it looks just like us. Building its little house. Always working." Tork laughs. “Remember Yuyu?”

Gunn laughs heartily.

“Yuyu was this beaver that set up a dam right by Beaver Hall,” explains Tork. “His dam was flooding the whole area. We took it apart one day. The next day, he had rebuilt the entire thing. We took it apart again and Yuyu rebuilt it a second time. And a third time. It was relentless.”

“We hated to kill it, having a soft spot for the clever little guy, so someone came up with the brilliant idea of setting up underwater funnels to channel the water right past his dam. That way, it wouldn’t flood, and he could still have his home. So, we did that and slapped ourselves on the back because we had outwitted the beaver. But within a day or two, Yuyu had clogged up all of our funnels and the flooding returned.”

“So what happened?” asks Esther, after a long silence.

“Well…we had to kill him. We made a hat out of him or something like that, didn’t we?”

“That we did,” agrees Gunn. “We just couldn’t beat him. “

After the three barrels are lifted onto the cart with much effort and sweat, it is Boo's task to pull the heavy barrels to the field. Boo struggles to pull the heavy cart all the way back. Then Esther helps Tork water the crops all afternoon long. He unstops a hole in the bottom of the barrel, and a steady stream of water runs out and dribbles onto the plants. Boo pulls the cart slowly, until everything is watered.

That night, it begins to rain, and Tork begins to curse in a loud voice. Tara finally makes him go outside until he is finished cursing, so he will not upset the kids. He goes outside and screams at the rain for another five minutes.

"Inconjunct," Bora whispers with a grin.

"What?"

Before Bora can explain his cryptic reply, Tork returns sopping wet and much calmer. He sits back down to dinner, his wet hair dripping all over the table.

"Oh well, what's another day wasted?" he murmurs to himself.

Beaver 11'

Wolf moon

"Today is the full moon," Tork says during breakfast. "Word is that some of the Wolf tribe are here for Polar Day."

"Oh wonderful," says Tara gleefully.

"Is there a celebration today?" asks Esther hopefully.

"This is a big planting day. Half the tribe wouldn't show up if there were. But there will be a party tonight in Beaver Hall. If we all work really hard, we'll get the planting done early and we can wash up and relax before dinner."

"I'll have to whip up something for the feast," says Tara, already thinking ahead.

Tork works them hard that day, and Esther plods along dutifully, thinking of sleep the whole time. She slept little last night, and if there is a feast, she is liable to sleep little tonight. They plant hemp and corn seeds most of the day, as is the custom on the Beaver / Wolf full moon, which is considered a lucky planting day. Even Tara comes out and makes one of her rare appearances in the fields. They finish a few hours earlier than usual, so everyone can wash up and get dressed. Esther puts on Bela's red dress again, so she will look presentable for a party.

This is the first time that Esther has been inside the Beaver House. The main room is magnificent, with a high 'A' frame ceiling soaring high, wreathed with smoke from the fire. Upon the walls, sit magnificent tapestries imported from China and India. A great stone fireplace roars with a huge fire and many candles light the room in a soft glow. Several long wooden tables with benches stand side by side, already set with appetizers and wine casks. They enter the room and lay into trays of smoked venison, corn cakes and fried mushrooms. The sip wine and begin to converse with all of their friends and neighbors whom they haven't seen since the party two weeks ago. That's the way it is with the Beaver tribe this time of the year. They throw huge parties so they can see all of their friends at once. Otherwise, they would be too busy to see anybody.

Esther wanders around, admiring the lush decor and the solid foundations of the room. She has never seen a room this big and beautiful, not even the mission church where she used to pray as a child. Soon dinner is brought out and the tables are filled with people from end to end. The room echoes with shouting, merrymaking and the smack of hungry mouths tearing into meats and breads of many varieties.

Esther eats and drinks to bursting point. She notices that she is filling out from all of the rich foods she has been eating, and she is surprised to see a little belly growing. She rubs it and giggles to herself, being a bit drunk by now. She hasn't spoken a word to anybody since she arrived here, so the only person she has to amuse is herself.

After dinner, everyone gathers in the dancing space. Benches are pulled up and people take a seat, still chatting amiably about this and that. Chief Mai stands up, preparing to speak. Instantly the crowd goes silent, so great is the respect awarded to this great woman. She smiles upon all assembled and nods slightly.

"The full moon...Beaver sun and Wolf moon. A time for all those who are Beavers to look into our hearts and recognize our own dark side hiding deep within. Find out what mysteries you are hiding and release them into the sun. In order to help us, our special guest, Ohona of the Wolf Tribe, is here. She will sing a song of power to help us to open our hearts. Here she is, accompanied by her tribesmen."

Ohona is a small woman with black hair that goes to her waist and piercing eyes underneath dark eyelashes and pale skin. Her body is lithe, flowing and covered in tattoos. She wears a black dress made from some sort of animal skin. Three people follow her, carrying instruments. They are dressed as savages, with animal skin clothing and strange masks. They begin to play a hypnotic drumbeat, mysterious, pulsing, and slightly menacing. Cymbals are delicately tapped and a horn wails out, a sound that chills the blood and makes the hair stand on end. And then Ohona begins to sing in a low wail that rises to a shriek. Her song is dark, and her voice haunting and strange. The three musicians sing along with her in deep, bass voices. The Beavers all stare at each other, wondering the same thing. What is this? Do you understand it? But then they turn back to watch, not wanting to miss anything. She dances like a body moving through jelly, slow and rhythmic, but always in time with the drumbeat. The song lasts a good half hour and many have strong feelings inspired by the music. Esther has a vision of Fernandez, leering at her from a fire, which consumes him. The song penetrates the most closed heart, and many find themselves becoming frightened by the feelings welling up inside of them. When it is finally over - and it does not end as much as die out - Ohona walks away without a word.

Everyone stares at each other, wondering how to respond to this music. It was strange, gloomy chanting with a dark heart, and nothing for a man of the earth to deal with. Esther, who has a dark soul, found it beautiful, and she wishes the musicians would go outside and Ohona would sing to the full moon. Finally, everyone cheers and toasts to Ohona, shrugs off the strange feelings, and goes back to the dining room for dessert and more wine.

Soon the Wolf tribe musicians begin to play more traditional dance music and the dance floor fills quickly. Esther sits with Bora and the kids, watching their parents dance with Bela and Kirth. Bela is a good dancer, although she obviously did not learn it from her mother. Of Tara's many wonderful qualities, dancing isn't one of them. But she tries hard, and that is the important thing. Tork has good rhythm, although he does the same moves over and over. They dance for a few songs and then Tork and Tara step off the dance floor for some wine and sweet corn pie.

"I heard the Bears were sending a whole shipment of moon pies," Tork mumbles. "What happened?"

"You know them," Tara says with a shrug. "They hate to travel." She takes a bite of his pie. "This isn't bad pie. Keli made it."

"Well I hate to travel," complains Tork. "But sometimes business demands it."

"You do like to travel," Bora cuts in. "At least the inconjunct part of you does."

"Now don't start," Tork says gruffly.

"What does inconjunct mean?" asks Esther.

"Inconjunct is when two signs don't work well together - like fish oil and water. Especially when the sun and moon are inconjunct. Tork was born under a Beaver sun with an Owl moon. The steady earth in him hates to travel, but the changeable fire in him likes the adventure. His earth is calm, but his fire is excitable."

"I don't understand."

"Inconjuncts are crazy," Bora says with a shrug. "There are stories of families of certain tribes abandoning or even killing babies that are born with inconjunct sun and moon. Because inconjunct babies grow up confused and useless."

Esther puts her hand to her mouth reflexively and gasps in disbelief.

"That's not true," says Tara, overhearing her son. "It's never been proven that anyone has done that."

"Some do." Bora argues. "Because inconjuncts are looked down upon. They can never be chief or hold a high position in the tribe."

"That doesn't mean that anyone would kill their own baby. That's a rumor. A sick rumor. Your sister, Bela, is an inconjunct, and we didn't kill her."

Bora shrugs. "I've heard stories, that's all."

"Nonsense. And your father is not crazy, Bora. He is a good man, and very useful."

Bora shrugs again and grins.

Bela walks over to join them. There is something lusty about her as she walks from the dance floor. She is flushed from dancing and there is a wild, sexual fire in her eyes.

"Kirth and I are going to his cousin's barn for a party," she says. "I'll be home later."

Tork and Tara exchange uneasy glances. They have definitely noticed the look in her eyes.

"Not tonight," Tork says a bit rudely. "Tomorrow is a busy day."

"Another night," agrees Tara.

"Tonight is the Wolf moon," says Bela angrily. "A full moon, too. I want to celebrate."

"All the more reason for you to stay home tonight," Tara says slowly. "You're not married yet, you know. It isn't proper for you to spend so much time with your husband until you are married. It reflects poorly on your value as a wife."

"What does that mean?" Bela asks suspiciously.

"It means that you are embarrassing us with your behavior," Tara says slowly.

"Think what you like. I'm going anyway."

"Why?" sputters Tork. "So you can go off to some barn with Kirth and - and -"

"And what," Bela says, eying him intensely.

He is at a loss of words. He takes a sip of wine nervously.

"And have sex," cuts in Tara quietly.

Bela glares at her mother, but her mother matches her gaze.

Bora begins to laugh, but his parents shoot him a look and he quickly shuts his mouth.

"Didn't you hear what the Chief said," complains Bela. "Tonight is a night to let go of things you are holding on to. Well, you are holding on to something. Me! You need to let go of me."

"When it's time," Tara replies. "And in the proper way."

"Well, it is time for me," Bela says bitterly. "I'm going with Kirth. And if you can't handle it, then I guess I won't come back."

"Fine," Tara says stubbornly. "If that's how you want it."

Bela turns and leaves, tears in her eyes. She walks over to Kirth and hugs him tightly. Kirth stares at the family nervously, not wanting to come between them and their daughter. All of a sudden, Tara begins to curse loudly and storms out of the room, making as much of a ruckus as possible. She knocks over a bench on the way out, just for effect. Esther has never seen her so angry. Everyone looks at her for a moment, and then they go back to dancing and having fun again.

Bela wipes tears from her red eyes, grabs Kirth's hand, and pulls him away with her. Kirth stares at Tork guiltily, and his eyes say apologies as he follows Bela dutifully out the door.

First things first - Tork drinks all of the wine down in one gulp. Then he gathers the children together and tells them that it is time to leave. The kids follow quietly, without protest. Esther thinks it is best to walk home alone, to give the family some space, so she stays at Beaver Hall. She tries to enjoy the music again, but it isn't fun anymore. She feels alone without her new family, so she finally goes outside and begins the long walk home.

The full moon lights up the night like a great lantern, and she can see everything around her bathed in a pale glow. She walks slowly, with Ohona's song weaving in and out of her head. It is warm enough that her bones are not chilled, and she begins to enjoy the walk. On the way, she stops to rest underneath a large tree. The tree feels safe, like a protector. She curls up underneath it, remembering what it felt like to sleep in hollow trees. She wants to fall asleep right here, sure that she will have amazing dreams.

But it is difficult to convince yourself to be uncomfortable if you don't have to be, and reason eventually prevails. She stands up, disobeying the moon, and walks back to the dirty barn she calls home.

Beaver 12'

In the morning, she is awakened by Tork.

"Up you go," he says brusquely. "Tara needs help."

He walks out of the barn without another word. Annoyed at his rude attitude, she stays in bed several minutes - silently fuming - before she finally rises. Still exhausted from last night, she walks to the kitchen. She is in a bad mood from lack of sleep, and she can already tell that it is going to be a very hard day.

"There you are. It's about time," Tara says with a disapproving frown.

Esther ignores her, and pours a bowl of tea for herself.

"You can make acorn bread."

So Esther starts putting the ingredients together for acorn bread. Tara is extremely irritable and keeps making comments about Esther's technique. Esther tries to ignore her, knowing how upset Tara is, but it is hard to take the long view when everything she does is picked apart. And her own patience is already on a hairline trigger as it is. She ends up acting like a neophyte from the mission, working really slow and pretending to be stupid to spite Tara. So breakfast ends up being really late and everyone is annoyed at everyone else as they sit down.

Bela doesn't come home at all today. Due to her absence, the whole delicate balance of chores is upset, and everyone is given extra work to do. Esther has to help Tara cook dinner and clean up afterwards, on top of her farm chores. As she stands at the dish bucket that night, her feet and back hurt and she barely has the energy to look at the huge stack of dishes - let alone clean them. She has to summon all of her reserves to finish and then she goes right to the barn - not even bothering to say goodnight. She is irritated at the whole family for being so mean today and for working her so hard. She considers just giving up and running away tomorrow, but she really has nowhere to go. So she goes to sleep and hopes it will be better in the morning.

Beaver 15'

Elk moon

Bela hasn't come home in days and the family struggles to keep up without her. Esther works from dusk till dark every day. She doesn't do anything any more but work, eat and sleep. It is a dreary schedule and she constantly dreams of her lost freedom to be as lazy as she wants. This place suddenly feels like the mission, dull and lifeless, where every minute of every day is scripted in advance.

Tork and Tara were always such fun in the past, but they have become grumpy and irritable - especially Tara. Ever since Bela abandoned them, all the magic has gone out of the house. The entire family is in a low level depression, only relieved by the heavy workload. They are too tired to feel sad, so they just walk around feeling nothing. Nobody laughs but the little ones.

After an especially long day, Esther is tired and weary. So it is to her surprise and delight, that Tara makes her a hot bath after dinner. She has often wondered why the family keeps a canoe in the back of the house. Now she finds out that it is used for bathing. Tara boils a large pot of water and pours it into the canoe and then adds cold water until the temperature is perfect. Esther melts into the bath, feeling that she has died and gone to heaven. She could swear that this bath is the best hour of her life. As it cools, Tara boils more water for her, and pours it in with a big smile. Esther looks up at the stars, thinking that when she has her own house, she will take a bath every single night.

"Everyone should have a hot bath once in a while," Tara declares, pouring more hot water into her bath. "It relaxes everything."

When Tara doesn't come with more hot water and Esther starts to shiver, she sadly has to admit that her bath is over. She climbs out of the canoe and dries off with a rag that Tara left considerately for her. She feels wonderfully relaxed and lazy, and her body feels as if it were made from jelly. Joining the family by the fire, she relaxes onto a tule mat with a sigh.

"I'll do the dishes in a few minutes," she promises.

"One should relax after a hot bath," comments Tara. "Take your time." Then Tara examines Esther's dirty clothes. "One shouldn't put dirty clothes on a clean body either. Come with me."

"If that daughter of mine wants to leave home, I don't see any reason why we should save all of her good clothes for her," Tara says, leading Esther into the bedroom. "I'm going to give you a few new outfits."

Soon, Esther is wearing a traditional Beaver dress, made from deerskin, and Tara smoothes out the wrinkles.

"A little big on you. You're thin, and Bela isn't. But we'll take it in a bit." She stands back to admire Esther. "There, I don't think I could tell you apart from any other Beaver daughter," Tara smiles a motherly smile. "Now, one more outfit I think."

She even gives Esther a pair of moccasins. The bottoms are made from cow leather, the tops from deerskin, and the laces are decorated with little shells. Esther has never worn moccasins before. She puts them on and walks around in them experimentally. They feel strange on her feet, because she has walked barefoot for her entire life.

"How have you come so far without shoes?" Tara asks, amazed.

"I'm just used to it."

"Well, we must change that," Tara says with a smile. "Look at your feet - so callused and dirty. From now on, your shoes will take the abuse that your feet have taken."

Esther surprises herself by giving Tara a hug. Tara laughs and wraps her arms around Esther. This is the first time that Tara has smiled in days, and the whole house seems to be cheered up by her simple grin.

"You never join us for family time any more," says Tara a little later. "You know that you are always welcome."

"Thank you," says Esther, truly moved by all of Tara's kindnesses on this night. "I'm just too tired after I finish the dishes."

"You'll adjust eventually," Tara says practically, looking one last time through Bela's things for something else to give to Esther. "I know you will."

Beaver 16'

Another long day of seeding, weeding, cleaning and other chores, and by late afternoon Esther is in a foul mood. She is weeding in the cold rain, on her hands and knees in the mud. To top it all off, she is menstruating. Esther usually has light menstruations, but today's bleeding is a bit more intense than usual. When Tara comes out with hot tea to combat the rain chills, she notices Esther's mood immediately.

"Esther, why don't you take a rest until dinner time," she says sweetly.

Tork looks up, preparing to argue, but she shoots him a look that stops him cold. He gives her an irritated look, but returns to his work without a word.

"Thank you," says Esther, as relieved as she can possibly be. She goes to her room, cleans herself up, gets under her blankets, and takes a long nap.

After dinner, Esther takes Tara up on her offer to join the family after dinner. Bora plays a beat on his drum and Anri and Sare sing in sweet, high voices. It is very cute and makes everyone laugh, and it seems that good spirits have returned to the household at last.

Bela picks this very time to make her triumphant return. She knocks on the door and Tara answers it, still grinning from the last song. But how her face falls as she sees her long lost daughter standing there. She turns cold instantly, returns to her chair, and picks up her knitting quietly. Bela steps into the house, looking extremely uncomfortable, and her eyes dart around the room nervously as she talks.

"I just came for some things," she says guiltily.

"Fine," says Tara flatly, never looking up.

Sare and Anri jump up and give their sister a big hug. At this act of childish simplicity, the tension in the room seems to drop a notch. Bela hugs them warmly and gives each a kiss. Then she observes the rest of the family, with one child holding onto each leg.

"Hey Bela," says Bora simply.

"Hello little brother. You're looking well," she says with a sad smile. "Hello Esther," she adds. "How are you?"

Esther smiles at her and says, "Hello Bela. I'm well. Thank you."

"Hope they're not working you too hard," Bela adds.

Then she turns and goes to the bedroom. Anri and Sare follow behind her, holding onto her hands. Grim silence replaces the joyful singing and laughing from just a moment before. Tork goes outside to smoke his pipe, and the house seems to sigh. Bela comes back in the family room a short time later, with a basket filled with clothes and other necessary items. The kids are still clumped around her protectively, as if to shield her from her parents' wrath.

"Goodbye," Bela murmurs.

Tork comes back in the house, and he seems agitated.

"Don't go," Sare says, tugging on her hand.

"I have to," Bela says, rubbing her head. "But you can visit me someday in my new house." She stares at her parents. "If Mom and Dad allow you to."

"This is absurd," shouts out Tork suddenly. "Of course we'll allow them. Look at how much they miss you. Sit down and let's talk this out."

Bela sits on a cushion, as far away from Tara as possible. She stares into the fire moodily, looking very much like her mother. Tara continues to knit sourly, and says nothing.

"We're not trying to take away your freedom," begins Tork. "We just want to remain a family as long as possible. It seems like only yesterday that you were my little Bela, sitting on my lap. Now you're all grown, and about to be married and going to a new village to live out the rest of your life. Why rush into it? Come back home and start your marriage in the right way on the new moon."

"You need to let go," Bela says firmly.

"We don't want to let go. We're your family. I'm sure Kirth wouldn't leave his family when they need him the most."

This seems to sting Bela. She becomes very uncomfortable.

"Come back and stay with us till your wedding day. You know this is a busy time of the year and we need you. We're struggling, Bela –"

"Is that all I am to you?" she asks angrily. "A farm hand?"

"No," he shouts, his voice going high with stress. "You're our daughter. Of course we love you. And look at the little ones. They miss you so much. We all want you here." He looks at Tara nervously. "Right Tara?"

Tara only stares at her knitting.

"Right Tara?" Tork repeats.

"Let her do what she wants," Tara finally says, in a calm, cold voice. "We have Esther. We can get along fine without Bela."

All the steam goes out of Tork's argument. He sags, defeated.

"Fine," Bela says flatly. "You heard Mother. You don't need me."

Bela stands up and walks to the door, Anri and Sare still in tow. She says her farewells and leaves the house, and everything is very, very quiet. Then Tork stands up and walks out of the house to smoke another pipe, slamming the door behind him as he goes.

Beaver 25'

Beaver moon

Tork wakes Esther up at the crack of dawn this morning. It is just barely getting light, as she drags her tired bones into the house to fix a large breakfast. Today, the family will try to finish all the planting for the year, so all of the little plants can be blessed by the new moon. Tomorrow is the big new moon celebration and Bela's wedding, so of course they cannot plant then.

All morning they bury little pieces of potatoes into the soft earth, which will grow brand new potatoes by the fall. Even Tara helps. Tork explains how potatoes grow extremely well when planted under the fixed earth sign Beaver, because they are very grounded and earthy themselves. After a quick lunch, they keep going until dark, because Tork wants to plant a lot of potatoes this year. To Esther's horror, he lights a lantern, and they continue by its feeble glow for another hour after dark. Tork is too tired to water them tonight, so he prays for a rainstorm and finally calls it quits.

They tromp into the house for dinner. Esther is dead tired and her back feels as if there are daggers digging in everywhere. Even the hardy farmer family seems exhausted tonight. They leave the dirty dishes in the dish basket, a rare thing in this house, and everyone goes right to sleep.

Beaver 26'

Tork allows Esther to sleep in late this morning before he finally wakes her. He has already been up for an hour, milking the cow and feeding the animals. Doesn't this man need any sleep?

"Tara needs help in the kitchen," Tork growls grumpily.

Esther dawdles over her tea, barely able to muster up an ounce of enthusiasm. She watches Tork and Bora water the potatoes with Boo. Finally Tara fetches her from her daze, and puts her to work on last night's dishes. Then she has to help Tara cook up some tortillas for the celebration today. By late morning, the work is finished, and everyone is given an hour's rest before they have to get dressed.

"Thank you all," Tork announces. "Now I can enjoy my daughter's wedding with a clear head. May the Great Beaver bless our crops and make them fruitful."

He pats Esther and Bora on their backs affectionately and gives Tara a little kiss. The tensions of the morning slowly melt away, and everyone falls into a dead stupor for the next hour.

Then the house becomes a frenzy of activity. Tara bathes the kids in the stream, dresses them, and fixes everyone's hair with a comb and a little grease. Esther bathes and puts on the brown party dress that Bela left for her to wear to the wedding. Tork walks in just as Tara is greasing Esther's hair, wearing his nice deerskin shirt and his cleanest pair of pants and a necklace of shells.

"Enough messing about. Get yourself dressed, Tara."

"I'm fixing Esther's hair."

"It is almost time to leave. Get dressed or we shall have to leave you here."

"Yes, I think you shall," she says, in barely a whisper. "I'm not going."

There is a long, uncomfortable silence as Tork digests this unbelievable piece of news.

"Woman, have you lost your mind?"

"No, Tork, I am clearheaded. Our daughter has acted selfishly and disrespectfully. She abandoned us during the crucial planting time and went off to play, with no regard to our feelings -"

"Tara, that's no reason -"

"- and she insulted me deeply with her callousness. It hurts me to do this, but Bela has not acted like a daughter should, and I will not attend her wedding. I will not go."

Tork is rarely at a loss for words, but he is now. He opens and closes his mouth over and over, but no words come. Esther takes this opportunity to leave them alone. But she overhears their argument from the other room.

"Esther sets a good example of how a daughter should act. Bela could learn a lot from her," Tara insists.

"Esther is not our daughter," Tork shouts angrily. "She's just the help."

"Don't talk about her like that," Tara shouts, showing a rare display of temper. "She's a better daughter than your daughter."

"My daughter! Now she's *my* daughter -"

The rest of their conversation is resumed in normal tones, but Esther thankfully can hear no more.

Some time later, Tork gathers the children together and marches them outside. The tension is so thick in the house that Esther is not sure she wants to be near any of them right now. Finally Bora comes to fetch her.

"Are you coming?" he asks with a grin.

"I guess so," she says sheepishly.

"Don't mind Dad," Bora says, waving his hands. "He's in a bad mood."

It is customary to give animals a vacation on the new moon, so they leave Boo to graze and they walk toward the Beaver House. They walk in silence until they arrive at the great assembly hall, which seems unusually magnificent today. The flowers are all in bloom and competing to give off their scents. The day is warm and everything seems happy to be alive. The whole tribe is gathered outside, drinking wine and chatting about the crops and the weather as they walk around the grounds in their finest clothes.

Tork leaves the family and goes in search of a drink, and Esther and the kids go looking for Bela. They find Bela and Kirth in the backyard of the magnificent house. Bela looks beautiful in a traditional dress made from antelope skin, with a wreath of flowers in her hair. She glows with the blushing radiance of a new bride. Kirth wears the traditional brown of the groom, a color that is said to bring good luck to a husband. He looks very handsome today, and Esther feels a slight touch of envy for Bela with her handsome man and the big house he has built for her.

Bela shouts when she sees them and runs over to give each a big hug. Anri and Sare tumble into her arms first.

"You look pretty," Sare squeals.

"So do you," Bela shouts back.

Bela hugs Bora with the calm acceptance each has for the other. Then she hugs Esther.

"Bela, you look so beautiful," Esther exclaims.

"So do you," Bela says laughing. "Where is the dirty girl in the stained sleeping dress?"

Soon Tork finds them, a glass of berry wine in his hand. He hugs his daughter and remarks on her beauty.

"You are so late," Bela says with relief. "They start the weddings very soon. And where is mother?"

Suddenly everyone is very quiet. Tork quickly explains the situation. Bela's blushing radiance fades quickly, replaced by pale sorrow. She seems crushed.

"I tried to talk her out of it," Tork says in a hopeless voice. "But when a woman with four planets in Beaver makes up her mind, nothing can change it."

"She hates me," Bela says to the ground.

When she lifts up her head, they can see that her red eyes are tearing up. She fights back an overwhelming sorrow.

"Don't cry," Tork says gently. "Your mother misses you terribly. It is so hard for her to let go. You are the first born - her little Bela - and you're leaving home. She cannot bear to say goodbye, so she gets angry instead."

"I was so mean to you all," Bela says, wiping her eyes. "I'm sorry. It wasn't right to leave during planting time."

"Forget it," Tork says, with a dismissing wave of his hand. "It's over and done with."

Esther detects a little flash of bitterness, which Tork quickly buries with a drink of wine. Kirth puts his arm around Bela protectively and she buries her head in his chest.

"Who will give Bela away?" Kirth asks.

"Maybe Aunt Tila can take her place," suggests Tork.

"We should ask Chief Mai," Bela says in a defeated voice, looking around for the matriarch. She sees the chief, standing near the wedding platform, wearing a beautiful cape of fine beaver fur that reaches almost to the ground. They walk toward Mai, who turns toward them and holds out her hands in welcome.

"Here we have the new bride and groom and their family," she says warmly. "Congratulations. You must all be very excited."

Bela quickly explains their situation to the chief, who listens silently until all have had their say. She examines their faces, seeming to gather much from them.

"I will not ask why your mother has refused to come today. That is your business. But Tara must give her consent to have Tila take her place. For without that consent, this wedding cannot take place."

"She is not against the marriage," Bela argues. "She didn't come today because she is angry at me."

"Nevertheless, you must obtain permission. Bring me a distinctive item of clothing from her, if she will give her consent. And you must go, Bela. You alone."

"But there is no time -" Bela cries out fearfully. "I'll miss the wedding."

"I will marry the other two couples first. There will be plenty of time."

"But-"

"I have decided. Do you doubt my resolve?" The chief looks upon her solemnly, and there is obviously no argument.

"No," Bela says, defeated.

"Then hurry off, child," Mai says, giving Bela a kiss on the cheek.

Bela walks away, Kirth in tow, and the family follows with many a respectful word and a smile for the chief as they part. Esther is struck by the respect all have for Chief Mai. She is quiet and thoughtful - a woman of few words - and when she says something, she means it.

"Better get going," Tork says to his daughter as they walk.

"Do you want me to join you, Bela darling?" asks Kirth tenderly.

"No, you stay here and keep an eye on things. I want a woman's company though." She gives him a kiss and then she turns to Esther. "Will you come with me, Esther?"

"Of course," Esther says, trying to be supportive, although she really doesn't want to face Tara right now.

So Esther and Bela walk to the house. Bela is quiet, but she seems to get much comfort from Esther's presence. When they arrive at the house, Bela turns to Esther and grabs her hand.

"Come inside with me. Mom and I won't fight if you are there."

Esther was hoping to stay outside, but she can hardly say no. As they walk into the house, she wonders why she is so involved in this family's problems. Is she to be an eyewitness to every argument and painful moment in their lives? Tara sits quietly by the fire, crafting a small pair of moccasins for Sare's growing feet. She looks surprised at the intrusion and stares at them both, wide eyed. Bela and Tara stare at each other a long time, saying volumes without speaking.

"Aren't you supposed to be getting married?" Tara finally asks, a bit coldly.

"Chief Mai told me I had to come here to get permission for Aunt Tila to take your place in giving me away," Bela says coldly in return. "I need an item of your clothing for consent."

Tara chuckles to herself.

"She's a tricky one - Chief Mai is. I know how she thinks."

She gets up and goes to her bedroom. She is in there a long time, and Bela and Esther sit restlessly by the fire, waiting for her return. She finally returns with a dress, which she hands to Bela dramatically.

"There you go. Now you better hurry back, or you'll miss your own wedding."

Bela takes it and turns to go, but she suddenly turns back around again.

"Mother, are you ever going to be my friend again?" she asks meekly.

Tara sighs. "Is now the best time to resolve this?"

"It's the new moon."

"True."

Suddenly Bela breaks down crying. "I'm so sorry, mother. I'm so sorry," she says over and over.

Tara stands up and pulls Bela close to her. She hugs the hysterical Bela tightly.

"Come to the wedding, mother. I can't get married without you."

She throws her arms around her mother's neck and buries her head in Tara's breasts.

"You just ran off, so excited to begin your new life," Tara says, fighting back her own tears. "And you left us when we needed you the most."

"I'm sorry -"

"No, that's not what hurts the most. You're my best friend, and you're leaving me alone."

And Tara begins to cry too.

Esther goes outside, the forgotten witness to so many dramas in this household. She sits on the porch, listening to the sobs of Bela and Tara from inside the house. Then Beggar comes up to her, begging for attention. She has to hold him down to keep him from jumping all over her, but she still gets a couple of mud streaks from his excited paws on her clean dress.

"Stop Beggar!" she shouts.

"If Beggar ever gives you trouble, just pick up a stick and he'll leave you alone," Tork once told her. She never could bear to do it, but now he is making a mess of her wedding dress. She grabs a stick and brandishes it over her head, and Beggar immediately backs off.

"Sorry, Beggar."

A short time later, Bela emerges from the house.

"She's still not coming," Bela says bitterly. "What a stubborn woman she is. After all that, she still won't come. She is acting so strange. You go tell her to come."

"She won't listen to me."

"Please, Esther. She respects you. Please...."

Esther sighs and walks back in the house. She has no idea what to say, but at least she can say she tried. She finds Tara sitting in her chair, her eyes red from crying. She looks lonely and miserable. She looks up at Esther and tries to speak, but she cannot. She wipes away a tear and stares at Esther miserably. Esther still cannot think of anything to say, so she just grabs Tara's hand and gently pulls her to her feet. Tara stands and her knitting falls off her lap to the floor. Tara stares at her, frightened and confused, as Esther begins to lead her outside.

"No -"

"Bela won't get married unless you come."

"I look terrible. I can't go to a wedding like this."

Esther goes into Tara's room and picks up her wedding dress, which lies uselessly on the floor. She smoothes it out, and then she goes back to the family room. Tara still has not moved, so Esther undresses her and puts the dress upon her as if she were a child. Then she combs her hair, and wipes the tear stains off her face before leading her outside. Bela sighs with relief, grabs her mother's hand tightly and leads her gently down the path. Esther walks a good distance behind them, letting them have their time together and avoiding more drama.

They arrive at the Beaver House as the second wedding ends. The benches from the hall have been moved outside and are packed with people. Esther is sure that the whole village must be here watching the weddings and she cannot believe how many old people are here also. She has never seen so many old people in her life. Very few people had a chance to grow grey hairs in Mission Santa Cruz. But here it is different. Many in the Beaver tribe live to a ripe old age, and old people just love weddings.

Everyone is very gentle with Tara, seeing what a state she is in, as they quickly get her prepared for her role in the wedding. Bela whispers something to Tork, who nods quietly. When Esther looks at him, he mouths a solemn "thank you".

And then Chief Mai announces, "The third and final wedding. Kirth of the Raccoon tribe and Bela of the Beaver Tribe please step forward."

Tara quietly takes her place next to Bela, and they walk slowly toward Chief Mai. When they get there, Bela whispers a 'thank you' to Mai, who nods seriously but says nothing. And then Bela and Kirth are married in the mellowing sun of the afternoon, and the golden shafts of sunlight make the wedding seem heaven blessed to Esther.

After the wedding, Chief Mai makes an announcement. "Mallie has just given birth to a baby boy," she says with a big smile. "Sun, Moon, Mercury, and Mars in Beaver, and Jupiter in Elk. A strong earth child."

There are loud cheers from the crowd.

"Of course, we send our prayers to the five other mothers who are hoping to give birth today. And now we will adjourn to the main hall for a feast and music."

This is the feast to end all feasts. The table is loaded with more food than Esther thought could ever exist in the whole wide world. Her nose is met with so many wonderful smells that she begins to drool. Although she promises herself that she will go easy on the food today, there are so many new dishes to try, that she has to eat a little bit of everything. And a little bit of everything adds up to a very full stomach indeed.

Everyone dances until late in the night to the music of Bear musicians. Esther allows Bora to take her for a twirl around the dance floor, and Bela and Kirth dance the entire night away, egged on by their family and friends who all want to dance alongside the happy couple. Everyone gets drunk and the party goes until very late in the night.

They go home in high spirits, weaving along the road in drunken weariness while singing in the darkness. Sare sleeps in Tork's arms. Tara is still quiet, but she seems in much better spirits, and she smiles the whole way home. When they get home, they stoke up the wood stove and sit down to soak up the last dregs of the evening. They are exhausted, but nobody wants the night to end. Finally, unable to stay awake a minute longer, everyone goes to bed with Tork's promise of a late rise the next morning and a lazy day of doing nothing.

Beaver 29'

Bear moon

Tara has been smiling at Esther all through dinner. But it isn't until they are all finished eating that she breaks the news.

"It's a Bear moon," she says.

"So?" Bora asks in his plain way.

"So...the Bear moon is a good time to make a home. It's a homey sign, isn't it? And somebody here has none."

"Who mommy?" asks Sare.

"Why Esther has none," says Tara, nuzzling Sare with her nose. "Esther has no home. She sleeps in a drafty barn. And we shall have to change that."

Sare cheers for Esther and looks at her excitedly.

"Esther," Tara continues, her grin returning, "we would like for you to sleep in the main house from now on. And we would like to offer you a place with this family for as long as you wish. We all adore you and would be honored for you to be a part of our family. You don't talk much about yourself, but we gather that you have no family of your own. Consider us your adopted family, if you wish."

Esther is speechless. She looks from one face to the other, and everyone stares at her with sparkling eyes and happy faces, eager for her to say yes. Esther smiles the biggest smile she has ever made in her life.

"I am so thankful. I don't know what to say. You are all so wonderful and I am so lucky to have met you."

"Is that a yes?" asks Tara.

"Yes." she says, and the whole family cheers.

Esther moves in that night. She puts her things into a basket and stretches out on a bearskin rug by the fire. It is as cozy as she imagined in all her nights in the drafty barn. She is so excited, that she squirms underneath her blankets. She now has something she has always dreamed of. She has a family and a home. Perhaps she will even have a husband soon. Esther is sure that she will be happy for the rest of her life.

Jay 0'

**Eagle moon*

Why is she having trouble sleeping tonight? Everything in this house drives her crazy. The warm, insulated room is stifling her. No sane person would leave a wood stove burning on a night this warm. Tork's snores from the next room grate on her nerves. And there are too many strange smells in here. She actually longs for her little bed in the barn tonight, with the comforting smell of moldy wood and dust. After an hour of tossing and turning, she wanders into the barn and lies down on her old bed.

She feels out of sorts, as if she is living somebody else's life. She has felt this way ever since she moved into the main house. While she was a farmhand, living in the barn and uncertain about her future, she was just happy to have a job. But now that she is part of the family, she is unhappy. She feels like a child, safe and protected in her new home, with Tara giving her a hug at night and Tork telling her what to do each day. And every day there is nothing to look forward to but work, work, and more work. Although the planting is done, there are still a million things to do each day. These people know how every day will start and end from now until the day they die. They like it that way. She understands now how Bela felt and why she felt the need to leave home.

Esther is surprised to discover that this life doesn't appeal to her any longer. It is too predictable. She wants to travel, see new things and visit more tribes, before she settles down in one place. She's been trapped in a tiny, ignorant corner of the world for so long, and suddenly she has broken free and there is a whole world out there. The paint on the new, independent Esther is still wet to the touch, but it is there and she's not about to wash it off.

"I finally found a happy place and I'm miserable," she thinks bitterly. She wants to pretend that this isn't happening. She is actually considering giving up her new life and all the security it offers. She has finally found a place where she is accepted for who she is and cared for, yet she wants to return to a life of uncertainty, danger, loneliness and wandering. Perhaps she is just uncomfortable because she is happy and safe, and she has never felt this way before. She doesn't know what to do with it.

Jay 1'

She sneaks out the window in the morning, hearing Tork in the barn. Tara gives her a strange look as Esther walks inside the house, beating the dust out of her hair.

"I was just in the outhouse," she lies.

Tara nods, and they both go about the morning chores. But Esther cannot concentrate at all. She burns the bread and sloshes milk all over the floor. During breakfast, she doesn't say one word to anybody. After the meal, Tork sends her out to help Bora clean the barn, and she hates every minute of it and works as slowly as possible.

By lunchtime, Esther has made up her mind. She is going to leave here and go off on her own. Where should she go? To see some of the other tribes, she supposes. The children are getting ready to go to the Jay tribe, where they will go to school for a month. Perhaps she can go along.

Esther decides that she should tell Tork and Tara as soon as possible, before they begin to think of her as a permanent member of the family. And she should make the announcement before she changes her mind or loses her ambition. She feels so horrible about telling them, that it takes her until dinner to work up the courage.

"I have to leave soon," she says in a quiet voice. "I have so much to learn and see. I was thinking maybe I'd come back later, after visiting some other tribes. Maybe I could come around harvest time. But while you aren't too busy, I thought -"

She trails off, knowing that she is partially lying to them. Making it seem as if she is just taking a leave of absence. But she is too afraid to just say, "I'm leaving. That's all there is to say."

She ruins dinner completely. The whole family gets upset. Tork is losing a farmhand, the children are losing a friend to play with, and Tara is losing another daughter. Tara takes it hardest.

"When will you leave?" Tork asks despondently.

"Soon...I don't know."

"Where will you go?" Bora wonders. He is the only one who takes it well. He takes everything well.

"I don't know."

"You're definitely not a Beaver," he laughs, trying to perk up the table. But nobody laughs.

"If you're going to leave, then leave soon," Tara says, getting up from the table. "I can't bear to have you around, knowing that you're leaving any minute."

Tara walks moodily into the kitchen and Esther stares at her aghast, feeling like a beast. She wishes she could take it all back, rush into Tara's arms and apologize and say she'll stay forever. But it's too late. Her path is set.

"Don't mind her," Tork says, with a dismissing wave of the hand. "She's still upset about Bela. This is about that as much as anything. You don't have to leave immediately. Think about it a while. See how you feel later."

"Yeah, so you can work me as much as possible," thinks Esther.

Jay 2'

**Raccoon moon*

The next morning, things are very uncomfortable between Esther and Tara. Tara hardly speaks a word as they make breakfast. Esther suddenly feels just like Bela. Last week she was the perfect daughter and now she is the bad seed.

"When are you leaving?" Tara finally asks in a defeated voice.

"I thought I might go with Anri and Sare when they go to Jay village."

"That's tomorrow," Tara says, sounding tired and old. She shrugs helplessly. "That's fine. It will be easier for me that way. I guess I've grown very attached to you. Probably because I'm losing a daughter and then I found another one to replace her. How silly of me to try to turn you into my daughter."

And no more is said all morning.

In the fields after breakfast, Esther is reminded of everything she loves about Beaver village. The calm, orderly way everything is run here. The feeling of satisfaction she gets from working the land, when she looks back over a whole row of plants and thinks, "I made this miracle happen. Food is growing right now, and I planted it." She realizes how much she is going to miss this place, where she has spent the first happy times since she was a little child. She forces herself to stop thinking about it and concentrate on her work, before she changes her mind.

At lunch, Tork says, "Esther, you cannot leave before I kill Boink. I will kill him this afternoon, that you may see it."

"Boink?"

"The pig."

"Oh, don't kill him on my account. That's not necessary," Esther stammers. She doesn't want to see them kill Boink.

"I'm not doing it on your account. I meant to kill him soon enough. Why not now, so you won't miss it?"

He turns to Bora.

"You must tell Bela and Kirth that we will kill Boink today. I know they won't want to miss it. And they may want to say goodbye to Esther as well."

"I'll go right after lunch, father," says Bora. "But don't kill him until I get back."

"Of course not."

Esther finds this talk quite disgusting and altogether strange, but she keeps it to herself.

That afternoon, Tork drags a squealing Boink by his hind leg into the center of the road. Bela and Kirth are on hand, as well as some of the neighbors. It is a community event here, killing pigs, and Esther finds that rather disturbing.

"Poor Boink," she thinks sadly. "Look at how they treat you. And you're so sweet." She says a little prayer for the pig, and then she covers her eyes as Tork holds his knife at the ready. There is a loud squeal that breaks her heart. When she opens them, poor Boink is dying, blood from his wound pouring all over the road.

Using torches, Tork, Bora, and Kirth burn off all of Boink's hair, until the skin is black from the fire. Then they scrape off the black with a knife, leaving the skin slightly cooked. They rub salt all over it and then Tork begins the process of skinning the pig. Everyone rushes in to take a big piece of skin. They all comment on how good it is and everyone has seconds. Only Sare refuses to eat it. Tork takes a piece and holds it in front of her mouth.

"Eat it. Try just a little piece. Come on, Sare. You have to try it. Mmmm. Good."

He finally threatens her with punishment and she takes a small bite. Then she spits it out.

"I don't like it." she says stubbornly.

"Now I'm ready to leave," thinks Esther.

He gives up and goes back to dissecting the pig. He cuts into the body now, giving the organs to Tara and Bela to rinse off in a bucket of water. Tara expertly rinses the intestines and wraps them into a tight bundle for sausage making. Then the head is cut off, and Tork uses it to scare the kids. He chases after Sare and Anri with the severed head and they scream and run from it. He laughs and laughs and does a little dance with it, and they giggle nervously as they stare at the decapitated pig head bobbing about in his hands. Finally, he tires of this game and leaves it lying in the middle of the road, where it stares at everyone with a creepy expression. There it will stay until some animal claims it and drags it away.

Fresh pork is served at dinnertime, which is also a going away party for Anri, Sare, Bela, Kirth, and Esther. This is Bela and Kirth's first dinner in the house as a married couple. It is a very uncomfortable evening, with two ungrateful daughters for Tara to feel badly about. She does her best to ignore her feelings and make sure that it is a nice dinner. Small talk is the order of the day.

After dinner, Bela and Kirth get ready to return to his cousin's house, where they are both staying. This is the last time that Bela will see her family before she leaves for her new home and it is an emotional farewell. Tara warns her about every little thing she can think of that could go wrong and the list of tragedies is endless. Finally, Bela hugs her mother quickly, before she can start a new topic, and she and Kirth are out the door. The little ones and Beggar run after them until they reach the road.

Soon Esther is alone in the main room. She stays up after everyone has gone to bed, savoring the house one last time. She drinks cup after cup of tea and keeps the fire well stoked all night long. Who knows when she will see such luxury again?

Jay 3'

During breakfast, Tork presents Esther with twelve shiny shells, smooth as glass.

It is her pay for a month of work. Her first thought is to buy something warm for the cold nights on the road. Maybe she can buy a cloak, one that she can sleep in or use as a blanket. After breakfast, she walks to the commons to go shopping.

She starts with the largest clothing sellers and is overwhelmed by all the things they have for sale. So many beautiful clothes displayed and her with only 12 measly tupas. She finally finds a brown cloak in her price range, made from deer hide, which is the cheapest of all skins because it is easy to get and the fur is not as fluffy as other furs. But it seems warm enough, as it goes down all the way down to her knees, and has a hood to keep her head warm.

"I'll give it to you for twelve tupas now," the man agrees, "though it is worth fifteen. You owe me three. Let's make an agreement. Next time you get paid, you just march over here and give me three more. Deal?"

"Yes," says Esther. She feels guilty, knowing she is lying, but she needs this cloak too much.

It is a grey day, with clouds blocking the sun, so she puts the cloak on and walks slowly back, trying not to think about how depressed she is to be leaving and how she just spent all of her money.

A large group of excited children are gathered outside, come to fetch Sare and Anri for the long walk to the Jay tribe. Tara and Tork quickly say their goodbyes and give each child a hug and kiss. Esther stands there, waiting for her turn, with a burden basket strapped to her back. She found a basket in the barn with back straps, and managed to stuff into it her new clothes, her cloak, her blanket, and finally her nightgown - which she could not bear to burn or leave behind. It is a heavy bundle, but Esther vows not to repeat her mistake when she left the mission without anything but the clothes on her back. She will be warm from now on - no matter what the weather.

"I'm sorry for being so harsh with you these last two days," Tara says, giving her a hug. "You will always be welcome in my home. Come back to visit soon"

"Thank you so much for everything." Esther says, prolonging the hug as long as she will allow. "You have given me so much. I will never forget you."

Tork gives her a quick and embarrassed goodbye hug and then he marches off to the barn to get some work done. Bora just grins and says farewell, then shrugs and follows his father. Esther goes out the door and hurries after the children who have begun to walk already.

She follows the gleeful children, who are led by three adults and two horses that carry all the supplies. The going is slow because the children giggle, skip, play and chase each other as much as they walk. They must examine every plant they see and argue about its name and scream at every animal and bird they pass. Esther learns a lot from listening to them. They certainly know more than she does about their land. Occasionally, one of the grownups in front turns around to tell them to keep moving, but this doesn't faze them, because they are too happy to be on the road and away from their parents for the month.

They stop for a quick lunch and then move on until dark. Finally, they stop for the night and set up camp, erecting two shelters from long poles and a thick skin tarp to protect them from the weather. The grownups get a fire going and cook a large pot of food for everybody. They refuse Esther's offer to help and tell her to relax. And then an early bedtime for all, with the children wrapped in thick blankets that the horses have been carrying. Esther wraps herself in her blanket and her new cloak and she is very warm. She stares up at the stars overhead as the children fall into sleep one by one.

As she watches the huge field of stars and hears the ocean pounding away in the distance, her fears and worries slowly fade. She remembers that she left Beaver village because she wanted to see the world, and here it is spread out before her, welcoming her. She decides that she is going to be all right. She falls peacefully asleep with the gentle snoring of the children for company, and dreams of a journey without end.

Jay Tribe

Jay 4'

**Swan moon*

Today is a warm day and Esther puts on her brown summer dress before continuing on. She pushes on through the morning and eventually finds herself perched on the top of the hill. All she can see are more green hills stretching on and on, and no sign of a village. The children are far behind her. A little boy twisted his ankle in a hole, and the group had to stop for a few hours to let him rest. Esther was in the mood to keep moving and get a little peace and quiet, so she left them behind and kept going by herself.

It is hot and everything is ablaze with life. Butterflies, insects, hawks, and hummingbirds buzz to and fro, and the air is filled with a chaotic swarm of movement. A snake slithers almost directly underfoot and Esther jumps out of the way quickly and escapes up the trail. There are squirrels and other small creatures scurrying everywhere, busy doing springtime things, and a herd of deer grazes nearby.

She flops in the tall grass with a sigh. Feeling wonderfully lazy, she strips off all her clothes and lies naked in the sunshine. What decadence! When was the last time she got to lie around in the sun doing nothing? She is completely happy and pats herself on the back for leaving Beaver village and traveling to these beautiful hills of tall grass waving in the breeze. She watches the hawks fly overhead and the clouds roll past and revels in this perfect moment.

Suddenly she feels a slight pain on her arm, where a fly has bit her. Esther has never seen a biting fly before. She shoos it away, but back it comes. She has to swat at it relentlessly before it finally goes for good. Then she closes her eyes again and sighs with contentment.

She wakes up from a sound sleep with a start, and looks around her. It is cooler now, and the slight breeze has strengthened into a heavy wind. She quickly throws her clothes back on, shoulders her burden basket, and starts hiking again. The path winds through a canyon and deeper into the mountains, and the sun slowly begins to drop into the ocean.

Her feeling of bliss is over, replaced by dull reality. She has several bites on her arms and legs from a source she cannot name, she is itchy all over, and her skin has splotches of red. Her stomach is growling too, and she has nothing on hand to appease it. She looks around for the band of Beaver children, but she can see them nowhere. Sighing, she steels herself for a long, hungry walk.

She begins to wonder if she should walk back and try to find the children and their guides. Just as she is about to turn around, she hears singing. A high, clear voice floats on the breeze - not a great voice - but a warm and friendly one. Soon she can make out words.

"The road winds on and on,
My tired feet they walk anon,
The trees keep cool my face,
The earth holds me from space.
The river winds on endlessly,
Onwards ho, until well met, mother, the sea,
But the river is not my friend sadly,
The river has nothing to do with me."

The singer walks into view, tromping through tall grass. He is a small, merry looking fellow, walking naked through waist high grass. He carries a small bow and a quiver of arrows on his back. He spies Esther suddenly and stops to stare at her from a distance, before he walks toward her. As he nears, she stiffens up and puts the basket on, preparing to flee at any sign of trouble. He stops in front of her and stares at her with twinkling eyes. His face is thin and gleeful with many laugh lines.

"A woman sits here, thoughtfully,
Full of doubt at the sight of me,
A woman beautiful and sad, seems to me,
Perhaps I should cheer her up, invitation to tea?"

Esther begins to feel at ease by his manner, and slowly relaxes.

"Well, say nothing stranger?"

"What?" she asks nervously.

"I just invited you to tea."

"Me?" she says, confused. "You did?"

"Me?" he repeats, laughing. "No the tree. Hello tree, come to tea." He steps up to the tree and pretends to shake its hand.

"Who are you?" she asks curiously.

At this he bursts into song again.

"I am a dreamer of words, walking free,
Dreaming my imaginary poetry, that's me,
This poem isn't wonderful, like Karbudde,
But I just made it up, spontaneously."

Esther is confused and doesn't know what to make of him or his strange speech. He seems to want her to say something, but she has no idea what to say to him.

"You have a way with words stranger. You really are a poet. The great Karbudde is jealous in his grave." He studies her. "Obviously you are a dreary Beaver. You wear their dress and speak in monosyllables."

"No, I'm not-"

"Then a melancholic Bear, perhaps."

"No. I'm nobody."

"Well, I haven't time to chat with a nobody. Good day."

He turns suddenly and walks away. Esther wakes up, as if from a dream, and curses herself for her dim-witted manner. He just offered to take her home to tea and probably a hot dinner, and she just stared at him like a stupid and fearful child.

"Excuse me," she shouts, hurrying to catch up with him. "I am sorry. Are you one of the Jay tribe? I'm going to the Jay tribe."

"You're slow," he says with a wink, "but I'll do battle with anyone who calls you stupid."

He starts walking up the path and waves his arm for her to follow him. She hurries to match his pace, and they walk together through a grove of trees, down a small hill and up a large one. As they walk, he chatters in his high, singsong voice about strange things that make no sense to her. She begins to wonder why she found him so frightening, when he is so silly. The funny, laughing guy is what she calls him from then on, at least in her head.

Suddenly, he stops, pulls out some clothes that he had balled up inside his quiver of arrows and puts them on. She is relieved that he is no longer naked, because now she is able to relax around him more.

"I have yet to introduce myself. How rude of me. I am Bodi of the Jay tribe. And you, my lovely mysterious stranger?"

"My name is Esther. I am a stranger to your land. I come from a Spanish town called Branciforte."

Her voice sounds hollow and cold compared to his lively chatter.

He chuckles. "How old are you?"

"I'm not sure. About twenty-one years old, I think."

"Twenty-one turns of the wheel. A good age to travel. Ah, to be young and never having seen the world before, then to go off and find yourself. My lady, that is a great thing indeed. I wish you much luck."

"Thank you. How do you know-"

"-that it is your first time away from home? It is obvious." He pats her on the back affectionately. "I have been around. This month I will be thirty-five turns of the wheel."

She stares amazed. He looks much younger than that.

"The Jay are a youthful people. We never look our age."

He spins around and begins to walk again. As he walks, he whistles a little tune to himself.

As darkness settles upon the land, they begin to see signs of civilization. Jay village is set upon five hills that form a rough circle. They walk up to the top of one of the hills to find several dingy houses set close together, with lights winking on and off in the windows. The houses are small and crudely made out of split logs and thatched roofs. Bodi leads her to one and they enter.

The house is no more exciting on the inside than on the outside. It consists of one room with a small fire pit, a small bed, and books and scraps of paper scattered everywhere. There are no chairs, only sitting mats made from worn tules. The kitchen consists of a small pot, a knife, and a few baskets of some strange grain.

"Make yourself comfortable." Bodi shouts, as he sets about getting the fire lit.

Soon the fire is burning strong and a pot of water is boiling. Bodi makes tea and pours it into little wooden mugs. Then he takes a few handfuls of the grain and puts it into an iron pot with some more water.

The tea is green and she recognizes the smell from the Hawk tribe. Bodi calls it bay nut tea. This time, she is brave enough to try it. It is not tasty, but it gives Esther a warm glow, a slight buzz, and makes her stomach do flip-flops for a few moments. She likes the way it makes her feel, once her stomach calms down. It is like a loopy version of the black Chinese tea she drank at the Beavers. Soon, the strange grain is ready to be eaten. Bodi serves her a little wooden bowl full of the mush and sprinkles it with seaweed flakes for a taste of salt.

"What is this?" she asks.

"It is called harti. It consists of six different seeds and grains. It is very nutritious, very delicious, and very...suspicious? Why do you look at it this way?"

Esther realizes that she is being rude and she takes a bite. It is bland and boring, just as it looks, and reminds her too much of the mission food. For a moment, she becomes depressed, realizing how much she already misses Tara's excellent meals. But she is hungry enough to eat anything, so she finishes the bowl without hesitation.

During dinner, Bodi quizzes her about life in a Spanish town. She is forced to make up a lot of lies so she can avoid mentioning the mission. Eventually, he starts to look at her strangely, and Esther realizes that she will have to come up with a better story if she wants to convince anybody she is from Branciforte. He seems especially interested in the Christian religion, and he is so nosy that she begins to wonder if he wants to get baptized himself.

After prying her with questions for three hours, he buries himself in his papers and books. Exhausted from her long day, Esther makes a bed for herself in the corner and gratefully lies down. The last thing she hears before she falls asleep is Bodi muttering to himself about rhymes.

Jay 5'

When she wakes, the first thing she hears is Bodi snoring gently. She stands up, yawning, and proceeds to get the coals of the fire going in the chilly house. Soon a small blaze has begun and she puts the teapot on. Her movements wake Bodi, who looks out at the pale dawn and groans.

"It is just the break of dawn. My stars, but you are an early riser."

He plops down, and returns to his snoring.

Esther suddenly realizes that she is no longer a farmhand, but a free woman. She can sleep as long as she wants, with no obligations to anyone. The thought makes her happy, and she exaggerates her whole morning in a parody of lazy decadence. Sipping the tea very slowly, she lies back in her bed and stares at the ceiling. She tries to find shapes in the wood and imagines that they are paintings.

"Esther, let's go. Time is wasting away," she says impatiently, imitating Tork.

"Not today, Tork. I'm just going to relax here by the fire this morning. I might take a nap. Maybe this afternoon, I could work for an hour."

Bodi mumbles in his sleep and rolls over, prompting Esther to stop talking to herself. She closes her eyes and takes a short nap, just as she promised Tork she would.

Bodi wakes disgracefully late. While he putters lazily around the house, Esther makes tea and harti for their breakfast. After eating, he takes her for a walk. In the daylight, the hills are beautiful, just as Bodi said. They are green and sparse, with clusters of large trees for shade and food. Oak trees and walnut trees stand side by side, along with several tall hemp plants. It is a beautiful spring day and the birds are singing.

"This is Acorn Hill," Bodi explains, as they reach the top and begin to walk back down. "The five hills of the Jay tribe are Acorn hill, Blackberry hill, Hemp hill, Walnut hill, and Apple hill."

In the middle of all the hills is the commons, which consists of several small buildings, a trading circle, and one very large house. Bodi takes her directly to the house and indicates for her to take a closer look.

"This is the Jeren library," Bodi announces, after giving her time to take it all in. "Biggest library in the Twelve Tribes. Have you ever seen anything like it?"

"No," Esther admits, thinking that it is nothing compared to the Beaver House. "It's nice."

"Nice? Nice? You have a decidedly bare vocabulary."

He takes her for a walk around the building, showing her various points and highlights. She soon sees that the building consists of two houses stuck together. One of the houses is older and more rundown than any Esther has ever seen. It is a rundown log cabin that has been renovated at least a dozen times, layered with bits of wood and split boards. Even the newest layers are all weathered and old, and threaten to fall apart at the first big storm. The other side is more beautiful, made from thick, rough-hewn redwood boards that have been well smoothed. Intricate carvings adorn these walls. The one that stands out the most is a large carving of several blue jays sitting on a branch, their mohawks ascending to the very top of the building.

"Why are you the Blue Jay tribe?" she asks. "Why did you pick such a little bird? It doesn't seem to do much."

"I might take offense at that, if I were not a Jay," Bodi says, laughing. "But Jays are flexible and light. They don't take anything seriously and they don't get caught in routine. They are not afraid of anything and they are unpredictable and clever - thus they are difficult to hunt or to capture. That is their power."

The tribe totem is the jay, which includes all jays, but especially the blue jay. This particular blue jay they speak of is called the Stellar jay today, but back then nobody had ever heard of "Mr. Stellar", who renamed the bird after himself. We will call it blue jay.

After circling the building, they end up back at the run down part. Bodi shakes his head and sighs, as he notices an old weathered board that has fallen down, exposing a great hole in the house. He proceeds to pick up the rotting board gingerly and stacks it on top of a jutting piece of wood, so it covers the hole again. He steps back and nods, satisfied, as if he had just completed a great task that required much effort.

"Why did they build it like this?" Esther asks. "With one part so old and the other so new?"

"A typical question that I have answered more than one hundred times. But I will answer again, as you are a traveler and have a good excuse for your ignorance. This 'old' house, as you say, is the exact house where Jeren did his life's research. This is Jeren's library, and of course, we cannot destroy it. It is a piece of history. But it is too small for our needs, so when we wanted to expand the library, we just added a new house onto the old one."

"Who is Jeren?" Esther asks curiously.

This is the first time that Esther has seen Bodi surprised. "Do you mean to say..." he sputters. "You don't - I know you're an outsider, but you have been with us over two months, you said. Well, I must tell you sometime."

Bodi leads her into the cool, musty library. She longs to go back outside in the spring air, but she hates to disappoint Bodi, who is so excited to show her the inside. There is a musty, antiquated air to the old part of the library. Several large shelves full of books, slanted heavily from water rot and old age, teeter on one side of the room. The books upon them are of uncertain condition. A few wooden chairs, weather beaten and old, and some hastily constructed benches, stand alongside low tables covered with candle wax. A few drippy, old candles are lit to supplement the two small windows that let in the daylight.

Esther walks around the library, which smells of arcane knowledge and secrets waiting to be revealed. She examines a display of various artifacts and writings belonging to Jeren, including his journals, his quill and ink, and a sketch of him. He is an old, crazy looking man with long, bedraggled hair and a long beard. His eyes are beady and piercing, as if he is looking into your soul from beyond the grave.

"This half of the library looks much like it did when Jeren lived here," Bodi whispers. "A few of these table tops actually belonged to him, and that bookshelf did too. And the painting of the strange beast on that wall there was actually done by him. Living history this is."

“When did he live here?” Esther asks, glancing briefly at the picture of a fierce dragon that Jeren painted on the wall.

“Our best guess is about three hundred years ago. Nobody is absolutely sure.”

An old man sits on a high-backed chair behind an ancient desk. He looks not unlike Jeren himself, with long white hair and a white beard, except his eyes are twinkly and light, instead of the devil eyes of Jeren. The old man is rail thin and wears a long hemp cloak. Bodi refers to him as the Librarian, caretaker of the Jeren library.

A few people read at the tables or browse through books. All seem lost in their own worlds. As they walk through an archway, Esther discovers quite a different library. It is clean, with large windows to let in the light. The newest books are housed here, along with several new chairs, benches and tables with paper, quills and ink. Several men and women drink tea around a large table, while chatting in a strange language. All are dressed in similar garb – shirts, skirts, and pants that are woven from heavy hemp fibers.

A few men Bodi's age greet him as he enters.

"Hillotosh mikow," they shout.

"Hillotosh mikow," he answers gleefully.

"Yayatuk mamamush hallalah."

They begin a long, animated conversation in this strange language, while Esther stands near the fire, waiting for something to do. Finally, Bodi turns to introduce her.

"I had almost forgotten. This is Esther. She's a traveler from strange parts."

They all say "Hillotosh mikow," and Esther repeats this phrase.

"So Esther may benefit from our conversations, let us speak in the common tongue." Bodi says.

"What language is that?" Esther asks.

"We speak the language known as Zwin, the easiest and most balanced language ever invented," answers a thin man with dark black hair and high cheekbones named Kulow. "It was invented by six scholars, including the great scholar and poet, Karbudde, one of the great geniuses of the world."

Kulow winks at Esther. "I can teach it to you if you like. I teach a class on Wednesday and Fridays. Or perhaps we can arrange private lessons?"

So light is his touch, that Esther doesn't realize that Kulow is making a pass at her. She doesn't notice the meaningful glance either. She smiles briefly and takes a walk around the room. Kulow watches her walk for a moment, but she continues to ignore him, so he turns back to the group.

"Heavy earth energy this month," says Bodi. "I am quite exhausted."

"Like the fly caught in the honey bowl," agrees Lad, a fat waddle of a man with thick curly hair that sits atop his head like a mop. "When things get into Beaver, you just have to be patient, for life moves slower than a yellow slug. Luckily, only one baby will be born this year."

There is much nodding of heads at this statement.

"Too much earth makes a dull child," adds Lad, nudging Bodi in the ribs. "A little is enough."

Bune, the tallest and thinnest of Bodi's three friends says, "Bodi, we were talking about the theory that there are other planets out there that affect our day-to-day lives besides the known ones. Planets that lie past Saturn, the farthest planet in our galaxy-"

"Impossible, right Bodi?" says Lad. "If there are other planets out there, then they can have no effect on us, for they are too far away."

"What about the newly discovered planet?" asks Kulow. "The one the old Spanish ship's captain spoke of to our traders. The one called Uranus."

"If it is does exist, it is too far away to affect us. If a planet cannot be seen, how can it affect our lives?"

"Spirits affect our lives, yet we cannot see them," Bune retorts.

"So does stupidity," intones Lad seriously.

"Lad, Lad argument bad. Wants to make it worse." Bodi jokes, messing up Lad's hair playfully. Then he turns toward Esther. "What do you think?"

"Me?" she stammers. "I don't know."

"Come on lazy head. Think it through and discuss it with us. That is the only way you will learn."

She tries to look away and fade back into the background, but Bodi walks over to her and drags her toward the discussion.

"I don't know anything about planets," she says, allowing him to lead her toward the group. "They all look like stars to me."

The others stare at her.

"She's an outsider," says Bodi. "From some Spanish town. What's it called again?"

"Branciforte."

They nod and stare at her strangely.

"How can a star have an influence on me?"

"Why don't you go ask the librarian for one of Jeren's books," says Kulow. "You need to begin to familiarize yourself with astrology if you are going to travel in our lands. Once you have a basic grasp, it will start to make sense."

"I cannot," says Esther, ashamed. She suddenly turns crimson.

"Why?" asks Bodi.

"I can't read very well," she whispers.

"Can't read?" he shouts. "Can't read?"

She can feel everyone's shocked and horrified eyes upon her. Esther's face is now scarlet red and she feels herself getting extremely warm.

"I know a few letters, but there never was much time for practice. And besides, you all use different letters than the Spanish do. I understand everything you say...mostly. But I cannot make out any of your signs."

"How horrible!" says Lad, shaking his head.

"Poor child!" shouts Bune.

"To think she lives in the dark," muses Kulow.

Esther starts to get annoyed. She cannot figure out why it is such a big deal. She has done fine all her life without it.

"You must enroll her in the basic reading class immediately," says Kulow. "And the writing class too. Go speak to Magdeli. She teaches basic reading."

Bodi takes Esther to a group of small log houses, sitting side by side. He peeks into the window of each one. Finally, he finds the right one and motions for Esther to follow him inside. A woman stands before twenty children, all between the ages of 5 and 7. She is a friendly woman, with a slight slouch and distant, darting eyes.

"Hai Magdeli. Can you take another student?"

"I suppose," the woman says. "From what tribe and how old?"

"From no tribe. And she's about twenty-one years old."

Magdeli stares at him as if her time is too important to be wasted on bad jokes. Then she catches sight of Esther, standing behind Bodi, trying to stay out of sight from embarrassment. She smiles slightly.

"She cannot read, Magdeli. Not everyone is as fortunate as we."

"Can't read at all?"

"Not a single sentence. But she is a friend of mine, nonetheless."

"Well, I suppose she may join the class for awhile."

Bodi turns to Esther and pats her head affectionately.

"Good luck to you."

Esther looks around, her face crimson again. All the children are staring at her. She cannot wrap her brain around the fact that she is going to be a student in a class of little children. And there are Anri and Sare, who are smiling at her with glee. Sare waves and shouts out Esther's name joyfully, motioning for her to sit next to them.

"Have a seat," Magdeli says, motioning for Esther to get on with it.

The children break into snickers and giggles. Esther is absolutely mortified to the point of tears. But it is too late to back out now, so she sits down near Sare and Anri and tries to be happy to see them.

"My name is Magdeli. And yours?"

She notices that Magdeli talks to her like one would talk to a little child.

"Esther." she says quietly, trying to sound disinterested, as if that will banish her embarrassment.

And thus Esther begins her first day of class.

Esther is soon reciting letters in front of everybody, and then she attempts to pronounce words with them. She stumbles over the strange symbols as the class giggles and laughs at her as if she is a clown to amuse them. Sare and Anri laugh too, not realizing the embarrassment their friend must be feeling. They all read much better than she does.

After a short lunch break, which Esther spends outside dozing in the sunshine, writing class begins. Soon Esther is creating dizzying swoops and sweeps with her feather and ink, trying to make words on a large piece of paper. This is something the fathers never taught her at all, because they didn't feel she had anything to say. Her writing is shaky and clumsy, and Magdeli has to show her how to draw each letter several times. Esther cannot see any end to her embarrassment on this day.

"Remember to write small, children. Paper is precious," shouts Magdeli.

After class, the children all file out dutifully and Esther and Magdeli are alone.

"How was your day? Was it helpful?"

"Yes, I suppose."

"Never mind the children. They'll get tired of teasing you soon."

"I hope so," she mumbles.

"So, shall we discuss payment?" Magdeli says. "I assume your parents won't be paying for this."

"Oh, I didn't realize -" says Esther. "I have no money. I guess I can't take the class."

She feels relieved.

"What have you got to trade?" asks Magdeli curiously

Esther thinks awhile, but nothing comes to mind.

"Well, I would love for you to read, but I must have some form of payment."

"I can work. Cook. Farm. Clean. Whatever."

"We have no crops, except for some hemp plants. I do not know of anything that needs cleaning either, and I have no need of a cook, as my diet is simple."

"Well, I guess I can't take the class -"

"Why don't you come back tomorrow and perhaps I will think of something. We get many children here and their parents pay in all sorts of strange and unusual ways."

"Fine," says Esther, already leaving the room.

"What is your tribe sign?"

"I don't know."

"Really? Well, see you tomorrow then."

"Yes, thank you," Esther says, hurrying out the door.

There are a few hours till dark, and Esther takes a walk in the mellowing sun, taking in the lay of the land. Soon she realizes that she is very hungry. She longs for a big Beaver meal, but it will have to be Bodi's house and dull harti. She makes the short walk to Bodi's house, but he is not home. His house is quiet and empty. Esther doesn't want to just barge in and cook, so she settles down to wait for him. It is dark by the time he arrives home, and he seems very surprised to see her.

"Hai. What are you doing here? Have you come for your basket and your things? You can just go inside and get them, you know."

It suddenly dawns on Esther that he has not invited her to live with him. She has gotten used to living with whomever she meets, and she has just assumed that these people are very hospitable. But perhaps not all of them are.

"Oh, I just -"

Embarrassed, she cannot think of anything to say.

"Come for tea, eh," he smiles. "Come on in."

Esther has tea and harti at his house again. But this time, she feels like a moocher. As Bodi dresses to go out again, Esther stares at the fire, wondering where she will live.

"Well, you can spend the night tonight," Bodi says to her.

"Are you sure? I don't want to intrude."

"Don't get me wrong. I happen to like you quite a lot. But I am working on an important and time consuming project, and I must have my space. So you cannot stay here all the time."

"Bodi likes to live alone,
He does not want to share his home,
Because he is so wild,
He has no wife or child."

"And besides," he adds as an afterthought, "my lover will not be pleased if you are living with me. She will assume the worst. But I am going to stay at her house tonight, so you can have the whole house to yourself. Just don't touch those papers."

"You have a lover?" she asks, blurting it out in surprise and wishing she didn't say it right afterwards.

"Why is it that everybody assumes that we Jays don't love sex," he exclaims in a loud, exasperated voice, "just because we don't love marriage?"

"Oh, but I didn't mean -"

"Oh yes, I forgot that you don't assume anything. Because you don't know anything. That is your best feature by the way. Don't ever lose it."

He winks at her, to show that there are no hard feelings.

Then Bodi adds, "As Gird the poet says, 'Relationships are like moon pies. They're delicious, but if you eat too much you get sick.'"

Jay 6'

The next day, Esther grinds through another day of class. Magdeli pushes her harder than the other children, trying to get her caught up to the rest of the class. Her head spins dizzily after hours of learning letters which all look the same. Magdeli seems nervous and jumpy during class today, as if all of her nerve endings are fried. Esther has noticed this as a common trait among these people, although Magdeli seems to have it worse than most.

When lunch time comes, the children walk to a large group of cabins in a circular shape. It is here where all of the children live when they come to the Jay tribe for school. Most of their parents live in other villages, so the children stay here under the supervision of local men and women. After the children are all gone, Esther finds herself alone with Magdeli again.

"So Esther," Magdeli says, "do you like to read so far?"

"Yes, although it is very hard."

"Of course it is. Anything worthwhile is hard."

"Yes, I am sure that's true."

"I have spoken to the Jay council and they say that we need someone to work at the Scribe's House a few days a week. You will work there when there is no school and they will reimburse me for my time. Do we have a deal?"

"Yes," says Esther.

"Good. Well, it is lunch time. We resume when the sun moves this much."

She shows Esther how far the sun must move before they meet again. And then she smiles and walks out of the room. When she is gone, Esther remembers that she has no food and no means to acquire any. Her lunch today will be sunshine, air and water, and dinner will be no more filling if she doesn't figure something out.

During the afternoon, her stomach growls loud enough to disturb the class. After class is done, she takes a walk around the village, hoping to solve the food problem. First she follows the sign to Apple hill, hoping that the name is accurate. She encounters several small apple trees there, but they are bare of fruit. The whole orchard seems deserted. Farther up are several houses just like the one where Bodi lives.

She walks down Apple hill and up Walnut Hill. After a ten-minute walk that leaves her exhausted, she finds the promised walnut trees are bare, and the blackberry bushes are the same. She can find nothing edible. She sees many more houses, but there are few people about.

By the time she returns to the center of the village, dusk has settled in. Esther is tired from her walk and her energy is low. She trudges to the stream that runs through the hills to drink some water, and then she follows the path that leads out of the five hills. Along the way she looks for food everywhere, like Dohr taught her to do. She examines every plant she sees, and looks for gopher holes, signs of quail or fish in the river. She finds a patch of thorny milkweed plants, and the thick leaves give her a little energy, but hardly satisfy her cravings for a big, hot meal. She feels too weak and tired to do anything else, so she just sets up camp and goes to sleep.

Jay 7'

Wolf moon

When she awakens, it is not even dawn yet, and she is soaked. A heavy dew has soaked her blanket until it is cold, heavy and completely useless, and she shivers underneath it. Cursing, she throws it off and puts on her cloak, which she has been using as a ground pad. Her cloak is somewhat better with the water, but now a chill wind blows hard on her bare feet, so she has to sit up again and put on her moccasins to warm them. She lies back down, hoping this time to fall back asleep, but the ground is hard and stony without a sleeping pad. Then she gets an idea. She puts the wet blanket underneath her and lies upon it, wrapped in her cloak. Much better. She ignores the twigs and dirt that have slipped inside her cloak and are irritating her skin. Nothing will make her move again.

But it is hard to sleep after being so annoyed for so long by matters of comfort. And she is very hungry, which makes it hard for her to warm up and relax. She feels quite thin and defenseless out here, so she finally gives up on sleep. She walks to the library, hoping to get dry and warm inside.

She spends the morning sipping tea in the new section of the library, which is nearly empty this early in the morning. The Librarian has kept the coals going all night long, so it is easy to stoke the fire into a hot blaze. It is a comforting morning and goes a long way toward improving her mood. She decides to come here every morning before class starts.

During school, she is unable to concentrate, and her nerves are frazzled. Magdeli seems a bit on edge too and the children have the attention span of a bird on a tree. One spastic boy keeps shouting out nonsense designed to irritate Magdeli, who is easily flustered and has no talent at discipline. She tries to ignore him, but that only makes him louder. Another boy moves to a different part of the room whenever Magdeli looks down at her book, and she has to tell him many times to knock it off. A girl keeps a running argument with Magdeli, her friends, and anyone else within range about whatever comes into her head. Esther slumps with her head in her hands, unable to believe how hungry she is and that she is sitting here enduring all this insanity instead of looking for food.

"It's a Wolf moon," explains Magdeli, desperate to make sense of the mess her classroom is in. "We are all a bit inconjunct today. Let us try to pull it together."

"Sare," Esther whispers, leaning over to talk to her. "Could you bring me some food from your lunch today?"

"I'm not allowed to," Sare says. "I tried to bring food to class and they yelled at me."

Esther nods, disappointed.

During lunch, Esther falls asleep in the hot sun, and doesn't wake up until well after class starts. When she wakes, she is covered in sweat and dirt, which forms an unpleasant grime. She cannot go to class like this. She has to go to the river to get a drink of water and bathe before going back to class. After bathing, she chews on some milk thistle. It is a bare lunch and she is hardly satisfied. A woman cannot live on leaves alone. Then she tromps to class, still ravenously hungry. By the time she arrives, class is almost done for the day.

"Esther, please get here on time. The whole class suffers when you are late. It throws everything off. Uyan? Understand?"

"Yes, yes, yes," says Esther, as uncooperatively as she can. In truth, the lack of food is driving her off the deep end. She cannot maintain a decent mood on an empty stomach. She feels like strangling everyone. Plus she cannot concentrate on her letters, and the teacher has to scold her several times to pay attention to instructions.

"Esther, you're not listening."

"I am trying- " she says miserably. "But -"

"I just showed you how to do it twice," Magdeli says, exasperated, "and you're still doing it wrong."

Esther begins to boil. Sensing her discomfort, Goldi and Miya, two Hawk children, begin to give her a hard time too. Goldi keeps poking her and when she turns around he pretends to be reading. She hears them giggling when she faces forward again. Finally, she refuses to turn around, but Goldi - or is it Miya - keeps poking her. When he pokes her too hard, she finally turns around and pushes him back. But she pushes too hard and he falls onto his back and hits his head. He immediately starts to scream and rage and tries to attack Esther. Esther escapes from the little raging storm and backs away, shocked and mortified that she has just attacked a little boy.

"Esther I think you should leave the class for awhile," shouts Magdeli, running over to pull Goldi off Esther and calm him down.

She feels tears well up as she walks toward the door.

"Esther, what is wrong?" whispers Sare, not understanding what is happening. "Don't go."

The children stare at Esther, suddenly liking her. Now, they can relate to her as an equal. She is somebody that cries as they do.

Esther runs out of the room, sure that she will never be able to show her face in that classroom again. She goes out into the sunshine and just lies down in the grass for an hour. The setting sun soaks through her and calms her down and she soon feels better.

When it gets cold, she goes to visit Bodi to ask him for some food, but he is not there. So she goes back to her camp, with a last ditch idea that she will carve herself a sharp spear to hunt for fish or gophers. She works hard at it, until the point of the spear is very sharp. Then she takes a long walk, looking for gopher holes, and she stands by the river, looking for fish. Eventually, she sees a little fish. It is barely a snack, but better than nothing. She stands the way Dohr taught her and holds her spear aloft. Then she thrusts as hard as she can. Her carefully sharpened point barely misses the fish, hits the rocks, and breaks.

Dohr was right. She is no hunter. She throws the stick into the river and curses her helplessness. Then she walks miserably back to her camp.

That night it rains, waking her up out of a sound sleep. She quickly gathers up her wet things and runs underneath a tree. She cannot believe how bad this day has been. She is so frustrated, that she begins to cry again. It is the only thing she can think of to do.

"These people don't care!" she screams. "They will let me die! I'll be a corpse who can read! What good is that?"

After a good cry, she walks into town and bangs on Bodi's door loudly. She screams for him to wake up, as rivulets of rain run down her face. He opens the door surprised, his mouth hanging open. There is another person in the room with him, a robust, pretty woman with a flat face and pleasant squinty eyes.

"Hai, Esther," Bodi says, surprised to see her.

She bursts into a fresh round of tears, as she tells him the whole story. How she hasn't eaten and she cannot concentrate in class. How she is soaked and cold and fears she will die of the shivers.

"The poor girl looks half starved," says the woman.

"You can tell that it is a Wolf moon tonight," says Bodi, as he finds her some dry clothes to wear. "What an inconjunct day it has been."

"I don't care what the moon is! I just want to eat!" Esther shouts, more at the whole town than him.

"See!" exclaims Bodi with satisfaction. "Exactly what I was saying. 'I don't care! I just want! That's a Wolf for you!"

He laughs to himself, as he puts a fresh pot of water on the stove. The woman, who introduces herself as Makki, gets Esther some dry blankets as she helps her out of her wet clothes.

"I hate Wolf moons," says Makki, laying a blanket over Esther's thin, shivering frame. "I can't wait for the full moon."

They don't seem to be too upset over her condition and this makes her even angrier. These people are so strange. They act like nothing is happening, when she is on their doorstep - half starved and crying. And Bodi thinks that she is only upset because of the moon. Esther misses the practical Beavers more than ever.

Bodi suddenly begins to sing a ridiculous song:

"The poor lass half starved,
So she uses her mars,
To yell at poor Bodi for food.
He'll make her some grub,
But here's the rub,
It will still be a Wolf moon."

Makki giggles and kisses Bodi on the lips. But Esther is speechless. She just cannot believe these people. They are making fun of her. She is starving and they are viciously taunting her! Food or no food, Esther is going to say something.

"Stop making fun of me!" she shouts. "I don't like it."

They stare at her as if she is a mad woman.

"We're not," says Makki. "You're feeling paranoia."

"It's the inconjunct sun/moon," says Bodi. "Creates paranoia and unreasonable behavior. And this is one of the worst inconjuncts there is. The stubborn vengeful Wolf can't handle the easy-going, light-hearted Jay."

Esther cannot make her point. They refuse to give her any sympathy, so she gives up with an exasperated sigh. Soon the food is ready and she eats quietly. She tries to concentrate on her harti and ignore all the irrational thoughts that are storming through her head, but it is difficult. Makki and Bodi read quietly, and Esther wonders about them while she is trying not to. What must they think of her? Storming into their house with tears and attitude, demanding food. Today, Esther has showered her bad mood on just about every friend she has here. She couldn't help it. They seem so simple and there isn't a devious or malicious bone in their bodies, yet they can be tremendously cruel by their simple callousness.

After dinner, when Esther is finally stuffed, she realizes that she has worn out her welcome here. She can never come back to Bodi's house again. This makes her very sad, because she has alienated the only real friend she has here.

"Thank you for the food. I'm sorry I bothered you. I'll be going now."

"Out in the rain. Nonsense," says Makki. "Sleep here. You've had a rough day."

They ignore her protests, and even go so far as to offer her Bodi's bed. Then they say a quick goodnight and are out the door before Esther can summon up an apology or a thank you. They have gone to sleep at Makki's house. They seem a little frightened of her and Esther cannot blame them. She feels a little guilty, but she is too happy to have a dry, comfortable place to sleep to worry too much about it. She lies down on Bodi's bed and falls into a deep slumber.

Jay 8'

In the morning, she fixes her last bowl of harti at Bodi's house - moving quickly before Bodi comes home. She makes herself a bowl for lunchtime too and puts it into a cracked bowl that Bodi doesn't seem to ever use. She is just getting the mess cleaned up, when Bodi arrives. She becomes very awkward and shy and starts to feel like a mooch again.

"Thank you very much," she stammers. "I won't bother you again. I'm sorry I was acting so crazy."

"No bother," he says simply. "Have fun in class."

That is all he has to say. He seems not to notice her extremely apprehensive and confused behavior at all. More confused than ever, Esther walks to school, dreading the thought of facing Magdeli too. But like Bodi, Magdeli makes nothing of Esther's behavior the day before. She does not even seem to remember it. Goldi and Miya sure do. They stay away from her. Other than that, it is business as usual in the classroom. Finally, Esther shrugs off the whole mess and tries to get beyond it.

"Esther, did you read about the adventures of blue jay? Wasn't that a scary story?" Sare suddenly asks her, waking her from her tortured musings.

"Mmmm. Yes Sare," she mumbles absently.

"That Goldi is scared of you," confides Anri. "I'm glad you did that. I didn't like him."

"Me either," says Sare.

"Me either," says Esther.

Esther watches Sare and Anri jealously. They look well fed. She considers asking them to sneak her some meat from their dinner, but pride stays her tongue. She fears that they will tell Tork and Tara that they had to feed poor Esther, who could not fend for herself, and she thinks that she would rather starve.

After class, Magdeli waves Esther over to talk.

"No school tomorrow or the next day. There will be a huge party to celebrate the full moon. I hear the Owl tribe is on their way right now."

"I'm sorry about the other day," Esther says in a humble voice.

"Oh, don't worry about it," Magdeli says with a shrug. "Wolf moon and all. Plus, perhaps you were bleeding. Many of us bleed near the full moon. I started bleeding today."

"That wasn't the problem. I wasn't feeling well yesterday…because I hadn't eaten any food at all," says Esther carefully, dropping a subtle hint. "I was really hungry."

"Oh, well why don't you just eat something then?"

Esther stares at her, as if she has just said the stupidest thing that anyone has ever said in the history of the world.

"Can't wait for tomorrow," says Magdeli lightly, looking away from her stern gaze. "The Owl tribe is fun."

She escorts Esther out the door and takes off toward her house. Esther sighs and goes to her little spot by the stream, thankful that it is not raining any longer. She makes herself a bed, eats some milk thistle, and goes right to sleep.

Jay 9'

Owl moon

The next morning, Esther is awakened by the sound of horses. She wakes, startled, as the ground shakes underneath her. Suddenly, twenty large horses charge right past her with the most tremendous thumping and pounding. She backpedals out of the way, sure that she is going to be trampled. Somebody yells, "Good morning!" and then they are past, riding down the trail towards Jay village. In a moment, peace returns to her part of the world. Esther sighs with relief and sits down again, letting her pounding heart settle. The horses and riders disappear around Walnut hill.

Sometime later, she follows the trail of the horses into town. She finds them on top of Blackberry hill, where the riders have begun to set up a little settlement. Some make tents from stretched hides, while others erect little shelters with bark roofs. Various members of the Jay tribe arrive every now and then to greet them and there is much shouting and back slapping as old friends meet. After things have quieted down and the excitement is over, Esther turns around and heads back to her camp to lie in the sun and wait for later. She is sure that a party is brewing, and that means food.

She lies in the sun all morning, trying to conserve her energy. She dozes for a while, until she is awakened by a group of deer grazing nearby. They watch her warily, reacting to her every movement and thought with a little tiny jump, until some understanding is reached and they return to their grazing. The only other disturbance of the morning is a fierce row between two blue jays in a tree above her head. She is awakened from her dozing by the racket. Above her head, two jays furiously screech bird curses at the top of their little lungs and thrash their wings and send leaves floating down onto Esther's head. They seem as if they are about to fight, but only end up shouting back and forth and making a great ruckus. Then one of them flies off and the other takes off after it, still screeching.

In the afternoon, she walks up Blackberry hill again to check on the progress of the party. By now, the celebration is in full swing. There is a large fire built and the smell of roasting game in the air. Several roasting ducks - fat and juicy – sit upon spits, and their juices drip into the fire and steam it up. Esther's stomach rumbles, and she hopes that they will serve the food before she has to resort to sneaking up to the fire to take it by stealth.

There is a game being played on a long grassy slope, which makes no sense at all to Esther. It is a very complicated form of tag, with several groups of people competing against each other. Children and adults all play together, while a small audience cheers from the sidelines. The game is called Pone, a local invention. Esther never does learn the rules, but it is fun to watch. Several Koko boards are brought out for a Koko tournament, and there are many other games and gambling going on also.

Then lunch is finally served, and it is so good that tears come to her eyes. She hasn't eaten like this in what seems like weeks. Juicy roast ducks, roast deer, and a sort of flat bread cooked in the coals of the fire. The bread is absolutely delicious, with a slightly charcoal flavor built in.

After the heavy meal, Esther walks to a secluded spot to lie down and relax, and she soon falls into a sound sleep. She wakes with a start, as another horse gallops past her and almost over her. It is getting dark, and she yawns and rises, feeling cold and stiff. She walks to her little camp by the river, puts on her warm cloak, and walks back for the full moon party.

She sits in front of a fire, and a boy appears as if on cue and gives her a cup of wine and a piece of burnt fire bread that tastes like charcoal. She throws the charcoal bread into the fire and sips the wine. All around her, people are shouting and laughing, so she sips the wine faster, trying to become as happy as them. The boy, who introduces himself as Jaan of the Owl tribe, sits down next to her and talks her ear off for the next hour. He offers her more wine, which she accepts gladly. Taking that as a sign of progress, he charms, jokes and works very hard to impress her. Then he tries to get her to come to see his teepee. She starts to get angry and closes herself off behind a wall of aloofness, and Jaan is chased away by a laughing man who has been watching them humorously for some time. He is the boy's father.

"Son, didn't I ever teach you about women? This ain't how you get 'em into your tent. Leave the poor girl alone. Go diddle yourself for awhile."

The boy's abashed reaction elicits howling laughter from the rest of the men and women around the fire. Jaan shrugs and walks away and Esther sighs with relief.

She meets a funny man with a huge smile who shows her how to make fire bread. He teaches her to make dough, mixing corn flour and water and kneading the whole sticky mass together - adding more flour until it is smooth and pliable and not wet and goopy. Then the man shows her how to pile red hot coals on top of the flattened dough - only on one side - until that side is brown and crispy. Then you flip the hot, steaming mass over, clear out a space, and pile coals onto the uncooked side until it is crispy too. Esther's first attempt at fire bread is a brown, charcoal lump. But she tries again and her second batch is a success. She is ecstatic. All she needs is flour and she will never go hungry.

"Write it down," the man says. "So you won't forget."

"I will," she agrees, proud that she is now able to do so.

After dinner, which consists mostly of leftovers from lunch, a man stands up. He is small, thin, and bony, with short, cropped hair and a pointed beard. He looks like a little dwarf from a fairy tale.

"I am Jasp, Poet Master of the Jay tribe," he announces in a high, fluty voice. "We of the Jay tribe have no chief, so our poets do the talking as they should. We welcome our esteemed friends, the Owl tribe, to our land. We hope they will be well stimulated during their visit. They have requested the 'Tale of Bunel' tonight," he shouts excitedly, "and I will not refuse. It has been too long since we read these stanzas aloud. They are wonderfully exciting and an important part of our history. Many young children here have never heard them before and they will get a great thrill tonight."

A young boy shouts excitedly, "What is it?"

"Ah," says Jasp with a grin, "it is the story of a great voyage across the ocean to see the strange lands in the east. There were many of the Owl tribe on this trip and a handful of the Jay tribe. The brave crew returned bearing teas, strange spices, art, pottery, and many other exciting things from foreign lands. That voyage changed our whole way of life."

A broad shouldered man, proud and handsome, stands up. He is very drunk and elicits much laughter when he stands and almost falls over.

"It is the same story as "The Asia Quest" by our Brin. Except it is a poet's version, which means it rhymes and is not funny."

There are a few chuckles in the audience.

"Thank you, Grym, chief of the Owl tribe, and a man of honor," says Jasp seriously.

"Yr' welcome," he shouts with a huge belch. "Now let's not run on with speeches until we fall asleep. Let's hear the damn story."

The chief sits down again. Jasp seems a bit put off by his behavior, but he swallows it and continues.

"I will now read the 'Tale of Bunel'. "

Two local women begin to play flutes to accompany the poem. Their playing is bouncy and light at times and serious at times, depending on the tone of the story.

This is a much shorter version of the epic poem, which was twenty pages long and rhymed much better. Unfortunately, everything loses much in translation.

Let us sing again of a great quest
A quest to explore strange lands
Like China, Japan and Russia
Exotic lands of many wonders.
The Twelve Tribes built a great ship
A ship called the Doce Tressessa
And assembled a great crew
For a most difficult quest.
For two new moons they traveled

Following the stars west
Across endless oceans
Of blue green water.
Two died of the dread typhoid
Three succumbed to scurvy
Such things happen
Even on a well equipped ship.
It was a most difficult journey
By the end all were weak and tired
Sun burnt, windswept, hungry, and sick
Only adventure waiting kept their will strong.
On a glorious summers day
'Land ahead!' cried the lookout
They beached upon a distant shore
A cold, harsh place called Russia.
A newly expanded kingdom
Life was hard there
They set up camp on the lonely coast
And began to regain their strength.
But they were soon besieged by a large force of soldiers
A short battle proved futile
Three more dead
And many put in prison.
There fell Coogin, Mikka, and Soot
Great warriors with fierce swords
But they took two men with them
Before being pierced by musket fire.
Billea and Mistu, two great scholars
Struggled to speak Russian
As most of the crew languished
In a desolate, ugly dungeon.
Then they spoke to Russian officers
Begged for mercy and kindness
And they negotiated their freedom
With persuasive words and a large bribe.
They were ejected from Russia forever
And they gladly left
To sail south along the coast
Until they reached greater China.
In China they finally landed
In the tail of summer
Harvest was upon the whole land
And it was rich with food and life.
They stayed in a city called Tianjin
Where they received a more proper welcome
No soldiers attacked them
They were treated as welcome guests.

They restocked their meager supplies
With amazing new foods
All manner of strange fruits
And rice, sugar, pork, and tea.
Regaining their strength
Their stamina and their sanity
They found peace and tranquility
In little homes of bamboo.
For many months they lived in great Shanghai
And gained much wisdom and knowledge
They spoke with all, from peasant to eunuch
They wandered the streets in a daze.
For great China was an old, old civilization
And the Twelve Tribes merely a child
They felt like little children in school
Little fish in a very big pool.
But finally it was time to leave
The travelers had worn out their welcome
There were problems brewing in China
Revolt and war were in the air.
The ships were boarded with many treasures
Pigs and sheep and rare plants
Silks and clothes and books and paintings
Sugar and soybeans and rice and teas.
But steel and metal were the real treasures in the hold
Cooking pots replaced hot rocks in a basket
Metal tools replaced bone and obsidian
Swords replaced spears.
They left China on the Raccoon new moon
And raced home to avoid the winter storms
It was a cold journey, and hard
But their ship was well stocked and they were hardy.
As winter approached, they hit their first storm
It almost ruined all
Two men washed overboard, half the horses and pigs died
And the ship knocked about like a ball.
But the storm soon passed
And the dead animals eaten for strength
For the last leg in a long journey
A journey that now seemed endless.
They reached home late in the month of the Wolf
Worn out past the point of tears
Would friends and family still love them
Would home even be here?

But all ended as it should
With a heroes welcome and all
Wisdom and treasure passed among the 12 Tribes
And Bunel wrote an epic song.

After the poem, there is a great cheer from all assembled. Great praises are shouted for the travelers, who brought so many new and marvelous things back with them. Some of the Owl tribe complain that the poem was a sadly dull version of a very exciting story, leaving out the gory details of the fights and the drama of the sea voyage and other exciting parts. Then there are shouts for more music, and a band of Bear tribe musicians who were assembled in secret begins to play.

Meanwhile, the full moon shines over all, setting hearts to madness and wild thoughts. Men and women of both tribes go off to secret places to have romantic sojourns. One of the highlights of polar day seems to be the opportunity to meet different men and women. She sees Bodi dancing with an Owl woman and later they go off together. Esther wonders about Makki and if she would be upset if she knew. But perhaps she is doing the same thing. It is that sort of night. There are no rules.

The music goes on until all hours. Esther is asked to dance many times, but she refuses. Lad is a little persistent, being drunk, and he keeps putting his arm around her. She finally escapes his clutches by telling him that she has to work tomorrow in the Scribe Center to pay for her schooling, and it seems wise to get some sleep. He nods, disappointed, and leaves her alone. She fills Bodi's cracked bowl full of leftovers and trudges back to her little camp to go to sleep.

Jay 11'

**Elk moon*

After school, Magdeli instructs Esther to walk to the top of Hemp Hill for her job at the Scribe's House. The Scribe's House is a place where books are copied down to paper to make new books. She walks into the house to find twenty men and women perched at desks, copying books down by hand on sheets of paper. She is required to wait on all the writers and get them anything they need, so they won't have to get up and disturb their work. Sometimes she walks down to the paper makers, where hemp is turned into coarse paper, and gets stacks of paper for the writers. Sometimes she has to clean up ink spills. She cooks for them too, which is the best part, because she gets to eat the leftovers. As soon as she finds out that the job includes meals, Esther volunteers to work every single day after school. It will mean that she will have no free time at all and will see very little sunshine, but she can handle that for a few weeks. The job is very easy and she gets a lot of time to just sit around and watch.

Esther is impressed by the speed and focus of the writers. Some of them are linguists, copying down books from foreign languages into the strange symbols of these people that sound like Spanish, although they do not look like it. Some of them are just copying popular books to make new copies to sell or give as gifts. But all of them write at lightening speed and they write all day long. At the rate they write, they can copy down an entire book in just a week's time, assuming it is not a large book. It inspires Esther to continue with her writing and not to worry about the fact that it is a children's class. The important thing is that she finally learns to do it.

Jay 13'

Once she gets the hang of the strange symbols that the tribe uses for letters, Esther learns very quickly. Today, she is asked to read to the class from a book called "Dariel the Deer and his Friends". It is a silly book, illustrated with crude drawings that make all the children laugh. Esther struggles along with the hard words and although she feels that her reading is poor, Magdeli seems very impressed.

"Very good Esther. There is air in you. I can tell."

Her writing is another story. She tries to copy down the recipe for fire bread in class. She works for a long time, trying to sound out the difficult words. When she gets frustrated, she draws pictures in the margins like all of the other children, trying to fill in every inch of her precious sheet of paper. Each child only gets one piece of paper every two days upon which to write, so Esther has to use every bit of it. When she shows her completed recipe to the teacher, Magdeli cannot make out a word of it. Sare and Anri cannot read it either. But Esther can read it and she wonders if that is enough.

Magdeli steps out for a bit and the children immediately forget about their assignment and stage an elaborate drawing contest. Esther joins in just to feel included. Considering how much older she is and how vast the canyon of experience that separates them, she feels like an outsider trying to enter a secret world.

She draws a picture of the beach in Santa Cruz and herself standing on it as a child, building a house out of wood. She works for a long time on it and she is amazed at how good it turns out. The children seem to think so too, because she gets "oohs" and "ahhs" when she shows it to them. It seems a good competitor for the title of 'best drawer'.

There are other good competitors though. Sare draws Boink and Mooloo and the other animals that her parents use for food, and the children are very pleased with that too. Many of the Jay and

Hawk children have never seen farm animals before and they ask many questions about them. Sare is soon involved in a long explanation about them and what they do all day.

Whether Esther or Sare would have won the "best drawer" award remains a mystery, because Magdeli walks in before they are finished looking at all the drawings. Magdeli puts on a stern face as she examines the fruits of the children's hour of solitude.

"You all know that you are here to learn to write. And our school's limited supply of paper is too precious to waste on drawings. Do you think paper grows on trees?"

"I like to draw," shouts out a Hawk child.

"Then draw at home, on your own paper."

Esther looks around at the children and feels the need to defend them.

"We don't have paper at home to draw with," she tells Magdeli.

Magdeli seems taken aback by Esther's sudden outburst.

"Well, actually, many of the children do. Perhaps only *you* don't."

Esther turns hot from embarrassment and says no more. Of course, Magdeli is right. But her cry of protest is picked up by the other children, who start to argue that drawing is more fun than writing. They try to show Magdeli their work to prove it. All of the noise drives Magdeli into a fluster.

"We are not drawing any more! Please children...."

Eventually the class quiets down, and they reluctantly start writing their daily assignments wherever they can find room on their paper. Esther writes her sentences along the waves of the beach and inside her driftwood house, which makes a nice effect. She ignores Magdeli's strange look, knowing that she was acting foolish and behaving just like a little child. She should have been writing, because that is why she is here. Esther is old enough to set a better example than that.

Jay 14'

Raven moon

"Esther! Esther!"

"Esther, look at my stick man!"

"Esther? Where do you come from?"

"Where is your mommy?"

The children are obsessed with Esther today. They want to know everything about her. They have finally decided that she is an equal. They can relate to her and they feel comfortable with her. Today, everyone tries to make friends with her at once. She is deeply touched by all the attention, although she is having a hard time concentrating.

She reads a children's book of poetry, while the class learns how to do arts and crafts. They make little stick men and stick women out of twigs and leaves and anything they can find on the ground outside. They craft the little people and stick them to a plank of wood with glue made from boiled sturgeon bladders.

Esther has to go around and look at everyone's art project before they will let her alone. Then she tries to read again. But soon she is pestered with another in a series of endless questions and she has to look up from her book again to answer them.

"Class, let Esther read," orders Magdeli.

They obey her for about two minutes. Then they forget all about their mandate, and continue pestering her. Magdeli sighs and tries to think of a way to deal with this.

"Esther, I have a special assignment for you."

Esther looks up from her book.

"I want you to go to the library and pick out a grown up book to read."

"Grown up books are hard," she complains. "I'm not ready."

"Esther, please -"

"I'm enjoying this book."

Magdeli gets flustered again and her eyes dart all over the room as she searches for a way to deal with a willful woman in a children's class. Magdeli is not used to dealing with grownups. It is not so easy to tell a grown up what to do.

"I think you can do it," she finally says lamely.

"Lucky," whispers Anri.

It suddenly occurs to Esther that she will get a chance to go outside in the sunshine if she does this.

"Fine," she says magnanimously, closing her book. "I'll do it."

"Thank you," says a relieved Magdeli.

"Yes, of course."

She stands up, towering over the little children, and walks outside.

Esther stands before the library, loathe to leave the sunshine to go get a book. It is too beautiful outside to be indoors, and she is hungry too. Then she gets the idea to try fishing again. Now that she is more grounded, she feels that she could do better. And then she won't have to go to the Scribe House today.

Esther suddenly wonders if they have any books on fishing. That would be a way to obey Magdeli as well as her stomach. She'll read for a bit and then she'll go put her knowledge to the test. She walks into the library, which is crowded today. Even the old librarian is wide awake, reading a book quietly at his desk. She stands before him until he looks up from his book and stares at her curiously.

"Sorry to disturb you. Do you know of a book about fishing?"

"Top shelf" he replies, pointing at a shelf. "Far right."

Esther goes to the shelf he pointed to, and grabs the first book with the word 'fishing' in the title. She attempts to read it herself, but the book is much too hard for her. She sits for a while in thought, wondering what to do.

"Excuse me sir," she says to the old librarian.

He looks up from his book.

"Can you read to me awhile?"

She quickly explains her situation.

Despite his crusty exterior, he is a kind soul, and he agrees to read to her. So she sits down opposite him, and explains what she wants to know. He reads to her for an hour, and shows her detailed pictures of everything, illustrated with great care. Soon her head spins with knowledge and she has come up with a plan. She thanks the pleasant old man, and even gives him a kiss on the cheek. He is pleased by the kiss and his eyes twinkle with glee. Then she goes outside and walks back to her camp.

Fishing with a net seems much easier than spearing the slippery little things with a sharp stick. The book she looked at went into great detail about crafting a net. The only problem is that she hasn't the proper materials. She needs some rope or at least strips of cloth or animal tendon. But where can she get such things?

She eats some old harti from yesterday, and then the sun lulls her into a stupor. While she rests, a blue jay lands on top of her bowl and begins to eat her food. Esther crawls over and shoos it away. But when she leaves her food, it comes right on back. She throws a stick at it and shouts at it sternly to get away. It merely jumps lightly out of the way and stares at her quizzically. Then back it comes for more. Esther is amazed at the courage of the small bird, and the gall. It seems to have no qualms about stealing a little of Esther's food right in front of her. Plenty to go around, it seems to say, and why would you stop me from taking some? And then, Esther has an inspiration.

The woman who runs the little store that sells tools is gone, as usual, because she only comes here on earth moons. Esther looks around guiltily as she walks up to the wooden fence and peeks inside. Should she do this? Then she notices a blue jay hopping on a branch and it looks at her and shrieks loudly, as if telling her to get on with it.

Go ahead. Take what you need. Why not?

Thanking the jay for the advice, she walks quietly into the dark and deserted shop. After a quick glance, she finds a long roll of hemp rope that would do the trick. Trying not to disturb anything, she cuts off a good length, trying hard to make the cut clean and unnoticeable. As she cuts, she knocks an axe to the ground, which sends a saw and a shovel crashing down, making a huge racket. Cursing, Esther stands them up again and tries to put everything back the way it was. Then she quickly runs to the door and peeks her head out to see if the coast is clear. Luckily the shop is on the outskirts of the commons and nobody can see her. Esther runs away with her stolen goods, pleased with herself.

She goes back to her little camp and spreads the stuff out on the ground. She stares at the hemp rope and her knife for a long time, trying to imagine it in her head before she begins. She makes a frame of twigs into a rough circle, cuts up the rope into small pieces, and ties them into a net. Finally, she attaches the whole thing to a long branch that she finds lying on the ground and ties it off with leftover strips of rope. It takes all afternoon, but the sun feels good on her back and she enjoys it. Then she stares at the finished net, very pleased with herself. It is crude, but it should work.

Jay 15'

Esther shows up three hours late to class this morning. It is silent reading time, but everyone becomes loud as soon as she enters class and they put their books down to see what she has been up to. Magdeli has to quiet everyone down and tells them to keep reading. She gives Esther a look of indignation. Ignoring her, Esther sits down in her spot on the floor.

"Where were you?" whispers Sare.

"Fishing," she whispers in her ear. "I went fishing this morning. It was really fun. I caught two fish and cooked them over a fire."

"Lucky!" whispers Anri, overhearing. "Can I go with you next time?"

"I can't -"

"Shhhhhoooook!" says the teacher. "Children, let's read."

"Esther went fishing," whispers Sare to all the kids.

Magdeli looks at Esther, wanting to tell her to stop disturbing class and take out her book and read already. Esther stares back proudly, feeling strong and accomplished from fishing and making fires and crafting nets. She wonders if Magdeli could do all those things. Esther would rather know how to fish than know how to read any day. Her gaze dares Magdeli to tell her different. Magdeli meets her eyes a moment but quickly looks away, not wanting to get into a battle of wills. With a satisfied smile, Esther pulls out her book of children's poems and starts to read.

Jay 16'

**Cougar moon*

Esther goes to the Scribe's House after school, but they don't need her and they ask her to work at the paper makers instead. After a quick lunch, she walks past the tall hemp plants to the house where they make paper and reports for duty. A tall, quiet man hands her a big wooden mallet and deposits her in front of a large wood bowl filled with water. Her job is simple. She will take hemp fibers and mash them into pulp in the water. It is hard work, and soon her shoulders are sore and aching and she is soaked. The weather is gloomy and windy, which is the worst weather for wet work, and she starts to shiver. It has been sunny all week and she has been stuck indoors. Now that she gets to work outside, the weather is not nice and she wishes she were indoors and warm.

When she has completed a big batch of slurry, two men lift up the bowl and carry it away. They dump the slurry onto little coarse hemp cloths, which are the size of a piece of paper, and the pulp congeals upon them into a wet sludgy sheet. They give it a quick press with a flat block and there is a wet sheet of paper. The paper is set out to dry and Esther is sent back to press more fiber.

By the end of the day, her shoulders are dead and she is covered in water and pulp. As a present for her hard work, the paper maker gives her two sheets of paper.

"Thanks," she says, without much enthusiasm.

Exhausted, she takes the paper and walks away in the late afternoon gloom. She goes back to the Scribe's House, eats some harti, and then returns to her lonely campsite. She lights a fire, using coals from an abandoned fire in the commons, and settles down to get warm and dry. As she stares morosely at the fire, she wishes she had somebody to share the evening with. This makes her wonder if there are any people with lives as strange as hers. She seriously doubts it.

"Bodi, can I read your poem now?"

Bodi looks up from his papers, to find Makki standing in his house watching him. He was so absorbed in his work, that he didn't notice her enter. The light of day is rapidly failing, and he didn't notice that either.

"No."

"When?" she says, sitting down next to him and putting her arms around him. She cuddles up close to him and nuzzles his ear. But her affections are merely a ruse to peek at his work and he quickly covers up his pages. She looks disappointed, but she doesn't say anything. She didn't expect him to let her look. He never shows his work to anyone until it is finished.

"I'm entering the Poet Master contest with this," he says at last. "I think I have a good chance this year."

"Really?"

"Yes."

"That's exciting," she says, staring at him with starry eyes.

He just shrugs and grins.

"If you win, you'll be able to afford a baby."

"Yes, I suppose that is true," he agrees hesitantly.

"Do you want one?" she asks, with baited breath. "A family?"

He shrugs. He hasn't really thought about it lately. It isn't high on his list of priorities.

"Let's talk about it after the new moon. I haven't won yet. It's still just a gamble."

"I want to marry you *on* the new moon. Before the other girls suddenly notice how handsome you are when you become Poet Master. I mean - I don't want..." her face falls. "You're just going to change, is all. If you win I mean...."

She trails off awkwardly and Bodi laughs at her pained expression. He stares at his lover, amused by her sudden intensity, and wonders how long she has been thinking these thoughts of babies and family. She has never mentioned such things before. Has she really been thinking about a family all this time, waiting for him to settle down and grow up? He told her a long time ago that he had no desire to settle down. It goes against all of his instincts as a poet.

"Bodi, you can tell me the truth," she says, her face crestfallen. "Are you planning to win the contest and leave me for a younger, prettier girl? I just want to know."

"Makki seems so sad,
Thinking that Bodi will be bad,
And the girl he left behind,
Will miss his funny rhymes."

"That doesn't rhyme very well, actually," she says in an irritated voice. "And it doesn't answer my question either."

"Suddenly serious Makki,
Doesn't look too happy,
The moon in Cougar is making her head swim-"

She is starting to become upset, and he quickly makes up a new rhyme.

"You know that a poet must be free,
For inspiration is like the leaves of a tree,
And a poet must always reach higher in search of the sun."

"Stop it," whines Makki. "Stop making poetry. Just talk to me."

Bodi shuts his mouth quickly, just as he was about to spew forth a particularly good stanza that would have summed up his feelings nicely. He resolves to write it down as soon as he finishes this conversation.

"I'm getting old, Bodi," Makki says suddenly. "I want to have a baby while I still can. I want to have *your* baby."

"But let me explain - " Bodi says desperately.

"No, I know what you're going to say. You warned me that you are like a trickster coyote, always on the run. But I don't need much help. I really don't. I'll raise it by myself. All you have to do is marry me, just for appearances, so the baby won't be shunned as a bastard. That's it. Plant your seed, and I'll leave you alone to run all over creation, thinking up interesting things to say. You won't have to do anything at all, except be my lover and visit the child sometimes."

He doesn't say anything for a long time. She has never seen him at a loss for words before. She squirms uncomfortably and wishes he would say something.

"May I say a poem now?"

Makki sighs and indicates for him to get on with it.

"If Bodi has a wife and child,
He will no longer be happy and wild,
But a quail caught in a trap."

Makki sighs and turns on her heels, a scowl on her face. Bodi watches her walk toward the door, hating to disappoint her. He feels a pain in his chest and guilt burns through his guts. And then he suddenly wonders if it would be so bad to give up just a little of his freedom. He could stand to be a little less idle, he supposes. And she is very generous to offer to raise the baby herself.

"But our baby would be cute,
And unless it were deaf and mute,
It could grow up to make me proud."

Makki stops just outside the door. She stands there for a moment, and then she turns slowly around and waits for the next stanza. He struggles to get the words out, as it is the most difficult three lines he has ever spoken.

Bodi does love her,
And though his freedom will be over,
He will marry Makki on the new moon."

A slow grin spreads across her face. Soon the grin turns into a huge smile that radiates throughout her entire body. Finally, she seems so happy, she doesn't know what do with herself. She just stands there, squirming and grinning maniacally.

"I liked that one," she says, running over to give him a big kiss. "Will you write it down for me?"

Jay 17'

Thankfully, Esther works in the Scribe's House today, and not in the paper makers. Her arms are given a rest, but not her nerves. The scribes are in a constant fluster today, and they make her run all over the place on every conceivable errand they can think up.

After work, she walks up to the top of one of the five hills to watch the sunset and get some peace and quiet. As she sits, enjoying the reddish dusk, she sees Bodi and Makki walking hand in hand. She wants to hide, but before she can get up, Makki points her out and Bodi lights up and waves at her. They come over, full of smiles and good cheer.

"Hillotosh mikow, Esther. What a pleasant surprise." Bodi says cheerily.

"Hillotosh mikow, Bodi."

"You say 'garinda hafilu' in reply."

"Oh. Garinda hafilu."

"Bodi and I are getting married on the new moon," Makki says with a grin. "I hope you'll be there."

"Mintall ess," Esther says, congratulating them.

"Ah," Bodi laughs. "She has learned to speak Zwin. Very good."

He locks hands with her in the Jay style, both hands grasping in friendship at once.

"And we're going to have a baby."

"You're pregnant?"

"Not yet. I will be soon," Makki replies.

"Jupiter will be in the sign of Raven," Bodi explains. "Astrologers speak very highly about next year's new moon."

"We are going to conceive in three months," explains Makki.

"Mintall ess," says Esther again.

"Zinta," says Bodi, beaming.

"And maybe we will have another when Jupiter enters the Jay constellation," adds Makki hopefully. "What do you think, Bodi?"

"We'll see," Bodi says, frowning.

A moment later his frown is turned upside down into a lopsided grin. Bodi stares at Esther with twinkling eyes and then looks at Makki for approval. He whispers something in her ear, and she smiles and nods.

"The moon is in the sign of the Cougar tonight. A good night for a segisti. Don't you think?"

"What is a segisti?"

"Segi - Zwin for sexual coupling. Sti - means many. A segisti is what you might call a sexual experience of more than two people. Makki and I are planning one tonight as a celebration. Are you interested? My friend Keroen is interested, which makes three, but we need another woman to balance everything out."

" We like you, Esther. We want you to be a part of our segisti very much," says Makki. "And Keroen is looking for a partner to conceive with. Perhaps you two will hit it off and you will be able to live here."

"Yes," says Bodi, pleased at the idea. "Jays are very good lovers. We do not get carried away by passion, thus we focus on technique and can last for hours and bring a woman to great ecstasy many times."

"That's a lie," snorts Makki. "I can name several -" she trails off, as Bodi hits her playfully. "But we three are all good lovers," she adds.

"I don't think so," says Esther uncomfortably. "But thank you anyway."

That night, in the library, she works on her assignment to write a poem for writing class. She feels empty and sad tonight. She is sure that it has something to do with Bodi and Makki and seeing how happy they are to be starting a family. And what a fun life they lead with their segistis, poems and childlike innocence. Her own bitterness pours forth onto the page before her. Her writing is spidery and childlike, barely legible, in fact. But it is legible to her and she decides that is enough.

Will I always be alone?
Alone, a walking skin and bones,
Through a land where I have no name,
Walking in shadows of pain.
Others marry and lie together,
In beds of feather,
I am completely lost,
My life is a permanent frost.
Once I wanted to die,
Now I just want to cry.

"Maybe Bodi can put this in his book," she says bitterly when it is finished.

Then she feels a little proud of herself for writing her first poem.

Jay 18'

In afternoon writing class, they share their poems for the weekend assignment. A Jay child, age five, reads from his paper.

"A bird is my friend,
I call him Gildered,
I like to play,
I play pone all day.

My friends and me,
We climb a tree."
He giggles shyly and sits down.
"Very good," says Magdeli. A bit more word variety is wanted. But a fine start. Clari is next."
Clari stands. She is a funny Jay girl with great curly hair done up in wild pigtails. She is a relentless class clown and everyone giggles in anticipation as she stands up. She pulls out her paper, ripped and stained from who knows what abuses, and begins.
"I made a zodie, (*poop*)
It plopped in the ferns,
My mother dug it out,
And checked it for worms.
She found one,
And now my zodie burns.
The class roars with laughter. Clari bows and giggles to herself as she sits down. Magdeli is ecstatic and she claps her hands together with glee.
"Excellent. Fine structure and use of irony. You will be a match for Karbudde yet. Next...Sare."
"My daddy is a farmer
My mommy makes dinner
My brother feeds the pig
My other brother goes to school."
"A nice try," says Magdeli. "But there is no structure, no rhythm. But a nice try."
Sare shrugs, not caring one fig whether it was good or not.
"Now...Esther."
Esther rises nervously. She reads the poem she wrote last night. She reads in a low, monotone voice that perfectly illustrates the hopelessness she felt. When she is done, the class is silent. They do not understand it in the slightest, other than knowing it is sad. Magdeli merely looks embarrassed.
"A good poem," she says hesitantly, although not with any enthusiasm.
Esther shrugs, not wanting to care.
"Fine rhymes. Good structure. The Bear tribe would love it, perhaps."
Esther can't help but feel disappointed, knowing that Magdeli did not like it. Magdeli sees this, and struggles to find words for her doubts.
"Poetry should not be too emotional or it loses its focus," she says softly, so the other children won't hear her. "That is what Karbudde teaches us."
One of the children makes a face at Esther and the whole class giggles insanely. She pretends to ignore the child, but inwardly she

feels frustrated and sick of this class. She sits down, but she fumes throughout the day.

"She liked that stupid poem about zodies, and she didn't like mine," Esther thinks. "How typical of them. They don't understand anything here. Not really."

By the end of the day, she has made up her mind to leave the class. Why should she waste her time here, when she could be fishing and enjoying the coming summer and all the beautiful weather they have been having? As she leaves class, presumably for the last time, Magdeli walks over and smiles at her.

"Your poem wasn't bad, Esther. I'm just a stickler for form and function, being a teacher and all. So you must take what I say lightly and not to heart. Remember also that you are a grown woman and I have to be harder on you than the other little children, or else you will not learn anything. You are much more stubborn and resistant than they are, and harder to teach."

Esther has to admit that Magdeli is right about that, and she decides to stay a few more days at least. To hell with what Magdeli or anybody else thinks. She isn't here for them. She's here for herself.

Jay 19'

Hawk moon

Esther skips class today because is too nice outside to be stuck in a little room all day. She goes fishing instead. She catches a small fish and cooks it. Then she lies in the sun lazily and naps.

She is awakened by a little insect tickling her nose. She waves it away, but it keeps on coming back. Finally she turns over and hides her nose, but the thing goes for her neck. When she tries to slap it, she finds herself grasping someone's hand. She jumps up, startled. It is Bodi, laughing gleefully, holding a feather in his hand.

"A girl sleeping soundly,
Fly on the nose,
Slapped it away,
I have ruined her repose."

"Hello Bodi," Esther mumbles sleepily.

"I have come to invite you to a party,
Care to come?
Mercury is in the sign of the Blue Jay,
Don't be a bum."

Esther is touched by the invitation and she apologizes deeply to Bodi for all the weird things she has said and done to him.

"Couldn't be helped," he says with a wink. "Mercury was crawling through Beaver - that's the determined earth sign. Communication was slow and stubborn. Now that it's in an air sign, we should communicate just fine."

It is a fun party, with lots of games and laughter. Upon finding out that Esther cannot play Koko, he shouts, "My stars, were you raised in a Beaver barn?" He insists on teaching her and proceeds to beat her three games in a row. She finds that she has a love of games and resolves to play them more. There is an amateur poetry contest too, where everyone reads a poem and then everyone votes on their favorite. At everyone's urging, Esther reads her sad poem and gets strange stares as a response.

"It's her first," says Bodi.

Everyone laughs and pats her on the back. They all agree that it is good for a first poem, although nobody votes for it.

"I like it," she thinks sourly. "Even if nobody else does."

After the contest, she asks Bodi why nobody likes her poem.

"You should read Karbudde's essay on poetic form and function. You would find it interesting. The basic philosophy is that poetry is an art form. It should reach for greatness. It is not for complaining. Complain to your friends, if you must. Not to your audience. Paper is expensive and you should treat it as such. Put sublime things on it."

There is a potluck feast after the contest, including deer meat, fire bread, fish, and a wild greens salad. It seems a feast by Jay standards, at least during this time of the year. Esther walks home after dinner with a full belly and a spring in her step. But in a little voice inside her head, she keeps wondering why nobody likes her poem.

Jay 22'

**Jay moon*

Everyone is tense and edgy at the Scribe's House today. Esther is told to sweep up this spill and that mess and to clean something that has been cleaned twice already. A woman snaps at her because she gets in her way and makes her drop a whole stack of paper. Esther is getting more and more irritated by the moment, but she bites her lip and keeps at it. After work, the woman walks up to her and Esther steels herself for a confrontation. But the woman only smiles and offers an apology.

"Reparations are sorely needed. The new moon is coming and everyone is on edge. Please accept my apology. By tonight, the new moon will have arrived and everything will relax again."

Late in the night, Esther is awakened from a sound sleep by a loud cheer, which echoes throughout the five hills.

"Jarela da! Hama fass da Jaya! Hama fass te la borali!"

Esther assumes that the shouts are for the new moon. She is beginning to catch on to the patterns of these strange tribes. The new moon means a big party. Which means no work or school tomorrow, and lots of food.

Jay 23'

The new moon festival begins with the parade of the fool. Everyone who is interested dresses up in the most ridiculous outfit they can find and lines up at the top of Blackberry Hill. A band of flutes, drums, and hand clappers begins to play a lively tune, and the fools do strange dances, shout obscene jokes and rude poems, tumble, prance, and run around like lunatics. Those that don't wish to perform just stand on the sidelines and laugh. Esther had not realized that the Jays held such magnetism. She cannot take her eyes off them and she laughs until it hurts.

After the parade, the games begin. For the youngsters and the young at heart, Pone is the game to play. Flying Birds is also an exciting and popular game. For the oldsters and the old at heart, there is Grimp, Moussai, Chess, Go, and other quiet games. Pone involves too much running and the other games are too sedentary, so Esther opts to learn Flying Birds. Flying Birds involves a piece of carved wood, which is roughly in the shape of a boomerang but does not return to its owner. One throws it toward a target that is very far away and sees how many throws it takes to strike the target and knock it over. The course winds throughout a heavily wooded area, which makes the game even more difficult. It takes Esther many throws to hit the targets, which are very small wooden carvings made to resemble various small animals. She ends up wandering all over the course, looking for her lost "Flying Bird" many times in bushes or up in trees. One time, she searches for a half hour before she finds it again. When she finally does locate it, she is scratched and bruised from wading in thorns and thick brush.

It takes Esther a few hours to finish one round, and she is constantly passed by more skilled players who play much quicker than she does. Some of the men have amazing aim, having played the game their whole lives. One man can hit the little wooden targets on his second throw. Esther is told that this man hunts small game with his Flying Bird.

Lunchtime proves that the Jay tribe can eat very well if they want to. There is quail (some of which was actually hunted with a Flying Bird), venison, shellfish, acorn bread, and seaweed salad. After lunch, some go off to play more games, but many people gather around a raised platform for the annual poetry contest. It is a heavy competition, as it results in the announcement of Poet Master for the year. Poet Master is a very prestigious position, and those competing take it very seriously.

It is one of the most competitive in recent memory. The first competitor is a tall, gangly woman who reads a story about the

Southern Zesti who live near the Mission Santa Barbara and a voyage across the ocean to a big island where strange gods live. Then comes a man who has collected stories of blue jay from ten different Zesti tribes. After that is an epic poem about the trading ship's journey to South America last year. It is a fascinating tale and generates quite a buzz. The author, who is none other than Jasp, the current Poet Master, is predicted to win the contest a second year in a row. Then everyone is tired of poetry and the competition is called until tomorrow.

There is a dance during the night, with music by a band from the Bear tribe. Esther has begun to recognize some of the songs of the Bear tribe, who seem to play at every big party. They are considered the best musicians of the Twelve Tribes – at least of the southern tribes - and are in high demand. One small wine cask is opened, but Esther cannot get near it. It is soon empty and many thirsty people curse the fates that made wine so scarce this year. Despite the shortage, the party goes very late into the night and everyone has a wild time of it.

Esther wishes she were having as much fun as everybody else, but she just feels empty and bored. She sits by herself and listens to other people's conversations moodily. She cannot muster up any enthusiasm about anything, and whenever somebody tries to draw her into conversation, they get bored of her quickly. She is not purposely avoiding people, she just cannot think of anything to get excited about. When the musicians stop playing, she walks back to her camp and goes to sleep.

Jay 24'

The next morning, there is another round of games. After everyone is tired out, the Poet Master competition resumes. There are three more works to be judged. Second to read is Bodi himself. He rises, with a stack of wrinkled paper covered in scratched and scribbled writing and stands before the crowd. Then he begins to read. His poem is about the legendary Jeren, who is somewhat of a religious figure to the Twelve Tribes. Jeren's books and discussions on astrology were the inspiration for the strange religion of the tribes. He is also known as the man who led the original founders to this land from South America. He was both chief and prophet to them. Nobody knows where he and his people's ancestors actually came from and it is the source of much speculation. Bodi's poem tells that the Twelve Tribes were originally South American natives under the thumb of the Spanish, and Jeren was a Spanish priest who broke from the church and led them to paradise. He speculates about how Jeren converted the people from the Catholic religion forced upon them to his own religion based upon astrology, and convinces the people that there are twelve gods that work in harmony instead of merely one. Esther notices that he mentions many of the things she told him about Christianity in it. It is an adventure, a speculative history and an astrological discussion in one - and it rhymes too! Bodi has been working on it for many years and it is quite involved. He can feel all eyes on him as he reads and he knows that he is winning the crowd over.

He finishes and stares around him with baited breath, wondering if they enjoyed it as much as he enjoyed writing it. When he hears the cheers of the crowd after he is finished, he knows that his nomination for Poet Master is assured. He humbly stacks his worn and wrinkled pages together and steps off the stump that was his stage.

Bodi is voted Poet Master for his superb work, a position he will hold for exactly one year. After a celebration lunch, it is time for the new moon weddings. This will be Bodi's first duty as Poet Master. Everyone gathers at the wedding platform and Bodi stands to address the crowd.

"As the new Poet Master, it is my duty to perform the marriage ceremonies of the new moon. But alas, I cannot perform all of them..." he stops for dramatic effect, "because I am one of those to be wed. Makki and Bodi will be wed. I hope that Jasp, our former Master, will perform that ceremony in our honor."

Jasp cheerfully agrees to do that. He seems to harbor no ill will for his loss today. He has said all afternoon that Bodi's work far surpasses his own this year, and that Bodi deserves the victory.

There are only two weddings this year. They are simple affairs, without the intensity or romanticism of the Beaver weddings. The couple first announces their intentions to form a partnership and then the Poet Master makes a long speech about doing the right things for themselves and the tribe. And then they kiss. Bodi's speech for the other newlyweds is rather vague and uninspiring, but he has only been Poet Master for a few hours, and everybody forgives him for his inexperience.

Jay 25'

Bear moon

Magdeli is very pleased with Esther's progress. Today, she shows her writing to the class and comments favorably on many aspects of it. Then she takes Esther aside to talk to her alone.

"I think you are ready to enter the next grade level. There are only five days left of school, but that doesn't matter."

"Today?"

"Yes. In fact, why don't I walk you there right now? I'll explain your situation to Mury."

Esther isn't sure that she wants to change classes. It seems to Esther that Magdeli is trying to rush her out of there just because she wants Esther to leave. She wants to deal with little children again. Esther feels a little sad about the thought of leaving all of her new friends, but Magdeli is already standing by the door. Esther suddenly feels sorry for the poor woman, who has had to put up with a lot from her. So Esther decides to do her a favor. She stands up nobly and puts on a brave face.

"Esther, where are you going?" asks Sare.

Esther gives her a little squeeze as she stands up.

"Bye Esther," Sare shouts and then she goes back to her book.

They walk toward another log cabin and Magdeli opens the door and motions for Esther to wait. She stands outside as Magdeli speaks to the teacher. Finally Magdeli returns and she seems pleased.

"Well, it's settled. Good luck. I have to get back to the children."

She waves and walks off.

"Thank you for all the help," Esther calls after her.

Magdeli waves again as she goes back into her classroom. And then Esther enters her new class. She is a little surprised to find a class full of young teenagers, ranging in age from ten to thirteen. She recognizes a couple of Hawk tribe boys from her days with them, including Dohr's brother Kahne, who laughs hysterically at the sight of her. She stares at the teacher, a dour, humorless man with a thick beard and beady eyes. Needless to say, she is very reluctant to enter this class.

"Please sit, young lady," he intones.

In a daze, Esther sits down amid strange stares and snickers from her new classmates. She hears a couple of whispered comments from boys behind her, laughing that here is a girl that they can finally sink their shaft into. The boys are hit by a couple of girls, who stare at Esther jealously because she is suddenly a spotlight of attention for the boys. Esther's face becomes flushed and she slumps in her chair. This is much worse than her last class.

"Class, let's keep going with our discussion of proper grammar," the teacher says, ignoring the ruckus.

He begins to talk about Karbudde, but nobody is listening. They are too busy goofing off. It is a beautiful day and they long to play games in the sunshine and flirt and do things a lot more interesting than sitting in this room learning grammar. They are suffering from the inactivity of the past month. The end of school is only a week away and they can't wait.

"Pssst. Hey you. What's your name?" says a boy directly behind her. He is a big, fat boy with a huge head and squinty eyes that are shoved way too close together.

"Esther," she whispers, not sure that she wants to talk to him.

"Hey, Esther, you want to have lunch together?"

"No."

The rest of the class busts up laughing as the boy gets rejected.

"You don't know what you're missing. You ever had a real man?" he asks, trying to save face.

"No," Esther says truthfully.

The class busts up laughing again.

"Shut up," a girl shouts out. "I'm trying to hear the teacher."

"Yes, please do try to pay attention," adds the teacher, who is trying to ignore the distractions.

He starts talking about grammar again, but Esther can only hear the drama going on around her.

"Bear boys are babies," says the squinty, fat boy.

"We'll see," says a Bear boy darkly. "You say that to my face later."

"I will."

"Shut up both of you," hisses the girl.

"What are you going to do about it?"

"Just shut up!" she shouts. "I'm trying to learn."

"Outside with you," shouts the teacher to the squinty Hawk boy.

"Why me?" he asks innocently. "She's been bugging me."

The teacher looks momentarily confused. He is not sure what actually happened.

"It was him," the girls shouts. "Wasn't it?" she asks Esther desperately.

Esther closes her eyes. She does not want to be here. She nods slowly in agreement.

"Liar," shouts the boy. "Ugly slug!"

"Out, now," says the teacher.

"Fine with me. I'll go hunting instead. Rather do that anyway."

"Can I go too?" asks Kahne.

"No."

"Why does he get to go hunting? He's supposed to be punished."

"Just be quiet, please. Don't you all want to go home and say you learned something this month?"

"No," sneers the squinty boy, leaving before the teacher changes his mind.

"Lucky," says Kahne jealously, watching him walk outside. "I want to go outside too."

Esther spends the whole morning listening to scenes like this, and she doesn't learn anything. The afternoon is no better. Mury gives the whole class a long lecture on how to deal with the heavy emotions that come up when the moon enters a water sign.

"Emotions can be a dangerous enemy," he declares. "They sap your strength and distract you from what is going on. Just let them pass."

A Bear tribe girl says, "That's stupid. Emotions are important."

"Now they are. Because everything is dramatic at your age. But when you are older, you will realize that they are not."

"You're just an air sign intellectual, like my mother says." retorts the girl.

"Thank you," Mury says.

As if to prove it, he proceeds to give a long, boring lesson on the movement of the zodiac and the mathematics of astrology. Following that, they talk about Jeren's principals of astrology. The teacher seems to think that this will interest the children, but they show no more interest in that than they do in grammar. After trying unsuccessfully to get a discussion going, the teacher gives up and dismisses the class for the day.

After school, Esther walks up to the Bear girl who has been so loud in class all day.

"What's it like in Bear village?" she asks curiously.

"Better than here. There's nothing to do here. We have dances and beautiful music at our village. We're right near the ocean and we go swimming nearly every day, and there is always something fun to do. I hate it here."

"Why?"

"The Jays are nice enough. I have friends here. But I hate going to school. We have to go to school during every air month until we are fourteen."

"What are the air months?"

"You don't know the air months?" she asks, a bit scornfully.

"No."

"What are you doing here anyway? You're too old to be here."

"You're right," agrees Esther.

"Is somebody making you go?"

"No."

"Then why are you here?"

Esther has to admit that she agrees with that logic. Why put herself through another day of this new class? She has learned to read and write at a beginner level now and she could care less about all the other stuff they are teaching. She's ready to move on.

"I want to go to the Bear village," she tells the girl. "How far is it?"

"A day's journey," she says, looking around for her friend.

"Is the food good?"

"Very good. Um...I have to go catch my friend," she says, and runs off.

Esther decides to go to Bear village. Before she changes her mind, she begins to walk up the path to get her things. But on the way, she decides to switch directions and head up to the Scribe's House first. It is only fair that she tells them that she won't be working there anymore.

The Scribe's House is full of the usual crowd, busily transcribing texts. Esther talks briefly to one of the girls she works with, and the girl nods slowly, as she continues to mix ink out of a mess of animal parts and charcoal. Esther tenders her resignation, and helps herself to a little harti to fill her stomach for the long journey. As she eats, she sees Bodi hard at work, transcribing his scribbled poem into a nice even hand for immediate display in the library. Esther doesn't want to disturb him, but she feels obligated to say goodbye and she taps him on the shoulder.

"Well, hello, my friend," he exclaims, rising to his feet and grabbing her hands in the local style. "To what do I owe this visit?"

"I just wanted to say goodbye."

"Where are you going?" he asks surprised.

"To visit the Bear tribe."

He laughs.

"Perfect. You'll like it there."

"Do you think so?"

"Will I always be alone?
A walking skin and bones,
Through lands where I have no name,
Walking in shadows of deep pain..." he intones in a dramatic voice.

Esther has to laugh at his funny reading, although it is at her expense.

"You memorized it?" she asks, surprised.

"Of course you'll like it there," he says with a twinkle in his eye.

"Congratulations on being voted chief," she says with a return smile, suddenly realizing that she is going to miss him a little bit.

"Poet Master, not chief. We have no chief. We have a council of elders, who make all the important decisions."

"Then what will you do?"

"I will make a lot of speeches and lead social events. That's what the Poet Master does."

She nods. They stand there for a while, just grinning at each other. She reaches out and touches his wreath of blue feathers, which is a symbol of the Poet Master. He laughs.

"Well, I'll let you get back to your work," she says, anxious to get moving before dark.

"I have to give you a present first."

He gets up and looks along the bookshelf at the newly completed volumes. He finally selects a very small book that cannot be more than ten pages long. With a smile he hands it to Esther. Surprised, she takes the book and attempts to read the cover.

"Zowe?" she asks. "Karb-"

"Karbudde, the great Jay poet. Zowe is one of his most famous poems. You'll like it. And it is good practice to have something to read."

"Mintall ess."

"Zinta."

And then she leaves him to his work and goes outside into the sunshine. Bodi sighs, as he picks up the quill again. He stretches his sore hands and stares at the blank page waiting to be filled. He is suddenly tired.

"Back to work..." he murmurs.

But then he suddenly remembers that he is Poet Master. He can certainly take a break if he wants. He stands up and walks outside into the sunshine. He'll come back when he feels like it.

Everything looks green and alert today, standing proud and lively in the bright sunshine, as Esther walks down the path towards her camp. It is a kind of sublime quality that one doesn't notice unless one is leaving a place and will not see it for quite a while. Esther quickly gets her things together, wanting to be well on the road by dark. She straps her new fishing net to her burden basket, but it is too bulky, so she finally pulls the long handle off the net and just straps on the net itself. Satisfied, she shoulders the pack and takes one last look at the five hills of the Jay tribe.

They look peaceful and serene in the fading light of day. The library stands tall and proud in the center. Wishing it all a fond farewell, she turns her back and begins walking down the path towards Bear village. She is surprised to find that she has very few doubts about leaving. It actually feels good to get on the road again. She thinks of what adventures lie ahead and she is glad.

Bear Tribe

Jay 26'

Bear moon

Esther has been hiking since the crack of dawn. The ground is rough, hilly, and rocky and Esther is weary from the long hike. Luckily, her strong Beaver-made moccasins are up to the challenge and her feet are well protected. It is misty, with a pale sheet of cloud covering everything, as if the sky wants to rain but is not finding enough water to do the job. She stops by a little creek for a rest and a drink of water. She nearly falls asleep, but forces herself to rise and continue walking. Ignoring her aching feet and her grumbling stomach, she presses on for a few more miles. She pushed herself hard all day yesterday and today to make Bear village by tonight. There is no point in stopping now because of a little pain.

Bear village was possibly located where Half Moon Bay stands today. It is possible to pinpoint the location of this village due to a strange coincidence. The half moon is the symbol of the Bear tribe, and was carved into rocks, trees and other eternal things. Since the origin of the name "Half Moon Bay" is a mystery, it is possible that it was named after runes left by this tribe.

The path comes in sight of the ocean again and Esther believes that she is getting close. As it gets dark, faint lights start to wink in the hills. The sight of lights urges her to move faster. There won't be much of a moon, but she can make it to the lights before it is pitch black. As she trudges in the gloom, she prays to find a hot dinner. She left Jay village yesterday with just a single bowl of harti and she is starting to really feel it. Her moods are starting to swing again and her temper is on a hair trigger. She knows she'll have trouble sleeping tonight if she doesn't eat something for dinner.

Just as night fully encloses the land, she finds herself at the base of one of the low hills that rise up from the ocean. Lights hit her from several different directions as the town emerges from out of the gloom. She becomes nervous as she approaches the first buildings of the village. Here she is in another strange land - a stranger with nothing to offer. What should she do? Barge in and announce her presence for dinner? She stands in the darkness for a long time, feeling sorry for herself.

Then a smell hits her nose. Fresh bread! Her stomach grumbles and she follows her nose toward the nearest house. Approaching the window, she can see shapes inside, and then she crouches down and peeks boldly into the window. There is a thin curtain partially obscuring her view, but she can make out half of a table with several people seated around it. The smell of the hot corn bread is too much to bear and she tries to work up the courage to beg for a piece. But she only just stands there, staring at the people as they tear into the food, her face a mask of desperation and longing.

Suddenly her view is blocked. A woman stares back at her through the curtain. Startled, Esther pulls back in fear. The face disappears, and a moment later the door opens and a woman pops her head out. She is a hefty woman with silver hair and a pleasant, if unattractive face, wearing an apron. Light shines behind her, giving her a homey glow. Esther notices a sign reflected in the light of the open door, announcing the 'Shelter of the Moon'.

"What are you doing sneaking around out here? Why don't you come in already?"

"Thank you," Esther says, very surprised.

"Do you want a room for the night?" the woman asks.

"You have one?"

"Yes." She looks at Esther strangely now. "Is this not a shelter?"

"I just arrived," says Esther, hoping that will explain everything.

"I know," says the woman impatiently. "And here you are. I have hungry guests to feed. If you want to eat, come on in."

She turns around and goes inside, leaving the door open. Esther wonders why she is so generous to offer a complete stranger dinner and a room without a second thought, but she is too excited to really care. She is not familiar with the concept of an 'inn' and doesn't know that a 'shelter' is one of those. Nervously, she enters the room and sits down quietly at a free space on a bench. Everyone stops eating a moment to stare at her, but nobody says anything.

To avoid looking anyone in the eye, she examines the heavily decorated room instead. The windows are draped with curtains made from woven feathers of many colors. Bearskin rugs lie upon the floor. But the real eye catcher are the wall paintings, which Esther admires at length. The one she really likes is a painting of a woman in a river, floating downstream. She has a round, open face with radiant eyes and long brown hair trailing behind her. River weeds cling to her body, twining around her legs and across her breasts. She seems to be floating with the river, almost a part of it. Her likeness is found in all the other paintings as well, and Esther wonders who it could be.

"Tea?"

"Hmmm?"

"Would you like some tea?" The woman hovers over her, a bowl of twiggy looking tea in her hand.

"Thank you. Yes, please."

"My name is Massie," she says, pouring her a cup. "Let me know if you need anything at all."

She puts another bowl of hot corn bread on the table, with real butter smeared on top of it. The hungry guests grab at the bread, dividing it up, and soon it is gone. Esther chews hungrily, as hot butter melts down her chin. The bread and the tea make a warm glow in her stomach that spreads to her entire body. Then Massie brings three plates of roasted fish smothered in herbs. As she sets the food on the table, she shouts "Kobe! Kobe!" A minute later, a young man walks into the room, carrying a Chinese made harp. He sets the harp near the window and pulls up a stool. He is chubby and soft, with a bland face like his mother's and hair that is close-cropped and so oily that it sticks to his head. Looking at nobody, he self-consciously sits down and plucks a few experimental notes. By the time everyone has their plates loaded with food, he is playing a sweet song to entertain the guests while they dine.

"Quite the best shelter in the Twelve Tribes, if you ask me," exclaims a tall, thin man named Zilt, who is of the Jay tribe. He sits back and sighs contentedly, as if he is a man who appreciates such luxuries.

"Except for the Beaver shelter, of course," adds his friend Lars, who is also a Jay. Lars has the biggest, most pointy nose that Esther has ever seen.

"That is a good shelter too, but it is not quite as homey. Music while you eat? Luxury!" Zilt laughs.

"It's plenty homey at Beaver village. And the food is much better. The food here is rather...simple."

A small, neat man with a tanned traveler's cloak and an impeccably neat appearance, speaks up suddenly.

"It is impolite to say such things as we sit here enjoying this fine hospitality. Let us think before we speak."

Zilt eyes him coolly. "That is fine for the Raccoon tribe. But we have no such limits to our freedom."

"Freedom? It's just plain manners. Does the Jay tribe not possess this virtue?"

"Jous..." a woman next to him says quietly.

"If by your talk of freedom you mean to say that the Jay have no manners or virtue, then they must learn some before they leave home," Jous continues, ignoring his wife.

Lars laughs.

"The honorable Raccoon will no doubt teach us all about manners. He knows what is good manners and what is bad, doesn't he? We have much to learn during dinner."

"I am always ready for a cultural lesson," adds Zilt. "Even one disguised as truth."

The wife of Jous sighs and glares at all of them in turn. She is a prim, proper woman with her hair in a bun and her body clothed in a simple brown dress.

"It would be better to pay more attention to our stomachs and less to our mouths. It is bad for digestion."

"An excellent suggestion, Tam," says Jous.

"I find that good conversation vastly improves a meal," retorts Zilt.

"But if they don't wish to converse, we may do so amongst ourselves," adds Lars.

"An excellent suggestion," agrees Zilt.

They begin to talk in Zwin, effectively shutting out the rest of the table. Jous shakes his head and tries to muster up support for his own point of view. Just then, Massie enters the room, having heard the commotion, and asks if anyone needs anything. Her tone is firm, as if she is really asking, "Is there a problem I have to deal with?" Even the Jays stop talking in her presence, so commanding is it. Under her watchful gaze, everyone returns to their eating in silence. Esther looks over at the harpist, who resumes playing now that quiet is restored.

After dinner, everyone retires to their rooms in preparation for the night's festivities, because there is a celebration tonight. Esther soon finds herself alone with Massie, who plops down at the table to take a load off. She absently munches at a small piece of bread and butter, mopping it in fish grease. Her face is plump with a huge flat, pudgy nose, and she has deep lines underneath the eyes, making her seem tired.

"So what brings you to the land of the Bear tribe," Massie inquires through a mouthful of bread.

"I'm traveling around," Esther says vaguely.

"Where are you from?"

Something in Massie's eyes makes her want to tell the truth, but she resists the urge.

"Branciforte. The town on the coast."

"By the moon, we have never had an outsider at this shelter before. How exciting." She doesn't look very excited though. Her face remains featureless. "You look tired. Let me get you to your hut. You must rest tonight."

“You really have a whole hut just for me to stay in?”

"Of course. This is a very good shelter. A whole hut for you alone. And for payment, we take tupas, dentalium shells or trade. As you like."

"I fear that I cannot pay at all," Esther says, her heart sinking. “I have no tupas or shells and very little to trade."

Massie nods slowly, but says nothing. Esther wonders if she should do something to pay for her meal.

"I could help you clean up, to pay for dinner."

"What else can you do?"

"I worked for a Beaver family. Cooking, farming, cleaning - that sort of thing."

"If you worked for a Beaver, you must be a good worker. Yes, you may help me clean up. That will cover dinner."

Esther is deposited outside on a stool, in front of two buckets of water and an old basket filled with the remains of food. She scrapes the food into the basket and washes the plates, as she did many times at Tara's house. She has the feeling that Massie is watching her the whole time and this makes her uncomfortable. After everything is done, Massie pulls up a stool and sits down with her.

"We may be able to help each other. My daughter is pregnant and is due to deliver in just a few weeks. The poor dear is having a harder and harder time keeping up, and she spends much time in her bed these days. And now that the solstice is coming, I will be swamped with visitors and I'll need an extra hand. Look at how late I served dinner tonight! If you are interested, we can do a work trade. I can offer you food and lodging and a few tupas in exchange for your help around here. Interested?"

"Oh yes," shouts Esther, very excited. "That sounds wonderful."

"I feel that you will do well here," says Massie. "Your temperament suits me. Come."

Massie rises, grabs a candle, and Esther follows her up the hill. Just above the main lodge are several simple huts made from tule, standing in a row. As they walk toward them, Esther can make out the sound of flutes on the wind, floating across the air like the songs of birds. She begins to feel very excited and happy about working here.

A few of the rooms are lit with candles, but many are dark. Massie picks out one for her and they enter through a tiny door that is only waist high. A little bed of thick furs and a few baskets are the only things that can fit into this little place. As Massie places the candle in a little holder, Esther sighs with contentment. It is perfect.

"I'll let you get some rest. In a few hours begins the moon dance. On the Bear moon, we always gather to worship. You must come."

"It sounds nice," says Esther doubtfully. "But I am tired and I think I should sleep. I must be rested, if I am to work tomorrow."

"To ignore the Bear spirit is not a good idea if you are going to be living here. You really should come. I will let you sleep through breakfast tomorrow. Yes? Good. So have a nap and I'll send someone to wake you in a while."

Massie doesn't look like she will take no for an answer, so Esther nods in agreement and Massie leaves her alone. She sits down on the soft bed and sighs. She loves her new room and feels instantly at peace. Soon she is napping contentedly.

She is awakened by an insect, buzzing in her ear. She slaps at it, but it continues to irritate her. She rolls over, hoping it will go away.

"What is love but a pipe dream? To smoke your deepest fears it seems."

She sits up, startled. Zilt sits beside her, reading from her copy of Karbudde. He tickles her ear and makes a buzzing sound with his lips. Then he laughs and Esther realizes that he was the insect.

"A scholar of Karbudde. I would not have thought a Beaver girl would read Karbudde. I'm impressed."

He closes the book and places it on her basket. Esther rises sluggishly, glances at her other Beaver dress, and decides that it looks cleaner than the one she wears.

"Well, the night grows late. Time to howl at the moon with the moon people."

She waves Zilt outside peevishly, changes dresses, and then follows him to the house where they ate dinner. Massie and the other guests are all gathered, waiting for her. Then they begin to walk down a path toward the beach. Esther's head is still bleary from sleep and she wishes she were back in bed. After a short hike, they hear the sound of drums, flutes, and cymbals. Then they see torchlight in the distance and hear the sound of many voices singing and drums pounding. The smell of burning sage wafts toward them on an ocean breeze. Suddenly Esther is not tired. She begins to feel excited and nervous.

As they reach the ring of torches, they see many women dancing. Long flowing hair wrapped in delicate scarves, heavy cleavage and fully formed hips are wrapped in transparent golintas. They wear shells on their ankles and wrists, which make a loud clacking sound as they move.

Golintas are made from silk and are imported from China. They have been altered to fit the tribal style and color combinations, which are soft blue, purple, and silver.

Their dance, raw and tribal, is the kind of powerful sexual frenzy that turns men into drooling, lusting dogs. No man can resist such a scene. As Massie's guests join the ring of grinning Bear tribe men clapping and stomping around the edge of the circle, the visiting men grow saucers for eyes and wide-open mouths. Esther just watches it all in awe. The music and excitement in the air are like a drug. Her pulse quickens and her blood boils.

Something awakens in Esther. A long dormant craving hiding in the darkest shadows of her mind comes to the surface. A primordial desire, the need to be beautiful and sensual, comes upon her like a crashing wave. The dancers bring tears to her eyes and her heart aches. She wants to dance like that. The feeling is so overwhelming and brutal, that Esther suddenly feels like screaming inside.

Suddenly the music stops dead and the women collapse on the wild grass of the plateau overlooking the sea. Their bodies heave as they struggle to catch their breath. The audience erupts into loud yells, whistles and screams, as the women stand up and walk off into the darkness.

Next, a trio of women comes out into the circle. Two are dressed as wood nymphs from some magical forest. The third is dressed as a bear spirit. They dance amongst the fallen bodies as flutes sing and a violin plays a sad strain. As they twirl, they begin to sing. The shrieking and yelling fades into attentive silence.

These dances are much different. They are sweet, sublime movements and the song is gentle and innocent. Desire softens into love. Esther has never heard a violin before and the music caresses her in this emotional state. She longs more than ever before for that long ignored impulse. She unconsciously plays with her hair and moves softly in circles, singing to herself.

Massie leans over and whispers, "Believe it or not, I used to move like that. I was a great dancer. Now I am stiff and clunky."

Esther is too far gone to respond to this cry for assurance. She nods distracted, and continues to sway softly.

When this new sublime dance is finally over, none are unmoved. The dancers run off into the night, and there is complete quiet. The quiet is more unnerving than the music. One can finally hear the ocean crash on the rocks below.

A single woman now comes out. She is dressed in an elaborate golinta and her hair is braided with bright blue shells.

"Now for a Zune," whispers Massie. That's a song to the great Bear spirit."

The woman begins to sing in a pristine, pure voice of honey. She sings and moves in slow but assured movements, and Esther melts. This is more than she can stand. All voices join in on a well-recognized cue and the air is bathed in a hundred voices singing. Hands are lifted to the sky, as if to sing to the glorious moon that they worship - the moon that is barely visible, just a tiny sliver. Then all voices stop and the woman sings the remainder of the song alone.

After the Zune, the circle breaks. The beating of the drums resumes, and everyone begins to dance. Meanwhile, the sweets are served. Most popular is the famous moon pie, a rich camas cake blended with cream and sweetened with honey and berries. It is the moon pie that is most often associated with Bear cuisine. Only five women in the Bear tribe know the secret recipe of the moon pie and they hide this recipe jealously from all prying eyes. Their secrecy is effective, as hundreds are exported to the nearby tribes every year. Blackberry wine flows freely and the night takes on a rosy, purple hue.

The dancing continues until late in the night and Esther begins to imitate all of the women's movements. She has never danced like this before, using dance as an expression of her spirit. At first, she feels like a rusted pulley, called into action after twenty years sitting idle in a wet field. Her joints creak and crack like a ship in a heavy wind. She feels foolish as she looks around, because all of the girls her age are great dancers. So she dances away from the torchlight in a dark space all by herself. She resolves to get good at it before doing it in front of people.

It has been a physically exhausting day and an emotionally exhausting night, and soon there is no mistaking it - she is dead tired. Her mind is numb, her feet hurt and her body is drunk and about to collapse. Although she cannot bear to stop, she knows that she must. She looks for Massie, but cannot find her. After a long search, she finds Jous, who is just leaving himself, and he leads her zombie-like form home to a welcome bed. She collapses into her soft bed like a dead thing and the music of the drums echoes faintly in her head as she falls into a deep sleep.

Jay 27'

Eagle moon

Esther is awakened at dawn by loud voices and laughter in the hut right next to hers. The huts are built much too close together and the walls are thin as tule reeds, so she can hear the noises of people talking and arguing next to her. It is only a little past dawn. She curses and prays that they go away soon. But they do not. They just keep getting louder and louder as the morning wears on and they assume everyone is awake.

She is afraid to go sleep somewhere else, because Massie is supposed to wake her when she needs her. So she just lies there in misery, half awake and half asleep, craving many more hours of rest. She curses her neighbors, who sound like Zilt and Lars, until they finally go away to breakfast. Then it is quiet at last. But she is annoyed and half awake, and it is getting very hot in her hut and she cannot sleep again. All too soon, she hears the noises of her neighbors on the other side, who return from breakfast, and she throws her cloak over her head in frustration.

Not long after she finally falls asleep again, Massie pops her head into the hut.

"Still asleep," laughs Massie. "You've slept enough, I think. I could really use your help for lunch."

Massie smiles at the sight of her struggling to wake.

"Be in the kitchen in a half hour."

Esther's heart leaps at the notion of a slow rise. Not like Tara and Tork's cruel efficiency at all. But she soon begins to doze off again, so she forces herself to rise and walks down to the kitchen. There she is put to work, with a head full of buzzing bees and a yawn every minute. She sips a cold cup of Chinese tea from breakfast and nibbles on cold corn bread as she works. Meal preparation is much like Tara's house, but on a bigger scale. Esther hauls water, cleans fish, washes bowls, and sets the table.

The guests slowly trickle in and sit down at their leisure, and Esther must now tend to their needs. It is a little strange to serve them, when only yesterday she sat with them as a guest herself, but they think it nothing strange. She runs back and forth from the outdoor kitchen and the main lodge, until they are all happy. Then she sits down, exhausted.

Massie hands her a plate of food and tells her that she must now eat outside in the kitchen, instead of with the guests. She is given clean up directions and then left to tend to things while Massie goes off on some errand. Esther hunkers down with a plate of fish and bread, slumped against the wall, thoroughly exhausted.

She is relieved to be eating regularly again, even if breakfast was the same as dinner. And she is thankful to be free from simple harti over and over again. After eating all she can stomach, she becomes very sleepy, and nods off. Massie appears a short time later and startles Esther awake. She remembers that she was supposed to have done the dishes. Guiltily, she rises and sets water to boil for the cleaning. Then she begins to scrape the leftover food into compost. Massie pretends not to notice the awkward moment and disappears into the dining room to collect wooden bowls and spoons for her.

Excused until dinner, Esther decides to explore the area a bit and find a nice patch of sun to doze in. The main path through town climbs up into gentle hills and she follows it. The wide path skirts the creek Aern, lifeblood of the town. As she continues uphill, she sees many cozy houses. Curiously, she peeks into an open window, drawn by a delicious smell. She sees a single large room, decorated with bright rugs and furs, and a large family eating at a table. An older woman turns to stare at Esther as her face appears in the window, and she glares angrily, as if to say "Don't peek where you're not wanted." Esther shrinks back guiltily and walks on.

After walking uphill a bit, she changes her mind and walks back down until she reaches the ocean. The beach is packed with people. Fishermen with great nets and baskets of sand dabs and clams and other ocean fish are working everywhere. There are many naked children splashing in the waves that lap the shore, the sweetest, most playful children she has ever seen. They hug each other, dance and laugh, with huge, blissful grins plastered on their faces. One child runs beaming to his mother, to be snatched up in her arms and given a big, warm hug.

"Hello, my beautiful baby boy," the mother coos at him and the child wriggles with pleasure.

The mother is topless, wearing only a skirt to cover the waist. It is considered bad taste to cover the breasts, so all of the mothers go topless most of the year. Only on cold days and nights do they hide the sacred bosom. The little child plays with his mother's breast and sucks at it joyously. Finding no milk, he laughs and runs back to play with the other children in the water.

The children aren't the only ones having a ball. The mothers are unabashedly doting as they watch their children, and make comments to each other about the eyes of this one or the smile of that one. "Look how they play together. Isn't that cute! Oh, your child has the most wonderful mouth for smiling!" And so forth. They gather close together, in a sea of bobbing breasts and glowing eyes of blissful motherhood. They assure each other of their wonderful children and how great it is to be a mother.

A small child suddenly screams as she ventures too deep to swim. She begins to paddle desperately, trying to keep her head above water. "Kibbie!" a mother screams, running toward her. The older children swim after Kibbie and pull her out of the deep water, still bawling. Soon Kibbie is surrounded by doting mothers and a few young girls, who make a circle around her. As one giant organism, they all pour their love into this child who got scared. It is so overdone, that it is almost sickeningly sweet, like a cake with too much honey. Everyone competes to be the most sympathetic, the most loving. Soon Kibbie is laughing again with baby eyes of glee.

Somehow, all of these beautiful moments only serve to make Esther insanely jealous. Watching these happy children receive in excess the love she never did, that is too much for her to bear. Her mood dives into sour memories of frightened, lonely children living with stern priests and sad neophyte parents with broken spirits. She remembers the first time she made a mistake and was whipped for it. This memory, long forgotten, surfaces in a dark cloud and blocks out the sun.

And the topless women, so free and happy as they sun their bosoms to a dark brown and watch their children play, while their men fish for their supper. How can Esther look at them without feeling bitter? She was forbidden to ever show a breast, under pain of a severe whipping. As these black thoughts surface, Esther feels more like an intruder than ever. She feels like a dark monster in a land of beautiful people. Overwhelmed by self-pity, she has to leave this happy scene and wander away down the beach toward solitude. But the laugher and shouts follow her, as if to mock her dark thoughts. Even as the sounds slowly fade away, their echo grows louder in her head. Wishing the dark thoughts away, she tries to concentrate on the sunshine and the crashing waves. Slowly, the sun and summer air dissipate the unpleasant feelings, leaving only a bitter aftertaste. She falls into a pleasant snooze on the hot sand.

Esther wakes with a start. The sun is not where it should be. It was above her and shining bright, and now it has dropped into the ocean and the sky is dark blue-purple and full of clouds. The beach is empty. She has overslept! And most assuredly, she has missed dinner preparation, the biggest meal of the day. Fears start to boil in her head. She'll be fired and kicked out of her room. Leaping to her feet, she runs down the beach toward the shelter.

By the time she reaches it, she is a nervous wreck. She bursts in to find dinner being picked at by satisfied guests with full stomachs and Massie sitting exhausted and grumpy outside in the kitchen. A dark cloud seems to hover over Massie, and when she sees Esther, she grimaces and releases her rage upon her immediately.

"Not a good start to your employment with me! I won't stand for missed meals! The customers won't stand for it! They pay well, and expect three meals. I had to cut corners on dinner today. Where were you?"

"I fell asleep," she says, her eyes downcast. "I am really sorry. I didn't sleep well last night and -"

Massie's eyes burn as Esther trails off, knowing excuses are not going to be welcome.

"Just take over and clean up. I don't even know what to do with you!"

Massie storms away, too upset to say anything else. Esther does the dishes and cleans everything as carefully and completely as she can, determined to make everything spotless. She feels as low as the ants crawling up the table to get at the leftovers.

Massie returns later with a sack of corn flour and a bucket of cream. Esther sets the cream in a large bucket of cold water to keep it fresh and puts the corn flour away. She continues to wipe obsessively at any piece of dirt or grime she sees, hoping to show that she is a good worker. Meanwhile, she watches Massie out of the corner of her eye and waits for her to get upset again.

But Massie looks around calmly, seeming to be in a better mood.

"That is clean enough. You can stop for the night."

"Thank you. I'm sorry I was so stupid. It was a dumb mistake."

"Just don't do it again."

Still obsessing over it, Esther goes to her room and tries to sleep. But she is too wound up, and the new couple two huts away begin to make love and they make as much noise as possible. And then Lars and Zilt return, very high on something. She cannot sleep again until many hours of tossing and turning are behind her and it is finally quiet. And tomorrow, she has promised to get up early. Esther cannot believe her bad luck and she wonders why things can never go smoothly for her.

Jay 28'

The next day is wet and cool, with a heavy coat of fog and mist that won't burn off. The Shelter of the Moon is quickly filling up in preparation for the Summer Solstice, and there is much going on. Esther and Massie make a huge breakfast to feed the twenty guests that are now residing here. Esther can hear them making a row in the dining room, munching on acorn bread and butter and sipping tea.

A solstice occurs on the first day of an agressive (cardinal) month, which is also the first day of summer, spring, autumn and winter.

"I'm afraid you will need to vacate your room," Massie says. "We have more guests than expected and more coming every day. We'll find you someplace to stay."

This is just fine with Esther, as it will only get noisier and noisier as more people come. Nothing could be worse than another night of no sleep. She has not slept well in three nights and she has kept a very grueling schedule. A fourth night would finish her off.

The summer solstice celebration is a huge draw and people make the journey for this party from all over the Twelve Tribes. The shelter is now filled to capacity and Esther works all day long trying to feed everybody. Kobe plays his heart out tonight, trying to entertain the rowdy crowd, but it is too much for him. There is a bottle of some strong liquor at the table and everyone is drinking and getting wild.

A group of drunk men start to clap and sing along with him in loud, grating voices. Those men eventually take over the room, when they all stand up and begin to sing "Great Forest", a popular tune that was written in ages past when the tribes were young. Everyone in the room joins on the chorus. Esther walks into the room to join the fun and it is so loud that she can barely hear her own voice as she sings along.

One man jumps up on the table, takes off all his clothes, and begins to dance. Then he must get all the other drunk men to do the same. Soon there are six naked men crowded on the table, stomping their feet and having a ball. They begin a medley of all of their favorite songs. As they sing, they form a circle, arm in arm, with their heads together and their rears facing the crowd. They shake their behinds at everyone and spin around faster and faster.

Esther escapes into the late night fog and drizzle after enjoying their antics for a while. She wants some peace and quiet before the dishes must be dealt with. She walks through the drizzle, feeling the drops on her face and not minding it. She walks down to the creek, where it fills into a little pool, and finds herself all alone there.

Feeling sticky and smelly from working all day long over a hot stove, she decides to take a swim. The night is dark and there is nobody about, so she strips off all her clothes, and places them underneath a tree. The drizzle feels good on her naked skin. She dips a foot into the Aern, and shivers slightly from the cold.

With a scream, she jumps into the river. Her body jerks in spasms with the cold, before it calms down and accepts the new temperature. It's the perfect temperature for waking up, but not for freezing. When she is used to it, she floats with her arms and legs outstretched in the dark, eddying current and stares up at the sky.

From high upon the hill, Kobe watches her silently. He ignores the light rain that soaks his clothes. If the rain doesn't bother Esther, then it sure won't bother him. He won't allow it. He wants to be like her. He stares at her breasts as she floats in the water. She has good breasts. They are not voluptuous, like many Bear women, but they have a nice shape. Kobe likes breasts, and he imagines suckling upon them like a baby. Then he feels the rain pick up, and notices that her clothes are in a bad spot. He feels them and sure enough they are becoming wet. Silly girl! He picks them up and wedges them into the tree.

Esther begins to shiver in the cold water. She decides to get out and go get warm in her hut and get under her blankets. But as she gets back to the tree, she finds her clothes are missing. Frantically she looks everywhere, before she finds them wedged into a hole in the trunk. How did they get there? She looks around fearfully and spies movement up the hill. Someone is there, and by the way he creeps, it is obvious that he is watching her. What does he want? She runs behind some bushes, so that she will not stand naked before him. What does he want? Sex? A peek at a naked woman? Then it occurs to her that everyone runs around here naked. Why would somebody go to all that trouble just to see a woman naked?

Kobe sees that she is scared and that he has awakened something dark inside her. Bears are very intuitive when it comes to feelings and Esther is an easy read. An open book of raw emotions and sizzling nerve endings, packed into a girl. He longs to run to her and comfort her, but he is scared to go near her. He will scare her and himself as well. He turns around and beats a hasty retreat, running through the rain towards home.

Esther puts her dress on over her wet body and feels the clinging, wet fabric stick tightly to her skin. No matter. She runs to her room as quickly as she can, and soon she is underneath the covers and feeling secure, warm, and safe. Massie has lit a candle in her room already and she watches the shadows dance across her wall till Massie comes to get her. She wishes she could just sleep outside on the beach, but it is much too wet.

Finally, Massie appears with the guests that will occupy Esther's hut. Esther throws her things together in a daze. The guests apologize guiltily as they watch her throw her burden basket on her back and walk out into the rain. Esther smiles and shrugs, and then follows Massie down the hill.

"You'll be staying in my house," Massie says. "Is that good with you?"

"I could just sleep in the main lodge," Esther says, preferring to be alone. "Then I'll be sure to get an early start on breakfast."

"It's occupied," Massie says, pointing to the light that burns inside it. "We're really packed. So it's my house, or outside."

Esther doesn't respond, so Massie leads her to her own house, which is dark but for bright coals burning in a fire pit. Esther lays out her blankets next to the fire and drops instantly into a perfect sleep in the quiet, cozy house. She sleeps so soundly that she doesn't notice Kobe, who sits down next to her and watches her half the night, with eyes that shine like a cat in the reflected glow of firelight.

She wakes in the middle of the night with a start. The dishes! She forgot to wash them. Massie will be furious if she walks into the kitchen in the morning and everything is a mess. With great effort and much bad humor, she rises and dresses. Then she walks down to the kitchen. At one point, she trips and stumbles over a rock. Her foot cries with pain and she hops up and down and curses the rock, the dishes and her job.

Finally, she makes it to the kitchen and it is worse than she feared. A complete pig sty awaits her. By the light of a single candle she works, scrubbing dishes, sweeping and setting everything to rights. The near darkness is soothing and the silence is comforting - with only the splash of water to disturb it. She scrubs diligently, taking her time, and watches a single candle cast dancing shadows. It brings back her peace of mind and she finds that she actually enjoys the experience of cleaning so late at night. Maybe she should do this every night? She returns to Massie's house and manages to get a few hours of sleep before morning.

Bear 0'

Raccoon moon

Massie awakens Esther early in the morning and then rushes out of the house. Esther takes her time rising, still tired from the night before. When she arrives at the main lodge, she gasps in disbelief at all of the people already gathered for breakfast. The inside table is full, two extra tables have been set up outside, and children sit on the floor because there is no room. Massie is busy tending to guests questions and problems, and she merely waves Esther inside impatiently. Luckily, they have some extra help today. Massie's very pregnant daughter is here and she has made all the bread already. But as soon as Esther arrives, she says she must lie down from fatigue, and Esther has to finish breakfast by herself. Organization be damned, she brings out each dish as it is completed. The shouts of some of the guests enrage her. "More food! More food!" She is so frazzled that she burns her finger. Cursing, she sits down to tend her wound. If they want to anger her, it will just take longer.

Eventually, Massie returns to help her, and breakfast is completed without further incident. Then the huge pile of dishes must be dealt with. It is nearly afternoon by the time Esther soaks and washes all the dishes and sweeps everything clean. She finally has time to tend to the plate she put aside for herself - now cold and stale from the long wait. She eats voraciously, although she has been snacking all morning. Just as Esther is mopping up grease with her bread, Massie appears at the door.

"Good work today, Esther. What say we skip lunch and just do an early dinner?"

"Really?" Esther asks, excited.

"Yes. We're both exhausted. This way we can cook up a huge dinner with no trouble."

"Great."

"I know it has been completely hectic, but the guests will be at the celebration all day tomorrow and you will have the day off to sleep late and enjoy it as you like."

Esther breathes a sigh of relief.

"Everything is very confused today. The celebration was supposed to be today, but the moon is void, so it was moved to tomorrow. But they tell nobody. The guests arrive today and there is no celebration and no food. So we must feed them all ourselves. And nobody comes to help."

Massie complains for a while about her unfeeling neighbors, and then she suddenly hands Esther seven tupas.

"We're doing very well today. Buy yourself something nice."

"Thank you." Esther says, amazed that she has made seven tupas in just a few days.

"Come by the house anytime and make yourself at home. It's yours until you get your room back," she says, as she sits down to rest her tired feet.

"I don't want to put you out," Esther says cautiously. "I can sleep outside."

"Outside? Nonsense."

"I like sleeping outside. I'll just be in the way in your small house."

"Esther, I won't have you sleeping outside during the solstice. There are a lot of strange people around, and there's no telling whom you'll run into. It can be very dangerous. And besides, it is my pleasure to have you stay with me. I insist."

Esther nods tiredly, not up to an argument, and it is settled.

That afternoon, Massie complains to the chief about her trouble with the extra guests, and in response the chief sends a woman named Hesja to help them fix dinner. Hesja is a good worker and an enormous help to the understaffed kitchen. With her happy talk, her dancing in the kitchen and her big smile, she is also a very fun person to work with. She even offers to finish the dishes by herself, seeing how tired her co-workers are, and orders them out of the kitchen to relax.

Free at last, Esther climbs the hill to watch the sunset. From the top of the steep hill, she can see the sun dipping into the ocean in the west. It is the same ocean where she spent her childhood, but somehow it seems different. She thinks about those early days and actually finds good memories lost among all the horrible ones that usually crowd her subconscious. Memories of walking along the beach barefoot, looking for shells and crabs. Swimming in the ocean in the summer and building sand castles. She notices that all her good memories are when she was alone, playing by herself. She wonders how much has changed.

The sun dips into the ocean and sprays red beams all over the sky. At that moment, Esther hears a flute borne on the evening breeze. It is accompanied by a voice, sweet and sad, singing beautiful words that are too faint to make out. Esther sinks to the earth, overwhelmed with amazement at the beauty of this place. As the sun sinks lower, lights begin to spring from dark windows and doorways in the hills around her. Esther stands up and wanders down the hill to the creek, which shines dully in the dim light of the stars.

"I feel truly happy," she tells the river.

She awaits an answer, but gets none. Then three high voices from above her begin to sing to the Great Bear spirit to welcome her to the world. Esther sings along with them and sways softly in the evening breeze. Suddenly, she laughs. "This is so unlike me." The wind swirls her dress, and she swirls with it. Whipping her head around, she lifts her arms up to the sky and spins. The wind springs up on cue and spins her faster.

Behind a tree, young Kobe stares silently, falling in love with every movement of this creature before him. This woman understands sorrow as he does. He feels dark waves of helplessness stir in him. How can this beautiful, mysterious creature ever love him? She is so different from the Bear women, a dark soul who moves through the currents below the light. He is possessed by the most intense feelings of lust and paranoia. He is very attracted to her, but he doesn't know what to do about it. He is shy, awkward, not very handsome, and he has a poor standing in his tribe. What has he to offer her, besides his heart with its intense desires? He thinks of his harp suddenly. His harp, which his mother says can soften the hardest heart. He can play songs that will make her fall in love with him. He knows which songs already. He walks back home to prepare himself for her coming.

As Esther walks back to Massie's house, she hears music coming from inside. It is Kobe, playing his harp. Kobe looks up as she enters. Gliding in on the wind, she seems so mysterious and wild, hair messed and thoughts untamed. Seeing her overwhelms him and he fumbles on the strings. He tries to play for her - to concentrate - but he cannot. He cannot think straight when she is near. He finds himself helpless and stares at her with wide eyes.

"Don't stop," she says. "You play beautifully."

Unable to look at her, he closes his eyes and tries to play a song to make her crazy with desire. He plays for a long time, and although he does not fan her flames of lust, he does put her to sleep.

Bear 1'

Swan moon

Of all the solstice holidays, summer solstice is the most popular among the Twelve Tribes. It is the one party of the year that you can expect to see most of the Twelve Tribes represented, because the weather is good for traveling. The tribes that live within a few days travel often show up en masse for the two or three day party. The Bear Tribe enjoy the crowds, because it is often the only time of the year that they get to meet new people - since they rarely leave home themselves. They love to play host too. Besides the crowded Shelter of the Moon, several families put up guests and some camp out in various spots around the hills. When Esther arrives at the plateau overlooking the ocean, she sees a massive crowd of people milling about.

There are tents and teepees set up, filled with food, crafts, games, and fun things for everybody. Esther peruses the various booths, looking for something fun she can buy. She finds some nice flutes, but the man won't take less than four tupas for the cheapest one. Despite the high price, a flute would be perfect for those long nights with nothing to do. She is just musing on whether she should buy one, when the sound of drums fills the air. Attentive crowds roar with excitement and Esther hears a shout.

"The Golai! It is time for the Golai!"

Soon the crowd takes up the call and passes it from mouth to mouth. All willing bodies crowd near the musicians, who are ready to begin. It starts with a spiraling, haunting drumbeat from a great bass foot drum and thirty supporting drums. Then twenty flutes begin to play in unison, followed by the chanting of hundreds of people. This is the Song of the Golai, written by the great Bear priestess Laeha, one hundred years ago. The song is so sacred, that it is forbidden to sing it publicly any other time than during the annual Golai of Summer. It is a song that is never ending and can last hours.

Most everyone dances, except for a few elderly people who can no longer dance. There are certain basic steps to a Golai, but they are simple and open to interpretation, so every tribe can bring its own sensibilities to the dance. Esther joins in, swept up by the excitement. She soon learns the simple steps and moves, which are circular in nature.

As the music intensifies and bodies start to sweat, clothing is shed. It is then that Esther learns that in a Golai, everyone starts fully clothed, and by the end of the song they are completely naked. It symbolizes the shedding of the clothing in the summer months and the shedding of inhibitions too. It pulls everyone out of their shells, where they have been hiding, and frees their bodies for the hot summer months when they can finally go naked or scantily clad all day and night. It is taboo to think of sex during the Golai, for all are as children while it is being sung. The mood is so safe and comforting, that even Esther, who was taught that nudeness is sinful, throws her clothes off in a surge of wild abandon. There is a moment when she is uncomfortable, and her hands unconsciously try to cover her private areas. But that seems incredibly stupid considering what is going on around her. So she forgets about modesty, and spins and twirls with everybody else, feeling like she has been freed of some horrible curse that has haunted her for her entire life. She smells the smell of hundreds of naked bodies around her and sees their skin making a patchwork quilt of brown textures. Her smile is so big, she is afraid she is going to split her face. She has never pushed a smile this far up her face before.

When one gets too hot, they run to the ocean and dive in. There are soon just as many people in the ocean, playing in the waves, as there are dancing. The Golai lasts for hours, but not everybody can keep up with it. Some wear out and lie down and some get something to eat. But a core group of Golai enthusiasts continue to do the dance with no thought of stopping. They will not stop until the last note is played.

Tired at last, Esther goes to get some food. She longs to dance until the music stops, but she has had a busy week and she is tired. She munches on potato pie, fish and acorn mush, and then lies in the sun, still mesmerized by the Song of the Golai.

The music stops near sunset and then it is time for the Sunset Procession. The Sunset Procession is a parade to the top of Brown Bear hill to see the setting sun. All children are given instruments and noisemakers of every type and variety, for them to make noise to their heart's content. No adult may make noise till the sun dips below the horizon. They must stand there and learn from the children.

After the sun sets, the adults may shout, scream, and act silly - as long as they act as crazy as the children and forget all of their adult seriousness. Then, the hills are filled with noise. Everyone beats drums and claps, sings snatches of song, and capers around until it is quite dark.

Dinner is served on Brown Bear hill, overlooking the ocean that is lit by a half moon. A feast has been prepared in advance and every tribe has added their own food. There are different meats from twenty animals or more, several types of fish and clams, bread, cheese, harti, seaweed, and finally moon pies and lots of wine. Esther tries to maintain control, but with all of this good food, she stuffs herself past the point of sanity.

The third act of the day's pageant happens after dinner. Many choose to skip it and go to bed instead - understandably tired from the long day and the heavy meal. And some come only to watch, for it is quite beautiful. Candles are lit and floated down the Aern, on little tiny boats crafted just for tonight. As they float, they drift and spin in the current, creating beautiful patterns. A procession follows the boats. No instruments are played, but many voices sing a sweet tune called "Little Boats". When the last candle washes into the ocean, all brave souls take a cold dip.

After a chilly swim, everyone climbs out of the water, and embraces on the beach. Their wet bodies form a great mass of clinging, gripping flesh and bones, slowly warming each other with shared body heat. This is also supposed to be completely non-sexual, although it is not completely - for it is difficult to fight human nature. It is a ritual of warmth, to appreciate the heat of the summer months. To welcome the heat that brings life with it.

Esther takes a dip in the water with the others, but she is frightened of the mass of clinging humanity, and refuses to join in. She throws clothes over her wet body and heads over to Massie's house to dry off and go to bed. The clinging naked ritual is interesting, but more fun to join in than to watch.

After a chilly hike, she finds the right door and knocks politely. Kobe opens the door, gives her a frightened cat stare, and then looks away nervously.

"You don't have to knock," he mumbles. "Just come in."

Kobe sits down on a cushion by the fire and Esther changes into her dry dress before joining him. There is a ratty old book open near him, with yellow pages tied together with strips of tule. He hands her a cup of tea, sits down next to his book, and fondles it nervously without picking it up. They sit in silence for a long time, each waiting for the other to speak. Finally, she takes the initiative.

"What are you reading?"

"Secret Heart, by Bhard. She's a Bear writer."

Suddenly inspired, she rummages into her basket and pulls out her Karbudde. She shows Kobe proudly.

"Ever heard of him?"

"No."

"The greatest Jay poet of all time. He is very famous. I was given this by a Poet Master."

He examines the book as if it is a piece of garbage.

"I don't like Jay poets," he says, and hands it back to her.

"Do you mind if I read for awhile?" she says, with a shrug. "I should practice so I won't forget."

"No."

He looks at his own book. Then he picks it up and begins reading himself. They read quietly and Esther falls asleep after no more that ten minutes of reading. Kobe stares at her sleeping form for a long time and then covers her up with a blanket. He is disappointed in himself for not being more aggressive when he had the chance. He got frightened and closed himself off, hiding in his book when he should have been talking to her.

He goes behind the bark screen that marks his own space, still upset, and collapses onto his bed. But he can feel her on the other side, and it drives him crazy to know that she is right there and he had a chance and he blew it and now he is sleeping alone. Kobe is sick of being alone. Tired of living with his mother. He wants Esther to be his wife and he wants her so much it hurts.

He sighs and rolls over, knowing that he is in for a long, restless night. In his desperation, he promises himself that he will do whatever it takes to win her love. He must follow his heart or else he might as well die.

Bear 2'

The next day is very busy again. Esther has to feed four very full tables for breakfast and lunch and she is busy until the late afternoon. Luckily, Hesja is there to help. She tends to the guests needs, while Massie spends most of her time in the kitchen, helping Esther. When Esther brings food out to Hesja to serve, she finds Hesja walking around in circles muttering angrily about a comment made by a Hawk man named Stur a few minutes earlier.

"I find Bear women very beautiful, although they could stand for a little more exercise," he said to her earlier.

She has been raging about this for the past few minutes, very upset. Esther tries to hand her the food, but she does not seem intent on serving just at this moment, so Esther does the serving herself. Meanwhile, Stur sees that Hesja is upset, and he tries to make things right, which only makes them worse.

"I was just joking," exclaims Stur.

"It is just like an Hawk to claim he is joking," Hesja says darkly. "When he isn't."

"Yes, I was."

"Well, then I will make some jokes about you. You are short, yet you try to act tough to appear taller. And you swagger around like you are a great hero to compensate for your lack of confidence and your cowardice. And make offensive remarks that you think are so clever."

Stur is stunned by her boldness.

"Woman, you have an ugly mouth."

"And your whole face is ugly!"

Stur stares at her, flabbergasted by the whole affair. This sort of thing is completely out of his element. Finally, he mutters "Kahn da kari" and returns to his meal. Hesja is now too angry to work, so she storms out of the dining area. Esther and Massie must finish lunch by themselves.

Hesja does not return until all of the guests are gone. She looks at Esther and Massie as they clear the tables and she can sense that they are angry with her. They ignore her utterly for abandoning them during the rush. Hesja stands solemnly before them, feeling very uncomfortable.

"Sorry," she says at last. "I will finish all the cleaning myself. You two may go relax."

This is the right thing to say, for she is instantly forgiven by a very grateful Esther and Massie. They go out into the sunshine to relax, leaving Hesja with a monumental pile of dishes to do by herself.

After a very long day, Esther relaxes by the fire with Kobe. She lies upon a bearskin rug, enjoying the feel of the thick fur against her body, with her feet propped up on a stone near the flames. Kobe watches her out of the corner of his eye, remembering his promise to himself. He cannot stop thinking about kissing her and he knows that he must try tonight or he will go crazy. But he cannot imagine kissing her here in his mother's house, with her snoring softly behind a thin bark divider. He needs to get Esther outside, where it is dark and romantic and he can be alone with her.

"Want to go for a walk?"

"I am very tired."

"We will go sit by the river then."

"I don't feel like moving."

Esther is naturally exhausted from working all day. Not that Kobe would understand that. He fishes for a few hours in the morning when he feels like it and then he plays the harp for guests. And that is all he does all day long. She has never met such a lazy man as this. She sighs, exasperated, that he cannot understand a simple thing like being tired after work.

"Come with me for just a short time," he insists.

To Esther's surprise, he grabs her hand and pulls her to her feet. He stares into her eyes and his look is very deep and penetrating. Her eyes dart to and fro, searching for escape from his gaze. Then he leads her out the door and down the hill. She goes along, suddenly curious about him, never having seen this side of him before. They walk to the Aern and sit side by side in front of the water. Kobe finally opens up and starts talking. He tells her of his people and talks of his feelings and his childhood. She tells him some stories of Branciforte in return - vague stories that don't involve her. They talk for a long time and the night grows old.

She feels his hand on hers. She is startled, but not frightened, and she sighs and grips his hand. They sit by the dark, peaceful river, hand in hand. The river sings a romantic song that is as old as the river itself. Then she feels warmth on her lips. He is kissing her. Her brain rumbles to life and she instantly defends herself. She pushes him away and turns her head from his. He turns to stare at the river, burning up inside. They sit for a few moments in uncomfortable silence and then he stands up in a deep sulk and leaves. She sits alone by the river and her thoughts drive her crazy. Finally, she stands up and returns to Massie's house, hoping by now that he is asleep behind his bark screen.

Bear 3'

Wolf moon

Things begin to calm down in the Shelter of the Moon, as many of the guests take off for other destinations or return to their homes. With the now solid team of Hesja, Esther, and Massie, the operation is smooth and efficient and the day flies by with a minimum of hassle. After dinner, Kobe invites Esther to go hear some music by the ocean. Esther is a little nervous about going out with Kobe after last night. But she wants to hear music and dance again, so she finally agrees to go. She walks with Kobe under the half moon and the stars to the sound of the drum, flute and violin that wafts on the wind. On a field overlooking the ocean, a celebration is happening. This not an organized Bear activity, but only young people out to have a good time without adults. A fire burns brightly and several young men and women dance up a storm around it.

They watch for a while, warming up to the music. Then the spirited playing gets to them and they begin to dance. Esther has to dance away from everybody, underneath a tree in the darkness. She is still too shy to dance in the firelight, as it seems like the whole world is watching her every move. She tries to get in touch with the long buried creativity within her and soon she is whirling, twirling and quite forgetting everything but the music and the movement of her body.

This is the first time ever that Kobe has been seen in public with a girl and he wants to show her off. But she dances by herself in the darkness and he feels like he is alone. He watches a boy kiss a girl underneath a torch, running his hands along the length of her body. Kobe's heart beats faster and he swears that he will have his own girl to kiss tonight. The moon is in the sign of the Wolf tonight and Kobe knows its power and intends to use it. It is said that the Wolf moon has a way of opening up the hardest heart.

Late in the evening, most everyone heads home to bed. Kobe and Esther are alone, except for a couple of lingering lovers a short distance away. Neither wants to leave the magic of the field on this summer night, with the crickets singing, an owl hooting softly and the moon's soft radiant glow on the beach and the stars. When Kobe puts his arms around her, she does not pull away. He holds her Bear fashion, which is like a bear hug from the back. They sit like that for a long time, while Esther stares at the moon, and Kobe strokes her gently.

"Most people think that the moon is romantic. Do you think that?"

"Yes."

"It's not. I know better. The moon is frightening. It can be devastating. I've been very aware of it my whole life and I'm scared of it. It makes me so sad. Constantly shifting feelings, up and down. I have too many planets in the sign of the Bear, I think. Sometimes I just can't handle all that water."

"I get sad too."

Kobe kisses Esther for the second time. As before, she draws away instinctively. But the moon stares down at her sternly.

"You need this," it seems to tell her. "This is what you need most."

A dam suddenly breaks inside her. Like a tidal wave it comes and a terrible longing fills her heart. She is aware of a desperate loneliness that needs filling and she pulls him to her and kisses him. He is so surprised, that it takes him some time to respond. It is a powerful kiss, like steam escaping. She is overwhelmed and dizzy by the rush. It seems to last forever, but it is not long before Esther has to pull away. Tears well up in her eyes, as repressed feelings all bubble to the surface at once. She cannot look at him. He tries to hold her and find out what is the matter, but she cannot answer.

He grabs at her desperately, but she squirms away. Then she moves toward him and kisses him again. Then she cries again and buries her face in her hands. It finally occurs to Kobe that everything is not well with this girl. She has problems. Normally, Bear people can tell such things immediately, but not when they are in love, for they become blind. This is not going quite the way he hoped it would and the only thing to do now is walk Esther home. They walk in silence. When they arrive at his house, her eyes are tired slits as she lies on the bearskin rug by the fire.

"May I sleep next to you?" he asks.

"No. Please...no."

So Kobe goes behind his screen alone, leaving Esther to stare morosely at the fire. She is exhausted, but she cannot sleep. She hears Kobe tossing and turning behind the screen and knows that he cannot sleep either. It has been a heavy night and Esther is now in full agreement with Kobe. The moon is a very intimidating force. Look what it did to her tonight.

Bear 6'

Owl moon

The world is full of promise this morning. Esther has her old hut back, some good rest, and she feels herself again. Her morning chores are done and she walks outside into the bright sunshine and thinks about what to do for the remainder of the morning. She decides to take a walk up the hill, looking for the huckleberries that are supposed to be ripe. She walks slowly, letting the sunshine wash over her like a shower of sun drops. Before long, she finds the huckleberry trees and eagerly helps herself. They are a little sour, but very refreshing.

As she begins to gorge, she hears a loud noise behind her. She turns around, thinking that she is caught raiding someone's private tree. But there is no farmer there. There is a big black bear instead, who has come for lunch. She backs away, thoroughly frightened. The bear rears up on its hind legs and Esther sucks in her breath and freezes. She watches the huge creature tower over her and feels as if she might faint. She wants very badly to run, but remembers never to run from a bear, or it might chase you. So she just stands there, holding her breath and shaking. The bear is such a commanding presence, that she doesn't move until it tells her to. Finally, the bear gets back down on all fours and ignores her. It is more interested in the berries than in her.

When bears stand up on their hind legs, it is said that they are getting a closer look. They are somewhat nearsighted.

Gaining confidence, Esther backs away slowly. When she has reached a safe distance, she watches it for a long time, marveling at its size and power. She remembers hearing at dinner one day that bears live off of mainly fruit in the summer and fall. They hibernate all winter by using the fat they stored from fruit eating. She marvels that a creature can grow so big eating fruit and still have enough fat left over to survive an entire winter. She wonders how fruit can make one fat. But then she remembers that bears eat flesh too and that is why she was so afraid a few moments ago.

The bear eats ravenously and Esther watches it curiously, wondering if she will get another chance at the berries. The bear stares at her every so often, wondering why she is still there. Finally it growls temperamentally. Esther leaves it alone to its gluttony and considers herself banned from the berries today.

She walks down to the ocean instead, thinking that she will lie on the beach. On the way, she passes a man who gives her a grumpy nod, mumbles "greetings", and continues on, hunched over as if he is admiring the insects on the ground. She passes many other people, but he is the friendliest of the lot. These people are very private, Esther realizes. Then she laughs, thinking that they are like the bear that didn't want her around.

Just before she begins cooking lunch, she sees six figures walking towards the shelter from the direction of the path. Due to their strange clothes, tattoos, hair and the baskets they carry they on their back, she realizes quickly that they are new guests. She walks forward to meet them, thinking she will find out their needs so she can tell Massie.

"Hello."

"Greetings from the Elk tribe," says a man. "We are looking for Massie."

"She's gone till lunch. But I work for her. Shall I go look for her?"

"Perhaps you may show us to our lodging. We are tired from our long journey and we require a dip in the river and clean clothes."

Esther considers what to do. She has not had to contend with guests yet.

"We could go look for empty huts?" she finally says, more as a question than a statement.

"Yes, good."

Esther finds three empty huts and then hurries to Massie's house to tell her the news, so she may get more lunch and dinner supplies.

"The Elk tribe," Massie exclaims with great surprise. "I didn't think they would show. Preparations must be made. Can you run up to the chief's house and tell her that the Elk tribe have come for Polar Day?"

"Is it Polar Day already?" asks Esther.

"Yes, the full moon comes," Massie says, distracted, as she rushes down to the shelter to greet the new guests. Esther follows her for a short time, until Massie stops and stares at her.

"Well?" she asks impatiently.

"Oh, the chief...where is his house?"

"*Her* house. Follow that road right there. When you see three cocoon shaped huts filled with acorns, turn right and you will find a large house. That is hers."

Esther nods, and trots off to the chief's house.

After a leisurely walk in the afternoon heat, she comes upon a large house, surrounded by a granary, sweat lodge, and a great burl statue of a bear with its paws raised threateningly in the air. There is an aura of wealth about the house, and she approaches nervously, wondering how to address a chief at her home. She notices a flute tied to a little rope and remembers watching someone blow a flute once to summon somebody inside of their house. She tootles the flute and then politely waits for someone to answer.

She waits the obligatory five minutes, but nobody shows. Just to be sure, she blows the flute a little louder. Just as she is leaving, she hears sniffling coming from behind a tree. Then comes a voice, choked and muffled, as if coming through a stuffed nose and great tears.

"What can I do for you?"

She follows the voice curiously and finds the chief herself, sitting naked underneath a tree, weeping great tears. Esther stands still as stone, not wanting to disturb the woman. She is struck by the beauty of Chief Shantie, even in middle age. Her beauty was legendary in her youth, and she had many admirers from not only the Bear tribe but all the Twelve Tribes. The chief of the Hawk tribe even bid for her hand in marriage once. In the flush of her youth, she would bathe naked in the river, and all the boys would come to admire her great beauty. She was reckoned to have the most perfect "full moons" - as breasts are often called in the Bear tribe - in the whole land. A song was even written about them.

Queen Shantie, blessed by the Goddess of Zunes
Wih two great, majestic, glorious full moons
As she bathes in the rippling stream
Her full moons, are they only a dream?
The deep rich color of the life giving Earth
They bring some to tears, some to song, some to mirth.

Shantie is now in her late thirties and she has an extra helping of fat from too much good food and silver streaks in her hair. But she is still a sight to behold even in the passing of her youth. Shantie looks up from her crying and stares at Esther without saying anything. She gives Esther a sad, sweet look from a tear stained face. In awe, Esther struggles to find her voice.

"I just came with a message," she stammers. "The Elk tribe has arrived. Massie sent me to see you with this message...."

She feels stupid for being so callous and business-like in the face of such a show of emotion, and she trails off.

"Why are you crying?" Esther asks awkwardly, after Shantie doesn't respond. "Is there anything I can do for you?"

"I am crying because I have five planets in the Bear sign. Is that not enough reason for endless tears?"

She has to stop speaking as her chest heaves and spasms with more tears.

"As for your second question, you may give me a hug."

Esther walks toward Shantie, as if in a dream, and Shantie rises and embraces her. As Esther's body is engulfed by Shantie, she feels a powerful rush of warmth. The embrace seems to find every empty space inside of her and fills all those spaces with heat. When Shantie releases her, Esther stands as if dizzy, unable to comprehend what just happened to her. Nobody has ever hugged her like that before. She marvels at the extraordinary woman before her.

"What is your name, sweet one?"

"Esther."

"I am Shantie. Go back to Massie, and tell her I will send for the Elk tribe at dinner time. They will dine with me in my home."

Esther nods and walks away as one who has seen a ghost. Eventually, she sits down underneath a tree and just marvels at all the wonderful and strange things that have been happening to her in the past few days. She does not stand up again until the afternoon begins to fade away and she has to get back home to deliver her message.

Bear 8′

Elk moon

Polar day begins with a big feast, followed by music and dance for those who wish it. But it is lacking in feeling and grandeur, compared with the other feasts and celebrations that Esther has attended here. It is poorly attended and there is nothing special about it. Esther begins to feel a bit sorry for the men and women of the Elk tribe, whom she has gotten to know a little bit. They seem a little nervous and uncomfortable, as if they want something that they are not receiving. Esther suspects that they know it is a poor party and she makes it a point to ask Massie.

"What do they expect?" Massie says in a frustrated voice. "If the whole tribe were here, then that would be something to celebrate. Or if they came only to see us, then we might be more excited. But a small group of them come to do business with all of the nearby tribes, and then they stop in and act like the returning heroes."

"Have you ever mentioned that to them?"

"No. It would not be polite. I am their host."

"Isn't this Polar Day? I thought the full moon was very special."

"Sometimes it is. But we are more sensitive to the moon than others and today is an Elk moon. It is a rigid, cold moon, and we do not love it. We put on a bit of a show for them, really, because it is Polar Day. But we find it rather sad and depressing, and we can do nothing to make it a great day. We would prefer they come for the winter full moon, the Bear moon that falls around the time of winter solstice. That would be a great celebration. But it is far to travel in the winter time and we always celebrate it alone."

"Why don't you visit them for Polar Day?"

"It is too far and cold for such a journey. But if you wish to make them happy, then you may go up there for the winter moon. Yes?"

By her tone of voice, it is obvious that she is annoyed by all the questions, so Esther goes off to the ocean to take a swim. As she walks, she tries to figure out why this moon is so bad, but she cannot feel any difference. Finally, she decides that the only thing rigid and cold around here is Massie.

After dinner, Kobe takes Esther for a long walk under the full moon. He kisses her again, and although she is resistant at first, she eventually gives in. She doesn't know how he does it, but he has this extremely passive way of getting what he wants. He isn't pushy, but he will go off in a mood if refused. And she wants him to stay, so she kisses him. After the kiss, she has a revelation. She is not really very attracted to Kobe. He is simply someone to shower her with attention, to ward off her loneliness. She feels guilty suddenly, for he is much smitten with her and she does not share his sentiments. She wonders if she should warn him, so he will not feel bad later. But she doesn't know how to break it to him, so she tells her brain to quit bothering her and she'll deal with him later.

They join a circle of musicians and dancers who are having a wild time of it. She looks up at the moon and wonders at Massie's strange comments again. Then she shrugs it off and dances with Kobe a little bit. Later, they both take a dip in the river, and then Esther announces that she is tired and going to bed.

"May we share a bed tonight?" he asks desperately, knowing the answer already.

"No, I want to sleep alone," she snaps, irritated by this constant query.

They both go off to separate beds. He wonders where this is all leading. She knows where and doesn't want to think about it.

Bear 13'

Cougar moon

Tonight, there is a large music jam on the beach, a wild, carefree, and spontaneous event with at least twenty musicians playing at once. There are none of the usual rules of how to dance, sing, or dress. All dance as they want to - naked, clothed, silly, or sacred. Some sing zunes and some sing nonsense. Shantie has even donated a cask of wine for the event and everyone begins to get very high. Esther sings loudly with the music and dances with carefree and wild abandon. It is a special night for her and she feels as if she is burning off another layer of the thick shell that keeps her from the world.

Long into the warm summer night, the party continues. The moon rises and sets and the ocean crashes to the beat. Even some birds sing along with the music, awakened from their slumber by the incredible energy of the night. The whole world seems to be one gigantic party and everyone is invited. The music often makes no sense, but nobody complains. And so it goes into the wee hours of the morning, until only a few remain, the faithful few who do not want to go to sleep and give up the magic to the daylight.

Long before that, Esther gets Kobe to walk her back to her room. She is anxious to get some sleep because she will have to get up for breakfast. They walk back, hand in hand and Esther sways in drunken bliss. Then they arrive at her hut and Kobe kisses her. It seems the perfect end to a perfect night.

Although he had planned to wait until the new moon to ask for her hand in marriage, he has been softened by the romantic night and he cannot wait. Watching her dance tonight, he saw that she was feeling the same and he senses that he should ask tonight. As she has no family that he knows of, he will not have to go through the usual process of going to her mother first and presenting himself. That will make things much easier.

"Esther," he says nervously. "I must ask you something. Do you like it here?"

"I love it," she says truthfully. "I never want to leave."

"Well, we love having you here." He stops a moment. Now comes the hard part. "I love having you here. I love you." He takes a deep breath. "I want you to live here forever…as my wife."

Esther finds her heart turning into butter. It isn't the "wife" part that gets to her, but the idea of living here forever. She wants to make a home here, in this land of music and beauty. The music and ecstatic dancing have softened her heart and blurred her judgment. The wine has taken her inhibitions. She hugs him to her, desperately wanting to crowd out any unpleasant realities that might get in the way of this perfect moment. He feels stiff against her, because he isn't paying attention to the hug. He is waiting for an answer.

She vaguely remembers something she felt several days ago. She saw this coming. And yet she cannot remember why she dreaded this moment. Tonight she feels as if she could spend the rest of her life in Bear village, with him as her loving husband. He will worship her as a goddess and she will be taken care of for the rest of her life. She will finally have a home. Who cares if she does not love him? She did not love Eunio, but it was far better to be married to him, than it was to be single.

"Yes, I will live here with you," she says quietly.

"Does this mean you will marry me?"

"Yes."

Kobe's heart soars and he swims in pools of bliss. This is the happiest day of his life. She lets him come into her room and they get into her bed together. He kisses her, and they lie entwined for many minutes. After a short time, she rolls over and falls asleep. This time he falls asleep along with her.

Bear 14'

Esther wakes up late the next morning, wondering why Massie didn't wake her for the breakfast meal. Kobe is gone and last night is a blur. Although she knows what happened in the pit of her stomach, she purposely pushes it aside. There is plenty of time to deal with it later. All she wants now is tea and something to eat, to soothe an upset stomach and a slight hangover.

Upon entering the dining room, she realizes why she wasn't awakened. Massie has prepared a congratulatory feast, having learned of the upcoming wedding. On the table sits corn cakes topped with fresh berries and cream, which are being devoured by the guests. When Esther enters the dining room, all the guests cheer. Hearing the noise, Massie and Kobe rush into the room. Massie hugs her tightly and then fusses over her. She sits Esther down in a chair and brings her a large plate that she has kept aside for her. Then she pushes Kobe down next to her, just so she can look at the two of them together. Everyone congratulates the happy couple, as Massie beams in the background and Kobe grins a huge smile from ear to ear.

"Welcome to the family," Massie says over and over.

Esther's heart sinks, as last night comes flooding back to her in a rush. She is now engaged to Kobe. In that sneaky way of his, he got her to agree to marry him.

"Please don't make a fuss," Esther stammers, her face turning red. "This isn't necessary."

"Not necessary? It isn't every day that my only son gets engaged. And to a lovelier young woman, I couldn't imagine."

"What's wrong," asks Kobe. "You look ill."

Grabbing her hand, he leans over and kisses her in public for the first time. Esther tries to smile and pretends to be happy, although she really wants to run screaming out of there. But she cannot do that with all these people watching. So she turns to her plate, her face red hot, and tries to ignore everyone and just eat in silence.

When Esther finally escapes, she runs to the hills to think. The big question on her mind looms like a frightening monster. Does she really want to marry Kobe?

"No," she says to herself firmly.

But does she want to live in Bear village, with all of the beautiful music and dancing? Does she want her own house and a husband who adores her? Does she want to stand on the beach naked with the other mothers of the tribe and watch her children run and play, and then receive a huge hug from her beautiful little child, kiss him or her gently on the forehead and profess her love, before releasing the dear child to play joyfully in the waves with the other children?

"Yes, I want that very much."

So if marrying Kobe will allow her to have all that, is it worth it? Is this her chance to have a good life for once? This time no answer comes and she feels as confused as she has ever felt in her entire life.

Meanwhile, Massie tells everyone about Kobe's engagement. A marriage is a big deal in Bear village and she wants to brag about it to everybody. As Esther walks back to the dining room for lunch preparation, she finds herself suddenly receiving a lot of attention. Before this, she could walk all the way across the village and nobody would look at her. Now, everybody looks her way. Some smile and shout congratulations, and one woman even grabs her hand and kisses her on the cheek. Esther has now become one of the family. It is a great feeling and the scales tip in favor of marriage.

"If only I loved him," Esther muses glumly, "this would be perfect. If only I was more attracted to him. But the more I get to know him, the less I like him."

In the evening, Kobe comes to Esther's room with two glasses of blackberry wine.

"Oh, it's you," she says quietly, opening the door for him.

"Hello, my lovely bride. Care to go for a walk?"

"I really need to be by myself for awhile. I'm new to all of this."

She speaks diplomatically, though she really wants to shout at him to go away.

"You like a lot of time to yourself. That's fine with me," he says, trying to be sensitive to her needs. "I understand your need for solitude."

This doesn't bode well, she thinks, as he leaves her alone with her doubts. She already can't stand him. She thinks of Eunio suddenly, and her heart grows hot with anger. Another Eunio - another husband of convenience whom she will soon grow to hate. She cannot bear to think of it.

Bear 15′

Hawk moon

Esther finally finds the courage to face up to the truth. She cannot marry Kobe simply to live here and be taken care of. He is quickly becoming repulsive to her and she must break it off before she goes mad. But how can she? Massie has already asked Chief Shantie to marry them on the coming new moon and she and Kobe have told the whole village the good news. It turns out that Kobe is something of a village idiot, and everyone is proud of him because nobody ever thought he would be married. So Esther is in a hell of a mess. She is sure that Massie will be so angry when she breaks her son's heart, that she'll fire her instantly.

"I'm so stupid!" she says over and over to herself.

After spending the night wallowing in heavy guilt, walking aimlessly and passing Massie's door several times without finding the courage to enter, she comes up with a very strange plan. One thing she knows about men is that after sex they seem to lose interest in the woman. At least she thinks she knows this to be the truth. After all, Miguel would always lose interest in her after he finished. He would just get up and walk away and not bother her for a while. Or he would fall asleep. And it was the same with Fermin. Even Eunio let her alone after sex. So she decides to have sex with Kobe and then break the news to him afterwards. Once he finishes, she can break up with him and he won't get hurt, because he won't care any more. He will have gotten what he wants - what all men want - and she can continue to live here and work and be a part of the village.

Bear 16′

Wanting to get it over with quickly, Esther shows up at Kobe's door and invites him to spend the night in her room. This is an unusually bold move for her, but he is so happy, that he doesn't bother to wonder what this about face in attitude could mean. He follows her like a puppy dog to her hut, a big smile on his face. As soon as they are in her hut, she starts to kiss him and takes off her clothes. She behaves as she did with Eunio, moving it along as quickly as possible to get it over with. Except this is not Eunio and Kobe wants to take a long time with everything. So she sighs and slows down to his pace.

Soon he is on top of her, his chubby body pressing her into the bed. After suckling on her breasts for a while, like a baby, he penetrates her. She closes her eyes, as she did a thousand times before, and waits for it all to be over. She wonders briefly if she should try to enjoy the experience, but decides that as long as Kobe enjoys it then that is all that matters. She never feels much during sex anyway, so the question is ultimately unimportant.

Within a few minutes he is finished, and he rolls over and sighs. She opens her eyes and sighs with relief. That wasn't so bad and she hardly felt a thing. Now she can break up with him with a clear conscience. She smiles and holds Kobe's hand, ready to break the bad news to him. He looks at her with slightly embarrassed eyes and smiles.

"I was a little nervous," he explains. "I know it wasn't so great, but that was only my second time. At least, I remembered to pull out, so you won't get pregnant -"

"Kobe," Esther says carefully.

"Yes, my little moon pie," he grins.

She smiles at the expression. "I can't marry you."

Just as she expected, he is detached enough not to flip out completely.

"I don't understand. Didn't we just…is it because I wasn't good?"

"No, no. Tonight was only a gift for you," she explains. "Because you are so nice and I'm so sorry to do this to you. But I can't marry you. I can't marry anyone. I have too many problems. I have a past."

This is the most she has ever opened up to anyone in her life and it is a relief to say these things to somebody. Her secrets seem a little less horrible when she speaks them out loud to somebody else.

"I was too hasty when you asked me," she continues. "And I did not tell you the truth about my life. I was married once. I do not love him, but I think it would be wrong to marry someone else so soon."

She holds her breath, hoping that he doesn't discover the real reason she will not marry him. But he seems not to catch the undercurrents. He is dense now. She put him in the right frame of mind. Now that he got what he wanted, he feels grateful and much more distant, so he can't lay his guilt trip over her. He tries to get her to say more, but she simply repeats the same things over and over.

"I don't care about your past," he tells her. "I love you. I want to marry you no matter what."

"I can't," is all she says.

Finally he just gets up, gets dressed, and leaves her alone. She sighs and lies back down, grateful that it is over and she can move on. But one thing runs through her mind. She cannot understand why people like sex. It is a tool for hurting people, manipulating people, or getting what you want from them. But what else? There is a base pleasure to it, she supposes, not that she has ever fully enjoyed that part of it really...but what's the point in putting up with all the pain and nonsense to get to it? She decides to remain celibate for the rest of her life, like a nun. This thought makes her feel a whole lot better. Sex has always been nothing but a burden to her and now she is free from ever worrying about it again.

She laughs bitterly, thinking that the fathers would be very proud of her. Ironically, now that she has left the mission, she is finally behaving in a way they would approve of.

Bear 17'

Beaver moon

Kobe visits Esther again. He has been drinking the shelter's blackberry wine and he stumbles a bit as he approaches her hut. He looks sad and confused, like a dog whose owner has just thrown it out into the cold and refuses to let it come inside ever again. He almost whimpers as he begs to come in. She reluctantly allows him inside for a few minutes.

He wastes no time in trying to convince her that he will love her no matter what her past is and who she is. He kisses her desperately, his breath smelling of some foul liquor and the sour taste one has after a day of drinking heavily and eating little. He looks so pitiful, that Esther wonders if she should give him one more night with her body. He isn't much trouble. But then she reasons that he will want a third and a fourth, and where will it end? She has given him already more than she thought she ever would. She must put a stop to it.

"I know I'm undeserving," he whines. "I am so unbearably sad sometimes, I want to kill myself. If you deny me, I may drown myself. That is how much I love you."

Esther is shocked. He really seems to mean it. She thinks of herself back in the old days. Overloaded by sadness to the point of madness. He brings back painful memories of that time, and his face, words, and whining throw Esther into a sudden rage. She doesn't want to see this. She's afraid it will contaminate her and she'll turn back into that pathetic creature.

"Get out of here! Go kill yourself then! What does it matter to me?" she screams. "Get out! Get out!"

She shoves him toward the door violently, her face a tangle of rage, disgust, and many other conflicting feelings. His is a pefect mask of surprise. He stumbles out the door, his thoughts of suicide suddenly banished by her tantrum. Soon he is facing a closed door and he turns around and walks down the hill.

"Now I've really done it," he says to himself. "I've pushed her too far. I'm such a whiny crybaby. I'm a worthless mess of feelings and emotions."

He walks down to the ocean and stares at it for a long time. Contemplates walking into it and never coming out.

I can't do that to Mom. She would absolutely die. And sister, with her new baby and all. To lose a brother now would be terrible.

Suicide begins to seem a bad idea. He ponders some more and his thoughts turn to Esther. He begins to find flaw with her. She's cruel, confusing, and withdrawn. She has no family, probably because she's a bastard child. She never talks about herself, and she used to be married and she didn't even tell him. And she is not even of the Twelve Tribes. The more flaws he finds, the more he cannot believe he was going to kill himself over her. He gets on his knees and prays to the Great Bear spirit for the power to forget all about her.

After a long while he rises and walks back home with new determination. He will not leave this earth. Esther will leave Bear village. He will force her to. Thoughts of revenge brewing in his guilty soul, he walks home to talk to his mother, who still thinks that Esther and Kobe are to be wed on the new moon. He will tell her the truth, emphasizing certain parts, and ask her to get rid of Esther as quickly as possible.

Bear 21'

Bear moon

Nothing has been the same since that day she threw Kobe out. Massie has been distant and non-communicative, except to order her around in a stern voice. "Esther, do the dishes. Esther, your bread is lifeless today. Throw that one out and make another loaf, Esther." Kobe has disappeared, and he won't come to the shelter to play the harp or get food or anything. And the rest of the tribe has stopped waving and smiling at her, and she is ignored again. The village she has grown to love has turned on her.

Today, Esther wakes to the sound of flutes and singing. As she rises and stretches her limbs, a wave of optimism comes over her that chases away the bad mood she has been in for many days. The new moon is here and there is rejoicing in the village. She has heard many say that the new moon washes everything clean. As she walks outside into the morning light, she hopes that is true.

By the time Esther makes her way to the kitchen, she finds four new arrivals come for the new moon celebration. Massie is nowhere in sight, so Esther gets them comfortably situated in their rooms and begins their breakfast. When Massie appears, she is pleased at Esther's initiative, and smiles at her for the first time in days. Esther hums to herself as she beats the dough for today's bread.

After lunch, Esther goes to Grizzly field, which is being readied for the big day. She walks around, watching people running to and fro with flowers and decorations. As she passes three small teepees, set upon a spot overlooking the ocean, she hears a sharp scream come from inside and then a woman's voice yelling for help. Esther is the only one nearby, so she runs toward it and raises the flap. As her eyes adjust to the gloom, she sees a very pregnant woman lying naked on the ground near a bed of bear fur, surrounded by various things to make her comfortable and medicines to keep her well. The woman looks sick, bloated, and very weak and unhealthy.

"Help me up dear," she wheezes, making a hideous cough. Then she wipes tears off her pale, chubby cheeks and tries to compose herself. She looks like a fat, old woman on her deathbed, although she cannot be older than twenty-five. Summoning all her strength, Esther helps the heavy woman rise to her feet.

"Lead me over to that table," says the woman in a throaty whisper, as she wipes her clammy hands on Esther's dress. "No wait, just put me on the bed, and then go get me that bowl of brown liquid over there." Esther helps her to the bed, where the woman crashes like a dead thing. Then Esther brings her the bowl, which is filled with a muddy brown liquid. The woman sighs and sits up with difficulty as she takes it. She drinks it down quickly and with a sigh crashes back onto her back.

"I was trying to get it when I fell," the woman explains.

"What is it?" asks Esther curiously.

"Yrra," the woman says, as if Esther should have known this. "Never been pregnant, have you?"

"No."

"I have taken mijorke for too long, I fear. I must give birth by tomorrow, but my body is weak now. I cannot get the baby out." The woman wheezes as she struggles to speak. "Why don't you sit down and keep me company till my husband comes back with the midwife?"

Mijorke comes from the root of a small tree, which only grows in a few places in the mountains. It is used to delay birth. Nobody knows how it delays birth, but it is very effective and very dangerous. The Zesti discovered it's strange effects quite by accident, but never found a use for it until the strange religion of the Twelve Tribes began. This tree is a mystery to the modern world.

Yrra is a tea made from a mixture of many herbs, which somehow acts as a counter to mijorke's effects. Within hours of taking it, a woman who is taking mijorke to delay her pregnancy will usually begin contractions. It is this combination of medicines that enable the women of the Twelve Tribes to plan out their births to coincide with the new moon. It is not a perfect system, but it is often effective.

A man soon walks into the tent with the midwife, who takes a long look at the very pregnant woman before her. Her face is an open book and she obviously does not like what she sees.

"It will not come," complains the pregnant woman, who is called Sara. "I feel bloated and very sick."

"Too much mijorke for too long has caused complications. I suspect your body is in shock," the midwife says darkly. "Nobody has taken it for 20 days and survived, as you have. Your body has shut itself down and refuses to give birth."

"What should we do?" asks the man with a worried face.

"Give her a triple dose of Yrra immediately," orders the midwife somberly. "I will massage her breasts. Then there are other things we may try. But the baby must be delivered tonight. The baby is in great danger and so is Sara. Look at her color. It is very bad."

The husband grimaces as he runs out of the tent to get more yrra. The midwife stares at Esther, who takes the hint, and leaves the two of them alone.

That night, a huge crowd gathers around the tent to lend support to Sara, who is struggling to give birth. They hold hands and sing the Zune of Birth to the Great Bear spirit for a safe delivery. Massie and Esther arrive at the tent, having just served dinner and left their guests to eat it alone. Esther finds it strange that the woman would choose to have her baby here, in the middle of this field in a teepee. She asks Massie about it.

"This part of Grizzly field is a place designated as a fertility spot. The legend is long and I do not wish to tell it now. But hundreds of babies have been born here. I gave birth here twice myself."

Esther nods and she and Massie join the circle to sing to the mother. An hour later, there is word that Sara has begun contractions. Then there is no word for a long time, but the faithful crowd never strays or stops singing. Esther is amazed at their dedication, as they sing the Zune of Birth late into the night. When somebody leaves, another soon takes their place. Finally the midwife emerges exhausted from the tent and beckons all to silence.

"The child is in the other world. A beautiful girl...she never took a breath." She says somberly.

There is painful silence as the news sinks in.

"And the mother, in her consuming grief, has followed the child to the other world," she says in a terrible voice. "There she will take care of her baby for all eternity. She has committed the ultimate sacrifice of motherhood."

The midwife hangs her head and kneels to the ground. No one dares to move or even to breathe. Then a woman begins to scream in anguish and something in the crowd is released. Many break down and begin to weep. Meanwhile, a big fire is lit in a large fire pit. The circle breaks and all move toward the big fire and form another circle around it. As soon as they are circled, everyone begins to sing the Zune of Mourning. It is a slow, eerie tune, accompanied only by one drum - always one drum and nothing else. The moon rises in the sky and the singers lift their heads and hands and sing to it. The song takes on all of their grief and sends it up in a cloud of beautiful, sad music.

Sara's husband, parents, and siblings all come to the center of the circle. Then one by one, everyone leaves the outer circle to give a hug to each of the grieving ones and express their sympathies. Meanwhile the song continues in softer voices. Like a low hum it seems sometimes, just a sad noise that you make with your mouth. Esther takes her turn and gives each a quick hug.

The song never ends, but goes on and on. Esther begins to yawn, but she cannot bear to leave, so she curls up underneath a tree to listen to the haunting music. When she can no longer keep her eyes open, she walks home to bed. The Zune of Mourning is powerful and she cannot get it out of her head. It sings her to sleep and then invades her dreams, which are dark and haunting all night long.

Bear 22'

Esther wakes up early, forgetting that she does not have to work today because it is the new moon. She walks down to the kitchen, but it is deserted. Last night's dishes sit in a gigantic heap near the washing tub, forgotten in all the excitement. She does them in a sleepy daze, sips some tea, and then walks over to Grizzly field to see what is happening there. The Zune of Mourning is still going, although only one voice still sings. That voice belongs to the husband of Sara. His voice is hoarse now, barely a whisper, because he has kept the song going all night long and into the morning. He looks completely spent, like a zombie walking the earth. Walking around the smoking embers of last night's bonfire, he sings the zune in a deathly whisper and bangs softly on a little drum.

Esther wants to comfort him, but she doesn't know what to say. So she just sits down and joins him as a silent witness.

"The babies are on their way! The babies are on their way!"

A man runs out of one of the tents, shouting this announcement and blowing a loud horn. The husband of Sara stops singing, a look of pure anguish on his face, falls to his knees, and cries.

People arrive quickly, some with eyes still bleary from sleep, and a circle quickly forms around one of the tents. The Zune of Mourning is over and now the Zune of Birth begins again. The Zune of Birth is an upbeat, joyous song with a repetitive hum to it. An hour later, the midwife comes out, holding in her hands a baby girl. The singing stops as she holds up the girl for all to see. The cheers are tremendous and the baby is trotted around the circle for a closer look. Then the baby is returned to the mother and the circle moves to the second teepee, where Massie's daughter lies. More people show up and the song grows louder.

Another midwife walks out a short time later, with a second baby in her hands.
The cheers are even louder, as the second baby is carried around the circle so everyone can see him. The death of Sara has left everybody anxious about the fate of the other two mothers and now everyone can relax. Massie comes out of the tent a few minutes later, her face beaming with ecstasy. She stands proudly at the entrance and tells everyone how happy she is.

This is a very small number of babies to be born for this tribe, but it is a poor year. There are only two planets in the Bear sign right now.

Soon everyone gathers at the wedding platform. Bear weddings are long, complicated affairs with all of the friends and the family involved in the ceremony. But the best part about them - besides the music - is the flowers. The wedding platform is covered with carefully gathered wreathes of wild flowers of every variety. The first bride of the day wears a headdress of flowers three feet tall. Esther cannot take her eyes off her, unless it is to look at Chief Shantie, who looks absolutely radiant and magnificent in her golinta, with flowers in her newly braided hair. Shantie leads the ceremony, with kindly old Hym, her husband, to her right, smiling and nodding blandly. He is fat and jolly, with white hair and a thick white beard.

Esther laughs to herself, trying to imagine her and Kobe up on the podium being wed. Then her laughter turns sour as she sees him with a miserable expression on his face. As she watches him, he suddenly looks up and stares right at her. There are tears in his eyes. She feels guilty for her mirth and tries to look suitably sorry. He wipes his eyes in an embarrassed manner and turns away from her. Then he suddenly storms off, jostling people in the crowd as he makes a hasty exit.

By the end of the day, Esther ranks this day as among the best in her life. The food never ends - meat pies, moon pies, roasted fish, clams and potatoes. Wine is served in great wooden cups. There is endless music to listen to or to dance to if you feel like it, and everyone plays games all day long. Then at dusk, a huge bonfire is lit, and the women dance in their golintas again, just like during the last Bear moon, twenty-eight days before.

"This is where I belong," Esther says to herself. "I want to wear a golinta and dance with them and sing zunes."

Everything has been washed clean on this new moon, just as they promised it would. She thinks back to all the things she has learned about these people's strange beliefs these past months. Voices inside her head told her to ignore all of it. It was for these people and it had nothing to do with her. But it begins to make sense suddenly.

After the zunes are sung, dancing goes on until very late in the night. When Esther is finally exhausted, she sleeps underneath a tree in Grizzly field. She cannot bear to go home and miss a minute of this wonderful night. It is warm out and the sky is the only roof she needs.

Bear 24'

Eagle moon

Many of the new moon guests have left for their homes and the shelter has grown quiet. When Esther arrives for breakfast duty, there are only a few guests left and they have already eaten a simple breakfast of berries and tea. So Esther makes herself some tea and nibbles on berries while waiting for Massie to show up. Finally, Massie does appear and she looks very depressed.

"Esther, there you are. We need to talk."

"About what?"

"I've been avoiding this subject for many days," Massie says, not looking at her. "But Kobe wants you gone."

Esther sighs deeply as her worst fears come to pass.

"I can't say that I blame him," Massie adds. "You led him on quite a bit. He's heartbroken. He doesn't eat or sleep and he refuses to come in here until you're gone."

This makes Esther very angry. She didn't lead Kobe on. She gave him all she could and more than she wanted to. But how could she make Massie understand that. Massie wants to believe her son.

"I have waited for many days to see if Kobe would come around and forgive you. But he has not and now I must do what is good for my son. You must leave here. I am sorry, but you cannot argue with a Bear in a mood, and Kobe is very hurt. You have been a fine worker, but he is my son and I must do as he asks. You must go."

Massie looks at Esther briefly, and then looks away with an embarrassed smile.

"I'm sorry," she mumbles again.

Esther wants to defend herself, perhaps even yell at her and tear up the kitchen, but she knows that it will only make things worse. Massie is right. You cannot reason with a Bear in a mood and Kobe is not the only Bear in a mood.

"I will clear out of my hut today. Perhaps you can recommend some other place for me to work."

"Not in this tribe."

"You're asking me to leave the Bear tribe?"

"Yes, of course. That is what I said."

"You cannot -"

"Yes, I can."

"I do not work for you anymore and you cannot tell me where to go," Esther says angrily.

"That is true. But I can make sure that nobody will hire you, when I tell them what an awful worker you are. And they already know what you did to my son. Who would want to be your friend? What good would it do to stay? You would be an outcast."

Esther stares at her aghast, unable to believe Massie would treat her like this. Massie's eyes rove this way and that, as if seeking escape from Esther's angry gaze. Then Massie begins to feel guilty and she sits down heavily in a chair.

"I do not like this," Massie says at last. "You have been a big help to me, so I'll tell you what I will do for you. If you leave, I'll give you fifteen tupas. I owe you ten for your work and I will give you five more just to leave. Go away for several months, and if you want to come back then, you may do so. I'll recommend you then to anyone who wants to hire you."

She hands Esther fifteen tupas. Esther considers silently for a few moments. Finally, she takes the tupas and walks out tight-lipped, without a word. She walks in any direction, feeling the tears coming. She cannot bear to leave this place where she has been happier than she ever thought possible. But then anger soon replaces her sadness. The only reason that Massie didn't fire Esther last week was because the shelter was packed and her daughter was about to give birth. Now that everyone went home, she can get rid of her without consequences. She didn't give a damn about Esther. She doesn't give a damn about anyone but herself and her crybaby son.

After some heavy thought, Esther realizes that she doesn't really have much choice. She goes to the main store to purchase supplies.

"Where are you going?" the storekeeper asks.

She considers her options. Return to the Jay tribe or the Beaver tribe? No, she cannot go back. It is not even an option for her right now. She can only go forward.

"Where is the next tribe to the north?"

"The Eagle tribe. But that is a long, hard walk from here. Water is scarce too. You'll need a lot of supplies."

The man is very helpful. He gives her dried seaweed, acorn cakes, and a large bundle of dried salmon strips, and promises that all of this food will last for days. He sells her two large water skins too and guarantees that she will need both of them. He seems to like her, because he smiles so much and then gives her the whole thing for only eight tupas. She takes everything gratefully and thanks him over and over again.

Going to her comfortable little hut for the last time, she packs everything into her burden basket until it is stuffed tight and then she takes a last look around her little hut. It has been a good home to her and she will miss it. She has grown very comfortable here.

Tearing herself away, she walks down the hill for the last time. As she passes the kitchen of the shelter, she decides that she needs a new bowl. Figuring Massie owes her, she creeps into the kitchen and shoves a clean bowl and some extra food into her basket. When she passes Massie's house, she sees her at the door, sweeping her house clean. Massie puts down her broom when she walks by and walks over to speak to her.

"Esther, I'm sorry. I hope -"

Esther ignores her. She walks right on past her and whatever Massie hoped is lost on the wind. Massie stands there confused for a moment and then she sighs and returns to her work.

It is a warm morning and Esther curses the sun and hopes for rain to go with her mood. But the weather is in no mood to cooperate and it only gets hotter and hotter. Her basket, stuffed with food and water as well as clothing and blankets, feels like a lead weight on her back. She stops walking suddenly and throws the basket to the ground temperamentally. She is not in the mood to go out on the road again, with all its uncertainties and difficulties. She considers returning the five tupa bribe and staying on, but that sounds even harder than leaving and Massie might make it so she could never come back. Sighing, she roots through her things, trying to find something to leave behind to lighten her load. But she can spare nothing, so she shoulders the heavy basket with a great sigh and keeps moving.

The path begins to head uphill and she sees that it will go uphill for a long time. She will have to walk over a mountain and down into a valley. The man told her she would have to walk for at least four long days before she arrives at the village. She walks on miserably and only her anger and stubbornness are left to make her put one foot in front of the other. But they are enough, and she slowly makes her way up the mountain. Only when she can no longer see the village, does she stop thinking bitter thoughts about what she is leaving behind. It occurs to her that she is simply fulfilling her destiny. She is only a wanderer now, for whom the road is the only home she will ever have.

The Eagle Tribe

Bear 25'

Raccoon moon

The road winds up into the hills. It feels good to be out here, alone with the hawks in the sky, the insects sucking on her sweat and the little animals that jump and hide when she walks past. She feels free out here, on this empty road with nobody around. It is just her and the world on equal footing.

It is a well-made road, which is good, considering it would be otherwise impassable terrain. She knows this after stepping through some tall green plants to get to a particularly tempting raspberry bush. She gets a sticky resin from the plants all over her legs and feet and little burrs stick to the hairs on her legs. She gets her fill of raspberries, but pays dearly. She is uncomfortably sticky afterwards and the flies have a field day on the resin, which must be sweet.

She walks up into the mountains and down into a valley, where she finds a sparkling lake. She swims and drinks her fill, and then eats dried fish and acorn cakes. Here she spends a few pleasant hours, hiding from the broiling afternoon sun. When it cools down, she walks on.

As evening approaches, she comes upon a large bay. There is a nice breeze here, and the temperature is absolutely perfect. She eats more acorn cakes, which already taste a bit spoiled from the heat, thinking of the food seller's promise that the cakes would last for days. She shakes her head in disappointment and stuffs herself with them before they go bad. As night falls, she lies down and muses on the glories of travel until she falls asleep.

Bear 27'

Swan moon

Esther sits underneath a tree on a dry, parched hillside, watching as the heat sends shimmering ripples across the valley floor. She is in a much different mood now, four days after leaving the Bear tribe on this long journey. Now she is not musing on the glories of travel any longer. She is exhausted, hungry, thirsty and anxious to get there. For the first few days, the walk was bearable. She had plenty of food to eat and water to drink. The bay was beside her and it was cool and pleasant to walk beside it. She was always thinking that Eagle village was right around the corner, because she knew that they lived on the bay.

Then the path left the bay and began to cut through a valley and life became very uncomfortable. The valley is hot, dry, windless, and stifling, with long stretches between water, and she has had to change her habits in order to survive. She walks from dawn until the heat of the day and then she takes a nap underneath a tree until late in the afternoon. Then she walks until late in the night, when it is cooler and she can conserve precious water. During the day, she has little appetite, and she doesn't eat much food, which only makes her thirsty. She snacks at dawn and then doesn't eat until late in the afternoon when it cools down. She has her main meal around midnight, before she goes to sleep.

Esther overslept this afternoon and woke up at dusk. To make up for lost time, she is forced to walk very late into the night. The moon is half full and spreads enough light for her to barely make out the path ahead of her. She watches her feet pad on the soft dust of the valley floor, kicking up little clouds with each step. Her moccasins, already old when she inherited them, are falling apart, and ripped flaps of deerskin flop on the ground with every step. She has bound them together with some reeds that she picked near the bay and this seems to hold them together for now.

Her mood is grim today. She is exhausted, her feet hurt, she is worried about her dwindling water supply, and she feels very alone out here in this endless, empty valley. She is used to being alone, but she feels the weight of her solitude very deeply tonight. In the three days since she left the Bear tribe, she has not seen a single person who could talk to her and tell her about this path which seems to stretch forever. She longs for someone to comfort her and tell her there is hope ahead. She came upon a family of Zesti this morning, who spoke no Spanish. She tried to communicate with them through hand gestures, but they just yelled at her and threw rocks at her until she ran away. Esther never did find out why they did that, but she was upset about it for hours afterwards. She has avoided all further contact with the Zesti she comes across.

Many of the free Zesti are scornful and afraid of the Mission Zesti, which they probably assumed Esther was. This incident took place in the San Jose valley and they probably thought she was from that mission. The San Jose valley was once populous and full of many tribes, but since the arrival of the Spanish, much has changed. It is now rather desolate and unfriendly.

The stars are beautiful tonight, clear and very bright, but she hardly looks at them. She mostly watches the faint outlines of the path and the dust clouds her floppy moccasins kick up. It is a flat path of hard packed dirt, winding through stands of oak and scrubby plants. It feels good when she comes to soft sand and her feet get a little massage. The occasional rocks she steps on are murder on her tender soles, and she treads softly so she'll detect them before putting all her weight on them.

She has been experimenting with different ways of walking, having nothing else to do. She finds that changing the way she walks gives her extra energy. Sometimes she rocks from side to side, using the edges of her feet. She'll stretch out and take very big steps, followed by small shuffling steps. She tries using her toes more and then her heels. Variety in walking is the only thing she has to while away the hours and keep her from obsessing on how tired she is.

A faint light comes over the horizon. She rubs her eyes, unable to believe that dawn is here and she has walked all night long. She sits down to watch the sunrise, which is absolutely beautiful, and wraps her cloak tightly around her body to ward off the morning chill. She is dead tired, but the colors in the sky offer her inspiration to stay awake for a little while longer.

Standing on shaky legs, she continues on. Although her legs are numb and she feels close to collapsing from fatigue, she will try to walk for at least another hour before going to sleep. Once she falls asleep, she'll have to sleep the whole day through, because it will soon be too hot to move. So she adjusts her burden basket upon her aching back and plods on through the dawn, wondering how many millions of steps she has left to make until the end of the path.

Bear 28'

Wolf moon

Today she has been climbing over hills, heading steadily northeast. She drank the last of her water last night, and her mouth, throat, lips, and nearly every other part of her body are now completely dry. In the morning, she had a little dew to wet her lips, but it was a tease and did little to satisfy her. Her life is at the mercy of the road now, which she hopes will kindly lead her to water soon. She is down to her last bit of food too, and there is nothing to eat along this trail that she can see. Nothing she can catch.

Sitting in the shade of an oak, she waits for the day to cool down. She tries to ignore the unpleasant dryness of her mouth and throat, and the groan of her hungry stomach. She is too thirsty to eat the last bit of dried fish, so she saves it for when she finds water. She has a nervous feeling in the pit of her stomach and she is too wound up to sleep, for she does not know how much farther she can go without water. She did not realize that it was so far to the Eagle village. Four days they said! Five days of walking, and still no sign that she is close. Every day she thinks that this will be the day that she sees Eagle village, and every day she collapses onto her blanket after a hard day, more tired than the day before, and more depressed.

She has begun to fear that she has somehow ended up on the wrong path, because she vaguely remembers seeing a diverging path on her first night hike. She is currently on a well-traveled path with a lot of horse traffic, and she has heard that the San Jose mission is near. She just hopes that this is not the road to that place, because she thinks that dying of thirst would be better than going there.

When it finally does cool down, she trudges on, her steps slow and laborious. She is going uphill now, into the hills, which is pure torture. Her feet feel like one big blister and her right foot is especially bad. With every step she takes on her right foot, pain shoots through her entire leg. But none of that matters, compared to her extreme thirst. She feels like a dried out cornhusk that has been too long in the sun. Her lips feel like frayed leather and even her tongue is dry. But still she pushes on, because every minute she rests is one more minute farther away from water.

Just before dark, she collapses to the ground, utterly spent. She never realized that there could be something worse than starving in the woods. But she has found it. Dehydrating in this barren valley is worse. She wraps her blanket around her and lies down in a daze. She licks her puffy lips with her dry tongue and stares up at the Milky Way, imagining it to be a river in the sky. She wishes she could dip her water skin into it and drink her fill. It seems the most crystal clear, perfect water she could ever dream of.

Suddenly she feels the ground tremor. A moment later comes the unmistakable sound of a horse. She cries out in relief, except her mouth is so dry that it sounds like the croak of a dying animal. She manages to sit up and then lumbers clumsily to her feet. Meanwhile, the light of a lantern, swinging madly back and forth, comes steadily closer. In a few moments, the horse and rider are right upon her. She tries to shout out, but her voice is so hoarse that it barely registers over the crashing hooves. So as the horse passes by, she brushes the rider's leg with her arm and grabs on tightly to his ankle. A man cries out in terror as he is nearly pulled off the horse. Brandishing his lantern as if it will protect him from the ghosts of the night, he swings it in wild circles. He tries to slow the horse down, but it continues to gallop as if it knows better than to stop on a night like this. In numb horror, Esther watches the light of the lantern swerve crazily as it disappears into the night.

Just before it disappears, the light seems to stop moving, and then swings gently back and forth. Esther runs toward it desperately, surprised that she has enough energy left in her body to run. The horse seems as if it is about to move again, so she claps her hands several times. The light slowly swings around and the rider points it at her. She comes up to the light and manages to croak out a single word.

"Water."

Then suddenly, her heart starts pounding in her chest. She feels dizzy, as if she might faint. She has to sit down, lest she topple to the ground and collapse. Closing her eyes, she hopes desperately that she is dreaming. But when she opens them again, she sees the man is still there. It is a man in a brown robe that holds the lantern. It is a Spanish priest.

A few moments later, Esther is drinking from the man's flask. The water is brackish and old, but it seems the sweetest, purest water she has ever drank. She feels only a momentary guilt as she empties the last of his water into her mouth. Then she takes a deep breath and sighs deeply. She can feel her body begin to flow and relax normally, now that it is lubricated.

"Thank you," she whispers.

"You gave me a fright," he says. "I thought you were going to die right here before me."

He keeps staring at her, surprised to see a woman all alone out here. But she doesn't look at him at all. She is afraid that he will recognize her and know that she is a runaway neophyte.

"Who are you?" he says at last.

"I am Esther -"

She stops speaking, wishing she hadn't said her name. It is a Spanish name after all - a biblical name. How stupid is she?

"Esther?"

"No, Estar," she says lamely.

"Estar? "

He stares at her confused, wondering who she is and what she is doing out here.

"Where are you from?" he asks at last. "Why are you out here in the middle of nowhere? Are you an angel, come to show me the way?"

He smiles, to show that he is joking.

"No," she mumbles.

He stares at her suspiciously, wondering if she is an escaped neophyte. That would explain what she is doing out here and why she speaks Spanish. But her clothes are not the clothes of a neophyte, nor the clothes of an Indian.

"I'm from the...Bear tribe," she says in a quiet voice. "I am going to the Eagle tribe, but I ran out of water."

"The tribe of the Eagle!" he says in a sudden flash of insight. "That is where I am going too. How lucky we are to have met each other. I am going to visit the tribe of the Eagle to learn all about your people. I will take you there and you can tell me everything."

For the first time, she looks at him. He believes her story and he his going to take her there on horseback! This turns out to be a lucky break after all, as long as she doesn't make any other stupid blunders.

"I will go with you," she agrees.

He nods his head emphatically.

"Are you tired? Do you need rest? Or are you ready to travel? I am sleepless tonight myself."

"I need a few hours rest. "

"Very well. I can try to sleep, I suppose."

She lays out her blanket and wraps herself in her cloak, preparing to sleep right there. He holds the lantern up to her face so he can get a good look at her and gazes at her intently. He is struck by her beauty, and feels a pain in his chest. Perhaps she is an angel after all.

"I have not said my name," he whispers in awe. "I am Pedro."

"Greetings Pedro," she says in a sleepy voice, as she lies down.

Soon she is fast asleep. Pedro finally recovers from his shock, but he moves in a daze as he puts the horse on a tether and unrolls his bedroll. He keeps stopping to stare at her. He lies down near her and tries not to think about her. Finally, he pulls out a flask, holding a different sort of liquid, and drinks deeply. The liquor soothes him somewhat and he is able to sleep at last.

Eagle 0'

In the light of day, Esther finally gets a good look at her rescuer. He is young for a priest, somewhere in his early twenties. He is also rather handsome and lively, with a thick head of black hair cut in the Jesuit style, with a fake bald spot at the top. He has several days' growth of beard covering a big smile, and a nasty scar on one cheek. She has never met a priest like him before, although that does not change the fact that he is one. He is from the San Jose mission, where he has recently been relieved from duty.

Pedro has a million questions about the Eagle tribe, the Bear tribe and all the other Twelve Tribes. He is on some sort of fact-finding quest. Esther doesn't know how much she is supposed to say, so she is vague about speaking of them. He keeps asking about their origins, which of course she doesn't know. She remembers Bodi mentioning something about how nobody knows where Jeren came from, so she just says that nobody knows for sure.

"I am going to leave this land soon," he explains. "I am relieved from duty, due to a serious injury that was inflicted upon me. Before I do, I have one more task to complete. I must open up a dialog between my people and yours."

"You mean you want to convert them," Esther thinks sourly.

"It has been tried before, by our soldiers," he continues. "But they are without the slightest trace of subtlety. I hope to succeed where they have failed. Perhaps you can get me an audience with the Eagle chief."

"I really don't know him too well. I don't come here very often."

"It is no wonder," he laughs, "as you nearly died upon the attempt."

She makes a face at him, although he cannot see it as she is mounted behind him on the horse.

"And why did you choose to make this journey alone?"

"Nobody else wanted to come."

By early afternoon, they come in sight of the village, and Esther is relieved to see that she was nearly there when she met Pedro. They begin to pass people, who stop and stare at Pedro and her as they ride past. It suddenly occurs to Esther that it might not be a good idea to be associated with a Spanish priest and she asks him to stop the horse.

"What is it?"

"This is where I get off."

"Here?" he says doubtfully. "The village appears to be just over there."

"I want to do something over there," she says, pointing at a small hut.

"Oh," he says, disappointed.

He helps her dismount. Then he keeps holding onto her hand until she pulls it away. He seems to want something more, judging by the way he keeps looking at her.

"Perhaps we may enjoy each other's company for lunch this afternoon?" he says.

"I am to meet my friend," she says quickly. "But I'll see you another time."

He nods slowly.

"Thank you for the help," she says. "I don't know what I would have done if you hadn't come along. I might have died out there."

"Died?"

"Of thirst."

"I have seen men severely dehydrated. You were no doubt very thirsty, but you were not what I would call close to death."

"That's good to hear. Well, goodbye then," she says, and turns and walks away.

He keeps watching her, so she has to walk over to the hut to protect her lie. Then she pretends to knock on the door, until he finally turns away and rides off. Some woman peeks her head out, and Esther mumbles something about having the wrong hut and walks away with an embarrassed smile.

She soon finds herself in the commons, which is a five minute walk from a large delta that flows into the ocean. She is pleasantly surprised to find that Eagle village is a very picturesque place. Six sturdy oak plank houses with roofs of thatch stand side by side. Each building has a brightly painted eagle carved in front of it, and there are many other burl statues of various animals like antelopes and salmon. There are a few people around, and loud shouts come from one of the buildings. After drinking about a gallon of water scooped from a large cask, Esther puts her burden basket down and sits on a bench to collect herself.

Esther's first thoughts are of food. There are a few old women with corn cakes for sale or trade, but Esther doesn't want to waste a precious tupa on a few corn cakes. She would gladly pay a tupa for a big lunch, and she wonders where the shelter is. Sighing, she puts her head in her hands and thinks of how tired and hungry she is. She hasn't the strength to deal with any more walking. Finally, she drags herself to her feet and goes to ask the old women where the shelter is.

A woman points toward the correct path. On the off chance, Esther asks for a free corn cake to appease her great hunger. Her request is granted. Smiling, she thanks her gratefully and shovels it into her mouth. Then feeling better, she walks toward the shelter.

The shelter is located right on a little hill overlooking the bay. The main lodge is a weather beaten house, painted with designs of red eagles and other birds of prey. Many little brown huts stand side by side, all of them with doors facing the ocean. Inspired by the smell of good food cooking, she walks right into the lodge. The house is empty, but Esther hears noise coming from the back door. She walks outside to the kitchen, where a fat woman with a sullen expression cleans fish. She looks up from her work as Esther walks toward her, and stares at her as if she were an intruder.

"Hello," Esther says with a smile, trying to charm the woman. "I was wondering the price of a room for the night and dinner."

Esther has learned from working in a shelter that you can usually make a deal if you ask first. She smiles again, but the woman doesn't smile back. She merely gives an expression that makes her appear to be sucking on sour grass.

"It free," she says in a strange accent, "if you pay for meals. One tupa for dinner and one tupa for two lunches. Or you just pay a tupa a night without meals."

"When is dinner?" asks Esther, sealing the bargain.

"Just before dark."

The woman goes back to her cleaning.

"Is there a place I can put my things?"

"You can have alap four."

"Alap?"

"Yes, alap four. Alap is right there," she says impatiently, pointing at a hut.

"Thank you."

The hut is filled with mosquitoes. They are so thick on the walls, that the wood looks moldy and black at first sight. Then the mold starts to move and she hears a familiar whine. Esther frowns as she sets her stuff down and a cloud rises around her head. She swats at the miserable creatures, trying to get them to go away, but they merely move around the hut and settle in new places. They are here to stay. So Esther turns around and marches back to the lady to ask for a new room.

"Light a fire," the woman says. "Smoke 'em."

"I just want a different hut."

"No other huts."

Esther frowns.

"Mosquitoes everywhere. Swamp attracts 'em."

"But-"

"You can take some coals from ova' there," the woman says impatiently. "Use green wood. Smoke 'em out. They go away."

By her accent, Esther wonders if this woman is a Zesti. She thanks the strange, sour woman, grabs some coals in an old bowl the woman gives her, and goes back to hut four. Then she begins to build the smokiest fire she has ever made and throws green, wet wood on top of it. Soon her hut is filled with a thick, unbreathable smoke, and she opens the door and walks outside to wait for the nasty bugs and smoke to clear out.

After an agonizing wait, dinner is finally served. Esther stuffs herself with fried fish, roasted roots, and hard disks of chewy cornmeal. The food tastes so good that she feels like dancing. She cannot believe that she is actually here, eating a hot meal with a bed waiting for her afterwards. Even a bed crawling with mosquitoes seems nice. The memory of the road is already fading and seems more like a dream with every bite of food.

After dinner, she returns to her smoky hut. The mosquito population has declined somewhat, but there are still many sticking relentlessly to the walls. Though it is too warm for a fire, she stokes up her "smoker" with green wood before passing out. She falls asleep with smoke curling all around her body and forming a thick cloud above her, then circulating lazily out through a hole in the roof. She prays that she will not wake up in the morning covered in bumps.

Pedro, the priest, sits up in bed, after tossing and turning for several hours. He swats ineffectually at the mosquitoes hovering over him in his own alap, and curses them in a loud voice. But the mosquitoes are not the reason he cannot sleep. It is much worse than that. He cannot stop thinking of the girl, Esther. It was that sad look she gave him right before they parted, that cut right through his heart like a cleaver.

He puts on his robes and walks outside. Dawn is nearly here and he knows that he will not sleep once the sun rises. His head buzzes from lack of sleep, as he takes a walk down the nearest path toward the delta that leads to the San Francisco mission.
When he first saw the girl, he felt a pain unlike he has ever felt before. At first, he chalked it up to lust. Pedro is no stranger to lust, because it is the biggest enemy of a man of the cloth. But he has never felt it so strongly before, such lingering anguish that won't go away. All night long, he has thought about her. He cannot stop imagining the way her hands felt on his back as she rode behind him. The smell of her still lingers on his robes, driving him mad. It has been a long time since he has had that much contact with a woman, let alone one that he is so attracted to.

And then he thinks again of that look she gave him. It was like...true love. He wonders if she felt it too or if he imagined it. Could it be true love? Why else can he not stop imagining kissing her? Why else can't he sleep? What a pity it is that he will never know whether or not it is true love, for Pedro has taken a lifelong vow of celibacy.

Not for the first time, he wonders what the forbidden fruit might taste like and if he is a fool to deny himself a taste of it. He thinks of the old proverb suddenly. 'What a wise man does in the beginning, a fool does in the end.' Sighing, he walks faster and tries not to think about it.

Eagle 1'

Owl moon

Esther wakes with a strong thirst and an even stronger urge to use the toilet, but she is too tired to move. When her needs become insistent, she finally rises grumpily, and stumbles out the door. She is stiff and every step is painful to her aching feet, as she walks outside barefoot in the bright sunshine, blinking rapidly. The outhouse is in easy view of the cabins, and she enters reluctantly. It is one of the dirtiest outhouses she has ever been in, because it sees so much use and is rarely cleaned by the troll-like keeper. It smells foul too and she holds her nose the whole time she is inside. Finally she escapes, and takes several deep breaths in the fresh air.

She goes to the large trough of water in front of the main lodge and fills her cup full, then sits down on a patch of grass and tries to clear her head of the fog that encases it. She doesn't want to go back to her infested hut, so she lies down in the shade of a tree and dozes the entire morning away.

"Would you join me for lunch, Estar?" asks a voice, waking her from her dozing.

She opens her eyes and sees Pedro standing there.

"Is it lunchtime already?" she mumbles sleepily.

"Yes."

"I'm not hungry," she says, closing her eyes again, and figuring that she'll eat later.

"It will be my treat."

She decides that she cannot refuse a free lunch. Forcing herself to rise, she accompanies him to the main lodge. As they walk in, heads turn to stare at them and glaring eyes accompany them to their table. Everyone seems to know who and what he is, and she hears some mumbled comments from people wondering what he is doing here. They must wait for a long time before the woman comes over to ask them what they want to eat, and she is unfriendly, cold and acts like she would rather serve a horse.

Esther wishes she had not joined him. He is nice enough, but he sticks out like a sore thumb, which makes her stick out also. She finds herself ignoring him, and hopes that everyone will notice that she is ignoring him. She doesn't want to be known as the missionary's friend or the people will shun her too. She feels bad, knowing that he saved her life, but she resolves to stay away from him from now on. It won't do to make a poor impression.

"I have a meeting with Chief Wendel in the next two days," Pedro tells her. "We're going to discuss opening a dialog between our people."

"That's exciting," she mumbles, looking around in a distracted way.

"I have so much to ask him. I feel that our people and your people can form a great alliance, to bring peace and prosperity to this land. We speak the same language, after all, and we share the love of reason. I am surprised to find such a high degree of civilization here. I thought your people very primitive, before I came. But already I can see that you have a grasp of reason and technology. I took a walk around the village square today and I was shocked to see that your people make your own books. The paper is poor quality, but that can be easily remedied. The instincts are there. You craft fine clothes too...although I think you all could stand to wear them a little more."

"It is hot out."

"True enough. Although there are hotter places, let me assure you. By the way, I have seen no church or temple here. Are there any priests in this place? What is your religion? Do you know Jesus, the Lord and Savior?"

Here it comes. He is going to try to convert her. It makes her angry and afraid at the same time. She squirms nervously, wondering what she should say. She knows very well what happens to people who say they do not believe. Then she remembers that he has no power over her here. Unless...he finds out that she is a runaway.

Just then, the lady arrives with their food. It is a bowl of some fishy smelling soup and a disc of corn. Leaving the question hanging in the air, she digs into the food.
Pedro watches her keenly for a few moments, finding her reaction to his last comment strange. But he decides not to press it for now and digs into the food himself. The soup is very bland and unappealing. These people seem to have no knowledge of spices or the art of cooking. He slurps it up half-heartedly.

While he eats, he finds himself staring at Esther more than he should. He cannot help himself. She is so beautiful. He tries to admire her beauty as one of God's creations, but that is supremely difficult. He has to close his eyes so he won't make her uncomfortable. Then he feels her radiant eyes burning into him and assumes that she must be staring at him, but when he opens his eyes to meet her gaze, he finds that she is not staring at him at all. She merely stares into space, lost in her own thoughts. He watches her, waiting for a clue to what she is thinking. The more he stares at her, the more his heart aches.

"I am tired," she says at last. "I must go. I'm sorry. Thanks for lunch."

"I understand."

She walks away, and it is as if all the life has left the room. He feels dizzy, giddy, and miserable at the same time. This woman is dangerous to him, because he has not felt like this since he was a young man, fatally in love with a serving wench. And this time it is much worse, for he is far away from home and feeling very isolated and alone.

There is a celebration tonight and Esther wanders down to the village commons, following the smell of food. In the main circle, they are roasting strips of antelope over a giant field of coals. The meat looks far from done, but there is a table filled with other kinds of food. Esther has a little cake made of corn and seeds and then sits down to wait for the rest of dinner.

Soon the circle is crowded with people, dressed in beautiful dresses of soft eagle feathers, snakeskin vests, buckskin skirts, and shell necklaces. They mill about eagerly, greet each other in loud voices, and compare stories of the day. And then the chief appears, wearing a magnificent headdress of eagle feathers. He carries a large cask, which he sets down with a grunt.

"The moon and the sun are on fire tonight and the month of the Eagle is here," he announces in a loud voice. "And best of all, the first wine of the season is ready. Let all have a cup and be merry!"

He backs away as the people rush to the cask en masse, cups in their hands. He basks in their praise and gratitude and then waves it off as if it is nothing. Everyone has wine, and there are many gasps of relief, as if they have not had a drink in ages. Soon dinner is ready and everyone lines up to fill their plates with food.

After dinner, the entire village moves to the assembly house. Esther walks slowly over. There is no bonfire, as it is much too hot, but there are many torches lit to provide light in the dark space. First, there are some ritual dances. Ten athletic men do a complicated dance with many difficult acrobatics. The women sing and clap along with the drums. It is a great spectacle. Following this, there is dance music. The men and women of this tribe do a very sexual dance, in which they gyrate their hips and bodies at lightning speed, with their bodies nearly touching. The drums are played at a galloping pace, and drive the dancers into a frenzy. Esther tries to imitate the movements of the dance, and of course, she soon has many males who are interested in teaching her how to do it right.

Later in the evening, when she is too tired and hot to dance anymore, Esther is bombarded with attention from a drunk man who insists on asking her every conceivable question in the universe all at once. She tries her best to appease him, but he is relentless, and his hands are groping everywhere. She finally has to excuse herself and explains that she has to visit her husband outside or he will get angry and come looking for her. The man lets her leave without further harassment.

Outside in the warm night air, Esther watches several drummers and a flutist play by the fire. The pounding is less severe outside, where the noise can evaporate, and her ears are given a welcome rest. The weather is perfect here at night. The hot valley combined with the bay breeze makes for a nearly tropical environment. Suddenly, she turns around to see a man standing right behind her, his face lost in the shadows cast by the fire.

"Hello," he says in a slow voice.

"Hello," she says hesitantly, hoping he is not creepy.

He steps into the light of the fire so she can see him better. He is tall and lean, with a wide angular face, a strong chin, and thick, wavy hair. He wears a beautiful snakeskin vest and a sort of kilt made from soft fur, and he moves with a self-assured grace. Esther finds him very handsome.

They talk for a bit and Esther flirts with him, which is something that she never does unless she is trying to get something from a man. But now she does it unconsciously. She smiles and laughs at his jokes and makes twinkly eyes at him.

"I am Garet," he says, touching her shoulder gently.

"Esther."

"And from what tribe are you?"

"None. I am a stranger from a Spanish town."

He seems pleased by this news. He tells Esther that he is of the Eagle tribe, and that he is a soldier and a fisherman, and one of the best divers in the tribe. His uncle is Chief Wendel and he may be considered for that position someday, if it is the wishes of the tribe that he becomes chief. They talk for a while and he offers to show her around. She accepts without thinking.

They walk down to the bay. A long wooden trail of boards has been built over the wetlands, stretching a quarter mile over the tall swampy grass. At the end is the large dock, with many boats tied up. There is nobody here now and he places the torch in a holder and sits down. She joins him, suddenly nervous about where this is going. She is prepared to jump up and run if he does something that she doesn't like. But he is not pushy or aggressive, and she soon relaxes and enjoys his easy company.

"You said that you are a fisherman?"

"I fish for salmon and smelt. And I hunt many creatures of both land and sea."

He seems very interested in her and asks her many questions. She tells him more than she wants to. She can't help it. He is magnetic, charming, and handsome, and she cannot stop smiling at him. He obviously has an eye for women and she is flattered that he has one for her right now. He seems to be a man that could get any woman he wanted. She begins to wonder what she will do if he tries to kiss her.

"Have you a man in your life?"

"No."

"Why not?"

"I am a traveler," she says vaguely.

"So you are without a man?"

"Yes."

"Good," he says with a knowing smile.

"And are you...without a woman?"

"I am...." He thinks about his answer for a while. "I am available."

He leans over and kisses her slightly. Esther is drunk enough not to be afraid and she kisses him back. It is romantic here in the torchlight, with the breeze and the waves lapping gently on the shore. Esther's usual reticence about men and sex is strangely absent, and she is pleased that it is going so well. Then he puts his hand to her flower and she moves nervously away from him. She has promised herself that she will be celibate, and here she is fooling around with one of the first men she has met.

"I'm tired," she says, realizing as she says it that it is true. "I need to sleep."

"And where are you staying?"

"At the shelter."

"I will walk you there."

Outside the door to her hut, he kisses her again. She feels her knees go weak, and she has to draw away after a few moments to gather her wits. She stares at him, feels herself melting, and fights to remain distant.

"I must sleep," she mumbles.

She goes inside before he can kiss her again. Then she sits down on her bed and tries to calm down. When she peeks her head out a few minutes later, he is gone. She trudges to the main lodge to get some coals and green wood to build a smoker and then stumbles back to her hut. After the smoker is going strong, she lies down, too drunk to stay awake and too excited to sleep. Finally, the alcohol wins and she passes out.

Eagle 2'

Pedro walks along the edge of the water, thinking about what he will say to Chief Wendel tomorrow. His official mission is only to study these people, but more was implied by Father Ulia. If possible, he is supposed to push for an alliance between the Spanish crown and the Eagle tribe and their allies. And he is supposed to suggest the construction of a church and the baptism of the chief. But it is not going to be as easy as he thought. Father Ulia thought that these people were primitives who just happened to speak Spanish due to some early Spanish influence. But Pedro sees that this situation is more complicated than that. For one thing, they are well armed with steel weapons, although he has seen no guns nor heard gunfire. But if they have steel, there is a good chance they may have guns, which makes conquest with force dangerous. They are technologically advanced and appear to be highly intelligent. Also, he thinks that they have some sort of religion, although he cannot make heads or tails of it. But if they have strong beliefs, they will likely resist any attempt at conversion and close their ears to the Word. It is a worthy challenge, and Pedro racks his brain to find a solution.

Suddenly, he sees Esther, standing in the river. She is naked, washing herself hygienically. His heart starts hammering in his chest and he cannot stop staring, although he fights to avert his eyes. He has seen some nudity here in the Eagle tribe, but this is different somehow. This girl is modest, unlike the carefree women he has seen flaunting themselves like harlots, and he finds that extremely exciting. She keeps glancing around to see if anyone is watching, which makes the experience that much more exciting. Unconsciously, he moves behind a tree and crouches down in the tall grass to remain hidden.

She turns around and walks out of the river and he feels as if he is going to collapse from desire. Then she begins to jump up and down in the sun, trying to get dry. Pedro finds himself gripping a branch so hard, that he might just wring the sap right out of it. Finally, he turns around and crawls through the grass on his hands and knees. He must not look upon that woman again. The sight of her naked body will drive him mad with lust. He must stay away from her at all costs.

Tonight there is another party and Esther unconsciously walks through a crowd of revelers, looking for Garet. She tries not to think about him and pretends that she is not looking for him, but he keeps popping into her head. A strange man walks up to her and hands her a cup of wine, and she welcomes the distraction from her thoughts. But he seems to want some form of gratitude for the wine and she quickly escapes from his designs and walks on.

Later in the evening, she sees Garet, sitting in front of a fire with a woman resting between his legs. She is a great beauty, tall, graceful and proud, and she strokes his legs lovingly as she talks to others around the fire. Garet glances around the fire, bored and listless, and then he notices Esther. He gives her a small, pitiful smile, but his eyes cry out for her to stay away, and he quickly looks away again. Just at that moment, sensing something dangerous perhaps, his woman pulls him to her and kisses him on the mouth possessively.

Burning from jealousy and anger, Esther walks off. She feels like a fool. Garet has a woman already! She wonders what was he was doing with her when he has a beautiful woman like that sitting in his lap? A little bit of fun on an off night? This burns her up even more and she is just happy that she didn't let him get any further.

She walks down to the dock, wanting to see the water. There are many lovers here tonight, kissing on the dock that overlooks the gently flowing river. It is not a conducive environment for sulking, so she wanders back over the long plank trail to look for a private place to do it. When she finally finds a private place under an oak tree, she slumps to the ground, puts her head in her hands and promises herself that she will stick to her pledge of celibacy and stay away from men.

Eagle 3'

Elk moon

It is quiet in the village, as everyone recovers from the revelry of the previous nights and prepares for the revelry of the nights to come. Esther spends the day hiding from the broiling sun in the shade of a tree overlooking the delta. She practices her reading and watches the world go by.

Meanwhile, Pedro sits cross-legged on the floor with Chief Wendel, watching a pretty young woman serve them lunch. She is naked and Pedro is trying not to look, but it makes him supremely uncomfortable anyways.

"Woman, put some clothes on," Wendel says, noticing the way Pedro squirms.

"Why?" she asks innocently.

"It is making our guest uncomfortable."

She smiles and flips her hips coquettishly as she leaves the room.

"I am told that you forbid your people to walk around without clothes," Wendel says. "Is this true?"

"It is true. We feel that it propagates lust and carnal infidelities."

"And what's wrong with that?" Wendel asks with a smile.

"We prefer spiritual love," Pedro says in a flat voice, without his usual enthusiasm.

"I'll take my wives over the spirits any day."

The meeting has not gone well so far. Pedro has been unusually murky and dense today. He can't seem to put together a single thought or explain himself with any clarity. He can see by Wendel's face that he thinks Pedro nothing more than a nuisance. Pedro is blowing this opportunity to gain an ally to the Spanish Crown and spread the Word of God. All over a heathen woman! He cannot stop thinking about Esther and it is driving him mad. Last night, he barely slept. He kept imagining her naked, bathing in the river. He has not had a case of the Lust this bad since he was a teenager, trying to rein in his libido in the monastery. Obsessed with the serving wench in the town pub, he would sneak off there at night just to stare at her and have a drink of wine.

It occurs to Pedro that his entire life has been lived in places designed to make life easier on the celibate. A monastery allows no women. There are Indian women at the mission of course, but they must walk around fully clothed at all times. Sexual contact is kept strictly out of sight, and then only among married couples. What a challenge to remain celibate in the real world!

An older woman walks in, bearing some meat in two bowls. She wears a skirt at least, although she is still topless. She hands Wendel the bowl and glances ever so briefly at Pedro as she hands him his food. She reaches all the way across the fire to give it to him, as if he is infected.

"Alat told me to come serve the meat. She said there was a problem. What is it?"

"She was distracting our guest," says Wendel, with a wink.

"Oh, so you told her to send me?" she says, flashing anger. "Cause I'm nothing to look at?"

"Woman, I told her to put on some clothes!" Wendel says, with a dismissing wave of his hand. "I didn't mention you at all."

She glares at him briefly, then walks out of the room. Wendel holds up his hands and rolls his eyes.

"Women," he says. "You know how they are. Always fighting for attention."

"Was that your wife and daughter?" Pedro asks.

"No," Wendel says, giving him a look. "Those are both my wives. Do I look that old to you?"

"No, no," says Pedro. "I'm sorry. We do not have multiple wives in our culture."

"One of the benefits of being chief," Wendel says with a wink.

Pedro tries to come up with something meaningful to say, perhaps a subtle lesson about the dangers of lust and the need for a church to set a moral tone, but he cannot get his brain to function properly. He takes a deep breath but nothing comes out.

"Alat was my younger brother's wife," Wendel explains. "But he was killed in a battle with some Zesti raiders. It fell upon me to take her and her child as my own. Believe me, it is quite a challenge. She and Tula fight like two bucks in a rut. Tula wasn't too happy about sharing me with a woman ten years younger."

"It must be hard on her," Pedro says, nodding slowly.

"Now, let's stop beating about the bush," Wendel says, after a tense moment. "You people need to keep those ugly beasts of yours away from our land. They are eating all the foliage, which chases away all the good game. What are those things called again?"

It is hot in here. Pedro wipes the sweat from his head, and tries to remain calm. But then he gets a vision of Esther naked again and he feels that he might pass out. He is sure that he is going to pass out.

"Well?" asks Wendel after a time. "What about it?"

"What? You mean cows? Oh yes, are they bothering you?"

"I just said that."

"I'm sorry," Pedro says, after a long pause. "I'm not feeling well. I have an illness, a fistula. I tend to pass out sometimes. I must go lie down, so perhaps we can continue this later."

Before Wendel can protest, Pedro is out the door and walking toward his hut as quickly as possible. On the way, a wave of dizziness forces him to sit against a tree. He sits there for a long time, breathing heavily. He knows that he is going to be ill for the rest of the day. This illness is the reason he had to leave San Jose. He was supposed to head south, so that he might receive proper treatment, but he took this disastrous detour instead. Now he sees that he shouldn't have come here. He is weakened and suffering from madness, and he is going to ruin everything.

Eagle 4'

Esther sits alone in a little wooden boat, floating on the delta. She has never been on a boat before and it seems to her to be the only thing to do on a hot day like this. She lies back and soaks up the sun with a sigh, as she trails her hand in the water. The boat sways with every movement and threatens to tip over if she merely leans too much in one direction, so she must make very small movements. Suddenly, a shadow blots out the sun. Surprised, she opens her eyes and sees a person hovering over her. She sits up with surprise, nearly tipping the boat over in the process, before she realizes that it is only Garet. He stands on the edges of his own boat, gracefully rocking back and forth with superb balance.

"I saw you floating out here and thought I'd come over and say hello," he says, with a big smile on his face.

She makes a face but says nothing.

"It is good to see you," he goes on, pretending that there is nothing the matter. "I was wondering what happened to you."

"Nothing."

"You seem upset."

"You didn't tell me you had a wife," she says sourly.

"I don't have a wife."

"I saw you with that woman."

"We are not married."

"You said you didn't have anyone at all."

"No, I said that I was available...which I am."

"But you have a woman," she says, confused.

"Before a couple is married, there are no taboos. They may romp with whomever they please."

She believes him. She has seen that young people in this tribe have absolutely no taboos against...almost anything they dream up. Still, she longs to kick his boat out from under him and send him into the water, just for argument's sake.

"Would you like to join me? My boat rides very smooth."

"Won't she be jealous?" she asks sourly.

"No."

Esther shrugs in a noncommittal way. He doesn't seem at all ashamed of himself, so she begins to wonder if he did anything wrong at all. Perhaps she is making too big a deal of this. Giving him the benefit of the doubt, she climbs aboard his boat, and he ties her boat to his. He sits across from her, watching her, but he doesn't say anything for a few minutes. He only trails his hands in the water, thinking of what to say. She stares off into the distance, trying not to look at him, and afraid of what she will do if she looks at him for too long. Finally, he begins to row with smooth and slow strokes. He rows toward the far bank, so they will not be seen from town.

"Are you angry at me still?"

"No."

"I find you very beautiful," he says, stopping his rowing and drifting in the slight current.

"Thank you."

He touches her on the shoulder and strokes her arm. After a few moments, she moves away from him.

"Are you looking for a husband?" he asks, choosing his words carefully. "Is this why you are jealous of that girl?"

"No," says Esther.

"Do you like me?"

"I did."

"Then why do you reject me?"

"I couldn't do that to your woman."

"She doesn't need to know. She doesn't want to know. She said that I must remain faithful to her when we are married...not before. Until then, she simply doesn't want to know about it."

"She said that?"

"Yes."

Esther feels that there is something very wrong in all this. She has a strong feeling that he is not quite telling the truth, and she doesn't trust him. But stronger than that feeling is the feeling that she is very attracted to him. Now she is more turned on than ever and she squirms in her seat, barely able to contain herself. Garet sees her discomfort and notices something in her eyes. And then he knows. She has heard him...and she understands. He leans over and strokes her arm again. This time she doesn't refuse him, so he runs his hands up and down her back and arms, exploring her body. She closes her eyes and enjoys the slow massage, promising herself that she will not let it go too far.

All this tension has made him very excited, hungry for this woman. He leans over to kiss her. But she draws back and the boat rocks terribly with the sudden motion, which sends his lips into her cheek. He boldly tries again. This time she is expecting it, and she kisses him back for just a moment. Just a small taste is all she wants and it is as nice as she remembers. But he is too ambitious. As he tries to climb on top of her, she moves the wrong way and the boat tips over. They are both thrown into the water.

They come to the surface and look at each other for a glum moment, and then burst out laughing. All the tension between them dissipates in this moment of shared hilarity. But the cold water extinguishes the flames of passion and Esther is done with him for now. She swims to her own boat and climbs aboard by throwing her body on top of it ungracefully, like a sea lion flopping on the beach. Garet frowns, disappointed, and then he rights his own craft and hops back in.

"I must go," she says. "I'm sorry."

"I blew that one."

She laughs and nods in full agreement. With a sober expression, he unties her craft and releases her. He sits in his boat and watches her float away, until she is swallowed by a shaft of bright sunlight in his eyes.

In the early evening, Esther walks along a dirt path that skirts the marsh, wanting to get to the dock before sunset. She stops to raid a huge wall of well-armored, thorny blackberry bushes that rises higher than her head and eats until the world turns purple. When she is satisfied, she makes her way to the path of boards that crosses the marsh. It is so narrow, that whenever someone is walking the other way, one of them has to back up to a wide crossing place, or else step into the water. There are many people on the boardwalk today and it is slow going. She arrives at the edge of the delta just in time to watch the sunset.

The world takes on a dreamlike quality. The weather is tropical again, with a soft breeze blowing gently. A small boat with a crude sail cruises past, in no particular hurry to reach its destination. The sky turns a gorgeous shade of red that deepens as the sun sinks lower. Esther sits down, trails her feet in the water, and thinks that this moment is just about perfect.

"Hello."

She looks up and swallows hard. Pedro is standing above her and he looks a wreck. His hair sticks straight out in all directions and his eyes are sunken like he hasn't slept in days. His mood is gloomy and vaguely pissed off and his eyes reflect madness.

"Hello," she says vacantly.

"May I join you?"

She nods imperceptibly and tries to hold on to the magic of the evening, which threatens to slip away.

"I thought we should talk. Would you do me the honor of joining me for dinner?" he says, sitting down beside her.

"No thank you."

"You are not hungry?"

"No, I just ate some blackberries."

She frowns, wishing she hadn't said that. Now she cannot go to dinner or else risk offending him with her lie.

"I understand. I am not very good company right now. But I'm not like this normally. I'm a very happy and fun person usually."

She has to struggle not to laugh.

"It's just - just this sickness. I am ill. I am due for treatment in Mexico, but I came here instead. I think I am suffering from -"

He stares at her bare arms and graceful neck, and fights desperately the desire to touch her.

"May I confess something to you?"

"You? Want to confess to me?" she asks, with a trace of a smile.

"Yes, why not?"

She remembers that she is pretending not to know anything about priests, and she quickly stops smiling and pretends to be interested.

"What is it?" she says, resisting the temptation to say "my son".

"Lust. Desire. I struggle against my demons. Forgive me for my weakness, Estar. This illness I have weakens me, and the devil is dancing inside of me."

She believes him, and wishes he would take his devil somewhere else.

"You must forgive me. Please. I have not felt these feelings in a long time."

He touches her gently on the arm and feels a spark go through his entire body. She draws away as if stung. But then she is stung again and she realizes that a mosquito bit her just as he touched her. Feeding time. Within minutes, they are both swarmed, and slapping at their arms, legs, feet, and face. A young boy at the other side of the dock starts shouting and doing a mad dance. Esther sighs. The sky is still gorgeous and the light shining off the river makes it glisten and sparkle magically, but the dock is crawling with too many pests. She rises.

"Yes, a good idea," he agrees. "We must escape these nuisances. Let us go."

She walks back the way she came, leaving all of the pests behind but the one that stubbornly follows her home. She finally shakes him at the door to her hut and he goes to dinner by himself. She goes to the kitchen and asks for a plate to eat in private, claiming that she is on her moon. She is given fried fish and a corn cake, which she takes to her alap to eat alone.

While she eats, she has a realization. She and Pedro are not that different and are struggling against the same thing. Both are fighting their desires. She promised herself that she would be celibate...just like a nun. Why should she deny herself the pleasures of sex if nobody else around here does? She is far, far away from the mission now, yet she continues to act like there are priests watching her and forbidding her to have any fun. Well, let them watch! Let Pedro watch and drool with desire, while she does what he only dreams of.

She promises herself that the next time she sees Garet, he is in for a pleasant surprise.

Eagle 5'

**Raven moon*

The village is becoming quite crowded, as the Raven tribe arrives for Polar Day. A new group has recently arrived by boat and they are setting up little huts, tents and teepees all over the place. The clearing in which the Eagle shelter is located is now a whole village of temporary dwellings and Esther has many new neighbors.

Someone has even strung a thick skin tarp from the back wall of her hut and moved in right under her very nose.

As it gets dark, drummers begin to pound the skins and the moon rises on a huge crowd, dancing around a big fire. It is cloudy today, so the moon is not visible, but it is still very bright out. Too many drummers create a tuneless noise soup, but everyone has fun anyway, screaming, yelling and thrashing around rhythmically. Esther dances wildly by one of the fires, trying to perfect the Eagle dances. She is drunk and doesn't care about anything. As the full moon rises higher, things get crazier and Esther gets drunker. She becomes bold and chats with everyone she meets. When she is asked to dance by a strange man, she twirls around with him.

Suddenly, she sees Garet staring at her. She can feel his eyes on her as she dances, although he isn't obvious about it because his woman, Gaela, is nearby. Esther likes the way Garet watches her. After a while, Gaela pulls Garet out into the crowd to dance. Garet is no dancer, but Gaela is, which makes them seem very mismatched. She tries to get him to dance freely, but he has too many hang ups, so she gets bored of him and starts dancing with one of her female friends instead. Garet stands there woodenly, until he and Esther lock eyes and smile at each other. He touches her arm, teasing her, and she nudges him back. Then he pretends to dance, just so he can keep on touching her. She begins to get bolder and rubs up against his back with hers. He pats her bottom. She lunges into his lap and then moves away. They continue to twirl around each other while pretending that neither one of them exists. They do not speak, but only exchange meaningful glances.

The music goes until very late in the night. A fresh breeze blows, cooling off the sweat from the tired dancers. One by one, people begin to fall to the ground in drunken, stoned dementia. Couples pair off and do as they please in front of everybody. Still fighting off persistent drunk men, Esther wanders home a few hours before dawn. She goes into her mosquito-infested hut and tries to light a green fire, but she is too drunk and tired. She finally goes to sleep unprotected from the bloodsuckers.

Eagle 7'

The full moon is here and Garet feels time coming for him, squeezing him. He stands by the edge of the water, next to his older sister and her two-year old daughter. His sister talks to him about something, but his eyes are not on her and neither is his mind. His eyes are on the three girls swimming naked in the water in front of him, beautiful young girls just coming into their own. Ripening flowers. And his thoughts are on what he could do with them if he were not going to be married in two weeks. Garet is one of the most eligible men in the Eagle tribe. He could probably have at least one of those girls, and possibly two.

He looks at his sister. She used to be beautiful like that. But age and childbearing have taken their toll. She is not a young, fresh girl any more. *And neither will Gaela be after our first child. Will I still want her?* He feels like mud for even thinking such things, but these thoughts bubble up constantly.

He skips rocks along the water, trying to clear his mind so he can think clearly. His little niece watches him and tries to imitate him. She can throw the rocks about three feet. He smiles at her poor attempt.

"Can you watch her for a minute?" asks his sister. "I'll be right back."

"Yes."

He watches the girls instead, but they don't look at him. He is engaged to be married - off limits. Nobody has looked at him with desire since he got engaged. But he has not forgotten the excitement of the chase and Esther awoke that side of him again. She doesn't know the taboos, and he knows now that she wants him.

He watches the girls swim past, his head lost in the movement of their flesh. He imagines one of them naked, sitting on his lap, gasping with pleasure as he penetrates her. Suddenly, he is awakened from his reverie by a squeal from his niece, and then he hears a shout from his returning sister.

"You were supposed to be watching her!"

His little niece has crawled far out into the water and is struggling to get onto a rock. She begins to get desperate, as the little waves threaten to carry her away, so she screams for help. Garet wades out guiltily and fetches her back.

"What if she had drowned?" intones his sister angrily.

"She was fine. I was watching her."

"You were not."

His sister starts complaining about how he is always daydreaming and Garet tries to ignore her. But it just makes him more stressed. This is just the sort of thing that he wants to avoid. Irritating conversations. Fights. The price of marriage. He suddenly realizes what his problem is. He doesn't want to get married.

There is a big feast in the afternoon, followed by dancing. Pedro stands at a distance, watching hordes of beautiful girls dance topless in the hot sun. He cannot go close for fear of losing his mind. His desires are so intense that can feel his body spasm. He finally has to take a thick branch and beat himself with it, just to calm down. The pain makes him feel a little better. He once promised himself that he would never be one of those priests who whipped themselves, but that was a long time ago. What's a man to do? Masturbation is a sin. Pain is the only quick fix available.

He walks down to the river, his legs bleeding from scratches inflicted by the branch. When he arrives at the water, he has to beat himself again to drive his desires away. Then he catches his reflection in the river, a gloomy face perched over hunched shoulders. His hair cut in the mission style, one big ring of tousled hair encircling his head like a halo. His haircut that makes him look as if he were bald, although he has a thick head of hair that he shaves once a week. Brown shapeless robes hide his body. He thinks of some of the older padres in the mission, covered in welts and bruises from constant whipping. Their faces, heavily lined and grim, speak of unfulfilled desires. It suddenly seems creepy to him and he begins to understand why nobody here talks to him. It is no wonder that Esther shuns him. He feels a desperate self loathing, followed by a desire to beat the hell out of himself again. Before he does, he jumps into the cold water, which cools the fire and makes him feel a little better.

Floating in the water, he suddenly has a strange thought. What if he shaved his head, ditched his robes, and became a regular man? Experience a normal life so he knows what he has been missing. Would God allow him to play hooky from the church and have a secret life among the natives? It would give him a chance to do all the sinful things that he has always dreamed of and get them out of his system. It might be just the thing to break this depression that has been strangling him.

It would all be in the name of duty, really. He was told to study the local wildlife- as Padre Ulia put it. Well, he has not done a good job so far. But if he became one of them, then he could really understand them. He crawls out of the water, his wet robes clinging to his body. They feel so heavy when they are wet and then he suddenly realizes that it is not only the water that makes them heavy. He is possessed by a sudden optimism that makes him yell at the top of his lungs, and then he takes off his wet robes, swings them around in a circle, and throws them into a tree. He laughs and dances like a madman in his bare skin. Then he walks back to his hut naked, not caring a fig if anyone is watching. He feels happier than he has felt in a long time.

The assembly hall is a good walk from the main village. It lies at the bottom of the dry hills, directly south of the bay. The Eagle and Raven tribes gather inside, out of the summer heat, waiting for the scheduled show to begin. Sweating terribly in the hot building, Esther gladly accepts a fan from a nice lady and fans herself. She adjusts her posture many times to make the most out of this uncomfortable seat. The Eagle tribe has built crude stadium seating out of rough-hewn boards, but the boards are too rough and bite into her rear. Torches and a large fire provide illumination, but they also add to the heat, and the air is so smoky that it is hardly bearable.

The evening's entertainment begins with women dancers doing an uninspired dance that goes on for far too long. Next come the fools, who do a hilarious skit with acrobatics and lots of bawdy jokes. There is a man named Bufo, who is painted from head to toe in red with black stripes. When he smiles, his teeth are black from the paint, making him look frightening. He is a superb actor who can make everyone laugh with the smallest expression. Everyone shouts "Bufo! Bufo! Bufo!" every time he does something funny. After Bufo leaves, his name is roared with delight for a long time.

Next come two women with lit torches who begin a complicated routine of juggling torches. They often interrupt their juggling act to light each other's pants on fire, sending the audience into howling laughter as they jump dramatically and run around with their pants smoking. By the time this act is done, Esther can barely stand the heat in the place. She is soaked in sweat and fanning herself furiously. She considers stepping outside for air, but the next act is too interesting.

A man comes out from the wings, carrying large bone needles in his hand, followed shortly by his assistant. He waves his hands and tries to incite the crowd into a frenzy. His expression is so proud, that it makes Esther laugh. After he has enough cheers (and he requires a lot before he will begin), he signals his assistant, who begins to push the needles through the skin of his arms, chest, and back. Next, the assistant attaches rope to all of the needles and this man begins to do amazing things. He lifts rocks with the ropes hanging from the needles in his arms. The skin stretches taut, but does not break. He drags rocks with the ropes attached to his chest. And for the grand finale, he suspends himself from ropes on the roof, using only the needles in his back. Esther gasps, as his skin stretches so far, she is sure it will tear. But it doesn't break. How that must hurt! Afterwards, the assistant helps him down, and the man stands proud as a rooster again, breathing in the roaring crowd. This time, Esther doesn't laugh, but cheers along with the others. The dancers return and Esther escapes outside to get some fresh air.

Bufo returns with a whole new group of clowns and she goes back inside to watch. After his inspired clowning, there are a couple of other unexciting routines, and then the show is over. Everyone leaves in good spirits and the crowd goes off to the commons, to begin celebrations that will probably last all night long.

Eagle 11'

Hawk moon

Pedro looks at his reflection in the water, unable to believe that his hair is completely gone. He shaved it with a rusty razor and some crushed soaproot, using the water as a mirror. A halo of white skin, where his hair used to be, runs around his sunburned head, making it seem like his head is an archer's target. Instead of his robes, he wears his linen undergarments and an antelope skin shirt that he bought from a man in the main circle. From solemn priest to wild heathen in one day! If only Padre Ulia could see him now! He laughs to picture the expression of disbelief on his face, as he barges in during Sunday dinner at the mission. He can picture Ulia choking on his beef and sputtering helplessly, as bits of beef and saliva fly from his mouth.

Pedro can already feel a difference in how people treat him. Nobody gives him that look anymore, that cold, frozen expression, as if his very presence had turned them into stone. The chief himself laughed when they passed each other in the commons, and his eyes seemed to say "at last you come to your senses".

Pedro takes a deep breath, feeling optimistic. He imagines hanging up his robes for good, marrying Esther, and raising a heathen family. The idea makes him laugh with glee and he does a little dance of joy. He can't wait to sample the life he has always secretly dreamed of. He wants to run to Esther and declare his love to her now, but he is struck with terror that he might screw it up. What if his personality is still too...righteous? He needs to wear this new garb a while first and allow it to saturate deeper into his personality.

Garet walks a little ahead of Esther, keeping a sharp lookout for anyone out walking or boating. He is taking her to an abandoned house very far from town, where they will be safe from prying eyes. He is a little paranoid that Gaela suspects him of infidelity, so he tries to be extra careful not to be seen by anybody. It is good to get away for a few days, while he makes up his mind whether or not to break off the marriage. And why not have a little fun while he is thinking?

Esther seems lost in her own world, tromping behind him on the long walk. That is fine with Garet, because it looks better if she is walking behind him, in case anyone should see them. And he prefers not to have to talk with her too, so he can muse on his worries in peace. After a long walk, they come to a deserted little house, made from bundled sticks and logs. They enter and she looks about the dusty hut doubtfully, while he goes about starting a fire. She sits down on a little bench and nervously plays with her hair, wondering why they have come here.

"Are you hungry now?" he asks.

"A little."

Garet spears some fish filets on a stick and places them a few feet above the fire to slowly cook. He pours each of them a welcome glass of wine he swiped from his uncle, Chief Wendel. After few sips, he begins to stretch his sore muscles, which are tired from practice today. He spent the morning training with the other warriors in the Eagle tribe, practicing sword fighting, bow fighting and hand-to-hand combat. As he stretches, he notices Esther watching him, and he smiles to show her that it is all right with him if she watches.

They talk of inconsequential things, each thinking of something entirely different, as dusk descends upon their little hideaway. When they run out of things to say, they eat in silence and finish the wine. A coyote yips plaintively from somewhere outside and they both peer out the dark window.

"I saw a coyote when I was a little boy and I threw rocks at it," Garet tells her. "When it ran away, I thought I was so brave. I said that I had scared a coyote and everyone smiled and told me how it was a sign I would be a great warrior or hunter. It was years later I realized that they were teasing me. Coyote's don't like to fight, unless it means dinner."

Esther laughs and the mood in the little cabin is lifted. As they make more small talk, she wonders when Garet is going to kiss her. Picking up on her feelings, Garet takes her hand and leads her to the bed. Without wasting any time, he pulls off her dress and stares at her naked body, admiring it. Without her clothes, Esther feels very vulnerable. She still does not trust him, but she finds that this only turns her on all the more. It seems as if being naughty makes her excited. He takes off his clothes too and they lock eyes for a moment. They quickly embrace, rather than have to stare at each other. It is easier to embrace than to look each other in the eye, for they hardly know each other. They have shared little more than a common attraction and some simple small talk.

They begin to kiss and explore each other's bodies. Eventually, he slides his hand down to her flower, and she feels a delicious surge of fear mixed with excitement. She doesn't pull his hand away, but allows him to continue. Next, he puts his lips to her flower, which feels tingly and makes her squirm. She is amazed, because nobody has ever tried so hard to give *her* pleasure before. She lets him do it for a while, just to see what will happen, but there is very little sensation down there. There is only a slight tingle that makes her uncomfortable. She decides that she would rather play with his than have him play with hers, so she pushes him away and fills her mouth with his shaft. And then, for the first time in her life, she gets an erotic sensation down in her flower. It is a brief feeling and she cannot get it to come back again, but she remembers it for a long time afterwards.

They have sex and then he falls asleep. She stays awake, thinking of the mission priests with their whips in hand, desperately trying to drive the sin out of her. They hoped that pain would drive all the desire out of her body. It didn't work though. It is fun being the object of men's desires and indulging in all of the naughty things that she was taught are sinful. If she is going to hell for giving up the teachings of the church, then she'll be in good company. She'll be joining all of these fine people from the Twelve Tribes, and she would rather be with them than with anyone she ever met at the mission.

Staring at Garet's sleeping form, she wishes that he would wake up and talk to her. She wants to know more about him. She lies down and puts her arm around his waist. She briefly touches his manhood and he moans and begins to stir, but doesn't wake. Removing her arm, she turns around and goes to sleep.

Eagle 13'

Beaver moon

Garet arrives back at the village late in the morning, after a day and a half alone with Esther. Before he goes home, he goes to the marsh and kills a couple of fat ducks. Then he scrubs his body with water and soap root to kill the smell of sex. When he feels reasonably sure that he won't be caught, he walks home and peeks his head in the door. Gaela isn't around, so he goes outside, lays the ducks down on a thick block of wood, and begins to clean them. A few moments later, Gaela appears, throws her arms around him, and gives him a big kiss.

"How was your hunting trip? What'd you get?"

"Just this," he says lamely.

"Two ducks?" she asks incredulously. "You go hunting for two days and you bring back two ducks?"

"I wasn't feeling too good. I slept a lot."

"You could have caught those right here and slept in your own bed. Why did you go all the way to the plains?"

"It was just a washout. That's all. I wasn't in the mood to kill anything."

He hopes that's all of the questions. He doesn't like to lie or make up stories, so he avoids it by telling half-truths taken out of context. But Gaela seems suspicious still. He may have to make up a story now, just to placate her. He told her he was going hunting with his friend Kuto, which means he'll have to involve Kuto in the lie.

"Is that why you've been acting so strange lately? You're sick?"

"No, just tired."

"Just tired? You've been acting this way for the past month!"

He frowns and realizes that he is going to have to tell her a little bit of the truth, or else she will continue to pry and come up with something much more damaging.

"I'm just anxious about the coming marriage."

Her stomach tightens into a knot and she loses all of her fire.

"Is it me?" she asks in a small voice that is unlike her.

"No, no," he says anxiously. "It isn't you at all. It is me. I'm just... nervous about things."

"What does that mean?"

"Being married. Having a family. It's a big step in a man's life. I'm not sure I'm ready."

"*Ready*? What does that mean? You are 25 years old, more than old enough to have your life in balance and ready for marriage. Most men your age are already married and raising a family by now."

A low blow. Garet starts to get annoyed and he struggles to explain his feelings without revealing what is really at stake.

"Just something I have to work out."

"What? Like whether you want to play around for the rest of your life? Remain a boy forever and have endless flings with young girls?"

"Not exactly -"

"Well then what?"

He cannot think of a way to say what is on his mind without ruining everything. His is extremely vexed and feels that he is about to explode from the pressure. He is on the spot now and he can't think of anything to say. This is a time for smooth talking, which is something that he can do quite well if he has to. But at this crucial moment, he is drawing a blank. Then he becomes angry that she is putting him on the spot. This isn't helping things. If she is going to scold him like a little boy who has done something wrong, then he is not going to discuss it with her.

"It's nothing," he says lamely. "Just pre-wedding nerves."

"That's all?"

"Yes. I just needed to get away for a few days. I guess I'm just having a little stress at the changes in my life."

Gaela sighs and walks over to Garet. She hugs him tightly and then kisses him tenderly on the lips.

"I am sorry I was hard on you. I just needed to know if you were going to break my heart. We won't talk any more about it."

Her touch reminds Garet why he loves her and wants to marry her. He looks at her, awed by her beauty, and guilt washes over him again. She is so beautiful and he hates to be such a heel. There are many men who think that Garet is marrying the best woman in the Eagle tribe, and if they knew the shenanigans he was pulling, they would say that he was a complete fool and didn't deserve her. And they might be right. She is funny, sweet and beautiful and she can cook great and is skillful with her hands. In many ways, she is the perfect woman, except for a few flaws. But why does he desire other women?

Within a few minutes, they are on the bed and forgetting about the argument and all their worries in the press of flesh.

"This is much better than if I told her the truth," Garet thinks, as he climbs on top of her. "Then she would be crying and I would feel like dung. There is no point in going through that until I am absolutely sure that I won't marry her."

Eagle 14'

Esther sits in front of another plate of fried fish, picking at it unenthusiastically with her fingers. The fish stares at her through deeply fried eyes. It seems that the shelter has a very limited menu, because the fat, bland woman serves the same kind of fish, cooked the same exact way, every single day. Always accompanied by the same hard, chewy disc of cornbread. The only other thing she makes is a stew made from whatever meat or fish she has on hand and boiled acorn mush. Although she wishes for more variety, Esther is not ungrateful. She is happy just to have a full stomach. Especially since she is out of tupas by now and is living entirely on credit that she cannot pay back. Luckily the woman never asks. She just continues to feed her, assuming she'll be paid eventually.

"Esther?"

It is Pedro's voice. Esther turns around slowly, preparing her excuses for leaving if he wants to sit down. But when she sees him, she is struck dumb by his appearance. His funny haircut is gone and he is completely bald. He wears a pair of Spanish linen undergarments with no shirt, instead of his robes. His skin is slightly red around the shoulders, because he has gotten more sun on his bare back than he has in a long time.

"How different you look," she says at last.

"Do you like it?"

"Yes."

"May I join you?"

"Sure," she says, her excuses for leaving forgotten in her amazement. "Have you stopped being a Father - I mean a Spanish medicine man - Pedro?"

"I may hang up my robes for good, but I have not decided for sure. In the meantime, I am sampling the life of a sinner."

He smiles, hoping that she gets the hint, that he is available now for romantic things. But he is too subtle, and she only continues to smile and nod her head enthusiastically. Pedro has no experience at seduction and he doesn't know the right things to say, so when she takes her leave of him, he just stands there with a stupid grin on his face and nods repeatedly.

In the nighttime, Garet visits her. This is the first time he has come to her hut. He comes dressed in a winter cloak of soft fur with a thick hood over his head. When he pulls the hood down, he is dripping sweat, as it is much too hot for such a warm outfit. Pulling off his disguise, he enters the house, grabs Esther in a hasty embrace, and leads her to the bed. He only has a little over an hour before Gaela comes home, so he'll have to skip all the preliminaries and get down to business tonight.

After they are finished, he lies with her impatiently, listening to her ramble and wondering how long he'll have to stay until she won't hold it against him for leaving. Time is running short for him already. She goes on and on about tupas and the fact that she has none. She wants to know when the woman of the shelter will cut her off and stop feeding her, and if there is any work that she can get. She wants to know if the woman makes anything other than fried squimm. After she has repeated herself a few times, Garet knows what she wants. He fishes around in his money bag, pulls out a handful of tupas, and counts them out. He smiles and hands her the shells.

"Here. That should keep you in fried fish for a few more days. How's that?"

"Oh, thank you," she says, with a big smile.

"Well, I really must run now," he says, standing up suddenly. "I'm sorry, but duty calls. I have to get home."

As he leaves, it occurs to her that she has just been bought off like a whore. Is that how she came across? She hopes that he didn't think that she *expected* anything for sex. She is about to run after him and say something, but she holds her tongue. She is too relieved to have the extra tupas and afraid he'll take them back. She would rather Garet have the wrong idea about her and continue to give her tupas, than have the right idea and give her nothing.

Eagle 16'

Jay moon

Esther walks in the noonday sun, loving the feel of hot sun on her back. She has gone to the southern hills for some peace and solitude, where the path winds through endless miles of yellow grass, dotted with green trees and shrubs. She has never seen so much yellow in her life, as she has in this place. And with the hot sun, everything is washed out and burnt, which she likes also.

She comes upon a swarm of dragonflies, hundreds of them, buzzing in a tight circle on the path. She will have to go through them if she wants to continue. She stands before them nervously, not knowing if they are dangerous. She has never heard of a dragonfly biting anyone, but you never can be sure. Finally she holds her breath and crosses into the vortex. She closes her eyes as she passes through the dense swarm. The buzzing is loud and insistent in her ears, and then she is through it and it is serene again.

A short while later, she nearly steps upon a rattlesnake that sits in the middle of the path. It is wound up into a tight circle, with only it's rattle sticking out like a tail. Stunned, she quickly backs away from it. She watches it nervously, but it continues to sit quietly, minding it's own business. It doesn't seem to notice her at all.

She suddenly has a flashback of a day long since forgotten. It was in Santa Cruz, when she was a little girl, in the days before she started talking and had to spend all day indoors. She was walking carelessly over a hill, chasing butterflies, when suddenly she heard a loud, hideous rattling noise. She jumped and stopped dead in her tracks. In front of her was a snake, sticking its neck out and its long forked tongue, searching for the source of the footsteps. She remembers backing away frightened, knowing that the weird creature was dangerous even though she didn't know what it was. And then running in the opposite direction, back to the mission.

Back in the present, Esther walks carefully around the snake, through the prickly, thorny grass, and then she continues on her way. She struggles to dredge up another memory from that long forgotten time when she was a child, but it has already faded back into the deep oceans of her consciousness.

In her third unusual animal sighting, she sees the most frightening animals of all. She spies the cows from the San Jose mission. There are about fifty of them, grazing peacefully, watched by a couple of neophytes and a single soldier on horseback. Esther quickly drops to her knees in the tall grass, lest the soldier see her and come to investigate. Her heart racing, she crawls backwards slowly until she is hidden by the hills. And then she turns around and walks quickly back the way she came.

Chief Wendel sees his nephew, Garet, sitting by the river lost in thought. He walks over to greet him and is rewarded by a grim smile, followed by an expression that makes him look as if he is chewing on river weeds. Wendel joins him and puts his arm around him.

"How goes it, nephew?"

"Not good."

"Tell me."

"I am having second thoughts about marriage. I fear that I marry only to please my family and make the people respect me. Not because I want to."

"You are not happy with Gaela?"

"I am happy with her. But I don't want to marry her. I do not want to be subject to the taboos."

"Ahhhh," says Wendel, nodding his head with a knowing smile.

"I feel guilty, but I think I might break it off."

He looks at his uncle desperately, hoping for a bit of wisdom. Wendel sits with his head down, contemplating his nephew's situation. Finally, he takes a deep breath and stares fixedly at Garet.

"You know I always tell the people that marriage is the right thing to do."

Garet nods tiredly, not in the mood for another lecture. He stares at his feet moodily.

"But there is something I do not say. This thing I will tell you."

He lets this sink in dramatically, but Garet doesn't look over and take the bait. He is too depressed. After waiting a while, Wendel plods on.

"I had the same problem when I was a boy," he says conspiratorially. "I did not want to settle down with one woman, so I played around. Over and over and over again."

Now Garet is hooked. He looks over at his uncle, curious about this new development.

"I finally met a beautiful young girl and I married her because my father told me it was the right thing to do. We were happy for a time. But then I grew restless and began getting the old craving. I started sneaking into other girls' beds. I thought I was being secretive, but she found out. She became jealous, moved away from the village, and never spoke to me again. It was then that I realized that I had loved her."

"That's what I want to avoid," says Garet.

"I was bitter and angry at myself. I spent a few years unhappily trying to find what I had already found and destroyed. I lost some respect with the tribe. It took a long time, and then I finally found it again with Tula. And this time I held on tight."

"If you learn anything from me, learn this lesson. You can go from woman to woman forever, looking for the thing that you already have in front of you. But you will eventually realize that what you were seeking was in front of you the whole time."

"That is true uncle," Garet says. "It is very true."

"Don't lose her, Garet. If you love her, marry her. You will see that one wife is enough for one man."

Garet nods, his mouth frowning so deeply it bends into a rainbow.

"But you now have two wives. Now that your wife is old and has lost her appeal, you have found a young one. So what is the lesson there?"

"My brother died. I am chief. I am just doing my duty, so my brother's family will be well cared for."

"Alat is attractive. That is a pleasant duty."

"This is true," he says with a little smile. "I will not deny it."

"But I have no brother. I have no hope...of pleasant duties in my lifetime."

With a smile, Wendel stands up and leaves Garet to his contemplation.

Eagle 19'

**Eagle moon*

During lunch, Esther overhears an interesting conversation between the glum, fat woman that runs the shelter and Gaela, the fiancé of Garet. Apparently the woman, whose name is Huoka, is an aunt to Gaela, but looking at the two of them, Esther cannot believe it. What she doesn't know is that Huoka is a Zesti who was adopted into the tribe when she married Gaela's uncle and there is no blood relation between the two women.

"I don't know, Huoka," Gaela confesses. "I'm having doubts. Maybe we shouldn't get married tomorrow."

"I thought you were happy wit' him?"

"Not lately. I don't think he really wants to get married."

"I warn you about that boy," Huoka says, shaking her head.

Esther's stomach does flip-flops. Married? Garet and this woman are to be married tomorrow! Her whole world shrinks down to nothing. She strains her ears to hear the rest of the conversation, which is beginning to drop in volume as they reveal secrets. Luckily, Gaela has a loud voice.

"Garet's a good man," Gaela continues. "He's attractive, he's a good hunter and fighter, and he's got connections and wealth. But I can't stop thinking about Neda."

"Who is Neda?"

"You remember that boy that stayed here a few years ago, the one from the Swan tribe? He was so beautiful. The sex, Huoka, oh it was - I couldn't describe it - you have no idea how good it was. I wish you could have sex like that, Huoka, just to see how great sex can be with the right man. But he eventually went back home and he took a woman from his own tribe. I met Garet -"

"I remember him," Huoka says with a frown, glaring at her for just a moment in regards to the subtle insult. "I didn't like that one. He was so lazy. And he had no money. He never pay me what he owe me for his stay here."

"I hear he is not with his woman any more. I wish I had gone up to see him. Just to know.... Maybe I should postpone the wedding and go visit him."

"That is a bad idea," insists Huoka. "He isn't worth the trouble."

"But do you think Garet is any better?"

"Garet could be chief someday."

"Garet?" Gaela laughs bitterly. "He would be a poor chief. He's not very motivated and he is terrible at politics. Why do I choose such unmotivated men?"

"I know one thing he is motivated about," Huoka says, nodding her head sagely.

Gaela looks hard at her.

"What do you mean?"

"He is a hummingbird."

A hummingbird is a man who jumps from woman to woman as a hummingbird flies from flower to flower.

"You haven't heard - he isn't having an affair?"

"No, no," says Huoka, shaking her head. "But I wouldn't be surprised. I know his reputation."

"Oh, he better not," she says, vehemently. "I would just kill him. I would bring down all of the spirits on his head." Her temper flares suddenly, as she thinks about it. "But what stupid woman would break the taboos? Everyone here knows better than to mess with me."

Esther stands up suddenly and walks out of the room. She tries to be subtle, like she was going to get up anyways, but she is so upset that she kicks a bench and knocks it over. Gaela and Huoka stare at her, as if noticing that she was in the room for the first time. Her face red, she quickly rights the bench and escapes into the night. She runs back to her hut, throws herself down onto her bed, and curses Garet over and over again. After calling him every bad thing she can think of, she decides that he is worse than all of them combined.

In the early evening, the moon enters the sign of the Eagle and there is yet another party. Things begin to get wild very quickly. But some are not in such a good mood, including Garet, who is in a miserable mood as he weaves through the crowd, looking for Esther. When he finally finds her, he drinks down his wine before approaching her. She glares at him, making him forget what he was going to say for a moment.

"I can't see you anymore," he says gloomily. "I'm getting married tomorrow."

"I know," she says in a small voice, her anger suddenly fading.

"I'm sorry," he mumbles. "I wasn't sure…I should have told you…. I was going to break it off, but - I just want to apologize and tell you we can't see each other anymore. It's better if I don't spend too much time with you in public. I hope you understand. Sorry."

And that is that. He turns around and walks off.

Esther is in a foul mood when Pedro finds her later. She is sulking on one of the logs outside of main circle and she barely looks up as he sits down. He notices a strong odor of wine on her breath and a dazed look in her eyes. She is very drunk off blackberry wine, which is fine, because so is he.

Pedro has been looking for her all night, ever since somebody told him that the new moon was a time of new beginnings. He has decided to declare his love for Esther tonight. If all goes well, he will ask her to marry him. He understands now that a heathen fling is not enough to hang up his robes for. But for true love, he will give up his vows. He carries some pink wild flowers in his hand, which he hands to her with a large smile when he finds her. She takes them as if they were a handful of weeds and holds them for about two seconds before dropping them on the log.

"Estar, are you well?"

"I'm fine," she says moodily, hoping he'll go away.

"Good. Because I have something important to tell you."

He feels his heart pounding in his chest, suddenly terrified. Once he opens his mouth, he knows it will all come pouring out. He will have no choice but to overwhelm her with his passion. But maybe his nervousness is a good thing. It will only show that he is sincere, because his love is so strong that he is helpless under its spell. And isn't that what love is for?

"I have decided to leave the priesthood for good," he says, taking her hand in his clammy one.

"That's great," she says quietly, trying to be happy for him.

"Because I love you," he says firmly.

She looks at him in surprise and withdraws her hand. He takes a deep breath, and continues.

"I have been thinking about you a lot. Trying to think of a way to tell you how I feel. Maybe I shouldn't tell you all this, but I can't hold it in any longer. Plus, I've had a bit to drink myself. When we met, I felt like I had taken a trip to heaven. You bring out a side of me that is sublime. I feel closer to God when I'm with you. When I see you, I feel so completely happy and at peace that I want to cry. I feel that we are soul mates, and God has put us together to be one on this earth. I love everything about you. Especially your smell."

He takes a deep breath, sucking in her smell, and he sighs with contentment. And now for the grand finale. Summoning all of his courage and praying to God for a miracle, he leans in to kiss her. It seems a lifetime, as he makes the boldest move of his life. And then...she turns her head. He is stunned as his lips are crushed against her cheekbone. He draws away and finds her with a cold expression on her face. He is stunned. It seems the cruelest gesture that a person could do to another. Let them pour their heart out, lay their love out on the table, and then turn their cheek.

"I'm tired," is all she says.

He stares at her miserably, waiting for something else that isn't coming. Finally, he wishes her a good night and leaves her alone. As he walks away, he feels as if he is sinking into the very depths of hell. He doesn't understand it. Isn't this the love he has always dreamed of? Isn't this the new moon? So why did she not fall into his arms? Why was she so cold? Did he do something wrong?

Eagle 20'

The weather is unusually cool and gloomy, which is just fine with Garet because it fits his mood perfectly. It looks as if he is going to go along with the flow of events in his life because he cannot bear to step out of the stream. He feels like he has to get married, even if he doesn't want to. It is expected of him. He is nothing more than a slave to the expectations of his family, friends, and ancestors.

And now he is putting on his best clothes - his finest deer skin shirt and rabbit fur vest - to do this thing that he doesn't want to do. He would rather be going through the Golden Eagle trials of pain than this. He would rather have red hot metal pins pushed through the skin of his body and the webbing of his fingers and toes and smell the burning flesh while he sits there gritting his teeth, than be put through this torture. But he is going to do it anyway. He is going to get married and give up all other women forever. The ultimate sacrifice...even to marry a woman as wonderful as Gaela.

Meanwhile, Pedro sits by himself, gloomily wrapped up in his blanket to ward off the strange morning chill. It just adds to his bad mood, this cold weather in the height of summer. The shelter is closed for meals today, not that he has much of an appetite. He didn't sleep at all last night and his stomach is too knotted up and queasy for him to eat anything.

He was always warned about this kind of love, and now he finds out what it is like for himself. He expected romance, flowers, and blissful kisses. He had this fantasy that Esther would fall into his arms and they would float away on pools of bliss. Instead he feels pains in his stomach and an agonizing feeling that he has ruined it. That look on her face last night turned his blood cold. The way she looked at him, after pouring his heart out, like he was the devil himself. Or is he being a little too sensitive? She was in a rather bad mood when he went up to her. Perhaps he was just careless and picked a bad time. He decides to keep an open mind and pray harder to God to deliver her into his hands.

He thinks of all the things the poets ever said about love. The plays of Shakespeare and the endless dramas of the heart his characters go through. All the things he read in books back home. But now they are not just words on a page. Now they are real.

Esther is not in a much better mood. She sits in a boat, rowing idly back and forth, numb to the world. She is so angry with Garet that she can barely stand it. She is angry with Pedro too, for no good reason really other than he is acting like Kobe. He reminds her of a lovesick boy, only creepier, because he is a missionary. She sighs, trails her hands in the water, and wraps her cloak tighter around her cocooned body.

Even Gaela is not in the best of moods. This is supposed to be the best day of her life, her wedding day, and she keeps thinking of a boy with whom she had an affair three years ago. She cannot stop thinking of Neda and how much she wants to see him. She takes a deep breath and runs a comb through her hair and tries to dispel all of the doubts in her head. She loves Garet. She can't give him up for a fantasy lover. She begins to twine Eagle feathers into her hair and tries to think only of him and the upcoming wedding.

The rest of the village is not so gloomy as these four. In fact, nobody else is even aware that anyone should be unhappy. They are too busy preparing for the day's excitements. A baby has just been born and the news is traveling all over the village. Two weddings are about to begin. There will be a great feast, followed by an afternoon of sports, games, theater, music and dancing. It will be a great day, for those who are not too hung over from last night.

It all goes quickly. As if in a dream, Garet stands before Chief Wendel and the rest of the tribe. He says the words of union, trying to mean them. Gaela says the words next, her eyes blissfully pooling with tears. Wendel finishes it off with a long speech. Garet maintains a stoic expression throughout the speech, trying not to dwell on the doubts he still feels. He tries to notice only how beautiful she looks with her hair twined with eagle feathers. He might as well enjoy the wedding, since he is going through with it. Wendel finally stops talking, Garet kisses Gaela, and they go off to their home to consummate the marriage. Everyone cheers and then the next couple steps up to the platform.

Lunch is a great feast. The tribe has really gone all out for this one. Antelope steak, roasted fish, duck stew, acorn bread, corn cakes, and a drink made from fresh blackberries. People eat until they can't move, and then they lie around chatting, digesting and waiting for the call to go to the theater. Esther leaves her bad mood in the river and tries to enjoy the rest of the day. Neither Pedro nor Garet are present at lunch, which makes things easier.

Soon everyone gathers in the assembly hall, as girls walk around pouring wine for everyone seated. When everyone is served, Wendel walks out before the tribe and raises his arms for silence.

"My friends, the Eagle tribe has had another great year. I am grateful for being the chief to such a wonderful tribe. Our hunters are powerful and they have hunted many bear, antelope, deer, and anything else that has offered itself. The Golden Eagles continue to patrol the lands, making sure that the Twelve Tribes are safe from our new neighbors, the Spanish, and any hostile tribes that seek to disrupt our way of life. The fishermen have had a great bounty from the great river and from the sea. Bushes are loaded with blackberries, which will make good wine. Two children were born on this new moon, a boy and a girl. The astrologers tell me that Jupiter has returned to the sign of the Owl just in time to give them a trine of sun, moon, and Jupiter. They will be an asset to the tribe.

"I have spoken to the priest from the nearby mission, whose slaves and soldiers are bringing those ugly horned beasts they call 'cows' near to our land. Many of you have seen them. They eat all the grass and scare away the game. They stand there and stare at you stupidly and don't run away like any sensible animal should. He has promised to keep these strange creatures away from our village."

Wendel talks for long time. He is an interesting talker. He praises his own deeds for the year and then praises the deeds of everyone who has benefited the tribe. Then he quickly moves on to more interesting things. He begins to tell horror stories about grisly and disgusting things that have happened to other people in the tribe that he finds particularly funny. He seems to take great delight in giving out as many disgusting details as possible. He is merciless and lets no one off the hook who has done something they might like to hide. Esther has never heard a chief give a speech such as this. The crowd loves it, laughing and hooting at their friends who have done the bizarre things that he speaks of. Two or three people storm out of the assembly house in embarrassment, hearing their secret stories told out loud to the whole tribe. Many cannot imagine how it was that Wendel heard these stories in the first place. He must have had some very effective spies this year.

After he has finished, the Bald Eagle troop, greatest of all Eagle performers, come out for the main event. Today, they are performing the legend of chief Gyle, one of the great chiefs of the Eagle tribe. In keeping with the mood that Wendel has set, they roast this great chief and tell all of his embarrassing secrets along with his great glories. It is a long, complicated piece, with many costume changes, set changes, dances and music. When they are finally finished, the applause and cheers can be heard echoing throughout the dry hills.

For those with enough energy, the night is just beginning. Those who want a raging party stay in the assembly hall, where drummers and musicians play all night long. But some opt for a quiet evening in front of fires, for as Wendel wisely said near the end of his speech, the Eagle new moon is not just about mayhem, but about living life with an open heart.

Eagle 26'

Wolf moon

Esther sits in her hut, idly running a comb through her hair. All the while, she thinks of Garet, whom she cannot get out of her head. She combs harder, trying to think of something else and knowing that she will fail. She tries to remember that she hates him, but she cannot summon up that emotion today. Finally, she puts the comb down and walks down to the commons, hoping to spy him from a distance without having to talk to him. He isn't hard to find. He sits by himself, mindlessly sharpening arrow points. She watches him for a while, fighting the urge to go up to him. Eventually, he sees her and his eyes widen. He puts down his arrows and casually walks over to her, as if he is just taking a stroll.

"I was wondering if you had left."

"No," she says, blushing slightly from the look in his eyes.

"Mmm hmm," he says, smiling slightly.

He is acting vague, as if to hide any ulterior motives. They make a bit of small talk about the hot weather and how good it feels to be in the shade. And then he gets serious for a moment.

"I apologize for the way I broke our affair off. I was under a lot of stress."

"I was really mad at you. You should have told me the truth."

"I'm sorry. I was afraid you wouldn't want to get involved with me if you knew I was getting married."

He looks around nervously, to see if anyone is watching him.

"Do you want to take a walk?"

She shrugs indifferently, although she is far from that. He takes her down a rarely trodden path through an oak grove and they talk of inconsequential things. The path passes near the shelter and Esther runs inside her hut to drink some water from her skin. Garet scans the area to make sure that nobody is looking and then he quickly ducks into the hut with her.

As she looks at him standing in her hut, she feels weak in the knees. She desperately wants to kiss him and she knows that Garet can see right through her. He stares at her, and his questioning look seems to ask if she wants to make love. Apparently her answer is yes, for he moves closer. Before she knows it, he is kissing her.

He removes her clothing and throws them in a pile on the floor. She pulls off his clothes in return. How she has missed this! How could she ever have believed that marriage would change him? He is still her dirty, secret pleasure - her married man now - and she likes it. She does not even think once of his wife. Just as their naked bodies embrace, the door swings open and they are bathed in daylight.

"Unhand her, you fiend!"

The two of them nearly jump out of their skins with surprise. Garet looks about the room for a weapon, fearing an attack. He is about to charge the man, but Esther recognizes the intruder. She puts her hand on Garet's arm to calm him down, while searching for a blanket to cover her nakedness up.

"Get out of here," she says in a very irritated voice, when she is no longer exposed.

Pedro feels all sorts of emotions tumbling though his head. Anger, jealousy, blind rage, righteousness, and sadness all compete for a foothold. Self pity takes the first victory, for the simple reason that Esther covered herself with a blanket so he will not see her naked. For this man, she will show every inch of her beautiful body. For poor Pedro, she covers up out of embarrassment. Pedro nods silently, turns around, and walks back out into the daylight.

He shakes his head, unable to believe his stupidity. When he stormed into her hut, he actually believed that a heathen was raping her. He saw the man enter and then heard strange noises. Acting instinctively, he didn't stop to consider that she was merely having some kind of affair. He walks to his own room in a daze. When he gets there, he is overcome with rage. He longs to run back there and pummel the man that is with her, but it is not in his nature to do that. So he pummels the door instead. He kicks his door in and slams it repeatedly against its rope hinges, until the frayed strands break and the door swings crazily to the side. He twists it and kicks it, until it crashes all the way to the floor. Then he stomps on the door with his sandals, just to make his point clear. Finally, when the door is no longer a satisfying target of his rage, he grabs a branch off the ground and beats himself furiously with it. He brings it down with a snap upon his legs, barely feeling the pain in his madness.

"What violence! Under the heavens, what do you do?"

It is the lady of the shelter, the fat, homely woman with the sour face. Pedro turns scarlet red, drops the branch, and stares at her guiltily, knowing that he made a mess of her hut. He wonders what he could possibly say to regain his dignity and then it occurs to him that he has none. His face is sweaty and sullen as he sits down and tries to keep his hands from shaking.

"What is wrong with you?" she asks directly.

"My love sits in yonder hut," he says in a whisper. "In the arms of another man."

"And that's why you tearing up me alap?" she exclaims indignantly.

"Yes. And the worst part is...she was with a man whom I just saw with my own eyes get married last week. He said his vows under the eyes of God and then he came and seduced my own love."

"Tall man?" she asks, forgetting about her alap in her great surprise. "Short curled hair?"

"That's him."

"Garet!" she exclaims. "In which alap did you see Garet?"

"Six."

"I knew he was a weasel," she hisses.

"He's a rat," agrees Pedro. "An immoral heathen! A no good rake!"

"Don't touch that door again!" she shouts. "Don't touch nothing!"

She turns around and waddles quickly away, marching resolutely toward the village commons. She moves faster than Pedro would have thought possible for someone so fat. Pedro has a sudden feeling that Garet is about to get his due and the idea is very, very pleasant to him.

Garet lies in bed with Esther, spent but not happy. She seems satisfied, curled up next to him, but his own mind is racing with worry. What is he doing? He has been married for one week and he has already broken his vows. Worst of all, he did it in the shelter, a very public place. They have already been seen by that strange Spanish man. Is he crazy? Does he want to get caught? What would Gaela do if she found out?

"I must leave," he says quickly, sitting up. "I'm sorry. I - I have to go now."

Esther nods, disappointed, but not terribly surprised. She rolls over and doesn't look at him as he stands up and quickly dresses. He peeks through the crack in the door, praying there is nobody about, and then he walks quickly and decisively away from the hut and ducks into some trees. He breathes a sigh of relief as he makes a wide loop around the village and heads towards an unused dock to take a swim and clean the smell of sex off of his body.

While he bathes, he watches an eagle soaring overhead. Suddenly it dives upon a hawk, stealing something from its talons. The hawk doesn't give chase, but lets the larger bird go. After its decisive victory, the eagle perches proudly on a treetop, tearing into a piece of red fleshy meat. Garet watches it for a while, awed by its power and beauty. The eagle, largest and strongest of all birds of prey, and totem of his tribe. Seeing an eagle is always a good omen.

He has not seen an eagle for some time. It reminds him of what is important in life. The Golden Eagles are important, as are the codes of the warrior and the thrill of the hunt. He cannot focus on all that, if he is so obsessed with this desperate need for new conquests. Fear of being caught and sneaking around are not the eagle's way. An eagle is proud and it does not creep in the shadows. It lives out in the open, according to its own rules.

Suddenly things are clear. He has jeopardized his standing in the Golden Eagles, his marriage, and his future with his tribe, over some strange girl. A girl who is not even as beautiful as his wife, just because he wants a little taste of new flesh. He makes a decision right then and there. He is going to be a faithful husband from now on. He makes a promise to himself that he will lay off all other women...if not forever, at least for a long time. Garet stands up and walks home quickly, thinking that he wants to make love to his wife right now to seal the bargain.

Late in the night, Esther is awakened from a sound sleep as her door nearly flies off its hinges. She struggles to wake up and adrenaline rushes through her body to help her. A woman stands over her, her chest heaving with anger. Esther barely has time to register that it is Gaela, the wife of Garet, and she has a large bone - the femur of a horse or a cow - gripped tightly in her hand.

"Where is he?" Gaela screams.

"I don't know," Esther gasps, rising to her shaky feet, and backing away from the grim, furious woman. "Where is who?"

"Dare lie to me?" the woman hisses. "Slut! Man stealer! Whore! I'll teach you to steal husbands!"

Gaela advances on her, the bone held threateningly in her hand.

"Where is my ass of a husband?"

"I don't know."

"Do you know what happens to man stealers in this village?" Gaela hisses. "They disappear into the river...forever."

Gaela swings the bone at Esther threateningly. Esther suddenly realizes that Gaela is serious and actually intends harm. Reacting quickly, she grabs the only weapon she can find. She grabs a little cast iron pot she borrowed from the shelter and brandishes it like a weapon. Gaela snorts in derision and swings the bone again. Esther holds the pot like a shield and feels her arm go numb as the pot deflects the blow with a loud clang.

"Why do you blame me?" Esther gasps, struggling to breathe. "Go kill him!"

"Don't you know the taboos, stupid girl? If a woman sleeps with a married man, then the slut may be killed by the hand of the wronged wife. I have every right to kill you. I'll smash your skull, whore!"

She lifts the bone again, prepared to do as she says. Desperately, Esther throws the pot at her exposed face. It hits her in the nose, making her drop the bone and put her hands to her nose. Quickly, Esther runs past her and out the door. Gaela screams with rage, grabs the bone, and runs out of the hut, waving her femur like a madwoman.

Gaela gives chase, still screaming like a banshee, and Esther runs as fast as she can to escape her. But Gaela is faster and quickly gains on her, so Esther desperately leaps into the marsh. She splashes through the waist high water, half swimming and half running. Gaela splashes behind her, screaming about dead whores and taboos.

After a desperate chase, they end up at the waters edge. Just as Gaela comes within arms reach of Esther, Esther throws herself into the river delta and swims out into deep water. Gaela tries to swim with the bone in her hand, but it is difficult. She finally tosses the bone away and begins to stroke. She is a fast swimmer and starts to gain on her. Esther realizes that she has put herself in even greater danger by going into the water. Gaela can easily drown her out here and float the body out to sea. No one will ever know.

In a panic, Esther dives down and begins to swim underwater. She swims as long as she can stand it, trying to stay as deep as possible so she will be invisible. When she pops to the surface, she fights the urge to gasp and catches her breath as quietly as possible. Then she drifts with the current, trying to be totally silent and still. It is too dark for Gaela to see her, and she screams ineffectually for Esther to show herself. Gaela swims in circles, trying to find her, as Esther floats slowly away with the current. Soon she is far away, and she swims quietly and slowly to shore. There she collapses, shaking so badly that she cannot walk for some time.

Eagle 27'

Esther wakes up underneath green leaves and blinks her eyes in defense against the bright morning. Her burden basket lies beside her. Last night, she cleared out everything from her hut and hid out in this grove of oaks on the far edge of the village. She slept late, judging by the heat of the day, probably to avoid having to think about last night. Now she is forced to deal with an uncertain future. She cannot stay in that hut again or that crazy woman might return. It is just as well, because she is out of money and can't afford to pay the fat woman for last week's worth of meals anyway. Better to just disappear and start over. She has burned another bridge and now she is being driven out of yet another village.

She takes a walk to the village commons, with a vague idea to find Garet and ask him for help. She wanders around the fringes of the commons for a long time, being careful not to be seen. Garet is nowhere about, so she returns to her makeshift camp to wait. She finally finds him a few hours later, skulking around the shelter, looking for her. He waves desperately to her when he sees her and beckons her to join him behind some trees for a private conversation. He seems very agitated and jumpy, as if he might leap out of his skin any moment.

"You need to leave here," he says, as soon as they are out of sight. "Gaela found out about our affair. She is furious and she threatened to take it out on you -"

"She tried to kill me last night!" Esther shouts angrily. "She tried to club me with a giant bone, and then she tried to drown me!"

His eyes bug out. He frowns and shakes his head angrily. He opens his mouth to say something, but he is at a loss for words. He just gestures frantically and keeps shaking his head as if trying to shake the guilt out of it.

"I can't believe it!"

"She said that she has the right to kill me because of some taboo."

"I'm such a fool. I'm so sorry, Esther. I had no idea...nobody believes in that taboo anymore. It has been years since any woman has done this." He laughs bitterly. "You better leave the village. Gaela is pretty good with a bow."

"Can you talk to her?"

"She won't talk to me. She came to the house this morning, packed a few baskets with her things, and left. I don't know what to do. I swore this was the last time. I apologized. But she's so angry. I think she'll forgive me, but -"

"I need money," Esther interrupts. "If I'm going to leave here, I must buy supplies."

She glares at him impatiently, not wanting to hear his problems. She has her own and they are partly his fault. She is supremely annoyed with him now, and just wants to get away with whatever she can get from him.

He nods guiltily, fishes into his money bag, and comes up with five tupas.

"It's all I have with me. This should buy you enough supplies to get to another village -"

She takes the tupas from him, cutting his thoughts off again. Then without another word, she turns away from him and strides off furiously.

"Goodbye Esther. I'm very sorry."

Garet walks off, feeling bad for Esther. The poor girl had no idea what she was getting into when she got involved with him. And then he thinks of Gaela, who will club a girl over the head to keep Garet for herself. What fire! She really loves him! Garet cannot believe how much she loves him.

In a sudden panic, he breaks into a run, knowing that he has to do whatever it takes to win her back. Now that he knows what passion she has within her, he is more attracted to her than ever. *She would kill for me.* He runs down the river road, past the village commons. As he runs past the crowded commons, he notices how the people stare and snicker at him as he passes. Someone shouts out a joke at his expense, which busts everyone up laughing. Many of the older women shake their heads in disappointment. Garet knows that he'll have to endure this ridicule for months. It is annoying, but he'll deal with it later. First, he has to get her back again. That will show the village that he's no fool. He'll have to go through hell first and really show her that he's learned his lesson, but it will be exciting to be that close to such white, hot fire. Such blind passion...just for him. And just think of the sex when she finally forgives him.

Eagle 28'

Owl moon

Early in the morning, Esther knocks on Pedro's door. Desperation has led her to this. She has no idea if Pedro hates her and she wouldn't blame him if he did. But she hopes that he has enough feelings left for her to consider her offer. He opens the door, very surprised to see her. His face is puffy and bloated and she can smell wine on his breath. He stares at her through slits for eyes, but he doesn't say anything.

"Hello," she says in a small voice. "I know you probably hate me, but in case you don't, I thought I could ask you something."

He nods slightly, giving her permission to continue.

"I want to know if you want to come with me to another village. I'm going to visit the Raccoon tribe. I hear they are close. I just don't want to go by myself."

She doesn't tell him the whole truth, of course. She has come to him because she wants a ride on his horse. She is not in the mood for another epic walk like the last one. After she finishes talking, she puts on her bravest smile and waits for him to refuse her.
He makes her wait a long time. Pride tells him to turn his back on her, but hope tells him to go with her, just in case she has softened her heart to him. He can feel the battle between them. In the end, hope wins, for it has always been stronger for him than pride.

"I will go," he says at last.

She laughs and gives him a grateful hug. His body is tense, edgy and awkward as he hugs her back.

"Will you be ready by this afternoon?"

By the time he tracks down his horse, which has been wandering in the nearby hills, it is late afternoon. He gave the animal to a boy who offered to care for it in exchange for hauling a heavy load, but instead of stabling it, the boy just let it go. It wandered into the hills, following the scent of the tribe's horses grazing out upon the slopes. He curses the boy as he chases down his mare, which has apparently gotten ideas from these free horses. He orders the horse back into service, but the horse likes its new life, and seems unwilling to go back to the old one. When they finally reach an understanding, horse and rider return to the shelter.

Esther has been sitting impatiently in his hut, waiting for his return. She peeks out of the door every five minutes, sure that Gaela is waiting right outside with a bow and arrows in her hand. Finally, she hears him outside and she runs out with her basket in her hands.

His horse is a small brown one, with the demeanor of a typical Spanish horse, quiet and subservient. Spanish horses are quite different from the horses of the Twelve Tribes, which are not trained quite so diligently. Pedro ties down their things with straps on the leather saddle and then summons Esther, who has gone back to hiding in the hut. She runs out and he helps her onto the horse, then he climbs on and off they go.

As they ride north, Pedro realizes that he is truly leaving it all behind now. Once he crosses this delta, he will be beyond the reach of the Spanish empire. Beyond the Camino Real, the golden road of the missions, he will be swept up into primitive California. Drawn into the strange world of this girl and the mysterious longings of his heart for the first time. Now he feels as if he is really in the New World now, and his old life seems just a dream.

They arrive at the dock, and she pays a tupa to the raft man, who has a great raft that he poles back and forth across the river. Pedro coaxes the unwilling horse onto the large, but shaky raft, and off they go at a snail's pace. He holds the frightened horse, so it won't be afraid, and thinks that he is like the shepherd who leads his flock across the river Jordan. He stares at the girl next to him, wondering what she is thinking, but her expression is inscrutable. Just as she is.

Raccoon Tribe

Eagle 29'

The path winds through a valley that has seen too much sun. The grass is brittle, yellow, and dead, and heat rises off the ground in waves. Even the large oak trees cannot protect them from the brutal, oppressive oven they have entered. Luckily the path follows a river, so they have plenty of water to cool off with. They are now camped by a stagnant pool, buzzing with flies and insects, hiding until late afternoon when the air cools down to a comfortable traveling temperature.

Esther takes a walk down to the river to wash the sweat off her body. As she nears the pool, she is startled by a loud flapping noise. Out of the corner of her eye, she spies the largest bird she has ever seen, which flaps quickly out of sight behind a large bush. She cannot believe that such a large bird exists, or imagine what kind of bird it might be. She tries to get a better look at it, but her way is barred, so she takes a satisfying plunge into the cool water instead. She dries herself in the sun, and revels in the fragrant, licorice smell that permeates the whole area.

Pedro waits for her by the grazing horse. He sits quietly, staring out across the land, lost in thought. Esther joins him, thinking about how nice it is to travel with somebody else. It alleviates the uncomfortable, nervous feeling she gets when she travels by herself. That feeling that something horrible could happen, and there would be nobody else to share in her misery.

At last the heat becomes tolerable, and they saddle up Quixote and continue up the path. The trail traverses under endless oaks and then returns into open air again. It passes near a Zesti village, and they see women carrying baskets on their heads and working busily near the river. The women stare suspiciously at them and someone shouts something in a strange language. Soon, many people come out to stare at them, men, women, and children with nothing better to do than watch them pass.

"Why do they stare so? Is this not a well traveled road?" asks Pedro.

"It looks that way."

"Perhaps they expect some sort of trade or offering?"

Esther shrugs, not caring what they expect, as long as the people leave them alone. She is not used to seeing people on the paths that she walks. Up until now, she has walked through land that has long been cleared by the Spanish. But they are entering *unconverted* land now.

Pedro waves and speaks a few words from local languages he knows, but nobody responds. The people only watch them silently until they are gone. Then Esther remembers hearing something about this path at the Eagle tribe. She heard that it is forbidden to veer from the path without invitation. The path belongs to the Twelve Tribes by mutual agreement with the Zesti, but the rest of the land does not. While on the path, they are under the protection of the Twelve Tribes, but if they leave the path without permission, they will be open to any sort of abuse the Zesti are in the mood for. And such things have happened.

They leave the boundaries of this village and enter another soon after. This village seems a bit friendlier, and some of the people even smile as they ride past. Then a man runs up to talk to them. He stops at the edge of the path, and does not trod upon it until they invite him closer. Using sign language, he asks them if they have any tobacco. He knows the Spanish word for "tobacco", although it is pronounced very badly. Then he picks up a twig and pantomimes smoking a long pipe.

Pedro laughs, digs into his pouch, and hands the man a small chunk of curly tobacco. The man takes it joyfully and waves at them to stay put, then he disappears for about ten minutes. He returns shortly after with some freshly baked seed cakes and bids them sit down on a log. He sits with them and hands out seed cakes. He even shows them a good grazing spot for Quixote, who is only too happy to try it out.

A few moments later, another man approaches. This man also seems to know the word for 'tobacco' in Spanish. Good-natured Pedro hands him another piece, and this man also leaves, and returns with some fresh fish he caught. He takes a little piece of wood in which he holds smoldering ashes, makes a little fire right there, and cooks fish for them. Then, the men pull out long, crude pipes, light them, and pass them around. They seem surprised when Esther smokes also, and the men laugh and point at her and talk to each other in their language.

When a third man appears and asks for tobacco, Pedro begins to worry that he will run out. He hands the man a smaller piece, just enough for two fills. The man takes it gratefully and returns with a basket of some rather sour berries to feed them. The three men seem to understand that Pedro is being stretched rather tight in his tobacco pouch, so they share what they have with the next one that comes forth looking for smoke. The growing group of locals spends the next hour watching them curiously, and commenting on their strange appearance and clothes.

Finally Esther and Pedro beg the forgiveness of the men, remount Quixote, and ride off. The men all wave at them and shout strange things until they are long down the trail. They have lost some precious daylight, but their bellies are full, and they have leftover berries and seed cakes for the morning too.

"It is strange how different they treat me," muses Pedro. "How much more comfortable they act, when I dress like this and travel with you. I have grown used to frightened stares when I wear my robes and ride with soldiers for escort."

It is a fact that seems painfully obvious to Esther, but she doesn't say anything. She merely agrees that it must be nice.

"It is a great deal nicer than getting shot at with arrows."

Esther smiles, liking the idea of priests getting shot at with arrows. She is glad she is behind him, so he cannot see her smile.

"Is that what happens when you approach villages?"

"Not often. But one time, I went to administer last rites to a group of sick Indians, and we were betrayed by one of our own party. The fog was very thick that day. He led us to the wrong village - a hostile one. It didn't go well for us. I lost a good friend in the attack and an arrow went through my cheek. Nothing more painful than an arrow in the cheek, trust me on that."

"I was wondering about that scar. Does it still hurt?"

"Yes. But the scars that hurt the most are on the inside."

He doesn't explain this cryptic comment, but it is enough to make Esther regret her mirth at his misfortunes.

"Sounds awful," she says, making a silent apology.

"It was. Of course, it went worse for them when we responded with a retaliation."

Esther takes her silent apology back.

The journey is stopped short for the day when Pedro suddenly seizes up, moans dramatically and slumps in the saddle. He nearly falls off the horse, and it is all Esther can do to stay seated. She groans, and struggles to hold him up.

"Pedro?" she shouts. "What's wrong?"

She grabs the reins out of his cold, clammy hand and stops the horse. With much effort, she manages to push him forward and then she jumps to the ground. He lies slumped on top of the horse, mumbling softly to himself. After a long, anxious wait, he is coherent enough to be helped to the ground. He sits slumped against a tree for a good hour, moaning slightly from the pain. Esther cannot get any explanation from him, other than some fragmented mumbling about an illness.

They camp for the night under an oak tree. The ground is covered in acorns, which may be good to eat but are uncomfortable to sleep on. Esther keeps discovering new ones underneath her blanket, and she has to remove them to get more comfortable. When Pedro feels well enough to move, he sets up his blankets a respectful distance from hers. He longs to curl up next to her, but he has no idea how to ask her for the privilege of her company. He lies there for a long time, wondering what to say. Finally, he decides that he will go mad if he does not try, so he takes a deep breath and screws up his courage.

"May I sleep next you?" he asks, with baited breath. "My heart is sore at the great distance between us."

"No," she says in a cold voice.

He sighs, and rolls over. He does not know what he is doing wrong, but the way she looks at him sometimes makes his flesh crawl. She can be very friendly, and then suddenly she looks at him as if he is a monster. He screws his own eyes up tightly, and prays to God to show him the way to her heart. He is resolved to get there, no matter how rugged and long the path is. Even though he needs medical attention for his illness, which almost pitched him off his horse today, he will not return to Mexico and risk losing her. He'll follow her to the ends of the earth if she wants him to.

Raccoon 0'

Elk moon

The next morning, they rise very early and eat a breakfast of sour berries, seed cakes, and cold water. Esther is so stiff, she has to walk for a good hour before climbing back onto the horse. After that, they make good time. They pass two more villages and some open ground, and then the path goes right to the water's edge. The timing is perfect, as it is unbearably hot out and they cannot possibly go any further until late afternoon. They drink and swim, and Esther naps underneath a tree. Pedro has never been a good day sleeper, unless he has enough wine, so he pulls out his last bottle of spirits and props himself against a tree. His face falls as he sees that he is down to the dregs already. A few sips left, and he'll be dry. He takes a swig and says a prayer that he'll be able to buy some in Raccoon village.

After an afternoon siesta, they continue on. Eventually, they come upon a little wooden statue of a raccoon sitting in a tree and Esther assumes that they have arrived. She is surprised to be here already, because she had mentally prepared herself for another epic journey like the last one. She is almost disappointed to be here so soon, because she enjoyed the trip more than she ever expected to. Not just because she didn't have to walk the entire way by herself. Pedro actually makes a nice traveling companion, when he isn't acting like a lovesick boy.

Soon, they begin to see people, busily engaged in a variety of projects. Pedro wants to go directly to the shelter, so they head that way. On the way, they pass the commons, which is quite busy, and they cannot resist going there first. The commons is very large, with many permanent structures. These houses are crafted with finely cut boards and much attention to perfection, which reminds Esther of the well-made buildings of the Beaver tribe. The circle has a busy charm to it, as many people walk to and fro, buying and selling goods at the many little carts and tables that stand in orderly lines.

They get off the horse, and Pedro ties him to a tree with a long rope. They agree to meet back at the horse after a brief exploration, and then they go their separate ways. Pedro goes to look for a bottle of wine, and Esther walks over to the fruit and vegetable sellers. Raccoon farmers converge here on designated days to sell and trade the fruits of the land. Esther is amazed by the variety of fruits, vegetables, and herbs. The farmers display blackberries, logan berries, raspberries, prickly pears, grapes, corn, potatoes, melons, peas, beans and olives. Gatherers sell wild plants they have picked. Wild lettuce, camus bulbs, mushrooms, dandelion greens, nettles, wild onions and strange roots of every variety. And there are many medicinal herb traders, with bundles and bundles of dried herbs. All of it looks so fresh and ripe, as if they burst off the tree or vine just this minute.

There are many traders from all the nearby villages. The Eagle tribe, Swan tribe, and Wolf tribe all come here to trade or buy during earth moons. There are even some Owl traders, come a long way for this great market. There are many carts already loaded up with multicolored piles of vegetables and plants. Others trade furs, tools, arrows, grinding stones and any number of things. Esther watches the busy trading with fascination. There is no haggling here, as one doesn't want to appear too greedy. A blanket is laid out, and whatever someone wants to trade is laid on it. Goods, foods, or tupas - whatever it is it goes on the blanket – and then the other person puts whatever he is willing to trade on the blanket. If the terms are satisfactory, then an exchange is made. If one person is not satisfied, the other has the choice to make it right. If terms are still not met after several tries, then the blanket is cleared and the haggling is over.

Esther is quite hungry, but she doesn't want to spend one of her precious tupas, and she has nothing else to place on the blanket. But there is so much food here, might somebody spare a piece of something? She walks around for a while, too shy to ask anybody, and then she spies a sprig of grapes on the ground that doesn't look too dirty. She picks it up, brushes it off tenderly, and quickly devours it.

"Woman, over here."

The man selling the grapes waves her over.

"Why not try some clean fruit? That was a bit unsanitary, don't you think? Didn't even wash it."

"I don't have anything to trade. I just got into town today."

"Beggars can't be choosers, eh? Well, I won't stand for it. Take a bunch. I've got plenty."

"Are you sure?"

"I've got more fruit than I can handle. And business is slow today. Go on. Take some. How about some fresh berries?"

She takes some grapes in her dirty hand, and then the farmer hands her a mess of blackberries on a piece of bark.

"Until you get your feet on the ground."

"Thank you very much."

"Gilda, can you spare a potato?" he shouts to a woman selling potatoes.

"Tell her to come over here!" Gilda shouts back at him.

Esther walks toward Gilda, who plucks a steaming potato from a small fire with two sticks. She hands it to Esther, who has to place it on a pile of leaves, as it is too hot to touch. Gilda also hands her a freshly baked seed cake that she traded for some potatoes. Esther keeps on saying thank you, thank you, thank you, as each new gift is laid upon her. She is amazed at the generosity of these people. And then, bursting with food, she goes over to a bench and munches and crunches on all the fresh, ripe foods.

Pedro soon appears with a glum look on his face, because he didn't find what he was looking for. Esther gives him some berries and grapes she saved for him, and he thanks her and makes short work of them.

"Where there's grapes, there's wine," he states matter-of-factly, shoving a handful into his mouth. "There's got to be something fermented around here somewhere."

It seems a good idea to get to the shelter soon or they might find it full, so they fetch Quixote and follow a stranger's directions. Now that she is well fed, Esther is happy to sleep outside, but Pedro seems anxious for a shelter. She accompanies him, hoping that he'll pay for it since it is his idea to go there.

"I have no more of your shell money," he complains as they walk. "I hope they will exchange some silver for shell money. A few pieces of silver and a single doubloon are all I have."

"How much shell money would they give you for a piece of silver?"

"The Eagle chief gave me a handful of shells for a piece of silver. Robbed me blind, if you want the truth of it, but I had no other choice."

They find the shelter easily, which consists of several large buildings in a rough semicircle. Esther points to a sign that says "Raccoon Shelter", and struggles to read the words. Pedro squints at the sign himself and shakes his head.

"They speak Spanish, but they do they not use Spanish letters," Pedro says, as he unloads the horse. "Why do they torture my language like that?"

Ignoring him, Esther goes in search of a keeper of the shelter. She finally finds a woman who is busy digging weeds out of a little herb garden. The woman stands as Esther approaches, a long knife in her hand covered with dirt. She fixes a scarf wrapped around her head that threatens to fall into her eyes and smiles pleasantly.

"I've been waiting for you. Follow me?"

She leads Esther over to small, dark shed that is stuffed with many baskets containing bundles of dried herbs. The woman quickly scans the baskets. There is a very strong odor of pungent herbs wafting out of the shed. Esther tries to see into the gloomy shed to see what the woman wants her to see.

"Echinacea, eucalyptus, jojoba, sage, nettles...." She stops and laughs. "Why don't you tell me what you need and I'll see if I have it."

"I am looking for a place to sleep," Esther says with a smile. "Not herbs."

"Well, why didn't you say so? I thought you were one of those visiting Wolf healers. "

She laughs pleasantly as they walk back to the garden. The woman wipes the blade of her knife and places it carefully back in its sheaf, and then she washes her hands in a basket of water and beckons Esther to follow her.

"My name is Jalia. I'm one of the hosts of this shelter. Anything I can do to make your stay here as comfortable as possible, you just let me know. We serve three meals a day in the lodge, and there is always tea there. This time of the year, there is always extra fruit also. Today is the first day of the Raccoon month, so there is no dinner tonight. But there will be a big feast at sundown, held in Hall of the Black Mask. You are free to attend, of course - as our guest."

She leads Esther to a small log house that is entered through an extremely small and narrow door. Inside are four neat beds and a fire pit in the middle. Two of the four beds have things piled on top of them. Esther frowns. She does not want to share her space with others. She rather likes having a private hut, as she did in the Eagle tribe and the Bear tribe. Even her barn at Tork and Tara's was more private than this. Her only roommate was a horse.

"Are there any private huts?

"There are. But they are for traders who have a lot of supplies and that usually requires an extra donation. Is that you?"

"No," she says, disappointed.

"Well, I think you will enjoy your stay here. We run a tight ship, as the expression goes, so you should have no problems with your hutmates. In that closet are a broom and rags and such. We ask that you please clean up any messes you make, so there will be no problems between hutmates. And no loud noises after dark please. People are usually very considerate here."

"And how much do you charge?"

"This time of the year we charge one tupa per day for shelter and meals. In the winter and spring it is more, of course."

"Oh, that's a nice price!"

"During the harvest time, we have so much extra food, that it is quite easy to feed everybody. We don't take advantage of our friends and kinsmen."

They walk outside, and Esther calls Pedro over. He walks slowly over, wiping at his pale, sweaty face with a handkerchief. He seems to be having another spell like the one he had yesterday. Collapsing against the wall, he struggles to catch his breath.

"This is Pedro," Esther says. "He's traveling with me."

"Hello," Pedro gasps.

"You don't look well," says Jalia, in a worried voice. "Are you feeling sick?"

"I feel dizzy."

"Let me get you some water. Or would you prefer tea? I think there is something suitable in the main lodge."

"Tea would be nice. Thank you."

She hurries off, and Pedro closes his eyes and takes ragged breaths as he struggles to remain conscious. A moment later, Jalia returns with a bowl full of warm tea. As Pedro gulps it down, Jalia feels his forehead and his hands.

"You may be overheated. A nice dip in the river would be just the thing. I'll make you a special tea too. I have just the thing growing in my garden."

"That's very nice of you. But it is not the heat. I have had this same problem for months. A fistula, it is called. It comes and it goes, like an unwanted visitor. I think the traveling just makes it hurt. The jarring of the horse, I expect-"

"This scar on your cheek?" she says, examining it closely.

"Yes. It is no matter. I'll feel better soon. If you would like to help, a glass full of wine would be just the thing."

"I don't think so. That would just make you feel worse."

"It soothes the pain," he says, wincing as if to prove his point.

"We have some fine healers here. Would you like to see one?"

"I'm fine," he gasps. "Perhaps, I'll lie down for a bit."

"Fine. Just please take off your dirty clothes and boots before lying down. Thank you."

With a 'cluck' and a 'tsk', she leaves them alone. Esther goes to get his blankets, which are still on the horse. By the time she returns, he has already lain down on the bed in his dirty clothes. Not wanting to anger Jalia, she makes him take everything off. He grumbles, but she keeps on insisting until he does it. Then she wraps him in the blanket and leaves him alone.

The sun is getting low in the sky and Esther decides to go over to the assembly hall, wherever that is, to get some dinner. She looks at Pedro, lying miserably in bed, who doesn't look in any shape to do any kind of a journey.

"I'm going to the celebration. Do you want me to bring you back some food?"

"No, I'll go with you. A celebration...bound to be some wine there. A glass of wine would be just the thing."

With a groan of pain, he stands up and begins to get dressed, and then follows her outside. He walks very slowly, and she has to keep stopping to wait for him. He leans on her often, and puts his arm around her to keep standing. She suspects that he only does it to get close to her, but she cannot refuse him support in this state, no matter what his intentions are. He drags his feet and groans with every step, so it seems to take forever to walk the short distance to the hall. She begins to worry that they will miss dinner and he will pass out somewhere, and she will have to stay with him all night long.

After wandering around the village, listening to Pedro's irritating groans and complaints, she discovers the hall's hiding place at last. It is a long, low, and narrow building hidden behind a grove of trees; a simple one-room building made from split cedar, with many holes and smokestacks sending out great plumes of black, billowy smoke. The assembly hall known to the locals as the Hall of the Black Mask, a nice, mysterious name.

Inside, about a hundred people sit cross-legged on the floor, discussing the state of the crops this growing season. There is no food in sight, although there are several speakers lined up to share recent news and ideas. They sit down in the back and listen to the speakers ramble on about tribe business. After listening to a few boring discussions about corn, Esther groans and goes outside. The meeting is not so irritating when one looks at it through a window, so she watches everyone talk and watches the sun set over the mountains. She is joined by a pleasant, slightly plump woman with a very beautiful face, who smiles in greeting.

"Hai, girl."

"Hai."

"Havi, of the Cougar tribe."

"I am Esther."

"I know how you feel, Esther," Havi says, looking in the window. "I was falling asleep in there too."

"I hope I have not missed dinner."

"No, they haven't served yet. They don't like to discuss things on a full stomach, in case there is a disagreement or bad news. So they hold the meetings first. They say it's bad for digestion to be upset right after you eat."

Dinner is worth the wait. From the back, people bring in baskets and bowls of food in a great parade. Everyone has brought their own bowl or basket to eat from, but there are plenty of extra for them to borrow. Before the food is served, many people walk around with great bowls of steaming water, and everyone washes their hands in the hot water. After washing, they place their plates politely down in front of them, and wait to be served. The servers come around and spoon little heaps of food onto plates. At first it is disappointing to get such small portions, but they begin to add up. Soon her plate is full of salmon, squash, corn cakes, boiled roots, camas cakes, potatoes, and about ten different salads.

As Esther stuffs herself, she notices that Pedro doesn't eat much. Just a little fish and a bit of squash, and he leaves most of the food sitting in his wooden bowl. Esther notices that everybody else eats their bowl clean, and she is a little embarrassed for him. But she has no room to help him, so she puts the bowl outside in a bush for him to eat later if he feels better.

After dinner, two musicians play soft music on the harp and flute, for everyone to relax after the meal. There is much soft chatter and laughter, but nobody stands up to dance. It is actually refreshing, after the lunacy of the Eagle celebrations, to just sit quietly and listen to music. Esther takes the time to examine the people more closely. Due to the hot weather, they tend to wear clothing made from hemp, embroidered with feathers and bits of shells. Grooming seems to be important here. Everyone has neatly trimmed hair and the women wear pleasant, soft perfumes. Tattoos or jewelry are rare.

The two musicians are soon joined by several other instruments, and to Pedro's utter amazement, they begin to play a classical piece that he recognizes. Tchaikovsky, isn't it? Even though he knew these people had some instincts toward the finer things, he is still shocked to hear such music. And then a woman steps out onto the dance floor, an older woman with a shrunken body and a big belly that droops like a sack. Her face is drawn and haggard, and she is dressed in a strange silk outfit that clings tightly to her body and shows off all of her sags and bulges. She stands there and smiles at the crowd of people, and then she begins to dance. Pedro is even more amazed than before, when she begins to dance a ballet. He cannot believe that he is seeing ballet in this village of heathens in the middle of nowhere. She wears moccasins that have been hardened with tree sap to make them resemble ballet shoes. She goes to point in them, standing on her tiptoes and spinning around as if defying gravity. She moves as gracefully as a deer, bounding across the room with her feet kicking high in the air. He is quite impressed with her dancing, and he only wishes that she were not so ugly, which rather spoils the show. She looks like a reanimated corpse in ballet shoes. He wonders why they don't get a young beautiful woman to dance instead.

The woman, Haisu is a local hero. Many years ago, she voyaged with her husband, an Elk sailor, to Russia to learn Russian dances and music. There she studied ballet and classical music. She returned with new instruments and a knowledge of classical music and ballet, which she began to teach and perform.

After the performance, a keg of wine is finally opened, to Pedro's great relief. He is first in line. The musicians are joined by drummers and clappers, and there is dancing. The dancing of the Raccoon Tribe is a little different than the dancing of other tribes. They have special choreographed dances with very specific movements. The movements tend to be complex and require great strength and flexibility to be performed correctly. Esther certainly cannot perform any of the movements herself, so she just sits back and watches them dance. She is embarrassed to dance her way, although Havi is doing that. It is more interesting to watch a whole group of people dancing nearly the same way. It makes a nice spectacle.

Finally Esther begins to yawn, and she is just not in the mood for being awake any more. She wants to leave, but Pedro begs for her to stay until he has just one more glass of wine. She agrees reluctantly. He has another glass and then stumbles drunkenly out the door.

It is still very warm and a pleasant stroll home. Pedro stumbles along with her and makes bad jokes about the 'heathen ballet' they just witnessed. Esther cringes at the word 'heathen', but she doesn't say anything. Pedro begins to sing Ave Maria in a loud, drunken voice, and he leaps about and dances with dramatic hand gestures. Esther sings along with him, pretending to learn the song from him, although of course she knows it by heart. It is one of her favorites. In the middle of a particularly passionate moment in the song, he stumbles and crashes to the ground. He roars with laughter and rolls around, holding his belly. Then he suddenly stops laughing and looks as if he is about to vomit. He retches, but manages to hold it in with great effort.

"I apologize, my lady," he whispers in a drunken lisp, as he rises to his feet. "Forgive me. I have lived with this illness for too long. It has made me very crude."

Somehow, he makes it home without killing himself or spilling his guts all over the ground. Crashing on top of his bed, he falls instantly asleep. Esther is grateful that he is silent at last, except for a slight snore that she can live with. She had feared that his drunken antics might continue all night long. She lays her blanket down on a freshly cut mat of tule that is so new that it is still soft, and goes right to sleep.

Raccoon 2'

Raven moon

Pedro wanders outside in the late afternoon, but he only makes it a few feet from the hut before vomiting again. Returning from a long walk, Esther finds him sitting miserably in the dirt, with splatter on his clothes. He complains of a ringing in his head, and being so disoriented that he can barely walk.

"I'm so tired of feeling like this," he complains. "I shouldn't have come here. I should have gone to Mexico City, like I was supposed to."

"Maybe you can see the healers here," she suggests.

"Maybe I should," he sighs. "Do you think they are any good?"

She helps him to his feet, and together they walk to the Healing House. At his pace, it takes them almost an hour to walk there. They finally find a ring of several small huts, right near the river. After waiting around, they are spotted by a young woman who walks over to greet them. She wears a shapeless hemp smock and her hair is pinned back with a carved bone. She takes one look at Pedro and instantly knows that he is the patient.

"My name is Tunia. Come with me," she says, leading him by the hand. "Let's get you into bed."

"Thank you," he sighs. "I need to lie down now."

He leans on her as they hobble slowly over to one of the huts. Before they enter, she takes a hard look at his dirty, vomit stained clothes and sniffs the air apprehensively.

"On second thought, let's give you a bath first."

Esther hurries back to the shelter for dinner. By the time she walks into the lodge, the food is already on the table, and the house is packed with people. There must be thirty people here, by Esther's calculations. She looks around for an empty seat, but she cannot find one, so she just stands there nervously until Jalia rises and comes toward her.

"You are late."

"I'm sorry. I had to take my friend to the Healer's House."

"That's fine. But try to be here earlier next time, as we like to be finished by dark," she says, looking around the room. "You'll need a stool. There might be some behind the building. Let's go look. And then you can wash your hands."

Jalia leads her to a large basin of soapy water and indicates that she should stick her hands into it.

"You must wash your hands very well, so any dirt or disease will wash completely off and not infect the food. Soak your hands in the cleansing bowl first and then wash it off with the fresh water."

"What's in this?" Esther asks, putting her hands into the strong smelling, warm water.

"Soap root, soapberry and chaparral," Jalia says. "The last two are very difficult to find in these parts. They grow in the southern deserts, where gatherers travel a few times a year."

Jalia instructs her to rub her hands together vigorously for at least a minute. After washing up, Esther takes the rickety stool that Jalia found for her, and carries it into the room. She squeezes her stool in between Jalia and another woman who looks like Jalia's sister. Before she sits down, Jalia makes her scrub her chair with a wet rag from the kitchen. Finally she is seated, and she gives dinner a hopeful eye. A huge bowl of multi-colored salad, with every vegetable that Esther saw in the market, sits directly before her. There are corn cakes, potatoes, a stew of acorn mush and beans, different types of roots, a basket of pine nuts, and a small bowl of olives, a delicacy Esther recognizes from the Santa Cruz mission garden but never was allowed to eat. It all looks so delicious. But there is no sign of the main course yet. Esther wonders if she missed that also.

"Is there any more of the main course," she asks curiously. "Or has it not come out yet?"

"What main course?" Jalia continues to whisper.

"This is all the food then?"

"Is it not enough for you?"

"Isn't there any meat or fish?"

"There is no meat here."

"None?"

"We do not serve flesh at this shelter. You will find that you feel light and energized after dinner, as opposed to feeling heavy and tired."

Esther nods, and returns to her food. As she chews, she notices that nobody talks to each other. The table is completely silent, as everyone concentrates on their food with no outside distractions. It seems strange, because a table with this many people should be loud and fun. But there is only mind-numbing silence.

She has to admit that it is one of the most interesting meals she has ever eaten. She loves the crunchy salad, with the tasty sauce poured all over it. She loves the olives, and has to struggle not to eat all of them. The soup is blander than she is used to, because it is not flavored with dried fish, but she pours sauce and seaweed into it until it tastes good. Esther stuffs herself and pronounces herself satisfied and pleased.

When everyone has finally finished eating, a low whisper starts, turns into a murmur, and finally grows into normal conversational tones. At that time, several people rise and begin clearing the table. Jalia rises with them and begins to help.
Before she leaves the lodge, Esther goes out to the kitchen to talk to Jalia. Now that she is well fed and rested, she will have to admit to her extreme poverty and risk being thrown out. Out in the kitchen, several people are busy cleaning up after dinner. Jalia is sitting in front of one of the three washbasins, which are a frenzy of

dishwashing activity. She looks up, and smiles at Esther, but it is a smile in a hurry, so Esther gets right to the point.

"My friend was going to pay my way, but he is now in the Healer's House, which I am told is rather expensive. I have a few tupas, but I would like to save them for emergencies. Is there some kind of work trade I can do for staying here?"

Esther quickly rattles off her resume of experience. Jalia nods seriously, but does not stop washing for one moment.

"I'll ask around. Talk to me tomorrow."

Esther agrees to do so, and leaves her to her scrubbing. One of the girls involved in dishwashing begins to sing a catchy tune called the "Work Song", and all the workers begin to sing while they work. Esther hums the tune to herself as she walks leisurely back to her house. She wonders if one is allowed to sing it, while engaged in lazy activities too.

Raccoon 4'

**Cougar moon*

Pedro lies in bed, depressed and miserable. He has been in this bed for two days, and he doesn't feel any better. Usually his symptoms come and go with a little rest, but this time they are getting worse. Here he is with a serious medical condition in the care of a heathen witch doctor. Tunia has examined him several times, and she cannot discover what is wrong. She gives him disgusting teas made from all manner of strange roots and herbs that make his face screw up with distaste as he drinks them. Then she returns an hour later to ask how he feels, and he always says he is not feeling better. Shaking her head in disappointment, she leaves to go make him more disgusting tea.

There are two others in the hut with him. On one side of the room is an old Indian man covered in tattoos and talismans of coyote paws, who keeps chanting a loud prayer in his native language. He suffers from a broken leg that refuses to heal. Apparently, he was old and crippled, and his tribe no longer wanted him. With that savage practicality that Pedro will never understand, they carried him out into the woods and left him to die. He managed to hobble into the Raccoon tribe borders and they kindly resurrected him. And here he lies - the old man that nobody wanted - stubbornly refusing to give up like he is supposed to. Next to him lies a young Indian with a stomach ailment, who groans all night long from the pain. His wife and children come to visit him sometimes, and they make a hell of a racket too.

"Good morning, Pedro," Tunia says, entering with a steaming bowl. "I brewed this especially for you."

"Tea," he says in a mocking voice. "Just what I wanted. More tea."

"This will soothe you," she says in a clipped voice

"I need something stronger," he moans. "Something for the pain. You must have some wine or other liquor…."

"I already told you no wine," she says sternly. "Wine is going to make you sicker. But perhaps I can get you some other medicine to dull the pain."

"Please hurry."

She begins to examine the old Indian man instead, as if to show him that she doesn't jump when ordered. Pedro curses under his breath and mumbles about stupid heathen nurses who don't understand anything.

In the afternoon, he is visited by a weasel-like man with a pinched up face. Pedro sighs with relief. A real doctor at last.

"Doctor, you have to help me," he gasps.

"I am not your doctor," the weasel says in a high, fluty voice. "I am a caretaker of the Healing House. I have come here to discuss payment."

"Oh," he mumbles, disappointed. "Very well, hand me that little pouch near my clothes."

The man hands him his dirty pouch with the tips of two fingers, as if the pouch were contagious, and then rinses his fingers immediately in a washbasin. Pedro reaches into the bag and hands him his only gold coin. He hates to part with the bulk of his riches, but there is no way around it. The man stares at the coin and sniffs distastefully.

"What is this?"

"Gold, sir. It is a real gold doubloon, I assure you."

"We do not take such things. What are we to do with gold? Tupas or dentalium shells please. Or in a bind, we'll take a trade."

"Gold is worth any amount of shells. You can use it to trade with just about any country in the world."

"We do not trade with other countries. Not at the Healing House, we don't.

"You must. You have iron stoves and steel tools that look foreign made. Where do these come from? Either you trade with somebody or else you have made a deal with the devil."

The man frowns, and examines the coin ruefully.

"Yes, the Twelve Tribes traders do business overseas, but we bring pelts and furs for trade, mainly. Especially otter pelts."

"Well, this is just as good as a pelt, I assure you. Give it to your traders, they'll know the value. I promise you."

The man frowns and stares at the coin again. He doesn't seem to believe Pedro. Finally he just shrugs.

"We'll, we won't refuse you care. How many of these things do you have?"

He makes Pedro give him the doubloon and every bit of silver in his possession. Pedro curses and argues, but the man insists, and Pedro finally gives in wearily. The man walks away, mumbling about how the Healing House has to stop giving out 'free healing' to every poor beggar that comes by or it will soon go broke.

Raccoon 5'

Esther awakens extremely late. Hearing muffled snoring, she peers about the room. Havi's boyfriend is the one making all the noise. He is a heavy man, with a thick beard and long, straggly brown hair that covers most of his face. He arrived last night with many others of his tribe, and he and Havi escorted Esther to a full moon party, where they danced for hours and drank lots of wine. Esther tries to go back to sleep, but the snoring is irritating, so she gets out of bed and heads to the main lodge for berries and tea.

There is a large gathering in the main circle in the afternoon. To Esther's surprise, a large deer is roasting over a roaring fire on a large spit. Three men walk around it, singing to it and basting it with some sort of herbal blend that smells wonderful. Many of the Cougar tribe, come for Polar Day, are gathered around the fire waiting for dinner. They play music with drums and flutes, and sing the deer song to bless the meat. Some of the Raccoon tribe dance with them.

Esther sees Jalia and Havi talking nearby and she joins them.

"Oh, Esther, there you are," exclaims Jalia.

"I thought you didn't eat meat," Esther says.

Jalia frowns and changes the subject.

"Good news. I found you some work. You'll be doing farm work."

She smiles and pats Esther on the shoulder, as if this is the best news that
she could possibly give her, but Esther's spirits sink at the thought of being a farmhand again. She imagines long hours spent doing menial tasks and hard backbreaking work. She considers refusing the opportunity and just sleeping outside, but that will mean begging for food or not eating. She finally forces herself to smile and thanks Jalia for the opportunity. Her gratitude comes out through clenched teeth.

"You're welcome," says Jalia, not noticing her hesitation. "You'll start tomorrow. Well, I must now get to work cooking dinner," she clucks. "By the way, we're a little short staffed today and there is so much to do. Could one of you help us out? We need help in the kitchen."

"I am supposed to help decorate the assembly hall tonight," says Havi.

"Esther?"

"Sure," Esther says unenthusiastically, with a face that says the opposite.

Esther is escorted into the kitchen, where ten or fifteen men and women are busy preparing a sumptuous meal. Jalia points to huge soapy bowl and another bowl of clear water. Esther dutifully washes, and then Jalia leads her to a table and gives her a large knife. Her job is to chop up a giant bowl of plants and herbs for a salad. Jalia watches her for a while and shows her how to cut every vegetable the Raccoon way.

"No, no, cut it like this or the thorns will remain," she says, showing Esther how to cut milkweed. "And do not put the root of the purslane in the salad. Only the leaves and the stem."

Men and women bustle around, their arms full of vegetables and bowls of seaweed and roots and baskets of herbs. They hand things off to each other and shout requests, forming a tight little group. And there is always talk, whether it's commenting on the merits of the salad and how the bread is turning out, or whether it is acceptable to mix certain roots and seeds. Every so often, someone walks by and hands Esther a bowl or a sprig of herbs and gives her a little nod of welcome. Esther likes the busy little camaraderie of the kitchen, although she wishes everyone would relax a little more, enjoy themselves and stop worrying so much about everything being perfect. As she cuts and chops, she absentmindedly nibbles on some of the vegetables in her bowl. Unfortunately, Jalia notices and begins fussing again.

"Now you must wash your hands, Esther. It is very poor hygiene to eat while you work. You'll get all sorts of diseases on your hands from touching your mouth. You've been going to the Healing House to visit your friend. Imagine if you catch sickness there. Everyone here could get sick."

Grumbling, Esther goes to the washing station and re-washes her hands. Then Jalia shows Esther how to make a dressing for the salad. They use a base of acorn broth and mashed olives, mixed with seaweed flakes and fermented berries. It is a long process, but Jalia insists that they cannot serve the salad without it.

They do not finish until late in the afternoon. Esther is upset that she has missed most of the day's activities, but at least she hasn't missed dinner. They load up a cart full of food and a horse draws it down the road toward the main circle, where the food is loaded onto several large tables. Dinner has been on everyone's mind for some time, and everyone comes over to eye the repast.

"You may do the honor, Esther," Jalia says, pointing at a salad bowl.

The way Jalia says it, it must be a great honor indeed to serve dinner, although it seems like just more work to Esther. But when the line forms to get food, Esther finds that whenever she scoops salad into someone's bowl, they are very grateful and they thank her, bow or smile to show how much they appreciate her. She feels a surge of pride that she cut many of the vegetables in her bowl and is pleased whenever a visiting Cougar remarks about the beauty of the salad heaped on their plate.

After dinner, everyone gathers in the Hall of the Black Mask for a long night of music and dancing. Cougar musicians begin to play and more wine is served. Esther gets drunk and crazy and teaches Havi the dance she learned at the Eagle tribe. She dances pelvis to pelvis with Havi, while her husband watches with considerable interest. Finally he gets bored of watching and jumps in the middle.

Soon the boyfriend and Havi begin to kiss, and Esther is excluded from the threesome. As she goes to look for more wine, she sees none other than Kirth and Bela dancing together. She runs up to them and they have a joyous reunion in the middle of all the drums and noise. They swap stories about their doings over the past months and Esther is invited to their house for dinner some night. Then, Bela and Kirth begin to dance with each other and Esther is excluded again.

The men here are far less aggressive than at the Eagle tribe and not a single person hits on her or even asks her to dance. The party goes all night long, but since Esther has nobody to dance with, she goes home long before that.

Raccoon 6'

Jalia awakens Esther at dawn, shaking her gently until she opens her eyes. Esther groans and throws her arms over her head. Why can farm work never begin at ten o'clock? Always at the crack of dawn, when any sane person should be sound asleep. She forgot that she was supposed to work this morning, and now she regrets staying out so late. She lies in a daze, wondering what would happen if she refuses to wake up. But Jalia doesn't leave, continuing to bug her until she finally rises and throws on some clothes.

"I'm going to walk you over there myself," Jalia says, stifling a yawn. "Are you ready to go?"

"Yes," Esther says miserably.

The farm lies near a small creek. A large section of land has been cleared of trees and there are many different plants growing. It is a sharp contrast - the neat rows of plants and tilled earth versus the wild and unkempt gardens of nature. Jalia leads Esther to a large wooden fence to keep out intruding animals and bids her a hasty farewell.

"Work hard," she instructs her. "And everything will go well."

"Will I be allowed to return home for lunch?"

"They'll feed you," Jalia says quickly. "Not to worry. So long."

Jalia walks away and Esther walks through the gate, stepping gingerly through a puddle of mud in order to get to the other side of the farm. A sturdy woman, with hair pulled back in a bun, walks out of a row of tall plants to speak to her.

"You are the girl who is sent to help us?"

"Yes. I am Esther."

"I am Nan. That's my husband, Beryl. He's the one you should talk to. He'll put you to work."

Nan returns to work deep inside the tall plants. A cart lies nearby, loaded down with neat piles of stalks ripped from the tall plants. Next to the cart is the man indicated as Beryl. He is tall and somber, with black hair that is graying slightly. He looks up from a large pile of corn that he has been eyeing keenly, as Esther walks over to speak to him.

"Ah yes, hello." he says quietly. "Welcome."

"Thank you."

"You've farmed before, right?"

"Yes."

"Good. Good. Then you know what to do. You can grab a knife and a burden basket and start harvesting corn. We have a large order to get out."

That's all he has to say. He returns to his sorting and pays Esther no more mind. Esther grabs a burden basket and a knife. She examines the tightly woven basket, admiring the weaving. Beryl stares at her a moment, wondering why she hasn't started working yet, but he says nothing. Esther smiles politely and walks out to the cornfield.

"Over there!" he shouts out. "That row there."

It is peaceful out here in this valley, and much more fun than farming at Tork and Tara's. There it was all planting and weeding, with nothing to show for it but rows of tiny plants that did nothing but grow. Now the harvest has begun and the plants are all tall and bursting with vegetables. Buried in the tall rows that go up to her neck, nobody can see her. She can go at her own pace and get lost in her own world. She brushes the plants with her arms, savoring the loud swish. She plays hide and seek with the ravens that are searching for lunch. She comes upon a scareraven, and she sneaks up on it and pulls down its pants.

Beryl eyes her suspiciously, as she comes up with only her third basket of corn. He has sorted and placed everything on the cart, *and* picked four baskets worth.

"Looks nice. Can you pick a bit faster, do you think?"

"Yes," she says irritably, thinking that she was doing just fine.

"Good."

There are two other men picking corn. One is an old man named Enri, a grizzled old man who turns out to be Beryl's uncle. He moves like lightening for such an old man, taking two baskets at once, and filling them as quickly as Esther fills one. He grins warmly at Esther, but doesn't pause for conversation. The other is a young man with long hair and a vacant expression. He is from the Swan tribe, come to work for the harvest season and bring back food for his family. His name is Yan and he is really strange. He talks to himself out in the fields, smoking while he works.

Lunchtime is a quick, hasty business. They eat around the cart, underneath a tree to protect them from the broiling noontime sun. Esther is given a wooden bowl filled with corn bread and roasted deer. She expresses her surprise when she sees the meat, which makes Beryl laugh.

"Not us," says Nan.

"It's those folk at the shelter that give people that impression," says Beryl, pausing to chew a bite of fat. "They try to force their beliefs on everybody that stays there and give everybody the wrong impression about us. They have even complained about our grape growing for the wine makers. They said in a discussion last week that it is wrong to grow perfectly good fruit just to ferment it. Can you believe that?"

"I heard about that," says Nan, shrugging her shoulders. "They can think what they want to."

"Just don't try to tell us what to do," grumbles Beryl.

In no time, Esther finds herself sent back out to gather more corn. They pick for another two hours and then she is called back in.

"That's a day. We've got to get a load of crops ready to be sent out to the Eagle tribe tonight, and another to the Swan and the Wolf tribes. One of our drivers didn't show up - so we have to find somebody willing to make a trip all the way up to Wolf village."

Beryl sighs irritably.

"The Swans expect regular deliveries, but ask them to show up on time and deliver the vegetables...and where are they?"

"You may have to take it yourself," says Nan with a sigh. "At least to the Swans. You can find someone there to take it up to Wolf village."

"I can't go tonight. There's so much work to do here and we don't have enough help."

"If we don't, all those grapes are going to rot."

"So be it."

"The Wolves really wanted fresh grapes."

"They can go talk to the Swans. Maybe that'll scare them. Imagine an angry Wolf mob showing up at your door, wondering why you didn't make their delivery? That Ulla will never be late again."

Beryl laughs.

"You can go," he tells Esther. "Thanks for the help. See you tomorrow."

Esther walks off, trouncing through the mud toward home, leaving Beryl and Nan to worry. She moves slowly in the afternoon heat, exhausted by the long day's toils. Her back is sore and aching. She knows that the only thing in her future tonight is a nap, dinner, and sleep.

Raccoon 9'

Beaver moon

"Beryl is here for you," Jalia says, shaking Esther awake. Better get up."

Yawning, Esther gets dressed and shuffles outside. It is warm out, even at dawn. Beryl sits on a horse, with a little homemade cart with three wheels tied to the back of it. His hair is a mess, he is unshaven, and he looks exhausted and irritable.

"Let's go," he says, indicating for her to jump into the cart.

She jumps in and off they go.

"How are you this morning?" she asks politely.

"Tired. I went up to the Swan village to make the delivery for that worthless Ulla, who never showed up like he said he would. So I gave him the delivery and turned around and came right on back. Just got back into town a few minutes ago. Figured I would pick you up."

"Did you drive all night long?"

"Some of it. Can't you tell?"

"How can you travel at night?"

He points to a lantern, sitting in the back of the cart. She touches it and finds it is still warm.

"You must be exhausted."

"Yeah," he admits with a sigh. "But it's going to be really rough by this evening."

They arrive to find Nan and Enri busy working in the cornfield. Nan stops working to give her husband a kiss and discuss yesterday's news. She hands him a cup of Chinese black tea. Esther asks for a cup for herself and Nan gives her what is left in the tea bowl. Once she is pleasantly awake and tingling from the tea, Esther is sent to work in the cornfield.

She hears Beryl complaining about Ulla, then he lays into Yan who has gone missing, and finally into all the Swan tribe in general.

"Why don't you get some sleep, Beryl," Nan says quietly, giving his hand a squeeze. "You look exhausted."

"I am."

"Go get some rest."

"Maybe this afternoon. I have to feed the horses and tend the herb garden, which is a mess of weeds. And then I must fill the order of medicinal herbs for that Cougar medicine man who came for polar day. And we must fill the order for the new moon celebration, which we have not even begun. We have to pick all those grapes and finish with the corn. Not to mention that huge order of hemp stalks for the Elks."

He trudges off, miserable but determined, and Nan watches him with concern. Finally she picks up her burden basket and heads out into the fields herself.

In the afternoon, Tunia makes Pedro get up and take a walk outside. As soon as he stands up, he feels as if his head is buzzing with bees and he is so dizzy that he has to lean on her for support. She helps him walk slowly out into the bright sunshine. He blinks several times, rubs his eyes, and feels the heat of the sun keenly on his skin as if he were standing too close to a hot fire.

They walk down a small path that winds through oak forest and then heads out into an open clearing. By now he is pouring sweat and feels as if he may pass out. They seem to be making for a bright plume of steam rising up over the trees and he wonders if they are going to a sweat lodge of some kind. He laughs to himself. The basic heathen treatment for everything is a sweat, isn't it? Well, he doesn't have much left to sweat out by now. He has already had his sweat just walking through this heat.

They stop by a tiny muddy river, thick brown like molasses. She smiles and indicates that he may sit down now, and he collapses gratefully in the tall grass.

"When you are rested, you may bathe."

He looks at the mud pit and laughs.

"That's funny. I didn't know you had a sense of humor."

"I'm not joking," she says with a straight face.

It is then that he realizes that she really doesn't have a sense of humor. She is quite serious.

"You want me to go in there?" he asks incredulous. "In that mud? It smells like...like a fart."

"It's healing mud."

He laughs at the absurdity of the idea. But she just sits down, prepared to wait until he actually goes in. He examines the muddy water more closely, trying to see how it is healing mud. He sits down by it and dips a finger into it. He is surprised to find that it is hot water. It must be a sulphur spring. He decides that a hot bath would be nice, even if it is a dirty hot bath.

Pedro takes off his clothes for a dip. He looks over at Tunia guiltily as he takes off his pants, feeling strange still to be naked in front of women, but she doesn't seem to care. Then he gingerly drops down into the water, and his feet sink down until he is immersed up to his knees. He wades out deeper into the water, each step requiring great strength to escape from the sucking sludge. Finally, he sits in a pool of hot water that is deep enough to go in up to the neck. It feels heavenly. He sits in the soft cushiony mud, immersed in hot, steamy sulphur water. He sighs over and over again. He could sit here all day long.

"Rub your body all over with mud," commands Tunia. "It is healing mud."

Pedro is now willing to believe anything she says. He rolls around until he is covered all over with the slimy stuff. Then he stands up in a shallow section and enjoys the feeling of mud drying on his body. He laughs heartily out of sheer joy and prances around like some sort of mud monster. When he begins to feel cold again, he plops back down into the deep part.

Soon the heat begins to get to him. The veins in his temple throb, he breathes more rapidly, and he begins to feel dizzy. So he clambers over to the bank, grabs a hold of some cattails, and pulls himself up onto the bank. He collapses in a heap, breathing heavily, as he struggles to regain his equilibrium. He feels on the verge of passing out and it takes him a long time to recover.

"I'm ready to wash off now," he says at last.

"Back at the Healing House."

"I'm not going to walk back naked, covered in mud," he says weakly.

"There's no clean water around here."

Pedro returns to the mud bath and struggles to clean off. He has about a foot or so of brown soupy water near the bank to wash off in. He manages it by sticking his hands deep in the mud and letting his body float until it rinses clean. Then he carefully pulls himself back out of the water, clinging to grass and cattails like ropes. He finally collapses in a reasonably clean heap and lies for a long time with his face pressed into the cool grass. He never wants to move from this spot. He feels very good, washed clean of his sins or something like that, like a muddy baptism.

He bounds up at last, ready to walk back. But the stress of walking soon wears him out again, and the last quarter mile is torturous. After a proper bath in clean water, he collapses back into bed almost as miserable as before.

There is much to do at the farm and Esther is kept until a late hour. Yan never shows up and poor Beryl must work all day long trying to make up the slack. He grumbles and groans, but manages to stay on his feet until most of the work is done. Then Nan insists that he go home with Enri. Beryl crawls into the cart and falls asleep almost instantly.

"I'll come back in the morning and finish up," says Nan with a sigh, looking at the setting sun. "You can go home."

Esther stands up and arches her sore back. She sighs deeply. "Thank you."

"I'll see you tomorrow."

Before returning home, Esther walks over to the river to clean herself off. She chews on a sprig of grapes as she walks. Her hands and clothes are caked in dirt, and she is covered in corn pollen and bits of twigs and leaves from head to toe. At the river, she strips off her clothes and prepares for a swim, but a hilarious sight distracts her. A raccoon is involved in stripping the husk off of a piece of corn that it managed to steal. It washes the ear fanatically, trying to get all the little corn threads off. But it is having a hard time, because corn threads are irritatingly difficult to remove entirely. The raccoon reminds her so much of Jalia and the others at the shelter that she starts laughing. Raccoon tribe indeed!

The raccoon doesn't seem to be afraid of her, so she comes closer to observe it. Then she sees two more standing behind a tree. Wanting to make friends with the curious creatures, she pulls out a couple of the little candies that Nan gave her. The candies are clever concoctions made from berries boiled down to a thick sugary paste and formed into little round balls. She makes the raccoons an offering of two berry balls, and steps back. One raccoon approaches boldly and examines them with eyes and nose. Then it takes one in its paw, goes to the river, and washes the little candy ball obsessively in the water. When it lifts the ball to its mouth, it finds that the ball has already dissolved. The raccoon seems confused and it goes for another ball. By the time it is through washing it, the same thing happens again. It stares at her, seeming to want another one.

Esther is not going to waste more of her precious candy on the raccoons if they are so stupid, so she gives up on them and jumps in the water. When she gets out, she finds that the two raccoons have brazenly gone into her little basket and taken more candies. And they are currently involved in washing them into oblivion. She shakes her head, laughs at the absurdity of it all, and leaves them to their bizarre rituals.

Raccoon 12'

Jay moon

Esther finally visits Pedro, and as soon as she arrives, she regrets it. He gives her an earful of all of his complaints about the Healing House - which he calls the Heathen House - berates her for not visiting him and begs her to get him some wine. She sits at the foot of Pedro's bed, slumped against the wall with her knees to her chest and her head resting on her arms. She sits like this not only because she is exhausted from work, but because she is avoiding him. She has had enough and wants to go home.

"I have to go," she says at last. "I'm tired."

"Please don't leave," he says despondently.

"I have to go," she says with a little shrug, as she rises to her feet.

"Don't you care anything for me? Sometimes I think you hate me. I can see it in your face."

"I'm just tired. I work every day at a farm. It's hard work. You couldn't imagine what it's like."

She smiles, wondering if he caught the subtle insult, aimed at priests who keep slaves to do all their work for them. But he has become far too dense to be open to subtleties.

"There's a bed right over there," he says, pointing to the empty bed where the young man with the stomach problems used to be before he left.

"They don't want me to sleep in here," she says, looking at the eternally sleeping old man with the broken leg.

"They don't care. You don't want to sleep in here. Admit it."

She looks away and wonders how to get this over with quickly so she can leave.

"That's alright. Go home. Don't worry about it."

"Fine. Goodnight."

"Goodnight," he mumbles, and he turns over and stares morosely at the wall until she leaves.

Raccoon 14'

Bear moon

In the afternoon, Tunia goes to see a learned man named Kuhl. Kuhl is the senior healer in the Healing House, although he is too busy with his research to take many patients these days. He spent two years in China and Japan, studying acupuncture and Chinese medicine, he is an expert on medicinal herbs, and he is very knowledgeable about the human body. She knocks on the door of his house nervously, knowing he is very busy and doesn't like to be bothered, and then she steps a respectful distance away and waits for him.

He opens the door after a good long wait and stares at her quizzically. No greetings or friendly hello, but only a curious stare, wondering what she wants. He is a tall, neat man with long grey hair tied in a ponytail down his back and a neatly trimmed goatee, that he first grew in China and has kept ever since. His stern demeanor has always made her nervous and she shuffles around uncomfortably as she speaks to him.

"I am sorry to bother you. I need your help."

"Now? Can't it wait? I am in the middle of making a tincture."

"Oh. Shall I come back?"

"Agreed," he says, and he turns around and goes inside.

She feels disrespected and that stiffens her resolve somewhat. She knocks again. He comes back out with a scowl on his face.

"What now?"

"When should I return?" she asks stubbornly. "When would be a good time?"

He sighs.

"Why don't you tell me the problem already?"

"One of my patients isn't doing well. I'm not really sure what is wrong with him, and I'm worried."

"What hut is he in?"

"Number eight."

"I'll be there in an hour. Is that all right? Or will he die by then?"

"No."

"Fine, I'll see you in an hour."

He turns without another word and goes back inside.

In exactly an hour, Kuhl walks into Pedro's hut with his healer's bag, and immediately goes right to work. He peers closely at Pedro's eyes. His tongue. Checks his pulse and the color and temperature of his skin.

"Hello, I am Kuhl. Who are you?" he says, looking into Pedro's eyes inquisitively.

"Pedro de la Cueva," the patient says weakly. "I'm a Spaniard."

"I can see that. Do you know what's wrong with you, Spaniard?"

"I have a head wound and ever since then I have had headaches, dizziness, nausea...that sort of thing. It has been called a fistula by a learned doctor."

"Is there anything else? Something that began recently?"

"There is pain here," he says, pointing at his chest.

"What kind of pain?"

"I don't know...it's not pain exactly...it's constricting."

"Have you experienced this pain before?"

"Not like this. It has bothered me for the past few days, and I can barely breathe. Make the pain stop...please. Thank God, you're here. A real doctor at last."

Kuhl frowns, making his mouth droop just like his drooping mustache.

"I am told you are not eating," Kuhl says, nodding his head at Tunia, who has just walked into the room.

"I cannot eat any more acorn mush. The texture disgusts me. And that soup made from those bitter roots I cannot swallow. I would like some meat, but the girl won't bring me any. Nor a glass of wine, which I desperately need for the pain."

Kuhl nods slowly and then peers suspiciously at Tunia, who stares at him with her mouth open.

"If the patient wants meat, you give it to him!" he says angrily, to an abashed Tunia.

They have gone outside to talk, or more likely for a lecture.

"But meat will interfere with his healing," she says in a small voice. "His body must remain *pure*."

"In certain cases. Digestive illness and the like. But remember that the patient must feel good in order to get better. If meat makes him feel good, give him meat. Better that than have him refuse food altogether. You've been listening to those fools at the shelter, haven't you?"

"Fine," she says in a flat voice.

"Did you know about the pain in his chest?"

"No."

"Why not?"

She stands there, stupefied again.

"He mentioned a pain in his chest over the past few days. Why did you not know about it?"

"He didn't say anything to me -"

"Don't you ask him for his symptoms daily?"

"No," she says weakly.

"I could tear my beard out! Why not?"

"I thought I knew what was wrong with him. He was shot with an arrow in the head. I thought he was just suffering from some sort of unhealed trauma from that wound. I gave him some healing teas, and kept his head elevated to let the blood drain."

"Never assume anything! Ask the patient! The patient always knows more than you. More than he thinks he knows. Get the information you need from him any way you can."

"I'm sorry."

"Don't be sorry. Learn something."

"Fine. But what do you think we should do for him?" she asks quickly, hoping to get the subject away from her.

"*We*? *I* am taking over this patient's case. First I am going to talk to him at length, and find out what the origin of this chest constriction is. I believe that the chest constriction is the key to this patient's condition. But I need more information to get a correct diagnosis. I need his entire personal history. Which I assume you did not get."

"No," she whispers, feeling about four years old.

"Then I am going to give him acupuncture, to increase his life flow. Maybe we can unblock his chest with his own *chi*."

"What should I do?"

He grabs her shoulders gently, and his face becomes kind at last.

"You will assist me. And together we will make him better. Now, go get the patient some meat and a cup of wine."

"You're giving him wine too?"

"He's got the shakes. It's a sort of withdrawal that people who drink too much get. Wine may give him relief…but don't give it to him until tonight."

Done with his lecture, the doctor pulls out his little bag of acupuncture needles. The needles were brought back from China by Kuhl, and they have seen much use since then. For this first treatment, he inserts twelve needles into Pedro's body, with an emphasis on the chest and the hands.

"Can you show me how to do that?" Tunia asks.

Kuhl stares at her.

"Why?"

"I want to learn."

"The study of acupuncture is very hard and takes a very long time. It can take many years. Are you now ready to begin such a journey?"

She hesitates, and Kuhl nods as if he knew she was not ready.

"How many years have you been studying healing?"

"Two."

"You have not come very far yet. You do not work hard enough. If you work harder, then perhaps I will take you as an apprentice. Ask me again in one year, if you are still interested, and we will see how far you have come."

She nods, irritated by his attitude.

Kuhl leaves Pedro to lie still and let the needles stimulate his vital *chi*. He promises to return in a while to remove the needles, and Tunia is instructed to keep close watch to see that he is sufficiently warm and does not move too much. She sits down to observe him and see if she can sense a difference in him, but it is a subtle process and she can see nothing.

Kuhl returns in an hour, carrying a small basket, and removes the needles one by one. Pedro moans quietly, which is the first sound he has made since the needles were stuck into him.

"A good sign," remarks Kuhl.

Tunia gazes upon his basket, which is filled with bundles of herbs and pieces of roots and other plants.

"What herbs have you decided on?" she asks curiously.

He quickly takes the basket away, before she can see what he has brought.

"What herbs would you prescribe?" he asks.

She thinks hard about his symptoms, wanting to make a good impression. Then she reads off a list of possible herbs and plants that she might give him. He thinks about her selections seriously.

"I agree with your choice of arnica. But I do not agree with the others. You are treating him for his symptoms, instead of for what is causing the symptoms. His constitution is very weak, so I am giving him herbs to strengthen the entire body. This must be done first, before we deal with anything else."

She nods and steps back to watch him work. Despite his irritating, know-it-all attitude, she knows that he is much wiser than she is. She decides that it will be worthwhile to work with him, although he will surely drive her crazy long before the patient is well.

Raccoon 15'

After the last disastrous visit, Esther decided that she would not visit Pedro any more, but tonight she is summoned to Pedro's hut by an errand boy who claims it is an emergency. She doesn't want to go, but she feels guilty about refusing, so she reluctantly walks over there after dinner.

"Pedro," she whispers. "Are you awake?"

Her smile falls when she sees him. She holds a candle up to his face, and finds it pale and drawn. He smells awful too. When the light hits his face, he murmurs and rolls around feverishly. He tries to speak, but only manages to rave a bit of nonsense. Mouth open wide in surprise, she sits down on the empty bed and just stares at him.

A while later, he comes to his senses and waves her over. She walks over nervously, and he grabs her hand in a tight grip and squeezes it. He pulls her head down so he can whisper in her ear. Being this close to him is uncomfortable and his breath is rank, but she endures it.

"When I die," he whispers, "you can have everything I own. Take good care of Quixote, please. He's probably run off again, but if you find him make sure he is well taken care of."

"You're not going to die," she whispers.

"Yes," he murmurs. "I am."

Pedro looks directly into her eyes, with bloodshot and red rimmed eyeballs, and there is a great pain mirrored in them.

"If I am going to die," he whispers, and his lower lip trembles as he struggles to speak, "I want you to know something."

She takes his hand gently.

"What?"

"You are the only woman I have loved in my whole life."

She doesn't know what to say. She looks down at the ground. She can't look him in the eye, not after words like that.

"Thank you," she whispers, and she stands there quietly until he lets go of her hand. Then she sits back down on the bed and feels sorry for all of the mean things she said to him.

A little while later, an old woman walks into the room. She is Usa, a senior healer at the Healing House, a kindly old woman with thirty years experience with tough cases like this one. Kuhl asked her to check up on Pedro at night, and summon him in case of emergency. Esther jumps up, happy to have somebody to talk to about Pedro.

"I'm worried about the Spanish man. He says he's going to die," she whispers to Usa, so Pedro cannot hear.

"He said that?"

"Yes. Is he?"

Usa stares at him, but says nothing for a long time.

"Perhaps he is."

"What is wrong with him?"

"We're not sure. Kuhl thinks he has a problem with his heart."

"Oh, that's not good."

"Yes," she muses. "But I'm beginning to wonder...."

"What?"

"He may be right," she says, staring at Pedro's face. "But maybe he's right for the wrong reasons."

Usa says nothing for a long time. She merely watches Pedro and paces the room. She dumps out his poop basket and washes it out, while Esther sits in a daze, musing on the fact that Pedro might die.

"Something can be done," says Usa suddenly.

"What do you mean?"

"We must summon Yatsa, the Ruok. I believe she can help this man."

"A Ruok?"

"Yes."

"What's that?"

"A shaman of the Twelve Tribes. The Ruoks are a very old and wise group of shamans, dating back more years than anyone can recall. They are wise in ways the rest of us are not. Yes, I think I will go to her. But Yatsa is a very great woman, and a woman like that demands a certain *respect*. We must approach her with a suitable offering. What does this man have to offer?"

"He has a horse," says Esther desperately. "I think that's all he has of value."

"That will do. I will go find her immediately and make the offer."

Raccoon 16'

Eagle moon

In the morning, Kuhl checks on Pedro, and he is shocked by what he sees. Pedro looks dead. Kuhl quickly runs over to check the body, but it is still warm. His pulse is weak and irregular, as is his breathing, but he is alive. Kuhl stokes up the fire and strips Pedro naked, and then he sticks him head to toe with acupuncture needles. Leaving him looking like a human pincushion, he goes to the Healing House kitchen for breakfast. He is in the mood for comfort food and he helps himself to a slice of berry pie with corn crust and Chinese tea. He sits down next to Usa, who is eating a fruit salad. Although he wants to talk to her very badly, he waits until she is finished eating, according to the custom of the Raccoon tribe, before speaking his mind.

"The patient is deteriorating rapidly," he says slowly, sipping tea between thoughts. "Did you notice anything strange last night? Did the patient complain of new pains? I need clues. I cannot discover why he is getting worse."

"I had a conversation with his friend," she says thoughtfully. "It was very enlightening. The patient believes that he is going to die."

"And?"

"Doesn't that suggest anything to you?"

"No. Enlighten me."

"He no longer wants to live," she says simply. "Perhaps he suffers from a wound of the spirit. That's why you cannot find anything."

Kuhl shakes his head.

"I don't think so. I believe the patient wants to get well."

"I think we need some outside help. I want to ask Yatsa, the Ruok, to help him."

Kuhl stares at her in disbelief, wondering if the old woman has lost her wits.

"Are you mad? Wands and mystical words and other nonsense? What will that accomplish?"

"Yatsa can help him," says the old woman stubbornly. "She is a great healer, and I think this is a case for her. I'll stake my reputation on it."

"I'll not have that witch in here," says Kuhl sourly.

"What is a witch?"

He merely waves his hand peevishly.

"You have had your chance. You cannot help him. He will die if we don't do something soon."

"I am not finished with him yet," Kuhl insists.

"But perhaps you could do with some help."

"Her methods are ridiculous."

"You are a good healer, Kuhl, in areas of healing that you understand. But this is an area of healing that you do not understand."

"Nonsense," Kuhl snorts. "A spirit wound."

"It can't hurt," says Usa diplomatically.

Kuhl glares at her. Then he stands and strides away purposefully, as if he has better things to do than to listen to such gibberish.

"His pride is hurt," says Usa to herself. "But that is no matter. I will proceed with the plan."

She stands up, slowly clears the remains of both of their breakfasts, and then walks quickly away on her mission of mercy.

Raccoon 17'

"Esther! Esther!"

"Mmmmmm."

"Wake up, sleepy girl. You're late to work."

Esther considers playing sick and not going to work, but she imagines Jalia hovering over her, pouring cup after cup of nasty medicinal tea down her throat. And then she will not be allowed to eat or leave her bed. Finally, she decides that she would rather work and she rises slowly to a sitting position. Looking around the dark room blearily, at the other cozy sleepers happily snoring, she curses all farmers and early risers in general. Stumbling in the dark, she accidentally steps on Havi's hand, who mumbles a curse in her sleep and rolls over.

Last night, she drank blackberry wine with Havi and her husband and some of the other Cougar tribe. Musicians played music late into the night, and she sat around a bonfire with them. Singing, laughing, dancing - how could she go to bed and leave all that fun to go on without her? A few of the Raccoons joined them to the bitter end, but most of them went to bed at a decent hour in order to be useful the next day. Esther begins to understand why.

She struggles to lift her head above the fog that encases it, as she wanders zombie-like out into the pink light of dawn and the din of a thousand cheerful, chattering birds. She shuffles languidly to the farm, tempted many times to just sit underneath a tree and go back to sleep. But her will is strong enough to get her all the way there.

Nan has kindly brought Esther a whole cup of Chinese tea this time. She thanks Nan many times and takes her time drinking it. When it is drained, she is put to work stripping hemp stalks and loading them into the cart. It is hard work and she cannot summon up any enthusiasm to exert herself. All this work for meals and a place to stay? It isn't worth it. She is still just like a neophyte, slaving away for no gain whatsoever. At the end of the day, she will be broke still. She works grumpily and slowly, and considers quitting.

Soon the sun comes up over the tall hill, the birds mellow, and Esther's buzzing head quiets down. She tries to keep up her spirits, by remembering that she is doing something good for many people. Because of her, people are eating well. And she knows that the overworked farmers are grateful for her help. As she watches Nan and Beryl bent over at their labors, she appreciates that more than ever. But she still can't help feeling that she is a sucker to do all this work for no reward.

Later that afternoon, she is so involved in loading corn into the cart, that she doesn't notice the small woman until she is directly in front of her. The woman smiles a large, toothless grin. Her teeth are all missing but three - three lone sentries in the wasteland of her mouth. Her breath is stale and rancid, from rotting molars.

"Hello," Esther says, cringing back slightly. "Can I help you?"

The woman just continues to smile, and she points to a pile of small, worm eaten corn. Esther finally figures out that she wants to take the rejects. She looks over at Beryl, to see if he minds. He sees the old woman, and indicates to Esther with a wave of his arms that she can give the woman as much reject corn as she wants. The woman roots around in the pile and picks out the best of the discarded ears. She puts them in a basket, still smiling all the while, and then walks off toward the grapes.

"That's Toothy," says Beryl sometime later. "She's a bottom feeder."

"What's that?"

"Like a sand dab. A fish that feeds off the bottom. Toothy takes all the ears that we can't trade or sell and she eats all the overripe grapes that nobody wants. I haven't any idea how she can eat anything with three teeth, but she manages somehow."

Esther laughs, because she cannot figure it out either. She watches Toothy shuffle off with her burden basket, and wonders if she too will someday be reduced to bottom feeder status. Wandering from village to village with three teeth in her head, begging for worm-eaten food. The idea scares her, and she realizes that she will end up just like that if she does not come up with a plan to improve her lot quickly.

At the end of the day, Beryl comes over to Esther and pats her on the back gruffly.

"We'll finish up. Thank you for all the hard work. We're glad to have you. Yan has disappeared for good, and Enri had to bring an order all the way up to the Owl tribe. Without you, we'd be sunk."

Esther nods slowly, wishing he hadn't said that. She has decided to quit today.

"I hope you're staying on a while," he says anxiously, watching her expression. "We really need you."

"I don't know," Esther says in a quiet voice. "I need to make some tupas, so I can buy some things."

"I'll give you three tupas a day on top of your deal with the shelter," Beryl says quickly. "How about that?"

He goes into a little piece of cloth tied to his waist and pulls out three tupas. It doesn't seem like all that much to Esther, and she gives Beryl a hard look as she stares at the small pile of shells in her hand.

"And here's some back pay," he adds, handing her a much bigger pile of shells. "Please stay. You're a good worker."

Esther considers. Three tupas a day seems rather cheap for all this work. But if she makes three tupas a day for the next two weeks, then she'll be in a much better position to quit if she still wants to. And besides, it makes her feel good that Beryl and Nan think she is a good worker. Coming from them, that is the highest praise a person could achieve. She decides to stay for a few more weeks at least.

"I'll stay."

"Good. Thank you."

"But I need some days off occasionally."

"Agreed."

She wraps her tupas in a cork husk and walks away in much better spirits.

Esther goes to see Pedro after work. He seems to be continuing his downward spiral toward death, and not even her face can cheer him up anymore. He just lies there, staring at the ceiling in a daze.

"We've been giving him a combination of herbs and jimm for the pain," says a voice behind her. "It seems to sedate him, but he doesn't talk much afterwards."

She jumps and spins around. Kuhl stands there, a basket of freshly picked herbs in his hand.

"He is worse than ever. What is wrong with him?" she asks.

"I suspect a problem with his heart, although I am not sure. He responds to none of the treatments I have given him. I will continue to work toward strengthening his vital chi and trust in his own healing process, but I am afraid that you must plan for the worst."

"The woman that was here the other night said something about a medicine woman who could help him. Where is she?"

"Mmm," he snorts. "Yatsa. We have not seen nor heard a peep from her. To tell you the truth, I am not surprised. She is worried about her reputation. She knows that she could not help this one."

Esther nods slowly.

"So he is going to die?"

"Most likely. I am sorry."

"Can Yatsa not come just to try?" she says suddenly. "I'll give her Pedro's horse just to try."

"Please, my dear," says Kuhl, sitting her down in a chair. He laughs to himself. "That Yatsa is a crafty one. She creates an aura of mystery and magic, and people think that she is powerful. Those that go to her believe that she will make them well, and then they do get well. That is positive thinking, not magic. You'll notice that she only takes patients who are going to get well on their own. Positive thinking is useful at times, I suppose, but then again, your friend doesn't believe in that kind of thing. He is not an ignorant who believes that the spirits of shamans can heal him like magic. And he is very, very ill, and so she will do nothing but gain a beautiful horse that is to be yours."

He points to the old Zesti man, lying in a silent daze in his bed.

"She might be useful to him perhaps."

Esther nods silently. There doesn't seem to be any hope for poor Pedro.

"Take some time and prepare yourself for the worst. And hold out a little hope - just in case. I have seen amazing things happen at the last minute. We are doing absolutely everything we can."

Kuhl lays the basket of herbs at the foot of Pedro's bed and leaves Esther alone with her thoughts.

Raccoon 18'

Raccoon moon

Esther is summoned to the hospital this morning by a young boy. She tells Beryl that she'll be back soon and walks there with a heavy heart. As she walks, she realizes that she has actually grown to care about Pedro, even though he is a priest and he usually drives her crazy. She arrives fearing the worst, but Pedro looks much the same as he did last time. It was Usa who sent the boy, and she rises from her chair when Esther enters and walks over to greet her.

"There you are. I have finally contacted Yatsa, who was meditating in a far away place. She said that her spirit friends told her that she was needed at home and she came as fast as she could. She will see Pedro if you still wish her to."

"Sure. I have decided to give her Pedro's horse, which is grazing in the hills. I saw it this morning. Should I go get it?"

"Yes. Do that. But remember, you must give her the horse as a gift. Not as payment, but merely as a token of your gratitude for the knowledge she has. That is the way you pay a Ruok."

Esther thinks of the doctor, and what he said about this woman.

"Do you think she can help him?"

"I don't know. But I know that the healers here cannot. She is his last chance."

Esther debates a few moments. She thinks about what Kuhl said about wasting Pedro's gift to her. She would love to have his horse in the event of his death. But in the end, there is really no room for argument. Pedro deserves a last chance, even if it turns out to be nothing.

Despite protests from Kuhl, Usa brings Yatsa to the Healing House later that day. She is the oldest woman Esther has ever seen. If anyone could ever be called an old crone, it is this woman. She looks as if she might have been beautiful once, except someone took all of her skin and stretched it until it hung limp and ragged over her frame. She is slightly hunched and thin, and her hair is stringy, grey and flat. However, she has the most intense, alive eyes that Esther has ever seen. And there is a deep power emanating from her that makes Esther step back as Yatsa walks past her.

"Yatsa, this is Esther. She is the friend of the sick man," says Usa by way of introduction. She doesn't bother to introduce Yatsa.

The old woman stares at her, which makes Esther extremely uncomfortable. Her gaze is much too bright. Esther looks away and stares at the horse tied up outside instead. Yatsa follows her gaze.

"I have no use for a horse. I am too old to ride," she rasps.

"Oh. Well...."

"Perhaps you will think of something else."

"I will try."

" Now, I must see the patient."

She hobbles over to look at Pedro. She takes her hands and runs them up and down his body. Checks his eyes. Puts her head to his chest.

"He was wounded by an arrow, as you can see," says Usa after several minutes. "He has complained before that it never healed properly."

"That is nothing," she snaps impatiently.

"You think it is something else then?"

"The wound from this arrow weakened him and gave him many problems, but the thing that consumes him is something much deeper."

Yatsa begins to hum softly to herself. She continues to run her hands up and down his chest. Finally, she sits down beside him. She closes her eyes and says nothing for a long time. Usa indicates for Esther to sit down and be patient. Esther sits all the way at the other side of the room and continues to watch Yatsa curiously. Yatsa's head nods a few times and then drops onto her chest. Her breathing becomes slower. She has fallen asleep.

An hour later, Yatsa finally lifts her head up and looks around her. The room is empty, except for Pedro and the old Zesti man. She stares at Pedro and nods her head slowly. Then she stands up and shuffles slowly outside. She finds Esther sitting against the wall, enjoying the sunshine. Esther has been out there a long time, wondering when Yatsa will wake from her nap.

"Where is Usa?" asks Yatsa.

"She went to do some rounds."

"Go get her."

Esther stands up and goes in search of Usa. When they return, they find Yatsa sitting on a bench in front of Pedro's room. She is asleep again. Esther begins to wonder if Yatsa is too old to be of any use, because she always seems to be asleep. Usa shakes her awake and whispers something in her ear. Yatsa seems confused for a second, and then her eyes become clear.

"What have you discovered?" asks Usa.

"He no longer wants to live."

Usa nods silently, as if it makes perfect sense.

"Does this sound right to you?" Yatsa asks, staring at Esther with those piercing eyes of hers.

"I don't know," she stammers.

"Don't know?" she laughs, as if it is such a stupid thing to say. "You know well enough! Speak up, girl!"

"He was a priest," says Esther quickly, shocked by the forceful tone of her voice. "But he no longer wants to be one."

"Yes," she whispers, "a man of spirit, who no longer believes in his cause. Go on."

"He and his party were attacked while trying to convert a village, and he was shot by an arrow. Ever since then he has lots of pains and he gets dizzy and throws up a lot. And he drinks a lot to kill the pain."

"Has he expressed remorse about anything?"

"He was sorry about destroying their village afterwards. And he mentioned something about seeing a lot of death since he has come here."

"What does that mean?"

"I guess it means that a lot of his slaves have died," she says, trying to keep the bitterness out of her voice.

"He has seen and done horrible things and he cannot escape the guilt," she intones in a dramatic hiss. " And so, weakened from his wound, he looked for strength in the usual place, his beliefs, and finds nothing to guide him."

"That sounds good," Usa agrees.

"And what else?" Yatsa asks accusingly. "There is something more. I feel it. What do you hide, girl?"

Esther shifts around on her feet uncomfortably.

"What is it?" Usa asks gently.

"He is in love with me," she says with a shrug, as if it is not a big deal. "I think that he gave up being a priest for me. But I don't love him. He saw me having sex with another man, and -"

Esther stops talking suddenly, surprised that she is sharing these things with the two women. Her face gets red from embarrassment. Yatsa sees her expression and chuckles. She glances over at Usa, who also has an amused look on her face.

"Don't be embarrassed," says Usa, touching Esther's arm. "Men have wept over me in my time. It is the way things are."

Esther is suddenly hit by a terrible revelation.

"I don't love him. Is that why he is dying?"

Yatsa muses quietly about this, while Usa continues to hold Esther's arm and rubs it in a comforting way.

"That may be one reason why he no longer wants to live," Yatsa mumbles, "but there is still more to this mystery."

The old woman is quiet for a long time. She closes her eyes and hums to herself.

"He was wounded once, by a black shaman," she finally whispers, so quietly that Esther has to crane her neck to hear. "I have felt that presence. It was a cruel, malicious man, who deeply injured him when he was a boy. A man of great power who used it for bad purposes. That darkness is still inside him and eats away at him. Now that he is weak from his head wound and no longer wants to live - the darkness has a chance to spread throughout his body and take over. It has waited a long time for this chance."

"Do you know anything about that?" Usa asks Esther.

"No."

Esther does think of something though. The words 'black shaman' make her think briefly of Father Fernandez. But she quickly brushes that thought aside. She is pretty sure that Pedro never knew Fernandez. Pedro is new to this land.

"Perhaps I can heal him," Yatsa says. "I will try. But I am very old and my powers have grown weak. I cannot do this alone. I will need help."

She stares at Esther, who straightens in surprise. Her eyes open wide.

"Me?"

"Yes. You."

"Why me?"

"Because he loves you. And there is a strong tie between you. I can see the bond. Your fates are intertwined."

"I don't think so," she says, frowning.

"Oh yes. Although you are not the one who has made him sick, you have the power to make him well."

"No, no," she says, shaking her head. "We cannot even get along."

"Then why do you ask for my help?" she asks, fixing Esther with a stern glare.

"I feel sorry for him, and a little guilty too, because I took advantage of him. I used his affections to get a ride up here, even though I knew he was sick."

Yatsa glares at her and shakes her head slightly, and Esther can see that this is not an acceptable answer. And then she suddenly understands the truth.

"He saved my life once," she informs Yatsa at last, as if the words are being dragged out of her. "I was dying of thirst in the hills…and he saved me."

"Perfect," she says, breaking into a sly smile. "So you owe him the greatest of all debts."

"Well, I don't know," she mumbles, "if I was actually dying, but…."

"I sense there is something important you are hiding," Yatsa says. "But I will not force you to reveal your secrets. It is settled. We will proceed on the Wolf moon, when the healing power will be strong."

"When is that?" asks Esther.

"Four days," says Yatsa. "Enough time to prepare myself for this task."

"Will he live that long?" asks Esther.

Yatsa grabs Esther's hand tightly and squeezes it. She has much strength for an old crone.

"You must stay with him constantly, comfort him, and take care of him. Be kind to him, although you do not love him. That will give him the will to live."

Esther feels her spirits sinking. She has no desire to spend three days in Pedro's hut. It sounds like slow torture. She is about to suggest that since she only causes him pain, she should stay away from him, but she is embarrassed to seem so callous when all of these other people are so willing to put so much energy into saving him.

"And Kuhl, the healer, may play his part also. I have seen that he has already lengthened the man's life, due to his wisdom and his knowledge of herbs and the Chinese needle cure. He must continue to do what he has done, and keep Pedro's body as strong and pure as he can."

"Kuhl is a good man," agrees Usa. "Except for his prejudices."

"Ah, I know. I know. He doesn't believe in my powers. That is too bad for him, and too bad for his patients. Attacking a problem from two sides is always better than one."

She finally releases Esther's hand, and she seems to slump.

"Until then," she rasps, in a tired voice.

Yasta slowly walks off. Usa, awed by the great Ruok, rushes to help her home. A little awed herself, Esther goes back to the farm. She smiles as she nears the fields, and sees everyone busy toiling. At least she has an excuse to miss work for a few days.

Raccoon 19'

Esther spends the whole morning with Pedro. It is a nice day, considering the circumstances. Pedro is feverish, extremely weak and quiet, so they don't fight or have any uncomfortable silences. In fact, he doesn't speak a word the whole afternoon, and she likes him better for it. She sits by his bed and reads to him from Karbudde, which she has not attempted in a long while. He seems to enjoy her company, for he squirms less and even manages a weak smile once or twice when she makes silly blunders. Tunia comes in the early afternoon to care for him, and the two women of similar ages quickly become fast friends. Esther helps her wash Pedro, and they make it into a fun game instead of the boring chore it usually is for Tunia. They splash him and giggle like little girls, and then the two walk outside in the summer heat and take a swim themselves.

Today is a holiday and Esther can feel the excitement in the air. There is a great celebration beginning in the late afternoon, and she expects a great feast and lots of good music and dancing. She bids farewell to Pedro as soon as the heat dies down to a more reasonable warmth, and walks over to the assembly hall.

The Hall of the Black Mask is packed solid. The whole tribe is here, bearing the fruits of their labor over the past mnths. Baskets are loaded with fruits and vegetables of all varieties and colors. Corn and hemp stalks hang from the ceiling. Flowers and herbs adorn the tables in intricate patterns. Some have brought clothes freshly made from the sewing rooms and hung them on the walls. Everything that came from the sweat of the Raccoon brow this year is gathered together in all its splendor. It takes Esther's breath away. Esther is proud to see grapes and corn that she helped pick sitting in a basket on the table. It makes her feel that she is part of this night, which is so much nicer than being a stranger observing tribal customs that have nothing to do with her.

Soon a hush falls over the crowd, as a woman stands up to speak. She is dressed simply, in a beige and brown dress that hangs limply from her thin frame. Her hair is plain and straight and tied with a garland of white flowers. But there is something special about her, something subtle, that Esther cannot quite figure out.

"My friends, looking around the room, we see the fruits of all of our labor this past year. It seems like only yesterday when we first planted the tiny seeds that have grown into the marvelous gifts before us today. It has been a good growing season. Everything looks healthy and strong. Sure, there have been some tough times. The cold snap in June that almost killed our precious baby sprouts before they became strong. The bear that got into the food traders-"

There is much knowing laughter among the crowd. They will never forget that.

Suddenly, Esther realizes that this is the chief of the tribe who speaks to all. It is she who will marry off the young couples. Esther is amazed at how humble she is. She does not wear anything to suggest that she is a chief. She dresses exactly like everybody else. In fact, she seems plainer than everybody else, except for that special something which Esther couldn't quite place until now. She makes a long speech about the harvest, and then the tribe sings the blessing of the Raccoon spirit. It is a short, simple song, but everyone sings it with feeling. And then it is time for the weddings. There are many rules and values that a newly married couple must adhere to, and the chief spells it all out for them.

"A married couple is a partnership from beginning to end. Anything that is not beneficial to the success of a marriage must be avoided. Pointless arguments, pettiness, and jealousy are examples of things that waste time that could be better used in building a successful union. There is little enough time in the day as it is, and we of the Raccoon Tribe have enough to worry about without the added pressure of having to worry about hurt feelings and anger. So avoid such problems by your humility toward each other, and by concentrating on giving as much as you can."

It is not a very romantic wedding, but it is sweet nonetheless. And then the couple kisses and everyone applauds. After the second wedding, dinner is served. Servers come around with big bowls of bean and squash soup, multi-colored salad, acorn bread, camas cakes, and corn cakes. Then comes the main course, which is raccoon stew. The servers sing the raccoon song as they serve their sacred animal. Esther notices that some decline this delicacy, but she has some and finds it delicious.

After dinner, there is classical music by the Broken Antler Quartet, which features dueling violinists, and everyone is free to mingle and enjoy the decorations and each others' company. The crowd is very lively and happy, long lost friends seeing each other for the first time in weeks, sharing stories of the past days and all the trials and tribulations and little excitements of the season. A keg of wine is opened and musicians from the Wolf tribe appear. A Wolf singer leads everyone into a circle and tells them to hold hands, and then everyone dances in a circle and sings a song he teaches them.

It is very late when everything winds down and everyone wanders home to bed. The hall is left a mess for the morning. Esther walks back to the Healing House, with a glass of wine for Pedro. She wonders if he'll come out of his near-coma for a glass of good wine. She walks under the tall oaks, swaying in a slight breeze, and breathes in gulps of fresh air greedily. She hears the sounds of the violins from the Broken Antler Quartet faintly in her head as she walks, and hums to herself in the balmy, warm night.

Raccoon 20'

Pedro has started speaking again, and his constant need for reassurance drives Esther mad. He keeps holding her hand and telling her things that make her want to vomit.

"I'm so happy you're here with me. You're my little angel."

"Your presence soothes me and makes it easier to know that I'm going to die soon."

"I hope I see you in heaven someday."

"I get the idea," she says unkindly.

"I'm sorry if I scare you. I know love scares you, and I don't blame you for your words."

"I'm not scared. You just say the stupidest things. Please stop talking."

She pulls her hand away and holds it like it is diseased from contact with him. He sighs and closes his eyes, and thinks that he can't wait to die and see heaven. Nobody would say anything like that in heaven. He is sure of it.

Esther sits on her own bed, trying to calm down and wishing she hadn't said that to him. She has spent too much time in this sick hut, and she doesn't know if she can take two more days it. She already feels like an eternal fixture in the smelly room - like the old Zesti man with the broken leg. Another broken piece of humanity, shuttered away from the world. As if on cue, the old man breaks into another round of hideous shrieking that is supposed to pass for singing. She feels the hairs on her arm prickle, and she has to walk out of there before she scratches his eyes out.

"Are you awake, Esther?"

"Hmm. Oh yes."

Esther rises sleepily and looks around. It is dark out, and a meager candle in Usa's hand is the only light. Pedro is sound asleep.

"How's he doing?" asks Usa.

"He's been a little better. He had some soup today and he has been able to talk."

"Good. How are you holding up?"

"This place makes *me* feel sick."

"I know the feeling. You must not become so obsessed with caring for another that you forget to care for yourself too."

"That is true," Esther agrees. "Perhaps I will sleep outside tonight."

"I thought you might like some food. I made it myself."

"Thank you."

In a large wood bowl is acorn bread, wild greens, and a piece of roasted salmon. Gratefully, Esther takes the plate outside into the fresh night air and sits down on a bench. Usa follows her outside.

"Before you eat, I wish to ask you a question. Have you decided what to give Yatsa as an offering?"

"No, not yet," Esther says, with a mouth full of food.

"You should present your gifts tomorrow. Then there will be no misunderstanding."

"I'll think about it."

"Good. I must go do my rounds. I'll see you later."

Usa leaves Esther to eat her meal in peace and quiet. After eating, she looks through Pedro's pile of possessions. Fire tools. Robes. Cooking pot. Wool blanket. All are everyday items, not suitable as a gift. But wrapped in his robes, she finds something good. Two beautiful books, obviously from Europe, with leather covers and thick, luxurious paper. One is a bible, and the other one is a handwritten book of poems, with elaborate drawings in the margins. She remembers him mentioning these books yesterday, as she read Karbudde to him. He said that these books mean a lot to him, because they are his sole link to memories of his home. It was a gift from an elderly priest or something.

She thinks that the books would be good gifts to Yatsa, because they are much nicer than local books. Anyways, they will have to do, for he has nothing else worth giving. She has nothing worth giving either, except her cloak, and she won't give that up. She won't mention this to Pedro just now. He doesn't need to know about it unless he gets well, and then he can be angry.

As she puts away his possessions, three raccoons boldly enter the room. They seem to hesitate, as if disgusted by the room full of sickness and bad smells, and then walk fearlessly over to the basket of berries that is supposed to be for Pedro and help themselves. Esther is so amazed by their bravery, that she allows them to eat a few berries before trying to chase them away. The raccoons ignore her until she gets right in their faces and nudges them with a broom, and then they leave slowly as if they know that she isn't really going to hurt them. It seems a strange omen, although she doesn't know what it means.

Raccoon 21'

In the morning, Usa shakes Esther gently and indicates that she should get up. She gives Esther a cup of tea and urges her to drink. After she has a few sips, Usa points toward Yatsa, who stands outside Pedro's sick hut.

"You should present her with your offering now," whispers Usa.

Esther gets the books and she and Usa walk outside.

"Esther thought you might want these books," Usa says, carefully avoiding any mention of payment. "They come from Europe. This one is a holy book, like the ones the Spanish priests read. It is a very old book. The small one is a book of poems."

"The small book is one hundred years old," Esther says. "That's what Pedro told me. The bible is new, but the words are thousands of years old."

Yatsa examines the novels curiously. She seems impressed by the pictures in the book of poems and the luxurious leather covers. Yatsa seems more wide awake than usual, as if she has finally gotten enough sleep.

"I like the feel of it," says Yatsa, stroking the paper with her fingers. "They are much nicer than our own books. My eyes are too weak to read, but I will enjoy looking at the pictures. Usa, perhaps you may read them to me someday?"

"I am interested to read the holy book of a far away land," says Usa. "Although I fear they are written in a foreign language I cannot translate."

"It is written in the same language as we speak," Esther explains. "But they use different letters."

"You can learn the new letters someday," Yatsa says. "Then you may read to me."

"Of course," Usa says with a smile, knowing that Yatsa will not live long enough for her to learn to read this book.

Both women stand over the sleeping Pedro, staring at him. He has grown very thin and drawn and his skin tone is bad. He seems on the verge of death.

"He is worse," Usa says solemnly. "But he is not dead yet."

"He looks like a spirit," says Yatsa.

"That is his normal color. He is of a race of pale men."

"That's not what I meant."

"Would you like to begin?" asks Usa.

"No, we will wait until the Wolf moon. I just wanted to look at him."

The two women walk slowly outside into the sunshine, holding Pedro's precious books in their hands. Esther follows them out. It is too beautiful outside to stay indoors watching Pedro sleep, moan, or complain. She decides to take a walk down to the river and go for a swim instead. Whistling a tune to celebrate her freedom, she leaves Pedro's deathbed and walks out into the riot of sounds and colors on this summer's day.

Raccoon 22'

Wolf moon

Yatsa comes in the afternoon, hobbling on her cane. Usa walks with her, holding a basket full of her things. They enter the hut and immediately begin to set up. Yatsa shows Esther two bracelets with little hard leather balls on them, and she wraps the bracelets on each one of Esther's ankles. Usa lights a huge bundle of sage and begins to sweep the room with a strong incense, and then she lights several candles and places them around the room.

Yatsa examines Pedro, who seems to be fading. She grunts and nods, as if seeing exactly what she expected to see. She puts her hands upon his face and mumbles to herself.

"Let us begin," Yatsa says after a time.

"What should I do?" asks Esther.

"You may dance."

"Dance?"

"Yes. I am too old to dance properly. You must do it for me."

Yatsa shows Esther a dance that is more like running in place slowly. Esther imitates her movements. The bracelets make a slight sound, as the seeds within them rattle. She makes the rattles go in unison, as she steps up and down. Yatsa sits down calmly and closes her eyes. She hums softly.

Kuhl walks into the room just then, holding a basket of healing roots and needles. He sighs, disgusted, when he sees Esther dancing, and glares at Yatsa, who ignores him utterly. Then he waves furiously at Usa to come outside and talk. She follows him outside, and soon their loud argument can be heard over the sound of the rattles and the humming of Yatsa. Esther can see Kuhl through the window watching her, as she dances self -consciously.

"Have you seen what is going on in there?" shouts Kuhl.

He does a ridiculous little dance, making fun of Esther.

"You've had your chance, Kuhl. You have done much for the man. But this is beyond your powers. Let them try."

"I will not. It is sheer nonsense. They are dancing and singing in there. How will that help him?"

"It can't hurt."

"No, he will be very amused until he is dead."

"When will you give up your silly prejudices and open your eyes? Healing is not done according to your rules. It is a very subtle art, that is beyond the understanding of anyone-"

"I do not need a lecture. I need to continue his acupuncture treatments. He needs another sweat and a rub of eucalyptus leaves and echinacea. We are finally making progress, and you are going to ruin everything."

They continue to argue, until finally Kuhl throws up his hands and storms off.

"I have better things to do than argue about dancing Ruoks!" he shouts out as he walks away. "I hope he enjoys the show!"

Yasta shows Esther new movements to add to her dance, including a strange back and forth motion with her hand, as if she is fanning the air. She instructs Esther to take off all of her clothes. She is only too glad to take them off, considering that they are becoming soaked with sweat. Then Yatsa begins to sing loudly, in a strange tongue. She seems a much different woman, as if she has just gained ten years of youth. Her energy is strong and she sits up straight - not slumped in her chair like before. Her eyes are clear. It is as if she is drawing energy from Esther's dancing.

Usa told her that Yatsa once danced over a patient for five days without rest. Esther closes her eyes and hopes that Yatsa does not have this in mind for her also. She doesn't think she could do it, and she certainly doesn't want to try. Not even to save Pedro's life.

She dances all day long, with only short rests for bathroom or refreshments. Then as darkness falls, Yatsa begins to dance next to Esther. She takes off all of her clothes, exposing folds of hanging, wrinkled skin. Yatsa steps softly up and down and begins to chant louder. Meanwhile Usa lights a great fire in the fire pit, sticks a bundle of herbs in the flames, and begins to fan the air with the smoke. The room is filled with a sweet, bitter aroma, and lots of smoke. When the herbs are all spent, Usa sits in a corner and beats a clapper stick slowly and languorously. The whole room seems enchanted now, charged with some kind of power.

Pedro is awake, and watches the women with awed eyes. He seems a little more lucid than usual, as if the dancing is having an effect on him also. He occasionally glances at Yatsa, but he cannot stop staring at Esther. The sight of her dancing naked in front of him hypnotizes him. She appears to be in a trance and there is something in her face that he has not seen before. It is like he is looking at a completely different woman.

Yatsa stops dancing, and she lights another bundle of herbs and bathes the room in fragrant smoke. She makes it a point to bathe Esther and Usa with the smoke also. Esther coughs, as she breathes in the thick smoke wafting under her nose. Almost as soon as she breathes the smoke, Esther falls deeper into her trance. Yatsa throws the herbs into the fire and chants rapidly. The sound of the clapper stick gets louder and faster, and Esther begins to move at its speed.

Finally, Esther stops dancing. She has no idea how long she has been doing this. She breathes heavily, noticing her exhaustion for the first time. Taking a moment to wipe away the sweat that stings in her eyes and wringing her hair out, she wonders why it is so abnormally hot in here. She feels dizzy and dehydrated and she drinks deeply from a water bowl. Meanwhile, Yatsa stops dancing also, as if Esther has made the decision to move on to the next phase. Yatsa walks up to Pedro and peers at him, and then she indicates for Esther to come forward.

"Do you see the darkness?" growls Yatsa in an unearthly voice. "It sucks his life away."

Yatsa seems transformed in the dim firelight. She seems to have lost another ten years in age. Her hair looks black in the dim smoky haze of the fire and not grey like before. Her skin seems smoother and more radiant, and her eyes shine brightly. She lays wet hands on Pedro's face and peers deeply into his eyes. Pedro is wide awake, and he stares at her like she is some succubus that will devour him. With a sudden cry, Yatsa rips his blankets off.

"Get on him!" she hisses.

"What do you mean?" Esther stammers.

"Climb upon him," Yatsa says, coming toward her and grabbing her in a tight bony grip that hurts her arm, "and heal him."

"H-how?"

"You will know," she says, releasing her grip.

Feeling strangely distant, Esther climbs onto the bed and straddles Pedro's naked body with her own. Pedro's eyes open wide with surprise and he and Esther lock eyes. But her eyes are too perfectly beautiful for him to bear, and he cannot look at them for too long. He is torn between wanting to recoil in terror and wanting to grab her in a lustful embrace. He does neither one, only lies there passively and waits for her to make the next move.

There is one part of him that makes the decision for him. That part stands up desperately, quivering in anticipation. Esther feels it against her pelvis, and she looks down at it curiously. Then she slowly raises her head and stares at him. She knows now what Yatsa wants her to do. Grabbing his shaft in slippery hands, she pulls it downward and thrusts it inside herself. She slides forward, engulfing him. Pedro gasps loudly.

"Oh my God," he moans. "Oh my God!"

Yatsa lays her hand on Pedro's chest. She begins to massage it while Pedro moans and writhes under the weight of Esther. While she strokes his chest, Esther moves slowly, rhythmically, like she is dancing on top of him. Her head is thrown back, her eyes are closed and her expression is calm and detached. Then Yatsa begins to scream in an unearthly wail that makes Esther jump with surprise and her pulse hammers like a woodpecker. Pedro screams "Oh God! Oh God!" over and over again, a desperate mantra against a coming explosion. He struggles to sit up, but Yatsa pushes him back down.

For a moment, Esther could swear that Yatsa is glowing with an unreal light, and pawing at a darkness on Pedro's chest. A great fear overcomes her, and she closes her eyes again, as if there is something happening that must not be witnessed by a mere mortal like her. She hears Pedro scream, and feels him come inside her powerfully. It is explosive, as if he had been saving it up for twenty years. When she opens her eyes again, everything changes. Yatsa's power seems to flicker and fade, and she slowly releases her pressure on Pedro's chest and steps away. Breathing heavily, Pedro sighs and lies still at last. Esther, who has been tightly clamping his body with her legs, slowly unclenches them and climbs off.

She puts a rag to her flower and cleans herself off. She still feels very strange, as if she were not herself. She wonders if she is drugged from the smoke they bathed the room in. Yatsa walks slowly outside into the cool night air, moving once again like an old woman. Usa gathers all of her things for her and takes a long time retying the remains of the bundles of burnt herbs, as if they were too precious to waste even the semi-burnt bits at the ends. She is quiet and withdrawn, and says nothing as she walks outside. With the two women gone, the energy in the room seems to slump and fall into a long quiet spell. Pedro just sits there, naked and dazed. His eyes are far away and distant, but they are clear. For the first time in weeks, there is no madness or sickness in them.

"What happened?" he whispers. "I thought I had gone to heaven, but I'm back again."

Esther doesn't answer him. She merely gathers her clothes and walks out of the hut stoically. She walks down to the river and submerges herself, and although it is cold, she doesn't get out until she feels herself again.

Raccoon 23'

Pedro seems much better this morning. He sits up in bed, and wolfs down plate after plate of boiled fish and acorn mush. Smiling for the first time in weeks, he jokes around with Tunia as she brings him more food. He even comments about the wonderful qualities of the acorn, which he just now sees for the first time.

"I feel wonderful," he gleefully shouts. "I feel like singing. Can I go outside and see the sun?"

"Are you sure you're up for it?"

"Oh yes. It has been too long since we laid eyes on each other. I could even go for another dip in that mud hole. Care to join me?"

"No thank you."

"And then I want to go to the sweat lodge. Like a heathen," he says gleefully. "I will walk there all by myself in the sunshine."

"Don't push yourself too far," says Tunia, laughing at his expression.

Esther sees Usa in the kitchen this morning and joins her for harti. It is good to have harti again, which she hasn't had in a while. It reminds her of the Jay tribe and her time there. She has learned by now not to speak to anybody until they have finished eating, so she eats quietly, although she is dying to talk.

"Good morning," says Usa, after both have finished eating.

"Good morning."

"Have you seen the patient?"

"No."

"You must see him. You wouldn't recognize him," she says, standing up and beckoning Esther to follow.

" I don't want to see him," Esther says uncertainly. "I couldn't face him. I can't believe what I did last night."

"What do you mean?"

"I had sex with him. Right there, in front of everybody."

"You did what you had to do," she says with a smile, taking Esther's hand and leading her out into the bright sunlight. "You healed him."

Esther laughs, because it sounds so ridiculous.

"Healed him? I don't think so. Yatsa healed him."

"Yatsa cleansed him of the black magic that was strangling his heart. But Yatsa herself said that you alone gave him the will to live. You made his heart strong again."

"How?"

"He really needed a romp," Usa says, with a cackling laugh.

When they arrive at the hut, Esther peeks inside, and sees Pedro sitting up in bed, talking animatedly to Tunia. She smiles, glad to see him well, although she still doesn't want to see him. She has fulfilled her debt to Pedro – and then some – so she figures they are even now. Backing slowly away from the door, she struggles to find a good excuse to leave.

"I have to get to work," she stammers. "I told Beryl I'd return to work today. I'll visit later."

"All right," Usa says, giving her a little pat on the shoulder. "I understand. I'll tell him you send your best and you'll visit when you can."

"Thank you."

"By the way," Usa adds. "Are you taking Barren Womb tea?"

"No," Esther says, giving her a strange look. "What's that?"

"It makes your womb temporarily barren."

"My womb?"

"You don't want to get pregnant with your friend's baby, do you?"

"Oh, I forgot about that," Esther says, in a panicked voice.

"When was your moon?"

"Just a few days ago."

"Oh, I wouldn't worry then. It is very unlikely, so near to your moon."

Esther walks away, thinking about how she will have to be more careful from now on. Getting pregnant would be a very bad thing for her at this time in her life. Especially with a priest's baby! She has enough problems as it is.

Raccoon 27'

Elk moon

Back in the daily grind of farm work, Esther walks back and forth, searching for good grapes among the overripe and shrunken remains of a thoroughly spent row of plants. By the time she picks a basket full, half of them have split from too much moisture, so she has to pick half the basket out again. Then she brings the rest over to show Beryl, who peers into her basket curiously.

"Not much there?"

"No."

"With you and Enri both gone, we were a little short handed. We waited too long to pick these plants and the grapes have gone soft."

"Should I continue?"

"Yes. We promised grapes to the Swan and Wolf tribes. We'll have to give them what we can," he says, stuffing some into his mouth.

"These won't last very long."

"I know. I'll have to make the trip very soon. Maybe day after tomorrow."

He sighs, thinking of the long journey.

"I'll have to go myself. There's nobody else to do it. "

"Can I come?" she asks curiously.

"You want to come with me?"

"Yes. Is that all right?"

"Well, Nan needs you here."

"Oh," she says, disappointed.

"Although..." he muses, "Perhaps I could use you. We could take two more horses, and we could sell off corn, hemp, potatoes and whatever else we can find."

He looks her up and down and nods to himself, as if appraising her usefulness.

"Can you ride a horse?"

"Sure," she says, although she has never tried to do it alone before.

"Let me think about it. I'll get back to you."

Pedro walks by the river, deep in contemplation about his experience, trying to make sense of it. Usa told him the entire story, about the involvement of the shaman and the black magic that was eating away at him and the ceremony they did to heal him. He is very upset about the loss of his two books, which were dear to him. And he thinks about the darkness that was eating him up, cast upon him by some black magician. Who is this black magician and why would he hurt him? Some angry heathen witch doctor who cursed him perhaps? Or was it a demon? Or the devil himself?

He can't for the life of him figure out why Esther had sex with him in the middle of the ceremony, but it was a wonderful feeling he will never forget. He keeps picturing the way she moved, as if in a trance, as she made love to him. It is like she was not even aware he was there. He wishes she would visit him again so he can talk to her about it, but she hasn't even come to see him yet.

"Ah, Pedro, there you are."

He looks up from his thoughts to see the healer, Kuhl, standing above him. Kuhl has a big smile on his face.

"It is good to see you up and about. We didn't think you were going to make it. And here you are, walking around all by yourself."

"I am feeling much better."

"You look very good. Your color is almost back to normal, although I must admit, it is a very odd color that you start with. I thought you were dead when I first met you, until Tunia told me that you were just that pale to begin with."

His friendly laughter shows that he is joking, so Pedro laughs along in a good-natured way.

"I know. I stick out among you darker skinned folk."

"There are some who thought you had died and were haunting the river on these walks of yours. I explained to them that you had pulled through and needed some time in the sun."

"Yes," Pedro says, laughing a little less than before.

"Well, you look fine to me," Kuhl concludes, giving Pedro a pat on the back.

"No small thanks to my good doctor. I thank you, from the bottom of my heart. God bless you."

"I admit that your case was one of the most challenging of my career. But I'm glad to see it all worked out in the end."

"Yes, I owe you a sizable debt in gratitude."

"That you do. But not to me only. To the Healing House and all the fine healers here, you owe a sizable debt. And not just gratitude."

Pedro stares at him suspiciously, suddenly understanding where the conversation is leading.

"I paid a gold doubloon and two silver pieces. That's a good sum. We had an agreement."

"Yes, you did. And that agreement was for a nurse, bed, and a week's care. But I would think that your situation was a bit more complex than that agreement covered. Many healers were involved in the end."

"So you are saying that I owe you a little extra in payment."

"I'm saying that you owe us a lot more. I myself spent a week with you. Tunia spent nearly the whole month caring for you, and Usa also. You were quite a handful. We deserve a fair trade in return, don't you think?"

But," Pedro says, in a lame, last ditch attempt, "it was not you who healed me in the end. It was the medicine woman. And I paid her well."

"Are you a mad man? That old crone says a few mystical words and her friend does a dance, and you think that is a substitute for the weeks of hard work we put into your health! Do you dare to insult me so?"

Kuhl is so angry that he slams his walking staff into the ground, crushing his toe with it. He yelps with pain and hops around on his other foot, cursing to himself. Then, feeling foolish, he glares at Pedro, challenging him to push him further.

"Forgive me for my foolish words," Pedro quickly sputters. "Go easy. I know it was you that healed me. I am just put out. I have not got a single coin to my name or any of your money shells. I am in a panic."

"Well, why didn't you say so?" says Kuhl, calming down. "Instead of raving on so."

"Sorry -"

"We have other patients in your situation. You can do a work trade. Perhaps we could find you some work here at the Healer's House."

"It would be an honor. I have some experience in the care and comfort of the sick. A little too much experience, if the truth be known."

"Good. I'll see what I can do. Excuse me for my cursing and my temper. It was uncalled for," Kuhl says stiffly, and then he turns around and hobbles off, leaning on his walking stick and favoring his sore foot.

Raccoon 29'

In the morning, Esther walks to Beryl and Nan's fields and helps Beryl load and saddle the horses for the journey. He has borrowed three extra horses, each with a load strapped to its back. The spare horse tied behind Esther's horse is loaded with huge bundles of hemp stalks that are destined to be made into paper at the Swan school. Esther sits down on her horse, a tall brown one, amid bundles of fragrant corn. This will be her first time riding a horse by herself and she is excited and nervous at the same time. She ties her burden basket behind her and then waits patiently while Nan and Beryl discuss the hundreds of little details that he needs to remember on this trip.

Finally, Beryl hugs Nan goodbye and climbs upon his horse. "Eeeyeeeyeee!" he shrieks, and kicks the horse, which begins to walk. Esther kicks her own horse and jumps up and down ineffectually, but her horse doesn't move. She shrieks like he did, but the horse still stands there. Finally, Nan gives the horse a smack and orders it to move, and it goes lumbering slowly forward, with the other horse following in her wake. Esther holds on to the rope nervously and prays that she won't fall off. Beryl urges his horse to move faster and Esther has to do the same or else fall behind. She wishes that Beryl would slow down their pace until she gets used to it, but she is too embarrassed to ask.

They travel toward the commons, where they will connect with the main path. As they pass through the trading area, Esther looks around the busy village, packed with traders and lively business as it always is during an earth moon. She is exhausted just watching them, and glad to be getting away on vacation.

Swan Tribe

Swan 0'

Raven moon

Fall has come, and with it, the downward procession of leaves. A brisk wind blows the leaves around their legs and sometimes into their hair, as they travel through warm valleys that are still sun drenched, despite the beginning of cold weather in other places. On they go, two and four leggeds walking in the late afternoon heat, on the road to Swan village.

Esther remarks to Beryl about how beautiful she finds the valley and how perfect the weather, and he agrees that it is particularly lovely this time of the year. She admires the brilliant yellow of the dead grasslands and the lush green of the oak trees, perfectly framed in the afternoon light. An untrained eye might notice only the similarities in the lands she has passed through - the sameness in color and the poor variety of trees and plants. Such things have been said of the land that is today called California. But to those that have grown up in it and know it well, the differences one finds every fifty miles is breathtaking. You just have to have the right sort of eyes, and Esther has those eyes today.

"There it is," exclaims Beryl with satisfaction.

"What?" Esther asks, from the bushes where she is peeing.

"You have to see this for yourself."

She hurries over to see a large plume of white water fly up into the sky. It reminds her of the spray that whales make when they surface. She wonders what other creature could make such a stream, ten times larger than the largest whale's spray. Some horrible monster, no doubt. It lasts a few moments and then slowly dies down.

"Is it safe to go down there?" she asks nervously.

"Why wouldn't it be safe?"

"What is it?"

"A geyser."

"Is it dangerous?"

"No, if you don't sit on top of it."

"What does it eat?"

"What are you talking about?" he asks with a smile.

It occurs to Esther that it might not be a monster or beast, but something else. And then it occurs to Beryl what she thought and he has a good laugh, while she blushes, feeling stupid.

Beryl makes a side trip to show her the great spray up close. There is a smelly, sulfurous pool of water that sits right in the middle of the valley. They meet three men there from the Wappo tribe, who have come to bathe in the mud baths. Communication is difficult, but there is no animosity between the strangers, just lots of curious smiles and hand gestures. The men point to the pool of water, and urge them to be patient.

Steam begins to build over the pool, like some dragon hiding in the depths, waiting to fly out and wreck havoc. And then the pool explodes, shooting a thick stream of water as high as a good-sized tree. Esther gasps, unable to believe her eyes. The hot water creates a rainbow in the sky, which quickly cools to air temperature. They are misted with water, which smells like a fart. After three minutes, the steam of water disappears as quickly as it appeared.

"How did it do that?"

Beryl shrugs, not caring at all how a geyser works. He is more interested in the Wappo, who are making indications that they would like to trade. Apparently they desire the tempting grapes in the baskets hanging from one of the pack horses. They seem unwilling to trade anything interesting though, so Beryl gives them a bunch of grapes each for free. They eat them with relish, one grape at a time, enjoying the strange food immensely. In gratitude, they invite Esther and Beryl to share some freshly caught fish, which they gladly accept.

There is no time to dally and enjoy a mud bath, so after lunch they say a hasty goodbye and continue on their journey north. Their path continues up into the mountains and Beryl pushes the horses until dark, because he wants to reach the summit by evening.

Swan 1'

Cougar moon

Swan village is located on a great lake, a shining blue jewel that stretches farther than Esther can see in the bright afternoon sunlight. The sun shines off the water, creating sparkles before her eyes, and she hears the cries of ducks, swans, and other lake birds. There are many tule boats out and about on this hot day, floating peacefully on this windless morning. This is Pomo territory, and there are many villages located along the lakeshore, each one with people fishing, boating, and soaking up the final dregs of summer before the cold days begin.

The Swan tribe boats are easy to tell apart from the other boats in the lake, because each is crafted to resemble a swan. Like a Chinese boat with a fierce dragon's head at the bow, except this is a simple tule boat with a gentle swan's head, with yellowed beak and black beady eyes.

Esther sees live swans too. Five of them float side by side in the tranquil water. Among the ducks, they seem like gods and goddesses. They are twice as large, white as snow, and bear a regal pride that the other ducks don't have. Esther gawks, open mouthed, at the beauty of the swans, as they walk onto shore and begin exploring the ground for bits of food. They show off for her, stretching their wings and craning their necks to appear large and grand. They never separate from the group. Where one walks, all of the other swans follow. Suddenly, they crane their necks to full height and begin screeching in obscene honks and unpleasant screams that fill the great valley with noise. Who knows what they are saying to each other, but it must be very important. And then they all take off at once, with a great beating of wings, on some important mission. They enter the water with a great splash, but then just sit there, floating serenely without a care in the world. Whatever it was they were looking for, they have apparently forgotten all about it.

The commons, located a short distance from the lake, is packed and teeming with people. A group of women crafts fine baskets, which they learned to do from the local Pomo tribes, who are renowned for their beautiful basketry. They coil and twine fine pieces of sedge root, tule, willow, or bulrush reeds so tightly together that the baskets can hold water. Esther walks over to see the baskets, amazed by their beauty. She looks at her ripped, old burden basket, and decides to buy a new one before she leaves.

Esther spends the day following Beryl around as he does his business. She meets many people, including the chief, and she is officially invited to the polar day celebration tomorrow about fifteen times. After a hearty dinner in a public house called the Obsidian Eye, which serves a big meal for a tupa, they make camp. The shelter is full and the night is warm, so they sleep out under the stars. It is too warm even for a blanket, until Esther begins to hear the familiar whine of mosquitoes, and she has to put the hot blanket back over her body to protect her from the bloodsuckers. She tries to cover her head with the blanket, but it is too warm. She may either sweat to death or be bitten to death - her choice. The bloodsuckers manage to get through her defenses anyway, and soon she is covered in bumps and lumps where she has been bit. She cannot sleep, imagining them feeding off of her, and she slaps at every noise she hears. Beryl sleeps peacefully. She watches him jealousl[illegible]ondering how he can sleep with all the buzzing around him. [illegible]ost dawn by the time she falls asleep, and then only because [illegible] too exhausted to fight any more.

Swan 4'

Hawk moon

In the morning, everyone arrives at the lake for the start of the full moon celebration. After a breakfast of berries and corn cakes in the commons, the games begin, including the famous Swan boat race. Twenty Swan boats will set sail, with three rowers in each boat, and race around the lower part of the great lake. Everyone gambles on the race by putting tupas into a big basket and placing a marker with the judge to show which boat they think will win. Those who predict the victorious boat will share the whole basket of tupas. There is a frenzy of betting on the shore, as the racers all stretch out and wait for the starting drum to pound.

When the starting drum sounds, the boats all go at once, with a slapping of paddles and much shouting and whooping. The thing that makes this annual race exciting is that the teams are allowed do anything to slow down their competitors, short of damaging a boat or hurting another player. So there is much shoving and pushing as they begin the race, with men leaning out to spin other boats around or pushing off them to get momentum at their expense. One team manages to steal the oar of another, leaving them with only two rowers. Laughing maniacally, they throw the oar far out into the water, making the other team paddle out of the way to get it.

Soon there are two teams tied for the lead, a co-ed Swan team and an all male Hawk team. Suddenly, a large Hawk man leaps out of his boat and lands on the edge of the other boat. He pulls down on the boat edge as he hits the water and the boat flips over. The Swan team is thrown into the water, with loud curses and shouts, and the crowd on the banks cheer or boo as the Hawk racer swims back to his boat, which will now have a big lead. But a very wet Swan man is a faster swimmer, and he grabs hold of the ruffian's leg and manages to hold onto it, while his own teammates right their boat and climb in. The Hawk eventually escapes and returns to his boat, but they have lost their lead to the rest of the boats that have now passed them.

There are many such shenanigans before the end of the race and almost every boat is tipped over at least once. It is a very funny sight, to see four teams swimming in the water, trying to right their own boats and prevent others from doing the same. There are oars floating all over the place. But despite all the drama, it is a friendly competition, and everyone is laughing and having a good time.

The last place team is a bunch of old Swan men who have been trailing behind everybody the whole race. They alone have not been tipped over, because they always stay in back where nobody is looking, and also because they are old and pretend to be feeble and nobody has the heart to tip them over. But in the last moments of the race, they put on a burst of speed, using all of their energy not wasted by fighting, and they suddenly skim into shore just ahead of the lead boat. Everyone roars with laughter and great delight as they win, and they laugh at the crestfallen and shocked faces of the young Hawk warriors, who thought they had earned a great victory, only to have it robbed by a bunch of old men from the Swan tribe in the final seconds.

The people say that the old men have taught everyone a valuable lesson, because they did not fight, but used guile to win. Such a thing has never happened in the history of this race. And best of all, nobody bet on the old men but themselves, so they alone split the big basket full of tupas. The old men are praised, and they receive a hearty cheer as they throw handfuls of tupas into the air, to show that they are gracious and generous with their winnings. Children run around picking up the tupas in handfuls.

As night falls, fish and ducks are roasted over fires and kegs of wine are opened. Three groups of musicians all play music at once. They are located just far enough away, so when you stand close to one band, you cannot hear the others. But if you are in the middle, you can hear all of the music at once. Soon Esther circulates in a maddening swirl of people, and her head spins with too much wine and too much stimulation. The music sways in and out endlessly, and she is not even sure where the drummers are or which of the three groups of musicians she is listening to. People dance everywhere, and Esther joins in like a shaman trying to reach an altered state. Someone shouts something in her ear, but she cannot hear him. All she can hear is her own heartbeat and the sound of the music weaving in and out of her fevered brain all night long.

Swan 5'

Esther wakes with a splitting headache. Where is she? She opens her eyes, shocked to find herself in bed with a stranger. Closing her eyes, she tries to remember the details of last night. She remembers dancing with several men until she was quite dizzy, getting extremely drunk, and walking home with one of them. She remembers crashing onto a strange bed and kissing a man with groping hands. She doesn't remember sleeping with him, but she is definitely not in the mood for early morning introductions, so she tries to sneak out of bed. Unfortunately, he wakes groggily at her movements and tries to wrap his arms around her. She squirms out from his grasp and he opens his eyes.

"What's the matter?"

She doesn't know what to say to that. She just stares at him.

"Come 'mere," he mumbles sleepily, offering her a space next to him.

Esther struggles to remember what happened last night. Did they have sex? Is he dangerous? Scary? Her head hurts too much for such difficult brain activity. She decides that she is too tired to go anywhere right now, so she turns her back to him and covers her face with her hair. Soon, she is sound asleep again.

She awakens to the smell of food some time later. Opening her eyes and removing her protective hair mask, she sees the man cooking fish in front of a small fire. He is of average height, with short curly hair, a bone earring in one ear, and a crystal worn around the neck. He is handsome and graceful in his movements, although there is something slightly feminine in them. She guesses his age to be somewhere in his late twenties.

He suddenly turns around and smiles at her.

"Good morning. Breakfast is almost ready."

"Smells good," she mumbles sleepily.

Soon they are sitting on the bed, eating fish and sipping tea. The food and tea go a long way to calming her stomach and grounding her after the night of drunken debauchery. She eats the entire plate in a few minutes, and gulps down the tea so fast she spills it on her clothes.

"Want more? I can cook some more."

"I don't want to put you to any trouble," she says, trying to remember his name. "How are you called?"

"No trouble. And I am called Vin."

He goes back to the stove, chatting about the wonderful party yesterday as he cooks. He asks her many questions about herself, but she is vague and tells him as little as possible. Soon another plate is put into her hand, and she eats until she is stuffed. He sits next to her as she eats, and she gets the uncomfortable feeling that he still expects something from her. It is the way he keeps staring at her. After finishing her breakfast, she stands up a bit rudely and walks to the door. She gives him a quick and confusing goodbye, then wanders out into the afternoon to look for Beryl.

While searching the commons for Beryl, she runs into none other than Kahne, the brother of Dohr. Fleeing from a friend during a violent form of tag, he bumps into her with a thud. He apologizes quickly, but stops when he recognizes her.

"It's you," he says surprised, as he looks around desperately for the friend who is chasing him.

"Yes. Hello Kahne."

"Hello -" he says breathlessly, spotting his friend in the distance. "I forgot your name."

"Esther."

"Yes, well I have to run -"

Is Dohr here?" she asks quickly, before he runs away.

"Yes, he's uh, at the Lily Pad, I think -" he blurts out, and then he is gone in a cloud of dust.

He has lost precious momentum, and his friend catches him and tackles him roughly to the ground. She can hear the breath whoosh out of him and a crunch and thud. He groans and hits his friend until he gets off him, and his curses ring in her ears as Esther walks away.

She finds Beryl soon afterwards, trading furiously in the commons. He is engaged in selling off everything he has left, and it will be a few hours at least before he is ready to leave. Not having anything else to do, Esther decides to go to the 'Lily Pad' to see Dohr. She asks around and gets some strange stares as a result, but they point toward a path and tell her to follow it out of town until she sees several little huts with large statues in front.

It is another pretty day, and she enjoys the walk in the sunshine, with a perfect light autumn breeze to add just enough coolness to the heat. The path leaves the village and winds up into the hills. When it reaches the highest hill, it drops down into a valley filled with oaks. It is a long walk, and she is just thinking of turning back, when she hears the laughter of many men in the distance. Walking a bit further, she finds several men sitting around a table of rough-hewn boards, smoking pipes and laughing uproariously at something. In an open area are eight huts in a large semicircle, and a larger house across from them. The house has a large sculpture in front of it, a fertility symbol of a woman with round hips and generous cleavage.

"Hey, here's another one!" one of the men shouts through a haze of smoke. "This one's for me!"

"I'll try that one also," says another, choking with laughter. "But I'll go first. I'll not go after you. We've tried that before."

They are Hawk tribe mostly, by the looks of them. Esther searches for Dohr's face, but he is not among them.

"I'm looking for Dohr," she says to one of them quietly, not wanting them to talk about her any more.

"Do y' hear that? Dohr is in trouble," the man shouts to his friends. "Someone's looking for him."

This starts another round of bawdy comments. Esther waits for them to finish so she can find out where he is.

"You can find him in that big house," the man finally says. "If there's anything left over after you're through with him, I'll take the remains home with me."

Confused, Esther goes toward the big house, which is a well-made structure of wood planks. Off to one side of the house is a steaming pool of water, with many burl statues of swans surrounding it. The pool sits empty now, but shows the scars of much use.

The inside of the house is dark and intimate, with candles set inside hanging gourds. It takes Esther a moment for her eyes to adjust, and then she sees several people sitting on soft furs. Two girls are dressed provocatively in some very beautiful and very transparent silk golintas that start very low in the bust and cling tightly to their bodies. Their hair is done up in a tight bun, with a stick inserted in the middle. Three Hawk men talk to the girls and stroke them with their hands. Esther feels that she has intruded on some private event and starts to back toward the door, when one of the girls waves her over.

"Anything I can help you with?" she says in an ordinary voice that is out of step with her dress.

"No, I'm just looking for somebody."

"Who?"

"His name is Dohr."

"He's in hut four," says one of the men with a grin. "Been in there a while. He should be back soon."

"You can wait if you like," says another girl, with a laugh. "But promise me you'll take the argument outside when he comes out."

Esther sits down on a crude cushion made from deerskin, filled with leaves and twigs. It is a very comfortable seat, if one sits upon it in the proper way. She looks around the room, trying to figure out what this place is supposed to be. It reminds her a little bit of a shelter, except there is a big difference that she cannot yet figure out to her satisfaction. A few moments after she sits down, Dohr walks into the room. He has a big grin on his face, and he laughs when he sees his friends and grabs their hands in celebration.

"I was great," he brags. "She should have paid me -"

His face falls as he notices Esther, and the words die in his throat. He slowly turns beet red and his mouth opens, but no sound comes out.

"Hello," she says, helping him to speech.

"What are you doing here?" he stammers. "How - I mean -"

"I came looking for you."

"How did you know I was here?"

She cannot figure out why he is acting so strangely. He appears to be very embarrassed to see her.

"Kahne told me."

He slowly regains his composure, and sits down to talk to her and find out what she has been up to. He seems very happy to see that she is alive and well, but his mind is obviously elsewhere, and although he asks a lot of questions, he is not listening to the answers. Esther becomes annoyed by his strange behavior, and begins to think about walking back to the commons.

Just then, a large, matronly woman enters the room, wearing a Japanese geisha robe that is different from the other girls' tiny golintas. She doesn't say anything for a while, just watches everything that is going on. After she has formed some opinions, she lets them fly in a deep, booming voice.

"What are you doing?" she asks one of Dohr's friends. "Trying to get a free feel without paying?"

The man guiltily pulls his hand out of the girl's dress.

"Why don't you do it right, instead of touching around it like a little boy who doesn't know what to do?"

His friends laugh uproariously, giving him as hard a time as possible. Even Dohr comes out of his strange mood to laugh at the spluttering man, who is fumbling for a quick comeback.

"I'm going to," he says haughtily, trying to salvage his pride. "When I'm good and worked up. But now I'm getting cold again, listening to your big mouth, and it will take me even longer."

"Care to put your tupas where your mouth is?"

He frowns a moment, and then shrugs and hands her a few tupas from his bag.

"Eight?"

Grimly, he hands her a few more, looking as if he would like to strangle her.

"Good. Get as worked up as you like. What about either of you men? Care to indulge or just waste my girls' time?"

"I'm waiting for that tall girl," says one.

"I like this one fine," says the other

The large woman takes eight tupas from him also. She nods, satisfied at last, and then turns to stare at Esther.

"Who are you? We don't generally allow women in here."

Esther looks around, confused by all the women lounging about in a house that doesn't allow women.

"What about them?" she asks quietly, in an irritated voice.

"They're not women. They're Ladies."

Esther is now really confused. She still has no idea what this place is, having never seen anything like it.

"I'm not a lady?"

"No, you're not. Who are you? You don't look like you're from the Hawk tribe."

"I'm not."

The woman stares at her a long time, making Esther really uncomfortable, and then she turns her gaze back to the men.

"I'm Lula, madam of the Lily Pad. I'll leave you in the capable hands of the Ladies."

As she starts to walk out the door, she glances sideways at Esther.

"Can I talk to you a moment, young lady?" she booms out.

Esther is so surprised that she nearly falls off her cushion.

"Follow me, please," Lula says in a quieter voice.

Esther looks at Dohr, but he just shrugs his shoulders, not having any idea what she wants. So Esther follows Lula outside and they walk toward a small rundown hut a short distance from the house. Despite the dilapidated appearance on the outside, the hut is lavishly and sumptuously decorated on the inside. Dark crimson bedcovers and a silk taffeta hang over a bed of bear fur, and two candles set inside Chinese lanterns provide soft mood lighting. All of it is obviously imported at great expense from the Orient, along with her clothes. This must be a very rich woman.

Lula bids Esther sit on the bed and examines her from head to toe. She seems to be making up her mind about something.

"I believe you have been a Lady before," Lula finally says, breaking the silence.

"What do you mean?"

"A prostitute."

Esther gapes, her mouth wide open.

"I'm right, aren't I?"

"No."

"Ever given your body away for a price?"

"No," Esther says spiritedly. "I have never done that."

But she thinks of Branciforte suddenly and remembers that she used to sleep with men for wine or other strong drink. Lula is right. She did prostitute herself once upon a time.

"I guess I was wrong," says Lula quietly.

"No you're not," Esther admits, finding no reason not to tell the truth. "I have done it. How did you know?"

"I have been the madame of the Lily Pad for eight years. Seen many girls come and go. I can see a certain…moral flexibility in you."

Esther feels ashamed suddenly, and looks away.

"What is your name?"

"Esther."

"Don't worry, Esther. I am one as well. All of my girls are Ladies of the Lily Pad - which we prefer to the word 'prostitute'. You will not get any judgments from me. There is nothing wrong with it. We are just fulfilling the role of seductress."

She stands up and swirls her body erotically, as if to show Esther that she too has received the call to seduce.

"This is a prostitutes' house?" Esther asks surprised.

"Yes. Did you think those girls dress and act like that for fun?"

"No. But -"

"The reason I called you in here was not to embarrass you. I have just lost a girl and this is our busiest time of the year. It really leaves us shorthanded -"

She begins chuckling heartily.

"It's a funny story actually. Her father, a surly man from the Hawk tribe, comes for polar day. He comes to the Pad and he just says, "Surprise me", so I point him to room six. Upon entering, he discovers his own daughter lying on the bed, wearing next to nothing. This makes him very upset, as you may imagine." Lula laughs heartily. "He starts cursing and screaming and slaps the poor girl in front of everybody and calls her a whore."

"That's terrible."

"Mmm. But if you could have seen his expression, you'd have laughed. Anyway, he took her away with him. I think she'll be all right. Just run away again, I'm sure. Show up on my doorstep eventually." Lula suddenly rewards Esther with her most charming smile and says, "So I need some help."

"What kind of help do you need?" Esther asks suspiciously, although she already knows.

"You saw all the men outside, waiting for a turn. The Hawk tribe will be here several days, and my girls are exhausting themselves trying to please all those men. We need someone to pick up the slack and take on a few of the extra men. We can pass you off for a Swan maiden, I think. You are very alluring, and I can see that the kiss of the Swan has definitely left its mark on you. You are wild and you are modest - a deadly combination. You will be very popular."

Esther smiles at the compliment, and immediately stops herself and tries to appear shocked.

"Plus, you have already worked as a Lady. That is the most important thing. It is very difficult to convince a woman who has never tried it that it is anything but reprehensible. But someone who has done it knows that it is just a job - and one that pays very handsomely. We pay six tupas a man. That man might take an hour, or just a few minutes. But you make the same wage nonetheless. Six tupas are nearly as much as our respectable teachers make in a day at the school. More than a fisherman makes most days. And you may make that in only a few minutes."

Esther finds herself getting angry and defensive.

"I used to be very desperate and in a bad situation. Now, I am no longer so crazy...and...no, I am sorry. No!"

"Crazy? I don't think so. You were smart. You used the only thing you had at the time, your body, in order to survive. There is nothing crazy about that. Have you got much money right now?"

"Some. I have a job already."

"So take a few weeks off then. In a week, you can make a hundred tupas or more if you are popular. That is a lot of money for a week's work. Men will pay through the nose for some discreet sex that their wives know nothing about. Half of these men have brought their wives - and obviously they cannot go about sleeping with any young woman they meet. There would be consequences.

But they have a huge taste for Swan women, so they come here for a few hours and tell their wives they are going hunting.

"I will throw in room and board free of charge," adds Lula after a long silence. "Although I normally take that out of your wages. Will you try it out, and see if you like it?"

Esther thinks awhile, and then puts on the most indignant face she can.

"No, I am not interested. Thank you."

Lula stares at her a while, sizing Esther up.

"Have you got any other skills?"

"I can cook. Clean."

"Then I will hire you to do that. Five tupas a day. Two meals a day for the girls and any men who order dinner. That price includes room and board."

"And that's it? All I do is cook?"

"And clean. But there is one more condition of the job. You must work in one of our sexy outfits. It goes along with the theme of the Lily Pad. Having an attractive girl serving meals adds to the atmosphere. What do you say?"

"Where may I stay?"

"You may use the empty hut, number 3."

Esther stares at Lula critically. She feels strange about this, as if there is more here than meets the eye. Lula is crafty and a smooth talker. But despite her reservations, Esther can think of no reason not to take it. She really has no desire to return with Beryl to Raccoon village. Why not stay on here a bit? She can make more money here, and it sounds as if the work is much easier than farm work.

Finally, she agrees to the job, and Lula congratulates her and hands her a golinta, just like the other Ladies wear. It is pure Chinese silk, crimson and black, and it is thin - nearly see through. It is wonderfully comfortable and feels soft and sleek on her. She walks around, admiring the way it clings to her body and feeling sexy and feminine.

Lula shows her the kitchen, which is outside the main house. It is a large, well-equipped kitchen, obviously meant to feed many people.

"Let's get going on lunch now, shall we? You will cook for all the girls and any of the men who have paid for a romp and want to eat."

Lula leaves her to her task. After exploring the kitchen a bit longer, Esther goes outside to ask which men want food. She likes the way the men out there stare at her in her golinta. They shout out things to make her blush, but it is a pleasant blush. She shakes her hips and struts around, enjoying the attention and the glamour.

But soon she is up to her elbows in a great bowl of fish, grease, and corn flour, and her blush turns into a flush. She has to make lunch for eight girls and seven men. It takes two hours to cook and serve all the food, and then she has to clean up and wash the bowls. She wears a huge, scratchy smock in the kitchen, so as not to mess up her expensive silk golinta, and the job quickly loses its glamour and becomes just hard work.

That evening, Esther finds Beryl in the trading circle. He is in a good mood because he sold everything he brought with him, but Esther quickly ruins his good mood with her plans to stay here and work.

"How am I going to get all four horses back myself?" he asks in an irritated voice. "Can't you come back with me and then return?"

"Then I'll have to walk back," she says, stating the obvious. "And they'll give somebody else the job. It pays very well. I want to stay."

"So be it," he says, sighing deeply. "Maybe I can pay that miserable Yan a few tupas to come back with me. He always needs money, being the worthless lump that he is."

Esther helps him load up the horses for old times sake, and then bids him a hasty goodbye. He is distracted by his troubles and waves at her absentmindedly, as she starts the long walk back to the Lily Pad. Luckily for her, the moon is nearly full and she is able to find her way back without too much trouble. When she returns, she hears the Ladies having a party in the main house, but she is too tired to attend and she goes right to sleep instead.

Swan 6'

**Beaver moon*

"Hey! Where's my dinner sweetie?"

"What?"

"I ordered dinner."

"No, you didn't."

"Yes, I did. Just because you weren't paying attention, doesn't mean I didn't do it."

"Why don't you lay off her? It's her second day."

One of the Ladies comes to her rescue - Kamie - a lovely girl, small and sweet, with a big old attitude.

Esther kicks the door open and goes back out to the kitchen to get this man some food. It has been a hard day and she is in a bad mood. She cleaned up after the Ladies all day long, and it turns out that the Ladies are slobs. She had to wash their golintas and soiled furs too, some sticky from dried sperm and all smelling of sex and stale sweat. And she has made a mess of lunch too - the fish burnt, the bread black, and the greens gone rotten. All the customers have complained and some of the Ladies gave her an unpleasant look as they ate the horrible food.

She goes into the main room to serve the man his dinner and then sits down on the couch heavily, with a plate of burnt food in her lap. She tries to enjoy it, but peace will not be hers, even now. A very pushy Hawk has been bothering her all night to give him a romp. He sits down next to her, as she tries to eat, and begins talking to her. She tries to ignore him and takes a bite into the bread, which is burnt and crunchy. She finally gives up on her meal, which was as bad as she has cooked in her life, and escapes from her desperate suitor. She starts clearing plates grumpily, throws out the uneaten food, and puts the bowls into the dish tub. She eyes the huge tub of dishes warily. The water is sluggish and brown, and bits of burnt food, grease and bones float at the top. She has no desire to stick her hands into that nasty soup.

She goes into the main house to escape from her fate and makes an excuse of looking for more dishes. She jealously watches Kamie and Kelli relaxing on the couch, giggling and flirting with the men. In an hour, they'll make more than she makes all day by working her ass off.

"You shouldn't waste your talents in the kitchen," her Hawk suitor says to her. "I'll show you what to do with them."

She stares at him critically. He's not so bad looking. How bad could it be? She has done it before, and for far less compensation.

"And everyone thinks I'm a prostitute - I mean a Lady - anyways," she says to herself, carrying a dirty bowl back into the kitchen and dumping it in the overflowing dish bowl. "Maybe I should just be one, and make lots of tupa shells, instead of slaving away in here for five tupas a day. I could do it just for a few weeks, and then I won't have to work for a long time."

Meanwhile, she puts on her huge baggy dish robe, which is stained and covered in grease. As she reaches into the overflowing dish tub, some of the bowls fall onto the floor with a clatter. She picks them up, puts them in a pile near the tub, and then sits down, staring miserably at the huge task before her. She is tired of working hard. Tired of dishes, cleaning, farming or weaving. She wants to be treated like a queen, even a dirty one. Suddenly inspired, she throws off her huge apron. Wearing only the little silk golinta, she feels beautiful again. Then she pours herself a cup of wine from the little wooden cask in the kitchen - for courage. The second cup is for luck. Then, pleasantly fortified, she goes outside, brushes aside a lock of hair, and smiles bravely. The man is still there, watching her.

"Let's go, handsome," she says, brushing his chest with her fingers, the way she sees the other girls do it.

Lula smiles as she accepts payment from the man who is going to be Esther's first customer. Her plan worked perfectly. She had a feeling that Esther would change her mind, after a day of slaving away in the kitchen for less than the girls make for an hour's work. She purposely overloaded Esther, just to make sure she got the message. It is for the best. Lula is too old to get much interest from the clients these days. She is better off as boss and cook, taking to bed the occasional older man who wants a more experienced woman. Esther is young, fresh and very alluring, and will bring in more business. And besides...it is obvious after tonight's dinner that Esther is not a great cook.

Esther lies next to the man, her heart racing. He snores softly next to her, having fallen asleep almost instantly after their brief liaison. She doesn't have the heart to wake him and ask him to leave, so she lies on the other side of the bed, trying to ignore him and avoid thinking about what just happened. Finally, she can stand it no longer. She leaves him to his snoring and goes out to the main house. Several of the girls are there, sitting around in their robes and enjoying the fact that all of the men are gone. As soon as Esther comes into the room, the girls cheer.

"Here's to our newest Lady!" Kelli shouts.

Kelli is a tall, rangy girl from the Jay tribe, attractive in a beat up way, who always seems nervous and moves her hands around manically when she talks. She pours Esther a glass of wine, almost spilling it on herself, but pulling it off at the last moment.

Esther meets the other girls, but she finds herself connecting most to Kelli and a girl named Mati. Mati is a short, husky Swan girl, and the youngest girl in the den. She has mousy hair and a mousy personality to match. She doesn't have the blatant sexuality of the other girls and is easily overlooked in this place. However, she has a quality that observant men enjoy and a wonderful smile and laugh.

Esther takes a deep drink from her glass, hoping to put the night behind her. The act of drinking the wine soothes her frazzled nerves. It seems appropriate to get very drunk tonight.

"The first one is the hardest," Mati counsels.

"Her first one was one of those Red Hawks. You know how hard those warriors are to please. They're a pain in the ass. Isn't that right, Esther?" adds Kelli, waving her hands.

"I suppose. He wasn't too much trouble. And he fell asleep right afterwards."

"You're letting him sleep in your bed?" Mati says with a frown. "He's a toad - that's what we call a customer. Never let a toad fall asleep on your lily pad."

"That's right!" Kelli insists. "Go wake him up right now and ask him to leave."

"Do you think I should?"

"Of course, you should. Are you crazy?"

"Go easy on her. It's her first night. You'll give her a panic attack."

"She's got to learn these things, and the sooner, the better. Unless, of course, she wants him to sleep over?"

"No, I don't."

"Then you march right in there and wake that man up or I will," Kelli announces, standing up to do just that. She looks serious too.

Esther does as she is told, and soon she is escorting a sleepy Red Hawk outside into the darkness. The full moon shines brightly overhead.

"I'm so tired," he complains. "Can't I just leave in the morning?"

He yawns and leans against a tree.

"I'm sorry. They told me that no men are allowed to sleep in the Ladies' huts. It's forbidden. But maybe I can find you a blanket if you want to sleep underneath this tree."

"That's all right. Thanks for the fun evening."

He tries to kiss her, but she gently pushes his lips away. He shrugs and begins stumbling back home. Esther wonders if he is capable of walking back to his camp in his condition or if he will get hurt. But then she realizes that it doesn't matter, because she doesn't care.

She returns to her wine and the pleasant company of her new friends. Lula has now joined them, holding a silk bag with Chinese writing on it.

"So how was it?" Kelli asks with a grin and a nudge.

Esther shrugs in a noncommittal way.

"Come on. You can tell us. We've all been there. Give us the details, Esther."

"Well, it wasn't as bad as I thought," Esther says, with a little smile. "I hardly felt a thing."

"Why? Was he small?" asks Lula.

Esther laughs. "No, I think it's because I drank so much wine. I was a bit dull."

"He wasn't small?"

"I wouldn't say he was small. I've seen bigger," she adds, trying to fit in.

The girls giggle.

"What do you feel?" Esther asks curiously.

"Not much, but I pretend to feel something so that the boys have a good time," Mati explains.

"He was drunk - and a Hawk - which makes for an easy customer," Lula adds, trying to instruct Esther in the finer points. "Drunk ones don't care too much how you act, because they're too drunk to notice. Hawks are good toads too. They are pretty straightforward. But if you have a Wolf toad, for example, or an

Eagle, then you better put on a good show for them. Or else they are disappointed and then they complain to me."

"How do you make yourself feel something?"

"Well, you can't have a real orgasm, because you don't feel anything for these men. But you can certainly feel something through the man's eyes - if you pay attention to what he is feeling - and then you feel through him. When he gets excited, you get excited. When he orgasms, you pretend to orgasm too. As long as you feed off of him, he won't notice that you're just acting."

"I just pretend I'm with my boyfriend," Kelli explains. "I think about him and I act like I am with him. But I'm a good actress. Some girls can't do that, and they have to learn Lula's trick."

"He was heavy and he squashed me pretty good," Esther explains, trying to remember what she felt. "He was a little aggressive, but he did not last long and then it was over."

"Sounds easy."

She shrugs.

"Did you take the Barren Womb tea on your table?"

"No."

"Well, did you put the sheath on his sword?"

"What?"

"The sheath…the little thing on your table that looks like a piece of shriveled intestine. That's to prevent him from pollinating your flower. I left it for you to use until the Barren Womb tea begins to work. It takes about ten days of daily use for that tea to make you temporarily barren. And then you must drink it every day, or you will surely get pregnant."

Esther puts her head in her hands, remembering that it is her fertile time.

"Come with me," Lula says, exasperated. "Hurry."

They go to Lula's hut, and Lula goes into a basket for her emergency supplies. First, she dips a rag in some foul smelling tincture, and tells Esther to stick it up her flower immediately to kill the toad's seed. Esther goes outside and does as Lula instructed. When she returns, Lula hands her a bowl of dark tea with a pungent aroma.

"What's that?"

"This is a very concentrated blend of Barren Womb for use in emergencies. It will probably make you ill. But it will ensure you do not get pregnant."

Without hesitation, Esther gulps down the tea, and she has to sit down on the bed as waves of revulsion wash through her.

"I'll take two tupas out of your day's work for the medicine," Lula says. "Wash out the rag for me please, when you are done with it. And remember that you must care for your sheath. Wash it carefully after each use. Always look for breaks, and if you see one, throw it away and I'll give you another one."

Lula leaves Esther alone to regain her equilibrium. Esther lies down on the bed, liking the feel of Lula's silk bedcover against her body. When she feels able to walk again, she returns to the main lodge. The Ladies are all watching Lula intently, as she loads a dark, sticky substance into a long pipe. Esther stares at it curiously, wondering what it is. Soon the pipe is being passed from hand to hand, and the girls suck deep puffs of smoke into their lungs. They sigh deeply as they exhale.

"Esther?"

Lula hands the pipe to her.

"What is it?"

"Lady Candy."

"What's that?"

"Opium. Imported directly from China."

"What's opium?"

"Heaven," says Kelli.

"You'll like it," Lula promises.

Esther stares at the pipe, remembering once again her experience smoking jimm with Bela. What a horrible night. She shakes her head emphatically.

"Are you sure?" asks Lula, taking a slow puff herself.

"I'm too tired."

"Another time then. You must try it. Once you do, you'll never want to stop."

"Never!" says Kelli with a sigh. "And now that you're a Lady, you can easily afford it."

"Speaking of which," Lula says softly. "Lady Candy doesn't grow on trees."

The girls all hand a few tupas to Lula, who nods her thanks as she puts them in her Chinese bag. Then the girls begin to nod off into their own worlds. Esther soon feels as if she is the only one in the room, so she waves goodnight and goes off to bed.

Swan 8'

Jay moon

Esther wakes up to the sound of a raven cawing right outside her window. She puts her cloak on over her naked body and goes out into the bright morning. The final sunshine of fall is here and she wants to enjoy it. All morning she romps through the forest, greedily sucking every last drop of sunshine she can find that filters through the trees. Then she returns to the Pad for lunch - thankfully cooked by Lula - and the camaraderie of her new friends. Besides Kelli and Mati, there are two other Ladies present. One is a quiet girl named Kassie who never talks. She could be mute for all Esther can tell. The other is a woman named Hesta, who is a bit older than most of the girls that work in the Pad. And there is something else that makes Hesta stand out from the rest. Most of the Ladies are average looking at best. Often, they tend to be outsiders, bastards, or rejects from their respective tribes, who have no other choice but to come here. Even the prettier ones are worn out like a mangy coyote. But Hesta is still beautiful. In her youth, it was said that her face could launch a thousand canoes. Now, it is still handsome, although a bit careworn. She is also blessed with lovely breasts and hips and smooth, creamy skin. Her manner is utterly confident too. Esther wonders why a woman like that would want to work here, when she could probably be anything she wanted to be.

Hesta is from the Swan tribe and she has her own house in the village. She only comes here a few times a week, but when she does, Hesta is the most sought after woman in the Pad. She usually works even when other girls cannot find a customer. Because she has worked here the longest, she pretends that she is the chief of the Lily Pad, even though she answers to Lula and secretly hates her. But she is better at dealing with the girls than Lula is and they look up to her. Some of the girls are very troubled, and Hesta helps them when they need it. She spends the afternoon getting to know Esther and giving her advice. She speaks fast, as if there is not enough time to get out all of the things she has to say.

"Don't ever get emotionally involved. Don't kiss on the lips or touch tongues. Stay detached. This is a job like any other, and it should be treated as such. If you want to feel love and passion and all of that other nonsense, you should take a lover. Don't waste it on a toad. They're not worth it."

"I don't feel anything for these men. I cannot -"

Esther is about to say that she cannot feel very much when she has sex with anybody, but she decides to leave that part out. No need to have her head examined.

"That's right. You cannot afford to and stay sane. If you are nervous, wine will help you relax. There is usually a little wine in the kitchen, and you just have to slip a tupa or two into the basket next to it if you want some. Also, you should keep track of your cycle, and make the man wear a sheath during your fertile period. Or tell the man to pull out before he releases. The contraceptive tea is good, but it is far from perfect, and you don't want a toad's baby."

Esther wants to ask about her cycle, but Hesta is still talking and interrupts her. She turns serious and fixes her eyes right on Esther, demanding her complete attention.

"The most important advice I can give you is this - pay attention - this is important."

"Yes?"

"Do not try opium. Stay away from it like small pox. That is how Lula hooks her girls. Once you start, you'll become a permanent fixture around here. You'll need this job with its high wages to afford the stuff, and you'll work as much as possible to feed your habit. Trust me, I know what I'm talking about. Do you understand?"

Hesta looks sternly at Esther.

"Yes."

"Alright then, we'll discuss it no further."

Hesta continues to instruct her in the finer points, until Lula joins them, bringing a book with her called "Excerpts from Chinese Erotica", which is a compilation of several old Chinese texts, including works from Hsiu Chen Yen I. Hasan, the Swan scholar, spent two years in China making translations of several ancient texts. Opening to the erotic art, she begins to show Esther pictures of various positions she could try and things she could do to please a man. Kelli brings a bottle of wine and the afternoon erupts into a big party with much jest and laughter, as they peruse the pages of this ancient Chinese text with all the funny pictures of cartoon Chinamen making love. Esther is entertained with many stories of positions failed and the embarrassments that they caused, and she giggles until she has to pee.

In the evening, several men from the Hawk tribe come inside the Pad, looking for some fun. Drunk and loud, they have come to see what trouble they can get into. There is a line of three waiting for Hesta, other girls get requested, and then someone requests Esther.

"Come sit down, Jahi," she says, inviting the man named Jahi onto her bed. He is an older man, a little fat, and not very attractive, but she tries to ignore that. She takes a sip from the wine next to her bed for courage. Then she teases his balding head, plays with the wisps of hair that spring like tufts of grass, and runs her hands over his face and across his broad, sweaty chest. She allows him to feel her up and kiss her all over her body. She finishes the glass of wine while he plays with her breasts. She is sufficiently numb from alcohol by the time he sticks his jade hammer into her jade gate, as the Chinese book calls them. She begins to float away from her body, just like she used to do in the old days. But she is too cool, and this makes Jahi annoyed.

"I am paying good money for this. Can't you get more excited? You lie there like an old Raccoon maid."

This makes her angry, but she stuffs the anger inside and tells herself to do whatever he wants like Hesta suggested. She moans, pants and thrusts her hips around in little gyrations like Hesta showed her, while making noises like she is having an orgasm. She really has no idea what a real orgasm feels like, but she has heard enough fake ones while staying here to know how a fake one sounds. Next, she rolls him around and mounts him like the Chinese book suggests. He begins to get extremely excited, screaming "Yes! Yes! Yes! Yes! That's what I want!"

She will have to remember this. This is what clients want. Now that she thinks about it, she is embarrassed for her performance with her first client. She just lay there like a dead thing. Luckily, he was too drunk to care - or maybe just too polite to say anything. Soon Jahi is done, and he sighs and stares at the ceiling for some time.

"You were pretty good, Esther. Not quite up to Lily Pad standards yet, but you tried and that is important. That's worth a lot."

Esther was in the mood to be generous and let him lie with her for a bit, but that last comment blew it for him.

"I'm glad you enjoyed it," she says flatly, standing up and throwing on her robe. "If you'll excuse me, I must get cleaned up."

"I said you were good. Don't take it so hard. You just need practice. Free that wild woman under there."

He smiles, to show that there are no hard feelings. As he leaves, she kisses him on the cheek like she has seen the others do. He grins again and gives her bottom a pinch, and then he is out the door. She breathes a deep sigh of relief.

Swan 9'

Dohr and his father Orym visit the Lily Pad in the morning. Orym is surprised to see her and stares at her for several moments with a shocked look on his face. She greets him, but he continues to stare at her with a strange, far off look on his face, like he has seen a ghost. Then he shakes whatever strange mood possessed him, and he seems happy to see her.

"You - you look so different," he says, by way of explanation. "So...beautiful."

"Thank you, Orym."

He chats amiably with her all morning long, while Dohr goes off with one of the Ladies. But Orym continues to act strangely around her. Every few moments, he gets that strange look on his face and seems almost sad, and then he shakes it off. She wonders what has possessed him. Maybe he is just shocked to see her as a Lady. Esther has a feeling that he came here to get himself a Lady for a romp, but that he changed his mind because of her. She is sure of it when Kelli comes by, greets him with a soft stroke on the cheek, and asks him if he wants another romp. He turns beet red and shakes his head quickly in refusal. Esther wonders if he wants *her* instead, by the way he looks at her, but she doesn't say anything about it and neither does he.

They talk until Dohr returns and then all eat lunch together. Dohr is in a good mood, and he inquires about all the things he taught her before she left him six months ago and if she did them. Orym seems quite curious about her too, and she has to tell them all of her adventures over the past months. Then the morning wanes, and it is time for Orym and Dohr to leave, because they are going to begin the long journey home today while the weather is still beautiful. Orym says goodbye and gives her a long hug, but he seems reluctant to leave, like there is something he has left unsaid. He insists several times that she return for a visit in the future and makes Esther promise that she will. Then he tears himself away at last, and he and Dohr walk off together.

The girls soak in the hot springs in the afternoon. There is a big pool near the main lodge of the Lily Pad where the girls usually go, but it is lukewarm today and barely warm enough to be comfortable. The girls get in anyway, but Hesta takes Esther to try their luck at the hot pool. The hot pool is a pond of boiling hot sulfurous water that has been lined with rocks. The hot pool is used to heat the main pool by a small trench that connects the two. Esther sticks her foot into it and quickly withdraws it. It is practically boiling water.

"I'm not going in there," she shrieks.

"It's not so bad," says Hesta. "You have to tough it out."

Taking a deep breath, Hesta enters the water. She makes a hideous face and then she is submerged. She begins breathing heavily in and out, as her body struggles to adjust to the deadly hot water. She arches her back and sighs heavily.

"It's so nice," she says in a breathy voice.

Esther struggles many times to enter. She gets as far as her knees, but her legs feel as if they are being scalded and she has to jump out. She does it over and over, but cannot manage to get in. Hesta gets out after a few minutes for a rest, and then she goes back in again. Bolstered by Hesta's courage, Esther determines to go in no matter what. This time, she fights through the pain, lets out a very loud shriek, and submerges completely. The pain is intense! Her skin tingles terribly, like it is blistering, and she breathes heavily, struggling not to jump out. She feels like crabs must feel when submerged alive in boiling water. But she did it! She entered what the Ladies call the "Kettle" and lived to tell about it. After about a minute, she has to get out. Her body aches all over, her skin is red and tender, she feels dizzy, and she has to lean onto a tree to keep from falling over.

Hesta jumps into the main pool now and Esther follows her in. This is where the Ladies spend a good part of most days. Besides the Ladies, two couples have come from Swan village to soak here. Both couples are wrapped sensuously together, limbs entangled, kissing and whispering sweet nothings into each other's ear. Esther sighs and floats in the warm water, feeling a wonderful sense of peace. She could stay in here all day long, and she probably will too. Her peace would be perfect were it not for the two couples, practically making love in front of everyone. She watches the couples with distaste, wondering why they have to do such private things in such public view. Because this is a place of prostitutes and they don't matter? Or perhaps it is just the way of the Swan tribe. The rest of the Ladies don't seem to notice, but then they are probably all high anyway.

Lula comes out a while later and asks if anyone wants to work. The Ladies all look around, nobody wanting to be disturbed in their meditations. Finally Mati agrees and she climbs out of the pool, her plump body gleaming in the mist and steam that surrounds the pool like an aura.

The rest of the Ladies stay here all afternoon long, listening to the songs of the birds and staring languidly at the branches of fat green leaves that hang like tendrils over the pool. Esther decides that this is where she will spend every spare minute while she is working at the Lily Pad. This is her house. Her room will just be for customers.

Swan 11'

Bear moon

Esther awakens late this morning, puts on her golinta, and goes outside to greet the day and see about a dip in the warm pool. She walks toward the springs, swishing along pleasantly in her sexy outfit, and feeling content about things. But she is in for a shock this morning, when she sees Pedro himself, sitting in the warm water smoking his pipe. Although he stands naked in the water like everybody else, he still stands out. Everyone stares at him curiously.

His eyes nearly bug out of their sockets when he sees Esther wearing the golinta. He doesn't know what to say. He just stares. Esther suddenly feels naked and vulnerable in his presence. She squirms under his gaze and it is a long, uncomfortable moment of silence.

"What are you doing in those clothes?" he finally says, as a father would speak to his naughty daughter.

"I found a job."

"I can see that with my own eyes. A job? Is that what it is called?"

"Yes."

She takes off her clothes and enters the water. She swims near him, but not too near, because she is mindful of the effect her nudeness has on him.

"Have you really become a prostitute?" he asks, watching her carefully.

"I am a Lady."

"Do you have any idea how unsanitary it is to be doing such work?" he whispers, so none of the other Ladies will hear. "Not to mention what it does to the spirit. Whoring is low work."

"Oh, but you don't mind spending an hour with one yourself," she retorts angrily. "Isn't that why you are here?"

"I just came because I heard there was a warm pool here. It is good for my treatment. Doctors orders."

"There are other hot springs in the area," she says grumpily.

They fall into an uneasy silence. He keeps glancing at her, his attraction for her at odds with his moral indignation.

"Whores are women of low character," he whispers at last. "That's hard, but it's true. And is that what you want for yourself? I only say that because I care about you."

Esther finds herself wanting to defend her new friends - the Ladies - whom she has just met and is already taking a great liking to.

"What do you know? You were a virgin until a few weeks ago. What do you know about sex?"

He opens his mouth, but has no answer for her. Instead, he remembers that Esther did indeed take his virginity from him. His mind wanders back to that night, which was one of the most exciting nights of his entire life. He has thought about it ever since, wondering what it means.

"I apologize," he says at last. "That was a little harsh."

"What are you doing here, Pedro?"

"I came to deliver some medicines from the Raccoon hospital. My horse and I have been of great service to them. I am working off my debt for my treatment."

He stares at her naked body again, and then takes a deep breath and tries not to think about that night any further.

"It occurs to me that I have a debt to you as well. You aided my treatment with your…kind attention." He wonders if he should say more and decides against it. "Why don't you come with me? I am going back to Raccoon village today on my horse. You can work on a farm as you did before and forget all about your recent mistake. Life is simple there, maybe, but it is good for the soul. This work is not good for the soul. It will corrupt your soul."

"No, Pedro, I am staying right here. I don't want to be a farmer again."

"Perhaps I can get you hired at the hospital then."

"No, thank you."

"So this is actually work you prefer to do?"

"Why shouldn't I do it? I am tired of working my behind to the bone and still nothing to show for it afterwards. I am tired of always being poor and hungry and at the mercy of others. I have a chance to make a lot of money and live as I want to, and the work is relatively easy."

"But not painless...it carries a heavy toll -"

"I have had enough of your preaching," she says angrily, beginning to move away from him.

"I am not preaching."

"Yes, you are. That is what Spanish priests do."

"But I am no priest any longer," he says desperately. "I have given it up."

"Yes, you are! Deep down, you still are."

"But-"

"Leave me be!"

He watches her get out of the water, amazed at the beauty of the female form and the power it has over men. When she is gone, he falls into a funk. That was the worst thing she could have said to him. That he will forever be trapped inside his religious shell, hiding from the world. That he will never be able to be happy with a woman in his arms. Since the night he lost his virginity, he has been convinced that she was an angel sent by God to take away his vow of chastity. But now here she is, telling him otherwise.

In the evening, Esther is summoned from the warm pool by Lula, who informs her that she has been requested by a toad. She walks over to the main house, thinking that she would like to return to the warm water after taking care of whomever it was that summoned her. She imagines the water cascading over her, lost in the hot sulfur steam. But her pleasant fantasy fades when she sees Pedro standing there in the darkness, too shy to even go into the house. He looks embarrassed and sad, stepping nervously from foot to foot and fidgeting restlessly.

"What is this?" she asks suspiciously.

"I have thought about your words, and I decided that I must experience sex again. It has been an unhealthy obsession for my entire life. It is the reason I no longer want to be a father. I must see if it is worth giving up my vows for."

"Why me?" she asks, her eyes flashing anger.

"Because I like you."

"Can't you choose somebody else?"

"I thought it did not matter to you," he replies, sounding confident and hollow at the same time. "I thought you were a whore. I thought the only thing that mattered to you is money. Well, I have paid the required fee."

There is a long, painful silence, as the impact of his words sinks in. Her wrathful fire is gone, replaced by numb shock. Frightened suddenly, he wonders if he has made a mistake. But there is no turning back now. He has played his final hand. If he will lose her to the Lily Pad, at least he will get to sleep with her again. If she breaks down completely, then he has won back her soul and she will come with him.

"Fine," she says, in a defeated voice. "My hut is over there. I'll meet you there in a moment."

Esther sneaks into the kitchen and drinks two cups of wine, trying to get as numb as she possibly can before Pedro gets back. She leaves two tupas in the cup near the wine cask to pay for it. Then she pours herself a third cup and goes back to her hut, feeling sluggish and dizzy from getting drunk so fast. Pedro is still there, waiting nervously. She takes off her golinta and throws it onto the stool, and then sits down on the bed. Her expression is dull and vacant.

Pedro nervously takes off his clothes and stands ashamed before her.

"May I have a bit of that?" he says, looking at her wine.

She gives him the cup, and he drinks most of it in a single gulp. She finishes it, although she knows he wants the rest. Then, feeling very tipsy, she lies down and lets the room spin. He sits down next to her and tries awkwardly to kiss her, but she pushes him away.

"You don't get to kiss me. You paid for it."

"Ah, I see," he says miserably, realizing that this was truly a monumental mistake.

"Not on my mouth. But you can kiss my body."

He kisses her neck and works his way down. At first she just sits there numbly, trying to punish him for putting her in this uncomfortable position. But as she watches him struggle to figure out what to do, she feels sorry for him, and decides to be a professional. She remembers that he is a customer who has paid well and deserves a nice experience. So she pretends to be excited. She moans as if she is enjoying it. She puts his hands on her breasts and shows him how to massage them. And finally, she strokes his shaft with her hand and hands him the sheath to put on.

"At last," thinks Pedro, as he tries to figure out how to put the sheath on. "At last, I am having real intercourse with a woman. I am officially a priest no more. I am only sorry that I had to do it this way."

He tries to insert his pollinator, but he is too nervous. He looks at her flower and imagines all the clients like himself that have been inside her. He feels ill suddenly. And then he realizes that everything is wrong about this moment. There is no love. No passion. She acts like she is enjoying it, but he knows that she isn't. He watches her eyes, but they are vacant, as if she is hiding somewhere else. He tries again to go inside her, but he just can't bring himself to do it. And slowly, his pollinator goes limp. Embarrassed, he closes his eyes, takes a deep breath and tries to get it to rise again. He sweet talks it, orders it and pleads with it, but it will not budge.

He sits up glumly and looks around the dirty, little ramshackle hut, as if seeing it for the first time. He looks at Esther lying there, naked and distant, waiting for him to enter her with only a slight hint of pretend interest. Suddenly, he thinks of the story of

Jesus and Mary Magdeline, and he laughs bitterly and shakes his head at the irony of this moment.

"What's so funny?" Esther asks.

"I am sorry," he mumbles thickly. "I made a mistake. Please forgive me."

"You don't want to have sex?"

"No," he says. "Not like this."

He looks in her eyes and sees that she is hurt. This surprises him greatly. She sits up, looking even more depressed than she did when he first paid for her. He would think that she would be happy to get out of it, but she doesn't appear to be.

"I do not please you?"

"No, no..."

"You don't want to have sex?"

"No, I cannot."

He rises and puts on his clothes,

"I am sorry if I humiliated you," Pedro says, dressing quickly. "But it is truly I that am humiliated."

He bids her a hasty goodbye, but she doesn't respond. She doesn't even look at him. Out in the comforting darkness, he lights a candle and walks back to the village in a daze. On the way, he tells himself that he is a blundering idiot and an insensitive lout besides. He has done nothing but hurt her, all in his agonizing, unrequited love for her. What a fool! What an utter fool he has been! He cannot wait for daylight so he can go home. He knows that he is not returning to Raccoon village. The only place he wants to go is back to Spain.

Swan 13'

The girls invite Esther to go to the commons to do some shopping and she is only too happy to go. She has been hiding out at the Lily Pad for the past week and she needs a break from it. She quickly gets dressed, fills up her water skin, and then she is ready to go. They start out on the long hike to the lake, where the main village is located.

It is another beautiful day, and Esther begins to wonder if they only have beautiful days up here. It is good to be out for a walk with the girls too. So often, the girls are off in their own private opium worlds and Esther cannot talk to them. But today, everyone is relatively sober, and they laugh and giggle their brains out about each and every thing.

They pass an older couple, and the Ladies all shout greetings, but they get no response. The couple completely ignores them and continues on their way as if they weren't even there. The others don't seem to mind, but Mati finds their attitude offensive.

"They didn't even look at us," she says sourly.

"That's right," says Hesta spiritedly. "They're jealous. Because we're the backbone of this town."

All the girls erupt into peals of laughter.

"Why do they act like that?" asks Esther. "Because we're Ladies?"

But Hesta cannot answer her, as she is laughing too hard.

"I'm not kidding. We are the backbone of this town," she finally manages to say with a shriek of laughter.

"Not quite," says Mati scornfully.

"Yeah? Who comes here for the school? A handful of children from the nearby tribes come three times a year. But how many men come here each year and go directly to the Lily Pad? And every time a man pays us, one tupa goes to our tribe as tribute. This tribe would be very poor, without us."

"They are happy to take our money as tribute," Mati says, nodding in agreement. "And then we are ridiculed and talked about behind our backs."

"I don't remember the last time I was invited to a party," Hesta adds.

"A party?" laughs Kelli. "I've never been invited to a party here."

"But you're not of the Swan tribe," Hesta explains. "These people were once my friends and family, yet now they ignore me to my face and talk about me behind my back."

They are so caught up in the ensuing discussion, that they don't seem notice the way people look at them as they approach the commons. Or maybe they are immune to it by now, judging by their conversation. But Esther notices. The people seem to stare at them like they would a bear invading their home to eat their dinner. And then she notices that Mati has disappeared without a word, as if she was embarrassed to be seen with them in public and went off to hide in the woods.

They come in sight of the lake and fall into quiet awe as they absorb its deep blue immensity, lit with sun sparkles. They make promises that they will take a swim soon, and then head over to the commons. The commons is extremely crowded, with many people out and about, engaged in bartering and lively conversation. Esther sees fortune tellers waiting for customers, huts filled with pretty clothes and artists painting wooden statues. Musicians play a lively tune to entertain everyone. There is so much to see and the girls have to see it all - so seldom do they come out this way these days.

The Ladies attract much attention as they walk through the commons. They walk like bad girls who have just blown into town to strut their stuff and cause some trouble. Most of the Swan tribe is dressed - if they are dressed at all - in local fashions like loose fitting skirts with swan feathers stitched on or light deerskin vests. But a few of the Ladies, like Hesta and Paila, wear very expensive, imported silk clothes from China. They dress to show off their wealth, which makes them stick out even more as they walk through the main village center. Esther feels strange and uncomfortable being the object of so much attention, as she is used to walking invisibly among people who don't know her.

They are soon waylaid by a group of boys, many of whom have been to the Lily Pad before.

"How about coming up to my house for a quick romp? I'll give you two tupas."

"I'll throw in lunch too!"

The Ladies act offended and throw some sass their way.

"I've been with you before," Hesta says. "You weren't worth two tupas."

"That's cause I didn't have much to get excited about!"

"Because it was over much too quickly."

After the boys stop laughing at their friend, they begin trying to seduce the Ladies in a more serious way and strike a bargain. Esther gets bored and welcomes the opportunity to drift away, eager to explore the market more thoroughly.

As she wanders through the clothing shop, admiring the fancy fur capes and the pretty summer dresses, it occurs to her that she has money in her pockets. She can afford to buy almost anything in the store. She looks down at the dress she is wearing, an old relic of Belle's. Why not buy a new dress? As she looks through the dresses excitedly, she is stunned at how much sex is worth. A few days work and she can buy anything she wants. As a farmer, it would have taken her weeks to make that much money. Sex pays better than farming and cooking and cleaning combined! And she would bet that she has more tupas in her pocket than most of the people in the entire village. What does it matter to her if it is demeaning work...or bad for the soul, as some might say? She figures that she is already damaged goods, so why not be rich damaged goods.

Feeling free and independent with her newly acquired wealth, she shops fearlessly. She is torn between a pretty white hemp skirt and shawl with frills of swan feathers and a tight deer skin dress that is a little wild and dangerous...and sexy. She decides on the deerskin dress, although it is more expensive. It costs her twenty tupas - the most expensive dress in the store - but she shrugs it off. What does it matter to her? She'll make more soon.

Inside the little draped off area, she changes into the dress to make sure it fits right. It fits so perfectly that it seems made for her body. Feeling like she is meant to own it, she buys it and goes to show the Ladies, her old dress draped carelessly over her shoulder. She is in such a hurry that she doesn't notice the man until he stands in front of her and blocks her way. Annoyed, she tries to go around, but he puts his hands on her shoulders and stops her.

"Esther?"

Surprised, she looks up. It is none other than Vin, the man she met when she woke up in his bed after a night of drunken revelry.

"I thought you'd left town without saying goodbye."

"No."

"I wondered what happened to you."

"I've been working."

"Good for you. You found work so soon. Doing what?"

"Nothing too exciting," she says evasively.

"Care to join me for lunch at the Obsidian Eye?" he asks hopefully.

Esther looks around for the Ladies. They have finally given up on the boys, and are beginning to shop.

"Um, sure. Let me just tell my friends where I will be. I'll meet you there."

"Sure," he says, and walks away.

She doesn't think they'll care if she disappears for lunch without telling them, but she wants to show off her dress. She walks up to them nonchalantly, as if nothing is different. Kelli's eyes get wide as she sees Esther.

"Oh Esther, what a pretty dress. You look so different."

Esther blushes with pleasure.

"Fetching," says Paila.

"Divine," adds Hesta. "Much better than that rag you were wearing before. I didn't want to say anything, but it was very ugly."

"That old thing," Esther says with a smile. "Glad to be rid of it. It's just something I picked up at the Beaver tribe from a farmer."

"Ahh," says Hesta, with a wise nod, as if that explains everything.

"I'll just be in the...Obsidian Eye," she says, "having lunch."

"Don't you want to wait for us?"

"I'm meeting a friend."

The girls agree to find her later, and she walks off.

They sit at the table of the Obsidian Eye, sharing a bowl of fish stew and laughing. Esther feels much more comfortable around Vin this time. Although he acts tough and macho in order to impress her, there is a sweet vulnerability about him. She finds him both charming and attractive, and he obviously is interested in her too. She begins to wonder if it would be a good idea to have an affair with him.

She recently heard the girls in the Lily Pad speak of something called an orgasm that you have during sex. Esther wants one, and she thinks that Vin might be the one to give it to her. He is several years older than her, and she can tell that he is experienced. But then she wonders why he isn't married. There must be something wrong with him for him not to be married at his age. She begins to imagine all the horrible reasons that he is single. *He's a criminal. He's crazy in the head. He's got some sort of disease.* She decides that she will ask the Ladies about him before she does anything.

While they are talking, the Ladies enter the Obsidian Eye, and the whole room turns to stare. Most of the men stare mainly at Hesta, infamous star of the Lily Pad, with a rumored one thousand men under her belt and a fortune hidden away somewhere. Her fortune is a favorite topic of speculation amongst the Swan Tribe, and many think she may be the richest woman in the entire Twelve Tribes. She struts into the room, with her purple silk robes, sleek black hair, and so many bracelets and necklaces of imported silver, crystals and other adornments jangling merrily. She really is a sight to behold - a dirty, sexy, tainted seductress with secrets to tell. These Ladies really enjoy the commotion they stir up and they make the most of it with everything they do.

"Hai Esther," says Kelli, waving at her.

Hesta comes up to Esther and gives her neck a soft stroke, whispers hello, and then stares at Vin a moment with a small smile. The smile seems to say, "See something you like?" He smiles back, suddenly nervous. Where did Esther pick up friends like these? And then he suddenly understands. Esther has been working at the Lily Pad.

Vin walks home alone, thinking about lunch today. As soon as he found out that Esther was a prostitute, he made an excuse for why he had to leave. He remembers the momentary look on her face - the sting of rejection - with a little regret and guilt. He doesn't know why he left. He doesn't care that she works at the Lily Pad. He has been there himself. Maybe he was just afraid to be seen in public with her, and people will all gossip that he is so desperate that he has taken to courting Ladies from the Lily Pad. The last thing his dwindling reputation needs is something like that to forever tarnish it.

His mind wanders back to his youth and the days of his great triumphs. Back when he was young, he had his fair share of the young girls in the village. Ahh...to be a young Swan in the summertime, and have his pick of all the single young girls - so eager to experiment! He would go to the summertime dances, pick out a young girl he wanted, and literally drown her with drinks and romantic words. That night, after the dance, she would melt into his arms in the warm, summer nights under the majestic trees. He would take them to his favorite place and seduce them until they gave in and gave him a romp. And they were only too eager to be seduced. It was so easy back then.

The young girls of the Swan tribe are eager to experiment, but they get bored quickly. So did Vin in the days of his youth. Sometimes it was he that got bored and sometimes them, but whomever it was who got rid of who, he would quickly get over it and move on to another that caught his eye. And so it went for many years.

These days, his love life has slowed to a crawl. He still attracts occasional young girls who are in their experimental stages, but those never last. All of the good women his age are married. Those that aren't married are either too unattractive to get a man or too crazy to keep one. And the young girls will not consider him, because of his lowly status as assistant teacher and janitor for the Swan school. Vin waited too long to find himself a wife. He couldn't decide which one he wanted to spend his life with and now he has nobody.

In the afternoon, the Ladies swim in the lake. There seems to be an imaginary wall around them, for though there are many swimming in the water and fishing with nets, there is nobody near them. Esther floats in the comfortably cool water and watches the beautiful swans again. She notices how the most beautiful swans - the pure white gleaming ones, the ones that seem like angels because they are so utterly and purely white - swim proudly side by side. And how the flawed swans - the dirty ones or the ones with feathers sticking at strange angles or other little flaws - are left to swim alone. The flawed swans are ignored by the more perfect swans. The swan's behavior reminds her of how the Ladies are treated.

Esther knows that she is a flawed swan, especially after being rejected by Vin this afternoon when he figured out that she was a Lady. She doesn't care if the other people of the Swan tribe ignore her. She doesn't even know them. But she feels bad that Vin, who liked her, ran away as soon as he saw her friends. Not wanting to care, she dives down into the cool water and stays down until she can't stand it anymore. By the time she comes up, she hopes to have forgotten all about him.

Vin has a house near the lake, underneath a black acorn tree. His house sits in the most crowded part of the village, close to the commons and the lake. He sits on the bank of the busy lake, with a fishing line in the water and a fishing net in his hand, and tries not to think about anything but catching fish. He watches the sun set slowly across the lake and listens to the lake birds make their noise. A vulture soars overhead, searching for carrion. There is so much going on right now, all around him, but he can't stop thinking about women. Specifically, he thinks of the one unmarried woman his age whom he still desires. A woman he has slept with many times, but never really had. That woman is none other than Hesta, the Seductress of the Lily Pad, who smiled at him today.

Vin has been in love with Hesta for practically his whole life. He first fell in love with her when he was a boy and she was a girl, but she didn't notice him. She was a rare beauty from a good family, and he was the son of a fisherman. He was two years younger than her and had nothing to offer her. In fact, they rarely spoke to each other, even though they grew up in the same village. And then she married the son of the chief, and he forgot about her and began having fun with the other girls in the village. He didn't think of her much after that, except for an occasional pang whenever she would walk by.

And then her husband died, drowned in the lake under mysterious circumstances. She was found at the edge of the lake, cradling his bloated body, which had washed up on the bank. Wrecked with misery, she wailed and cried for many days. She singed her hair off, as is the custom for the mourning of the dead. But she didn't stop mourning, like one is supposed to do after a certain time. She continued to mourn, rarely coming out into public, long after the required time.

One day, she began to work at the Lily Pad. She completely disappeared from regular village life and stopped talking to her friends. Her family was so upset that they stopped talking to her too. And so she was rarely seen, except in the hot springs or in the Lily Pad. He remembers seeing her in the hot springs one day, a short time after she began to work there. He tried to talk to her, but she kept nodding in and out and her speech was unintelligible. She was obviously under the influence of some drug. He stared at her with chills, watching her strange behavior for a long time.

After another year, she began to regain some of herself. She would come into town with the other Ladies and strut around. She began showing off her wealth, buying expensive imports from China, Japan, South America, and other places where the trader ship of the Twelve Tribes ventures. Finally comfortable in her new life, she didn't care anymore who approved or disapproved of the once proud Swan gone bad. She dropped out of society altogether, except for an occasional visit to her mother, with whom she was once again speaking.

Then Vin's own love life dried up, as he became too old for flings. In desperation, he went to the Lily Pad and purchased Hesta for a few hours. That night, having sex with her, he fell in love with her all over again. It was a strange night. She was very high and open and they stared into each other's eyes for a long time. Just for a moment, she kissed him on the lips, and then she remembered that he had paid for it and didn't do it again. The sex was amazing, too - at least for him - he imagined it was amazing for her but it was hard to be sure.

He tried many times to start up a relationship with her after that. He paid for her services a few times and tried to talk to her in the hot springs, where she spent many hours. But she was unreachable. Lost in her own world, which was fueled by some strange Chinese drug, she was vacant and uncommunicative. And he was just another man who paid to have sex with her. She called him a 'toad' once. So he gave up and moved on.

He has dreamed of her often lately. The lack of love in his own life has just fueled that fantasy into an unhealthy obsession - an obsession with a beautiful, crazy and unrepentant whore.

Mati reappears and joins the Ladies in the lake with a guilty glance around town. As the Ladies swim, all the real swans gather around curiously, as if wanting to see what all the fuss is about. A little girl appears, walks up to one of the swans curiously, and tries to touch them. Mati quickly runs up to the girl, grabs her arm, and pulls her away.

"We must be careful around the swans," Mati warns the girl. "They are very strong."

Esther laughs at Mati. Imagine being afraid of giant ducks.

"I think you are being a little paranoid," Esther says to Mati later. "You think a duck could hurt a person."

"It's not a duck. It's a swan."

"What's the difference?"

Mati gives her a sly smile and rummages around in her basket for a piece of corn bread left over from lunch.

"Go on. Feed the ducks, brave woman."

Esther does as she is told, having an idea that she is being tricked. Especially since the ladies are now watching her with big smiles on their faces. She holds the bread out to a nearby swan, who stands up on its legs and begins walking toward her. It snaps at the bread with its beak. Standing upright, the swan seems much more powerful. Its beak is quite hard and suddenly seems dangerous. She withdraws her hand as it snaps and drops the bread, which is quickly devoured.

Seeing this, all of the swans start walking toward Esther. Standing up to their full height, with necks extended, they come up to her chest. They quack up a storm, demanding to be fed too. They beat their large wings and the wings make a lot of noise. Esther backs away from their extended, impatient beaks, which now seem strong enough to gouge a hole in her body.

The ladies are laughing hysterically as Esther runs away from the furious, quacking white terrors. She laughs sheepishly, knowing she walked right into that one.

"They seem pretty, but they have a mean streak and a powerful bite," says Mati to Esther, after the swans leave them alone.

"Their wings could break your arm," adds Hesta. "They're quite dangerous if you piss them off. Never piss off a swan."

Once the fish he catches are cleaned, Vin carries the fillets home, stokes up the fire, and sets the fillets on sticks so they will become smoked and be able to last the winter. He rubs his own secret blend of herbs on the fish, which gives them a nice flavor. There they will sit for two or more days, until they are completely dried.

Vin begins to think of Esther again. He ran from her because he didn't want to be seen with her in public, but now it occurs to him that he could have some fun with her in private. She is obviously interested in him and he still finds her attractive. She is definitely strange and a bit of a head case, but she is rather sweet too. The more he thinks about it, the more excited he gets. He stands up, inspired at the prospect of having sex tonight, and decides to go into town. He hopes she'll still be there, but if not, maybe he'll walk all the way to the Lily Pad.

He finds the Ladies involved in some last minute shopping. Hesta is determined to buy herself a new rabbit skin blanket for the coming winter, the biggest and most beautiful one she can find, and she is walking among the traders looking for the perfect one. Esther wanders idly along with her, gloating about how she can buy almost anything she sees. Vin surprises her, and before she has a chance to ignore him, he invites her to dinner. She thinks about it a bit, and then excuses herself to go talk to her friends.

"That man over there," she says to Hesta, pointing at him. "What is he like? Is there anything wrong with him?"

"Him? Isn't that the one who was so rude to you earlier?" says Hesta in a whisper.

"Yes. But he is being nice now."

"I'll bet I know why too," she says in a huff.

She marches up to Vin and throws her hands to her hips.

"Trying to get a free one?"

"Just because you've decided never to have a normal relationship again, doesn't mean that nobody else should."

Hesta opens and closes her mouth, unable to believe he just said that. She is very offended now, and soon they are embroiled in a long and heated argument. She wants him to leave Esther alone. He cannot figure out why she is upset, and tells her it is none of her business. But instead of walking away, he continues the argument past the point where it makes sense. He likes the way her chest heaves and her face flushes when she argues. He likes that she knows he is alive at last, and talks to him as if she cares what he has to say.

"Come on, Esther," Hesta finally yells, breaking off the debate. "He's not worth it."

"I'm going to go have dinner with him," Esther says with a shrug. "I have nothing else to do."

"Do what you like," snaps Hesta bitchily. "Try to help a friend and they ignore you."

She stalks off to look at more blankets, washing her hands of the whole thing.

After a dinner of fresh fish, he sits next to her and stares into her eyes. He thinks of kissing her and leans a little closer to her. But as soon as he does this, Esther gets up and goes to the window to look outside.

"Can you read the stars? What do you see?"

He gets the point and backs off. He grabs his little guitar instead, which was handmade in South America by mission neophytes in some jungle somewhere.

"Do you sing?"

"Yes."

"I'd like to hear you sing."

"If you'd like."

"I would."

It takes them a while to find a song they both know, but finally they agree on a Bear tribe song that she knows, and he begins to strum the chords and sing. He finds her voice very unique, sweet and intense, and he is that much more attracted to her upon singing with her. As they get comfortable, they begin to develop a harmony and soon they are making good music. When the song is over, he fights back the overpowering urge to kiss her.

"I love your voice."

"Thank you. We sounded good together."

Suddenly, they hear a shout of approval coming from Vin's neighbor's house.

"Let's hear 'Light of Venus'!" shouts the neighbor.

"They never encourage me when I sing alone," says Vin with a smile. "They always come over and tell me to stop."

"I think you sing very well."

"Not compared to you. You sing like a thrush in the morning. I sound more like a loon - I make people's hair stand on end."

Esther giggles. She is now off guard, and Vin takes the opportunity to press his lips to hers. Esther kisses him back tentatively. After a moment, he pulls back to observe her reaction. She smiles nervously, but says nothing.

Esther paces restlessly about the little house, allowing Vin to sleep peacefully. She made love to Vin, expecting no money in exchange. And what did it get her? Nothing. It was exactly the same feeling as when she gets paid - she pretends to be excited and

Vin has fun. Where was the mythical orgasm that the girls talk about? And to what purpose should she take a lover if she cannot have one? The intimacy is nice, but sex just gets in the way of that anyway, and it was much nicer between them before they had sex.

How does one have an orgasm? She hasn't the slightest idea. Her flower is numb and it always has been. She wants so badly to feel what other women feel, but how does she awaken her sleeping sex?

Swan 14'

Raccoon moon

Vin is frustrated. Esther left this morning without saying anything. Then in the afternoon she returns, obviously in a bad mood, and asks him to make love to her. Not asks - insists! After kissing for a while, she urges him inside of her, and began slamming and grinding against him forcefully. It catches him off guard, and he doesn't know what to do. This goes on for some time, and then she suddenly bursts out crying and rolls away and hides her head. And then he sees, for the first time, the scars on her back. The whipping scars - though they are faint, she has many of them.

He has been asking himself why she is here ever since. She has been getting progressively more and more upset for the past two hours. She won't say much, but she won't leave either. Any time he touches her, she withdraws as if stung. Her mouth is sharp and mean, and it makes him feel awful.

"What's wrong?"

"Nothing."

"You're obviously in a foul mood. Do you want to talk about it?"

"I'm just not - Do I have to explain everything? Just leave me alone."

"Fine."

He wishes he were the kind of man who could ask her to leave, but that's not his way. Instead, he leaves her alone in his house, and goes down to the river to get away. He fishes, but his mind is not in it and the fish are staying away from him.

Besides being baffled by Esther's behavior, he is baffled by his fight with Hesta. That argument they had was very exciting for him. It is probably the first time she has ever showed even the slightest interest in anything he has to say. And the fact that she got so upset, gets his hopes up that she might actually have an interest in him. He laughs, thinking about how excited he is over a fight.

Esther sits in Vin's house, stoking up his fire and making yet another cup of tea. Making tea is one of her favorite things to do when she is stressed or tired, and she has made five cups already. While she waits for the water, her mind races with thoughts of her life and the things that have led her to this place. She had a dream about the mission fathers last night. She was naked, and they whipped her with a whip with wire at the end and became excited by her screams. Fernandez whipped her bloody, and then tied her up and began to kiss her wounds and suck upon her dripping blood. He then stuck his shaft inside of her and it hurt terribly, like his shaft was a whip with wire at the end of it. He kept telling her that she deserved nothing less, because she was a bad girl. And then he turned into Him, and He laughed and laughed while she screamed. What does He want with her still? She had thought He was long gone, but for some reason He has returned to haunt her again.

This afternoon, she had sex with Vin, and the feeling of that dream kept running through her head the whole time. The more she tried not to think about it, the more she thought of it. She felt like a very bad girl for wanting to have an orgasm and it made her angry. She just couldn't get past it, and she ended up having violent sex and freaking Vin out, so he ran away as soon as it was over.

And no orgasm, of course. This time, neither of them was satisfied, and she cried after it was over. What is wrong with her? Why can't she have a normal life? And what can she do to get those horrible images of Him out of her head?

Vin wants to go home, but Esther is still there and he is still avoiding her. It makes him angry that he has to hide from her while she stays in his house. Why won't she go home? Soon he has built up a head of steam. He'll march right in there and ask her kindly but firmly to leave. He goes home to find her staring at the fire with tear stained eyes, and her face is a mask of misery. His temper dissipates immediately when she offers him a cup of tea and smiles through her tears. He accepts the tea and asks if she wants to talk about it, but she just shakes her head emphatically. He cooks the fish for dinner, along with some acorn mush. He decides to be kind and lets her stay as long as she wants to, even though it makes him really uncomfortable to be around her when she is like this.

She sleeps over, despite the fact that they have hardly spoken all night. As they fall asleep, he puts his arm around her waist and she grabs his hand and clutches it tightly to her chest. He is appeased and decides to give her another chance.

Swan 15'

Two men show up tonight and both request Hesta. The other girls, not having anything to do, retreat into their magical opium shells. Though they are all in the room with her, Esther feels like she is alone, so she spends the night looking through the

Excerpts from Chinese Erotica book and thinking about having an orgasm.

When the two men leave, Esther knocks on Hesta's door. She wants to talk to Hesta about orgasms. Hesta opens the door, stark naked and exhausted. Her face is flushed and her hair goes all over the place.

"Is this a good time? I wanted to ask you something, but I can come back."

"I'm fine," she snaps impatiently. "Come in."

Hesta gets back into bed and pulls the covers up around her chin. Esther notices a freshly packed opium pipe by the bed. She must have disturbed Hesta right before she was about to smoke.

"I hate men," Hesta says, making a face. "After they finish, they look at you with those sad, pathetic eyes. They want you to tell them how incredible they were. So you lie and tell them they were incredible, and then they don't believe you. And then they're hurt that you lied."

"That's true," says Esther with a laugh. "I know that look."

"I hate being sober when I'm with them. But Lula wasn't around and I was completely out of dragon's blood, so I had to smell their smell and hear their grunts and then tell them how magical they were. It's an impossible thing to do."

"Dragon's blood?"

"Yes, and now that Lula has returned...."

Hesta stares at the pipe upon her table longingly. But she doesn't smoke yet. She fixes her bright eyes on Esther, wanting to be present for her.

"I wanted to ask you a question," Esther says quickly, knowing that Hesta is distracted. "I want to know how to have an orgasm."

Hesta stares at Esther strangely.

"Don't tell me you've never had an orgasm before."

"Never. I just recently learned about it."

"It's absolutely lovely. All of your tension and pain drops away, and you are engulfed in this incredible feeling of bliss. By the silver moon, haven't you ever had great sex -"

"I've never had great sex."

"That's awful. An orgasm is almost as much fun as dragon's blood. You've got to have one."

"How do I do it?"

"First, you must have one by yourself. You must play with the upper petal of your rose and think erotic thoughts, until you can successfully have an orgasm by yourself. Once you can do that, then you will be ready to have one with a man."

"Do you have orgasms with your customers, Hesta?"

"No. Only by myself."

"Don't you have a man?"

"A man?" says Hesta with a grin. "Certainly not."

"But don't you want one? I bet you could have your pick."

"I don't want one," she insists. "I don't need them anymore." She lays a finger sensuously on the opium pipe. "I have discovered greater pleasures. I have discovered an orgasm that lasts many hours. It's an orgasm of the spirit -"

She suddenly stops talking, not wanting to give Esther any ideas about taking opium herself.

"But never mind that, because you're not going to try opium ever in your entire life. You should have an orgasm though. You'll love it."

"By myself?"

"It is best."

Hesta gets a pained look on her face, that makes it crunch up like a raisin. She is about to say something more, but she falls silent instead.

"Just play with my...upper petal, until I have one?" asks Esther, after a long silence.

"But you must put yourself in the mood by thinking erotic thoughts. Just rubbing is not enough. Your imagination must also be involved. Now you march right into your room and don't come out until you have yourself an orgasm. I don't care if you're trapped in there a month. You keep trying."

Esther realizes that she has been excused, and Hesta wants to be alone. Esther leaves, feeling disappointed. She has a feeling that Hesta knows more about orgasms, but she is too preoccupied with her pipe. Esther likes spending time with Hesta more than the other girls in the Lily Pad, and she wishes that Hesta were present more of the time. But Hesta tends to drift in and out, floating through her own secret worlds on the wings of a dragon. She is quite moody too, and you never know if she is going to smile or snap at you.

Esther enters her room nervously. She has never attempted to play with the 'upper petal' of her rose before in a serious fashion. She lies down on the bed and wonders where she should begin. Perhaps her clothes.... She takes off all of her clothes and lies back down naked, and then she begins to touch her clitoris, gently probing. She touches her lower lips and gently sticks a finger inside her flower. For about twenty minutes she strokes it, trying to awaken sensation. She attempts to think erotic thoughts, but it doesn't help much. It is as if she is completely dead down there and she can feel nothing. Finally she gives up, rolls over and goes to sleep.

Swan 16'

Swan moon

The entire village is teeming with energy, as people from nearby villages come to celebrate the Swan new moon. This is a particularly busy day for the Swan tribe, because there are four planets in the Swan constellation, which means that besides the large crowds to be taken care of, there will be four weddings and seven babies due to be born. There is much activity in the village, but Esther doesn't expect to see much of it, because the Lily Pad is packed today. She puts on her Lady outfit bravely and prepares herself for a long day. She gulps down enough water from the spring to make her belly stretch out, knowing that she gets really thirsty while she is working. She washes herself in the cold spring and then a quick dip in the warm pool to finish the process off.

When she walks into the Pad, she finds all of the girls eating breakfast, and gladly accepts a bowl of roasted deer meat and acorn mush. Lula comes in from time to time, to tell them that men are massing outside and will be allowed in as soon as the Ladies are finished eating breakfast. She makes a big show of allowing them a private breakfast, as if it is the height of graciousness. Three packed pipes of opium are ready and waiting on a little table already. The girls are just beginning to light them, when Lula enters in a rush, waving her big, bracelet-covered arms wildly.

"Mati. Your father's outside!"

Mati stares at her, a pipe in her hand and smoke pouring out of her surprised mouth.

"What's he doing here?"

"I don't know."

"Did he ask for me? Did he seem upset?"

"He seemed calm."

"He knows," she whispers.

"He was bound to find out eventually. This is a small village."

"I have to get out of here," she says, making for the back door to the kitchen. "I wish you had told me before I smoked."

"Maybe he's just here for some fun," says Hesta helpfully.

Mati stares at her with disgust, the idea suddenly occurring to her. She shakes her head, as if the very idea is too disturbing to contemplate.

"I don't know which is worse," she mumbles, as she flees out the door.

Esther finds Mati cowering in the kitchen, when she brings her bowl in to be washed.

"Are you all right?"

"Oh yes," breathes Mati in an angry whisper. "They don't know I work here. They're so stupid. They think I'm just a nice, quiet girl, always out weaving baskets by the river, like some Raccoon girl preparing to be a good wife. They don't know I come here during the day - my *other* life. I wonder if they found out, would they ever talk to me again? Oh, curse him, for ruining my flight with the dragon today. Now, I'm so nervous."

Esther leaves Mati mumbling to herself in a dark cloud and goes back into the main house. She soon hears someone whispering that the father did indeed come for some fun, and he requested Hesta. Esther goes back out to the kitchen to tell Mati, thinking she'll be relieved. Instead, Mati begins cursing in a breathy whisper, calling her father many unpleasant names, and Hesta too, for indulging his sick, perverted pleasures. Then she begs Esther to get her another packed pipe, as her first attempt doesn't seem to be working quite right.

By early afternoon, Esther has serviced two customers and she is exhausted and irritated. The men are sweaty and smelly because it is an unusually hot day, and so is she by the end of it. And they take forever to finish, so she must endure a lot of abuse to her sore flower. She refuses any more customers for the day and for the first time seriously considers her sanity in taking this job - no matter how much it pays.

She walks to the hot springs, but it is packed with people, including the two men she has been with today. She doesn't want to look at them, so she takes a quick, painful dip in the kettle instead. Once sterilized by the hot water, she walks grumbling back to the Pad to see if there is any lunch made.

There are several more men at the Pad, and Esther is bombarded with requests when she walks into the main house. Being in a bad mood, she just brushes them aside irritably and goes out to the kitchen to get something to eat. She finds leftovers from the lunch she just missed, and makes herself a plate of corn bread and deer meat. She sits down to eat gratefully, but before she can take a bite, Lula enters the room.

"Don't be so distant and grumpy with our clients. We have a reputation to consider as Ladies."

Esther shrugs and ignores her.

"You should act like a Lady at all times. As if every man you meet is the most attractive and wonderful man you have ever seen. Touch them intimately and giggle at their jokes and make wide eyes." Lula demonstrates this behavior on Esther. "Shake you hips," she says, giving her wide berth a shake. "Bat your eyes and open them very wide. Even if the sight of their naked body makes you gag, you must still pretend they are the man you've been waiting for all your life."

Esther nods agreement, hoping she'll go away and let her eat, but Lula is persistent.

"And after you eat, you can take that young Raccoon boy. He's very shy and embarrassed to be here. It's his first time. I think he'll like you. You're sweet and will go easy on him."

Esther shakes her head morosely.

"I'm done for today."

"You can't be done. There are too many men in there. This is the biggest day of the year, Esther. We need you."

They argue for a while, and Esther begins to lose her appetite. She is just about to scream 'I quit!' when Lula suddenly stops arguing and leaves. She returns a few minutes later with the opium pipe.

"Let me make a suggestion, Esther. Smoke some opium, and then you can service a hundred men and it won't make any difference to you. They'll just come and go, and you'll be lost in your dreams and won't notice. One day, a long time ago, I was the only girl working, and twelve of the Raven tribe showed up at once. I smoked dragon's blood and took care of all twelve men. I was a champion that day. Think of how much money you'll make if you do the same."

Esther stares at Lula like she is the devil herself.

"I don't want to."

"Try it. If you don't like it, then don't do it any more. Try it just one time, and by tomorrow evening, you'll have enough tupas to get through the entire winter comfortably."

Lula takes a drag herself, to demonstrate how easy it is. Then she hands the pipe to Esther. Hesitantly, Esther takes it from her and takes a small puff.

All night long, men tromp through her room, but she isn't aware of any of them. She is in another world now, a world far above and beyond this world of Ladies and Toads, and her body acts out the mortal part without her having to be there to endure it. She is vaguely aware that she is sweaty and sticky and sore, but it seems far away, like a bad dream. Meanwhile, the little wooden circles (each one worth six tupas) continue to pile up in her payment basket, and she can't even remember half of the customers that deposited them. The firelight spins her brain in circles, and the shadows on the walls turn into spirits that are watching her. She moans and sighs, as if she is having a great time, but her moans make her feel very strange, as if she is living in a cave with shadow ghosts who shriek like the wind.

Who is this man on top of her? Is he finishing or just beginning? Where did he come from? There was a different man, a fat man, on top of her a little while ago. This one is much slimmer. He stands up and kicks the wall cruelly.

"That wasn't worth eight tupas," he growls. "It was too short. I want a free one."

Esther giggles to herself, at the contortions his face makes. He is upset because he only lasted five minutes, and she knows that isn't her fault. She is soaring so high that his anger cannot reach her. He is just an angry face in the shadows that has nothing to do with her. She comforts him and tells him it will be alright and he shouldn't worry. Then she kisses him on the cheek, gives him a squeeze, and tells him to come back soon and next time it will be better. Chagrined and flustered by her confidence and her strange eyes, he apologizes and leaves her alone.

Lula was right. It is much better on opium. Alcohol only makes her numb, but opium makes everything so much more interesting. The fire is brighter and the shadows are deeper. She walks naked to the fire pit and puts some more wood on the little fire. The shadows are so thick, that she feels as if she is swimming as she moves through them, and the flickers of light are like waves in a strange hot springs of her mind.

Another man enters a while later, and Esther greets him with her customary amorous glances, strokes, and squeezes. She takes off his clothes and admires the rolls of fat that seem to shimmer before her eyes. She laughs to herself as he pulls her to bed with him and begins to kiss her all over her body. The little touches of sensation feel good, yet she is not really aware of anyone else being in the room but herself. It is almost as if she is making love to herself.

As it goes on, she screams and moans as if she is enjoying him, while actually enjoying the sounds she makes which vibrate through her entire body. Waves of bliss envelope her, carried by her screams. Hesta was right. This is divine. Who needs an orgasm? This is much better, and simpler too.

Swan 17'

In their golintas, all the Ladies sit in the main house, flirting with the men who have come for a morning romp. They are waiting for breakfast, after which they will begin working. Lula has asked them to work this morning, and then they will close the Pad in the afternoon so everyone can go to Swan village and enjoy the new moon party. They will miss the morning weddings, but nobody seems to mind. This is not a wedding crowd anyway.

A man grabs Esther's breasts playfully, and she teasingly lets him touch her for a few seconds before pulling away. She is getting good at this. She whispers in his ear in a sexy voice to wait until after breakfast, then she smiles, sits on his lap, and asks him how he likes it. He says that he prefers to show her in private. She smiles again, never missing a beat, and acts as if she can't wait. Meanwhile, she is thinking of something quite different. She thinks of smoking more opium instead. Before the men start flowing through her bedroom, she wants more dragon's blood, so she can go back to that place in her mind.

Lula brings the Ladies tea, sweet corn cakes, and blackberries. Esther feeds blackberries to the man who has asked to be with her. Following Hesta's lead, she puts a purple berry between her breasts and allows him to bury his face into her chest and suck out the berry. He tries to lick her purple lips with his purple stained tongue, but she pushes him away with a laugh, never losing her smile or composure. She is proud of herself for maintaining the air of a Lady, which is a casual indifference mixed with supreme confidence in her sexual prowess. It is an easy act to play, knowing that she is merely playing a role. None of these men will ever find out what she is really like. They are not real. They are merely there to serve as magic mirrors so she can look into their eyes and see herself as a beautiful, desirable seductress. She goes around the room, staring at this reflection of her that emanates from all the men. As soon as she sees that woman reflected, she moves on before it disappears and is replaced by a different one.

After breakfast, Lula gathers the girls into her bedroom and packs a pipe full of opium in preparation for the day's work. Everyone is allowed one small puff, just enough to get them through the morning. Everyone chips in some tupas, and then they all chase the dragon into the morning. Hesta is upset to see Esther take the pipe and smoke from it, and she opens her mouth to complain, but by then it is too late already.

Esther wakes late in the afternoon and stumbles to her water pot to get a drink of cold water. How long has she been in this hut? She counts the little wooden chips in her bowl. There are three chips, which means she has been with three men today. She can barely remember a single one of them - nothing but fleeting glimpses. She can tell that her flower is extremely sore from all the hard use, but the pain is far away like a bad dream.

She wanders into the entertaining room, to find most of the girls ready to go out and party. The girls all gather around her and touch her fondly, glad that she is up and about.

"Esther is here! How are you girl? What happened to you?"

"I was...working," she says in a far away voice.

"We're all ready. Get ready to go," Hesta urges, anxious to be off.

"I'll be ready in a few minutes."

"Hurry up. I want to go," Hesta whines.

"Esther, I'm very proud of you," Lula says, putting her arm around her. "You have been a real champion, and two men even praised you for your skills. You're becoming a true Lady."

"Thanks," Esther says to the cheering Ladies, feeling genuinely pleased. Although it is not her goal to be a great Lady, it always feels good to be praised by your peers.

Lula smiles to herself as Esther hurries off to get dressed. Esther is now one of them.

They make the long walk to the lake, where they can see the lights of candles and torches flickering gaily. They arrive at the commons to find a huge crowd gathered and the commons sparkling. The Swan tribe has spared no effort to make this a night to remember. They have placed candles inside small wooden boxes with designs etched into them - creating patterns of light, which reflect off the lake and all over the buildings and trees. One hundred little carved swans, painted white, are hung from every possible tree and overhang for good luck. Little boats with candles float in the lake and there are hundreds of other little touches that are too numerous to catch in one glance.

There is a basketry contest too, and the winners are displayed for all to see. The number one winner is a huge basket with swan feathers stitched into a complex design of a woman dancer. It is an amazing work of creation that must have taken months. The girls all cluck over the basket and compare handiwork and make comments about stitching, shape and texture. The second place winner is a baby cradle basket, lined on the inside with multi-colored feathers for the babies' comfort. The cradle basket is complete with back straps, and those too are lined with feathers for the mother's back comfort. A couple of women start a fuss, complaining that the baby basket is a far finer work, and the judges are biased in the matter because they are males and don't have to carry baby baskets. The judges ignore them as they pass out the prizes.

Everyone is dressed in their finest. All women have carefully groomed hair, some with tight braids, and as much jewelry and necklaces as they can wear. Men prance around bare-chested with capes of rabbit fur, deerskin pants, and fresh haircuts. Three women are dressed from head to toe in suits of pure white swan feathers. They flap around and waddle like the big white birds they are dressed to represent. But the absolute biggest spectacle is a group of men dressed as Ladies from the Lily Pad. They wear old, discarded Lady outfits and flowers in their hair. Hesta throws some sass their way, and is soon sorry for it. The men all surround her and flirt with her as the Ladies do. Hesta curses at them and escapes their circle, but not without getting laughed at by a large crowd, all gathered to see her and the other Ladies made a fool of.

They have not missed all the weddings after all, for everything is running late today. The fourth wedding begins soon after they arrive. It is a very romantic one, with the families of the married couple making speeches about how much they love each other and how their marriage will surely last forever. Then the wife of the chief, who presides over the weddings, makes a beautiful speech.

"Dearest children, as you enter into this sacred union, do not worry if you argue. All couples argue. You cannot spend every day with a person without hating some things about them. Do not expect a life of peace, without fighting. There are many of our young people today who think that if a marriage is not happy, then it should be dissolved in the ocean on a stormy day. This practice is meant only as a last resort, but it is being used more and more often for trifles. The children of the broken marriages suffer, and our village is thrown into chaos with new waves of old ones – especially the men - mixing with the young ones of marrying age. This is not good. Strive for harmony. Suffer a few faults."

It is a Swan Tribe custom that when a marriage cannot work, the couple must travel alone to the ocean and throw themselves into it on a stormy day. This is the only way of breaking off a bad marriage. It is done this way so a couple must make a journey of many days, stuck together through many hardships, and they may work out their problems before the journey is complete. Once they reach the ocean, they must wait for a day of heavy waves and perhaps even storm clouds - a day to match their moods - before the rite is finally complete. Once this is done, they must travel back together, so there will be no hard feelings. This is the only way it is done, and many couples stay together rather than go to so much trouble.

When the couple kisses, a man begins to sing a love song that makes hearts melt. Soon Esther's own heart grows soft, and she starts dreaming romantic dreams that are at odds with the wild, devil-may-care lifestyle she has been leading the past few weeks. She dreams of having a husband who loves her and gives her orgasms every night. The soft lights and music make her long for partnership and for someone to kiss. She longs to find Vin and kiss him at the first opportunity.

Then comes the dancing, and Esther first sees the dance called the Varen. The band plays a swaying, sweet rhythm and a woman sings in a soft voice. The Swan women, wearing grass skirts, begin swaying softly and waving their arms and swinging their hips in circles. The soft, warm breeze and the music creates such a perfect mood, and Esther stands with her mouth open, watching so many beautiful people doing this graceful, undulating hip-swaying dance. The lights cast shadows everywhere, and the whole scene looks like a great gathering of tree sprites come to dance in an enchanted forest.

The Varen was created by a Swan woman named Luthia who spent several months in Hawaii. She was a dancer and musician of great renown who went to Hawaii to learn their dances and music. She adapted many Hawaiian songs to her own language, adapted the dances and then called the whole thing 'The Varen', which is a word meaning 'balance' in Zwin, the language of the Jay tribe.

The Varen goes on for a long time and everyone is almost completely in sync and doing the same movements at the same time. Luthia, who is now an old woman, still leads the dance, making sure that everyone knows exactly what move to do next. Esther decides that she must learn the Varen, which is the most beautiful dance she has seen since the Golai of the Bear tribe.

Later in the evening, Esther walks around the edge of the dance floor, looking for Vin. She searches everywhere, craving someone to talk to besides the Ladies. After a fruitless search, she goes down to the lake instead. There is an empty swan boat with an oar inside, and she gets into it and pushes off into the inky blackness. She rows out on the black lake until the sound of the oar plunging into the water drowns out the distant music of the party. Once she is out a good ways, she lies down to get a better look at the stars. She longs to soar in her swan boat up into the night sky and float gently through oceans of stars forever.

Esther could not find Vin because he is avoiding her purposely. He is stalking Hesta, who wanders all by herself on the edge of the crowd. She seems very sad tonight, and he wants to cheer her up. Now that they have finally made a connection, he wants to see if he can become somebody she thinks about. If it doesn't work out, he'll find Esther later in the night and take her home with him. But first he has something more dangerous to pursue.

As he walks nervously up to Hesta, he realizes that she has been crying. She stares at him with a tear stained face and red rimmed eyes, and he wonders if he is going to make her feel better or worse.

"I want to apologize, Hesta, for my harsh words the other day. I had no cause to offend you so."

"Thank you," she sniffles.

And that is all. He was prepared for her to give him attitude and he doesn't know what else to say, now that she is acting so helpless.

"Let me know if there is anything I can do for you," he finally says.

"Thank you. You are kind. But there is nothing...."

"I know you are a Lady, but you are also a woman. Do you never desire to be held in somebody's arms? To be caressed? I - I would -"

"You would what?"

"I would hold you. That's all. Comfort you, so you won't cry anymore."

She feels the tears well up again, more strongly at his kindness. She goes to him, puts her arms around him, and clings tightly to him as she cries tears from the deepest, darkest pools inside her. He wraps his arms around her and tells her that everything will be fine. He says that she can cry all night long if she wants and he'll stay here with her. He knows he is selfish and really doesn't care why she is crying. He doesn't want to know. He just wants to hold her.

Hesta has always known that Vin likes her. She could tell by the way he avoided her eyes when handing her the little wooden circle in her room and the way he would stare at her while they were having a romp. She didn't give it much thought. He's a toad, and she would never date a toad. And besides, he is poor and of little worth in the tribe. He is attractive enough, but he has never made anything of himself. She is not even sure what he does for work. What could he possibly offer her? She is a very beautiful woman, a sexual goddess and the richest person in the Swan tribe. She was once married into the son of a chief, and now she is a Lady that men will pay a lot of money to have sex with. They will pay it over and over again. Four chiefs of the Twelve Tribes have paid for her. Why should she give herself to a nobody like Vin?

But tonight, she feels differently. She has wandered around the commons for an hour, desperately fighting an overwhelming empty feeling. She began crying, and nobody came up to her or even cared that she was crying. They looked embarrassed for her. Not that she would ever tell them anything. Tell them what? That the wedding moved something inside of her that she thought was long dead. That she suddenly and desperately wants a real lover again.

She thought that her passion for love was gone forever, buried deep in the lake with her dead husband. She hasn't had to think about it for a long time, because opium satisfied that craving. But it doesn't anymore. And she has learned something else about herself. She has always assumed that she could get any man she wanted, if she ever decided she wanted a man again. But tonight, she realizes that although many men will sleep with her, when was the last time someone cared about her as a person? She is a drug addict and a whore, and her body is ravaged from hard use. She is moody and vain, and people laugh at her behind her back and make jokes about her, like those men in the Lady outfits. She understands now that she is lucky to get anyone at all. As she holds Vin tighter, she hopes that he will still want her, once he gets to know her better.

Hesta and Vin spend the night together at his house. And they kiss, although they do not make love. Hesta has no desire at all for that. It is a kiss that is special for her. Vin tries to push it further, but she gently refuses and explains to him how very important it is to her to wait. He nods sympathetically, although he is a little disappointed. It is considered good luck to make love on the new moon. In fact, he can hear orgasms going on all around him from his neighbor's houses. It is like a symphony tonight, all these orgasms coming from everywhere. Vin hopes that the symphony will inspire Hesta in some way, but she remains unmoved.

After her boat ride, Esther goes back to the party. A man with a concertina is singing a bawdy song called "I miss romping with you". He does a whole naughty concert, and she gets re-drunk and laughs crazily the entire time. After the concert, there is more music and the dancing area is filled with couples kissing and hugging. Esther decides to walk over to Vin's house to see if he is there. Where else is she going to sleep? It takes her a while to find the place in the dark, but finally she does. She recognizes the shadows of his crazily thatched roof, the one that looks like it was built by a madman. The fire is lit inside and sends out a flickering glow.

As she approaches, she hears soft whispers and giggles coming from inside, and her heart sinks into her moccasins. She wanders off, thankful that she is too drunk and tired to really care that he is with another woman. She'll get pissed off tomorrow. All she wants to do tonight is find somewhere to sleep. She ends up making the long walk home in the dark. She is very drunk and it seems that she is floating home on her buzz. She sings songs as she walks and wobbles musically. She trips on roots and twigs, but barely notices the pain. She can feel the pain in her feet tomorrow, along with everything else.

Swan 18'

Wolf moon

Esther wakes late and spends the morning in the hot springs. The rest of the girls arrive early in the afternoon, ready for work. Lula makes a big lunch for everyone, in preparation for the large crowd of men waiting for the Pad to open in the afternoon. The girls have a quick meeting after lunch and are informed that a rich man from the Elk tribe has made a special request. It is his desire to have two women tie him up and have very rough sex with him, and also to play with each other while he watches. He will pay handsomely for this special request. Lula told him that two women will cost him twenty tupas and he agreed. So Lula asks for two volunteers to make eight tupas each to double up on this man. Hesta immediately volunteers. She seems to be in an unusually good mood today and she whispers in Esther's ear that she should also volunteer because it will be great fun. She tells Esther what fun they could have making this man squirm and playing with each other instead of with him. They can totally ignore him and make easy tupas. Esther laughs, liking the way Hesta describes it, and agrees. She wouldn't do this thing with anybody else at the Pad, but she would do it with Hesta.

After Lula gives everyone a quick afternoon smoke of Dragon's Blood, Esther and Hesta go off on their little adventure. The man is a neat, nervous looking man wearing a leather outfit he got from some Spanish trader and silk stockings from China. He tells them to be rough with him and tear his clothes off, but not to tear his silk stockings, which are delicate. They go to Hesta's cabin, which is richly decorated with imported silk and lace, and Hesta takes off his clothes and ties him to the bed. Then she takes off Esther's golinta, while Esther does the same for her.

First, Hesta climbs up onto her bed and jumps onto him, crushing him roughly with her body. She does it again and then Esther does the same thing. He moans, loving it, and begs them to play with each other before doing things to him. They get lost in each other for a while, totally forgetting about him as they sensuously touch each other. It is a very erotic experience, playing with Hesta in the light of the candle in the haze of dragon's blood. Hesta licks her all over and Esther gets tingly. She licks Hesta's large breasts, watching her nipples stand erect. It is like they are two huge babies, rolling around and climbing on top of each other. Esther suddenly remembers some strange sensations of a happy childhood when she was a very little girl. She struggles to remember more, to picture her parent's faces, but she cannot. But she can feel them somehow, tumbling her up and down as she laughs with glee.

After what seems like hours, the man begs for some more attention, waking her up from her trip down into the bowels of childhood. She cannot remember much of what happens afterward. She vaguely remembers Hesta having rough sex with him, bouncing up and down on top of his shaft so hard that Esther is sure that it will break off, while shouting obscenities at him. Meanwhile, she wraps her hair around the man's face so he cannot see anything. Many bizarre rituals, lost in time, fade in and out of her consciousness. And then Hesta unties him and kicks him out of her house with a curse and a laugh, and throws his clothes after him. As she closes the door, she and Esther start to laugh uproariously. Making jokes at the toad's expense, they go off to soak in the warm pool, ignoring the other men waiting for their turns.

In the evening, Vin takes a walk down to the Lily Pad, hoping to surprise Hesta. He is in for a shock, after a two-hour walk, when he discovers that she is with a toad. He had somehow got it into his head that because of last night she was going to give up being a Lady. He feels very stupid for assuming this, and also hurt and angry that she is now having sex with strange men a day after their little affair. As he begins to overflow with jealous rage, he decides that he is allowed to do the same thing if he wants. If she wants to have an open relationship, then he might as well take advantage of it.

He knocks on Esther's door, who is surprised to see him, but not at all disappointed. She is still high and feeling quite open from the dragon's blood. Vin sits down on her bed, his face easy to read with simple desire, and then she knows that she doesn't care if he was with a woman last night. She was with several men today and yesterday. It isn't important. All that is important is that she has an orgasm and tonight she feels ready to try.

They have sex, and due to the lingering opium buzz, Esther is more relaxed than usual. She can feel that elusive place of pleasure right in front of her, although she cannot reach it. She still feels numb, except in this state of heightened awareness, she can almost feel the wall that keeps her from entering that orgasmic place. And try as she may, she cannot get around it. It is so intense, seeing that wall that keeps her from her own pleasure, that she begins to cry. She continues to grind and thrust desperately, as tears stream down her face. Vin watches her, strangely attracted to the tears that stream down her face and mingle with the sweat on her nose. It is a sort of turn on, almost as if he is so good that he makes her cry.

He leaves before dawn, creeping out in the darkness. He walks in the darkness because he doesn't want Hesta to know he has been here. He has a sinking feeling that he just made a big mistake by sleeping with Esther, and he resolves to stay away from her from now on. Once he is out of the Lily Pad, he relaxes and walks home, enjoying the dawn light. It is something he rarely sees, being a late sleeper by nature.

Swan 20'

Owl moon

The Lily Pad is finally slowing down, as the influx of men come for the new moon run out of tupas and head back home. Esther has a lot of time to think on this cold, gloomy day with nothing to do but soak in the springs and hide from the world. She has much on her mind and she can find no solution to it. She cannot stop thinking about how she is incapable of enjoying sex, and she is frustrated with her body for being so numb. So she eventually finds herself knocking on Hesta's door again.

As usual, Hesta listens carefully. Even if she is a little short of sympathy, having heard this particular question many times already, she is still a good listener. Esther tells her of her experiences with sex recently, not naming names, and how she discovered the wall that keeps her from having an orgasm.

"This profession attracts women with…disturbances," Hesta says, choosing her words carefully. "Many of the Ladies have serious emotional or sexual problems, and that is why they are here."

"That sounds right," Esther sighs.

"Why is it so important that you have an orgasm right now?"

"I am afraid that I am completely numb and I will never enjoy sex. And that I will never find a man because of it."

"You must be patient," she implores.

"But I don't want my flower to be dead. And I think my work at the Lily Pad is making it worse."

"You have tried all my suggestions?"

"Yes, but I cannot break through the wall. What can I do?"

Hesta sighs. What does Esther want her to say? Hesta, problem talker of the Lily Pad. When she retires from being a Lady, she wants Lula's job. She could do a much better job managing the girls than Lula. All Lula ever does is keep them hooked on opium. If Lula occupies the position much longer, Hesta will use her influence with the girls to force her out. Hesta suddenly jumps with excitement. She has an idea.

"I know what to do. You must visit a Wolf healer. They understand things of a sexual nature - if it's a sexual problem, then you need Wolf help.

"The Wolf tribe?" Esther asks doubtfully.

"That is my advice to you, although I would not recommend this course of action to some around here. Some of the Swan tribe have had bad dealings with the Wolves."

"Why do I need to see a healer? I'm not sick."

"Well, I can't think of anyone else who can help you. You could go see an astrologer or a problem talker in the commons, but I don't think they can help you. You need...deeper help."

"What would they do to me?" asks Esther nervously.

"I do not know."

"Would they want to help me?"

"I do not know that either. Although, a purse full of tupas is powerful incentive."

"Where is the Wolf tribe?"

"On the other side of the lake and inside the forest. The easiest way there is by boat, although there is a road that winds around the lake also."

"I will consider it."

And then it suddenly occurs to Hesta that something is wrong. Because she suddenly remembers who it was that Esther had sex with last week. She feels a sinking feeling in her stomach, because the answer is already obvious. But she has to ask to be sure.

"By the way? Is this a toad you discovered this with?" she asks hopefully. "Yesterday, I mean."

"No. You told me to take a lover," she says innocently, having no idea of the trouble she is about to cause. "Vin was here yesterday. Remember him? That man you didn't like."

Swan 21′

It has been a busy day for Vin. He worked at the Swan school for many hours, supervising all the little children who have come to study while the sun is in an air sign. Today, Vin was asked to take the children out and watch them play games all day. It was unbearably hot out, and he had to stand on the unsheltered beach for hours while the children played every game ever invented by the Twelve Tribes. After school, he went to the market to sell a whole mess of fish that he caught to an old woman whose husband died, and then he bought some arrows with the tupas. He hasn't been hunting or gathering as hard as he should be, and he will suffer for it this winter if he doesn't get back to it. Finally, he went to the black acorn grove and filled his basket with acorns. So he is quite tired by the time he returns to the commons and sees Hesta shopping. He walks up to her innocently, puts his baskets down, and his arms around her. But she squirms out from under his grasp and glares at him.

"What is wrong?"

"You are a maggot ridden vulture!" she shrieks. "Picking at carrion with your repulsive head! Any dead carcass in front of you is fair game, I see."

"What are you talking about?" he asks, shocked, although he knows the answer well enough.

"Don't play stupid with me! Just because I was busy, you had to bury your beak in my friend's flower."

"You were with a man," he says irritably, deciding to tell the truth. "You were with three men, actually. I got hurt, and I...well, I guess you know the rest."

"To think I opened myself up to such a stupid, air headed maggot! I am so embarrassed. It was a moment of weakness only. Stay away from me please, I'll have nothing else to do with you."

"But you were with three men last night," he repeats. "How can you make such a double standard? I figured we had an open relationship."

She stares at him, shocked that he would say such a thing.

"That's not the same thing at all. That is just work."

"And what's the difference?"

She finds herself smiling at the question, because it is so stupid, and this just throws her into a fluster.

"What's the difference? What's - I - I - what a stupid man you are! You don't see the difference between work and pleasure? Of course not, why should you? You're a toad yourself. I should have known better than to trust a toad. I must have lost my mind."

"I am so surprised by this attitude. You are a Lady, aren't you? Since when are you so uptight about sex?"

Again, she finds herself laughing - so pathetic is his argument.

"I didn't think you'd mind," he says lamely.

"Not mind? Me? Of course I don't, because you're pond scum. Excrement of lake ducks. I wouldn't expect anything else of you."

She kicks his burden basket over dramatically, spilling his gathered acorns all over the ground. Then she storms off, pleased with herself for that last touch. He follows her and grabs her with both hands, but she squirms out of his grip.

"How is it all right for you to have sex and not me? Tell me that!" he shouts.

She stops, puts her hands on her hips, and looks very much like an angry swan.

"It's my job! I don't enjoy it. I do it for money. I didn't make love to those men. I let them use my body. But you made love to Esther, my friend, and only a day gone by since we were together. How can I ever trust you?"

"I didn't make love to her. It was just a romp, a jealous reaction -"

She shakes her head, exasperated.

"This is all a misunderstanding. A mistake - please, let me make you dinner, and we can talk about it."

"You've got that right," she says, slapping at him in her haste to get away from him. "A bad mistake. Go away!"

"Talk to me," he pleads. "I know we can work this out."

And then he stops dead. He is begging her, and that means it is over. He has been here before, on both sides of the fence. He stops talking and just stares at her with his heart wringing itself dry in his chest. Waiting for what he knows is coming. At least he can do this with a little dignity, instead of begging like a little boy who wants a treat.

"It's over then?" he asks. "You don't even want to talk about it?"

"You are not so dumb after all!" she calls over her shoulder, and then she is gone down the road. He watches her miserably for a moment, and then he goes back to his spilled burden basket to pick up the acorns, which have rolled everywhere. He notices many people staring at him, trying to hide their smiles, and making notes for later gossip. He grits his teeth and ignores them.

Swan 25'

Raven moon

There is a birthday party tonight. Mati is a Swan sun with a Raven moon, so there is a party in her honor. Lula makes cakes and pies and other sweet things in celebration, and the girls all gather to eat, drink and be merry.

The calendar birthday is never celebrated in the Twelve Tribes. Astrological birthdays are celebrated instead. That is when the sun and moon are aligned as they were on the day a person was born.

Esther has been drinking wine all night, so it comes as no surprise that she begins to feel a little strange. But when the feeling grows stronger, she begins to wonder what is happening to her. Soon, she begins to feel as if she is floating through the party, instead of walking. She feels creative tonight, and when the ladies begin to make music, she bangs on the drums and sings at the top of her voice. She sings a couple of bawdy songs with them and accompanies herself with her own drumming.

Soon she begins to feel very, very high, and she cannot take the music or any sort of stimulation any more. She must be extremely drunk, though she hasn't drunk *that* much. She walks to her hut, sits down on the bed, and attempts to catch her breath. Her head begins to buzz and she lies down on the bed, hoping to go to sleep before she gets sick. But lying down is very uncomfortable, so she sits up again.

Her room is a mess! Her clothes and other possessions are scattered all over the hut. Since when did she become such a slob? In the candlelight, she notices that the walls are moldy and rotting and the roof is covered in spider webs and dust. Her room disgusts her and she wants to clean it from top to bottom, but she cannot muster the energy right now. The smell in the room is bad too - sort of stifling and rancid.

She is going to leave and go outside...soon. Not now, but when she gets the energy together. She sits cross-legged on her bed, aware that her brain is overloaded. It seems to be zapping information all over the place, at such a rapid pace that she cannot follow it. Her head is moving so fast, she is sure it will explode. It is like a horrible lightening storm in her skull. This is not drunk. She doesn't know what is happening to her.

She is thirsty too, but the water barrel is so far away. Soon she will have to get water. She sits there for what seems like an eternity, dreaming of drinking water, until she can stand it no longer and she has to get up. Some of the ladies are outside, laughing hysterically at something. They call out to Esther to come join them, but she merely waves and moves in a beeline for the water. She drinks two cups of the wonderfully cold and refreshing water, and then goes back to her room. She just wants to lie down now and go to sleep and wake up normal again.

She lies down, but it feels wrong. Her whole body is wound up like a spring and ready to pop, so she sits up again. This feels better. She'll just sit cross-legged all night long. She begins to wonder what is going on with her. What did she eat? Opium? Of course...there must have been opium in one of the foods! Can you eat opium? She must have eaten a lot of it, and this is a bad side effect of doing too much. She heard stories from the Ladies about people overdoing opium, until they went insane. One Lady had to spend the rest of her life with her parents, unable to live by herself anymore. Esther doesn't even have parents. She can't afford to go insane.

She thinks bitterly that she has been sort of normal for the first time in her life these past few months, and now she has ruined it. She has gone too far and there is no turning back. She is now back on the road to insanity. Why does she keep coming here, down this miserable road? What is wrong with her?

For the next hour, she embarks on an introspective nightmare of epic proportions. She breaks down all the thoughts in her head, realizing how stupid and pointless they are. Then she thinks of all of the decisions she has made and how she made them all for the wrong reasons. She tears her entire life to shreds, until it seems the only thing worth doing is sitting cross-legged on her bed and doing nothing until the day she dies. She has no personality left and there is nothing left to do or say. There will be no more fun for her. Never any orgasms. She will never be normal again.

Finally, she can stand it no longer. She goes outside into the night, hoping to escape from herself. It is late now and most of the ladies have gone to bed, but she sees Mati skulking around.

"What did I eat?" she asks desperately.

Mati shrugs.

"Was it opium?"

Mati just shrugs again and walks off, lost in her own world. She must have eaten it too!

Esther drinks some more water, and then takes a walk. The night air is crisp, cold, and comforting. She tries to push all the frightening, chattering thoughts out of her head. She desperately fights them off, as if something she could do would make them go away. But she knows, deep down, that nothing can help her but time. The drug has to wear off sometime. It better wear off.

She sits in her room, waiting for dawn. She knows that when dawn comes, she'll be able to sleep. It's like a beacon of hope - the light of day - that will signal the end of her horrible night. I'll never do opium again, she thinks. Never. She makes a promise to herself to clean up her life and get her head straight. She feels like she can see the part of her mind that is bad, a great mess of twisted thoughts. And she could get rid of those thoughts, just throw them out, if she were not so afraid to go near them. And she is even more afraid of living without them. Whatever they are, however bad they are, they are more comforting than the unknown.

Swan 26'

Esther wakes up from a deep sleep, slowly sits up, and stares at the wall as her head clears. She can feel sanity returning. She is no longer spinning in that vortex of madness. Sighing, she goes outside, desperate for water. She has a splitting headache, and she knows water will help. To her surprise the sun is already setting. She slept the entire day away! But she doesn't mind that so much. She is just relieved that the ordeal is over. She sits down on the forest floor and enjoys the hard earned peace and quiet in her head.

"Lula, do you know what I ate?" Esther asks, when she sees her. "I ate something bad."

"There was jimm in the pie. The green pie."

"Jimm? That's all?"

"Yes. Why? Did you like it?"

"No. I had a horrible night."

"I'm sorry. I should have warned you. You did eat quite a big piece, didn't you?" Lula smiles sheepishly and walks off. This is the second time that Esther has had jimm and it was even worse than the first time. It makes her so crazy and paranoid that she cannot figure out why anybody likes it. She makes a solemn promise to herself to recover her sanity and clean up her life, and then goes to the warm pool and sits in it all night long.

Hesta goes to town to buy the nicest rabbit fur blanket in the village. Walking toward the main circle, she sees Vin sitting by himself, idly strumming his Spanish guitar. She quickly turns away, hoping he won't see her. But it is too late. He looks sharply up and the guitar falls into his lap. He freezes for a moment, and then recovers and begins to walk slowly toward her.

"Mud," she hisses, invoking a childhood curse.

She starts to walk away, but he shouts out her name in a loud voice. There are many people about, so she turns around and faces him in order to avoid a scene. She would prefer that nobody knows she was ever involved with Vin.

"It is good to see you," he says, trying to keep his head, while his heart hammers in his ribcage. "Can we talk?"

"I'd rather not."

"Please."

She sighs in resignation and follows him to a little sandy beach by the lake, where they can talk in private.

"I don't get it," he finally says, confronting her when they are alone. "Did we not share something wonderful together? Something that is gone with the wind, like a dandelion tuft?"

"Yes, we did. So what does that mean?"

"I don't want to lose it. It meant a lot to me."

"It was nice for a few moments," she says with a slight sneer. "Like a flower that wilts in your hand when you take it into the sun."

She has that haughty look again. The one that seems to say he is no longer worthy of her attention. It infuriates him.

"Look at you. Acting like the queen bee again. Don't you know what you are? I wish you could see yourself the way you really are."

"And how am I?" she asks accusingly.

"A plaything. A toy for men. A fantasy. For a single night, you were something else, a real person with real feelings. But now you're back to the way you were."

"You think you're so much better?" she shouts back. "You're just like all the other toads. You create the fantasy and then you accuse me of creating it! You think I am a beautiful woman just to play with your mind."

He tries to wrap his brain around this new argument, but suddenly, he doesn't care. He is sick of her. She is physically beautiful, and yet her personality is almost the opposite - grotesque in its vanity. He cannot believe he has loved her for so long like a fool.

"Well, I might be alone tonight," he says bitterly. "But you will be too. The only company you'll have tonight will pay you for it. Eight tupas a night."

He pulls out a little cloth bag.

"By the way, how much do I owe you for our night together?"

"Go away, toad!"

However brave she tries to sound, her voice cracks, and her face betrays her. But he doesn't notice. He just turns around and walks off. She watches him go, wishing she could just kill the pride that keeps her from running to him and telling him that she doesn't want it to end like this either. She stands there frozen, hoping he will turn around and come back, but he doesn't. He is proud too.

Swan 28'

Cougar moon

Esther quickly puts her things together, before she changes her mind. She can see now that she has to get out of here. Ever since her ordeal with the jimm pie, she has seen this place in a new light. All of the girls are strung out on opium, in and out of reality, and lost in their dreams. Esther doesn't want that kind of life for herself. Yesterday, she craved opium, and she could feel the desire deep inside her body. She has heard the ladies talk about opium withdrawals and how painful they are. Hesta warned her about that trap already and Esther knows that if she stays here, she'll fall deep into it and never get out. The experience with the jimm scared her enough to give her a window of sanity that she can use to escape, but she has to go now. She has a feeling that this is her last chance. There is no escape for many of these girls from the 'dragon' and perhaps they are too far gone to even care.

She doesn't want to say goodbye to anybody but Hesta. She is the only one who won't ask her to stay, and Esther can't handle that right now. On the way to Hesta's hut, she sees Lula, walking in the distance, and she quickly hides behind a tree. Lula will definitely try to get her to stay if she knows that Esther is leaving. At the very least, she will probably try to get some tupas out of her for opium or wine or the golinta or rent or whatever. Luckily, Esther turned in all her little wooden disks a few days ago, and she has all the tupas she is owed wrapped in a piece of fur in the bottom of her burden basket. She is free and clear and she wants to get back on the road again without hassle.

Hesta is in her room, heavily sedated. She stares at Esther with glassy eyes as Esther explains how she has to go away and she'll come back for a visit soon and how she'll miss all the Ladies and all the other things she has to say before she goes. Hesta nods slowly, although Esther isn't sure how much she'll remember later. Finally, Esther gives her a hug and leaves her alone. She feels bad that she couldn't say a proper goodbye, but it seems a proper omen. But now she has to tell Mati she's leaving, so somebody will know and remember where she has gone, or else they will all worry about her.

Mati is very understanding, wishes Esther well, and tells her to come back for a visit. Then Mati has to fetch Kelli and Paila, so they can say goodbye too, and Esther ends up saying her goodbyes to all of the Ladies. The Ladies all decide they want to walk into town with her and go shopping, so Esther gets an escort into town. They are barely on the road, when they see Hesta chasing after them, struggling to move her sluggish limbs. They stop to wait for her.

"I want to come," she mumbles quietly, when she catches up to them.

They all walk into town to see Esther off, and she is glad that she was thwarted in her attempt to sneak off like a shadow. It is better this way, walking bravely forward in the sunlight, with friends at your side.

The village commons is busy today, but Esther cannot remember a time when it hasn't been busy. Everyone seems to spend as much time as possible in the commons. There is always music playing and everyone has something to sell, and it doesn't phase them that nobody is buying. They just come to enjoy the camaraderie of the market. Even Mati joins them, although it means being seen in public with the Ladies and risk being discovered by her still clueless parents. Now that she has some dirt on her father, she is less worried about them finding out.

After a swim in the lake, the Ladies start haggling for a ride across for Esther. They finally find a young boy, who cannot be older than twelve, who agrees to take her. She hands a tupa to the young boy, who borrows a little Swan craft for the long ride. While he fetches the boat, she gives a quick goodbye hug to all of the Ladies. Then she climbs aboard the boat of tule and the boy paddles out onto the lake. It takes about an hour to the trailhead. These tule boats are very fast and she helps him paddle, so they zip across the lake in no time. When they arrive, the boy demands another tupa, because he has to go back now by himself. She refuses, and he gets upset and throws a little tantrum. He demands a kiss instead for his trouble. She finds him cute, in his little rage, so she gives him a little kiss to placate him. He smiles and waves to her as he zips on home again, probably to tell his friends that he just had sex with the Lady he took across.

Deposited on the trail, she begins to walk. It feels good to be on the road again, off on new adventures. As usual, she will miss the friends she has left behind, but each time she does it, it gets easier. She has accepted by now that she is determined to keep moving until...when? She doesn't know. She knows that the time for stopping is not yet at hand and the wheel continues to turn.

The Wolf Tribe

Wolf 0'

Hawk moon

The days are getting shorter and night creeps up quickly. Esther crashes through thick brush, looking for the path she was just on. She took a detour through a grove of trees, following a herd of elk, but realized she was getting lost and turned around. When she finds the path again, she sighs with relief and continues.

It begins to get dark, but she does not stop for the night. There was a sign nearby, welcoming her to the boundaries of the Wolf tribe territory. Just a little farther and she'll find a hot meal and a bed tonight. Soon the path becomes pitch black underneath the thick roof of foliage. The path is not well maintained, but is covered with fallen branches, rocks, and holes that she can fall into. She moves very slowly, her eyes wide open and still not seeing a thing. The hooting of an owl catches her ears, and she stops and stands still as stone. She feels a strange calm come over her, and remembers that a nearly full moon will be out soon. She will be able to see well enough to walk on.

After a long wait, the moon finally makes an appearance and bathes the forest in its glow. Confidently, she walks on. After an hour, she sees lights in the distance and she quickens her pace. Soon she comes to a bunch of houses with lights peeking through windows and doorways. Esther wanders around in a daze, until she finally asks somebody if there is a shelter nearby that might be serving dinner still. She is pointed in the right direction and off she goes.

She comes to a round building with cheery lights peeking through windows. The smell of fish is overpowering, and nearly faint from hunger, she follows the smell inside. In the round room, a great fire sends smoke up to the ceiling. Many men and women are gathered around tables, talking and laughing, with the remains of dinner piled in front of them. Esther guesses that many of these people are locals – not guests - by their dress and attitudes. The main dress of the Wolf tribe is furs and hides, often dyed black as night and covered with various symbols and crests of their lineage. They also wear totems around their necks and arms. Some have necklaces with various bird feathers and bones entwined, bracelets made out of real wolves fangs, or the tail of an elk or marmot tied to a necklace.

The tables are full tonight. A man moves back and forth, waiting on everybody. He spies Esther standing at the door and walks over to her. He is a stout, swarthy man with a thick beard. Sweat and grime are smeared on his face and clothes, and he looks as if he has been slaving away over a hot stove all day long.

"Welcome to the shelter. My name is Temu," he says, with a little smile. "What can I do for you?"

"Have you any food left, please?"

"Have a seat," he says, and hurries off with the pile of dishes in his hands.

She cannot find any open seats, so she sits by the fire, hoping she will be fed there. A moment later, the man returns with a plate of food for her. He walks over to the fire, but doesn't hand her the plate.

"What are you doing over here?"

"There were no empty seats. I can just eat here."

"Intolerable. I'll make room for you. Hold on."

He walks up to a boy of about fifteen years and murmurs something in his ear. When the boy shakes his head, Temu grabs his arm and gently pulls him out of his chair. Esther overhears a few words of his explanation.

"-paying guests. You'll have to sit on the floor."

The boy protests and sits back down, but the look on Temu's face is firm and he pulls more insistently on the boy's arm. The boy gets angry and tries to shake him, but Temu keeps a firm grip and doesn't allow him to. There is a brief moment of tension, but finally the boy curses and stands up. He sits down morosely by the fire and glares at Temu. Temu smiles in a satisfied way and indicates for Esther to sit.

Everyone now stares at Esther, to see whom it was that the boy was booted for. The boy glares at her, as if it was her request that he be moved. Esther is very uncomfortable with the whole situation, and she doesn't want to take his seat. She just stands there, unsure what to do. Temu's expression becomes strained, as if she is embarrassing him now by refusing to sit. He places her plate down at the table and glares at her impatiently. She finally gives in and sits down. She keeps her head down and looks only at her food, not wanting to look anyone in the eye.

"Enjoy your meal," Temu says kindly.

"Thank you."

He nods and goes back to the kitchen.

Dinner is a seafood feast, freshly brought back from the bountiful ocean. Clams, mussels, seal and many varieties of fish, all of it freshly caught and prepared many different ways. It is a huge plate of food and more than she could eat in an entire day, but she does her best. A friendly young man next to her talks her ear off while she eats, and she cannot get out a single sentence before he starts rambling again. But she is happy for his attention, as annoying as it is, because it keeps her from thinking about the resentful stares of the boy on the floor.

After dinner, Esther sits by the fire, feeling full, warm, and satisfied. It was a great meal, although she wishes there were some kind of grain or roots to go along with all the meat. She chats with an old man with long stringy hair, who seems very intoxicated. Then she receives another visit from the shelter keeper, who has washed up and seems more relaxed.

"Will you be staying on tonight?" he asks.

"I will. How much to stay here?"

"Tupa a night gets you dinner and a bed. Two tupas gets you three meals a day and a bed. If you have no tupas, we can make other arrangements."

"That sounds fair. I'll take a bed and dinner for now."

"Good."

He grabs her basket from the doorway, puts it on his own back, grabs a candle and leads her outside.

"You didn't have to make that boy move," she says, as they walk in the darkness.

"Don't worry about him. He just got angry because he doesn't know his place yet," he says firmly. "Accept and move on. That's what I say."

They reach a small hut, and he opens the door and puts her basket down. Then he lights a candle and examines the room.

"It's a little dirty," he says apologetically. "I'll have the girls clean up tomorrow. I'm sorry about that."

"It looks fine."

"It's hard to get good help," he says, not really hearing her. "They're all larva."

"It looks fine to me," she insists, hoping he won't be too hard on the girls.

"The man who runs this shelter only hires young girls he wants to sleep with. He's useless. His father gave him this place and he's determined to run it into the ground. It's me that holds it together." He waves it all aside, making mental notes for later. "Make yourself at home. Let me know if you need anything. The fire goes all night in the main house, and there is plenty to smoke if you want it. On the east wall of the main house is the wood pile, if you want wood for your fire pit."

He gives her a warm smile, and leaves her to settle in. She sits down on the bed, which consists of a bearskin laid over a flattened tule mat. She spreads out her blanket and cloak and soon falls into a deep sleep.

Wolf 2'

Esther is depressed. It is gloomy out, nobody is about, and she wanders around the nearly empty village commons trying to find something to get excited about. And she has this itch for opium that won't go away. Opium would cure her poor mood instantly, and she could discover all the fun things about this place. She kicks herself for forgetting to buy some from Lula, even though she knows deep down that she is better off without it. It runs through her mind all day long, and it frightens her that she is so obsessed with dragon's blood after such a short time using it.

She goes into the shelter and hangs by the fire for a while. She chats with Temu, who sits with her and smokes endlessly from a long, clay pipe. She asks him offhandedly if he has any opium and is immediately embarrassed about it. But he takes the question seriously, as if it is a question he hears everyday.

"I don't, but I might be able to get some for you," he says after some thought. "I'll look into it."

He asks her about her experiences with opium, and she tells him all about it. She finds that her depression immediately lifts as she tells him some of her adventures with the drug. He offers her some jimm to tide her over, but she refuses. Then he brings two plates of leftover fish for lunch and sits down to eat with her.

"Have you any acorn soup or corn cakes or something like that?" she asks, craving something more than more fish.

"I don't generally bother with that sort of thing," he says, nodding his head at his own wisdom, as if agreeing with himself. "You are better off living on meat alone, if you just get used to it."

In the afternoon, she takes a sweat, which cheers her up somewhat. There are a few moldy old men and an old woman in the sweat lodge, sitting in a deeply meditative state. She sits with them, enjoying their wise silence. She emerges feeling fresh and new again, and her mood is much improved. She jumps into a cold stream to wash off the sweat and feels relatively human again.

Afterwards, she goes back to her room and takes a nap. When she wakes, it is dark and she is depressed again. She cries for a while, but she doesn't know why. After crying her eyes out, she sits in her room until her eyes lose their redness. She is embarrassed to go into dinner with tear stained eyes. When she feels and looks better, she goes into the main lodge. Thankfully, it is less crowded today, and she is able to find a seat without a hassle. Temu brings her a small piece of fish and a big bowl filled with acorn mush.

"I got this for you," he says with a smile. "My brother's wife made it. Enjoy."

"Thank you," she says gratefully. "You're very kind."

"You deserve it," he says with a nod, and leaves her to eat.

Wolf 3'

Beaver moon

In the morning, Esther walks to the village commons, which is packed and noisy. Drummers pound ragged rhythms for early morning dancers, and everyone does their daily chores with an excitement that seems far beyond the chores themselves. Esther's gloom is gone, replaced by an incredible sense of unfulfilled desires all competing for attention. She feels the urges piling on top of one another like planks of wood stacked for burning, and the very air seems to be sparking and snapping with them. There is something large looming on the horizon. She can feel it coming.

Later, she eats lunch in the main room of the shelter, when a striking woman enters the room. All heads turn when she enters and Esther hears somebody say, "Chief Vayanna is here". Vayanna is slender, beautiful and radiates a fierce sexuality, with a large smile that lights up the room. She is commanding and her presence lacks any hint of weakness. She wears a skirt of tight deerskin, dyed black, and snakeskin vest and boots. A long tattoo of snake scales runs up one hand. Vayanna walks briefly around the room, greets everyone gathered for the full moon and welcomes them to the village.

"Welcome to the Wolf tribe," Vayanna says to Esther, with a serious expression. And who are you?"

"I am Esther?"

"Which tribe are you from, Esther?"

"I am not from any tribe."

Vayanna stares at her suspiciously for a moment and then her smile returns. But this time it seems a mask and Esther feels no warmth from it.

"Not from any tribe?" she asks, as she looks Esther up and down. "You don't look like Zesti. Who are you and what is the purpose of your visit?"

Esther opens her mouth but nothing comes out. She is rather taken aback by the question, and unwilling to speak about her business under such direct compulsion. Vayanna glares at her impatiently, as if it is a simple enough question and she is surprised that it takes so long to answer. Finally, Esther comes up with a proper response.

"I am Esther, a traveler in your lands. I have no home or people. I am merely looking for a healer to help me with a problem."

"What sort of problem?" Vayanna asks, nodding her head slowly.

"I'd rather not speak of it, except to the healer."

"Well, how may I recommend a good healer if you don't tell me the nature of the problem?"

Esther swallows and sucks on her tongue.

"It is a woman's problem," she says at last, in a quiet voice.

Vayanna nods again.

"Then it is a woman healer you want, I presume."

"Yes."

"And you understand you will need to pay her?"

"Yes, of course."

"I will send somebody to visit you, if you wait here," Vayanna says, grabbing her hand in a friendly way, as if to show her that things will be better now that she has revealed her business. Then she quickly moves on to the next person.

Two hours later, another woman enters the room. She is a tall woman with long straight hair and eager eyes. She wears a black deerskin cloak that wraps around her dense frame like skin and her body is covered with many tattoos. She walks in purposefully and scans the room.

"Who asked for the healer?"

"I did," Esther says quietly.

"Come with me and we'll discuss your problem," she says, indicating for Esther to rise and follow her.

They walk into the afternoon sun, which is mellow, warm, and pleasant. They settle against a tree, and Esther sighs, enjoying the late sunshine. For some reason, the sun makes her not want to discuss her problems, and she begins to wonder if she should just forget it.

"My name is Numei," the woman says at last. "And your name is Esther. Isn't it?"

"Yes."

"Do you want to share your story? I hear you are not of the Twelve Tribes."

"I grew up in a Spanish town on the coast."

Numei's eyes open wide in surprise.

"Really?"

"Yes."

"Tell me about it."

Esther doesn't say anything at first, and Numei waits impatiently. Finally, Esther mumbles a few basic facts that don't mean much. Numei seems to sense that she is avoiding the question, but she doesn't comment on it. She waves it aside and gets down to business.

"And what is your problem, may I ask? I was told you have a woman's problem. Is it a problem with too much pollen in the flower?"

'Too much pollen' means a yeast infection.

"No," Esther says slowly. "I don't think so."

"Well, are you going to have me guess all day long or will you just tell me?"

"It seems stupid now to worry about it. I don't think it's really something you could help me with anyways," Esther stammers. "Let's just forget it."

"I came all the way down here," Numei insists. "What is it? If I can't help you, I'll tell you. I won't pretend I can help if I can't."

"I have..." Esther says carefully. "I mean, I cannot...um, I don't know how to say it-"

"Let us walk to the river," Numei councils, grabbing her by the hand again and pulling her to her feet. They begin to follow the path toward the river. Numei lets go of her hand and sings quietly to herself, ignoring Esther, who follows along behind.

"Spit it out," orders Numei, after a long silence.

It is easier for Esther to speak, now that she can concentrate on walking and doesn't have to look Numei in the face.

"I can't have an orgasm," she blurts out.

Surprised, Numei stops and turns to stare at her. A faint smile plays across her lips.

"I mean - I haven't - there is this wall there -"

Esther stops talking, feeling suddenly foolish.

"That is why you have come?"

"I know it seems silly," Esther stammers.

"A lost orgasm."

"It isn't lost. I have never had one."

"Tell me about where you have looked for it."

Feeling bolder, Esther speaks about her flower being numb whenever she has sex. She speaks of Vin briefly, and the wall that she discovered somewhere inside of her. She talks on and on about the wall, and how she feels it every time she has sex. She believes that this wall keeps her from feeling pleasure. She is sure that on the other side of this barrier is a whole world of sensation that she wants to experience.

They have reached the river, and Numei stops to watch the water swirl past. She stares at the sky and listens to the sounds of birds. She takes particular notice when a woodpecker is heard overhead. For a long time she is lost in her own thoughts, and then she turns to look at Esther again.

"I believe I can help you."

"You can?"

"Yes. First thing we must do is to find you a man to practice on. Come, let us return to the village and enjoy the full moon festival. I'll point out some single men who can help you and you pick out the one you like. It will most likely have to be a young one, as the old ones are all married. But the young ones are cuter anyway and a few are quite talented."

She grabs Esther's hand and leads her back the way they came. They walk toward the commons, where lunch is being served. Several fires are going at once, lit in a semicircle, and bubbling pots send delicious smells of all kinds. Most of the village is already here, but they seem subdued, as if the party hasn't yet started.

"Excuse me, Esther. I will see you later," Numei says.

Numei goes off to do something, and Esther goes to the food tables for something to eat. She gets a small glass of some thick, sweet blackberry wine and a plate of deer meat topped with a delicious mushroom broth. She skips the second pot of food, which has a strange smell and a layer of thick, greasy fat bubbling merrily at the top of it, and takes her food over to a lone tree and sits by herself to eat.

After lunch, she listens to a woman with an impossibly deep voice sing in a strange Zesti language, accompanied by hand drum, split stick clappers, and a flute. She cannot take her eyes off the riveting woman, who never looks up from her feet as she sings. She seems too intense to look anyone in the eye, as if her gaze would instill fear in the heart...or perhaps madness.

After that, two women do a very intense dance. Never dropping their gaze, they encircle each other like two warriors in a fight to the finish, and do a dance with a sharp, dramatic flare. They swing their arms high and twirl with faces scowling, then drop to the ground like battling cougars and circle around on their hands and feet. They always seem to be about to attack each other and draw blood with a bite to the neck, but they never do. They do the same dance for over an hour, without rest.

Numei finds Esther late in the afternoon, and she seems to be in good spirits.

"I have found you four men who have agreed to help you. You have only to pick the one you want."

"You mean you told them?" Esther gasps.

"Well, I didn't say much," Numei says defensively. "All I said was I need help for my friend, who wants to learn about sex."

"That makes me sound like a little girl who has never had sex before," Esther says.

"Well, if you cannot feel pleasure in your flower like you say, then you are that little girl. Now do you want to meet these men or not?"

Esther shakes her head.

"How do you expect me to help you if you don't listen to me?"

Esther nods, defeated, and agrees to look at the men, provided Numei only points to them from a distance. So Numei takes her on a tour, and points out four young men whom she considers good lovers. Two of them she has tried herself, and she speaks highly of their skill at lovemaking, although she speaks ill of some of their other qualities. Esther agrees to think about it, and Numei leaves her to it, promising that they will get down to business soon enough.

The night brings a trip to the Ring of Snakes, a place of great significance to the Wolf tribe. Off they go, torches in front and behind, on a tough journey along a poorly made path. Were it not for the full moon, the journey would be a nightmare of tripping over stumps and fallen logs. It takes over an hour to get there, but upon arriving, Esther declares it worth the trip. The Ring of Snakes is a large, oval shaped clearing, surrounded by dense forest on all sides. The tangles of branches and roots encircling the clearing makes it look just like a ring of snakes. Torches are set up at five points, and everyone sits down to rest in the center of the circle. If somebody speaks, it is in whispers.

After a short rest, everyone makes a large circle, but still nobody speaks. Esther spies Numei, whom she did not recognize at first, among the crowd. Numei is dressed as a wolf woman, covered from head to foot in furs, including a frightening hat that is made from an actual wolf skull. Great claws are attached to each finger of her hand. Numei notices Esther and locks eyes with her, smiling slightly.

Then Vayanna appears, and all eyes turn to her. She walks purposefully into the center of the circle, carrying a large jug of some foul smelling liquid. Her entire body is painted yellow green, with black scales drawn on. She wears no clothes, except for a necklace of real snake fangs. As she appears, two women begin to sing a mysterious and frightening song, wailing and shrieking in unison, accompanied by a single drumbeat. Vayanna takes a sip from the jug solemnly and then passes it around the circle. Everyone takes a deep drink.

The jug comes to Esther. She hopes briefly that this might be something like opium, but as she stares into the brown, stinking liquid, she decides that she doesn't like the look of it. She is about to pass it, when she notices Numei staring at her again. Esther asks a question with her eyes. *Should I drink this?* Numei answers with her eyes. *Yes, you should drink it.* Numei indicates that she should take two sips. Esther puts the jug to her lips, still watching Numei for her approval, and Numei continues to stare at her until the first drop hits Esther's lips. It tastes bitter and pungent, but not too horrible. Esther takes two mouthfuls and then passes it to her left. She is nervous now. What did she just drink? Judging by the ceremony involved, it is strong stuff.

The drink that Esther tastes is called Tulum, and nobody but the Wolf tribe knows all of its ingredients. There are probably hallucinogenic mushrooms boiled into it, as the Wolves prize them above all other intoxicants.

Later that night, as she stares up at the night sky in awe, she begins to feel the effects of the Tulum. She reaches her hands into the air, trying to smear the stars across the sky. She never realized how close the moon, stars, and planets are. She feels like she could just reach up and touch the glowing orb of the moon that hovers right above her head. In fact, the whole sky seems almost flat - not real - like a painting of the sky. She likes the thought that the sky is so close that she can almost reach up and touch it.

She stands just to the left of the drum circle, as a massive wave of sound fills up the whole valley. The drummers are mad, throwing their arms up and letting them crash onto the drums. Their hair splays wildly in the night sky, spinning around and around as their heads bob up and down to the syncopation. The wall of sound drives the singers, who scream and wail at the top of their lungs, thrashing their bodies and gyrating crazily. Sometimes the singing is softer and more musical and sometimes it is raw and pure. Esther has never heard singing quite like this.

From a few feet away, Esther watches Vayanna dance. She has rattles on her wrists, which she uses to imitate a rattlesnake in time to the music. She seems to be in a trance, and Esther is sure that if she were to approach too close, the woman would bite her. Suddenly Esther gasps involuntarily, as Vayanna seems for a moment to turn into a giant, green serpent. She could swear that Vayanna is staring right at her, with sharp fangs and glittering eyes that bewitch her. Esther feels numb and the queasy feeling in her gut grows stronger. Then Vayanna looks human again, but her eyes are still snake eyes, and Esther feels that they are sucking some part of her. Vayanna finally looks away, the spell is broken, and everything returns to normal.

Not quite normal. Now Esther feels very strange, and there is a tingling sensation throughout her entire body. The tingling seems to heighten all her senses, so the slightest movement or noise is one hundred times as loud or vivid as before. The drums pound away at her head like her skull is the drum. As if in a trance, her body begins to dance, and she has never moved like this before. It is as if she is a rag doll at the mercy of all the forces of the universe. Her body shivers and undulates and her arms flay about wildly. She sings as loud as she possibly can, but it is so loud in this circle that she cannot hear herself.

The music has stopped. The people howl to the full moon, holding hands and raising up their heads to the great, yellow moon. After awhile, they hear an answering call from a nearby wolf pack. The people cheer. They are blessed for the year.

But Esther is not in the circle any longer. She wanders through the woods in a deep trance. Somewhere in her head, a voice keeps telling her to go back before she gets lost, but she keeps walking anyway. She follows a small path that is barely a path, until she hears a great howling and stops to listen. At first she thinks that it is wolves, but then she realizes that they are human howls. She sighs with relief and starts walking again. A few moments later, there is an answering call from a pack of real wolves, and it sounds much closer than the human cries. Esther stiffens and hides behind a tree, all of her bravery leaving her at once.

She hears panting on her left, the rustle of a foot crushing a leaf on her right, and a snort. She feels the sticky wet spot on her leg, where she cut herself when she tripped over a log. She knows that wolves are attracted to the scent of blood, and though they rarely attack a human, they might if the human is wounded. She begins to back away warily. Was that an eye she saw glinting in the dark? She hears a low growl, and she completely loses her nerve and turns to run away. She runs desperately, back down the path, and the gasps of her own ragged breath going in and out sound like the breathing of some insane lunatic that has taken over her body. There is a crashing directly behind her, getting steadily louder. As she runs, it occurs to her that the steps remind her of human feet and not wolf pads. And then a human hand grabs her and Esther screams.

Terrified, she spins around to face her pursuer, and what she sees makes her nearly faint from terror. It looks like a giant wolf, standing on human legs like a werewolf. She screams, but the thing holds on and grunts as it struggles to keep a hold of her. Then she realizes that the beast is laughing at her. It towers over her, laughing hysterically, pearly, white teeth gleaming in the dark. Her heart racing, Esther discovers that it is Numei, still in her wolf costume.

“Come, Esther,” Numei says, after catching her breath from both the chase and laughing so hard. “Let’s go before you scare yourself to death.”

Still trembling like a leaf in the wind, she follows Numei back the way they came. She struggles to make her jelly-like legs work like normal, but she doesn’t really feel herself again until they are back at the fire and much time has passed.

It is cold now and the night is nearly over, but the fire still burns brightly, warming Esther and Numei against the wet and chill of the coming dawn. The drums are finished, but a few still sing and dance in the silence. Numei seems much her old self, but Esther still feels strange.

"I saw you run off, chasing something, and I followed you. I wanted to see what you would do, so I could get to know you better. And then I heard wolves in the woods, and I had to have a little fun with you. How do you get along with wolves, generally?"

"There was a time when I almost died, and the wolves sang to me."

Numei looks at Esther suddenly, with many questions in her eyes.

"That is a powerful omen. Perhaps you should have faced them tonight. They might have given you power, and not had you for a snack."

As dawn spreads its fingers against the sky, Esther lies down near the fire, wrapped in her warm cloak. Most of the revelers have already gone home and only a few remain, unwilling to see this night end. Next to her, Numei listens to the sounds of the forest, trying to hear a pattern behind them. She looks over to Esther to remark on an interesting noise, but Esther has finally fallen asleep.

Numei watches her sleep, wondering what to do with her. The woman is a puzzle, and her request is even stranger. She has never heard of this problem before. Numei has certainly never had a problem having an orgasm – not since she was fifteen - and she has no idea how to explain it. How does one teach such a thing? Nobody ever taught her. She just figured it out.

If she could not help, she promised to admit it, but she needs money too badly to give up this job. And her reputation as a healer is poor right now, due to several recent failures in helping clients with their problems. Only because Chief Vayanna is her cousin does she continue to get work. She needs to prove herself again, and finding this lost orgasm would be just the thing.

Wolf 4'

Esther gladly drinks the tea that Numei hands to her, a sweet and fruity blend, with the essence of fresh berries. She and Numei are the only ones who remain in the ring of snakes now. There is a strong wind this morning that throws up piles of leaves and whips them into little yellow and orange leaf storms. The air is wet and humid, and threatens to storm. Everything is supercharged and crackles with life. She watches Numei's hair floating in the air above her head, and it seems to signify something.

"Are we going back to the village soon?" Esther asks, warming her hands over the steaming tea.

"Not yet. First we will get to know each other out here, where it is quiet. And we will begin a cleansing. You really need one. You look awful."

Numei laughs at Esther's expression, and touches her on the arm to show that she is exaggerating a little bit.

"You look tired and unhealthy," she explains. "Beaten by the elements. That is where we must begin. I am putting you on a special diet. Eat only what I give you. If I am not around, you may eat a bowl of acorn mush for dinner if you like."

Numei lets her words sink in, and then she stands up and urges Esther to follow her as she begins to gather plants. She sings quietly to herself as she walks along, filling her basket with weedy looking plants and freshly dug roots and tubers. She shows Esther a few plants that she knows which have healing properties, and explains how they will help Esther.

Afterwards, Numei cooks the food the old fashioned way. She fills a basket with water first, takes rocks from the fire pit, cleans them in water, and then throws them into the basket, along with some herbs and a few chopped pieces of dried fish for flavor. While she cooks, she keeps up a running commentary on the various properties of the roots and plants they'll be eating. When there are enough hot rocks in the water, it boils, and the weeds and roots cook into a sort of soup. It is a bitter soup, and makes Esther feel slightly ill.

They spend the rest of the day sitting by the river quietly. Numei asks Esther many questions about herself. She wants to know where she came from and who her parents are. Esther is vague as usual, and Numei soon grows irritated by her mysterious, elusive responses to every question.

"Can't you give me more than a few words about anything?" Numei finally asks gruffly. "You are so vague. I have asked you question after question, and I still have no idea who you are."

"There isn't much to tell. I'm just a traveler -"

"Nonsense. That may be enough for everybody else, but not for me. I need some real answers if I am going to help you. Not these mysterious half sentences."

Esther falls into a troubled silence, while Numei waits impatiently.

"Do you want my help or not?"

Esther nods.

"Then you have to talk to me. I challenge you to tell me something personal about yourself. Something that you have never told anybody else."

Esther thinks awhile.

"I am not very good at dealing with people," she says at last.

She looks at Numei as if this is the revelation of the century. Numei chuckles upon seeing her satisfied face, which seems to suggest that Esther has told her something of great importance.

"This is going to take longer than I thought," Numei says, leaning over and grinning a mischievous grin. "I can see I'm going to have to get a little rough with you."

Wolf 5'

Jay moon

A heavy rain soaks the village and the wind howls all day long. Esther spends the entire day in the shelter, eating Temu's wonderful, greasy seafood meals and sitting by the fire with all the other guests. Numei doesn't appear at all, so Esther forgets all about her mandate to purify herself. She gets drunk off of Temu's house wine instead. And that night, she ends up in Temu's bed.

It begins when Temu asks for payment for her time so far at the inn. Including wine, breakfasts, and other luxuries, he suggests that she pay twelve tupas. Esther doesn't know how much Numei's help is going to cost her, but she thinks that she should save as much money as possible. She looks at him, standing there with his hair all blown about by the wind outside and sprinkled with rain, and she says something which surprises him and her both.

"I could pay you in tupas. Or perhaps you would like to make a trade?" she says, touching him on the arm gently.

"And what have you got to trade?" he asks playfully, guessing her intentions.

"I could think of something."

"What a little whore I have become," she thinks later, as he sleeps soundly next to her.

But it makes her feel independent to have a job that she can do anywhere. And she is her own boss. She doesn't need the Lily Pad to be a Lady. She could be a Lady anytime she wants to be. And then she could hand pick her clients...the ones that she likes. She imagines what the Fathers would say and how shocked they would be. How Quintana would set his jaw and gnash his teeth in frustration, because her soul is tainted. She smiles with satisfaction, because she does whatever she wants now and thinks for herself. Somehow the idea of hell isn't as scary as it used to be. Without the Fathers constantly talking about it and showing her frightening pictures, it has just faded from her mind.

She listens to his soft snores and smells the stale tobacco smell emanating from his little house. And then she falls into a deep sleep.

Temu wakes and stares at the sleeping form next to him. He smiles with satisfaction, because it has been a long time since he has been with a woman. It is good to be with somebody again, and such a strange and sweet beauty she is. He doesn't mind that he has to trade for it. It doesn't matter. She was kind and giving, and he suspects that she enjoyed it despite her Lady from the Lily Pad act. That was just a defense. The more he thinks about it, the more he is sure that she enjoyed it.

Temu almost got married a few times and then he came to his senses. He is not the marrying type. He doesn't want to share his life with anybody. Although he can be very giving and would never turn his back on a friend in need, he knows that he is selfish and likes living alone. That is why he is such an outsider in the Wolf tribe. The people of Temu's village are marrying fools. Everyone here is married, and to be alone is to be an outcast. This doesn't mean that he dislikes sex or romance. Temu loves both and he has missed its absence. But he is old and he is not rich, so he has learned to take what he can get, even if he has to trade for it.

The last time he had sex was at the Lily Pad, two years ago. He paid for it then too, but it just didn't do it for him. The woman, Hesta, was definitely beautiful, but she was too much the skilled actress and it didn't seem real. This girl has real truth hiding underneath her Lady act, and he enjoyed it so much more because he could look inside her and see that truth peeking out at him - even if the truth is not so pretty. He can tell that this girl has been broken and bent by some cruel twist of fate. He can smell it on her.

He rolls over and sighs, wishing she would go sleep in her room. He is too used to sleeping alone to sleep comfortably with another person. He feels bad about asking her to walk home in the rain tonight, but in the future, when the weather is nicer, he'll ask her to go home after sex. After all, he is paying for it.

Wolf 7'

Bear moon

Numei finally comes to get her on a clear day just after the rains have ended. The tops of the mountains are white with new snow, the air is heavy and full of moisture, and the temperature is crisp and chilly. Numei urges Esther to bring some warm clothes, because they are going to spend a few days out in the forest. She knows of a little hut far out in the middle of nowhere, where they can sleep, cook and get away from everybody for a few days.

Everything feels renewed after the first big rain of the fall season. The green is extra green and the plants are fresh and alert again. They crunch along the path, over fallen bits of trees, crashed branches, and thousands of tumbled leaves. Numei sings bits of song, but otherwise she is quiet. There is something pressing on her mind today. That much is obvious.

"Numei," Esther asks after awhile, "what are we going to do out here?"

"We are going to fast and get your body clear, which I see you have neglected to do as I instructed."

"There wasn't any acorn mush in the shelter-"

"And then we will do a spirit journey," says Numei, not acknowledging her excuse. "I believe that this wall that you say is inside of you is a bad spirit of some sort. So we are going out into the wild to call upon the aid of helpful spirits to cast it out."

Esther doesn't say anything after that. She is frightened by the idea that she is invaded by evil spirits, and her mind starts to race with worry. She begins to wonder if this is a good idea. What if she makes this spirit angry? What if she cannot cast it out?

"We will stay out here for the Bear moon," Numei adds. "When the Eagle moon comes, then you'll go back and get yourself a man and have yourself a great time."

"Are you sure?"

"Yes," Numei says, glaring at her as if insulted. "Of course I am."

Later in the afternoon, the sun comes out. Esther hasn't seen the sun in three days and she takes off her cloak with great relief. Numei takes off all her clothes, throws up her hands to the sun, screams joyfully and runs down the path. Esther is in a grim mood and does not share her enthusiasm, so she walks at the same slow pace, moodily musing on evil spirits.

Eventually they arrive at their destination, a small, run down hut in the middle of nowhere. Numei begins to clean the hut, complaining in a loud voice about the slobs who last used it. Esther just casts herself down in the sunshine, closes her eyes and tries not to think about what is coming.

Wolf 8'

Esther wakes up in the morning, famished with hunger. After a search of the hut, she remembers that she has no means to appease her stomach, because Numei has brought no food with her. They are both going to fast. The hut lies a short distance from a river and Esther walks slowly across the wet, chilly ground to fill up her water skin to make tea. She returns to the hut and sparks up the fire. Numei is still asleep, being a night person by nature, and Esther brews herself several cups and sings softly to herself to pass the time until Numei wakes. She sings many songs before Numei finally opens her eyes for the first time, and it is a long time after that before Numei opens them for the second time and actually sits up.

When Numei finally rises, she doesn't waste much time. She has a cup of tea and then she gets right down to business. She pulls a long wooden pipe and a little pouch out of her small basket, and sits down to fill the pipe with a strange mixture from the sack. Esther watches her with trepidation, as this is obviously meant for her.

"You have not cleansed yourself for three days as I said, so this will be a little more painful than it would have been. You might even throw up your insides. I can see that your life force is sluggish and poor."

"You can tell that?"

"Yes. You had an indulgent couple of days and now you will pay for it. I was unable to check on you and I had hoped that you would take responsibility for yourself. But you didn't and so it goes. You will learn."

"What is that?" Esther says, trying to change the subject.

"It is called Yalum. A cousin to Tulum."

Numei hands the pipe over to Esther. Esther takes the pipe and examines it. It has a stone top and a wooden shaft, carved with many strange symbols. She smells the mixture in the bowl, but the only smell she can discern is white sage.

"Take this pipe and smoke deeply. Do not fight it. The sacred smoke called Yalum will show you many things and together we will try to interpret your path from the signs."

"Can I eat something first?"

"No. You will just throw it up."

"I'm really hungry."

"You have feasted enough. Now is the time for empty stomachs and clear heads."

Numei takes a branch from the fire and holds it over the bowl. Esther reluctantly takes a puff and breathes in dense smoke, tasting cool sage. She begins to cough savagely, and it is awhile before she can take a second puff.

Numei takes a small puff herself. She knows she probably should stay sober and watch Esther, but she cannot resist just one small puff. Just for fun.

Esther is a small child, running along the beach. She looks down at her tiny feet, crunching wood and small shells as she pads along. She stops, watches the breaking surf and crashing waves and then continues to run.

Why is she so scared? What is chasing her?

She hides under an old tree as an old Zesti man walks past, singing a strange song. She watches him, wondering what would happen if she were to go to him and show herself. She longs to touch him, look into his eyes and find out what he knows. He reminds her of somebody she used to know. But she is afraid and she continues to hide.

She feels as lonely as a person could possibly be, like there is no place for her in this world. There is nobody that loves her and cares for her and there never will be. She doesn't feel like dancing, drawing pictures, making sand castles or singing. All she wants to do is cry. But she doesn't dare, because she knows that nobody will be there to comfort her if she does cry, and that is the whole point of tears. She tries to remember her mother and how she would hold her when she cried and whisper soft words to her, but she cannot even remember her face.

Esther opens her eyes, suddenly back in the present. She feels as if that painful memory of her past was not a memory at all, but that she lived through it again. It was clearer than any memory she ever had. She was actually there - could smell the salt and feel the wind. She never knew that she carried such complete pictures of her past inside of her. Esther falls onto her knees, overcome with misery. What a sad little girl she was! On her knees, she looks down at her hands. They are not the same hands that she knows. They are old hands, calloused and used. She walks over to the river and looks at her reflection. Just as she thought, her face is old and haggard - the face of an old woman.

I am an old crone at 21 years of age.

She feels as tired as she has ever felt in her life. She is dying slowly. She can actually feel her limbs stiffening, her muscles tightening, and her body withering away. Her face seems to be sagging at this very moment and becoming a little more wrinkled and ancient with every breath. As she lies down on the ground, she feels her life slowly dribbling away and she is powerless to stop it. There is absolutely nothing she can do to halt her death. She sees now that it began as soon as she was born.

"The child is stupid. She cannot talk. She is only a dumb heathen, little better than an animal."

She can hear the words in her head. They have always been there, but the voice that speaks them has changed. It used to be her voice saying these things, but now she hears them spoken in their true voice. It is the voice of the Fathers and the soldiers that speaks through her. They learned to speak in her voice. They have done this for so long, she forgot where the words began. She sees now that they made her what she is.

"Do not speak back, child! The fathers only do what is best for you."

She hears other voices too. The words of the old Zesti woman who took care of her.

"Hold your tongue, girl. To speak your mind or think for yourself is dangerous here. Be quiet, do what they say, and you will not be whipped and beaten."

And the words of Miguel.

"You are a little whore! You are stupid and worthless and only good for sex. Can you not clean up after yourself? Can't you cook anything edible?"

She tries to think of words that are her own and come from her alone, but she cannot think of a single one.

"Where are my words?" she whispers to herself. "Don't I have any words?"

She swims in the river now. The river is good and washes all of it away. She felt so contaminated by all of those people in her head that she had to jump in the river to wash it all off. She watches the light filter through the water in tiny golden shafts, as she sinks to the bottom and runs her hands through the thick mud and rocks. It is cold, but the chill doesn't bother her. She hardly notices it, in fact. It exists outside of her and it will not bother her as long as she does not let it. And why should she? She has only a little time left and none to waste. She knows now just what she has to do.

I must find my own words. Words spoken only by me. I must think for myself before I die. And I must get all of these people out of my head forever.

She finally has to come up for air. As she pops her head above the water, she sees Numei watching her. She smiles, takes a deep breath, and dives back down to the comforting golden shafts which wait for her.

They walk back to the hut in silence, and Esther is struck by the serene beauty of the forest around her. The lush green leaves look as if they are dripping on top of her. Gold sunlight glints through the foliage and pink shafts of light ripple as the sun slowly sets behind the clouds. The musty smell of rich earth fills her nose. There can be nowhere else on earth as beautiful as this place. She sings a Bear song of gladness, feeling suddenly blissful. Numei laughs, knowing this song, and joins her. As they sing, walking turns to skipping and then to dancing. Later, Esther remarks to Numei that she has never felt so comfortable singing with another person and Numei thanks her for the compliment.

They eat dinner at the cabin, a simple dinner of acorn mush and seeds. Numei allows Esther to eat in peace, refraining from questions until she is done. Esther feels light and happy, now that she is back from her hellish journey into her past. It was a difficult day, but she feels as if she gained a great deal from it.

"What did you discover today, Esther?"

"I must get these horrible people that are inside my head out of it. I just want me in there. Nobody else."

Numei nods and thinks about that awhile.

Finally she says quietly, "That is a very difficult thing to do. Very few are strong enough to do that."

"Why is that so hard? It doesn't sound so hard."

"Because you must leave everyone and everything behind you and go on a long journey into your own heart. Into other realms and worlds. And you must go alone. It is something that I have never done, because it means leaving my people and all whom I love and love me."

"I don't have any people," Esther says quietly.

"None at all?"

"None."

"That is a curse and a blessing. It's lonely, but it's also freedom. You can fly as far as you want, without thought of all those left behind. Do whatever you want. As I said, this has been a tough thing for me to do. It is not easy to be both a healer for my people and also a wife to my husband. I must often leave them all behind for days or weeks or even longer, and that is a difficult thing because I love them all dearly. Even though I know it is good for me, I hate to be apart from Horim, my husband, for even a little while."

This last is said with so much passion, that Numei's eyes smolder from the feeling. Numei looks like she wants to elaborate on her own troubles, but Esther changes the subject back to herself instead. She wants to tell Numei some things about herself before she loses the courage. She wants to speak her secrets for the first time to another person.

"Numei, to tell you the rest of my vision, I must also tell you about myself. I must tell you all about my childhood. But that is a difficult thing for me. I have never told anyone these things."

"Good. It's about time," says Numei, forgetting about her own problems in her excitement to hear Esther's secrets.

Esther speaks for the entire time that the candle on the table takes to burn down. She tells of her entire life, from the Santa Cruz mission, to her time in Branciforte and how she came to run away. At first, the words come slowly, but as she becomes emboldened, she remembers things and begins to elaborate.

Numei sighs deeply and tries to remain strong for Esther. It is difficult, as she can feel the woman's pain in her bones. She holds Esther's hand when Esther talks of particularly difficult things and urges Esther to elaborate as much as possible.

"I am a liar," Numei thinks, "acting calm and strong, when I want to scream with rage for you and throw things."

Numei sees that Esther carries around a venomous past inside of her that is far worse than Numei could ever have imagined. Numei can almost feel a poison cloud over her head, from all the anger that Esther is harboring inside. Esther is unusually detached right now, the result of the smoke leveling her mood to an even keel, but Numei can still feel hatred oozing out of Esther's skin and infecting her own hand and body which holds onto Esther's.

Finally, the candle burns out and Numei decides that she has heard enough for today. Esther has been indulging in self-pity for the past ten minutes and Numei doesn't think she can take any more. It is a good time to stop. She gives Esther a long hug, and then declares time for sleeping. They set up their blankets on the worn tule mats in the little hut and lie down.

As Numei lies there, Esther's stories revolve in her head. They are like a stain on her formerly clean brain, coloring everything black. She has heard of slaves being tortured by northern Zesti tribes and horrible illness brought by the Spanish that decimated whole villages. Vicious stories of barbaric cruelty among tribes such as the Paiuti and the Klamath tribes are well known. But Esther's stories of the Spanish mission beat them all for sheer twisted perversions. She cannot imagine that anyone could even dream up such a warped, bitter reality. She wonders why nobody ever speaks of these missions. Probably it is a tale too ugly to make good gossip.

Numei is no longer sure that she can help Esther - not in her own muddled state. She would need to cleanse herself and take her own journey deep inside a place of power just to tackle this mess. It seems that many evil spirits are residing inside of Esther, and it will take a whole harem of spirit guides to lead Esther out of the darkness she has been in. It gives Numei a chill to think that she has been chosen for such a task, because it shines a bright light on her own failures as a healer. She has not done anything to increase her own power in a long time and now that she needs it most she finds it lacking. As the Ruoks say, ‘The Flow works in mysterious ways’.

Wolf 9'

**Eagle moon*

Numei and Esther have been going over Esther's history all morning, looking for clues to the present. Numei has forced Esther to recall everything she possibly can, even the most painful memories. Esther even talked about Him. Numei found that story very interesting and made Esther recall every detail of her experiences with Him. Esther is grateful for Numei's unflinching ability to hear the most horrible stories without batting an eye and then to offer comfort and guidance. Numei has been her rock, without whom she could never have gone through some of these memories, which have been hidden for a long, long time.

“Is that the evil spirit inside of me? Him?”

“I believe it is,” Numei says, nodding slowly. “What do you think?”

Esther doesn’t answer. She is overwhelmed and exhausted. She did not sleep last night and she cannot stop thinking about her childhood and how horrible it was. She wishes she could just erase it all and start over.

"You seem distracted, Esther."

"I don't want to think or talk about my past any more. I want to just forget everything in my head and start over."

Numei smiles.

“That would be nice, wouldn’t it? Erase the past? The Ruoks say that this is possible. I wouldn’t know. I haven’t done it.”

“Do you think it would be hard?”

“It is very hard,” Numei admits with a frown. “I studied with a Ruok for awhile and one day he told me I was holding onto the past. I told him there is nothing wrong with the past, and then I never went to see him again.”

Esther nods and begins to feel hopeless again.

"That doesn't matter," Numei says, waving it away peevishly. "I've an idea I'd like to talk about that will help you."

Numei stares hard at Esther, wanting to be sure before speaking her mind.

"I want to talk to you about your parents."

"My parents? I can hardly remember them. I don't know anything about them."

"I do."

Esther stares at her in shock. The whole world suddenly shrinks, until it exists only in Numei's next words.

"You do?"

"I cannot believe it didn't occur to you or anybody else. It is obvious who your parents are."

Esther feels dizzy, but she cannot move to sit down.

"I don't think that you are Zesti. You bear little resemblance to a pure blood Zesti."

Esther gapes at her. She has always assumed that she was from some Zesti tribe near Santa Cruz, like everyone else at the mission.

"You are a mix of different bloods. There is some Zesti blood in you perhaps, but you are obviously not full-blooded. And most importantly, you only speak Spanish. As a child, you didn't remember a word of any other language, right? The only language you could ever speak was Spanish."

"I guess I hadn't learned to speak yet."

"I don't think so. You were at least four or five years old when you came to the mission. Right?"

"I forgot my first language, or maybe I never learned to speak."

"I don't think you forgot your native language."

"I don't understand."

"I think you do."

Suddenly Esther understands and she nearly faints from surprise.

"My parents were from here? From the Twelve Tribes?"

"Exactly. Your features are similar to our people. I would never be able to tell you were not of the Twelve Tribes until I got to know you."

Numei smiles at Esther's expression, as she sits numbly on a fallen log and stares at her feet. It takes her a long time to recover from the initial shock upon hearing this, but she doesn't think to question it further. Deep in her heart, she is sure that this is the truth. She just knows it.

'Our people'! Esther has always thought of herself as a girl without a people, and a traveler without a home. But all these people she has met *are* her people. Esther feels tears come to her eyes, but for once they are tears of happiness. She feels a great weight lifting from her shoulders as she realizes that she has been home all along.

"And before too long, we may find out from which tribe you came and who your parents are."

"How?"

"Are there any tattoos on you?"

"No."

"I don't know how. I will think about it."

"Thank you," says Esther, feeling overwhelmed all over again. "Thank you so much for telling me this."

"Now that you know, how do you feel about your parents?" Numei asks.

Esther looks up at her, surprised.

"What do you mean? I told you, I don't remember them."

"You must have some feelings about them."

"How can I? I remember nothing."

"Do you love them? Do you hate them for abandoning you? Do you long to see them?"

"I don't think about them much. I guess I regret not knowing them."

"And?"

"And...maybe I am a little angry at them. Because -"

Esther stops, unsure of why she should be angry.

"Don't think. Just say it!" Numei orders in a sharp voice.

" - they didn't come for me when I was kidnapped. They didn't come to find me. They never came to get me from the mission."

Esther struggles not to show how upset she is getting.

"Do you hate them?"

"No. Of course I don't -"

"Are you sure?"

"How can you tell me how I feel?" Esther says, getting angry. "You don't know how I feel."

"I can see you are bitterly angry at them. I don't blame you for it. You have been through a lot."

"I don't hate them," she insists stubbornly.

"Are you sure? I hated my father for a long time. I felt like he let me down, and my troubles are tiny compared to yours."

"I need to be alone for awhile," Esther says suddenly. "This is too much."

Esther stands up and walks off quickly. She cannot listen to this anymore. She is afraid that Numei is right and that she does hate her parents. How awful of her. And then she has a flash of memory from her childhood. She remembers sitting on the beach of Santa Cruz as a child, cursing her parents with great venom.

They left me alone. They abandoned me and I was left to fend for myself. They weren't strong enough to take care of me or rescue me. They must have been very stupid and weak people.

Esther suddenly feels her whole body go numb. She no longer wants to be alone. She runs back to Numei and grabs onto her as if she would tackle her to the ground. Numei holds her quietly, until she stops shaking.

Wolf 10'

The morning sky, covered with dark clouds, threatens to pour a deluge upon the waiting village. Everyone works hard, getting things done in preparation for an afternoon's hermitage. Meanwhile, Esther stuffs herself with meat in the shelter. She has nothing to do today, except sit by the fire and stay warm. At least, until Numei shows up with a head full of ideas.

"Look at you stuffing yourself like a starving coyote," she says, buzzing into the room full of energy, "when I have a whole list of things planned for today. And you're supposed to be on a cleansing diet."

"I need to eat," Esther says, defending herself. "It's too cold out to starve myself."

"Well you're headed right for a nap at this rate," Numei insists. "Slow down. We have much to do."

Numei takes some time to chat up the room, before returning to Esther's side. By this time, Esther is stuffed beyond reason, so she pushes the plate aside and sits down near the fire. Numei was right. She is ready for a nap.

"Let's go," Numei says, returning to her side.

"What do you want to do?" asks Esther, stifling a yawn.

"We're going to work on your orgasm today."

With all of the incredible experiences and revelations of the past few days, Esther had forgotten all about her original reason for visiting Numei. She really doesn't know if she cares right now, because she would rather figure out who her parents are and which tribe she is from. But she asked Numei for help and now she can't refuse it, so she stands up with an effort and follows Numei out into the cold morning.

"Numei," Esther says, as they walk, "we have not discussed payment yet."

"I haven't decided that yet. It all depends on how difficult you are to treat," Numei says, turning around to glance at her. "And so far, you don't have enough money in your purse to pay me what I deserve."

Numei smiles to show that she is joking and turns around again to think about it as they walk.

"Let us say thirty tupas," Numei says at last, "provided that you do what I say from now on so this will go faster. I would charge more, but I know you are a single girl alone in the world and you have had many challenges. Being poor is not one you need also."

Esther's eyes bug out when she hears this figure. She has a large purse right now, but that would cut it down to a small one. She doesn't respond right away, wondering if Numei is worth such an extravagant sum. She has seen nothing in her travels that costs thirty tupas. Then she remembers that Numei told her about her origins and promised to tell her what tribe she is from and she decides to pay whatever she asks for. She has already earned her fee for that information alone.

"I will pay you thirty tupas," Esther agrees.

"Good. Then today, we will work on your lost orgasm."

Numei stops walking just before the main circle and turns around. They stand just off the path, so they are able to see people without being seen themselves.

"Now Esther," Numei begins, "I want you to think of an orgasm like a flowing river. The Ruoks talk of the Flow, which is the movement of all life, and it is the same with an orgasm. If the path of the river is clear then the orgasm will come naturally. Yours is blocked by something, and that is why you are having problems. Perhaps there is a spirit beaver inside of you, building a large dam in your womb. I believe we can start by increasing the force of your 'river of orgasmic pleasure' to destroy whatever blockage is damming you. Remember that no dam can withstand a great flood. If your passion is intense enough, then you will burst through any wall. Does that make sense?"

"A little bit."

"Good enough. Now tell me, do you have to pee?"

"Sure," Esther says, laughing.

"Then do it now, stop in the middle, and hold it."

"Why?"

Numei doesn't answer her, so Esther goes behind a tree and does what she says. A moment later she shouts out that she is holding it and waits for further instructions.

"Now, let a little go and then hold it again. Keep doing it until you are dry."

"I'm dry," Esther shouts out, after stopping and starting three times. "Except for my leg. I peed on my leg a little bit."

"Good work," Numei says laughing.

"What was that about?" Esther asks, when she comes from behind the tree.

"That was the muscle you can use to increase the power of your orgasm," Numei explains. "Maybe yours is weak, and you must strengthen it. Pretend you are holding your pee and then release it.

Do that over and over for the next half hour. Relax your entire body, except for that muscle. I'll return in a half hour."

She laughs at Esther's expression, and then turns around and walks off to the commons to talk to some friends. Esther gapes at her, and then sits down to do as Numei says. As she does it, she has to admit that the exercise feels pretty good.

"Did you do it the whole time?" Numei asks, upon her return.

"Yes."

"We will now practice with a real person. I just spoke to Buiti over there. He is available now. He will massage the petal of your flower and I will watch and give you pointers. "

"I don't think I want to do that," Esther says, in a quiet voice.

"Why don't you give him a chance? He gave me the most intense orgasm once."

"I want to figure out who my parents are. Can we do that instead?"

"That's not why you hired me," Numei says. "You hired me to have an orgasm. And that's what we're going to do."

"But I can't do it with somebody I don't know."

"Are you shy, Esther?" Numei asks teasingly. "Didn't you tell me you worked at the Lily Pad?"

"But that was just work."

"So is this."

"No," Esther says stubbornly.

"Then you'll have to do it yourself," Numei says with a dramatic sigh. "Come on. Let's go into the trees."

"I will do it," Esther says. "But I want to do it alone."

"If you could do it by yourself, then you wouldn't have asked for my help in the first place."

But Esther is firm about needing privacy, and finally Numei acquiesces. Esther goes off by herself to her hut and Numei wanders back to the commons.

During her first few attempts, she just can't do it. She feels shameful for playing with herself and angry with herself for feeling shame, which she now sees as something the priests gave her. It reminds her of Pedro and it makes her crazy to think that she is like him. Now she is determined to get past this stupid guilt.

She stokes up the fire to a blaze, until it threatens to burn down her hut. The heat somehow helps to melt her inhibitions. Then she closes her eyes, fantasizes, concentrates on that feeling, and works on that muscle that Numei showed her. It takes a long time for her to get past the guilt and and focus only on her flower, but soon she is actually wet and she begins to feel something. It is alive! She has awakened her flower, and it has begun to open its petals up to the sun. The wall is not there! Time slows and she is sure that she is getting close. She moans, deliciously afraid and exhilarated at the same time.

She suddenly opens her eyes, thinking that she heard a noise in her hut. She looks around wildly and gasps with shock. The demon that she knows only as Him is here. He stands in the fire, leering at her from the flames. His hair is a bonfire and she can smell burnt hair in the hut. Her own smell changes from pleasure to fear. Then she feels the wall come crashing down upon her, and He disappears behind it. She screams in frustration and shouts out to him to leave her alone and never come back. She pants and struggles to stop shaking.

After a little while, she touches her petal again, but the wall is now firmly in place and she is numb again. With a sigh, she crawls underneath her blankets and curls up into a little ball. She lies like that until the fire dies down into coals and then she wanders over to the shelter to see if they have any wine there.

Wolf 12'

Raccoon moon

Esther and Numei sit by the river, enjoying the afternoon sunshine.
Esther throws pebbles absentmindedly into the water, trying to hit fish with them. Numei meditates quietly, cross-legged, trying to absorb all that Esther has told her. They have just had a long talk about Esther's experiences in trying to have an orgasm over the past few days. Esther tried again yesterday, but she felt like He was there watching and she couldn't concentrate at all. She has been in a deep funk all day long, barely able to crack a smile. She thinks about her parents a good deal, trying to remember their faces and anything about the tribe she grew up in. But try as she may, all she can remember is life in the mission. She wishes she could forget those times, and just remember when she was a little girl with a home and family.

"I told you there was a bad spirit following you," Numei reminds her, trying to cheer her up. "Remember when I said that? This spirit has shown himself to you and now we know who put him there. Don't we?"

"The Spanish fathers," Esther says moodily.

"If you want to call them that."

Esther nods, scratches her head, and stares at the ground as if the blades of grass hold clues to this mystery.

"Do they control Him?" she asks finally.

"I don't know who or what this spirit is. But it follows you of its own free will now. Or...perhaps it is you that have chosen it, and it only comes when *you* call."

"Me?" Esther says, offended. "Why would I call Him?"

"That is a good question. Why would you? But often times, spirits only follow us when we want them to."

"I don't want him to follow me," Esther insists.

Numei shrugs.

"How do I get rid of all the bad things that the fathers put in me?" Esther asks.

Numei doesn't speak for a long time, making Esther think she didn't hear her. She is just about to ask again, when Numei looks at her keenly.

"To erase the past is very hard. I tried once, but I was not strong enough. I am too attached to my memories. They connect me to my home, family and my tribe."

"I have to do it. I hate my memories."

"Then maybe you will."

"I am more myself than I used to be," Esther says in a soft voice.

"Why?"

She shrugs.

"I don't know. I just feel more like myself."

"Because nobody is chaining you with their thoughts."

"What do you mean?"

"It is very simple. In the mission you were a slave, and could never be anything else in the eyes of those people. They refused to see you as anything but a simple primitive, and you came to believe that you were who they thought you were. In that town you used to visit, you were considered just another mission slave, good only for prostitution or sex, and you could never become something else in their eyes either. That place was a trap too. But once you went out on your own, nobody knew who you were for sure, and you were suddenly a mysterious stranger with no past. How did that feel?"

"It felt great."

"Because you had a chance to grow and become who you wanted to be. And you want to be a free human who thinks for herself. So you have kept moving, and nobody can tie you down and make you who they want you to be. That is the best thing for you now. Until you learn who you are, you should keep moving."

"What about you? Are you free?"

Numei looks sad all of a sudden. Esther has not seen such a look on her before.

"I come from a good home, among people that love me. I am well thought of in my tribe and in a position of respect. But good people can chain you just like bad people can. They see me a certain way, they think they know me, and I am trapped by their thoughts too."

They sit in silence for a long time, both women lost in musings that take them far away from the river they sit in front of.

"So all I have to do is keep moving?" Esther asks finally.
"No, you must also change yourself."
"How?"
"There is only one way I know of."
Numei suddenly begins to sing.
"Free your body, and your mind will follow.
Free your body, and your mind will follow.
Free your body, and your mind will follow.
And that is the only way I know."
Esther smiles for the first time all day, liking the song.
"Our past is stored all over the body, in secret places and in our flesh and bones. For example, your spine is bent and twisted with all of your pain and always looking down out of shame like you were taught to do. And so you slouch and you are tight everywhere."
"I'm not that bad," Esther says, although she does not sound convinced.
"Yes, you are. Release all of that tension and make your body supple and relaxed and all of those problems will slowly float away like a feather in the wind."
"But that is so hard."
"It could take your entire life, so there is no time to waste. Start now. Dance a lot. Walk differently. Teach yourself everything all over again until you feel free."

The women walk through the woods, guided only by Numei's sense of direction, looking for a special place that Numei knows where a special plant grows. At least, that's what Esther thinks they are doing. The truth is that they are wandering aimlessly. Although Numei is supposed to be paying attention to where they are going, she is not doing that at all. In fact, her mind is racing with worry, thinking about what a hypocrite she is. She is telling Esther to do things that she is not doing herself. How can she give advice that she is not following?

When she studied briefly with the Ruok healer, Tumock, he told her to release all ties to the tribe and go to a place where nobody knows her. He suggested that she live with a Northwest Zesti shaman for a while, as he did. There she could continue her training, unfettered by the family and friends who inevitably hold her back from her full potential. He suggested that only by releasing all the binding ties of her life, could she make the next leap forward in her evolution.

But she is afraid of the Northwest Zesti, who are so fierce and warlike. And she does not want to leave her husband, whom she loves deeply, and her many friends and family who love her too. So she scorned Tumock's advice, which she felt was extreme, and decided not to continue studying with Ruoks. She learned from a

Wolf healer instead, who taught her Wolf healing knowledge. Wolf healing knowledge is good, but it is limited in its own way. Since that time, she has slowly grown more and more comfortable and lazy and has not continued with her training at all. And now that she needs specialized knowledge, she finds it lacking. Numei has no idea how to cast out a spirit, especially a foreign spirit like this one.

Wolf 13'

"Esther?"

"Yes."

They sit by the river, watching it glide gently past. Numei chose this particular spot because it will help soothe the girl. What she is about to say is going to be a little brutal, and she wants a nice environment to make it easier.

"I've had some thoughts I want to discuss with you. Is that all right?"

"Sure."

"It's about you. Things I have noticed."

Esther nods reluctantly. She has a feeling that Numei has some unpleasant things to say by the way she tiptoes around the subject.

"I want to talk about your habit of closing yourself off. You had a miserable childhood. Because of this, you have closed yourself off inside a shell of protection, like a clam. You were taught not to speak your mind, and so you don't. I want you to understand that things are different now. You can change who you don't want to be now by opening up and speaking your mind."

"I think I speak my mind when I have to."

"You don't do it enough. And as long as you don't stand up for yourself, you are at the mercy of anyone who wants to do harm to you. Men or spirits. They can see that you won't fight back and you are an easy target. That's why those priests of yours were so brutal to you. To scare you into being passive, which makes you easy to control."

"I speak when I have to. And I do stand up for myself."

"Do you? How long did you live with those monster Spaniards before you gave that one the beating he deserved? Why didn't you run away before that? You should have run away long before."

"They would have tracked me down. They found many of the runaways, and they were returned to the mission and then they were whipped and shackeld with chains."

"But you did get away, didn't you? In the end?"

Esther stops arguing, realizing that Numei is right.

"You put up with their abuse for years before you finally had enough. Wouldn't it have been better to risk it all as soon as you were old enough to get away? Better to die free than live like one of Hoja's wolves."

"Who is Hoja?"

Numei laughs.

"Let me show you."

They take a long walk down to the edge of the valley, where the mysterious Hoja lives. She is a hermit of sorts, who lives far away from the rest of the village. Esther marvels that Numei can waste so much time walking across the entire valley, just to make a point.

She is even more amazed when she sees what a run down, dirty shack they have walked so far to visit. It is a large house, but it is so trashed and surrounded by junk, soot, and dead animal carcasses, that it makes Esther feel unclean just to be standing next to it. Numei sneaks over to the door and opens it, and then she quickly runs out of sight behind some bushes. She urges Esther to follow her rapidly before they are spotted.

Two massive wolves run out of the house. They are dirty looking scoundrels, their beautiful coats soiled and filthy. They caper around joyfully, happy to be outside after spending so long indoors. They prance and play and jog happily after a squirrel, who just barely avoids being eaten.

A few moments later, a woman waddles out. She is immensely fat, with jowls that run down her face and into her neck, and a light moustache. She could be the ugliest woman that Esther has ever seen.

"Watch this," Numei whispers.

"How'd you get out?" snaps Hoja angrily.

She waddles after the wolves and grabs one by the scruff of the neck.

"How'd you get out?"

She looks around suspiciously and then starts dragging it into the house. The wolf growls and barks and Hoja screams back at it in a loud voice. She hits it with a stick a few times, until she finally she manages to drive it into the house and closes the rickety wooden door on it. Then she goes for the other one.

Finally, the two wolves are secured and the fat woman waddles back inside and closes the door. They hear her screaming again and the wolves yelping as they are beaten.

Esther stares at the closed door in shock.

"That's horrible."

"Isn't it?"

"How could you permit her to treat those wolves that way?"

"I don't permit it. That's why I let them out. I've been letting them out for years."

Numei gives her a mischievous smile, as they stand up and walk back the way they came.

"But they keep on coming back."

"Yes. Those wolves are not ordinary wolves. They were captured by her when they were pups, and she raised them. They see her as their master. She is top dog. Although she beats them every day, they come back to her. Although she rarely lets them out, except to hunt when the food is low, they come back. Although she is a miserable woman, they follow her."

"They could kill her. They are so much stronger than her."

"But it is not in their nature. They are followers. She is the leader."

Esther feels really bad for the wolves, and tries to think of ways to help them. She wonders why the Wolf tribe never does anything about this.

"Why can't you help them?"

"I already told you I have tried. But they always come back. What can I do? This misery is all they know."

They walk for a while in silence. Numei knows that the hard part is coming. She can feel it. She hardens her will, knowing that she has to be strong in this moment. But it is Esther who first makes the connection.

"You think I am like the wolves, don't you?" Esther says quietly.

"Yes. Not as much as you used to be, but you still are."

She looks over and sees a look of numb horror on Esther's face. Numei feels like a beast, but she cannot back down from this.

"I'm not like them," Esther insists, although her protests are empty.

"No?"

"The wolves are bigger and stronger than her, and they are faster. She could never track them if they ran away. But I was only a single girl, imprisoned by many, many men."

"A single girl? There were many more Zesti than soldiers and priests," Numei adds. "Enough to put up a good fight. Why did they never fight back?"

"The Spanish soldiers had guns."

"It would not have been easy," Numei says. "I know that. I'm not saying that I would have been different. I'm just saying that you must recognize your faults and try to change them. You were a follower for most of your life. Just like the wolves."

"We were taken as children," Esther complains bitterly. "We had no choice. If I did not do exactly as they said, I was whipped."

"That's why they took Zesti children and converted them, instead of their parents. Easier to train. Once you put the fear into a child, then it is easy to maintain. The child will chain himself up eventually, and then you have a slave for life. Even now that you are free, you are still their slave."

Esther stops walking, as tears come to her eyes.

"You are being very mean to say these things and show me these things."

Numei shrugs.

"What right do you have to say these things? You had a happy childhood. You were loved and cared after in your home. I was ripped away from mine and given to strangers who mistreated me and cared nothing for me. How can you dare to speak as if you understand what I went through?"

"My childhood is not the issue," Numei says sternly. "You are the issue. You came to *me* for help, remember?"

"You don't even understand what it was like. You couldn't possibly know. It was so horrible."

"I felt how horrible it was the night you told me, and I feel for you now. But this is a new day and there are no men with whips and guns here. You can wallow in self pity, and say that because you had such an unhappy childhood you have the right to remain a sad, miserable victim of others' whims all your life. Like those wolves. Or you can take responsibility and change."

"I am not miserable and a victim -"

"Yes, you are. You just don't know it because you have been it for so long that you have grown to like it."

Esther sits in a numb state for a long time, unable to say anything more. She hates Numei suddenly. Hates her with a passion. She is the meanest woman she has ever met. She stares at her face and sees a cruel monster there, and she cannot look at her or talk to her for a long time. Finally she rises, unable to stand her presence anymore. She feels tears come to her eyes and she curses herself for showing her weakness now.

"I'm leaving!" she says dramatically.

She begins to walk away, steaming from the ears. She will scream if she stays here any longer. Numei watches her go, feeling guilty. But she pushes the guilt aside quickly, because she has no time to indulge in guilt, which will help nobody. She has to ride this out and stand firm. 'Nice' will help nobody right now.

"Leaving won't help you. Stay and face me."

Esther ignores her, only walks further away.

"What are you feeling right now?" Numei calls after her. "What do you want to do? Whatever it is, do it! Don't hold back! Let it out!"

Numei sighs, as Esther continues to walk away. She is struggling to keep the lid on the building pressure of her emotions, but Numei can see that it is about to burst. It is inevitable. Numei will have to turn the heat a little higher though, just to make sure.

"Don't be such a baby! You're not a child any more! Time to grow up, Esther!"

Esther releases a piercing scream that hurts Numei's ears. She falls to her knees and begins tearing up the grass in large handfuls. She screams louder and beats the ground with her hands.

"I hate you! I hate you! Go away! Get out of my life forever!"

"You came to *me* for help," Numei says in a numb whisper, shocked by the force of her anger.

"I hate you! Look what you did to me!"

Suddenly, Numei realizes that Esther is not really talking to her, and she feels great relief. It worked. Numei takes a deep breath and tries to calm her nerves. Brutal honesty is not fun. It wasn't fun when Tumock did it to her. But it is very effective.

Numei walks over to Esther and calms her down with gentle and soothing touches. She leads the spent girl back to the river, and gently splashes her face with water. Esther wipes the tears from her eyes and apologizes to Numei for yelling at her. Numei apologizes for being so direct and mean. Both fall down over themselves being nice to each other and the grim mood lifts.

"What should I do?" Esther asks at last. "To change all those things you said? I'll do whatever it takes."

"You just did it," says Numei with a smile, and she gives Esther a big hug.

The whole village is out and about, making huge piles of dead branches and bushes and lighting them on fire. There are great fires burning all over Wolf village. The smell of burning wood is strong, and smoke arcs into the sky and creates manmade clouds. People gather around the fires, watching them carefully to make sure that they do not get out of control. Numei and Esther stand by one of the fires and the heat hits them full blast like an oven. You cannot get too close to the great mound of burning logs and brush, for they create an unbearable wave of hot air that is overpowering. They stand a good distance away, enjoying the warmth and not saying much. It feels wonderful to be so warm and toasty after spending so many chilly days out and about in the weak sunlight.

The Zesti of California have always kept the land open and park like by burning, and the Twelve Tribes took up this practice early on. It makes it easier to get around, for both the people and the animals. Grazing is better, which attracts plant-eating animals, and hunting is better as a result. The plants and trees always come back stronger every year too, so everybody wins.

Eventually, Numei bids Esther farewell and begins the long walk home. She lives on the outskirts of the village, on the other side of the valley, and she wants to get home before dark. She has a feeling that Horim is upset that she has been gone so long and she wants to see him and make him at ease again.

Esther stays where she is, waiting for the sun to set. She wants to see this great bonfire at nighttime. As it grows dark, the great pile of burning wood resembles a little volcano with a bed of hot lava. It is a whole bonfire and light show, just for her.

She is tired already of the scene at the shelter. She just wants to be alone tonight and it is impossible to get a moments peace there. It is a place to gather for the Wolf tribe and they tend to get very wild when they are together. There are too many people there, having intense conversations in loud voices. But as night deepens, Esther begins to realize that she is hungry and thirsty. Sighing, she rises on her very warm, relaxed bones and ventures forth into the cold night, where she slowly stiffens again. She goes to face the crowds, the noise, and the drama in exchange for a meal, fire, and something hot to drink.

Wolf 14'

Swan moon

Numei watches her husband anxiously, lying on his side in bed with his back to her. She wants to put her arm around him, but gets such a cold and distant feeling from him that she refrains. He is obviously not asleep because she can hear no snores and he is completely silent. Which means he is angry with her. Her husband is not a very communicative man when something bothers him, although he talks a great deal about things of no importance. Numei likes this about him. It is too easy when a man tells you everything. She likes a little mystery. She does her usual trick of twirling his hair in her fingers, knowing that he hates it and will be forced to react. He simply takes the blanket and pulls it over his head. She reaches underneath it and tries again. He does nothing, but she can feel him smoldering under there.

"Numei," he growls, when she refuses to stop.

"Mmmm," she mumbles innocently.

He says nothing more, but she stops stroking his head. It would not do to push him too far if she wants to find out what is wrong. For a long time they lie in silence, while Numei broods quietly. She hates that she cannot be detached or strong in Horim's presence. She is still at the mercy of his moods. When he is in a bad mood, then she cannot help but be in a bad mood herself. When he is happy again, then she becomes happy again. When they fight, she is miserable until they make up, and she knows that he is the same way. The only way she can escape from this endless cycle is to get her space and go off on her own. But as time wears on and their marriage becomes more and more tense, she finds that she needs more and more space. She knows her faithful Horim has been very confused lately by her behavior and he has been getting more strange and distant himself, which just makes things worse.

"What is the matter?" she whispers into his ear, when she cannot stand the silence anymore.

"Nothing."

"Fine," she says grumpily. "Don't tell me."

She rolls over and sulks. Although his behavior is annoying, she knows that she likes being submissive to him. She gives away all of her power to him because it makes her excited to be dominated by him. In public, she is a powerful presence in the tribe. She is a healer and midwife and her cousin is Chief Vayanna. Her husband is a quiet hunter and fisherman, taking little heed in society at all. He mostly keeps to himself. Everyone thinks that he does whatever she tells him to, but when they are alone, it is he who is the dominant one. And she likes it. She likes feeling like a little girl.

"Horim?"

"What?" he mumbles sleepily.

He must have fallen asleep while her brain was spinning.

"I'm sorry, I woke you. I didn't know you were asleep."

"We'll talk later," he grumbles.

"Go back to sleep then," she says, disappointed.

She cannot sleep herself, and eventually she rises and walks over to the fire. Horim must have gotten up sometime during the night and put on fresh logs, for there are still burning embers. After throwing more wood on, she brews some tea. She is hungry, but she gives a distasteful look at the remains of last night's corn mush, which have congealed into a strange glossy membrane overnight.

As she stares at the fire, drinking her tea, she thinks back over the years. Back when she first met Horim and how different things were then. She had dreams back then, of a perfect life and a perfect love and everything in between. When Numei first met Horim, she was young - sixteen to be exact. She fell madly in love with him instantly. It took him a bit longer, but he eventually became very attached to her. Within a year, they were married. For the longest time, she remembers hanging on his every word. He was older than her by four years and he seemed to know how to do anything. He could hunt, fish, cook, build things with his hands, walk long distances, or live outdoors for weeks without a shelter. She was so madly in love with him that she made him crazy after awhile. He began acting distant and disappearing on long hunting trips, which nearly drove her insane.

One spring, he decided to walk up to see the land of the endless rain, where the Chinook live. She wanted to go, but he refused. He said she wasn't tough enough and couldn't make the rigorous journey on foot. She got extremely upset and they had some big arguments. Many tantrums later, he finally agreed to take her. He figured that if she was too much trouble, he would leave her in the Cougar village and she could stay there or return home at her leisure. They made the trip up to Cougar village in twenty days, which is rather slow for Horim. By then, he knew that he was leaving her there. Traveling with her was a nightmare. She whined and complained constantly and wanted a lot of attention from him because she was so uncomfortable. He had to build shelters for her every night, so she could have a roof over her head, and they had to sleep in the shelters at Elk and Raven village for several nights, using his valuable tupas on wasteful extravagance so she could rest and relax.

They had a huge fight in Cougar village over him going on without her, but in the end she just let him go. She really didn't want to go with him anyway. They said a gloomy goodbye and off he went. She was miserable for a month afterwards, moping around Cougar village, thinking about Horim and missing him terribly. She kept kicking herself for driving him away and worrying that he would not come back. He was going to a dangerous place to see a dangerous people. What if he died?

Then she met Tumock. At first, he was just the strange man who liked her singing and would come to watch her sing at the assembly hall. She could tell he liked her and wanted to sleep with her, and she enjoyed teasing him. But on a strange night during the full moon, she drank a potent tea of hallucinogenic mushrooms and they spent the night romping around the forest in the dark. She learned that he was a Ruok, one of the last of an old cult of shamans. He told her of the powers of the forest and led her to a power spot, where she had intense visions. He was so much more masterful than Horim, and that night she became incredibly attracted to him, even though he was so much older than she was. She kissed him and they made love right there on the scratchy leaves. It was unlike any other sex she ever had.

Later, she began introspecting, and it was a very difficult night from then on. When they watched the sun come up, she told him she didn't like what the mushrooms had shown her about herself. She realized that she was a silly girl with silly dreams. She wanted to change her life and do something fulfilling and she decided that night to become a healer.

His response was to teach her a little bit about the path of the Ruok. He taught her diligently all summer long. It was a hard summer, but it was exciting. She did many things she had never done before. He taught her the movements to change the body and how to toughen up her will so she could do anything she wanted to. He taught her to take responsibility for her life and follow the Flow. They took long walks in the forest for many days, and she lost several pounds of baby fat and became strong and limber. They had a passionate romantic affair also, with the understanding that it was to be kept a secret and with no strings attached.

Horim returned in the fall, but he didn't find the woman he had left. He was surprised to see a completely different woman greet him in the woods on that rainy morning.

"You waited for me?" he asked breathlessly, watching her stand in the rain without flinching.

"I've been learning new things," is all she said, and then she grabbed him and kissed him and told him that everything was going to be different from now on.

When she said goodbye to Tumock, he surprised her by asking her to stay and become his juwanna. But she refused because she wanted to be with her family, friends and Horim. She returned to the Wolf tribe and Horim built a long house in the style of the Chinook people for them. They planned for a family.

But Numei soon discovered that something inside of her had changed and she began to feel penned in. Horim is very possessive and jealous and so is she. They were inseparable, but it became uncomfortable. She thought that a close union was what she wanted, but it was like Tumock had planted a seed within her that threatened to split her open and destroy her. He showed her a part of herself that she wanted to know better - a wild and free self. She became more independent and free spirited after that and Horim found himself more and more attracted to her every day. And slowly, over time, the roles reversed. He became the desperate one and she the one running away. And now, she finds herself sitting by a fire with congealed corn mush and a cup of tea, thinking about how she should have followed Tumock's advice and not gone home with Horim at all. And about how much more painful it would be to separate now, after all this time.

Horim pads in a short time later, sits down next to her, and has a bowl of tea. To her utter disgust, he eats a few bites of the congealed corn mush like it is the most delicious thing in the world and then he kisses her, his breath smelling of old corn. He suddenly wants to talk and make things right. Numei no longer cares why he was angry, but he has to tell her all about it anyways.

"I have hardly seen you since I got back from my fishing trip to the ocean. It's been a month since we have spent any time together. I miss you."

"I have a client. A very difficult case who needs healing."

"I always make time for you, even when I am busy."

"I make time for you too."

"Not much time anymore."

He feels her detachment and the distance between them and he gets very sad. He is losing her. It looms over their heads, like an axe about to swing down and chop them off. He immediately feels that familiar stubborn feeling coming on and knows that he is not going to let go of her. Not if he can help it. He stands up, determined to win her heart back right now. He walks over to her and picks her up in his arms. She is heavier than she has ever been before, but he can still carry her to the bed. After throwing her down, he pins her down with his naked body. She protests, just to make things interesting, and then they kiss as two people who have not seen each other in a long time would.

"Soon you must stop drinking the Barren Womb tea, so we may have a baby," he says, spooning next to her after sex.

Numei sits up, frowning, and reaches for the bowl of bitter contraceptive tea that she left by the bed. She puts the bowl to her lips dramatically and finishes it off. Then she lies down again and strokes his chest with her fingertips.

"I, too, want a baby. But I am not ready," she says after a long silence. "I am still training as a healer. This healing I am doing now has shown me how far I have to go. It has shown me how important it is for me to seek out spirit guides and gain more power and knowledge. A baby would take up so much time and energy, that I would never do that. I need another year to get to where I want to be. I need to heal myself if I am to heal others. I need to - "

"You need to think about your priorities," he insists. "Your dedication to healing is good, but there are other important things in life. Our family. Our tribe. The future of our people."

"Improving my medicine skills will benefit the tribe."

"Do you not want a family?" he asks suddenly, his eyes narrowing to slits. "Is that what you are saying?"

"I think about having a family all the time. I dream of babies often."

"We missed a wonderful opportunity two years ago, when Jupiter was crossing the Wolf constellation," he says. "You said you weren't ready and I granted you that year to do as you wanted. We missed our chance this year, with Saturn in Wolf. You said you were still not ready and I gave in again. I have been very patient with you, but Saturn will be in Wolf only one more year and I want my first born to have that great gift. Saturn is a strong planet to be in the home sign. This is our last chance and I will not give in this time, Numei. I want a child."

"The time of conception is not until the month of the Cougar," she reminds him. "So why argue about it now?"

"You have the luxury of a few more months of indecision, I suppose, but I want an answer soon. You have been of childbearing age for ten years and that is a long time to be barren."

"I am not barren. I have simply waited."

"The people talk about us. They laugh at us because we are childless. I hear things they say. I don't care what they think about me, but I don't like what they say about you. I won't stand for it."

"The people can say what they want," she says grumpily. "They'll come running when they need my skills. I can promise you that."

Despite all this talk of high ideals, what is really going through her mind is a little different than she has admitted to Horim. Although she does want to live up to the great ideals of a Wolf healer and continue with her training, that is not what really makes her hesitate. The real dilemma is that if she has a baby with Horim, then she will have to give up that precious freedom that she has been craving lately. She will have to hang up her wild and rebellious ways and be responsible for the rest of her life.

"I will think about it," she promises, turning around and facing away from him. "Just give me some time."

Wolf 16'

Wolf moon

Esther wanders aimlessly down to the village, looking for distraction. It is too painful to be alone with her moody, racing thoughts, which threaten to drive her insane. There is much commotion in the village commons today and she wants to be entertained and forget about everything. She spends the afternoon wandering back and forth, watching people involved in preparations for the new moon celebration. The trading tents are packed with people getting ready, and she takes a look inside one of the tents, wondering what is going on.

Inside this tent, a mysterious little man with hair that goes all the way down to his knees sells all sorts of potions, rattles, amulets, wands, and masks. He has a gnarled face twisted into a sneer and slits for eyes. Many people examine the merchandise intensely and he hops from person to person and tells them stories about the objects they are looking at. He claims that every single thing has some magical property or another and whispers conspiratorially to each one about the powerful things they could do with his special items.

Esther sees Temu there, examining a rattle, and she goes over to greet him. He smiles as he sees her, and waves the rattle in her general direction.

"Hello, it's good to see you. How are you?" he says.

"I'm doing well."

"Good."

"What is all this stuff?"

"That little man is called Fang. He calls himself a snake magician. Nobody remembers his real name - just Fang - the snake magician. He's Chief Vayanna's little toy. She uses him for various things. Spying. Mischief. Errands. He takes care of all the...unpleasantries. He's a vicious little weasel, but he serves his purpose."

"Snake magician? "

"That's what he calls himself."

He puts the rattle down and walks away from the tent. Esther follows him. He lights his eternal pipe and they take a walk over to the Hall of Wolves.

"Are you enjoying your stay here?"

"Yes."

"Wonderful. Tomorrow should be quite a day. The new moon is here. Several more people have arrived. The shelter is packed."

Esther nods politely, although her attention is drawn to the men going in and out of the hall. They are dressed in strange costumes of animal fur and skins, with painted faces and pierced ears and noses. They seem like beast men, unkempt and dangerous. Esther gets a chill as she examines the men in their primitive finery. They seem shadowy and mysterious with dark purposes, probably bent to tasks that no sane man would dare.

"What are they doing?"

"They are getting the hall ready for a ceremony to welcome the Great White Wolf. Tonight is an ancient ceremony."

"Why are they dressed like that?"

"They dress to please the Great White Wolf. It's all a show really, to amuse the foolish. Keep them entertained so they won't get into trouble. But it's worth watching. It's a great show."

Temu invites her to share his lunch back at the shelter and she gladly takes him up on it. They go back, eat lunch and have a glass of wine. Then he takes her upstairs to his room and she pays for the wine and her room bill in the way that they have grown accustomed to.

Numei watches Horim silently as he works in the drying hut. He has been drying fish in there for a few weeks and now packs the last of the smoked fillets into large leaves. Once wrapped, they will be buried under the earth in wooden boxes, where they will last for the remainder of the season. The smell of cedar wood burning is strong. She helps him pull down sticks pierced with smoked halibut and tastes a piece, pronouncing it good.

All morning long, she's been considering dissolving their marriage and going up to see Tumock again, but she cannot imagine it as she works silently beside Horim. She enjoys even the small chores they do together. It is good to work beside him, wrapping smoked halibut for the winter months. Sighing, she decides to leave it up in the air until tomorrow. She hopes that she can store enough power tonight, at the Hall of Wolves, in order to make a decision before she drives herself crazy.

Esther hasn't seen a soul around for a long time, and she becomes restless and moody sitting in front of the hall, waiting for the celebration to begin. Some dark mood is descending on the village and it makes her feel creepy. Strange singing and chanting can be heard from inside houses and in secret places in the forest. The wind howls through the trees, creating a symphony with the voices.

Eventually, she gets up and walks to the main lodge for a hot drink and a snack. The lodge is silent and lonely, except for a few small candles on the tables. Esther sits by the embers of a long burnt fire and munches morosely on the leftovers from tonight's dinner, which nobody has bothered to clear.

When she returns to the Hall of Wolves, it has taken on a much different character. People are arriving en masse, dressed in the strangest costumes. Some have mud caked faces and bones of animals tied to their hair, horns glued to their heads and grim spears in their hands. Others are dressed in animal furs with their faces painted up to look like beasts from some nightmarish jungle. A few are covered in something like dried blood - from who knows what dead thing - and they carry bloody arrows tied around their necks. She sees several people dressed in black robes- their faces and hands painted to look like a skeleton. They even walk like a skeleton might walk, and strange rattles made of bone on the arms and legs make a sound like an army of skeletons walking in unison.

Rattles are shaken violently, ghastly horns blow off-key notes, and drums beat slowly, as if something dreadful is approaching. The music is grim and brooding. Esther feels like an innocent child who suddenly wakes up to find herself trapped in a nightmare, surrounded by demons all pushing past her - late for a meeting. The ghastly revelers pay no attention to Esther as they all file past her and into the hall.

Soon everyone has gone inside, and it looks like they might close the door. Esther decides to enter, excited to see what strange things will be going on inside. As she walks in, she sees Fang, the snake magician, standing on a stool at the door. He is covered from head to toe with mud and draped in a robe of snakeskin. He holds a gourd filled with what looks like Tulum. Solemnly, he hands it to Esther and waits for her to take a sip. Esther doesn't want to drink it, but he doesn't look like he will take no for an answer. He stares at her with cold, mischievous eyes as she takes a small sip. With a sneer and a chuckle, Fang tips the gourd and forces more of the vile potion down her throat, making her choke. He laughs at the look of rage she makes, and it is all she can do not to hit him and pour the vile mess over his head in her anger. She curses at him as she backs away from him and his nasty gourd.

It doesn't taste like Tulum- in fact, it tastes even worse. As the liquid burns down her throat and into her stomach, she shivers in revulsion. Her stomach does flip-flops and she struggles not to vomit. As she stands there dizzy, with her hands on her knees, Fang holds up a mask for her to put over her head. The mask resembles a fierce bird, bloodthirsty and deadly, ready to kill. She doesn't want the hideous thing, but a woman caked in mud takes it from him and walks over to soothe Esther with some kind words and a gentle touch on the shoulder. Esther reluctantly allows the kind woman to put it over her face and attach it with ropes. It fits pretty well, except it makes it hard to breathe and see, and makes her feel even more like vomiting. But the woman looks at her and pronounces herself satisfied.

It is extremely dark and smoky inside, with a great bonfire burning wildly in the middle. Esther is shocked at the size of the assembly hall. She didn't realize how big it was from the outside. Smoke pours up to the ceiling and flickering shadows dance across the crowd, who slowly dance around the great fire. Many musicians are gathered in a tight bunch near the blaze, playing a morbid tune.

The decorations are equally bizarre. Scareravens hang from the walls, skulls sit on top of poles, and skeletons of real human bones dangle from the ceiling. Wolf heads are stuffed, mounted and hung from the ceiling. The most prominent decoration is the great serpent that snakes across the roof, around the beams and winds its way to the floor in a great heap. It is painted red and yellow, with the red symbolizing danger and the yellow symbolizing thunder. Esther examines the head in amazement, with real, genuine razor sharp teeth and claws that must have been pulled from a great beast.

Esther is starting to feel suffocated from the heat and the crowd and she moves closer to the door where a fresh breeze flows. Also she reasons - easy escape. As she jostles through the crowd, they begin chanting. This is the song to awaken the great White Wolf, protector of the tribe.

The song of worship frightens Esther. With the great heat and light of the bonfire, it reminds her of slaves chanting in unison to a great volcano, spewing forth fire and brimstone in the center of the room - pictures of hell she was shown in her youth. The singing grows in volume, until it is so loud that Esther begins to swoon. That is when she begins to have powerful, hallucinatory visions. She becomes ill and paranoid and tries to jostle through the crowd and get outside. But the door has been shut and barred and she cannot escape. She is trapped.

Suddenly the singing stops and there is dead silence. The silence is so complete, that Esther feels like screaming just to break the spell. There is a platform, suspended several feet off the ground, and mysterious minions crawl up ropes toward it. They have torches in their mouths. When they reach the ledge, they set down the torches, and slide down the ropes. A hideous creature walks out of the shadows and into the torchlight.

It is like a giant bloodthirsty wolf and a human fused in the black cauldrons of hell. It has a great head with giant fangs and bloodshot eyes and its fur is pure white as fresh snow. Huge claws extend from its hands and feet. It seems to be a wolf, yet it stands upright. The crowd gasps and falls to its knees. Esther is the only one left standing, and she becomes panic stricken that the hideous beast might see her and order her thrown into the fire as a sacrifice. Her head filled with paranoid visions like these, she drops to her knees. She struggles to catch her breath, with her heart beating wildly in her chest.

Three women begin to chant in some demonic language that only they can understand. Their voices are impossibly loud and piercing and they fill the hall with a sound both terrible and beautiful. The musicians play a slow, throbbing drumbeat with lots of rattles and the revelers begin to dance in a trance. In terror, Esther finds herself dancing with them -afraid not to. She is sure that the White Wolf - whoever it is - will kill her if she does not act like a slave too. As soon as she gets a chance, she resolves to flee far from this land and never return. The mask has been pulled off this place and its core is pure evil.

She sees a man with one arm dancing next to her - its zombie-like flesh rotting away as it hops around like a maniac. A woman has a face like a slug, with slime dripping off it and onto the floor. Skeletons dance and clatter away, doing a bony sort of maniacal dance as if they are marionettes being controlled by the great power of this White Wolf. Esther feels that she is going to throw up. She pushes forward toward the fire desperately. If she throws up, she will vomit directly into the fire so that she won't do it all over everyone.

It is extremely hot next to the bonfire and Esther begins to drip with sweat. She can almost feel the fat and hair and skin melting off with the drops of sweat, so that soon she will be a skeleton with the rest of them. She hears the rattle of bones in her ears and she backs off, terrified that she will be melted away to bones like the others, with her skin melting and boiling at her feet.

She doesn't know anything any more. She is not even sure who she is. The bitter drink that Fang poured down her throat has taken over her entire body and she can feel it throbbing in her skull and creating hideous visions. Desperate, she tries to focus on the music, which threatens to drive her mad with mesmerizing menace. She watches the White Wolf dance wildly and leap about. Eventually, she loses her terror and enters some sort of dream state. She begins to dance as if her life depends on it, believing that the faster she dances, the faster she will become sane again. She spins around like a dervish. She feels a terrible heat and suddenly a hand reaches out and grabs her and yanks her backwards. With a gasp, she realizes that she almost danced right into the fire.

She moves to the back of the crowd and joins the skeletons in their jerky, marionette dance. She is now accepting of her fate. She will become one with the skeleton slaves and worship this beast that dances above them all. Only in acceptance of everything, no matter how strange, will she survive this night.

I will become one with them. And I will never escape from this horrible pit. That is my punishment for my sinful life. The Fathers were right. Hell was real. I didn't believe it. But it was real all this time.

One of the torches goes out and the White Wolf seems to grow bigger and more terrible in the shadows. Suddenly Esther realizes that it is not the White Wolf at all up there. It is actually some sort of hellish demon. She is truly dancing with the denizens of hell. She can almost hear the screams of the damned wailing in abject misery. Writhing and spinning, the satanic creature dances, as the flames rise higher and higher. The creature puts its hands in the fire of the remaining torches and its hands are suddenly aflame. The crowd gasps as the beast waves its arms in the air, the flames making trails above its head. Sparks fly down to the crowd below. There is an explosion, bright sparks shoot everywhere, and the whole building seems to turn to bright red for a moment. There are more explosions and the wolf waves her flaming hands in the air and wails in a horrible voice, while everyone screams along with it.

Suddenly Esther gasps. There is a spirit standing right in front of her. It is a beautiful woman, with a long shadowy dress that goes to her feet and hair worn in a bun on the head. Esther feels her blood run cold. It is not just a woman - it is her mother. She is sure of it, from the way she wears her hair to the way she moves slowly and languidly in the flickering light. Her face is blurred, but it seems familiar somehow. The ghostly woman looks at her with faded eyes and bows her head silently. She seems sad and humbled, as if her experiences have been hard and she has learned tough lessons. In her bowed head seems to be an apology of some sort.

What does this mean? Is her mother dead? What if this is her spirit, come from beyond the grave? Esther feels an overwhelming sadness for the poor woman. All the anger she ever felt for her fades instantly, and she wonders how she could ever have been angry with her.

The shadows seem to shift and turn into something else and the spirit vanishes into the other flickering shadows. Esther's mind reels. Was that her mother's face? She is sure that it was. It feels right. Did her mother go to hell after she died? Has Esther been sent down to hell to see where her mother has been for all this time, trapped forever in this place of unending torment and pain? Esther buries her face in her hands and shakes with horror.

"Don't live in hell, mother," Esther rasps in a broken voice. "I am sorry I hated you. Go to heaven...where you belong. Please, I want you to go to heaven. I'm so sorry. I know it wasn't your fault." She thinks of her father suddenly, and wonders if he is also in hell. "Father, if you're dead, I want you to go to heaven too," she says desperately.

She pushes through the crowd, knowing he is somewhere in this horrible place, wanting to see his face as she saw her mother's face. But she can't find him anywhere, so she puts her hands together desperately and prays.

"Please God," she whispers, "release my parents into the light of heaven. Let them out of here."

The torches surrounding the While Wolf suddenly flare up and disappear and the mad monster disappears into the darkness. The crowd screams its final farewell, bidding it a good journey back to the spirit world. The door to the hall flies open and cool air comes rushing into the stifling hot room. Esther breathes a sigh of relief and fights to be the first one to escape out into the cool night air. There she struggles to catch her breath and clear her head of the madness that has engulfed her.

Slowly the cool air calms her racing heart, and Esther lies down on the wet grass until her dizziness clears. Meanwhile, the revelers file out of the Hall of Wolves, screaming, howling and hell bent on destruction. Demons and monsters of all types are suddenly loosed on the world. She hears screams and yells and then the sound of splintering wood and things crashing to the ground. Some hideous native in a frightening mask jumps over Esther, turning to scream at her before scuttling off. A fight breaks out between a snake woman and a wolf woman and their bloodcurdling shrieks pierce the ears. Another fight breaks out between two skeletons and they swing real live human leg bones at each other like clubs. Esther feels that she is going to throw up if she doesn't get out of here. She jumps up and makes a run for the woods. On the way, some hairy beast man trips her and she falls onto her face. The man laughs and laughs, before disappearing into the night.

Esther finally makes it to the safety of the dark woods, where she sits down behind a tree to catch her breath. She can hear mayhem going on all around her and her head is spinning wildly so she couldn't get up if she wanted to. What madness has taken hold of this village? Eventually, the noise spreads beyond the Hall of Wolves as the monsters spread out over the entire territory. She is glad to be away from them.

She runs desperately under the trees, trying to outrace the demons that are following her. She can hear screams and cries in the night and they are fuel for her mad panic. She runs and runs, but even as the cries fade out, she can still hear them in her head. She slows to a walk, and rambles aimlessly down a pitch-black path. It is not easy to follow a dark path on a new moon but at least she is not afraid of the dark tonight. She has been through too much horror tonight to be afraid of a little dark. She takes deep breaths and tries to calm herself down.

Suddenly, she comes upon Hoja's house. She doesn't know how she got here but she knows instantly that she is here for a reason. She must let the wolves out. She tiptoes to the door, puts her hand on the jagged wood and pushes it open.

Two large forms jump out almost instantly. The wolves run up to her and nearly knock her down in their excitement. One licks her face affectionately and the other one licks her hand. And then they prance around, cavorting in the night. Esther watches them, amazed. They are such beautiful creatures.

Then fat Hoja appears and begins screaming at Esther.

"Who are you? Why have you released my wolves? Come here!"

Esther runs away, easily outdistancing Hoja who puffs slowly after her, shouting for her to stop. Finally Hoja gives up and begins a mad tantrum. She shakes out of pure fury, as if she is going to explode and spray fat and blood all over the forest. An impressive string of curses spews from her mouth. And then, when her rage is more tolerable, she chases after the wolves. But they are in no mood to go to her. She runs in circles, shouting their names, but the wolves scamper off into the night, easily evading her.

Esther slows to a walk and the screams of Hoja slowly fade away. She feels the buzzing in her head subside. The evil drug has worked its way through her system at last and she is slowly returning to normal. She feels an immense wave of relief pass through her, as she heads back to the winking lights of torches flickering in the distance. This time she walks towards the screams of the village and not away.

Numei slowly takes off the White Wolf costume, piece by sticky piece. It is a long process. As she peels the thick furs off her body, which are soaked with perspiration, she breathes in deep gulps of cool air. She almost passed out in there tonight, with the heat and the hot outfit. She takes a deep drink of water from a skin and tries to regain her equilibrium. She will need to drink a lot of water or she will get sick.

She is happy with her performance today. Her recent confusions have only made her passions more intense. Judging by the noise and commotion around her, the people are pleased as well. She hears screams and yells coming from somewhere nearby and the sound of running feet and maniacal laughter. Two skeletons run past her, sprinting from a thoroughly soaked and miserable bird beast.

A few moments later, Vayanna finds her. She comes up to her and gives her a big hug.

"You were wonderful tonight. The people loved it."

"Thank you."

"I don't know what we would do without you."

Numei stares at her, surprised at her foresight. How did she know Numei was thinking about leaving?

"I hear you and Horim are having troubles."

Numei laughs. Although she has lived her whole life among the Wolf tribe, she is still amazed by the eyes of the gossip hounds, which miss nothing.

"I need to bathe," she sighs, peeling the final piece of the costume off.

"I will go with you."

They walk over to the river. Numei stands naked before the stream but she doesn't jump in. She just stands there and watches the water swirl past.

"What is wrong?" Vayanna asks, as she stares at Numei's confused face.

"I want it all," she shouts loudly, and jumps into the water.

After washing herself clean, she feels more herself again. She walks back over the cold riverbed stones to the bank and Vayanna helps her dry off and get dressed.

"You're trapped in your head," Vayanna says, watching her face. "I know the feeling. Don't think so much. Everything is fine."

The White Wolf celebration used to be held on the full moon, but when Vayanna became chief she switched it to the new moon because she felt it was more powerful. There is still a running argument that the White Wolf ceremony is more appropriate to the lunacy of the full moon and should be switched back.

Wolf 17'

Esther wakes late, hung over and bleary, and wanders out into the gloomy morning, shrouded with clouds, to find the ruins of the night before. Gates have been smashed and food from the trading post pilfered and scattered. Everyone is out, thankfully dressed as people again, cleaning up the mess as if nothing out of the ordinary had happened. As they work, they share stories from last night and burst out laughing.

All Esther wants is food and warmth. She goes to the main lodge, but the fire is out and there is no food in sight, so she walks back outside to look for Temu. After a long search, she sees him on the roof of the main lodge trying to get a frightened goat down. The shelter keeps two goats for milk and Temu has been trying to breed them. Last night, somebody managed to stick one of them up on the roof. He whistles, offering it food, but the goat continues to back away from him in fright. He reaches for it and misses, nearly falling onto his face, and he has to hold on tight to keep from falling off the sloped roof. He slowly gets back his footing and then his panic turns to anger. He curses the stupidity of his tribe and their foolish traditions and holds the food out once again for the poor animal, which still backs away from him.

Esther walks around in a daze, her eyes glazed and her mind still soggy, pondering last night's experiences. Everything is still vivid in her mind, especially her mother's face. She wonders if that was her mother's spirit and if she is really dead and burning in hellish torment. She wants to find Numei and talk to her about it, so she searches the commons for her, but Numei is nowhere to be seen.

In the afternoon, begins the traditional new moon weddings. There are no less than five marriages scheduled for today and two babies have been born on the new moon so far, which has four planets in the Wolf constellation to make a powerful Wolf child. A great feast is laid out in honor of the newly married couples and the new parents, although nobody is eating yet because they are watching the weddings. Esther finds Numei there and she goes up to her just as soon as there is a break between couples.

"I wanted to talk to you," Esther says, her eyes desperate for understanding.

"About what?"

"I want to tell you what happened to me last night."

"What happened? You had an orgasm?"

Esther shakes her head and leads Numei over to a quiet place to talk. She tells the whole story and then waits for Numei's wisdom. But Numei seems distracted and depressed and her thoughts have no cohesion.

"I think my mother might be in hell," Esther says miserably.

"Hell is that place the priests told you about? A place that is always on fire?"

"Yes. It is where the damned are sent for eternity."

"That's ridiculous."

"Do you think so?"

"This hell that you speak of does not exist," Numei says irritably. "Your parents are not burning forever in a world of endless punishments. It only shows all the resentments and anger that you hold inside of you, that you think your mother might be in such a horrible place."

This makes sense to Esther, but it still leaves many unsolved mysteries in the air. She tries to discuss it further, but Numei has nothing more to say about it. Numei soon wanders off, leaving Esther with a head full of unanswered questions. She finally decides that thinking about it endlessly won't help and goes to watch the next wedding. When her brain starts thinking about it without her permission, she ignores it and tries to focus on Vayanna's speeches to the married couples instead.

Wolf 23'

Raven moon

For the past three days, Esther has been hibernating in her hut, recovering from a sickness. She emerges for meals when she can stomach them and then returns to her little cocoon right afterwards. Once a day, she goes to the sweat lodge to relax. This evening, Esther feels a lot healthier, although she is not yet in the mood to go out and see the world. Dinner holds no appeal for her at all, because Numei has put her right back on an acorn mush diet, claiming that Esther's sickness is a sign that she has deep poisons in her body that need cleansing. Esther doesn't mind acorn mush, but she suspects that Temu is giving her the same batch day after day, because he doesn't want to prepare it more than once. And that batch is getting stale and old.

She begrudgingly rises to get some fresh wood from the pile outside the main lodge, takes a pee, and then goes right back to bed. It is boring being in this hut by herself day after day, but she entertains herself by trying to figure out which tribe is the one she was born to. She has come up with all sorts of theories but none of them hold water. She thinks about the vision of her mother and tries to find clues to the mystery in that. She tries to dredge up old memories, but they are not there.

Her hand absently strokes the petal of her flower, without her even being aware that she is doing it. Suddenly, she realizes that she feels sensation down there. After a momentary hesitation, Esther keeps going. She clears her mind and tries not to think about what she is doing, although she keeps an eye out for Him, just in case her tormentor should make another appearance. She doesn't know how long she does this, because she feels like she is floating in a void in time, where she has no name and nothing to do or worry about. Every so often, her brain dredges up some memory of sin and shame, but she ignores it and keeps going. After all, what is sin to someone with no name? And then...there is a sudden, unexpected explosion. Waves of pleasure course through her body and she moans loudly as her body arches. After the initial explosion, she lies still for a long time, feeling tingly and enjoying a lingering bliss.

It takes her several minutes to realize that she just had an orgasm. Then she laughs out loud. It was so easy! She cannot believe that she had so much trouble and stress over it. She doesn't know what she did differently today, but now that she knows what it feels like, she can surely have another one.

"You all can go to hell," she whispers to all the Spanish Fathers who told her that playing with her petal was wrong.

Wolf 26'

Cougar moon

Numei walks through the woods, looking for mushrooms and wild greens for dinner. The woods seem boring and lifeless today. She has walked for an hour and not noticed anything along the way, which isn't like her. And worse, she went the wrong way entirely. She will have to backtrack to find the little trail that heads up the mountain. She walks back to the trail and starts walking up the hill to the place where mushrooms grow, but again she zones out and loses the trail. Then she trips on a stump and falls flat on her face. Cursing, she stands up and keeps walking, limping a little from the pain in her knee when she fell.

She manages to get up the hill without further incident, but she finds no mushrooms. She walks around, searching everywhere, but she cannot find a single one. She tries to summon up her power but it doesn't work. She finally gives up, noticing the lateness of the day, and turns back empty handed.

Numei sits in front of the fire in a half lotus position, trying to meditate unsuccessfully, while her mind keeps wandering into gloomy thought patterns. Meanwhile Horim cleans the house around her. He sweeps the entire floor with a broom twice over, then stacks all the loose tools and clothes into their proper baskets and places them outside so he can clean the benches. And still she just sits there. He glances at her from time to time, wondering how she can just sit there while he works so hard. When he has to put more wood on the fire, although she is sitting right by it, he becomes very angry.

"You could at least put some more wood on the fire," he says grumpily.

She ignores him, hoping he will leave her alone before she takes out her mood on him.

"Never mind, I'll do everything myself, as usual."

She looks up, about to defend herself, but with a great effort she keeps her mouth shut. He continues to work, sweeping the benches, walls, and ceiling free of dirt and ash. Then he returns the baskets of things to their places, takes the bed apart, and beats it clean of dust and debris. He glares at her, but she still hasn't moved a muscle.

"Could you at least help me with dinner?"

"I'm meditating," she says firmly, speaking at last.

"I know. It's quite convenient. And when dinner is ready, then you'll be relaxed and peaceful and eat a hearty dinner, and I'll be exhausted from doing everything myself and too tired to enjoy my food."

"So don't cook then. I don't care."

"Fine, I won't," he says in a loud voice.

He goes into the smokehouse to get a piece of dried fish to eat. He craves a hot meal, but refuses to cook if Numei is not going to help. When he returns, he finds her sitting in the same exact place, but now with her eyes open. He sits down on the other side of the blaze and chews the fish. He is in a bad mood now and very angry with her. He keeps giving her looks, and the fact that she doesn't respond indicates to him that she is also in a bad mood and is ignoring him on purpose. So they both sit like that for a long time and the air in the house turns sour and brooding.

After awhile, he starts sharpening his sword, which he has been meaning to do for some time. He rubs the sharpening stone back and forth, trying to get a better edge. He chants a song quietly to himself as he works. Numei looks up, irritated at the interruption in her peace and quiet.

"Could you do that later?" she asks annoyed

"It needs to be done now," he grumbles. "It's so dull, my sword couldn't cut through pond scum.

"Then do it somewhere else, please."

"I'm not going to go out in the cold just to sharpen my sword. It won't take long. I'll be done soon."

"I can't believe how inconsiderate you are. I feel achy and tired and my head hurts and you can't do me a simple kindness and be quiet for a while."

To her utter horror, he begins to sharpen his sword again.

"Stop that!"

"No. This is my house too!"

He continues to sharpen and sing louder.

"Eat dung! Beetle!" she snaps.

"I'm not giving in this time. I'm tired of you taking out all your bad moods on me. I've had enough."

"Fine, I'll go out into the cold to meditate. I'll freeze my bones and let my ache get worse and get sick. Just so you can sharpen your stupid sword which you can do anytime."

"Your eyes are open. You're not meditating anymore."

She squeezes her eyes shut dramatically.

"What if somebody came tonight and tried to hurt us? I need my sword sharp to protect us."

"Oh please," she hisses. "You couldn't protect us anyway. When you're not around, all the men say that you don't even know how to use that thing. They say you're useless with a sword in a real fight."

"No they don't. They *wouldn't*."

"They do. Not to your face, but they've all sparred with you, so they should know."

"I'm still not giving in."

"Maybe we should dissolve our marriage," she says quietly. "It obviously isn't working anymore."

There is deathly quiet in the room and neither one speaks for a long, poisonous silence. And then, there is a crackle and spark from the fire, and as if on cue, the anger lodged deep within Horim bursts to the surface all at once. He grabs a log that is only burning at one end and throws it as hard as he can at the wall. It explodes in a rain of sparks that showers over their heads and falls smoking to the ground. Numei cringes as some of the sparks burn her skin. He screams with rage as he throws another, harder than the first, and the shower of sparks falls all over him and not over Numei, who has gotten out of the way by now. A chunk of burning coal lands in his hair and starts smoking and she can smell burnt hair. He brushes it aside wildly, then turns to her, his eyes blazing brighter than the sparks and a little wisp of smoke coming from his head.

Shocked by his sudden display, she runs outside. She wanders around in a rage, hating him and feeling helpless. She realizes that she has become that immature girl again, whom she thought she had banished so long ago. That little monster is back. She starts crying, which seems the proper end to this miserable day.

She comes back to the house a while later and her face is a mask of misery. She sits down next to Horim, who is sharpening his sword again as if nothing out of the ordinary has happened. Only a drawn, tense look in his face indicates the stress he has been through. As she curls up into his lap, he puts down his sword and sighs. He strokes her hair and kisses her forehead. She smiles and curls up tighter.

"I'm sorry. I didn't mean it. Any of it."

"Good."

"I know I've been difficult lately. I guess I deluded myself into thinking I am somebody I'm not." She sits up and looks him deeply in the eyes with a very serious expression. "I am ready to have a baby."

"That would be wonderful," he says, giving her a kiss. "I'm glad you came to your senses."

Late that night, Numei lies next to Horim in a state of utter bliss, their bodies still warm and wet. They have just had the most wonderful sex - perhaps the best sex of their entire marriage. She floats on a high cloud way above the earth - not just because of the sex – but because she has chosen. The mind-blowing orgasm was merely her reward for making a decision. She will stay with Horim, stop drinking the Barren Womb tea and start a family.

Wolf 27'

Esther hasn't seen Numei since the new moon, so she decides to walk over to her house and see what she is doing. She gets directions to her house from Temu and then makes the long walk in the cold morning mist. Numei's house is square and long, with a beautiful statue of a wolf guarding the front door. A pile of fishing tools, nets, and other useful things lies in a heap near the front door, as if they are needed any minute for an emergency fishing expedition. She shakes the seashell chimes that hang near the door and steps back to wait.

"Numei!" Esther shouts, trying to imitate her bold manner.

Numei comes out a few minutes later, wearing no clothes.

"Come in," she says, and walks back inside, shivering.

Numei's house is built and decorated in the 'Flathead' style. Benches surround the entire length of the one room house, loaded with baskets filled with all of their possessions. One wall is carved and painted in a very elaborate crest called a juja, upon which is painted the face of a wolf, a great snake, and an owl. Another wall has a giant Eagle painted in red and black. The ceiling is pointed, with strong beams running across the length, and three holes for the smoke from the fire to escape. Esther has trouble seeing the roof, as the whole ceiling is completely filled with smoke from the great fire burning in the center of the room. A man sits by the fire on a tule mat, wrapped in blankets and utterly motionless.

A juja is a family crest that includes all the protectors and spirits that guard the family.

"This is Horim," Numei says, introducing him.

Horim is tall, thin, quiet, and unassuming. He seems an odd choice for somebody as strange as Numei. Esther sits down by the fire and Numei brings her tea and cakes made from corn and dried berries, then sits down next to Horim and curls up with her head in his lap. It makes Esther feel uncomfortable, like she is intruding on their family time by coming to their house uninvited.

"I have some good news," Esther says, although she doesn't say what the news is.

"What is it?"

When Esther still doesn't answer, Numei nods and waves her outside. Putting on her cloak, Numei follows Esther outside. They walk around the house toward the back wall, which is bathed in weak sunlight. Numei takes a deep breath, savoring the fresh air. She didn't realize how smoky her house was until now.

"I had an orgasm," Esther says dramatically.

"It's about time," Numei says with a big smile. "How was it?"

"It was nice."

"Who gave it to you?"

"I did it myself."

"That is a good way to begin," she says enthusiastically. "So the spirit is gone?"

"I don't know," Esther says, getting a chill just thinking about it. "I don't think so. What should I do about Him?"

"I don't know," Numei admits, after a long, pensive silence. "I have no experience in casting away spirits."

"I understand," Esther says, trying to hide her disappointment.

"You should go see a Ruok," Numei says. "You can visit Tumock. He would know what to do."

"A Ruok?" Esther says, thinking of Yatsa.

She realizes suddenly that Yatsa would have known what to do about Him and she curses to herself for not mentioning it to Yatsa when she had the chance.

"Tumock lives with the Owl tribe these days," Numei continues. "At least, that's what I last heard. He could help you. I am sure of it. You should go see him."

"I don't know if I want to do any more traveling," Esther says, dreading the idea of another long walk during this cold weather. "This weather is not good for traveling."

"Stay on until the spring and go then."

Esther nods vacantly.

"You can stay here through the winter. I'll talk to Vayanna if you want and ask permission. I'm sure she'll let you."

"I'll think about it," Esther says pensively. "And before I forget, I have brought your fee."

She hands Numei a large pile of tupas, which Numei gathers in her cloak.

"Thank you," Numei says. "Let's go back inside now."

"No, I'll leave you two alone," Esther says quickly. "I'm sorry I intruded."

"No intrusion," Numei insists. "You can stay the morning with us, if you want."

"No thank you. Another time. But I want to thank you for all your help, Numei."

"You're welcome," Numei says, as they walk back around the house. "And congratulations on the orgasm. Just don't forget to play with your flower often, to keep it in practice. If you don't use it, you lose it."

Wolf 28'

Hawk moon

Esther gets dressed quietly, leaving Temu snoring softly next to her. He always falls asleep right after sex, which is convenient for them both. That way, she can just slip out afterwards and go about her business without either one having to say something. Today, she felt uncomfortable with him and their arrangement. Now that she is not completely numb, somehow her flower seems more precious and she's tired of selling it for currency. She sort of likes Temu and that has made it easier to continue, but there is nowhere for it to go. It has run its course. She is paid in full now and she wants to move on.

All day yesterday, she thought about holing up here for the winter, but somehow it just felt pointless. She has a feeling deep in her gut that she should move on because there is nothing more for her here. She will go north to the next village and perhaps she will look up the Ruok that Numei told her about. It seems a better idea than just hanging out here all winter in this hut, trading her body every so often for the privilege of staying here and eating their food. She has a feeling that there is a better place for her and it might be her last chance to find it, before it is too cold to travel.

Temu told her that the Owl village is probably near, but it is hard to say for sure because they move seasonally. He has heard that they have already set up winter camp along the main road and he thinks it likely that they are already there, but the only directions he can give are to follow the main road until she sees a sign that points to the new location of their camp.

In the dim light coming from the coals of the dwindling fire in her own hut, she packs her things together experimentally. Her basket is stuffed tight and unraveling from everything she has been collecting on her travels, but she cannot think of anything to leave behind. As she looks fondly at her burden basket full of possessions, it occurs to her that this basket is her only home. She touches her things tenderly. They are her things. They go wherever she does.

Before going to sleep, she goes out into the bright moonlight and takes a look around the village. Everything is covered in fall leaves, forest grime, and fallen branches from the last big wind. It is nearly deserted, as everyone is holed up in front of eternal fires, keeping warm and safe. The sound of a soft flute pours from an open window. She spends a long time just soaking up the ambiance. Her experiences here have been so intense that she has not taken the time to enjoy the small things that make Wolf village unique.

She likes it here, but she feels good about leaving. She is tired of traveling, but she wants to move on. What are a few days more and a little farther north? She decides stubbornly right then and there that she'll keep moving until she finds what she's looking for – even though she is not sure what that is anymore. Home? Family? Perhaps she is searching for something else entirely. But only when she finds it will she stop and settle down. And if she never does, then she'll just wander forever. A burden basket strapped to her tired back. Worn out moccasins on the dusty road.

Owl Tribe

Owl 0'

Beaver moon

There is something in the air tonight. The moon is an eye, staring down on the world. Strange things are happening that don't make a bit of sense. Her big, wide-open camp space feels haunted by a thousand different creatures. Esther sits upon a log, listening to the sounds of animals walking around in the darkness. Every loud noise she hopes is only a deer. She wonders what a deer would look for at night. Big, fat leaves and juicy twigs? Water? Lost friends? Or maybe they are all looking for that mysterious and elusive power that she feels so strongly tonight.

She pulls her hood tighter, as a brisk wind blows across her neck. Nestled in her little hood cocoon, she looks out upon the world. Then she hears a noise, a rustling, and a sound of steps. She has a momentary panic, cranes her neck, and looks about wildly. Then she forces herself to calm down. She doesn't have any choice, a woman on her own has to stay calm. The thing disappears, but she doesn't like this spot any more, and she decides to walk on and find another. She walks down the path, staring wide-eyed at every nook and corner. A cloud passes over the moon and she feels a momentary chill that has nothing to do with the temperature.

She finds a new spot and sits. The ground is wet, although there has been no rain lately, and not that much moisture in the air. She spreads out her blanket and sits upon a grassy area in a loose ball of limbs. She scrunches up tighter inside her cloak and decides that she needs to figure out what to do with herself. She needs a place to hole up for the winter. That is obvious.

Owl 1'

It is a perfectly beautiful day for this time of year. Fall creeps slowly toward a close, but it is still warm during the day. For a full five minutes, she is even hot and she takes off her dress and continues on naked. Then a chill wind begins to blow, the clouds partially cover the sun, and she has to put it on again. It is like that all day long. The sun breaks through for a short, hot spell, and then it cools again.

She looks at the tatters of clouds that cover the sun and they are beautiful even though they are annoying. Then she has one of those moments that she treasures. A moment of perfect happiness, when nothing else matters but to be out here in the middle of these empty hills and watch the sun play off the trees. The glow from that perfect moment lasts a long time, even when the moment is long gone.

The path follows the hills now. She can feel that this is a whole new land. The air is different and so are the smells. The people she encounters on the path look different, taller and fiercer than the Zesti she is used to. She wonders if that is why the path follows the hills. It avoids most of the settlements, which are in the valley, as if it would not be safe to go down there. In that case, she doesn't mind a little extra climbing. Plus the views are exquisite. She crunches along on an ever-present carpet of fallen leaves of all shapes and sizes and keeps her eyes on the wide world spreading out in all directions.

In the afternoon, she comes upon a quail lying in the middle of the road, flapping its wings but not moving. With a start, she realizes that it is wounded. The timing is perfect, because she is very hungry and here is dinner lying right in front of her. Then she notices a boy staring at her and a large rock next to the bird. She realizes that he must have hit the bird and wounded it, but the bird managed to crawl over to the path, which indicates the boundary of his village, and the boy was afraid to get it. Or perhaps he was going to and she is just in time to claim the bird for the Twelve Tribes. She bends down to get a better look at it and then she looks over at him. She smiles at him, hoping he'll give her the quail. He stares at her with slits for eyes. When she doesn't leave, he just waves his arms at her and shouts something unintelligible, then turns around and walks away. The bird is hers.

The hardest part is killing the bird, which is not yet dead. She tries hitting it with a stick, but that doesn't seem to hurt it. She gingerly places her foot on its neck and pushes slightly, hoping to break it. It still keeps flapping. The bird seems indestructible. She steps harder, closing her eyes and cringing as she leans all her weight on it. There is a crunch and the bird stops moving at last. When she picks the bird up, a whitish fluid pours from its beak, and she is surprised that it has white blood and not red blood. She pulls out all the feathers and the wings, then ties it to her basket with a small string and walks on.

That night, Esther builds a fire to roast the bird. She bought a bow drill in Wolf village before she left, on the off chance that she would have the energy to start a fire on some cold night. Tonight, she tries it for the first time. She pumps up and down on it, trying to start a spark to light the kindling. It is frustrating work and the effort hardly seems worth this small quail. But she does it anyway, because the very presence of the bird seems to demand it. It takes her over an hour to learn to use the bow properly and then she finally gets the thing to start spitting out little sparks. It takes another hour of solid concentration to nurse the sparks into a small blaze, but at the end of that time, she has a small, precious fire going.

Smiling and proud of herself for this minor miracle, she props the bird on a stick and holds it over the fire. Starting the fire took up most of her patience and she has very little left for cooking. After an agonizing wait, she tears the meat off the breast with her fingers and eats voraciously. There are feathers mixed with the meat, but she doesn't care. It is delicious. Then, she accidentally smears the contents of the intestines all over the meat, which gives it a bad taste. It is that taste that sticks in her mouth for a long time afterwards.

Owl 2'

**Jay moon*

In the afternoon, she comes upon a sign stuck on a tree. It has no words, only a painting of an owl with an arrow pointing east. She follows that road, which goes up a hill, following a wild, churning river. There is evidence of much horse travel on this path. Soon she sees white blotches in the distance, and as she continues on she realizes that the blotches are the village. Perched on the edge of this wild monster of a river is Owl village. It is a beautiful sight and she has to stop a moment to savor it. Then she does the last little bit of the journey with a proud smile on her face. She completed this last walk between tribes with ease and she is not even very tired. She is a true traveler at last.

The Owl tribe's camp is much different than any other village she has been to. Forty or fifty teepees are set up in a large circle, with all the doors facing inside. A great fire burns in the center of the circle, and many are gathered around it, engaged in various pursuits. A few men stop what they are doing to watch her as she walks to the edge of the circle and puts down her basket. Someone shouts out a greeting to her and she waves back. Many eyes rest upon her and she feels like the center of attention, as she stretches her stiff back and massages her aching feet. As she stretches her legs, she notices how different they look. There are muscles popping out all over, when there was once just smooth calf. This past year, she has walked hundreds of miles, and it shows.

The Owl tribe learned the craft of teepee making from the Plains Zesti far to the east, then made revisions to allow for wet weather. These teepees are more circular and less conical, made with double layers of skin. Other than that, their design is similar to the traditional teepee of the plains. It is a rarity to find such shelters in the California area and they are proud of it.

Owl village is a lively place. Before she has even finished resting her feet, she has met at least two or three people who are curious about her. A young man instantly takes her under his wing and walks her to the kitchen to look for food. The tribe has a communal kitchen set up to cook dinner for everybody. Among several cook fires and a clay oven, three women are gathered together to grind acorns and corn. Another skins a freshly killed deer. There are many young boys nearby, playing drums tunelessly in a large group for the entertainment of the kitchen help. A few young girls dance enthusiastically to the drums, even though they are supposed to be cooking. They ignore the irritated shouts of the older women grinding grain who want their help. It is a chaotic scene and she is not surprised when she hears that there is nothing to eat now. Her protector promises that there will be a meal prepared sometime soon and he takes her on a tour of the village while they wait.

There are many horses grazing around the camp, and none of them are tied, stabled or bridled. They just wander around, free to eat or roam as they wish, and the surrounding hills are dotted with the grazing beasts. They are large creatures, grander than any horse she has ever seen. She thinks about the little Spanish horses and remembers how they used to keep them tied up all day long or fenced in these little areas. It was all so neat and orderly. This is chaotic, much like the kitchen, but the horses obviously appreciate it. They can go to the best clumps of grass and walk free as nature intended. Some men tend to them, brushing them and talking to them in low voices. A few men ride past, just for fun, with the wind in their hair and big grins on their faces. They ride on top of horse blankets with makeshift bridles.

These horses are from a stock that came from the plains Zesti in the middle of North America, who got them from the first pilgrims. They are bigger and swifter than the horses of the lower Twelve Tribes, which were traded or stolen from the Spanish missions.

Esther examines the teepees more closely, which are made of tanned skins skillfully woven together and painted with crests and symbols. The most popular is the design of a very fierce owl, which stands upon a branch and stares with wild eyes. Some have designs of horses galloping and others have pictures of flames and burning arrows. Next, they walk past several men constructing a large sweat lodge. They build a framework from strong sticks, which will be covered with blackened skins stacked nearby. There are no permanent dwellings here. It is a village designed for mobility. The Owl tribe wanders the land, following food and game or wherever their whims take them. And judging by the cleanliness of the site, they have just arrived.

"Dinnertime!"

The sun has set and Esther has been anxiously looking toward the kitchen, waiting for the communal dinner. Finally the cooks shout out that dinner is nearly ready and people begin to make their way toward the fire, carrying bowls, cups and wooden spoons. Esther goes into her burden basket for her bowl and spoon and then makes her way toward the circle. She feels lost in the strange crowd, but it is a familiar feeling by now, and almost comforting in a way. These people are very friendly, so she soon finds people to talk to and wait for dinner with. And wait...and wait...and wait.... Where is dinner? She has been here for a long time and nobody has brought food. Many are having a wild time, playing drums, singing in loud voices, dancing, smoking pipes and chatting quietly. The children run around like maniacs, playing Pone and other games, and young boys wrestle. There is so much energy here, but none of it seems to be going toward dinner. As the night grows dark, many begin to grow impatient.

"What the hell are they doing over there?" somebody shouts.

"Haven't eaten all day," grumbles another. "They've been taking their sweet time, haven't they?"

Finally, food is brought out to the relieved crowd - deer meat, burnt on one side, and acorn mush. The only thing to drink is water. For all the time they spent cooking, the cooks did not bother to season the meat or the mush with anything other than a little seaweed. Esther is disappointed in the quality of the food, but she is too hungry to pass it up. She eats all that she has in front of her and seconds of the meat.

After dinner, she goes to the communal dish basket to wash her bowl and spoon, but the water is so dirty that she cannot bring herself to rinse it in there. She will have to walk down to the river or wait until morning. Since she wants to drink tea from her bowl, she makes the walk to the river. It is so dark that she slips and sticks her foot into the river by accident while she is cleaning. She has to walk up the hill on one dry foot and one soggy, cold foot and she marches directly to the fire to warm up again.

As befitting their totem animal, the Owls like to stay up late. Especially tonight, which is the night before the full moon. The drummers pound their skins and everyone smokes pipes and dances. These are not a musical people, as the drumming is offbeat and chaotic, but they have more energy than anyone Esther has ever met, and that makes up for it. Esther tries to keep up with their energy, but she is tired from her long journey, and she really doesn't care to talk to anybody tonight. She takes a walk around the camp with her burden basket, looking for a distant, abandoned fire to curl up next to. She finally finds an empty fire pit, its coals slowly burning out. Throwing some more wood on it, she stokes it up to a small blaze, lays out her blanket, wraps herself tight and falls asleep with the sound of the drums still in her head.

Owl 3'

Esther wakes early. The camp is dead quiet and not a soul is moving about. She stumbles sleepily toward the big fire, hoping that it is still burning, but it is a smoldering pile of ash. People are passed out around it, wrapped in blankets and oblivious to the rising sun. Esther has a feeling that she has the whole place to herself all morning and she doesn't mind at all. She returns to her fire pit, builds herself a fire, and goes into the kitchen to look for a pot to cook with and tea of some kind. She finds a small basket of bay nuts and a pot and goes back to her fire to make a morning beverage.

Things get off to a very slow start in the village, but by noon, everyone is up and about. The cooks begin to get lunch started but it should be another two hours before it is ready. Esther feels the urge to do something, so she wanders into the kitchen and offers her assistance.

"Here is all the food we have to work with. What would you like to make?" a little woman shouts, her size not at all proportionate with her large voice.

"I could make acorn bread."

"That's ambitious! Have at it. You can use that oven over there."

Esther greases up her hands, buries them in yesterday's acorn mush, and begins thickening it and mixing it with corn flour. Soon she has several piles of dough ready and waiting. She looks around at all the other cooks and understands why the meals are so slow to happen here. All of the cooks, mostly women, take their sweet time, spending as much time chatting and laughing as they do cooking. They wouldn't last five minutes in a Raccoon kitchen or a Beaver kitchen. At this rate, Esther will have finished the entire bread making before anyone else is done. She feels proud of herself and the skills she picked up from the earth tribes, and a little scornful of the disorganized cooks in this tribe.

Two ovens have been built over a large fire pit, made of stone and dried mud. A large rock is moved to insert the food and then put back as a cover to trap the heat from the fire inside. Esther puts four loaves into the oven and settles down to watch and make sure that it won't burn. The oven is larger and less hot than Esther is used to and the bread takes a long time to cook. The fire boy is too busy talking to a pretty girl to pay much attention, so the fire keeps dying down.

"Look at you. How quickly you cook," exclaims a young woman, who has been skinning ducks next to Esther and putting the feathers in a large pot.

She and Esther begin to chat while they work. While they are talking, someone hands them a pipe. The woman wipes her bloody hands on a piece of disgusting, blood soaked fur, takes a deep drag and hands the pipe to Esther. The smell of jimm and tobacco is unmistakable. Esther is used to getting strange looks when she refuses a pipe that is handed to her, so she takes it this time and pretends to smoke. She holds it in her mouth, pretends to inhale, and then blows it out. Sure enough, the duck plucker is pleased and rewards her with a big smile.

Esther soon learns that even if you don't inhale jimm, it can still get you high. She fumbles with the first pan of finished bread and nearly drops it, then has trouble forming the next loaves and drops pieces all over the place. She looks around guiltily but nobody seems to care. She fits right in here. She struggles to act normal but that proves impossible, so eventually she stops trying and just acts foolish. Once she gives herself that freedom, it becomes kind of fun. The girl next to her joins Esther as an assistant and they whip out many more piles of dough. The girl is small, cute and endlessly smiling, with a delightfully weird mind that cannot keep up with a single thought for more than five seconds before changing the subject. Esther smiles from sheer exhaustion as she tries to keep up with her stories. She begins to laugh so hard that she nearly pees in her skirt and she has to take a walk to the bushes. As she pees, she plays with a little bug that runs away from the yellow waterfall that mysteriously appears from nowhere. Then she realizes that she is actually enjoying being high from smoking jimm, and she finally understands why these people smoke so much of it. She skips back to the kitchen and returns to work with a smile on her face.

After a few hours, the cooks finish preparing lunch, which is acorn bread and a rich stew of duck, wild mushrooms, and potatoes. Lunch is called and everyone gathers in the eating area. After a quick speech from Chief Grym welcoming the visitors who have come for polar day, everyone digs into the food. The stew is a bit bland but very hearty and everyone cheers the cooks for their good work.

After lunch, it is time for games and competitions. The most popular game for the men is Lost Arrow, which is a form of Flying Bird with bow and arrows instead of a boomerang. Every participant gets a special arrow with a certain feather combination on it, which they must aim for a very distant target, a wooden statue of an animal. It takes about three or four tries to hit the target with the arrow because it is so far away. The tricky part is that the arrow cannot hit the ground and the archer must plunk each shot into a tree, log, or something above the ground. Every shot is worth one point to your total score. If your arrow hits the ground or becomes lost, then you must start over at that target's starting point, while keeping your point total. The person who completes the course with the least shots is the winner.

Esther gets a girl to teach her how to shoot a bow, hoping to play, but she is so bad that she decides against it and watches instead. The course is packed with deadly serious archers competing for a big pot of tupas, and her ears ring with vile curses and triumphant cheers, depending on the fortunes of the archer. By the end of the tournament, two men named Gito and Hiot are tied for the lead. Esther joins the growing crowd following them around the course, waiting to see who will win between these two excellent archers. Everyone starts gambling on the two men and cheering them on. The two men put a large wager on the game themselves and the pressure builds higher.

Gito sends his arrow into a grove of trees on the last target and he cannot find it. He searches for a long time, knowing that he will probably lose the competition if it is lost. Many people help him look, but the arrow cannot be found. The other archer searches along with them, as is expected of him, but he quickly becomes impatient.

"You have gone over the time limit," Hiot exclaims. "It is a lost arrow. Start at the beginning."

"Not yet," argues his harried competitor. "I might find it still. It was a strong shot."

"You have gone past the count of five hundred. It is considered 'lost'."

"I will keep looking a while longer," Gito declares. He seems stressed to his limit, as if any moment he's going to explode. "It is such a close game and all of these people have money on me. Give me another count of five hundred."

"There are rules to every game."

"What kind of a man are you?"

"A man who sticks to the rules of the game."

"It is an informal rule. An honorable man would give me another count of five hundred without a second thought."

The crowd gets involved in the argument and things get hot quickly. Finally, everyone turns to an old man named Yasu who has been watching the argument silently. Yasu has no wager on the match and he is known a wise man, so Hiot and Gito agree to let him decide.

"The loser is only a loser if he worries about being inferior and complains that the game is unfair. Then he is a true loser. The winner is only a winner if he is gracious, letting his talents speak for himself. In this case, you have both ruined the game by arguing and getting personal. I say that you are both losers."

Yasu walks slowly away without another word and the crowd laughs and declares this to be a wise judgment. However there is the matter of the large sums of money that have been bet already and there must be an ending. To the great grumbling of those who bet on him, Gito declares his arrow lost and starts over from the beginning of the target. He does his best, but his concentration is already shattered and he cannot catch up. Hiot wins and it is deemed a fair match, but the game feels tainted somehow. There is much grumbling as money is passed from hand to hand.

It is late in the night by the time dinner is ready and everyone is already completely drunk and high and having a crazy time of it by that time. Esther wanders into a sea of wildly swaying people, singing silly songs to the moon and dancing to the ever present drumming of young boys. Another cask of wine is opened and she stands among drunken fools fighting to get their share. She finally gets a bowl full of wine and she takes it to the fire and grabs a seat as close as she can get to the flames. She drinks it quickly, so she can use her bowl for food.

Dinner is a heavy affair involving venison, duck, salmon, and something called goop. Esther eats everything but the goop, which looks disgusting. In addition to the meat, there are corn cakes dipped in some kind of animal fat. It is a rich, heavy dinner and Esther is soon stuffed beyond words.

Goop is a stew of organs - liver, brains, eyes, and whatever else the cook cares to throw in. It is considered a delicacy, although not to everyone's taste.

The heavy food combined with the wine makes her very sleepy and she begins to think about a warm, cozy snooze in front of a hot fire. She considers the noise in camp tonight and wonders if she could sleep even if she wanted to. Nobody else seems to be tired. There is drumming and dancing by the biggest fire. The drummers and shouters seem determined to wake up the whole world with their noise, if nothing else. Men are drunk by now and singing in loud voices. A group of several men strip off all their clothes, lock arms, and begin chanting in a loud, singsong voice as they spin in a circle. They sing a bawdy tune about all the girls they have had and begin drumming on each other's rear ends, laughing hysterically whenever there is a particularly good, loud slap. Soon they all have red asses.

There are men running back and forth, grabbing women and swinging them around or grabbing their breasts and biting down. The women shriek and yell as they fight off their male attackers. A group of girls are having a screaming contest, trying to see who can be the loudest. They scream themselves hoarse and then they keep going anyway. Several young boys keep hitting a camp dog, just to hear him go crazy from barking. Esther wonders how these people could be called the Owl tribe, creatures known for utter silence, mystery and subtlety. They should be called the loon tribe, she thinks.

She is soon to change her mind about that. Late in the night, she wanders away from the village, searching for some peace and quiet. She settles down underneath a tree, curls up under her blanket on top of her cloak and closes her eyes. She is almost asleep, when suddenly she is awakened by a noise above her.

"Whoo! Whoo!"

There is an owl above her. It repeats its call and then another owl flies up to join it.

"Whoo! Whoo!"

Esther is amazed. She has seldom been so close to an owl in her life. It is right above her, a creepy black shadow, framed by the glow of the moon. It is a great horned owl, which is the largest of all owls, and this one is as big as a raccoon. There is an air of mystery and wisdom about it, as if it holds secrets she can only guess at. Her heart catches in her throat as she stares at it. It seems to be staring back at her and that fills her with dread. What is the great bird thinking? Is it wondering if she is an enemy? She feels as if it is staring right into her.

"Whoo! Whoo!"

"Whoo! Whoo!"

It seems to be hooting to her now. Her blood freezes. She wonders if owls ever attack people. Only if a baby is nearby, she has been told. Could an owl hurt her? Why would it? She's too big to eat. It is only communicating.

Two of the owls begin to fight suddenly, rattling the tree branches and slamming into each other violently. Esther jumps up, frightened out of her wits. She moves to another tree and settles underneath it. The owls pay no attention to her movements. They are viciously sparring with each other and too obsessed to notice her.

"Whoo! Whoo! Whoo! Whoo! Whoo! Whoo! Whoo! Whoo!"

There is another one. Or is it four? She has found a whole village. They are all going at once, singing their weird, spooky song as loud as they can. They hoot and holler and flap and fight. Esther is mesmerized at the show before her. She laughs at her earlier judgment, that owls are quiet and secretive. These owls are louder than the Owl tribe.

One of them leaves the tree and flies right over her head and its great wings make it look huge and menacing as it descends. She throws up her hands in fear and backs up against the tree, but it flies harmlessly over her head. It is probably hunting some juicy mouse somewhere, not that any mouse would be crazy enough to hang around here, with the owl orchestra singing away in the trees.

Her peaceful repose is shattered. She can get no rest anywhere. She gets up and walks to a spot far from the owls and sets up camp there. Finally she has a little peace and quiet, but her nerves are shot and it takes her a long time to fall asleep.

Owl 7'

Eagle moon

Esther sits alone by the fire, bored and restless. It is too easy here, with free food, a free place to sleep and no need for work. These people are so generous, that she wants for nothing, which makes things really dull. She is used to a steady stream of challenges to occupy herself and now there is nothing to do. And she has many other complaints. The weather is gloomy and there is no sun to lay out in. The food here is not interesting and the sweat lodge is *still* not finished. She has been moping around for the past few days, wondering what to do with herself.

The man in whose teepee she has been sleeping is hardly there. He is a strange man named Elso, with tight curly hair and a little boy's face set upon a man's body. She met him the day after the full moon party and when he found out she was a visitor with no place to stay, he insisted she stay in his teepee. She assumed he expected something in return, but he was so cute and nice that she didn't mind if he did. But he left that afternoon and didn't return until yesterday. He said a few words to her and went right to sleep, as if he hadn't slept since the day he left.

She watches him all morning, as he helps them finish the sweat lodge. He clings precariously to the roof, lashing sticks together with a stout rope that he wove himself. It seems certain that the roof would cave in with his weight on it, but he is so skillful and nimble, that he seems to defy gravity and every other natural law.

She asks a couple of people about Numei's friend, Tumock, but nobody has seen him. Then she wanders over to the kitchen to see if help is needed, but nobody is cooking. She walks to the fire instead to watch a large group of people obsessively involved in a great chess tournament. They play for a big rabbit fur blanket. While she is watching, Esther meets a young girl who teaches her a game that is more or less "guess the hand the rock is in". It is a popular gambling game learned from the Zesti. The winner, who will be paid a tupa by the loser, is the first one to collect ten sticks, which means you have won ten times and the other player has lost ten times. The best part of the game is that one must sing a song while moving the stone from hand to hand behind the back. Each player has their own special song, that nobody else may sing without permission. So while they play, Esther begins to come up with her own unique 'luck' song.

As soon as she begins to develop a good song, her luck begins to get better and better. It is like magic. She wins several games in a row, thanks to her special song, and she is three tupas richer. She makes sure to remember that song for the future. Then she spends the rest of the day learning all of the games that everyone plays. Her favorite is a game played with little stones on a woven reed mat. It is called Bu and she is told that it is a very popular game in China. She wishes she had a deck of cards, so she could teach them all poker. She used to spend many nights watching Miguel and Fermin play poker, and she knows the game well. She could make a lot of money quickly, before everyone caught on to her tricks.

Bu is known today as Go.

Grym, chief of the Owl tribe, sits in front of his teepee, watching the happenings of the village. He absentmindedly whittles an arrow while he watches the sweat lodge being finished. He has just gone over the winter provisions and everything is stocked and full for the coming winter. The tribe is prosperous and they have found a perfect spot for winter camp this year. A small piece of unclaimed land with river access is a great find in this crowded land, even if you have to hike down a steep hill to get to it. Everything is going well and that worries him, because he believes that when things go well for too long, then eventually they must go sour. That is a bitter lesson he has learned from too much gambling.

It doesn't take long for his prophecy to come true. It is almost as if just by thinking it, he makes the bad luck instantly happen. It starts this afternoon, when three Zesti appear in camp. They stand outside the village for some time, just staring. The tallest has an air of leadership. He wears a cape of deerskin and a simple skirt of tule grasses. There is a smaller man standing next to him who is very strong and carries a long spear. The third man is the strangest of the three. He is an old man with long, grey hair, covered from head to toe with animal talismans of all types. He has an aura of power and malice, judging by his eyes, which are not friendly.

Everyone comes from their teepees or their chores to see the Zesti. They try to communicate, but of course neither speaks the other's language. Every few miles, one comes upon a different language in this land and it is hard to find a common tongue that you can share. The taller one shows several people his headdress and they all nod and remark on what a beautiful headdress it is. Finally someone understands that he wants to speak to the chief and a search begins for Grym. The Zesti are usually very formal with strangers and they ask to speak to the chief first before speaking to the rest of the people. Chief Grym is found and he comes forward and welcomes them. He speaks in a manner that is typical of the local Zesti.

"Come friends, come by the fires, and warm yourself on this cold day. Let us offer you some fresh meat we have caught."

They just stare at him.

"Ah, yes...Yasu! Yasu! Where is Yasu?"

The old man who spoke up during the game of Lost Arrow is summoned. He hobbles from his teepee slowly, using his cane to walk. Yasu speaks the Pomo language, which is often used as a local trade dialect among the central coast Indians. (Lucky for him, because he is old and crippled and of no other use to the tribe.) Yasu walks up to the visitors and speaks slowly to them, trying to pronounce the words correctly. They smile at his accent, but they seem to understand. The two younger ones nod politely and enter the camp, but the old man refuses to come. He stands near the back, mumbling to himself and shaking his head.

"What's with the old one?" asks Grym. "What's he saying?"

"Cursed if I know what he is saying," mumbles Yasu, "but it can't be good. He's not what I'd call friendly."

"Ask him what is the matter."

Yasu speaks to him a moment. The old man stares at Yasu coldly, but he says nothing. Yasu seems afraid suddenly and he turns away and walks off.

"This is very strange," Yasu muses. "That old man is a shaman. He wears a string of snake fangs and a bear's claw. His very presence suggests that this is not a friendly call."

Grym shrugs.

"He's just a grumpy old man, as far as I can tell. I don't buy all that shaman stuff."

"I warn you. Be careful what you say to this chief."

Grym leads the two Zesti over to the fire and hands them some meat. They sniff it and eat. The taller one nods and says a string of words.

"He says thank you for the meat," translates Yasu. "He says that he is pleased to meet the chief of the new tribe that has come to this land. He is the chief of the tribe who lives upriver. His name is Veekta. He wants to meet his new neighbors and find out about them."

"Tell him I am chief of this tribe and I too am pleased to meet him."

Yasu tells Veetka, who nods politely, but offers no smile to match Grym's. Veekta eats some more meat and continues to examine the village quietly. He takes particular note of the swords and steel knives hanging from the belts of the men. He steals a quick glance at the old shaman who stands outside the village and then quickly looks away.

Veetka speaks to Yasu again. Yasu nods and translates.

"How do you like this land to which you have come?"

"Fine, fine. It's a beautiful spot," Grym says absentmindedly.

Yasu tells his offhand reply to the chief, but Veekta doesn't seem satisfied with the answer. He shakes his head and says nothing. Grym looks at Yasu suddenly and nods his head slowly, understanding the truth of the situation. This is not simply a neighborly call. Veetka is fishing for something.

"Where does your tribe come from? We have not seen dwellings like these in this land before," Veetka says to Yasu.

"We are from this area. We are one of the Twelve Tribes. The Owl tribe."

Upon hearing the name of the tribe, Veetka becomes noticeably frightened. He stares at Grym as if he claimed to be a demon from the other world, come for Veetka's children.

"Owls are fearsome creatures," says Veetka, after a long silence. "They work bad magic on the land. How can you be a friend of the Owl spirit?"

"I assure you, we do not work...bad magic," explains Grym, having heard many Zesti speak of the owl being a bad spirit. "We merely seek to embody the fine qualities of that great bird. Owls are fearsome hunters."

"A great hunter is owl," agrees Veetka. "They hunt at night and fly as silently as a soft breeze. They are difficult to see or hear. But we have seen and heard *you* many times."

Grym's eyes turn to slits. He stares at Veetka, who looks as innocent as he can.

"Tell this man to speak plainly. What is it he wishes to say?" growls Grym.

"No, Grym -"

"I want to know what is going on," Grym says angrily. "Ask this chief why he has come here."

Yasu shakes his head.

"More tact is required, Grym."

"Tact? Tact be damned! I am a plain man."

"You don't know these people like I do. We cannot just discuss these things openly. We must speak politely and of things which do not pertain to the true purpose of their visit. That is their way. It is not polite to 'get to the point' with these people."

"It is a strange way, and I do not see the purpose in it," retorts Grym. "It certainly is not our way. Tell him that. Tell him to speak his mind."

"But, Grym -"

"Tell him!" Grym shouts angrily. "I order it."

Yasu says something to Veetka in a quiet voice. Veetka stands up in a huff and begins to yell angry words, shouting and waving his arms dramatically as he speaks.

"He says that he is insulted. He says that we come to his land and set up our village without asking permission of the neighboring tribes. We make noise at all hours of the day and night. He does not know how the tribe of the owl - the silent hunter - can make so much noise. We scare away the fish in the river and the deer in the hills, which are the main food of their people. They come here to see what we are about and perhaps to discuss matters between tribes. They are curious about us and try to talk to us and then he is insulted. He will certainly remember how he has been treated here when he returns to tell his people about us."

Veetka slowly backs away, with his warrior flanking him. Finally, they come to the place where the old shaman stands. The shaman starts speaking in low tones to the chief and Veekta nods unhappily. Then he speaks to Yasu one last time.

"They will be back," Yasu says, translating. "He must think and discuss with his council of elders."

"Tell him that he is welcome anytime," says Grym spiritedly. "We are not a stubborn people and are willing to listen."

Yasu tells him. Veetka nods and then walks away with his party.

"That didn't go well," says Yasu unhappily.

"It takes time to make friends," says Grym. "Next time, it will go better."

Tonight, Esther relaxes in Elso's teepee, sitting cross-legged on a mat. She stares at a reading candle, not doing anything in particular other than trying to stay awake. When she cannot stand the boredom any more, she struggles to read a book he loaned her. It is a book on the local Zesti, a compiled study written by several different members of the Raven tribe. It is interesting, but difficult reading for her limited skills. At least the pictures keep her entertained.

The candle soon goes out, but to see the book well requires both a good-sized fire and a candle held up right underneath the page she is reading. There is only a piece of the little candle left, so she lights that little piece and sticks it into a crack in an upside down basket that he uses for a table. She has to lean really close to it to see the book and then she continues to read until she becomes too tired and the words start getting all fuzzy. Then she gives up and just glories in her ignorance for the rest of the night. She makes shapes with shadows in the candlelight and wishes she had a child handy to laugh at her shapes. Perhaps she should go borrow one from somebody.

Later, she goes out to see the night. She wanders around in a daze, staring at the stars, before she finally settles by the large fire pit. She stares at it in a bored stupor, wishing there was somebody interesting around to make the night fun. Unwilling to sleep, but too tired to do anything else, she just sits there vacantly.

Then a bright glow from Elso's teepee catches her eye. It looks like Elso came home and stoked up the fire, but that seems strange to her somehow. Elso went inside the newly completed sweat lodge and that door is still barred. Nobody has come out of there yet. The glow grows and Esther begins to get a nervous feeling in her stomach. She runs to the teepee to see what it is.

The basket is on fire! The candle must have burnt down and torched it. She stares at it, stunned, and then watches the teepee skin catch fire. And then it dawns on her in horror that she is burning Elso's teepee down.

She looks around wildly for something to put it out with, but she cannot find the water bucket anywhere. She begins to panic, as the flames crawl higher upon the walls. She doesn't call out for help, because she doesn't want everyone to have to run out of their warm homes and panic and scream. Then the whole village will know how stupid she is! She looks around wildly for inspiration, and realizes that she isn't quite in control of her body right now. She runs around like a panicking squirrel, until she finds a basket that can hold water, and then she runs out into the night at top speed. She has only a few seconds to spare before the fire is out of control and she looks around desperately for some water.

"Oh my god!" she moans. "I need water now! Where's water? Water!"

Finally she sees a bucket outside a nearby teepee that is full of water. Throwing down her basket, she grabs the bucket and runs into the teepee. The flames are crawling higher as she desperately releases the dirty water onto the wall of the teepee. The fire explodes in a hiss of steam and then snuffs out. Smoke rises to the sky and there is an unpleasant aroma of charcoal, burnt animal skin and guilt mixed together. But the fire is out! Breathing a sigh of relief, she drops the bucket numbly and falls to the ground in a daze. She sits there for a long time, watching the smoke slowly dissipate and trying to calm her screaming nerves.

Elso returns an hour later, to find a thoroughly ruined teepee. She tells him what happened in a shaky voice. When he finally speaks, his response is typical.

"You can't just leave a candle sticking in a basket like that. That basket was easy tinder."

"I know it was stupid. I don't need you to tell me that," she snaps.

He examines the teepee more closely and sees that it is easily repairable with a good craftsman. The basket is done for, but easy to replace.

"Could have been worse."

She agrees wholeheartedly.

"I'll patch it up," he says. "Easy."

"I'll pay for whatever materials you need," she says glumly.

"Don't worry about it. I have some extra strips of elk hide that will do nicely."

He throws the basket out the door and begins to clean up the ash that has lighted everywhere.

"You improved the smell in here," he says with a smile, trying to lighten the mood.

She nods, not really hearing him. She has been feeling stupid for the past hour and she is not going to laugh and ruin that feeling. But as she watches him clean up, it occurs to her that there is nothing to feel upset about. The fire was put out easily, Elso isn't angry with her and she doesn't have to pay him or repair it herself. So she shrugs it off and helps him clean up the ash on the ground.

Owl 9'

Raccoon moon

On this freezing cold morning, Grym finally gets a chance to use the new sweat lodge. He strips off his clothes and stokes up the fire, which has nearly gone out. He will have to talk to the old man in charge of keeping the fire going about sticking to his duties. No sooner does he get the sweat lodge hot, when Hyu, the blacksmith, storms into the lodge in a rage and begins shouting.

"We were robbed last night! That dirty toad went into my shop and took everything! Took my own sword too!"

He starts reciting all the things that were taken. It is a long list, which includes five swords, four knives, a steel shield, a few tools and a pot. Whoever stole them knew just where to go, for Hyu, the blacksmith, repairs all of the steel for the tribe. Grym frowns more and more as the list goes on, for he will no doubt be asked to replace some of those items from his own storehouse. But he patiently allows Hyu to finish.

"Your own blade was taken also," Hyu says finally. "I just finished sharpening it and did not have a chance to return it."

"No!" shouts Grym, his eyes opening wide. "Who did this? I'll have their head on a pole for this! I'll strangle the miserable skulking thieves with my own hands!"

Grym thinks of the recent visitors from upstream and hopes it was not them. That would be extremely bad news. It could mean a war.

"I have an idea," Hyu growls. "We believe that Wilu is back. A strange man came upon a young girl and tried to seduce her last night. He grabbed her and began to suck on her neck. Luckily she screamed and there were men nearby. Viril was nearby and he chased him off. He swears that it was Wilu he saw running away."

This makes Grym frown even more. It certainly sounds like Wilu and if that scoundrel is up to his old tricks again, then he will have to be taken in hand this time. Grym promised the people that if

Wilu was seen in the area again, he would be hunted down and dealt with once and for all.

"Go around to your neighbors and ask them if they saw Wilu by your tent. Ask them if they saw anybody strange in camp last night. Return to me and if we are sure that it is Wilu, then we will hunt him down like the coyote hunts the rabbit. Swiftly and without mercy."

Hyu runs off and Grym sits down and puts his head in his hands. This is upsetting news. He loves that sword. It is the perfect height and weight for him and it has saved his life in battle. He can beat almost any man in the tribe when he wields it in a practice battle. It is a truly personal loss for him and he swears that he will get it back. Once he has made this oath, he tries to forget about it and just concentrate on the sweat. Now he really needs it, because he can feel his muscles knotting up from the bad news. He is so upset, that he doesn't even bother to greet the three beautiful young girls who come into the lodge for an early morning sweat.

Wilu's sad story began many years ago, when he fell in love with a girl who didn't like him. He had grown up with Jula and she was a beauty, so it was not surprising that he loved her. Unfortunately for him, she liked Utai, who was a craftsman with great potential. They joined in marriage and Wilu was expected to get over it. But he did not get over it. He brooded on it.

The boys in the village had always been mean to Wilu. He was never good at anything and they laughed at him and pushed him around. Losing Jula was the last straw. Wilu started following the girl around desperately, trying to win her back. No matter how many times she rebuffed him, he would show up at her house when Utai was gone. Eventually Jula got upset and told Utai about Wilu. Utai went to find Wilu, knowing that he was a pushover, and told him to stay away from his girl. Then, to be sure that his point was made, he pushed Wilu to the ground and smeared a dollop of horse dung on Wilu's face.

This was the last straw for poor Wilu. As soon as Utai's back was turned, he grabbed a rock and hit him over the head with all the rage he had kept inside for his entire life. The rock had a sharp point, which opened a big gash in Utai's head. Utai was knocked unconscious and his head was bleeding. Wilu hit him twice more in the head before his rage subsided.

Suddenly realizing what he had done, Wilu panicked. He tried numbly to stop the bleeding, but he could not. He eventually ran for help, but it was no use. Utai died that afternoon. The village was in an uproar. Wilu was tied to a pole and the people threw rotten meat and small stones at him. He sat there numbly, in a state of shock, as bits of rotting flesh clung to his face and stones cut his cheek. He didn't seem to care. He was simply unable to believe that he had killed another member of the tribe. The people were angry and bitter and they all hated him. They had loved the dead boy and his wonderful hands, which produced such great crafts. They felt no such affection for Wilu, who had always been a loner and produced nothing.

It was one of the few times that there was one hundred percent consensus in the council and the tribe. Wilu would receive the harshest penalty in the Twelve Tribes. He was to become an outcast. Nobody in the Owl tribe would ever speak to him again or help him in any way. Also, word was sent to the other tribes that this boy was a killer and should not be taken in. Wilu was sent away with only a small basket full of supplies and the people turned their backs on him. He walked off alone into the wide world, devastated and feeling utterly alone.

He didn't come near the tribe for a long time, and the people slowly forgot about him. After a year had gone by, he began to show his face near camp. He would watch them, mostly the women. He stole many things that he needed. He had learned to be quiet and sneaky and he was hard to catch. The people put up with his thievery and his spying for a long time. Every now and then, he would come upon a little girl and try to seduce her. He never raped them, he just tried to kiss them until they ran away.

And now he is back again, stealing the tribe's precious steel. Steel is the key to the tribe's survival and he has taken much of it. Why would Wilu need so many swords anyway? Is he selling them? Perhaps he is outfitting an army? Or maybe he is just being irritating? Either way, things are going to go very badly for him.

A horn sounds to signal a tribal meeting. Esther stands up and stretches her aching legs. She has been sitting cross-legged for some time and is stiff from lack of movement. She has been quizzing Elso for hours, trying to learn everything he knows about the history of the Twelve Tribes. He has graciously answered all of her questions, while sewing a new flap of skin onto the burnt section of the teepee. The sun set and she didn't even notice, so absorbed was she. But now there is something exciting happening and Esther walks outside to see what all the fuss is about. She hopes that dinner will be served at the meeting. It will feel good to do something physical, even if it is just stuffing food into her belly.

Outside, many of the people are gathered together in a circle around the fire, having an open council about Wilu. Esther walks toward the fire to listen to what they are saying. Hyu, the blacksmith, is telling all of the things that were stolen. Many of them belonged to the gathered people, who are very angry.

"He is a dangerous nuisance," Hyu shouts. "The people are tired of him. Tomorrow, we ride out to find him. If we find him, we will end his miserable life."

There is agreement from many and protests from a few. Meanwhile, Arasu, brother of Wilu, sits quietly, with a pained expression on his face. He looks around at all the angry faces and knows that he must say something. He slowly stands, prepared to inspire the wrath of the entire tribe.

"He is my brother. My blood. Although he is a disgrace to the family, I wish him to live," he says grimly. "I will take responsibility for dealing with him."

"Arasu has spoken," says Grym. "Arasu pleads for his brother's life. Despite the seriousness of the charges, we cannot refuse to hear his plea. Arasu wants to take responsibility. Does anyone care to challenge this?"

Nobody speaks at first. Arasu is well liked and his request is heartfelt. He has pleaded for mercy for his brother and everyone understands his predicament. But Hyu looks around angrily and feels great annoyance at the sudden shift in mood.

"He will never stop until he is dead," Hyu insists vehemently. "We have tried to run him off before."

Many people mumble their agreement, although nobody looks Arasu in the eyes.

"He will stop," Arasu says grimly. "I will get back what he has taken and tell him to stay away from us."

"That is not enough," says Hyu. "He must be punished if he is to learn a lesson. Find the stolen goods and bring him back here for punishment. And that will be enough."

Most of the men nod approval at this action. Arasu sees the anger in his people, and knows that his brother is in danger.

"I will do this. Provided that it is not too harsh."

"Very well," Grym says. "Arasu will lead a hunting party in the morning. He will do whatever is necessary to get back what his brother has stolen. He will bring him back here for punishment. And then, we will see what happens."

"We will see what happens!" the men shout, agreeing with this age-old philosophy.

"So who will go? I suggest a party of four."

Elso has always liked Arasu, although he doesn't know him very well, and he stands up before anyone else and offers to ride with him. Arasu gladly accepts, glad to have Elso along. Elso is cool-headed, skilled with his hands, and very useful. Ysu, the best tracker in the Owl tribe, offers to go and his help is gratefully accepted also. Grym makes a special request that his son, Viril, a brave warrior and hunter, also goes. Arasu agrees reluctantly, but he is a little worried about Viril's hot temper and wishes he wouldn't.

They agree to leave tomorrow at first light and then there is nothing left to say. The meeting is disbanded. Dinner is nowhere near completion, so Esther wanders over to the kitchen to help. But instead of preparing dinner, they put her to work roasting recently gathered bay nuts for breakfast tomorrow. The old women who run the kitchen take their sweet time preparing the acorn mush and roasting the birds and it is a few hours before dinner is finally served.

Arasu sits in the newly completed sweat lodge, trying to purify himself for the difficult day tomorrow. He smells the charcoal smell of the fire and the rancid smell of the burnt hides that encloses it like a cocoon. He brushes a frayed root against his body in the way of the Zesti and watches the sweat drip in rivulets down his body. He tries to clear his mind as his tight muscles loosen. He sits in silence, all alone in his little womb. He has never been much for sweat lodges, but today it seems the only thing to make him feel better.

His thoughts spin in a whirlwind of confusion. He knows that he is partly to blame for this situation and he is now responsible to fix it. Against the strict orders of the Owl council, he has seen his brother many times. Although, he never got along well with Wilu, his mother had always been very close to him. She was always much closer to him than she ever was to Arasu. She was devastated when Wilu was made an outcast. She sat around miserably, losing joy in everything, while Arasu had to take care of her. Just to make his own life easier, he tracked his brother down one day and brought him to see their mother. It lifted her spirits greatly to see him, made her much more pleasant and optimistic and her health improve. It made Wilu feel better too and he began to show up on his own.

At first, Arasu didn't speak to his brother much or give him anything at all. He tried to keep to the spirit of the law, if not to its word. But then he began to feel sorry for Wilu and helped him out in small ways. A bag of food here and there. Some arrows to help him hunt. They even started speaking to each other again and his brother began to hang around more and more often. For a while, Arasu was practically taking care of his poor brother, who was having a difficult time living on his own.

But then his brother began to spend more and more time away. He learned to live by his wits and became proud and difficult. Every time Arasu saw him, he was more and more strange and withdrawn. He developed a hatred for the Owl tribe, whom he felt abandoned him. He developed many uncouth habits, including approaching young girls who didn't know his face and trying to seduce them. Worst of all, he began stealing. One day he was caught and beaten with a stick and then he disappeared for a long time. Why does he return now? Arasu wonders if he knows that their mother is now dead.

After awhile, Arasu becomes dizzy and dehydrated and he cannot sit in the sweat lodge any longer. He bathes in the creek and then goes to the dinner gathering. Everyone is nice to him and tries to cheer him up by telling him that they will not be too difficult on his brother for his sake. Their kindness only makes him more stressed and his stomach begins to ache and his back gets very tight. There is nothing to do but go back into his warm womb again. Back in the sweat lodge, he sits while others come and go. He does not speak to anyone, only brushes himself with a frayed sedge root and revels in the simplicity of heat.

Owl 10'

Early in the morning, Elso puts the finishing touches on the repairs to his teepee. It looks pretty good. He has sewn and patched the hole so well, that it is difficult to tell from a distance that it had been damaged at all. Esther watches him and compares notes on sewing techniques. She has never met a man who is as handy with a bone needle and sinew as Elso is. He teaches her how to make a repair waterproof, by smearing it with a resin of boiled brains, the standard Zesti fix all. After he finishes, he packs his things together quickly in preparation for his adventure.

"I'll be gone a few days at the most," he tells her. "But probably only two."

"Is it going to be dangerous?" she asks.

"Dangerous?" he laughs. "Four men looking for one man?"

"But isn't he a killer?"

"Well yeah, but it was a cowardly murder under stupid circumstances. This fool is no threat to anybody but himself. We're just going to get back what he took from us."

"Oh."

"Want to come?" he asks suddenly.

"With you?"

"Sure. Why not? There are some beautiful mountains east of here and we can do some rock climbing. There's good rock in the mountains."

"Are you sure it won't be dangerous?"

"Wilu is no threat. Trust me."

"Isn't it going to rain?"

He looks up at the sky and shrugs.

"Is it far?"

"We'll be on horseback."

Esther considers. She planned to spend the day winning back all the money she lost gambling yesterday. She gambled on Bu, which was a mistake, because she's not that good at it. But last night she found herself a powerful rock and she is going to play 'guess the hand the rock is in' and sing her power song and win it all back. She has been looking forward to games by the main fire all morning. But she sees that Elso really wants her to come and she hates to disappoint him because he has been so nice to her. And he looks so cute standing there with his stuffed burden basket, packed tightly with more tools, weapons and gear than he could ever use.

"Sure," she says after a long pause.

"Great," he says with a grin. "Get ready. We leave shortly."

They set off on four horses late in the morning. Esther gets strange looks from the other men in the party when they see her strap her basket to Elso's horse. But after Elso makes introductions, they welcome her to the adventure and it is settled. They mount up and thunder out of the village at a fast gallop.

Because the Owl tribe moves around so much, Arasu does not know exactly where his brother might be camped. Back when his mother was alive, Wilu used to follow the migrations of the tribe at a distance and set up suitable camp as he went. Arasu guesses that he might use an old camp a few miles from here, at the base of a hill that looks like an ocean wave. It is the best guess they have, so they ride off in that direction.

The Owl tribe horses are uncommonly swift as well as large and they tear up the road as they race up a narrow path into the mountains. Esther has never ridden a horse this fast before and she holds on tightly to Elso as the large horse crashes through brush and foliage. She nestles against him and tries to relax and enjoy the speed. This is hilly country and the road sometimes races along a cliff's edge. Esther looks down at the long tumbling gorge that falls into a rocky river and gets dizzy with fear. She finally has to ask Elso to lead the horse to the other side of the path, for she feels that she is going to pitch over at any moment.

Late in the afternoon, they arrive at the little nook described by Arasu, which is located near a tiny creek. They have to get off their horses and climb down a hill to get to his camp. The ground is slippery and they slip and slide down a mud streaked trail, holding on to roots of trees as they make their way to the bottom. Here the stream bubbles merrily into a still pool and they find traces of recent fires and a few squirrel carcasses. It certainly seems as if Wilu is here.

"He lives off squirrels," muses Viril. "How pathetic-"

Arasu shoots him a look and Viril immediately shuts his mouth.

Ysu does a lengthy examination of the surrounding area. He finds a couple of broken arrows and bits and pieces of things that were once useful. He spends a good deal of time examining his tracks and even tastes the ash in the fire.

"He has been here at least three days ago," he pronounces at last.

"Then he must have followed us from the summer camp," mumbles Viril, looking around as if the man might suddenly appear out of the brush.

"He's close," Arasu says. "I can feel him."

Arasu kicks the squirrel carcass, thinking about what life must be like for his brother.

"He likes to sleep in the same places over and over," Arasu adds. "We're alike in that way. He probably did follow us here and he used this old spot because he feels comfortable here."

"You've been in contact with him, haven't you?" Ysu says in a quiet voice. "That's why you knew he would be here."

Arasu looks away guiltily, but says nothing.

"I'm not judging you," adds Ysu. "It is no easy task to banish your brother. I don't know if I could do it either."

They all fall into a long, moody silence, punctuated only by the cry of nearby hawks and other twittering birds. Nobody knows what to do next. Ysu starts examining the ground, looking for a pattern to the footprints that might suggest where he has gone. Viril stabs at bushes with his sword, as if he might find Wilu crouching in one.

"Is it possible that he heard our horses and fled?" Elso asks, breaking the silence.

They all look at him and nod in agreement.

"There's an old trick," says Ysu, after a long silence, "that I've used to hunt deer. It is quite effective. Two of us ride off with the horses and two stay here quietly. If he is here, then he'll return when the horses leave. And then the two remaining men nab him. It's either that, or I try to track him."

"The horse idea sounds much simpler," Elso says. "I like simple."

"You and Viril go," Arasu says. "Me and Elso will wait here. And Esther too, if she wants."

"Viril should stay with you," Ysu says, looking at Viril, who nods in agreement. "He's the best with a sword and Wilu now has a blade."

"My brother is no great warrior," says Arasu. "I could beat him alone."

Agreeing, the two men ride off with the four horses in tow. They will not return until they hear the sound of the shrill whistle in Arasu's hand or until many hours have passed. Soon Elso, Arasu, and Esther are alone in the deepening twilight. Elso begins to set up a tarp by stringing it up between trees. Arasu rummages around in the food supplies and finds some cold venison for dinner. He passes it around for everyone to take a piece.

"Can I start a fire?" Esther asks.

"No," says Elso's voice, floating from high above the ground. "Wilu would see it."

She looks up and sees Elso, hanging from a tree with a rope in his hand. He is busy angling the tarp for the best rain protection.

"Good point," Arasu says. "But it's sure going to be a cold night for us."

"It's not cold out," the voice from the tree intones and then a body drops from a high branch and hits the ground with a thunk.

"It will be."

"Cold is a choice," Elso says, repeating his favorite saying.

Owl 11'

Swan moon

It drizzles all day long and they huddle underneath a tree miserably, trying to stay dry. Elso took the tarp down early in the morning, as it was too easy to spot from a distance, so they are forced to sit uncovered, enduring the trickles of water pouring down from the leaves and onto their heads. They do not talk much, except for a few whispered complaints. Time passes slowly when you're waiting in the rain for someone that may never show up at all.

"I've had enough," Arasu whispers. "We should call the others and set up camp somewhere else. I want a hot fire and a little protection from this rain."

Elso nods in agreement. Arasu is just about to blow the horn, when they hear singing off in the distance, coming steadily closer.

"Is it him?" asks Esther in a whisper.

Arasu strains to listen to the voice and then nods slowly. They hear someone walking and then the sound of a burden basket falling to the earth.

"Let's go," Arasu says, his mouth set.

The three of them crawl from out of their hiding place in the bushes and face Wilu. Wilu startles and looks from one to the other with wild, panic stricken eyes. Once he identifies his brother, he relaxes considerably. Wilu is a funny looking man, with a big nose and wild, staring eyes. He has long hair and a thick beard, covering a grimy, dirty face. His clothes are stained and tattered and he smells strongly too, which leads Esther to conclude that hygiene does not seem to be a major need in his life. He wears several talismans around his neck, such as a coyote paw, a squirrel's tail and vulture's feathers.

Arasu stares in great surprise, never having seen his brother look this wild before. He seems like another person altogether. These are not the eyes of his brother, but seem possessed by some other person. This lean, strong body is not his brother's pudgy frame. He has grown hard and tough from his adventures in the wild. He wears a sword at his side now and seems more dangerous than any of them suspected. Arasu wonders if his brother would draw it against him.

"Hello Wilu," Arasu says quietly, his shock slowly fading.

"It's been a long time," says Wilu in a nasal voice. "The brother, who has not come to see Wilu in a long time."

"How are you, Wilu?"

Wilu notices them all staring at his sword and he puts his hand upon it self-consciously.

"I know that the brother has only come to take from me what is mine," he says with a cockeyed smile, as if he sees through his brother's pathetic act quite easily. "He has not come to bring me to my mother because he has stopped caring. I, who am the eldest. Unfairly cast out and abandoned. But do not worry about me. I live a good life out here. I have many friends."

He shows them his talismans, to show that he has friends or at least pieces of friends. Then he shuffles nervously, blinking his eyes over and over again. Arasu feels his heart sinking as he watches this strange behavior and listens to this strange speech. He sees that his brother has gone truly crazy at last. He doesn't have the heart anymore to take him into town to be laughed at and punished. He also doesn't have the heart to tell his brother that their mother is dead. Wilu has obviously suffered enough.

"I need the things you took," Arasu says, in a voice meant to be comforting. "The tribe is angry. They want to punish you. Perhaps I can protect you, if you return everything."

"What more could they do? What else? I hate them. I hate them all. I answer to none of them. These things are mine."

Wilu stares at Esther, as if seeing her for the first time. A glint comes to his eyes and he continues to stare at her greedily, as if Arasu has brought her here as a present for him.

"I'll give you my own things in trade," Arasu says. "Whatever you need. Just give back what you stole from Hyu, so the people won't be angry."

"No! I care nothing for him," he says angrily, putting his hand to his sword and backing away. "I will not -"

"Wilu," says Arasu gently, "I'm here to help you. Give us what is not rightfully yours and we will give you what will be rightfully yours. You will be taken care of."

"I found those things. They are mine. It was my power that found them. Hyu is nothing. I have the greater power now. I have grown strong. I have been trained by the spirits to find whatever I need. I am guided by the spirits that help men."

"We found you," says Elso suddenly. "What does that say about 'greater power'?"

"I will trade this sword for the woman," Wilu says suddenly, without a trace of irony.

Arasu sighs, knowing that he cannot talk to his brother like one talks to an ordinary man. Wilu has left sanity far behind. But since he is not rational, he might easily be tricked.

"Mother wants to see you," he says, as one who talks to a young child. "I will take you to see her. Will you come to see our mother?"

Wilu blinks rapidly many times.

"How is Mother?"

"She's good," he says guiltily. "She misses you. She always talks about you. Every single day."

"She misses her Wilu. I want to see her."

"Yes, we'll go to see Mother. I must call my friends back, who have horses. They will take us all to see Mother."

Wilu's eyes narrow.

"You think I am stupid, that I will fall for that trick. When your friends come, they will hurt me. I will not go with them."

He grips the sword tightly, to show that he is not kidding around.

"I will go by foot under cover of night. I will visit her in a few days. And you will keep my secret. You will not betray your own brother. You will not tell the men on horses."

"Only if you bring back everything you have taken from us."

Wilu considers this.

"Some things. Some things I will bring back. Not all."

"Everything," Arasu says firmly. "I'll give you my own sword and knife but you must return everything you have taken."

He looks at Elso with questioning eyes, to see if Elso will go along with his risky plan. Elso nods slowly.

"Thanks," whispers Arasu.

"Do you think he'll cooperate?" whispers Elso back to him.

"Wilu," Arasu says firmly, "Understand me. I cannot protect you unless you bring me everything. And what do you need with four swords anyways?"

Wilu just stares at him suspiciously.

"I need an answer, Wilu. Or we must take them by force."

"They are not here. You'll never find them. I'll never tell."

Arasu stares at Elso helplessly. Elso shrugs, not having any idea what to do. So finally Arasu pulls out the horn and puts it to his lips. He is just about to blow, when Wilu begins gesturing frantically and waving his arms.

"Wilu will bring everything to Mother's house. Don't call the horses," he shouts. "I hate them all. I don't want them here."

"Good," Arasu says with a sigh. "Thank you, Wilu."

"I will see you at Mother's. Don't tell anybody else you saw Wilu."

"You promise you'll come? With *everything?*"

Wilu nods rapidly. Arasu sighs, realizing that he'll have to trust his brother. Then he indicates that they can go now.

"What about the girl," Wilu asks desperately. "How about a kiss for poor Wilu?"

"She's mine," says Elso in a stern voice.

They start to scramble up the hill. When they are near the summit, Arasu blows the horn. They wait up there for a long time, wanting a fire and a hot meal desperately. The sun starts to set and a chill wind blows. Finally, they hear shouting off in the distance. They stand up and follow the sound to its source, where they find Viril waiting for them in the wrong spot.

"Any luck?"

"No," Arasu says quietly. "We didn't find him."

"Too bad," Viril says, shaking his head. "Slippery weasel, isn't he? We're camped over there. There's a fire and some fresh meat. Follow me."

Owl 12'

Elso spends the day hiking with Esther up to some rocks he likes to climb. They scramble up, down and around the rocks, and he shows her how to find purchase on the smallest toe or finger hold. He is an amazing climber. He can climb nearly vertical faces without slipping. She watches him climb and wonders if he likes her. She cannot tell. He has made no moves yet, although they have been up here alone all day. She thinks about when he said "she's mine," and she likes the sound of it very much.

When they return, the others are itching to get home. Ysu spent the day trying to track Wilu, and Arasu wandered around with him and Viril as if he had not seen his brother at all. He felt guilty about leading them on like that, but it seemed the only thing to do to save his brother. If they knew Wilu was coming to see his mother, there would be an armed posse camped in front of his teepee twenty-four hours a day. Finally, Ysu gives up and pronounces the cause lost. Wilu has learned how to avoid leaving a trail. They get their things together and ride home.

They ride through the night, a sliver of moon their only light. Nobody seems worried about crashing into a tree or a large rock. Horses and riders know this land like the backs of their hands and they stay glued to the path the whole way back. This is the Owl tribe after all, and sunlight is apparently a luxury that nobody needs. Nobody speaks on the ride home, lost in musings and looking forward to a comfortable night at home.

Owl 14'

Wolf moon

When Arasu wakes, a quick glance around the room shows that Wilu still hasn't arrived as promised. He sees now that his brother was not to be trusted. It has been three days since they saw him and obviously Wilu would have come by now if he was so desperate to see their mother. Arasu washes up, gets dressed and walks outside to see if breakfast is ready in main circle. He resolves never to help his brother again in any way.

As he walks to the kitchen, Arasu stops dead and gasps in horror. Wilu is tied to a post near camp. He is covered in mud, rotten food and bits of dead flesh. A couple of boys use him for target practice, flinging handfuls of horse dung at him and laughing hysterically. The mother of Utai, the boy Wilu killed, screams curses at him and spits on him. Utai's brother whips him sadistically with a long branch. A good portion of the village seems to enjoy the spectacle immensely and they laugh and shout taunts at Wilu. Only a handful of people, mostly women, try ineffectually to calm everybody down and rescue the poor wretch.

Arasu feels his temper grow hot. He runs to the two boys throwing horse dung and pushes them to the ground in mid throw. He runs toward his brother and steps between him and Utai's furious relatives.

"Back off!" Arasu shouts.

They start screaming at him to get away. Arasu screams back. Then he scoops some of the horse dung off his brother and throws it at Utai's brother, Himtu. Himtu roars in anger and Arasu gets into fighting position, with fists forward and a scowl on his face. Things are just about to turn very ugly, when Grym appears with two men who step between Arasu and Himtu. He shouts at the top of his voice for quiet and the two men restrain the furious Himtu. Everything quiets down at last, although the tension is so thick, you could stick an arrow into it.

"What's going on here?" shouts Grym.

"I will not watch this happen to my brother again!" shouts Arasu. "The next person who throws something at my brother will face my wrath!"

"Agreed," says Grym. "Somebody fetch some water and clean him off."

"He's a killer!" shouts Utai's mother, a withered old woman named Mita.

"He's been punished already!" shouts Arasu in return.

"He should be killed!" Himtu screams.

"Over my dead body!"

"That can be arranged!" shouts Himtu.

"Let's dance!" roars Arasu wildly, getting back into fighting stance. "Let's dance!"

Grym shouts again for silence. Meanwhile, two women run up with buckets of water, dump the water over Wilu's head, and start scrubbing him down with sedge brushes. Arasu relaxes considerably when he sees his brother clean again.

"Let us talk this over," Grym shouts. "Untie the outcast and bring him to my tent. Let the council come, for there is much to discuss. Arasu will come also. And Mita, to speak for Utai's family."

Viril cuts through Wilu's bonds and shoves him in the direction of Grym's tent. Arasu bristles, but says nothing. He senses that everyone is angry with him and he begins to fear for himself. Soon they are all gathered in Grym's large teepee. There are six members of the council gathered, all tribal elders, along with Wilu, Arasu, Mita, and Viril.

"Your brother came to see you last night," Grym explains as they walk. "Luckily he was spotted by the ever vigilant Ysu, apprehended, and brought to me. I talked to Wilu late last night. He told me that you saw him a few days ago. You told him to visit his mother."

"He promised to bring all that he had stolen," Arasu says, his head hanging in shame at being found out. "I thought I could resolve this quietly."

"He didn't bring anything but the sword on his belt," scolds Grym.

"You let me track him all day long," snarls Ysu, who is one of the council, "when you knew exactly where he was. You are a shame to your tribe."

Arasu says nothing. He only glares at his brother, source of so many of his problems for his whole life. He wishes he didn't feel compelled to defend his pathetic brother, who certainly doesn't deserve his help.

"Wilu," says Grym seriously. "I'll ask you again. Where are these things?"

"Wilu will never tell," Wilu sneers. "He hates you all. Where is justice for Wilu? Wilu gets no pity and so he has no pity for you. Or your questions."

"He'll tell if we force him to," says Bua, a creepy old man with deep-set eyes in a drawn face. "I say we beat the information out of him."

"No!" shouts Arasu.

"Young man," intones Bua. "I would keep your mouth shut, if you know what is good for you. This is a very serious problem. Unless you would like to join your brother in the wild."

"Yes," hisses Mita. "A good idea.

Arasu stares at them in horror. He looks around the room and there are no friendly eyes gazing at him. Not even Grym, who is usually a very fair man, seems inclined to come to his rescue. Arasu becomes terrified at the thought of being an outcast like his brother, and he says nothing more, even after hearing the next thing to come out of Grym's mouth.

"Take him out back," he says to Viril. "And give a shout out for Hugu. Hugu is quite talented at persuading the tight lipped."

Wilu gasps and stares at his brother in horror. Arasu looks down at his feet. He feels very cowardly, but he's not about to risk becoming an outcast for the sake of his uncooperative brother. Wilu begins quaking with fear, and then he begins howling. He screams and curses and makes such a racket, that Viril has to whack him repeatedly with a stick to get him to stop. He finally stops screaming and starts whimpering pathetically and wringing his hands together.

"Get him out of here," Grym orders.

As Wilu is escorted away by Viril, Grym lights a pipe and passes it around the room. Arasu is relieved when the pipe is passed to him. They don't hate him after all. He smokes and then hands it to Grym, who accepts it with exaggerated gratitude.

"Arasu, we know he is your brother," says Grym, smoking thoughtfully. "We all sympathize with your concerns and we don't begrudge you for trying to help him. But you must understand that we will do whatever it takes to get back what he has stolen. Whatever it takes. You know what I mean, too. If you have any influence with him at all, get him to speak. Go talk to him. Be his friend. Perhaps you can stop this before it goes too far."

Arasu goes outside, where his brother stands sullenly with Viril. His hands are tied behind his back and his tattered shirt has already been removed. He is close enough to the council tent where everyone will hear him scream. Arasu wonders if the men in the council get some sort of thrill from listening to men being beaten behind their teepee. He wouldn't be surprised.

"You're in a heap of trouble," Arasu says quietly, so Viril cannot hear. "If you tell me where all of that stuff is, then I can help you."

"Wilu's whole life is trouble," Wilu says, staring bug eyed at Arasu. "Wilu is an outcast."

"I can't protect you if you don't help me. You'll be on your own. They'll torture you."

"Wilu is always on his own. Brother is not there for him. Never was. Brother let Wilu become an outcast."

"I've always helped you as best as I could."

"Wilu has no brother any more."

Arasu doesn't bother to reply because he can't stand the sound of his brother's arguments. Wilu's habit of referring to himself in the third person is extremely annoying. And he hates the way he never uses anybody else's name but his own. He wonders if Wilu even remembers his name.

"Why did you do it?" he asks, after a long silence.

"Wilu needed a sword to protect himself -"

"No!" Arasu says through clenched teeth. "Why did you kill Utai? Remember that?"

His brother's face works spasmodically, as he struggles to remember that long ago time.

"Wilu needed to kill the bad man," he finally says. "The bad man who stole Wilu's girl."

"She wasn't your girl! She didn't even like you!" Arasu shouts, wishing he could control his temper.

"She loved Wilu. Wilu loved her. But the bad man changed all that."

Arasu sighs deeply. This person who stands before him isn't his brother. His brother is already dead. It is only a madman tied to a post. As he muses on this, Viril returns with Hugu, a huge man with a perpetual sour expression. He is shirtless, exposing powerful arms that are crisscrossed with tattoos. Arasu gulps and feels very sorry for his brother. He himself once felt the sting of Hugu's fist, when they were boys. Even then, Hugu was a terror. But now he's a good deal meaner...and he has carte blanche to do whatever he wants to Wilu.

Neither Viril nor Hugu look Arasu in the eyes, as he walks slowly back to the main circle. He doesn't look back, not even when he hears Wilu cry out from the first blow.

Esther has been watching Wilu, ever since they brought him back from the council meeting. His face is covered in blood and a huge open gash on his head leaks blood into his eyes. His body is covered in black and blue marks too. He is tied with his hands behind his back and his feet bound together, totally defenseless from any further abuse and unable even to wipe the blood from his eyes. People walk by him and spit on him, and the spit mixes with the blood. It's been an ugly scene here all morning long, but this is too much.

She feels like she can relate to him somehow. Back in Santa Cruz, she was an easy target for anyone's rage. The soldiers were always taking out all of their bad moods on the neophytes. Miguel used to hit her too, when he was in a bad mood. And she remembers how the soldiers would jeer at her after whipping her and call her names. That was almost worse than the actual beating. So she feels that she should say something to him to cheer him up...something soothing.

"Hello."

Wilu doesn't answer. He just blinks his eyes.

"Are you hungry?" she asks in a soft voice.

"Wilu is thirsty," he says with a breathy hiss. "Wilu needs water."

She goes to the water barrel and fills a bowl with water. She walks up to Wilu, feeling the eyes of many upon her. As she puts the bowl to his lips, it is slapped from her hands. Esther turns furiously and stares down the man who did it. It is Hyu, the blacksmith.

"Don't contaminate our bowls with that filth," Hyu declares. "The prisoner gets no water."

She can feel all eyes upon her now, and she struggles to fight down the fear of making a scene. Her heart pounding rapidly, she picks up the bowl and walks over to the water jug again. She fills it up, feeling Hyu's glowering eyes on her back. She knows that she cannot back down from this. This man reminds her too much of Miguel, perhaps. She stiffens as she walks past Hyu again, who grabs her wrists cruelly and once again knocks the bowl out of her hands.

"Are you going to tie me up too?" Esther asks loudly. "Perhaps you would like to have your way with me? Perhaps you just want to slap a woman around? Is that how you like it?"

Embarrassed, Hyu lets go of her. He looks around at the people laughing at him. Esther takes this opportunity to get more water from the jug. She laughs inwardly, thinking that she just used a tone of voice she learned from Hesta and the other Ladies. And it is a very effective tone too. She walks back and this time Hyu lets her alone. She helps Wilu lift his head so he can drink some water.

"Thank you," Wilu gasps, after he has had his fill.

"Who are you?" Hyu asks angrily. "What right do you have to interfere in tribe business?"

"What right do you have to grab me?" she retorts.

"If you get in our way, it won't go well for you," he sneers. "Woman, you don't know what you're doing."

"Neither do you," says a voice behind her.

It is Elso, standing next to her. He doesn't say anything else, he just stands there protectively. Hyu glares at him and his mouth opens and closes spasmodically as he searches for a particularly good rebuke. He looks around, but he suddenly has no allies. He turns and stalks away, mumbling to himself. Elso looks at Esther and smiles. She smiles back.

That night, Esther sits by the fire in Elso's teepee, watching him make rope. He expertly twines different strands of stout hemp fibers around each other in a painstaking process. Next year, he plans to go to Awani and explore. He is going to climb to the very top of the highest mountain known to the Twelve Tribes, which is along the same range. He wants to look down and see the whole world stretched out before him.

Awani is known today as Yosemite, and 'the highest mountain' is probably Mount Whitney, the highest peak in the lower 48 states.

He teaches her to make rope and soon she begins her own strand. She twists the fibers around and around, her fingers remembering years of weaving at the mission. Elso comments on her speed and technique, and she quizzes him on various techniques and which fibers make the strongest rope and which are the most flexible. She learns some knots while she is at it, so she'll have something to do with her rope when it is finished.

Sometime later that evening, Esther peeks out of the teepee to see the poor prisoner still tied to his miserable post. He is shivering in the cold night air, while his warm clothes lie in a heap at his feet. Esther wants to go put a blanket over his shoulders, but she is not feeling quite as brave as she was this afternoon. She decides to wait until later, when most people have gone to sleep.

"How long will they leave him like that?" she asks, coming back into the teepee and resuming her work.

"They once left a man tied like that for a week. But they hate Wilu much more than that man."

"Is there any way to get them to let him go?"

"Sure. There are a few ways."

"What are they?"

"During the talking circle before dinner, you can make a motion to free him. If more than half the assembled crowd agrees, then he will be freed. That will eventually happen, when everyone is sick of looking at him, but that could take weeks."

"Is there another way?"

"Sure."

"What?"

"You can speak to the council on his behalf. If the council decides to overrule popular vote, they can free him. But they don't do that very often."

"Why not?"

"If the people get angry at the council, they will ignore them. If the council are ignored for long enough, a new council will eventually be appointed. Those old men won't risk that unless it is really important. They've been on the council a long time and they're all rich. The only one who might risk it is Grym, because he's a gambler. But he couldn't convince the council."

"But he's chief, isn't he?"

"For now. But he probably won't be chief for too long. He's a serious gambler. Eventually, he'll go broke or make a poor decision and they'll find a new chief."

"Then there's no way to help him?"

"There is one more way."

"What is that?"

"We could free him ourselves. Just cut his bonds and let him run away. That's the simplest way."

"Won't we get in trouble?"

"Not if they don't know it was us."

"Would you do that?" she asks hopefully.

He thinks awhile and then shakes his head in refusal.

"I saw what he did to Utai. I liked Utai."

"Oh," she says, disappointed.

"But I won't tell anybody if you do it."

"But what if they blame me," she says, after some thought. "Everyone saw me give him water."

"That's true. They might. Unless you walk past him and spit on him when everyone is watching. That will deflect suspicion from you."

He smiles to show that he is kidding. A few minutes later, he walks over and sits down next to her. He rests his body against hers and continues to weave his ropes innocently. She boldly reaches out and plays with his thick, curly hair. It doesn't take long before they are curled up by the fire, with their bodies entwined sensuously. Not long after, they are removing clothes and move to his bed and get underneath the blankets to get warm. Soon they have forgotten all about Wilu, shivering relentlessly in the cold, and they only have eyes for each other.

Owl 15'

**Owl moon*

Wilu eventually did sing out about the missing stash. It turns out he sold it all to the Zesti tribe directly down river - the same tribe who visited them a few weeks ago. Grym doesn't know if they knew the steel was stolen or not, but he assumes they didn't care either way. The council decides that the best course of action is to send a small party to speak to the Zesti chief and see about getting everything back without further ugliness.

Grym, Viril, Yasu and his son Ukko go to the Zesti village early in the morning. Yasu rides a horse to the edge of the village, because he is too lame to walk such a long distance by himself. Outside the village, Yasu dismounts and leaves Ukko to guard the horse. Then Grym, Viril and Yasu walk toward a village of huts made from tree bark and wood, with roofs of earth and grass. They are lightly armed with walking staffs so they won't be perceived as a threat, but will be able to defend themselves if absolutely necessary. Except for a few young girls gathering wood for the fires, the village seems deserted. The girls move out of sight and peer at them from behind their homes.

"Look," Grym says in a loud voice. "Over there. Look familiar?"

Sitting on a bed of coals is none other than the steel pot that was taken from the blacksmith. They all stare at it and then they stare at each other.

"They must know we are coming," Yasu says thoughtfully, "yet the village appears deserted. We should proceed with great caution and do this the right way. I will walk into the village alone and call out the chief. Tell him that our chief wishes to talk to him."

"Agreed."

Yasu hobbles into the village and calls for the chief. He calls many times. Just as he is starting to get nervous, a man comes out of a hut and walks toward Yasu. He speaks to Yasu and then disappears again. A few minutes later, he returns and says something more. Yasu returns to the party.

"Veetka says that we approach in the right way and he will speak to our chief."

The three men stride purposefully into the village, where Veetka waits next to a man who looks as if he might be his brother. Veetka looks nervous for a moment and then he composes himself and puts on an air of might and power. He nods respectfully to the visitors and begins to speak rapidly, while Yasu struggles to translate.

"The Owl tribe has come. The Owl tribe comes finally to pay their respects to us. This should have been done long ago."

"Yes, it should have."

"Come sit with me. We will eat together. Come. Come."

Grym looks at Yasu, who indicates that they should eat first before discussing business. Grym would rather get right to business, and he has a head of steam built up already upon seeing their stolen property in camp. But Yasu insists and they follow Veetka and his brother toward Veetka's hut. It is a simple hut, reasonably large, made of thatch and strips of bark. They sit outside, in front of a roaring fire, while Veetka shouts out for his wife and daughters who are inside the hut. The wife appears a short time later, a large boned, attractive woman, with striped tattoos across her face. She nods quietly to Veetka's orders, comments briefly, and hurries off to bring the guests food. She is never introduced. Yasu doesn't follow what they say to each other, as they speak their own language to each other. They only speak the trading dialect when they speak to him.

The chief asks all sorts of polite, inconsequential questions and Grym answers all of them. He gives in to Yasu's request that they discuss nothing important before lunch. Grym asks some questions in return and learns a bit about this tribe. They are called Huchnom. They are not included among the Pomo or the Yuki, although they rest somewhere in between those two large tribes. Their people consist of three small villages, bound by a common language. The Pomo pay them to fight with the Yuki, because they are better fighters than the Pomo. They are mercenaries, trading Yuki scalps for strings of dentalium.

Soon the wife and one of the chief's pretty young daughters bring them lunch. Lunch begins with acorn bread mixed with some kind of red earth that is dug up nearby. The earth adds a sweetness to it and a strange consistency, which is not unpleasant. Then the women present a soup that is a great delicacy among the Huchnom. It is an oily soup made from angle worms that have surfaced during the recent rains. The faces of the three visitors fall as they stare at it. They will have to eat this soup or risk offending the chief. It is a challenge comparable to any of Grym's trials this past month to hold down this soup without gagging. But he does manage to stomach it, as long as he doesn't look at what he is eating. Yasu has eaten this sort of thing before and does all right, but Viril eats a few bites and claims not to be hungry any more, because he is ill.

After lunch, Grym gets right down to business. Yasu wants him to wait awhile, but Grym will not be deterred any longer.

"We come about some stolen property. Many weapons and tools were stolen from us," Grym says to Veetka and his brother.

Veetka seems offended by the abrupt accusation. His mouth opens and closes with surprise. He stares at his brother, who shakes his head, not understanding why such a thing would be said.

"There are many thieves in the land," Veetka says after a short spell. "The Yukis are thieves. Perhaps it was a Yuki. We fight Yukis. The Yukis are bad thieves. Do you wish to hire us to fight Yukis?"

"We know who stole these things. It was no Yuki. It was a man named Wilu."

He stares at Veetka, looking for a flash of recognition.

"Then why do you speak to me? I am sorry that it happened but I know nothing about it. Do you think we have done this? We know of nobody named Wilu. But there are many unwanted strangers in this land these days."

Veetka seems to insinuate that the Owl Tribe are unwanted visitors. Grym is now the one to be offended and he decides that the time for holding back is gone.

"We saw a pot in your village that was stolen from us," Grym replies. "Wilu told us that he sold everything to you. We have come to claim what is ours. We're not angry, but we must have these things back. They are...valuable to us."

"We have not traded with this man," assures Veetka.

"We saw our pot in your village. Our steel pot."

"How do you know it is yours? There are many hard-as-stone-baskets - or 'pot' as you call them - in the land."

"Do I look stupid to you?" Grym asks in a loud voice. "Obviously it is our pot. You people have no iron or steel. Obviously you have bought our things from this man."

"I recommend against saying that," councils Yasu, expecting to be overruled once again.

Grym waves him on and Yasu reluctantly translates. Sure enough, Veetka becomes agitated. His eyes dart wildly back and forth for a moment because he is not used to such direct accusations. He seems as if he is about to explode from the pressure building inside him. He chats with his brother for a while, before turning to them and answering.

"We bought them from a trader of your own tribe. It was a fair trade."

Nobody speaks for a long time. Nobody knows what to say. The cards are on the table now and the situation is potentially dangerous. Grym doesn't care about the pot. But he does care about the swords, shield, and knives. Those swords are especially important to his tribe. Although nobody will admit it out loud, swords and steel are integral to the safety of his people. The Twelve Tribes are surrounded on all sides by large villages of dangerous Zesti warriors who would not hesitate to take their wealth of horses, steel tools, and many luxuries if they saw the opportunity. The sight of the long, deadly steel swords, shields and horses has deterred more than a few hostile enemies. It is in the best interests of all the Twelve Tribes if the steel is recovered and there is no hint of weakness in his tribe's defenses. It is also in the best interests of his tribe and people if the Zesti don't have these weapons themselves. That would even out the score, and the Twelve Tribes don't have the numbers to compete on an even playing field.

"These things were stolen from us," Grym says after a long silence. "We want them back. We will pay a reward for their recovery."

"These things were sold to us at a fair price," says Veetka, after conferring for a moment with his brother. "It was a fair trade from one of your tribe to our tribe. These things are ours."

"Ask him what they paid for them," says Viril. "I bet the little worm sold them for next to nothing."

Yasu asks and listens to a long rambling reply. When Veetka finishes, Yasu's face is a mask of amusement.

"You don't want to know."

"What did he say?"

"A couple of furs, some meat, some dried fish, a chunk of cinnabar, a coyote paw, a magical talisman of vultures feathers, and a hat made from blue jay feathers."

"Wilu," sighs Viril, "should be killed."

"Wilu is not of our tribe," Grym explains hopelessly to Veetka. "He is a crazy man. He stole those things and sold them for almost nothing. We are not satisfied with this arrangement. We will allow you to keep a few of the tools and the pot for your help in this matter, if you will return the rest."

"These things are ours. It is not yours to take. You try to cheat us," Veetka's brother says in an agitated voice, while Veetka nods emphatically.

"It is you who try to cheat us," says Grym angrily.

"You make a trade and then try to take it back. This is the way of the coyote, not the owl," insists Veetka.

Although he is a great kidder, Grym doesn't smile very often. When he smiles even slightly, like he is right now, it means he finds something very funny.

"That's right, chief," he says. "We're the Owl tribe. And you know what that means. It means don't fool with us, if you know what is good for you."

Agitated, the two Huchnom men withdraw to discuss the situation. Grym watches them with annoyance. This chief is crafty and cagey, and Grym wonders how far he is prepared to go. It may come down to a fight in the end. He knows that his men would back him up if it came to that. They would fight like wild beasts and show the Huchnom that the Owl tribe is a fierce enemy to double cross. He's pretty sure the Owl tribe would win without too many deaths on their side.

The Huchnom would be an easy target for another reason. The Zesti take family obligations seriously, and a battle usually means a long, drawn out cycle of revenge by the slain warriors' family members in other villages. A single battle can make waves that might last years. But the Huchnom is only a small village with a small extended family. They may be brave warriors who can fight Yukis, but they don't have many allies. It would be a clean victory, without entanglements.

Veetka and his brother are getting antsy as they discuss rapidly among themselves. Finally, Veetka suggests a compromise. He promises not to buy anything more from the crazy man, Wilu. The tribe of the Owl will come for a feast, given by his tribe, and gifts will be given by Veetka to even the score. The tribes will engage in fair trading from now on and everyone will profit.

It seems a reasonable request and very typical Zesti logic, but Grym knows that it won't do. A few rabbit skin blankets won't cover the cost of all of that steel. The Huchnom don't really have anything to offer that would make it worthwhile to accept losing that much precious steel, imported at very great expense from China. Not to mention the reputation of the Owl tribe, which is priceless. If they are soft on thieves now, then there will be no end of grabbing hands until everything valuable they own is gone. Their horses will begin disappearing from the hills next. So he finally shakes his head.

"Can't do it, Veetka," he says sadly, shaking his head. "I'm sorry. But we're going to need our weapons back. If you won't give them up, we'll simply have to come back and take them by force." He smiles again. "Like the owl does."

Veetka has another long discussion with his brother. Grym can see that he is angry and thinks the Owl tribe has no honor. They have a long and heated argument. Eventually Veetka stands and his posture is proud once again.

"The way of our people is not to march into villages and burn them down and kill women and children," Veetka says. "We will fight you if that is what you want, but we hope that we can do this in the right way. Our warriors will meet your warriors on the battlefield. We will look each other in the faces and then we will fight. That is the best way."

Grym considers this. It seems an honorable way to settle a dispute. More honorable than launching a raid with superior weapons and killing everybody in the village for the sake of some steel. Grym sees a way to get what he wants and still maintain the dignity and honor of the Owl tribe.

"And if you lose, you will give us our things back?"

"Yes. And what will you give if you lose?"

Grym smiles again for the second time that day. He likes this chief despite himself. He's a sly one.

"A couple of horses. Those are the tall beasts that we ride. How about that?"

"Agreed. A man horse and a woman horse of young age."

"We will meet you in two days for this battle."

"Not enough time. We need five days at least. There are many preparations to make. Our warriors must seek their guardian spirits. Some are hunting and we must wait for their return."

"When is the Hawk moon?" asks Grym of Yasu. "If we cannot fight on the Owl moon, then let us fight on the Hawk moon. Our luck will be stronger if the moon is on fire."

Yasu does some figuring on his fingers.

"Ten days."

"Tell him ten days then," says Grym.

The date is made and then the meeting is over. Everyone wishes each other luck and the three visitors return to their own village. Veetka immediately goes to visit the old shaman Yutu'taka, to ask him to put a curse on the Owl tribe for the coming contest. Perhaps the curse works instantly, because on the way home Grym begins to feel quite ill. All of a sudden, he falls to his knees and throws up worm soup all over the ground. He curses all soups made from insects and larva and promises to refuse such entrees in the future, no matter how much their guest is insulted. It takes him a while to get home after that and then he must lie down and rest while Yasu and Viril fill the tribe in on the big news of the day. Grym misses the opportunity to tell the story, which he would have enjoyed doing, as it is very dramatic. He also misses the beginning of the new moon celebration, which is also upsetting.

There are many men willing to fight. Some are upset that the tribe will fight a battle over something as stupid as this, but those are mostly women. They can whine all they like, because the tribe doesn't need them to fight. From his sickbed, Grym orders Viril to open a barrel of wine from his dwindling storehouse, to kick off the celebration of the new moon. He stumbles out to make an appearance and he is given cheers to show that everybody is behind him. They make a toast to a quick and easy victory and the men all promise to fight like Owls. Nobody can ask for more than that.

The barrel is sucked dry before dinner, and Grym is forced to open another one. He expected as much, because the Owl tribe loves to drink. Dinner itself is nothing special. Nobody put any effort into making something special. It's just another meal to line the stomach, so the wine doesn't burn though an empty belly.

Somebody debuts a giant xylophone that he built from heavy planks and he bangs upon it with giant mallets to the great joy of those who hear it. He is pretty good on the thing and he makes some nice music. It is one of the more gentle and refined things Esther has seen in this tribe and it is enjoyable for that reason alone. When he is finished, a band of musicians from the Wolf tribe begin playing.

Things get way out of control quickly. The upcoming battle lends a surge of aggressive energy to the whole party and there are men running around the camp in mean, drunken stupors. Some prance around naked, shouting lewd things and grabbing the opposite sex. There are people coupling right out in the open. Bawdy songs are sung in loud voices. Several drunk men and women wander over to the boundary between the Owl tribe and the Huchnom, and one obnoxious man screams curses at the village and threatens a bloody battle. He is pelted with a stone from some unknown hand, which throws him into a rage, and it is all his friends can do to keep him from running over and engaging the entire village with his own bare hands.

Esther gambles for a while, playing 'guess the hand the rock is in' and 'throwing stones'. Her luck is poor tonight and she begins to lose. Disappointed, she gets a big bowl of wine and works on her gambling song as she drinks by the fire. She starts getting too much attention from men and when someone grabs her forcefully and tries to plant a kiss on her lips, she goes into the teepee to hide for a while. The beasts are wild, they are rutting, and any single, young filly is fair game. Elso is out drinking with his friends, so she spends the rest of the evening watching the teepee spin in circles. She has drunk too much. When she passes out, it is still just as noisy as it was several hours ago.

Owl 16'

The new moon celebration peaks today, with the usual assortment of weddings, ceremonies and a single birth early in the morning. The mother wakes everybody up with her screams and Esther has to laugh when a man begins to howl back at her.

"Get it over with already so we can get back to sleep!"

"Come on over here and make me!" she shouts back.

She eventually quiets down and when everybody wakes next, there is a new member of the tribe.

Esther spends the entire morning lying in bed, hung over and exhausted. She is not the only one having a rough morning. Many are hung over and some find themselves sleeping next to people they wish they hadn't. There are few smiling faces this morning, and the day is dedicated to recovering from last night. But there is a hardcore element that will continue to party as long as they can move. About ten or twelve of them stand in front of the fire, desperately keeping the new moon celebration going. They egg on anyone unlucky enough to walk by them, proclaiming how they have been a hell of a lot more hung over and tired than this and still managed to keep up with a hundred mile hike. They urge the 'little babies' to quit whining and join the celebration. Esther looks so miserable when she walks out, that she doesn't get any taunting at all. They take one look at her and just shake their heads.

Elso stayed up all night drinking and he is hung over and tired, but he refuses to lie down and sleep. He spends the morning twining rope, practicing knots, fetching wood for the fire and food from the kitchen. Esther is impressed that he can even move, much less keep up all this work.

"Aren't you tired?" she asks, as he carries a heavy load of firewood inside.

"Yeah," he admits. "But exhaustion is a choice."

He throws the wood down and sits down to let his head stop spinning.

"I want to go to China on the traders ship. You have to be able to work hard through seasickness, cold, wet, heavy wind, exhaustion, disease.... If I give in now, I'll never make a good sailor."

"You plan to go soon?" she asks.

"Yes, after I climb the mountains of Awani. Next summer, perhaps. I want to see China very much."

"That's nice," Esther says, trying not to sound disappointed.

Esther has begun to have fantasies of living with Elso. She has already decided to stay on for the winter, but she has secretly thought that perhaps Elso would make a great husband. He can build things and repair things and he is very athletic and useful. The people respect him. And he is very cute. But somehow, he doesn't seem the marrying type. And without him, she doesn't know if she would like living in the Owl tribe. These people are a little too intense for her. In fact, they never stop to rest, unless they are sleeping.

In the afternoon, when everyone is feeling better, there are two weddings. Both are extremely strange. During the first wedding, the groom is drunk and swaying slightly as he stands there. He even holds a glass of wine in his hand during the ceremony and sips it whenever he gets nervous. He asserts in a loud voice that he couldn't do this sober and his woman has to get him falling down drunk in order to get him to go through with it at all. His wife agrees that this is definitely the case and then Grym begins his typical wedding speech.

"Do you agree to love each other even when your husband gets drunk and winds up in bed with your sister," he says in a voice meant to be humorous. "Do you agree to love her even when you wake up next to her in three years and she looks like a half-dead buffalo with your baby in her belly?"

Everyone laughs as the couple agrees wholeheartedly that they will still love each other.

"Do you agree to love her when she screams at you to fix the teepee which is leaking and calls you a waste of flesh who is better off as meat for the wolves than as a husband? Do you agree to love him when he disappears for three weeks on a drinking binge at the Swan tribe and you know he has spent all of your money at the Lily Pad?"

They still agree to love each other. Others call out their own suggestions for things that can go wrong and the couple must endure ten or twelve people's worst marriage nightmares and insist that they will still love each other before Grym will declare them married. Esther laughs heartily, thinking that Grym will be her first choice for minister if she ever gets married. Then she looks at Elso again and wishes he were a little less restless.

Grym complains that his storehouse is running low on wine and he will run out if this new moon lasts much longer. So it is decided to take a break from drinking until a time when a barrel of wine may be much appreciated. Those in the mood for a mind bender get high on whatever else is at hand, which is an assortment of things from jimm to mushrooms to tulum brought by the Wolf tribe musicians. Everyone goes off on their own strange adventures, which is a little more appropriate to the new moon anyway. Elso takes mushrooms and goes on a quest to the top of a nearby hill that he has not scaled in at least five months. He invites Esther along, but she is still tired and has a headache, so she just hangs out in the village and watches everyone else act crazy.

Esther's lower back begins to hurt terribly. The pain comes on suddenly, and it is sharp and very uncomfortable. She walks miserably back to the teepee to lie down and every step she takes is agony. She tries to sleep, but her back hurts too much to make that possible. She lies there in a daze, wondering what is wrong with her. Finally, she walks slowly and painfully over to the healer's teepee. The healer is a big, fat man with wild hair, who is sound asleep at his post. Esther enters the teepee and shakes him gently awake, mumbling apologies as she does it. Lifting his bleary head, he stares at her.

"Yes?" he asks with a sigh.

"I just have a question."

"What is it?"

"My lower back is hurting. I've been hung over all day long and I had a headache earlier. But now it's my back that hurts. Why is that?"

"Probably your kidneys," he says without a moment's thought. "Drink lots of water. That's what I recommend."

"Do you have anything for me to end the pain?"

"I'm out of tincture. But you don't need it. Remember, pain is a choice."

"Thank you," Esther says, annoyed to hear Elso's favorite quote. "But I choose to take something to make me feel better. Are you sure you don't have anything?"

Grumbling, he goes to a dark corner and searches for something to give her. He finds a small bowl that looks promising and pours a bit of whatever is inside it into a cup. He hands it to her with a yawn.

"What is it?" she asks, staring at it doubtfully.

"I'm not sure. I think it is a medicine for cleansing the body. Tumock made it."

"Tumock?" she asks, surprised. "Is he here?"

"I don't know where he is. He gave this to me a few months ago."

"Is it still good?"

"I think so."

She looks at the dark brown sludge in the cup and makes a face. She gives him a look and he shrugs again, as if it isn't worth bothering to ask what's in it. She doesn't really want to drink it, but it is Tumock's potion, and Numei spoke very highly of his skills. She takes it from him hesitatingly and takes a sip. It tastes as bad as it looks and she nearly gags. But she manages somehow to stomach it and she quickly hands the cup back to him and goes to look for some cold water to wash the taste out.

At first, the potion makes Esther ill and she has to struggle not to throw it up. But as it begins to absorb into her body, it gives her an incredible rush and makes her float on clouds. She goes back to the teepee, but she is too wired to sleep now. Propelled by surges of energy, she lights one of Elso's homemade torches and takes a long, restless walk. Along the way, she passes an owl, sitting high on an overhanging branch. It seems to be watching her, curious about her movements. She spends a long time just staring at it, wondering what it is thinking. She could almost swear that it glows with an unreal light, like some sort of beacon of the forest. Then she continues to follow the faint path until it dives into the woods.

She hesitates for a moment and then pushes forward. The path starts off wide and slowly grows narrower and narrower until she has to turn sideways to move through some parts. And then she comes to a place that is like a dream. The trees are all bent and twisted and they bend over and drape moss and leaves to the very ground. It is so thick that one can barely move.

Suddenly, she stops dead in her tracks, on the trunk of a fallen tree she was attempting to climb. She feels something in the darkness, waiting for her. Not an animal or another person, but something else. In her usual state, she would dismiss it as paranoia, but in this altered state she accepts it as real. A thrill of fear runs up her spine, as she looks around for the spirit that seems to be lurking, but she can see nothing but shadows dancing in front of her eyes. Then some strange shape makes her pause, or is it some trick of the light? She sees a dark shape in front of her that seems to blot out everything else in the world but Esther and itself. It resembles a large bird, made up of shadow and it is staring fixedly at her. She has never felt so terrified in her life.

The shape seems to move toward her and Esther is frozen with fear. A strange energy suddenly flows through her, as if something has just entered her body. She begins to move like a bird, as if possessed by one. She perches on a small branch with her arms inside her dark cloak like wings. When she sees her shadow against a tree, it reminds her of a bird woman. As if in a dream, she screeches loudly, and the sound makes the rational part of her quake with fear.

She dances in the shadows made by her torch. In her bare feet, across the mossy floor of the forest, she spins and moves in a trance. She dances for the spirit, knowing that it is pleased. She sings to it, and her voice is high and coarse. Then she hears the hoot of an owl from somewhere close by and knows that the owl is aware of this power and is watching.

The torch begins to sputter and fade. In a dream, she watches it slowly die out, until with a hiss, it sparks and dies. She stands in total darkness and begins to panic. With that sudden shock, she feels the bird spirit leave her and she is alone in the pitch black.

Somehow she finds her way back out of the thick forest. She feels as if her escape is guided by this bird spirit, because she could never find her way out in this darkness on her own. So it is a friendly spirit, at least. She breathes a deep sigh of relief as she sees stars again and the dark, claustrophobic feeling leaves her. Then she heads toward the lights of the village.

When she passes Grym's teepee, she sees Wilu slumped in a sitting position against his pole, with his hands tied behind him. He has been moved away from the main circle so nobody will have to look at his face on the new moon. His face is covered with scabs and half healed wounds and he has burn marks on his arms. Someone cut his hair off, leaving it in tufts to make it look especially bad. Wilu cannot sleep, because it is too cold and he has no blanket for warmth, so he is forced to shiver all night long and then try to sleep during the day. His head lolls sideways like a rag doll and he looks half dead already. It makes Esther furious to see him humiliated and beaten like this and she feels the bile rise in her throat.

She walks up to him and taps him gently on the shoulder. He looks up and stares at her with numb eyes that have no hope left.

"Can I get you anything?" she asks. "Water? Food?"

"Water," he whispers. "And food."

"I'll get you some," she promises.

"No, no," he insists, as she begins to walk away. "Let me get it. Cut me free."

She has not heard him speak in the first person before and it touches her. It seems that all of this suffering has made him sane again.

"No, I can't," she says sadly.

"The mean people want to kill me."

She frowns and looks away guiltily.

"They will kill Wilu," he pleads. "Please help me."

"No," she whispers. "I can't do that."

"I don't want to die," he whines. "Please...."

She looks around carefully and sees that nobody is about. Perhaps she could cut him loose and nobody would know. She has a sudden feeling that she is meant to help him, that whatever spirit she met in the woods today has given her the mandate to free Wilu. She wonders what would happen to her if they found out her treachery. She can think of any number of possibilities and some of them are very bad. But she thinks she would feel worse if she did nothing to help this poor wretch than if she suffered any one of them. So after a long deliberation, she decides to gamble her future with this tribe.

She finds a knife stuck in a pile of wood near Grym's teepee. Knife in hand, she creeps up behind him, walking like the bird spirit still possesses her. She examines the rope, which looks like the rope Elso makes. It is strong rope and she has to saw at it to cut it. Wilu shouts with surprise when she tugs on the rope and she hisses for him to be quiet. In moments it is completed and Wilu stares at his freed wrists in great surprise. He moans with pleasure and he rubs them until the feeling comes back. And then he notices she is leaving.

"Hey wait!" he shouts.

"Shhhhhhh," she hisses, as she quickly walks away.

To her great annoyance, he begins to follow her. How stupid is he? She turns around and waits for him to catch up with her.

"You'll get me in trouble," she whispers. "Leave me alone. Get out of here before somebody sees you."

"Come with me."

"No," she orders, shaking her head violently. "You have to go now."

"You are Wilu's friend."

He wraps his arms around her and embraces her. She gives him a quick hug, but then he won't let her go. To her great surprise, he begins to suck on her neck. She cannot believe his gall. She just risked her life to help him and now he is acting like this! She shoves him violently away, realizing for the first time why everyone here hates him. Now, she hates him too, and she wishes he were still tied up. She struggles to get away, but he holds tight.

"If you don't let me go right now, I'm going to scream. I'll scream for everybody to come tie you up again. I'll say you had a knife and you tried to kill me."

He gives her a bitter look and then he lets go. With a sad look on his face, he turns around and runs off. She quickly scuttles home before somebody sees her. As she walks, she scans the village furtively, sure that a thousand eyes just saw her do it. When she gets into the teepee, she breathes a deep sigh of relief.

"Elso," she whispers, shaking him awake.

"Mmm, what?" he mumbles.

"Move over," she says.

He scoots over and she lies down and wraps herself in his arms where she feels safe again. Still, she tosses and turns for an hour before the adrenaline subsides and she can finally fall asleep.

Esther awakens in the middle of the night, feeling sick to her stomach. She can taste Tumock's medicine in her mouth and it makes her gag. She lies still, struggling not to throw up. Her head spins. But finally, she cannot fight it anymore. She gets up, runs outside, and barely gets her head out the door, before she falls to her knees and throws up the foul medicine and her dinner all over the outside of Elso's teepee. She stumbles back to bed and lies down with a spinning head. She fights the nausea that makes her want to throw up again, mainly because it means moving. Then she has a miserable hour of feverish tossing and turning before she finally falls asleep.

Owl 17'

The next day, Wilu is discovered missing and the village is in an uproar. Ysu is immediately called to examine the evidence and he spends a good deal of time examining the cut ropes and the footprints around the pole. Esther watches him with fear in her heart, knowing what a good tracker he is. But he finally declares that there are just too many footprints around Wilu's pole for him to tell who cut Wilu free. He thinks he can track Wilu if he starts now, and he begins to assemble a tracking party. Then Grym calls an emergency meeting of the tribe and demands to know who cut the thief and murderer free.

"It was Arasu," shouts Hyu.

"You're a horse's ass, Hyu," retorts Arasu.

"It is obvious to me that you had the most reason-"

"I had every reason to help my brother. But I am ashamed to say that I did not, because I knew I would be blamed for it."

"Did anyone see anything?" asks Grym once again.

Nobody saw who did it and they cannot be sure who it was. Esther can barely sit through the meeting, so frightened is she that they will know it was her. Only when she thinks of the spirit from last night can she keep from running away. She still cannot believe she did it. She must have been very high last night to even consider it.

"Ysu and Viril are already on the trail of our eternal pest," declares Grym at last. "When we find him, we'll beat the information out of him. We'll discover our traitor soon enough."

Esther is terrified when she hears this and she thinks about leaving the village immediately. But if she runs away, then everybody will know it was her. After deliberating a good long while, she cannot decide what to do, and she decides to do nothing. Instead, she goes to the main fire to play Bu. Once she does this, she instantly feels better. At one point, Hyu comes over and stares at her suspiciously, but she ignores him. She feels as if the spirit she met last night is happy with her and gives her strength to endure his gaze. Soon she becomes too obsessed with the movements of the little white shells on the reed mat to think much about it. And then she wins her first game of Bu and she is sure that everything will work out just fine.

Owl 21'

Raven moon

In the morning, Esther sleepily walks out into pale daylight to use the toilet. It is cold, with sunlight spread thin by too many clouds, and her bare feet freeze on the hard, wet ground. Then she sees a sight that makes her blood run far colder than the morning air. Wilu is back, once again tied to a pole, and covered with fresh bruises. She asks a woman standing near the main fire pit and gets the entire story. Apparently Wilu came back on his own, looking for his 'girlfriend'. Esther doesn't have any doubt that Wilu meant her. She remembers the story of Hoja's wolves, and realizes that it has come back to haunt her.

Esther quickly returns to her teepee and spends the entire morning waiting for the executioner to come and chop off her head. Late in the morning, Elso appears from a morning sweat, and he stares at her strangely. He doesn't say anything for a long time, and then he grabs her hand and sits down next to her.

"Your presence has been requested," is all he says, in response to her questions.

"Elso, it was me," she whispers, as if the whole village were listening. "I freed him."

"I know," he says. "The council just called me in to ask questions about you. They wanted to know who you were and why you might have done it."

"I'm afraid," she says.

"Don't worry."

"What will they do to me? They won't tie me to the pole, will they?"

"I won't let them hurt you," he says protectively. "Not if I have to draw my sword against the whole tribe."

Holding her hand, he drags his unwilling charge outside to attend the upcoming meeting. She walks like the prisoner walks to face the firing squad. As soon as they reach the main fire, where the entire tribe is gathered in a circle, Hyu walks up to her furiously and drags her toward the center of the circle. She stands there mortified, feeling the eyes of the whole tribe upon her. Hyu holds onto her, as if she might run away if he only lets go for a minute.

"The villain Wilu has named this girl as his accomplice," Grym shouts, trying to be heard by all. "This morning, the council met to discuss what to do with her. But before we pronounce judgment, we will let the girl speak. She may tell us who she is and why she did it. Why she cut the thief and murderer free."

The whole circle falls silent. Esther stands there numbly, not wanting to say anything. What could she say that would lessen her punishment? Eventually she falls back upon her old neophyte instincts to blame somebody else for it.

"The Owl spirit told me to do it," she says, in as loud a voice as she can muster. "I drank some medicine from Tumock and I met an Owl spirit in the woods and he told me to do it -"

As she speaks these words, she realizes how crazy they must sound. She blushes and stops speaking. Everyone shouts out for her words to be repeated and Grym repeats her words in a skeptical voice, as if they are too ridiculous to be worth repeating. But many do not agree with his opinion and arguments erupt all over.

"Whether or not she was high on some of our resident Ruok's special medicine when she did it, the council will stick with its opinion," Grym says at last, waving aside all other protests. "The traitor will be banished from the tribe like the traitor she mistakenly freed. It is more than fair, considering the severity of the crime -"

"Nonsense!" shouts out an old woman suddenly. "You'll do no such thing!"

Esther looks at the voice surprised, and sees one of the cooks from the kitchen. She cannot remember her name, but remembers her being very friendly.

"The girl only did what we all wanted to do. We were all sick of looking at him. Sick of his cries and his whining. I wanted to cut him free myself, but I didn't out of respect to Mita."

To Grym's great surprise, several of the women of the tribe shout out in complete agreement.

"The council has spoken!" intones Hyu solemnly.

"Well, I'm un-speaking it!" the woman insists. "Let go of that girl now, before I come over there and make you!"

Everything erupts into chaos. Hyu screams and shakes Esther violently and demands justice. Arasu and Elso run over to Hyu and pull Esther away from him. Hyu resists, Viril steps in to help him and there is almost a fight, but several people rise and pull them apart. There is chaos for several minutes and nobody can be heard over the shouting. Finally, things calm down enough for a few people with loud voices to be heard.

"We have more important things to think about!" shouts the woman who first came to Esther's defense. "We have a battle in a few days in which many may be killed. And here we are wasting time over this. The girl is very brave and she should be rewarded, not condemned. Has the council become this useless and shortsighted?"

"The great Owl told her to do it!" shouts a little old man with long grey hair and an incredibly loud voice. "It was the will of the Owl spirit! Does the council dare to go against our protector's will? And right before a battle too! That is incredibly stupid!"

The drama goes on for a good while, but in the end the council is overruled. Few want to see Esther banished, especially if it might mean angering the great Owl before a battle. Hyu is publicly humiliated and he storms off in a fury. Grym tries to get order back, but passions are strong today and there are many arguments going on at once. He cannot get any kind of rational discussion going. Finally, he just throws up his hands and walks out of the circle and goes back to his teepee.

After the close call, Esther goes to hide in Elso's teepee. She stays there for a few hours, until the meeting is disbanded and everyone has scattered. She feels mortally embarrassed and considers just leaving the village today and not coming back. Elso checks on her and tries to comfort her, but she is moody and he leaves again. She mopes some more and then begins to pack her burden basket. But then she is struck with the realization that if she leaves this village, then that cruel blacksmith will get what he wants. She will not give him that satisfaction! Eventually, she gets the courage to go back outside and look for Mani, who was one of those who spoke for her. Esther thanks her and asks her to play a game of Bu. They sit down to play. She can feel all eyes upon her once again, but she focuses on the game and ignores them. The movements of the little shells magically dispel all of her problems and she thinks no more on it.

Owl 25'

Cougar moon

The night before the battle, the men of the Huchnom tribe prepare themselves for war in this way. They cover themselves in mud and pitch and sprinkle eagle feathers over themselves. The drums start the war beat and they begin the war dance. They will dance all night long, for courage in battle the next day. The war drum pounds and all the men chant, roar, scream, hold their weapons aloft and make a horrible racket. The women all gather around them and sing in shrill voices and dance beside them. The women will dance all night long and all the next day as well, until the battle is finished. They believe that as long as they dance, their men will not get tired.

While the Huchnom village is loud and boisterous, Owl village is rather subdued. A deer is killed and roasted to give the men strength for battle. Everyone goes to sleep early, that they will be well rested for tomorrow. Wives and girlfriends nestle in bed with their men, enjoying what could be their last night on earth together.

The wife of Grym gives a speech to all the women during dinner. She says that it is good luck to make love to a man the night before the battle, because it makes him strong. Esther is glad to help out any way she can and she makes love to Elso as many times as he likes, in case this is his last night on earth. She massages him and treats him like a chief. Late that night, she curls up next to him and tells him to get some sleep so he will be healthy and well rested tomorrow.

"This is a stupid conflict," he says in a low voice, so nobody else can hear.

"You don't want to fight?"

"I don't mind a fight," he sneers, "but not over a few swords and tools. Grym is a new chief and he has a lot to prove. He wants the men to think that he is a strong chief."

"Then why are you fighting?" she asks. "Don't fight."

"I have to," is all he says.

Owl 26'

Hawk moon

At dawn, everyone silently begins to get ready. Esther follows Elso out into the cold dawn, crisp with moisture. She shivers underneath her cloak, as she joins the tribe gathered silently around the fire. The women have roasted some deer meat for the warriors, and each one eats a small portion for strength. The women are not supposed to eat today, as some sort of gesture to the men. Esther doesn't understand it, but she agrees to follow the taboos.

The men wear armor over their torsos, made from three layers of elk hide, which is supposed to repel arrows. They wear helmets of the same material. Each man receives a steel shield from the armory and they are loaded down with bows and arrows and swords and knives. Once attired, they scream out a war whoop that echoes throughout the village. Then somebody blows a horn and the men jump upon horses and race off to the battlefield. The horses sense the urgency and the excitement and they race full speed ahead with every ounce of strength that they possess. Esther watches Elso ride off with a big grin on his face, displaying none of the doubts that he showed last night. She fears for his safety and knows that it is going to be a long day of waiting.

Soon the horses arrive at the battlefield. The Huchnom are already there, waiting patiently and dancing slowly in place. They have not eaten this morning nor slept the night before, and they have the clear, focused intensity of the hungry and deprived. They are in a trance from dancing all night long, so they will feel no fear and not dwell on death. But even these brave warriors are momentarily subdued by the approach of the great horses, whose hooves sound like thunder as they crash upon the ground. They stop dancing for a moment, shocked by the noise and confusion. When the Owl tribe dismounts and they are facing men and not great beasts, they begin a racket and brandish their weapons and give fierce cries. The spell is broken.

The two sides observe each other. The Owl warriors stare at the Huchnom warriors with great surprise. They are much larger than expected, tall and brave men painted from head to foot in black and red and loaded down with talismans like bear claws and wolf fangs. All wear great feather headdresses that make them appear huge and menacing, and wear no armor but elk skin loin cloths to protect their most sacred body parts. They carry bows, spears, and obsidian knives. A few carry the swords, knives and axes recently stolen from the Owl tribe. The biggest of the Huchnom warriors holds a steel shield and sword and he is a fearsome sight. There is nobody that large in the Owl tribe. He will be a holy terror in the upcoming battle.

Each member of the Huchnom shares a momentary fear as the Owl tribe lines up. Each man is equipped with the stone-like weapons and shields that shine like water reflecting sunlight. These are magical weapons that are much stronger than the weapons of the Huchnom. Although they now have a few of these weapons too, they have not had the time to learn them properly. The Owl warriors are well armored and carry large bows. The spies have said that they are good with them. Although they are not huge men, they seem fierce and fearless.

Veetka, the chief, watches the Owl warriors with the greatest anxiety, for he bears the greatest burden. If his tribe is victorious, he will have to pay the Owl tribe for their lost warriors, so they will not be angry any more. If they are victorious, he will have to pay his own tribe's families who lost their men, because he doubts that this strange chief Grym will pay for the dead properly as he should. He fears that his people will lose, he will be shamed by the poor showing of his tribe in battle, and the Yuki will not be afraid of their warriors any more. Then Veetka decides that there is no need for pessimism. His warriors are strong and brave and the shaman Yutu'taka swears that they will be helped by many great spirits. So the chief shrugs off his fears and joins in the warrior's dance to get his mind off the coming battle.

Ysu, appointed battle leader, stares at the brave Zesti, all lined up and ready to fight. After long observation, he turns to Grym, who stands nearby.

"How do you suppose this battle works?"

Grym shrugs.

"Like any battle I guess. We kill as many as we can."

"I know. But what are the rules? Did this Veetka mention any rules?"

"Rules. I don't know. I guess we'll figure it out as we go."

Ysu shrugs and turns to his men, who are all clustered together, staring at their opponents.

"Line up like they are. Bows in the hands and swords at the hip. The first part of the battle will be the dangerous part. We're evenly matched when the arrows start to fly. But if we can get a few swords inside their ranks, we will have no more problems. Most of them still carry obsidian and clubs, which is no match for steel."

"Who is the best with a sword?" asks Grym.

"Hugu is probably the best. Ruian is good." Ysu calls the two men over. "You two should be ready to charge at the first opportunity. We'll cover you when you do."

"I am ready," says Ruian, staring in disgust at a man wearing a gruesome talisman. "Is that a dead hawk's head he's wearing? The tall one, over there?"

"Let him wear it," growls Hugu. "We'll be wearing their heads for talismans by tonight. I'll make a bed from their feather hats."

"And I'll cut off their hands and wear them around my neck," laughs Ruian.

Arasu and Elso stand side by side. Arasu grips his sword firmly and makes a few practice swings. His face is set in a ferocious scowl and his practice swings are strong and decisive.

"Let's dance," he roars, with a sadistic grin.

Elso stands quietly, watching the enemy closely. He is trying to decide which to take down with an arrow first. They all seem fierce and fearless and he cannot decide who is the most dangerous, so he finally decides to just pick his target according to size.

Suddenly a man walks across the field, a tree branch in his hand, and he makes a beeline for Grym. Grym calls to Yasu, who walks out from the line of spectators to translate. Yasu is too old to fight, so he stays with the horses.

"Veetka wishes to speak to the chief of the Owl tribe," the man tells Yasu.

"About?" asks Grym.

"Just speak to him," says Yasu, hitting Grym on the arm.

"Yes, yes of course. I will meet him in the middle of the battlefield."

The man returns to tell Veetka. Meanwhile, Grym watches the Huchnom warriors scream and yell.

"What are they saying?" he asks Yasu.

"I don't know. They don't curse in the trade dialects that I speak. But I can guess."

"Do they say they will tear out our entrails and feed them to their women?"

"I do not think so."

The Owl warriors begin mumbling, wondering when the battle will begin. Meanwhile, Veetka approaches the center of the field and Grym and Yasu walk to meet him. Grym is shocked to see that Veetka has his very own stolen blade bound to his waist. It stuns him momentarily, and he feels a great rage build inside of him. His sword in the hands of the enemy! The sword Grym holds in his hand is no substitute for the great blade that Veetka holds. It is like Veetka has stolen a piece of him. He longs to just take it from Veetka right now, and he has to struggle not to.

"Grym of the Owl tribe," begins Veetka. "Your men are brave. They are ready to die. My men are brave. They too are ready to die. Here is my offer. I will give two dentalium strings for each Owl tribe warrior killed in battle."

Grym laughs.

"He's serious," explains Yasu.

"He is?"

"Among these Zesti, it is customary to offer money for any warrior killed."

It suddenly occurs to Grym that this man is serious. He and his men are ready to die, and a man's life is worth two strings of dentalium. It is a savage form of justice to count out a man's life in money. Grym begins to wonder if he has a taste for this. He has a hideous moment of reflection and deep insight into himself. He begins to see that this is a personal matter for him and he is threatening the lives of his tribe over it. And then he recovers and realizes that Veetka is waiting for his counter offer.

"Veetka, you are a brave warrior," he says at last. He speaks slowly, with many pauses. "This is a fight started by a man we cast out of our village, because he killed another man. We bear no grudge against your people and only want what he has unfairly taken. Our people feel cheated by this trade, because they did not profit from it. Look at the sword in your hand. This sword was once mine, Veetka. It has saved my life many times and I know it well. It is my sword and I would never have traded it. The blacksmith was sharpening it for me when it was stolen."

Veetka stares at the sword at his hip. Grym holds his breath, hoping that Veetka is going to be moved by his passion for his blade and will come to his senses. Veetka almost seems moved, and Grym can see the war in his eyes. Then his eyes are dazzled by the shining steel, and they lose their compassion and become steel like the blade.

"I understand," he says insolently. "But it has chosen a new owner now."

"I will fight you for it then," Grym says hotly, putting his hand on his sword and drawing it out. He shows it to Veetka and indicates for him to draw his sword. "If I win, I get my sword back. If you win, you get my horse. No reason to get all the men killed over this battle that is really between us. Let us fight."

"This can not be," Veetka says, shaking his head mightily. "It is not the way it is done. The tribes will fight. What is your offer for our men?"

Grym sighs hopelessly. His efforts to avoid bloodshed have been unsuccessful. He always pegged Veetka as rather confused, but the man is eerily crafty underneath his surface behavior. He knows that Grym is better with a sword than he is. He would rather risk the lives of his entire tribe, than engage in a fair combat that he might lose. He knows his only advantage is his own stubbornness and his men's willingness to die. Grym begins to realize how much he has misjudged this man. He is used to dealing with the high-minded Pomo. The Pomo are a noble people as a whole and easy to reason with. But these men are different. They are the ones the Pomo pay to do their dirty work. They are professional mercenaries, and this is pure business for them. Each man is worth two strings of dentalium shells. A sword is worth much more than that.

The day Veetka first came to visit, he must have seen the steel of the Owl tribe and been dazzled. Grym begins to wonder if Veetka somehow put Wilu up to the task of stealing the weapons. The more he thinks on it, the more he is sure that he did.

"I do not pay thieves," Grym says bitterly. "Tell him I offer nothing to a thief. We will kill the Huchnom and take back what is ours."

Yasu reluctantly translates. Veetka becomes very agitated. He knew that this man would not do the right thing. He sees that this chief does not know the ways of the land. He is an outsider. And he sees that he is a dangerous outsider, who may upset the delicate position that the Huchnom is in.

"I am no Yuki," Veetka says. "Veetka does not steal. The Huchnom did not steal from the Owl tribe. If a Huchnom had stolen these things, then I would return them. But it was a member of the Owl tribe who stole them. It is a member of the Owl tribe that is the thief."

"This is true," Grym admits. "But I think that you asked him to steal them."

"No," Veetka says angrily. "This is not the right way to do things. Veetka is no Yuki."

"I say that Veetka is a Yuki!" roars Grym.

"That is a nice killing weapon too," Veetka says suddenly, changing the subject. "If Owl chief loves this one so much, then perhaps he will trade that for this one. Veetka sees no difference between killing weapons."

Veetka shows Grym the sword in his hand and holds it in front of him. He has that same crafty look in his eyes.

"Agreed," says Grym quickly.

He hands his spare sword to Veetka. Veetka takes it and gives Grym back his favorite blade. As soon as it enters Grym's hand, he feels his body relax noticeably and he feels whole again. He hefts it and nods satisfied. Light and well balanced...this is a blade! The heavy, unwieldy blade that he traded is not worth the handle of the blade in his hand now. He stares at Veetka, and suddenly he has an idea.

"Veetka," he intones solemnly. "There are still two men who have lost blades that they love. I will offer the same trade for their weapons. A sword for a sword."

Veetka nods.

"This is acceptable."

Grym nods and tells Yasu to engage Veetka in conversation while he goes to look for replacements. He goes to speak to his men, who have grown very impatient. He quickly explains the situation. He asks them if they want to fight or if someone will offer their blade for the blades of Hyu and Bua. There is a long silence. Nobody comes forward.

"Then there will be battle," says Grym solemnly.

"I will offer my sword," says Arasu suddenly, stepping forward. "I will offer my sword and also my father's sword, which is in my mother's house."

"Arasu has made a generous offer," Grym shouts. "Is this acceptable to Hyu and Bua?"

The two men nod.

"I have an extra shield in my storehouse that I will give to Hyu in exchange for the one he lost," says Grym. "And then we may forgive the theft and we will not have to fight."

Grym walks up to Arasu and puts his arm around him warmly.

"Arasu is a good man," he intones, leading Arasu in front of the assembled men. "Arasu has sacrificed for the tribe."

"But I ask something in return," Arasu says loudly. "I ask for my brother's freedom. He has suffered greatly for this crime he committed. He is a madman now and he will never be sane again. I ask that you do this for me in exchange."

Grym waves down the protests of several members of the tribe.

"This is acceptable to me," he says. "Let it be done."

He takes Arasu's sword and goes to speak to Veetka. As he walks, he feels a new sense of purpose. For the first time since he became chief, he feels like one.

They make the trade and agree to end hostilities. Veetka invites the Owl tribe for a potlatch where they will finalize the trade of property and the two tribes will make peace. Veetka suggests that the two tribes can trade together like friends. Grym smiles, knowing that Veetka has his eye on more steel. He is a very crafty man and he won the battle of wills today, without a single arrow being fired. Veetka won because he got what he wanted, which was three swords, a shield, and several tools. Grym got what he wanted too, but on Veetka's terms. But he feels fine being the loser. It was an enlightening battle of wills and Grym has learned from it. Both sides were willing to compromise. That is all that matters.

A potlatch is a party given by a tribe, where the chief must provide the feast as well as gifts to all the guests. A good potlatch shows the wealth and power of a tribe and their chief, and creates strong alliances.

They agree to a potlatch in ten days time and then they part company. Grym and Yasu return to their warriors and tell everyone to mount up and leave. Some of the warriors are moody and some complain that they went to all this trouble for nothing. But most seem satisfied just to have had this little adventure. They all mount up and return to their village, where a great rollicking celebration begins as if they had actually fought a battle.

Owl 28'

**Beaver moon*

Wilu has been freed and allowed to stay in Arasu's teepee until his wounds heal. He is a very demanding patient, and Arasu has spent much time fetching him the many luxuries that he craves during his brief respite from solitude in the wild. But as Wilu begins to feel better, it is suggested to Arasu that he release his brother back into the wild. So this morning, he sits down with Wilu to have a little talk.

"It is time for you to leave, Wilu," Arasu says firmly. "The tribe insists on it."

"I will not leave until mother comes," Wilu insists. "I had a bad dream about her. She was very ill. When will she return?"

Wilu has demanded many times to see their mother and Arasu keeps insisting that she has gone to visit her cousin to avoid breaking his brother's heart.

"She is not visiting our cousin," Arasu says in a soft voice. "Mother is dead. She died last year."

"You lie to me," whines Wilu. "I don't believe you."

"I'm sorry, Wilu."

Wilu begins to sob. Tears stream down his face and glisten on his beard, as he struggles to catch his breath between sobs. Arasu watches him cry, remembering that he himself did not cry when their mother died. It is not that he was not sad. He mourned as one mourns when their mother dies. But he did not cry. He did not cry until the night before the narrowly avoided battle a few days ago, when his mother came to him in a dream.

"I had a dream about you," Arasu tells his brother, his eyes watering once again as he remembers it. "I dreamed that you died. There was a funeral and mother came to see you buried. She told me that she is happy in the other land. She looked strong and brave as she was when she was young, before she became old, weak and sad. She said in the dream that she would take care of you in the other land, and I was not to worry." He doesn't say that the people rejoiced when Wilu died and they danced and played games all day long in celebration. No need to say that. He also doesn't say that he was the one who killed Wilu in the dream, and in a very obscene way. He will never speak of that, because he can barely stand to think of it. Wilu stops crying when he hears this dream about his mother, and he wipes his eyes with a dirty hand, smearing smudge all over his face.

"I will not return here," Wilu says at last, when he can finally speak again. "I have nothing to come back for."

"Where will you go?"

"I don't know," he says, his expression inscrutable. "But I know that Mother will watch over me."

He stares at Arasu for a long time with a somber expression. Then his eyes suddenly twinkle from under his bushy eyebrows, and he says something that Arasu will always remember.

"Goodbye...Arasu."

Arasu smiles. Wilu remembers his name. It comes as quite a shock, and it is strangely touching. Not wanting his brother to notice that he is touched, he gives him a quick hug and then turns his back as Wilu walks away. Arasu has a feeling then that he will never see his brother again, but he knows that he will dream of him.

It is a fine morning and not as cold as usual. Esther sits outside the teepee, helping Elso make rope for his journey to Awani. She is in a bad mood this morning, because things are just not going well for her and Elso. He has been withdrawn for the past two days, ever since the narrowly avoided war. They have slept apart and not touched each other. And he hasn't spoken a word all morning, and Esther feels like an intruder in his private space. She knows that Elso has a generous heart and wouldn't say if he wanted her to leave. But she feels like he does by the way he looks at her sideways, as if checking to see if she is still here. She decides to ask him and get it over with.

"I'm not sure what I'm going to do," she says, broaching the subject carefully. "I'm not sure where to go next. But I'm thinking about it."

He nods, but says nothing.

"Is it alright if I stay here until I figure it out?"

"Sure," he says woodenly, not even looking up from his rope twirling.

She frowns. This is getting nowhere. She throws the rope down dramatically and sits down on her knees to better address him. She glares at him, and when she speaks it is in a loud voice.

"Have I done something wrong?"

He seems surprised by the outburst.

"No."

"Why are you ignoring me?"

"I'm not," he says quietly, still looking at his ropes.

"I can leave if I'm not wanted. I can find somewhere else to stay."

"If you like," is his cryptic reply. "But I have not asked you to."

"Fine," she says loudly. "I will."

"As you like."

He's being vague still, which makes her want to pry the truth out of him.

"What do you want me to do?"

He stares at her suddenly, as if he has decided to be straight with her.

"I don't want anything," he says slowly. "I'm not telling you what to do. But I'm not looking for a wife, if that is what you are asking. I am going away soon and I will be gone many months. Then I plan to sail away for another year's time. I don't want someone at home, worrying about me."

"I didn't ask you that," she insists. "I don't want a husband. Just a place to stay...where I feel good."

"I already said you could stay. You can stay until the spring, if you want. You can stay longer if you really want to. You can live in my teepee while I am in Awani, as long as you don't burn it down."

He smiles at his little joke, but she does not share his mirth.

"Thank you. That's very nice of you," she says in a clipped voice.

It seems settled, yet Esther doesn't feel that anything is really settled. He seems more withdrawn than ever and she has a feeling that he is going to stay that way for a while.

That afternoon, a party of strangers arrives in the village. She doesn't think anything of it at the time, being heavily involved in an intense game of Bu with a young girl. Later, she hears someone shouting that guests from the Wolf tribe are here and she starts scanning the area in between shell movements on the board. She wonders if it is anybody she knows. After beating the young girl, she asks around and learns that the Wolf travelers have gone to take a sweat, to loosen up tired muscles after their long journey. Esther decides to take one herself and she throws off her clothes and crawls into the round sweat lodge, thick with green, smudgy smoke. The smoke is so thick that she has trouble seeing anyone at first – not to mention breathing. When she finally adjusts, she sees the Wolf tribe all gathered at one end. To her utter surprise, Numei is among them.

"Numei!" she shouts, tripping over sweaty legs in her mad dash to greet her old friend.

"Hai Esther," Numei says with a big smile, as if she were expecting her to appear out of the smoke any minute.

"What are you doing here?"

"We're on our way to the Elk tribe. They've requested midwives. It's a big year for them and I hear almost the entire village is pregnant."

"You're going this far north to deliver a baby?"

"Yes. A few of them, probably."

"There's a baby being born right now," a woman says, from behind a wall of smoke. "Did you know that an Owl baby is about to be born? Maybe one of your midwives could help her."

"Three planets in the Owl sign," says a male voice next to her. "And Hawk moon."

All the Wolf tribe agrees that it is a great blessing, and an old woman sitting next to Numei agrees to help immediately. As she rises, Esther takes her wet seat and she and Numei share stories of the past month. Esther tells her about the battle and Wilu, and how she was almost banished from the tribe. Many of the Wolves shake their heads as they listen to the tale. One remarks that it is a shame that such things have to pass in this world. And then Numei suddenly touches Esther's arm with a wet hand and stares at her through the smoky haze.

"Want to come along? The Owls have agreed to loan us three horses. There are only five of us, so there is room on the back of my horse if you want to come."

She leans in close to Esther and whispers in her ear with hot breath.

"It's much nicer than it is here. Trust me."

After her conversation with Elso this morning, there is no doubt in Esther's mind that this is a great opportunity. The timing is almost too perfect.

"Sure," she says firmly. "That's a great idea. When do we leave?"

Elk Tribe

Elk 0'

Beaver moon

Esther is sick. She coughs every two minutes and has a runny nose and a headache. She tries to ignore her symptoms, because this is no time to be sick, but she keeps having to stop and rest. They have to get off the horses and walk often, due to the uneven and steep terrain, and she has been truly miserable.

"The wind is not your friend," says Utani, a wrinkled old stump of a woman with wise eyes. "It has blown this sick into your body."

Esther nods distractedly, thinking Utani is making a joke, but then she sees that she is serious.

"You should wrap your head like mine," Utani insists.

Esther notices that she has a scarf wrapped in many layers around her head so it covers her ears, neck and mouth. Only her eyes and nose are uncovered.

"The wind carries sickness with it," Utani explains. "It blows too strong and it feels bad. You cannot let it into your body. Put on your cloak this instant. And wrap one of your dresses around your head."

"It isn't that cold out. I'll get hot from walking."

"Look at you, covered in goose bumps. It isn't helping your health any."

As Esther puts on her cloak and wraps a dress around her head, Utani puts her basket down and begins rummaging around in it. She pulls out her medicine bag and unties it. Esther notices that the old woman won't let her look into it as she looks through it herself. She tries to peek over Utani's shoulder, but the old woman gives her a dirty look and turns her back to block her view. Utani eventually makes a decision and shows Esther her palm, which is filled with an assortment of strange roots, twigs and leaves.

"I will make you a tea when we stop for the night."

They have fallen behind the group, and Esther reluctantly starts walking again. Onward they go, two shapeless beings in cloaks and head wraps, sheltered from the bitter wind that sends up huge piles of dead leaves and blows the grass around their feet.

After another two hours of walking, they reach the top of the mountain and stop for a rest. They eat a snack of smoked deer meat and stale acorn cake, then they mount the horses again and off they go. The path runs along the eastern side of the mountain, which is less heavily wooded. The horses travel slowly and carefully, because the path is muddy and weakened. They often have to get off the horses and walk over particularly treacherous parts.

Whenever they look up at the sky, it threatens to rain. This makes them push on harder, knowing soon the journey will be a lot less comfortable. Sometime during the late afternoon, the sky makes good on its threats. Everyone bundles up and hunkers down against a light rain. The horses neigh and complain, but they keep moving at the urging of their riders.

They camp for the night in a grove of oaks. The men set up two large tarps and everyone huddles underneath. The horses go off to graze by themselves. Hopefully, they'll find a good tree to sleep under. The men are coaxed to start a fire, although it means using the last of the dry wood they have carried for emergencies. One of them shows off his skills as a fire maker, rapidly spinning the stick until he has a little blaze going. He keeps it well sheltered from the wind, as he struggles to dry pieces of wet wood to make the fire last longer.

Esther heats up water in her little pot and Utani seeps her herbs in it. It takes forever to boil and then she pours it for Esther to drink. She makes a second pot to put into her water skin for later. The drink is spicy and bitter, but she feels a warmth rush into her body as she drinks it. Her nose clears up a little bit and she can breathe again.

"What is it?"

"Ephedra, cinnamon, and perilla leaf," the old medicine woman answers in a soft, husky voice that is full of exhaustion. "And of course, a little Oota."

"Today is the winter solstice," muses Numei, smelling the tea deeply. "I'll take some of that, if you don't mind. I have a feeling that we have some bad weather in our future."

They manage to cook some roots and they eat those along with an oily piece of dried fish. Then, they all nestle close to each other in their fur blankets and watch the fire slowly die. Nobody has the energy to keep it going. By the time it is out, everyone is sound asleep.

Elk 1'

Jay moon

Numei walks out into the chilly morning, looking for her horse, whom she calls Timid. She carries hay in one hand and a horse blanket in another. She knows that Timid must be somewhere on top of this plateau, but she is not sure where he went to. She whistles a tune as she walks. After a long walk, she sees all the horses clumped together in the distance. They graze peacefully, oblivious to her desire to get a move on. As she approaches, they nearly trample her to get at the hay in her hand. She saves the hay for Timid, because that is the one she wants to like her. She learned this trick from the Owl tribe. Let the horses roam free all night long, grazing as they like. The horses will stay close to camp, on account of the hay they will receive first thing in the morning. It is so much nicer than tying up the poor animals, like they are friends rather than master and servant.

After Timid chews up all the sweet hay, she throws the horse blanket on him, attaches the reins, and mounts. Getting on top of a tall Owl tribe horse requires a huge leap and quick reflexes, and she has been slowly learning the skill. It only takes a minute of struggling and falling off to do it this time. She finally manages to climb upon the huge beast and then she gives it a kick and a "Geeeeeaaaaaahh!"

They gallop off. The other horses come to the conclusion that there is hay waiting for them at camp and they start galloping alongside as she leads Timid to camp. The excited horses set a rapid pace and Timid races after them, practically throwing Numei from his back in all the excitement. She struggles to hang on as Timid joins the stampede and pulls on the reins to slow him down before she falls and is trampled to death.

The others wake at the sound of thundering hooves. All the horses want hay and they insistently stomp around until the men rise and give it to them. Soon everybody is up and bundled against the weather. A hasty breakfast is wolfed down and then it is time to go.

They spend the morning pushing north over the mountain tops, but are soon stymied by a heavy rain. As the deluge begins, everyone agrees that they should stop and wait for the rain to let up. The men set up the tarp again and they spend the rest of the afternoon hiding from the weather. The men cannot get a fire going, as all of the dry wood is gone, so they bundle up inside their blankets and gather close together to avoid the rain pouring over the edges of the tarp. Esther feels sorry for the horses, eating morosely in the pouring rain, and she wonders if they hate the rain or if they don't mind it too much. Either way, they don't have any choice and they deal with it as best they can.

Elk 2'

The rain is not too bad today, but the ground is soft and muddy and it is slow traveling. They descend into a valley and the path begins to follow the river known as the Yashi. Then they come to a small marshy spot at the base of the hill. As the horses walk across gingerly, they begin to sink. Numei urges Timid on desperately, but it is no use. The horse can find no purchase. It struggles onward in the muck.

Soon Timid is half submerged. He pushes on, neighing pitifully, but it is very difficult to move. The two women pick up their feet to avoid getting wet, but the horse lurches and they fall off Timid and land in the soft, weedy mud. Esther's entire body is drenched and Numei's is not much drier. Esther curses and shrieks and beats the swampy water with her fists, but Numei only laughs.

"Walk through it the way I am," she yells. "Like this. With your arms and hands spread out on the surface of the muck."

She does as told and manages to move through it well enough. The horse makes it on his own. Soon they are all on the other side of the marsh, soaked and miserable and covered in mud. The horses behind them learn from their mistake and manage to find a way around the marsh without having the same problem.

The two women scramble down to the river to clean themselves off. But when Esther feels the freezing water, she refuses to jump in. She tries twice, but she cannot bring herself to even step up to her knees. So she simply strips off her clothes and washes herself off with little splashes of water until she is clean enough. When she steps out, her feet are completely numb. Numei braves a quick swim and then she quickly crawls out and jumps up and down on the bank until she can feel her body again.

As they put on a change of clothes, Esther notices a Zesti man standing on a cliff side watching them. She points him out to Numei. Numei knows the reputation for thievery that some of the Zesti in this area have and she gets a little nervous. Urging Esther to hurry, she starts scrambling up towards the rest of the group so they can get moving before this silent watcher gets any ideas. But the man only watches and stands still as stone until they have moved on.

From then on, Esther could swear that the man is following them, although she cannot see him. They are forced to walk up a steep, muddy hill and she feels prickles in the back of her neck as they walk, as if the man is following her and boring a hole into her head with those piercing eyes of his. But every time she turns around, there is nobody there.

The path turns west and they cross the tops of the hills for the remainder of the afternoon. It begins to pour again, but the men insist on pushing on through it. As evening approaches, they reach the other side of the range and see a whole valley shrouded in mist and fog. The temperature drops to freezing, and the sky grows blacker than it was before. Esther shivers, soaked and completely miserable. She is angry with the two men for making them ride all day through the rain, but she changes her opinion when she learns why. The men are worried that it is going to snow tonight and they don't want to get caught in it. They want to get down the hill before they are trapped in a snowstorm.

They ride fast down the mountain, racing against the daylight and the weather. But they do not ride fast enough, for it does begins to snow. One moment it is driving rain and the next moment, soft white flakes fall peacefully. Esther yells for Numei to stop the horse. Numei manages to coax Timid to a stop and then she turns around impatiently.

"What?"

Esther stares at her hand, where little flakes are appearing and disappearing. She stares around her in amazement. It is beautiful. The sky is filled with little tiny feathers all falling to earth.

"I've never seen snow before," she whispers.

Were Numei not so cold and wet, she might be in a more generous mood. But her cloak is wet from the dip earlier and she is soaked through and through. She gives Esther an impatient thirty seconds and then urges the horse forward again. Esther just stares at the falling snow in a daze. She is so amazed, that she forgets to be cold.

Soon it gets dark, but nobody wants to stop moving. The path quickly disappears underneath a blanket of snow, but lights appear in the bottom of the valley, so they have a beacon to make for at least. Numei sighs, hoping that it is Elk village making these lights and not some strange tribe of Zesti. It is so foggy out, that she cannot be sure.

"We'll have to walk," Gora says. "It's too dangerous to ride in the dark without a clear path. We could get knocked off the horse by a branch."

Gora is a know-it-all, but he is right a lot of the time, so they usually listen to him. They hop off Timid and Esther's feet land on a soft carpet of cold snow. She reaches down and scoops some up and the cold burns her hand. She puts some on her tongue and sucks on it experimentally. Then she stares up at the sky, at the thousands of tiny flakes falling, and feels like she is dreaming all of this.

"Where's that moon?" Numei grumbles. "I can't see anything."

They don't have long to wait until the nearly full moon rises and bathes the night in a soft glow. Moonlight reflects off the snow to create a perfect illumination. Esther is sure that she is in heaven, as they sluff their way through the powder and the trees. The oak crusted hills, so familiar by now, are turned into the most eerie and hauntingly beautiful landscape she has ever seen.

After an hour of walking, she is no longer thinking about how beautiful everything is. Her only consuming thoughts are of dinner and a hot fire. Her feet are numb and her moccasins are stiff as a board with the consistency of ice. She realizes that she needs new moccasins very badly. Numei has fur-lined moccasins, which look very comfortable. Her own shoes are Beaver made and not designed for this cold weather. Plus they are patched, stretched, worn and cracked from hard use. At least Elso patched the holes for her. Were it not for him, she would have snow in her shoes and serious frostbite.

They have been walking for what seems like hours and progress has been painfully slow. Everyone is dead tired and freezing and they have gone off the path completely, which makes things much more difficult. By some miracle, they keep managing to find little trails through the trees and down into valleys. And still the lights of the village draw closer. Esther stumbles after the others, watching her breath, which is visible like the smoke from the Thunderserpent who breathes fire.

The snow disappears as they descend deeper into the valley and they walk in the rain again. The rain is much less pleasant than the snow. The night is foggy and they cannot see lights any more. Everyone is very nervous and they begin to worry that they will be lost in these woods all night. Esther is already sick and she knows that this cold and wet is going to make it much worse.

One of the men thinks he knows where the lights came from and he begins to go in that direction. They walk for another age, through a nightmare maze of fog, trees and rain so thick they can barely see in front of their faces. All have given up any hope of getting into the village tonight. The women all climb upon the horses again, having figured out that if they ride flat on their stomachs they won't get knocked over by branches. They ride in mute silence, dejected by the endless journey. The men cover the women in tarps and lead the horses on foot. They are mandated to take care of the midwives on this journey and they do their best to keep the women comfortable.

Esther huddles underneath the tarp with Numei, trying not to move and knock the tarp off. It seems like she sits like that for hours, which gives her a lot of time to reflect on her situation. She realizes that as bad as this night is, she is just happy to have company. It would be a nightmare of epic proportions if she were doing this alone and on foot.

"It's that way," Numei shouts. "I thought I heard something for a moment. Music, I think."

"Are you sure?" asks Gora.

"No."

"I think it's this way," he says, pointing in nearly the opposite direction.

"That's not right," she says, peering out of the tarp. "The lights were that way."

"No, I don't think so."

They argue for a while. Nobody wants to make a mistake this late in the night. The others wait helplessly, not having any energy to join in the discussion. Numei's face is determined and she is sure that she is right. Eventually, Gora gives up the struggle and decides to trust her. They go off in the direction she pointed to. After awhile, everyone can barely discern the same music, a faint whiff of noise floating through the night air. After a short ride, they see lights ahead of them, floating out of the fog.

"You were right," he says, giving her frozen hands a grateful squeeze. "I'm glad we listened to you or we'd be totally lost by now."

"I've had a lot of practice being lost," Numei says triumphantly.

Finally they reach the source of the light. The center of town is lit up with two torches, flickering underneath an overhang. Lights come from lighted windows in solid, cozy houses. Nobody is out on a night like this, but they hear loud singing and drumming coming from one of the houses. As they pass, they all shout out a grateful thanks to the singers who unknowingly led them in the right direction. After a short search, they locate the Elk shelter, which is called the Den. They are so exhausted, that they cannot muster up anything more than a pitiful cry of joy. The Den has a stable for the horses and the men search for it as the women run into the main lodge to get warm. But their hope fades as they enter. There is no fire and it seems deserted, or perhaps everyone is asleep.

"Hai!" Numei's voice echoes through the deserted inn. "Anybody here?"

She continues to shout, not being a woman who cares much for politeness or manners even when she is in a good mood. Meanwhile, they make themselves at home. The women strip off all their wet clothes and then go about starting a fire in the big fire pit. A large stack of wood is piled neatly in the corner and there are a few buried coals with which they can light tinder. Soon the fire is blazing and the women begin to thaw out their numb fingers and toes. The men gratefully join them, having found the stable and fed the horses. They too strip down naked and hang their clothes from two lines set right over the fire.

"A wonderful shelter," exclaims Gora. "They think of everything."

"What are the chances that the sweat lodge is hot?" asks Numei.

"That would be wonderful," agrees Cira, the other midwife.

"Almost no chance," insists Gora. "But you're welcome to walk out there and check it out."

Numei thinks about it and decides that she will wait until tomorrow. Meanwhile, the men decide to make *this* place the sweat lodge. They light up the wood stove too and feed it until it is so hot that they all have to back away. Soon numb bodies are toasty and warm, and the night's ordeal seems like a long forgotten dream.

"Anyone hungry?" asks Gora, although he doesn't offer to move.

After a quick search, it is discovered that their food supplies are soaked and ruined.

"Come on, Esther," Numei sighs, rising to her feet. "Help me find some food. I'm starving."

Lighting a candle, they walk into the kitchen area. It is well stocked and Numei becomes excited about all the things they could make with a little effort. She points out many exotic spices with great zeal and plans a banquet in her head. But both women are too tired to actually cook anything, so they settle for leftover deer meat sitting in a pot. And of course, they hang an iron pot for tea.

Almost as soon as the meat is eaten, everyone begins to drift off to sleep. They would like to wait until their soaked bedding is dry, but it is a torture to remain awake. They all drift off to sleep naked and the forgotten pot of tea boils itself dry. Esther wakes up an hour later and notices that her blanket is nearly dry. She pulls it off the fire, still damp, and wraps herself inside it. Her last thoughts as she drifts off to sleep are of the beautiful snow, which she can now enjoy in her dreams from the comfort of a warm bed by the fire.

Elk 3'

Bear moon

Esther does not wake up until the following afternoon. The wood stove has been blazing all night long and the room is incredibly warm. She peels her blanket off her sticky skin and sits up in a daze. Except for Numei, everyone is awake and gathered around the small fire in the fire pit, with iron mugs in their hands. The shelter keeper appears from the kitchen a few moments later. He is an interesting looking man with a huge flat nose and a toothy grin, which he flashes at Esther when her sees her awake.

"I come in last night to find the lot of you passed out on the floor. Thought I had me a den of bears come to hibernate for the winter. Then I peel off these bear blankets of yours and find people under them. Imagine my surprise."

"That's funny," she murmurs, wiping the sleep from her eyes.

"Sure was."

"It's hot in here," she says a moment later.

"That's right. That's the wood stove. Keeps the place real toasty, don't it? We only use the fire pit for cooking, so everything don't get saturated in smoke. Most people around here smell like smoke."

"Mmm hmm," she says, not really listening.

"Seen one before?"

"Yes."

"I'll get you something hot to drink," he says, checking on the huge iron pot bubbling over the fire. "I can see you need a jolt of wake up."

A few moments later, he returns with a steaming iron mug full of a dark, strong scented tea. He takes a little bag of some brown, powdery substance and sprinkles it in. Esther stares at it, amazed. It is sugar. She has not seen sugar since her days at the mission, when she would get a treat of sugar about once a year or so.

"Careful," he warns, as he sets it down next to her. "It's hot."

Esther has also not seen an iron mug since she lived at the mission. The cup holds the heat much better than a wooden one, and the tea burns her lips as she tastes it. Soon she is wide awake and chats amiably with the innkeeper, who pummels her with questions as she drinks his sweet elixir. It is too early for such animated conversation, but she does her best to placate the wide-eyed man. He drinks three cups of tea as they talk and after each one he gets louder and louder. Esther has never met such a loud person in her life.

"My name is Lem," he finally shouts, handing her another cup of tea as he helps himself to a fourth. "Welcome to the Den. Best shelter in the twelve tribes. Imported tea in the morning - all you can drink. With sugar."

"What kind of tea is this?" Esther asks.

"It's imported from China," Lem exclaims. "It's called 'Red Tea'."

"It's good," she says, finishing her mug.

"Let me get you some more," he exclaims.

He pours another steaming cup and sprinkles more sugar into it.

"Breakfast is late usually, but good once it comes. My new girl is a beast in the morning, and it takes her a long time to get going. But she's quite nice once the afternoon rolls around."

"How much do you charge?" asks Esther.

"This time of the year, we charge three tupas per night per person, which includes breakfast and dinner."

"*Three* tupas?" Esther asks shocked.

"We ask a bit more than some shelters," he says with a shrug, "but we offer a lot of luxuries to compensate. And it is winter now, so we have to charge more than usual. Come back in the summer and we'll only charge you two."

Esther realizes that her money will not last long if she stays here. Three tupas a night will break her completely in no time. She begins to think about finding a cheaper place to sleep, while Lem continues to speak of the endless virtues of his shelter. Suddenly Numei sits up, awakened at last by Lem's loud voice.

"Welcome my friend," booms Lem. "The last of the den of bears is awake. Care for some imported tea?"

She nods affirmatively.

"Can you put some sage in my tea?" asks Numei.

"Sage and red tea? I don't think they would go well together," Lem says with a frown.

"On the contrary," says Numei, never taking her eyes off the fire, "they do."

"You got it," says Lem with a shrug, as he places a kettle on the stove in front of them. "A woman of distinction, I see. Fine with me. Say no more."

After bringing her a mug, Lem goes to locate the cook to start lunch. Numei curls up next to the wood stove by herself and sips her tea silently. She is a slow riser by nature and is usually grumpy until a good hour has passed. Esther has learned to wait until Numei starts talking first, to avoid getting snapped at.

A group of other guests soon enters the room and Lem hustles to get them tea. The guests are all noisy and keep up a witty banter with Lem, who hovers around the pot of tea as he talks. When the pot is dry, he pulls out a giant brick of dried tea leaves and makes more. Soon a young willowy girl enters the room with a grumpy look on her face. Lem introduces her as the cook. She doesn't say a word, but sits down with a cup of tea and stares at the fire.

"It's hard to get any peace and quiet around here," Numei observes.

"It's noisy," Esther agrees.

"If it weren't so cold out," Numei says, with a wistful look at the mist through the window, "then I'd go outside."

"Do we get our own room?" asks Esther.

"No, they have three big houses for guests to sleep in. The lot of us will get one of them."

"This place is expensive," confides Esther. "And we don't even get our own room."

"We're not paying anything to stay here, so what do you care?"

"We're not?"

"We are the midwives. We came all this way to help. Of course they will not charge us."

"Yes, of course...but what about me?"

Numei shrugs.

"We can just tell that man you're a midwife too."

"Oh, that's a good idea," exclaims Esther with relief. "And then I won't have to pay anything."

"Lunch is prepared," announces Lem at last. "My daughter usually does the cooking, but she's pregnant. The new girl is slow, as you can see, but she's a decent cook if you're patient enough. I've had to learn more than a bit of patience."

"You're a slow learner," retorts the girl.

"That I am," he retorts. "I won't argue with that."

Esther sits down at one of the tables with great joy. She is powerfully hungry after last night's strenuous efforts and the tea has only made her hungrier. Numei looks up from her vigil by the wood stove, where she sits naked and cross-legged, and eagerly stands and joins them. The benches at the table are lined with various pelts, and she sighs as she sits down on the soft fur with her bare butt.

"Best shelter in the twelve tribes," she announces, rubbing her bottom all over the bear pelt that she sits upon.

Lem brings loaves of coarse bread, which resemble Beaver Bread, deer meat, and a piece of smoked salmon for everybody. Then he brings a little pot of melted whale blubber to smear on the bread.

"There's no dinner today," he announces, when everybody has food. "As you all know, this is the full moon, and there's a celebration tonight. I hope to see you all there."

After lunch, they all bring their things to one of the sleeping houses. It is crafted in the northern style, low and long, with two fire pits. Lem shows them around and explains to them that they'll be required to get their own firewood from the large storage hut near the stable. Then he brings up financing, and he is rather surprised when he finds that none of them expect to pay for lodging.

"I won't make the midwives pay," he says, suddenly serious. Then he looks at the men with wide eyes. "But the rest of you...I don't know about that."

"We're all midwives," Numei explains, pointing to all of the women, "and these two men are our escorts. It's a dangerous land for a woman to walk alone. We need them and you need us. You would make them pay for the service they do for your tribe?"

"I'll have to discuss it with the council," he announces. "If they agree to sponsor the lot of you, then that's fine with me. If not, then we'll talk further."

The way he speaks, it seems clear that he wants to get paid one way or another. He smiles his toothy smile as a sort of apology and disappears out the door. They all get comfortable and get the fires going to warm up the hut. Then there is nothing to do but wait for evening. Esther falls into a state of lethargy and naps the afternoon away.

Early in the evening, Esther wakes reluctantly. Rain patters on the roof once again. From her bed, she watches Numei hustle about, getting ready for the party. Numei puts together a costume of furs and a great hat of various feathers, whistling while she works. But the rest of the group is not as cheery as she is. Apparently, nobody but Numei is in the mood to go outside and get soaked and cold to go to this polar day celebration.

Although Esther is in full agreement with the group mind, she allows herself to be coaxed into getting dressed. If she can muster up no enthusiasm, at least she can look the part. She wears her sexy deerskin dress, drapes furs about her body, and even allows Numei to adorn her in a hat of blue jay feathers. The rest of the group dawdles by the fire, so Numei suggests that they meet at the party. Esther puts on her cloak and goes outside with Numei, knowing that if she doesn't then she'll likely not go at all. The cold and rain are a shock and the girls hunker down and start walking.

"Do you know where it is?" shouts Esther.

"I think so," Numei says, looking around suspiciously. "But it's not easy to see right now."

They walk through the village commons and then Numei stops under an overhang to get her bearings.

"Our hats are getting ruined," she complains. "And I'm not sure which way it is. The rain drowns everything out."

Numei gives her hat to Esther and runs back to the shelter to ask Lem for directions. She returns ten minutes later, thoroughly soaked. Her face does not give Esther any hope.

"He's gone already. We'll have to find it ourselves. The whole village is already there."

Esther dutifully follows the very determined Numei back out into the rain. They make a wide loop around the edge of the commons, looking for the path that Numei knows leads to the assembly hall. She finally locates it, and she and Esther start running down a muddy path through an impossible deluge that threatens to drown them.

"Didn't we just do this?" Esther asks, as they run.

Numei laughs, but doesn't reply. They run faster, as the feathers on their heads droop and fall. Esther realizes suddenly that her reluctance to leave the shelter was simple foreknowledge of the future. Her body didn't want to do this. Her poor, overworked body is not in the best of shape right now, having just gotten over a sickness and a rigorous journey. If it weren't the full moon, she'd turn right around and go home.

Eventually, they see a great structure ahead of them and many lights. It is a huge building, but so hidden by trees that it is hard to see until you are right upon it. They race into the hall and sigh with relief when they are no longer getting poured upon. Numei peels off all her clothes, forgetting how much work she put into her costume and prances over to the fire to dry off. Esther wants to do the same but she feels self-conscious. Although there are a few naked people drying off, this seems to be a tribe who generally values clothing. Everyone is dressed in very elaborate clothing and costumes. So she endures her wet clothes and goes to sit by the fire.

The room is filled with people, swirling around with fancy China teacups filled with wine. Many wear Chinese robes. Some wear elaborate Russian costumes with big fur hats. Some are dressed as Spaniards. Esther later finds out that it is a costume party and you must wear clothes from another culture. Numei knew this and she tried to make her and Esther appear Zesti, but the rain ruined it.

They dry off by the fire and sip wine from a big wooden cup. Numei chats with everybody, seeming to know many faces. Somebody hands them two wooden bowls and points at a great table filled with food. They take the bowls gratefully and go get something to eat. Esther helps herself to a stew of roasted venison with mushrooms, corn bread, sweet roasted roots, seaweed salad, and some brown smudge that she cannot identify.

There is a great clay oven with a fire burning in one end. A man and a woman stand before it, making corn cakes and having an argument about who makes better ones. He points to the charred ends of her cakes and she points out the oblong shapes and uneven lumps in his. When Numei and Esther try to take a few cakes, the woman stops them.

"Those are no good. They're old and dried out...and lumpy," she says, with a sideways glance at the man.

"So?" asks Numei, not getting the joke. "We're really hungry and we don't care."

"They only take a minute," she insists. "See I'm already making them."

She quickly makes two patties and throws them into the oven. True to her word, the patties cook quickly. They begins to bubble and morph shape almost as soon as they hit the clay base. Numei reaches her hand into the oven and pulls it out immediately.

"How do you get it so hot?" she asks. "I can't even reach in there."

"It's simple," exclaims the man, happy to show off his tribe's superior oven. "It all boils down to where you put the hole. You have your hole in the top of the oven, am I right?"

"Yes."

"That's dead wrong. You have to put the hole right in the front - just before the entrance. Then the heat in the oven builds up."

"That's clever," agrees Numei, taking two corn cakes and returning to the fire.

Esther accepts the woman's superior corn cakes and returns with Numei. True to their word, the corn cakes are great. So is everything else on her plate.

"It is good to eat well again," Esther says, with a mouth full of venison. "The Owls are the worst cooks."

"I told you this was a good place," says Numei, licking a finger full of the brown smudge. "Mmmm."

"What is that?"

"Coco bean."

"What's that?"

"The Spanish call it chocolate," a man next to them says.

"Try it," Numei says, sticking Esther's finger into the paste.

Esther tastes it. It is bitter, but sweet and delicious. She can't help but eat the rest of it immediately. As she eats, she hums with pleasure. After cleaning her plate of the rest of the good food, she goes back to the table to look for more coco. It is all gone, but she scrapes the bowl with her fingers and then licks them clean. She wants to lick the bowl too, but she is afraid that people will see her and laugh.

As she walks back to the fire, she sees yet another pregnant woman. The woman is dressed like a southern Zesti, with a huge belly sticking out of her grass skirt. That makes at least ten pregnant women she has seen so far. And there is another one by the fire, leaning against her husband. This one seems exhausted and tired, and she is so big that Esther is amazed that she even made it out tonight. Then she sees Lem sitting near her, and realizes that it is his daughter. He waves when he spies them and walks over to talk to her and Numei.

"Are you enjoying the party?" he asks.

"Yes."

"Where's the music?" asks Numei, from across the fire. "And the dancing?"

"Most of our women are with child, as you can see," Lem explains. "You don't want to see a woman nine months pregnant dance. It's not a pretty sight."

"What about the rest of us?"

"I heard that Cougar tribe sent some musicians," he says with a shrug. "They should start playing soon."

"Good."

"Now I understand why they need midwives so badly," Esther says. "The whole village is pregnant."

"The upcoming new moon will have sun, moon, and Jupiter in the Elk constellation," explains Lem. "The big three - not to mention Venus floating among them somewhere. Four planets...that's a stellium. And Mars in the Raccoon sign. That's a powerful child in our tribe. One of these new babies will be chief someday. Everybody wants a chief in the family."

"Having a chief in the family is nice," says Numei. "But it's also a pain. Trust me."

"Why should I trust you?"

"My cousin is Chief Vayanna."

"Really," Lem exclaims, a radiant smile lighting up his face. "I didn't know that. Chief Vayanna...that's a beautiful woman. I met her once. She stayed in my very own shelter. And you're her cousin?"

He stares at her, drinking her in. His smile grows bigger.

"Are you married?"

Soon the Cougar musicians begin to play, and Numei excuses herself to dance. Lem follows her to the dance floor and she gives him a suspicious eye, wondering if he is making a move on her.

"I wish my husband were here to dance with me," she says, trying to be subtle. "I miss him."

"You're just horny," he says quickly. "It will pass. In the meantime, I want to ask you something." He turns serious. "Would you do me the honor of being my daughter's midwife?"

She finds the request touching and decides to ignore the horny remark.

"You have no other midwife yet to attend to you?"

"There are four midwives in the whole village to attend to about twenty mothers. Nobody has committed to our daughter's birthing hour and Siyle and I would very much like you to be that person."

"I would be glad to," says Numei.

"Thank you."

"I will give her a full examination tomorrow," she says, her eye roving to the dance floor. "But for now, if you will excuse me-"

"Wait a minute," Lem says, waving her over to speak to his daughter. "We must tell Siyle." Then he hurries to tell her the good news.

"I am very happy," Siyle says to Numei, gripping her with a clammy hand. "It would be an honor to be under your care. We are ever so fond of the Wolf tribe and your cousin, Vayanna, who has made so many visits to our tribe. I am sure you will be a wonderful midwife."

"I will be a wonderful midwife," agrees Numei. "But now there is music and I will go dance. We will discuss everything tomorrow."

"Yes, go dance," agrees Lem, pawing at her with his hands. "Dance your little heart out. We'll talk tomorrow."

Esther follows Numei to see the musicians. Walking to the south corner, where the musicians play, she is suddenly aware of just how large this assembly hall is. It is the biggest one she has ever seen, rivaling even the massive Beaver hall. It has four wood burning stoves at each corner of the room and a massive fire pit in the center. The ceiling is extremely tall and smoke from the fires has plenty of room to gather and dissipate. She wonders at the amount of wood it must takes to keep a place like this warm all night long. It must take an entire tree.

The music of the Cougar tribe is very nice, but rather unorganized and chaotic. This is because the Elk tribe has been rather distracted, and more worried about finding midwives than hiring musicians. In fact, nobody hired musicians at all this year. These four just happened to come by for the party and they agreed to play some music. A couple of Elk tribe musicians round out the group with a violin and a bizarre instrument that looks like some sort of cannon inspired by demons with hideous imaginations. It plays deep bass notes. When Numei asks about it, someone calls it a tuba and claims it comes from Russia.

Many drunk men begin to dance and sing and those women who are not bursting with child join them. Numei dances with all of the men, as she likes to do, and she is the life of the party. Another barrel of wine is opened and the men all pounce on it. Soon they are rip roaring drunk and the party really starts to cook. But all at once, the pregnant women become tired and order their husbands to take them home. The poor husbands, who are just starting to have a great time, have to leave and walk their wives home in the late night drizzle. Many promise to return, but few do. Eventually, it is down to a small handful of diehards.

Numei plans to stay up all night and dance, but Esther is not up for such a long night. Numei tries to get her to stay longer, but Esther only yawns and waves goodnight. The rain has died to a drizzle, which makes it much easier to find her way back to the shelter. She only gets lost once, which seems a minor miracle, and she doesn't step in a single puddle on the way back.

Elk 5'

Eagle moon

In the afternoon, Esther explores the village thoroughly. It feels good to be up and about, after sleeping most of the morning away. The houses are quaint and sturdy, made with thick, even redwood planks and thousands of little black rocks set in a mud plaster. Little wooden statues of various animals stand proudly in front of each house. Almost every house has a little garden in front, in which herbs and useful plants are grown. The gardens are all overgrown this time of the year, with only the hardiest perennials able to live.

The village is located in a little valley in the heart of the redwoods. Not much sunlight gets through, due to a constant mist that surrounds the valley and the high trees that act as an ever-present umbrella. There are three good clearings in the whole village, including the commons. The commons is a busy little place, with many different shops and buildings. Nobody trades from under a tarp or tent. All goods are sold in enclosed shops. Esther walks among them, admiring the variety of goods and services available. One cute little building has a sign announcing that she must come experience the Exotic Goods Store. She peeks inside and instantly a droopy old man walks out of the shop and orders her inside to see it.

The Elk tribe is notorious for it's closed trading system. With the exception of food, all goods must be sold to a shop, which then resells it at a slightly higher price. There has been much debate about this system, which is understandably unpopular among the other tribes.

The place is a clutter of exotic things from all over the world, gathered during the travels of the Twelve Tribes trading ships, which the Elk tribe has a large investment in. Everything from old books in various languages, rugs, paintings, foreign made weapons and clothing from various cultures are all strewn about. The place makes one feel as if the whole world could exist side by side on shelves and piled on the floor. Esther spends a long time searching through the various artifacts, imagining the people who crafted them. She considers buying a little Chinese bag made from delicate silk, until she remembers she needs new shoes first.

She goes to a clothing trader, who has a handful of pre-made moccasins in stock, all used and in various states of disrepair. The trader, a serious man with two deformed fingers, offers to make her a new pair, custom made for her feet. She considers. But one of the used pairs fits her feet perfectly and as a bonus is lined with soft rabbit fur. The shoes are a little cuffed and worn, but otherwise in good shape. She tries to bargain with him, but the dour man is stubborn and difficult to talk to. He finally agrees to nine tupas for the shoes, which is a whole one tupa less than he wanted for them. It seems a lot for used shoes, but it will be a whole lot cheaper than paying him to make her a new pair. So she forks over the shells and the shoes are hers. Gratefully taking off her tattered shoes, she puts these on. Instantly, the world is a nicer place. Her feet sink into the soft fur and she grins with delight.

Forgetting about the money she just spent, she bounces out the door and hops about like she has brand new feet to go along with the shoes. She takes a long walk in her new slippers and wiggles her toes joyfully in the soft down. Every step is a chance to sink her feet deeper into it.

Elk 7'

Raccoon moon

The Wolf midwives prepare to go to a big meeting of mothers and midwives today. Each has a client already, but all midwives will be given at least one more today. Because many of the mothers will try to give birth on the new moon, two clients could potentially give birth at the same time. So they will try to determine which mothers are likely to be early or late and pair them with ones likely to give birth on or around the new moon.

Lem has a big breakfast prepared to give them strength. Ever since Numei accepted his daughter as her client, he has been especially generous and fussed over her and her friends. He even talked to the council himself and got them to sponsor the two men, so nobody has to pay anything.

"I know somebody that needs a midwife," Lem tells Esther over breakfast. "You're the only one that doesn't have a mother to care for yet, aren't you?"

"Well yes...I mean, no...I mean...I'll see at the meeting," she says vaguely.

"As you like."

He gives her a strange look, but says nothing. Esther tries not to look guilty, but she has been feeling bad about lying to him. She considers telling the truth, except her little bundle of shells is rapidly shrinking and she could easily go broke here, as everything is so expensive. So she keeps her mouth shut, which means she'll be accompanying the women to the meeting to keep up appearances.

The gathering of midwives and mothers is in the assembly hall. When they arrive, they can see that it has already started. Esther floats away from the group, not planning to go inside, but Numei waves at her impatiently to follow them in.

"It's cold out here," Numei insists. "Just come in and watch."

"This is a private meeting, isn't it?"

"Don't worry. You're with me."

After a moment's hesitation, she accompanies Numei inside. The room is not much warmer on the inside than on the outside. Only one wood stove burns, and the fire pit is burnt down to coals. A huge group of pregnant women sits side by side, wrapped in nothing but furs. Around the wood stove are all the midwives. There are three midwives from the Cougar tribe, one from the Raven tribe, three from the Elk tribe, and now three from the Wolf tribe. When Numei, Esther and the other Wolf midwives enter, all eyes turn toward them. Numei walks confidently inside and takes a seat with the other healers and midwives. Esther follows uncertainly and sits next to her. Introductions are made, although most of the older midwives know each other already.

"I am Numei, a Wolf healer. This is Esther, who is my juwanna."

"You are all very welcome here," sighs an elder Elk midwife. She is Ruala, rail-thin and wrinkled, with a no nonsense air carved into the lines of her face. "Now the meeting may begin. We are pleased to see that the Wolf tribe has sent so many midwives. Thank you very much. We will remember this favor in the future."

"What's a juwanna?" Esther whispers.

"An assistant."

Esther nods, impressed by Numei's wisdom. She now understands the plan. Numei will pass Esther off as an assistant. This will certainly fool Lem, who might think it strange if she did nothing for any of the births. Plus she will possibly get to help out with the births, which could be fun.

"That makes ten midwives. We are doing better. And now, let us move on to our discussion for the day. It is time to discuss postponement and induction of pregnancy."

Everyone agrees that it is a good idea to discuss this and the room falls into a serious, hushed silence.

"There are eight days until the new moon. I would assume that you all hope to give birth then. I judge that many of you are ready now and have done the necessary things to delay birth. Let us go over them again. Take mijorke twice or three times a day. Drink lots of water, so the mijorke won't make you ill. Cut out all meat except for fish oil, which you should be drinking regularly. And stay cool. I know this is uncomfortable when it is this cold out, but we must stay cool. If we only keep our house too warm, we will hasten birth. The temperature in this room right now is perfect. Your house should be kept this temperature or less. If your husband complains, remind him what is at stake."

All the mothers laugh, picturing their husband's faces when they announce that there will be no heat allowed in their houses until the new moon is done.

"As you know, slowing down a birth means bigger babies being born. This makes it harder to give birth and increases problems. So we wish to see each one of you personally and decide if there will be any problems we need to deal with. Some of you will have to be bound. Some will have to stand a certain way for many hours. We will check you in the order in which you are sitting and decide by committee what is best to be done.

"As for those who are not yet ready to give birth, you must do the opposite of what we have described above. You will not take mijorke, of course. We will check you and we may offer more suggestions in order to hasten your birth. Please listen carefully to our instructions. We will do our best to make all of your babies into new moon babies. But if we feel it is not a good idea to force it, then please do what is best for your child and take our advice. A Beaver moon or Cougar moon will be a good moon for your child also."

"Just make sure it's not a Jay moon!" a mother shouts and there is much laughter.

"Of course, we wouldn't want that," Ruala says, chuckling. "Now, let the first mother come forward."

A woman leaves her bear fur blanket by the iron stove and lies down on a thin table, lined with a rabbit fur blanket. Two of the elder midwives come forward to examine her. One gently probes her belly and the other examines her flower. They both ask a lot of questions about pains and sensations and if she has felt any contractions. Finally, one of her examiners asks all of the other midwives to feel her belly and see if they agree with her opinion. Esther is offered a feel and she gingerly touches the rock hard belly, but she says nothing.

Most of the midwives agree that the baby is too high in the womb and must be lowered. But there is a little disagreement about the way it should be lowered. After a heated argument, they agree that she should be bound. A skin is taken from a pile and wrapped around the top of her belly.

"This will push the baby slowly downwards into the lower part of your womb," says an Elk midwife, fitting it tightly while the next woman gets naked. "It should have been done sooner, but better late than never. Wear it all day and night and tighten it whenever it becomes loose."

"Why?" asks the mother nervously. "I don't understand."

"It will make for an easier birth."

The next mother is given a wrap for the underside of her belly, because the consensus is that the baby is in a poor position. Esther is amazed at how they can tell just from looking at the big swollen belly. All of the mothers look the same to her.

Finally all the mothers have been seen and most of them are pronounced fit and ready for birth. One very pregnant mother is told to stop taking mijorke and fish oil and to do everything she can to make the birth happen as quickly as possible. This makes her very mad. She jumps up from the table and puts her clothes back on, steaming with rage.

"I know I can make it to the new moon. I can wait eight more days."

"Be warned, we think it is dangerous," says her examiner. "You may hurt the child or yourself by waiting. You are too ripe."

"I can make it," she says hollowly.

"It's your life."

"Can I have your attention?" asks Ruala, waving a hand in the air to stop the chattering mothers. "We will meet again on the Wolf moon to go over induction of pregnancy and final birth details. You all know the correct diet and things to do - so please do them. Now, we will assign midwives. There are ten midwives present and twenty-three mothers who need them. This is an unprecedented number of births in one month, but then it is a special year for the Elk tribe. Therefore, this is what I have decided. Each midwife will have two mothers. Those with juwanna's will have three, and the juwanna may assist to take the pressure off her jodhai. In an emergency, the juwanna may even perform the duties of a midwife herself, using her jodhai as a guide."

Esther's eyes open wide in astonishment and she and Numei share a quick glance. Numei's eyes are no longer confident, but are as nervous as Esther's. As Ruala assigns mothers to midwives, Esther whispers desperately in Numei's ear.

"What do we do?"

"We can't do anything," she whispers back.

"Tell them I'm not a ju - a whatever it was,"

"No, I will not."

"But-"

"Shhhhh," she hisses. "We'll talk later."

"Numei," intones the ever serious voice of Ruala, "who are you promised to already?"

"Siyle, the daughter of Lem will be one of mine," Numei says. "It is already arranged."

"Very good. Do you think that you can handle two more with the help of your juwanna? And do you think she is competent to deliver a baby in an emergency?"

Numei glances at Esther briefly and again Esther sees the fear in her eyes.

"Yes," she says slowly. "In an emergency, yes."

"Excuse me-" Esther says, her eyes bugging out with fright.

Numei hits her hard in her side and glares at her. Esther falls silent, the protest dying in her throat.

"Then you will be given two more. You will have Viana and Hasa. Good luck to you both."

"Thank you," says Numei.

"Juwanna, what is your name?"

"Esther," she says in a tiny voice.

"Esther, heed all your jodhai says," Ruala intones solemnly, and then she laughs at Esther's terrified expression. "And don't look so worried. You will do just fine."

When the assignments are finished, the midwives and mothers begin to circulate. Numei glances at her two assigned mothers. She wants to talk to them, but first things first. Grabbing her panicked young apprentice, Numei pulls her aside to talk to her privately.

"Numei, I don't know how to deliver a baby!"

"I'll teach you."

"But I can't learn that fast."

"You'll have to," she insists. "Don't worry. You won't have to deliver a baby by yourself. You'll just be my assistant. It will be fun."

"I just think you should tell them the truth."

"Tell them that I lied to them in order to get you free room and meals. That I pretended you were my assistant and brought you here just to fool Lem. Imagine what they would think! You don't know the Elk tribe. They'll remember that forever. This is a great opportunity for me, Esther. My first midwife assignment outside the Wolf tribe. I will not ruin my reputation and this opportunity over something so stupid as that. If they want me to take three, I'll have to take three. And you'll have to help me."

"I just don't think I can."

"It will be a rewarding experience. Watching a baby being born is magical."

"I want to help. I just think that they would rather have an experienced woman."

"They are just happy to have anybody. You saw the shortage of midwives in there."

"But what if something bad happens? What if I do something wrong?"

Numei grabs Esther's hand and gives it a squeeze.

"Don't worry. I'm not careless or stupid. I'm going to keep a very close eye on you. I'm going to teach you everything you need to know beforehand. I'll be there with you always and if something goes wrong, I'll be there to fix it."

Esther falls silent, seeing that Numei is determined to do this. But her eyes still show much confusion.

"Just be quiet and do what you're told. All right?"

"All right," she finally says.

"You're my juwanna now. Remember that. You have to do whatever I say from now on."

She smiles, amused by the stern voice she is using. Then she leads Esther to meet and greet the new mothers who wait for them. The two new mothers, Viana and Hasa, couldn't be more different. Viana is a big, bossy woman with a deep loud voice. She has assisted midwives herself and she already has two kids. She is very confident about the whole process and assures Numei that she will not cause her a bit of trouble. On the other hand, Hasa is her exact opposite. She would normally be a very tiny woman, except she is pregnant, so she is small and skinny with a very big belly. She seems confused, disoriented and very nervous about the whole process. She has a million questions about everything and Numei must work hard to put her at ease.

Eventually, Siyle, the daughter of Lem, draws Numei away and Hasa starts asking Esther questions instead. Esther has no idea about anything she is saying, so she resorts to saying "I'll ask Numei" over and over again. Viana watches her silently, which makes Esther very uncomfortable.

"How long have you been training?" Viana asks suddenly.

"Not long," she admits.

"But you have assisted before? In a real live birth?"

Esther hesitates and then forces a 'yes' out of her mouth. She looks away, so Viana cannot see her guilty, lying eyes. She is sure that the game is already up. But Viana only nods quietly and they fall into an uneasy silence.

After chatting for a while, all the mothers make the long journey home. Soon only the midwives are left. Someone puts on a pot of tea and the conversation turns to strange and unusual births they have experienced and different techniques for dealing with them.

"Pay close attention," whispers Numei. "Listen carefully and learn. Do not say that you have no experience or are afraid or anything stupid like that. Act like you know what you are doing. Better yet, try not to say anything at all. If someone asks you a difficult question, I'll interfere."

"Cause they'll know -"

"Yes, they certainly will. You're a terrible liar."

Esther sits quietly and tries to learn as much as she can from the collection of old, wise and powerful women before her. Numei simply refers to Esther as her 'juwanna' a few more times and nobody questions her abilities further. In fact, they are very supportive and strive to make her comfortable. But as she hears the horror stories of some of these midwives, she wishes that someone would discover her inexperience and take the job away from her. She doesn't know what she would do if a baby got tangled up in its own 'lifeline'.

Elk 9'

Swan moon

Esther is awakened in the darkness by a gentle hand. She yawns and tries to turn over, but the hand shakes her awake harder. Finally, she opens her bleary eyes and looks upon the face of Numei.

"I cannot sleep. Come, let us go see the sunrise this morning," whispers Numei. "From a certain spot, we are supposed to be able to witness a stunning sunrise."

"No, no," mumbles Esther. "I want to sleep."

"Come on," Numei insists. "Sleep is overrated. We are going to be keeping very strange hours these days and we need to get ourselves prepared."

"Prepared for what? You're the one who cannot sleep."

"Come on, juwanna," Numei insists with a little smile. Then she turns resolutely and walks outside.

Esther rises groggily and searches in the darkness for her warm clothes and her coat. She sniffs her clothes questioningly as she puts them on and realizes that it has been too long since she has washed any of them. She will have to do it soon, before she offends everyone within smelling range.

It is miserably cold and pitch black outside. Not a star can be seen underneath the heavy cloud cover. The cold stings Esther's cheeks and numbs her body. She sighs and trudges after Numei in the darkness. She has a strange sense of deja vu, as if she has been here before. Trudging after this strange woman in the darkness, toward some inexplicable goal that only Numei understands.

Up and up and up they walk, along a thin path that winds through redwood trees. They pass over rocks and across little streams. Soon they tromp over a thin layer of snow, their feet making a crunching sound as they crush the delicate crust. Numei is surefooted as ever, expertly making her way uphill toward their destination. Esther wiggles her toes in her new shoes and is glad for them. They really keep the cold out.

Suddenly Esther slips on a rock and falls hard on her left hand. The sting is worse because of the cold and she curses and holds her bruised hand tenderly, until Numei comes over to look at it. Numei holds her hand gently in her two gloved hands, until it warms up.

"Wiggle your fingers. Can you move it?"

After testing it out a number of times, Esther decides that it isn't permanently hurt. Numei graciously takes off her gloves and hands them to her.

"You wear these until we can get you some of your own."

"Thank you."

They continue to walk and Esther is more careful than before. They get lost for a while, because the path is hard to follow with the snow. After going back and forth a number of times, Numei is able to locate the correct route. They navigate a particularly large boulder and suddenly find themselves on a ridge overlooking the whole valley below. A sharp wind blows cold from the east, where a barely discernable glow can be seen.

"Lucky the clouds are so high," Numei says happily. "Or we would not see anything."

Soon a pink ribbon of light appears in a dark blue sky and then the colors gradually emerge bolder and bolder with approaching day. Reds, yellows, and oranges all smear against the sky haphazardly. The whole valley lights up below, framed in soft light. Esther sighs and sits down on a rock. It is beautiful. But she will only admit that to herself. She doesn't want Numei to know that she is glad in any way that she was awakened to come here.

But Esther doesn't have to say anything. Numei knows that she is happy by the peaceful look in her eyes. After the sun rises and the day becomes warmer, Numei begins to explain the basics of being a midwife. Her plan works well. In this beautiful spot, far from the chaos of the village, Esther's mind is quiet and better able to concentrate on the many things that she must learn to become Numei's assistant.

Elk 10'

Numei gets Esther up at dawn to hike again. This time they hike through thick western woods, upon a poorly kept trail. The trail follows a beautiful stream, breached by fallen logs along its length, creating a thousand tiny waterfalls. It is a peaceful place, with the music of water in your ears and the smell of mulching wood overcoming all other senses. Even the trail is exciting. Some parts are marshy and they sink up to their ankles. They jump on logs and balance precariously on small branches. Many little adventures keep them on their toes. Finally, they come to rest on a large log overlooking a shallow pool in the stream. There they sit, legs dangling, and listen to the quiet chattering of the water and the loud mutterings of birds up in the tallest trees. Esther stares in awe at the immense redwoods that are bigger even than the redwoods she encountered outside the Santa Cruz mission. One tree is so impossibly thick and high that she is sure it must have been growing since the beginning of time.

"This is an old forest," Numei tells her. "Some of these trees were here before people ever came to this land. I thought it would be a good place to talk."

"It's a good place to do anything," agrees Esther.

Numei begins to tell Esther everything she can think of about pregnancy. For someone who has no children, she knows an awful lot about it. Today, they discuss what would happen if Esther were forced to be alone with the mother for an extended period of time during the birth process. Esther's head is filled with every conceivable thing that can go wrong and what do about it. Numei draws crude and funny pictures in the mud to explain various things.

"Is that supposed to be a baby or a coyote?" Esther asks.

"It's a baby," Numei says, laughing.

"What do I do if a coyote comes out instead?"

"Run."

Esther starts laughing hysterically, which busts Numei up too. When they stop laughing, Numei decides that they need a break. Esther has been steadily losing focus for the past hour, and shows signs of cracking up completely.

"I want a sweat. What do you think?"

Esther agrees wholeheartedly, glad for the break from learning, and they both rise and walk back the way they came. A sweat would be just the thing on one of these cool, wet afternoons and she wonders why she didn't think of it first.

Back in the village, they make a beeline for the sweat lodge. On the way, they pass many who smile and greet them, knowing who they are. It makes Esther feel important and she walks taller and smiles at everyone. She begins to feel as if she could handle all of the new responsibilities that she finds herself stuck with.

Outside the main circle, they are approached by two small Zesti men, dressed in thick furs. Esther wonders what they are doing here. Traders perhaps? But they merely hold out their hands and stand there silently. They must want food. Or tobacco? Esther and Numei try to communicate with the men, but get nowhere.

A few moments later, Lem appears and comes over to say hello. He greets the Zesti too, but gets no smile in return for his smile. He shrugs and ignores them.

"What news?" he says.

"Who are these men?" asks Esther.

"They live on our land."

"What do they want?"

He shrugs.

"Anything you want to give them. Just watch yourself around them. They are thieves and don't like us all that much."

As if to prove it, he smiles again at the men, but gets only fierce stares as a result.

"See," he says, with his same goofy smile.

"Where does their tribe live?" Numei asks.

"Nowhere. They used to live here in the time of my grandfather. Their tribe was small and weak and they were pushed out of this valley many years ago. There was a bad war with the Wailakki tribe and they were nearly decimated. The survivors were driven over the mountains, where they went into hiding. This valley was a perfect place for a village, with trails already made and lots of good clearings, so we stepped in and took over."

"And nobody tried to stop you?" asks Numei.

Lem laughs.

"A small battle. Some retaliations. Nothing too horrible. The Wailakki sent some families to habituate this valley after they beat - what's their name - that little Zesti tribe. They planned to expand their territory, of course, except we got here first. We had set up camp and were already comfortable here. They sent back some warriors to take it, but the Owl tribe was here helping us clear trees and our two tribes beat the elk armor they wore to pieces and sent them howling home."

He looks at the Zesti men and waves to them.

"Ain't that right, men?"

They merely stare at him, stony faced.

"You took their village away?" asks Esther, feeling suddenly sorry for the poor men.

"No we didn't. The Wailakki took it. We took it from the Wailakki."

At the mention of the Wailakki, the two Zesti spit on the ground and utter a foul stream of curses.

"See? They still hate them and that was back in my grandfather's time. They were decimated by the Wailakki. Killed down to a few women and children. We were there to help them survive. If not for us, someone would have probably killed them off entirely or turned them into slaves. We are a lot nicer than some of the tribes around here. We invited them back to live here and let them stay in huts on our land. Give them clothes and food sometimes, as long as they don't steal. They used to steal from us all the time, until we threatened to throw them out. Now they beg instead and do a little work for us when we have some."

"Can't you adopt them into the tribe?" asks Numei.

"They won't learn our language. They're a proud people, despite the fact that they don't have much to be proud about. Old Gui married one of their women many years back. She never did learn much Spanish, but she bore him a couple of strong children.

"Are they hungry?" asks Esther.

"I don't know," Lem says with a smile. "I never can figure out what it is they want. I just give them a tupa every now and then and let them buy whatever they need."

He tosses the men a tupa, as if to demonstrate his generosity. The taller of the two catches it, examines it briefly, and then puts it in the sheath in which he carries his bone knife. He continues to glare at Lem silently, offering no hint of gratitude.

"I have never seen those men smile and I've known them since they were boys. If they would only smile and say 'thank you', perhaps I'd give them four more."

"Well, we were going to the sweat lodge," says Numei, looking at them for an uncomfortable moment.

"I won't keep you. Dinner will be a little late today, but it will be very good. None of that dried bark that the new girl usually cooks. We're eating some excellent elk meat that my good friend killed just yesterday. He's a great cook. He's making potatoes too. I told him about what a good job you were doing with my daughter and insisted he make you all a good dinner for a change.

"You're cook is good," says Esther. "I like her food. Except for that soup she keeps serving over and over."

Numei makes a face just thinking about that soup.

"Is that stuff horrible or what?" Lem asks, with an embarrassed shake of his head. "I have no idea what she put in it. Tastes like a rotting carcass. I told her to throw it out. You'll never eat it again, I promise you that."

On that note, they go their separate ways. The women go to the sweat lodge, Lem goes to the shelter to throw out the soup and the two silent Zesti walk to the commons to buy some corn with their tupa before the food trader goes home.

Elk 12'

Wolf moon

The mothers and midwives meet again to discuss the finalities of birth. The new moon will be here in four days and babies will be popping out all over. The chief of the Elk tribe has also come for a visit. She is a beautiful woman, although it is a cold beauty like a sculpture made from ice. She is stately and tall and moves with consummate grace. She is of a serious frame of mind and there is no trace of anything frivolous in her personality, although her smile is heartfelt. As she greets all of the midwives personally, she rewards them with that smile as if it were a great treasure that she often keeps under lock and key.

"Hello, I am Nadria," she says, as she meets Esther. "Thank you for all your help. Welcome to the Elk tribe. I hope your stay here has been welcoming so far."

"I am Esther," she says, trying to speak to Nadria as if she were a regular person and not the chief. "I have enjoyed my stay here. Thank you for the hospitality."

"Not at all," she says. "Thank you for coming. We are very grateful for your presence."

After a few more brief words, she moves on to greet the other midwives. Esther watches her go, feeling honored to have met her. There is something about Nadria that makes one feel special to have merely spoken with her. She is the most 'chiefly' chief that Esther has yet seen. And she just thanked Esther personally for her visit to the tribe!

The mothers and midwives meet and greet briefly. Esther greets the three mothers more confidently, feeling much more comfortable now that she knows something about pregnancy. Numei speaks with Hasa first, as she is the most nervous. But when Hasa starts pestering Numei with too many questions, she turns her over to Esther and whispers to Esther to talk to her.

"What do you think about a water birth?" asks Hasa. "Would that be possible for me?"

Esther thinks about it. She wants to run over and ask Numei her opinion, but she knows Numei would just snap at her to think for herself. So Esther struggles to remember everything they discussed.

"A water birth is comfortable for many people. Sometimes it is not recommended for certain problems. And your feet can prune up a lot."

Hasa laughs. Esther smiles, knowing that it was a silly thing to say. Who cares if her feet prune? But Hasa is smiling and that is good.

"I'd rather not do a water birth. I don't like swimming very much. Unless you think it's less painful."

Esther remembers that water births are better for inflexible women.
But Hasa is petite and thin and Esther assumes that she could pretzel into any position she wanted to. So she doesn't need a water birth.

"I think we should try squatting. That's the best way, for it opens up the flower. You seem flexible enough to handle it."

"Will I be able to squat for that long?"

"Yes. You should be able to. If not, we can support you somehow."

"How do you squat?"

Esther shows her the way that Numei showed her. Hasa does it and seems comfortable enough in that position. They work on variations together and practice doing them, until it is time to join the group again.

"This will be the last meeting of the midwives," announces Ruala. "All questions will be answered today. But before that, let us go over the induction process. Yes, that time is coming soon."

The mothers struggle to sit down on the furs, which have been set on the floor. Some of them are so pregnant, that they need help just getting down. Esther has to help Hasa sit down and it is a very ungraceful process.

"This room is a little less crowded than before, as you can see. Oiki has already given birth, as you well know, to a beautiful Swan moon boy. Yalla, our youngest mother, is in process as we speak. We have word that it is going as well as can be expected."

Everyone claps and laughs with delight. Ruala wishes her well and then waves aside all questions about her and gets right down to business.

"After tonight, you are to stop taking mijorke and stop drinking fish oil. Then you must wait until the morning of the Elk moon. The first thing we want you to do that morning is to blast the heat in your homes and have sex with your mate. The man should massage your breasts for at least ten minutes. Then do what you can to have an orgasm. The contractions of an orgasm are similar to the contractions of giving birth. You may trigger the birth in that way. And your man should spill his seed in your womb. A man's semen is an excellent inducer of birth. For those of you who fail to attract your husband with such a fat belly, tell him to do it himself and bring you the seed."

Although the old woman is dead serious, the mothers all burst out laughing so hard, that they might go into labor from it. All the midwives are laughing too, except for one Cougar midwife, who looks very upset.

"No, no, no," she shouts. "The mothers must not have sex until at least six months from now, when the baby is stronger."

"Semen has been known -"

"I know. I know. But sex with a man sours the breast milk. That is the reason for that rule."

"Superstitious nonsense," snaps Ruala.

"It's true," the Cougar midwife growls. "Ideally, we should not have sex until we wean the baby, but few can last that long."

"Especially the Cougar tribe, considering how long it takes some of you to wean your children."

The Cougar midwife bristles and prepares a nasty comeback. But the other midwives all jump in and ask for peace. Such is the power of all the midwives, that she finally backs down and even mumbles an apology for her outburst.

"You have heard both sides," says Ruala. "What you do is up to you. Semen is only a primer. It is not our main kick to the womb."

Looking around the room, Esther guesses that all the mothers will be glad to give it a chance.

"Those of you who are extra ripe, bursting out and ready to give birth immediately, take mijorke tomorrow and don't have sex until the following night. Ask your midwife if you are not sure. You will receive a visit from your midwives early on the morning of the new moon. Then there will be four steps. First, your midwife will perform the loosening of the womb ceremony. She will massage the breasts and then give you an enema with red raspberry tea. And then you will drink yrra."

There are groans from several of the mothers. Yrra tastes horrible.

"I know. I know. We will sweeten it as best we can. But yrra is the magic ingredient to this process. Within twenty-four hours, you should all be in labor if your baby is ready. From then on, as you know, anything goes. There are many things that can go wrong and our brave midwives know most or all of them. They will help you through anything."

In the evening, Esther and Numei relax with a cup of tea and a plate of sweet corn in front of the fire in the main lodge. Ever since they became midwives to his daughter, Lem has been doing everything in his power to spoil them. Esther decides that she likes being a midwife. If only she didn't feel like such a fraud.

Suddenly, the door slams open, the force of the wind slamming it into the wall. They both jump, startled. A man stands there, his hair blown all over the place and his cloak dusted with moisture.

"I hate to burden you ladies at this late hour. But which one of you is Esther?"

"Me," says Esther, rising to her feet with surprise.

"My wife is Hasa. She is in a state and I can do nothing for her. She has asked for you to come talk to her. Perhaps you can spare a few minutes."

"Me? What is the matter? Is she having contractions?" Esther asks nervously.

"No. She's just very upset."

Esther looks at Numei. Numei smiles briefly and waves her hands for Esther to get on with it and go see Hasa. She looks pleased that Hasa asked for Esther and not for her.

"Don't you want to come?" Esther asks Numei.

Numei smiles again and shakes her head negatively. She looks too comfortable to move. Esther knows how she feels, as she grabs her cloak from the hook.

"Oh, thank you. We both really appreciate it. She was very nervous about disturbing you at this hour of the night and with this weather. It is so foggy out, we can barely see a thing."

"Nonsense," Numei insists. "Esther is only too glad to help. Our job is to help your wife through all parts of her labor. Not just the birth. Anything that comes up, a midwife must deal with."

"That's great," says the man, impressed by her words.

But Esther knows that Numei is talking to her and not to the husband. She is telling Esther to go out there and make this woman feel better. So Esther follows the man out into the deep fog, which is so thick that she cannot see a thing. He leads her down the path to his house and she stays close to him. It is not a night to get lost. Too many things can hide in the fog.

Hasa's house consists of one room, which is a complete mess. Baskets lie knocked over and clothes are scattered everywhere. Esther somehow got the impression that this tribe valued cleanliness, but here she finds that she was wrong. It is very warm inside, breaking the rule about keeping the house cold to delay birth. Hasa lies in her bed, pale and miserable, when Esther walks in to see her. She dabs a wet rag into steaming water periodically and rubs it all over her face and neck. Esther also notices a pipe by the bed that looks as if it has been recently used.

"Hi," says Hasa meekly.

"What is the matter, Hasa?"

"I don't know."

"Hasa, Esther came all the way out here in this bad weather. Tell her what is the matter."

"Go away!" screams Hasa. "I want to talk to Esther alone."

The man glares at his wife briefly, but he does as asked. Esther is alone with Hasa now. And somehow, she has to find a way to calm her down. She sits down in a chair and they both sit in silence, neither knowing what to say. Esther's mind is racing, trying to think of what Numei would do in this situation. She thinks back to their conversation.

The most important ingredient for a successful birth is courage.

The thought bubbles up into Esther's head and seems to fit. Hasa is afraid. It seems simple enough. Esther thinks about when she is feeling scared and not wanting to face a situation. She appreciates boldness. Someone to just open the dam by force. At least, it is the only thing that seems to work.

"Tell me what you are afraid of," Esther says, surprising herself with her firmness.

"I don't want to do this. I changed my mind. I'm not ready to be a mother."

Esther cannot believe what she is hearing. The woman is two days from giving birth and she wants it to all go away.

"You can't change your mind. You know that already."

"I'm not good with pain. I've listened to all the other mothers talk about how much childbirth hurts. I don't want to do it...."

"Don't think about it. Try to relax. When the time comes, you just go through it until you reach the other side."

"I know...but...is there any way that I can be drugged and then you can just pull it out of me while I'm asleep?"

"No."

"It's just...the pain. I'm not a strong person."

"You are afraid."

"Yes. I am scared I can't do this. I'm so scared, that I want to kill myself rather than go through it."

Esther is suddenly speechless. She thought that she was doing well in comforting Hasa, but now she has no idea what to say. They sit in silence for a long time, the import of those words poisoning the very air around them. Esther wonders if there are any herbs that would help with this. She will have to ask Numei about it.

What would work on you in this situation?

Esther suddenly realizes that she has also been here before. So afraid, that she would rather die. It scares her that she could be so frightened that she would rather die than fight. Now that she sees the same behavior in another person, she is revolted by it. She suddenly sees herself as Dohr and his family must have seen her when they called her a 'suicide'. It is a sad thing to see someone so afraid that they are paralyzed.

How did Esther ever get over her fear? She thinks about it and realizes that she never did. She is still scared. She just stopped paying so much attention to it.

"It's alright to be afraid," she finally says. "I'm afraid too."

"You are?"

"Yes."

"But you seem so brave."

Esther smiles.

"What are you afraid of?" asks Hasa.

"Many things. Right now, I'm afraid that I won't be able to help you. That I'll leave here and you will kill yourself."

Hasa looks down, embarrassed, but she doesn't say that she won't.

"I'll have to stay here then. To make sure that you don't."

"You don't have to do that."

"Yes, I do."

Hasa fidgets with her wet rag nervously. She looks positively miserable.

"Thank you."

"You're welcome.

"Tell Balik to make up a bed for you."

"You should drink something. I'll make you some tea."

Esther makes her a tea of chamomile, raspberry leaf, thyme, and nettles from a bag that Numei gave her. The raspberry is supposed to strengthen her uterus and the nettles and chamomile are supposed to relax her and strengthen her immune system. As Hasa sips the hot liquid, Esther sings softly her. It just occurs to her to do this. Hasa's eyes slowly soften and she allows herself to be calmed and relaxed.

"You have a nice voice."

She sings a few Bear lullabies and then a few mission songs. Hasa closes her eyes and the hard line of her mouth softens. Soon her breath becomes even and pronounced. She has fallen asleep.

Elk 13'

Numei visits her two clients to check on their progress. The first one is Viana, the large woman who has two children already. Viana's husband greets her at the door and takes her into the house. Viana sits in bed, sewing booties for her new baby.

"Ah, Numei, I wanted to talk to you," she says in her husky, booming voice.

"Have you been well?"

"Yes, I am just fine. Don't worry about me. But I hear that my friend Hasa is having troubles. How is she?"

"She is well. Esther has been keeping a close eye on her."

"Esther? That strange juwanna of yours? Why her and not you?"

"I have been busy caring for three mothers. And Hasa seems to like Esther."

Viana does not seem satisfied with this answer.

"What is the matter with Esther?" Numei asks suspiciously, although she guesses what is on Viana's mind well enough by her expression.

"She doesn't know what she is doing, does she?" she says flatly.

"Why do you say that?"

"Do not lie to me. I have been an apprentice to midwives. And I have given birth twice. I know what I am doing and I know when somebody else does not."

"I will not lie. Esther has never delivered a baby by herself before. She is my juwanna, as I have said. But I can vouch for her competency."

"Where does she come from? Who is she? I am certain that she is not one of the Twelve Tribes. Her accent is strange and so is her manner."

The woman is a hard case and a smart one too, and she has apparently been watching Esther closely. Numei realizes that she will have to be straight with her.

"She was born to the Twelve Tribes. But she grew up a slave in a Spanish mission. From that prison, she made a daring escape and found her way home. Now she is my juwanna."

"A Spanish mission?" Viana says, her eyes opening wide. "What a horror!"

"Yes."

"Well, I will go easy on her then, but I still balk at letting her care for Hasa at such a critical time."

"She knows what to do," insists Numei. "I would not have let her do this if I did not think she was highly capable. She is much more than she appears on the surface."

"That doesn't answer my question," Viana says with a frown. "Why do you let your juwanna handle things alone?"

"Is Hasa not happy? Has she complained? Please tell me and we can make other arrangements."

"Hasa is my friend and I love her, but I wish she was stronger. She tends to be melancholy and fearful. And she is an inconjunct," she adds, as if that explains everything. "And so is her good-for- nothing husband. He won't be any help."

"Esther is perfect for such a woman," Numei says, suddenly inspired. "She understands such behavior better than you or I do. That's why they get along so well."

"Perhaps. But I fear she will have complications that require experience and not merely *understanding* - well intentioned as it may be."

"I will be at the birth of Hasa, handling things to the best of my ability. She will be very well taken care of. I promise you."

Viana begins knitting furiously. She doesn't say anything for quite a long time. When she speaks again, she speaks in a quiet voice with her head down, as if speaking to herself.

"This is not my first child and I am very good at labor. I can probably do my part without anybody's help. I have a great womb, which has delivered two children to this world already, and my midwives were bored out of their minds. I did everything myself. If she and I go into labor at the same time, I'd rather you were with her than with me."

"Or perhaps you two can give birth in the same room. You can give her strength and I can keep an eye on you both."

"If Hasa feels comfortable with that, then it is fine with me. I'll even walk over to her house myself. It doesn't matter to me. I could give birth outside in the rain if I had to."

"Whatever you prefer," says Numei with a smile.

"Yes, yes. All jokes aside, just make sure you are present and watchful during Hasa's birth. I think you are careless and you do not take your job seriously enough." She glares at Numei challengingly for a moment. "But you seem knowledgeable enough and you are the cousin of Vayanna, who is a great friend to the Elk tribe. That counts for something."

Numei bites her tongue and says nothing. Then she bids Viana farewell and leaves her to her sewing. She is now irritated and insulted, but also a little relieved that Viana didn't threaten to go to the other midwives. Numei could be in a lot of hot water if they choose to investigate this further. She suddenly feels guilty, wondering if she *is* careless. It is a nagging feeling that stays with her the rest of the afternoon.

Elk 14'

Owl moon

Esther sits outside with Lem, drinking tea early in the morning. He brought her out here at dawn to show her the family of foxes that lives near the Den. He wears his artic fox fur hat - his pride and joy – for the occasion. While they wait, he gives her a lecture about foxes, assuming she is interested. She really isn't, but she pretends to be because he is so excited about it.

"Some of us Elks use the fox for a helper totem. I take after fox myself. Know much about foxes?"

"No."

"This is the month that foxes do the wheeooo wheeeooo wheeeoooo," he says.

"What's that?"

He pretends to have sex on a rickety wooden plank like the kind that guests sleep on in the shelter.

"Oh," she says, smiling.

"They live alone happily half the year, and then in the winter they miss their homes and family and come home to their burrow and their loved ones and do the wheeooo wheeeoooo wheeooo. Three months later you have little fox babies."

"Do they have easy births?"

"Don't know. Never been invited to one."

"Well, how do you know they have sex this month?"

"Cause this is when daddy fox comes home. Obviously, he comes for some tail."

They watch for a while, but nothing happens. Finally, Lem goes inside to get a persimmon. He lays it out on the ground and they wait for the fox to show up for one of its favorite foods. Suddenly, Esther realizes that Lem is rubbing her shoulders gently and stroking her neck softly. Then she guesses the real reason he brought her out here. She has to admit that he tricked her. She never even guessed that he was interested.

"Lem," she says, using her Lady voice. "I'm not in the mood for this now."

"I can wait until later."

"You might wait a long time."

"Oh look," he says, changing the subject. "It's been there the whole time, watching us."

The fox is nearby. It is a grey fox, missing a piece of its tail. It begins to creep forward and then suddenly begins to act very strange. It rolls around on the ground as if scratching its back. Then it bounds up and leaps into the air and as it lands it goes into a back roll. Spinning in a circle, it chases its missing tail.

"What's it doing?" she asks.

"I'm not sure."

Suddenly, it dashes toward the persimmon and grabs it in its mouth. It quickly dashes toward its burrow and disappears inside. Lem laughs and claps his hands.

"It charmed us."

"What do you mean?"

"It's a sneaky hunting trick the fox has. We use it on elk all the time. It will dance to fool its prey, and when the rabbit or mouse or whatever gets distracted by its movements, it goes in for the kill. I've never seen them do it with my own eyes. It must be the magic fox hat I'm wearing."

"But that's just a piece of fruit. Why would it charm fruit?"

"Foxes love persimmons. I think it started dancing so we would watch it and not notice the persimmon on the ground. It assumed we were competition for the fruit. Then when we were distracted, it made its dash and grabbed it."

"How cute," she says, not sure if she believes his theory.

"I'm a good charmer too," he says.

To prove it, he leans in and kisses her on the mouth, and then backs off before she can protest.

"Fox got his forbidden fruit and I got mine," he says.

Chuckling, he walks back inside. Esther smiles and shakes her head, although she doesn't follow him inside right away. She doesn't want to get charmed a second time.

Late in the morning, a strange person walks into the main room of the shelter, where Esther sips tea alone. He is tall and very thin, with long hair matted in dread locks and tied with squirrel's tails. He has a dirty face and a beard caked with mud. He wears a dirty cloak of squirrel furs, and carries a small bag made from the same material on his back. His appearance is so strange, that Esther cannot stop looking at him.

He sits down and warms his hands by the fire. There is a mist sprinkling his hair and beard, which he wipes on his cloak. As he begins to warm up, he sighs with relief.

"Would you like some tea?" Esther asks, pointing to the pot that Lem left hanging over the fire.

He nods and smiles at her through all his facial hair. She pours him a cup of tea and he takes it in rough, weather beaten hands and takes a sip.

"Good," he mumbles, his voice cracked as if he hasn't used it in awhile.

He doesn't say another word for a long time. Esther keeps glancing over at him, wondering who he is. Then Numei walks into the room, having just woke up. She stares at him in surprise and then she smiles.

"Hello Squirrel," she calls out.

He looks up at her surprised and then laughs loudly.

"Hello," he says, grabbing her arm in a weak grasp.

"What happened to you?" she asks, examining the many cuts and bruises on his face. "You look like a recluse."

"Well, it's a long story," he says in a raspy voice. "But I have traveled many miles in the past ten days and haven't had a thing to eat in the past two that has done me any good."

"Let me make you something," she says in a worried voice. "Esther, can you help me please? What do you want to eat, Squirrel?"

"Everything," he says with a laugh.

"What are you doing here?" Numei asks, after he has been true to his word and eaten just about everything in the shelter.

"There's a gathering of Ruoks. Ulupi sent me to spread the word as far as I could. I went down all the way to the Swan tribe before turning back. On the way, I spent a few days with the Pomo, and then I took a canoe to the coast to gather seaweed. I tried to take a short cut here and got lost."

"Same old Squirrel," she says with a smile. "Can't do a single task without wandering off somewhere."

"I forgot all about you, Numei," Squirrel says, stirring the fire with a stick and taking a coal to light his pipe. "Would you like to come with me to Cougar village?"

"Oh no, I can't," she says.

"All Ruoks have been summoned. When was the last time that happened? I even sent word to the Raccoon tribe and beyond, although I could not make it that far myself."

"Nobody is going to come," she says. "It's the middle of winter."

He shrugs.

"Why now? Why not in the spring?"

"The meeting takes place during the month of the Cougar. Almost spring by then."

"I can't," she repeats absently. "I promised Horim I'd be back by then. I'm going to get pregnant."

"Is that so?" he says with raised eyebrows.

Changing the subject, she starts telling him about the incredible number of women trying to give birth on the upcoming new moon. He laughs when he hears about it and puffs on his pipe.

"It's ridiculous," he snorts.

"Why?" asks Esther, who has been listening to their conversation with half an ear.

"All these babies induced artificially on the same day. Doesn't that seem a little stupid to you?"

She has to admit that it does.

"Everyone is so obsessed with their baby being born on the new moon. But new moon babies are very single minded. And they're boring."

He starts ranting about the insanity of the whole Twelve Tribes system of birth, until Numei cuts him off.

"Ruoks don't believe in the Twelve Tribes way of giving birth," Numei explains to Esther. "They want us to go back to the regular way of birth."

"Most Ruoks don't believe in it," Squirrel says, correcting her. "But Numei does. That's why she wants to skip the Ruok council meeting. She wants a super Wolf baby. That's why she has to get pregnant by the month of the Cougar."

"Don't start with me, Squirrel," she warns him. "And I'm not a Ruok."

"You were."

"Not really."

He shrugs and packs his pipe with jimm and tobacco. Numei puffs on it contentedly and then hands it back to him.

"Can't smoke too much," she says. "I'm a midwife. I may be called at any moment."

"No you won't," he says. "It's not the right *moon* yet."

Elk 15′

Two mothers go into labor today and there is nothing they can do about it. One has a very quick labor and the baby is born in less than an hour. The other mother has a long labor. Part of the reason her labor is so long is that she is reluctant to give birth on the Owl moon, which is considered a mild inconjunct. There is only one more day until the new moon and she tries vainly to slow down the inevitable. But nature proves stronger than her wishes and eventually the pain grows so great that she decides that she doesn't care any more. Moon be damned, she is going to get this child out of her now. Her husband is upset when she decides to stop fighting, but she clubs him in the head with her fist.

"Ow! What was that for?"

"If you want to carry it for awhile, then we can wait another day. If not, then shut up and help me! I'm giving birth, now!"

Taken aback, he quickly jumps to her aid.

"Yes, of course. Of course, you should give birth now! I'm sorry."

She delivers in just over an hour and when they hold the little girl in their hands, they forget all about the new moon.

"A little fire is good for the young one," the husband says. "She'll be a happy child."

"Of course she will," sighs the mother.

By nightfall, things are very tense in the village. Tomorrow is a powerful day for the Elk tribe and everyone wants powerful children to be born. So obsessed is everyone with the drama of nineteen mothers fighting to push their babies out in a short two day span, that they almost forget that tomorrow is supposed to be a celebration of a successful year and a brand new year to come. Only a few people are left to organize the new moon celebration.

Esther and Numei talk late into the night about childbirth and Esther has a million questions about everything. But finally Numei yawns and shakes her head, indicating that she is done talking.

"Let's go to sleep."

"Just a few more questions."

"Esther, there really is nothing more to say. There is no way you can be truly prepared for this. Every birth is unique. Surprises are going to come from everywhere and you never know what will happen until it does. Sleep is what we both need now. Any moment, we could be summoned to the birthing room and you'll wish you were well rested then."

"But what do I do if the cord is wrapped around the neck? I don't understand."

"If that happens, neither one of us is ready to handle that. We get one of the old women to reach in there and pull the baby out by hand."

"And what -"

"Esther, stop worrying. You are not a midwife. You are only a juwanna. You will assist me and fetch me anything I need. And you will concentrate on making Hasa comfortable, keeping her focused and not letting her give in to her fears. I will handle everything else."

"As you say."

"Good. Let us go to bed then."

Esther struggles to sleep after that, but it is very difficult. She is too wound up. She lies in a daze for a long time, vainly trying to talk herself to sleep. Strangely, she begins to dream, although she is sure that she has not fallen asleep yet. She dozes in a half-awake state and has vivid and intense dreams. Eventually she does fall asleep for real and the dreams continue for the rest of the night.

Elk 16'

**Elk moon*

All of the mothers that are considered 'ripe' are made ready for the inducing of labor. Their houses are heated for the first time in days and wood is piled on fire pits and into wood stoves until the houses cook. Husbands have sex with their wives, making sure to massage the breasts and spill their seed into the womb. Midwives loosen the womb, massage the breasts, and give enemas of red raspberry tea. And finally, all are given a dose of yrra, which is one of the most foul drinks in creation. The village is filled with groans of distaste as mothers try to stomach this potion, which makes them want to vomit.

Nobody knows the exact ingredients of yrra. The best guess: Black and blue cohosh, castor oil, evening primrose oil, red raspberry leaf, motherwart, and possibly semen (the husband adds his own).

Two mothers begin labor immediately, including Viana. Numei is summoned and she rushes to Viana's house immediately. Esther comes along to watch and assist, and she sits quietly out of the way, except when fetching something for Numei. It is hot in the house from a huge bonfire in the fire pit. Viana walks around naked, singing to distract herself from the pain. She seems powerful and strong, as if she is an athlete whose time has come for glory. Her focus is intense and her eyes are wild.

She leaves the house for a little bit and everyone waits patiently. While they wait, Esther looks at her husband and wonders what he is thinking. He is quiet and taciturn by nature, and sits in a dark corner of the house, his thoughts inscrutable. Then Viana returns and she is soaked in water and her hair is wet. She is now ready to give birth.

Just as promised, Viana is a champion. She balances on two benches in a squatting position, for a good part of the labor. Deep in concentration, she sings to herself and rocks quietly. She doesn't seem to want anybody's help and she reluctantly takes Numei's orders when she gives them. When the pain is intense, her song turns into a deep groaning. She strains against the benches, which rattle and shake, and she seems no longer a human woman but something fierce and primal. It gives Esther the chills just watching her. Then Viana screams, gives one mighty push, and the baby pops out. Esther gasps and puts her hand to her mouth, as the bloody little thing slowly drops out of her womb and falls into Numei's hands. Another little contraction and a bloody mess follows it out. That bloody mess was the babies' breakfast, lunch, and dinner for the past nine months.

After a few tense moments, the baby starts crying. Viana shouts out with joy, grabs it from Numei's hands, and gives it a big hug and kisses all over its body. Eventually, Numei has to wrestle the baby away from her, just to clean it off and give it a check up. Viana sits down, suddenly exhausted. She is smeared from head to foot with a grime of blood and sweat, but she is too tired to clean herself off.

Oddly enough, the husband never emerges from his little dark corner to see the baby. His face remains in shadow, but Esther can just make out a big smile from the darkness.

Meanwhile, the village readies for a celebration tonight. There will be three weddings, speeches, music, feasts, and discussions of the future of the tribe. Esther is asked by four different people to help out with the feast or the decorations, but she claims that she too busy helping Numei and gets off the hook. The village is so hectic, that Esther escapes into the sweat lodge just to get some peace and quiet.

She has just gotten comfortably situated in the broiling sweat lodge, when a familiar face appears at the door. He smiles in an apologetic way as he waves at Esther.

"Hasa wants you," he says. "Sorry to disturb you. Numei told me where to find you."

"Is she getting ready to give birth?"

"I don't know. She just yelled at me to get you quickly."

So Esther gets her clothes back on and walks with Balik to his house. Balik makes jokes about his wife on the way and keeps smiling at her. She finds Balik to be very funny, charming and cute, and she feels a little guilty for her thoughts as they walk over to see his pregnant wife.

Hasa is lying in bed, clutching her stomach and groaning in utter misery. When Esther enters the room, she cries feebly and waves her over to talk.

"I think I've been poisoned," she groans. "That stuff you gave me to drink is making me ill. I've already thrown up twice."

"The yrra?" asks Esther, looking at the empty glass before her.

"Yes, of course. I feel like my insides are having an earthquake."

"I think it is supposed to do that. That's how it makes you give birth."

"I don't want to!" she shrieks.

"You can do it," says Balik supportively.

"What do you know?" she shouts. "You have no idea what pain I'm in."

"Walk around," Esther says suddenly. "It will make you feel better."

Esther doesn't know why she knows that walking around will help, but she does. At first Hasa complains that she cannot possibly stand up, but she manages to get to her feet with a little help from Balik. After walking for a while, her head stops spinning and she is able to breathe normally. She sighs and sits down again.

"You should walk a little more," Esther says.

"I'm tired," complains Hasa.

"I'll get Numei."

"Don't leave me," Hasa implores, grabbing her arm with a white-knuckled grip.

"She knows more than I do."

"Send Balik then."

By nightfall, two women have already given birth - including Viana - and another is having a long labor, which is attended now by two midwives. Esther hasn't left Hasa's side since the afternoon. Numei has been in to see her twice, but she doesn't stay long because she also has to check on Siyle and Viana.

"She needs to give birth as soon as possible," Numei says. "You might give her more yrra and even put some up her flower. I'll get you some."

After she leaves, Esther walks over to speak to her miserable patient.

"Hasa," Esther says, "have you done everything we told you to do to make the baby come?"

"Yes," says Hasa.

"Don't lie," complains Balik. "We didn't do anything except drink some of that Yrra. We didn't have sex or massage the breasts or anything else. And she refused the raspberry tea enema."

"I'm not going to have sex with you," Hasa shouts. "Not like this!"

"You need to make this baby come," Esther says. "Not just for the new moon. Your baby is ready to come out now. If you don't do this, you will put yourself in danger."

Hasa says nothing, but her eyes bug out with fear.

"Hasa, Balik told me how attracted he is to you right now. He wants to have sex very badly."

"That's true," says Balik with a smile.

This gets a laugh from Hasa, which is just as Esther hoped. She and Balik go into a long, rambling discussion about how much Balik loves fat women and how he has longed his whole life to make love to one. Hasa laughs heartily and the tension in the room is much relieved. And then Esther wisely leaves her and Balik alone. She indicates to Balik that he should massage her breasts and the rest of her body, and perhaps even have sex with her if the mood hits them.

She goes to look for Numei and finds her at Viana's house. Viana and her husband are cooing over the baby like a couple of lovesick doves. The baby is covered in a little fur blanket and suckling on her breast. Esther fills Numei in on the situation with Hasa, and Numei tells her to go back to the shelter and relax. They will meet in the house of Hasa in one hour's time and see what is happening there.

"Esther, wake up. Esther...."

It is Lem, shaking her gently.

"What?" she mumbles.

"Your girl is in labor. Everyone is looking for you."

Esther jumps out of bed like a woman with a snake in her underwear. In a total panic, she runs around, desperately trying to find her cloak and moccasins. She cannot find the shoes anywhere and is beginning to seriously panic, when Lem finds them by the fire where she left them. She puts them on and runs over to Hasa's house as fast as her feet will carry her.

By the time she arrives, Numei is already there and trying to keep Hasa calm. Hasa is lying down, screaming in agony and clutching her stomach. Esther has to hold her hands over her ears as she runs over to Numei.

"What is wrong with her?"

"She's in a lot of pain," Numei shouts in Esther's ear.

"I can see that."

"She's a fearful one. Talk to her. You have to get her to fight. She refuses to help herself."

Esther stares at Hasa, wondering what she could possibly say that would make a difference to her.

"Where have you been, anyways?" Numei says, giving her a push toward Hasa. "That was more than an hour."

Esther quickly walks up to Hasa and grabs her hand. Hasa stares at her with crazy eyes.

"Help me," she moans.

"I brought a stick," Esther says. "I'm going to stick it up inside of you and the baby will grab hold and we'll pull him out."

This gets a small laugh from Hasa and she stops moaning.

"Baby, you hear me? It is time for you to come out. Hasa, it is time for you to get it out of you!"

"How?"

"First you have to be strong. You have to be ready for anything."

"That's easy to say. But I can't do it. I'm an inconjunct. I'm not strong like everyone else here."

"You are strong," urges Balik, holding her hand.

"No I'm not!" she screams. "And neither are you! You're an inconjunct too."

"That's just an excuse," Esther insists. "But if you won't be strong for me, then I can't help you. I'm going to leave you alone."

"What?"

"If you won't help me by being strong, then you'll just have to suffer here alone. I'm going to leave and so is Numei."

"You can't," gasps Hasa.

"Goodbye," says Esther.

She starts to walk away and she indicates for Numei to follow her. Hasa suspects that they are bluffing, but she is terrified nonetheless at the thought that they might leave her alone.

"I'll do what you want," Hasa groans. "Don't leave me. Please."

"Good one," whispers Numei.

Sometime later, they find themselves in a strange position. Balik holds Hasa like a sack of potatoes, as she has a furious round of contractions. Hasa screams and claws at Balik's arms with her fingernails. Already, he has bloody scratches all over his forearms.

"This girl is very weak," complains Numei. "She has not done the stretches that she was taught to loosen up the body for birth. She does not get enough exercise, and her body is unhealthy and in poor condition in general. She is going to have a long, unhappy labor."

"How can we help her?"

"Years of laziness can't be erased in a day, Esther. Her hips are tight and her muscles are weak. She's going to have to work with what she has and so will we."

Suddenly Balik groans. Hasa has pooped on his bare feet. When she sees the look on his face, Hasa starts laughing uproariously. She tries to apologize, but she is laughing too hard. Still chuckling, she stands on her own two feet and steps away from him so he can wash his feet off in the water bowl.

"I'm sorry," she says, still giggling.

"She's on her feet," Numei whispers. "And in a good mood. Let's get her into a squatting position, before she falls back into her swoon again."

"Squat like this," Esther says, showing her what to do.

Hasa continues to giggle as she does just what Esther says. Everytime she looks at Balik's face, she starts cracking up all over again.

"Just don't poop on *my* feet," Esther says.

"I only poop on my husband's feet," Hasa says with a giggle. "He likes it."

Hasa tries squatting for a while, but she cannot seem to maintain it. She spends forever trying to find a position that suits her. She prefers to lie down, but Numei forbids it. Finally, Numei suggests a position. Balik sits down on a stool and Hasa sits on top of his legs. This seems to work pretty well and everyone seems satisfied. Everyone except for Balik.

"Just don't poop on my lap," says Balik.

Hasa laughs like a madwoman.

"Say more funny things," she giggles. "When you do, it doesn't hurt so bad."

Meanwhile, Numei binds a cloth around Hasa's stomach. She explains that whenever the baby drops, Numei will tighten the sheet so it will not rise up again. She urges Hasa to start pushing, so she can start tightening.

"Don't you want it out?" asks Esther.

"Yes," she pants.

"Then push. Or would you like me to push for you?"

Esther grabs her belly and threatens to push down on it and pop the baby out.

"I will," she groans. "Just don't do that."

"You're a ruthless midwife," laughs Numei, giving Esther a pinch. "I didn't know you had it in you."

Hasa gets down to work at last and things go more smoothly. Suddenly they hear shouting from outside. Esther runs to open the door. From out of the fog, Lem appears, running toward their house.

"Siyle is giving birth!" he shouts excitedly. "Right now!"

Everyone stares at him like he just shouted that the whole village was on fire.

"Sorry to interrupt," he says abashed. "But I don't know what else to do."

"I'll be done here shortly," explains Numei.

"We don't have a 'shortly'!" he shouts desperately. "She needs you now! She's screaming in pain and she's panicking. We're afraid that there is something wrong. Seriously wrong."

"Get out of here!" screams Hasa.

Numei frowns and glances around the room. She stares at Hasa and then at Lem, sizing up the situation.

"Esther, take over!" shouts Numei suddenly. "I'll come back as soon as I can."

"Me?" Esther shrieks.

"I'll see to Siyle," Numei says quickly. "Lem, you go find another midwife to come here and help Esther finish."

"Right away!" he shouts, and he runs out the door.

"You can do it," Numei urges, pulling Esther aside. "Finesse the baby out. I'll come back as soon as I can."

"You can't leave," Esther gasps, grabbing her hand and refusing to let her go.

She turns to Esther and looks her square in the eyes.

"You're Hasa's midwife, Esther, as much as I am. You practically did it all yourself up until now. We knew this might happen, and now it is, and you'll have to deal with it!"

Numei quickly runs out the door and disappears into the fog. Esther watches her slowly fade away, open mouthed, until Hasa's screams bring her back to reality. Esther turns around and marches resolutely toward her fate.

Hasa's screams sound like shrieks in a cave of bats. They have been doing this for hours now. They make some progress every now and then, followed by another round of noise and chaos. She has tried every position under the sun, yet she is getting no closer. Hasa complains that she can't make it much longer. She asks if she can take a break, but Esther assures her that there are no more breaks until she has given birth.

They are soon visited by Ruala, the senior midwife, and she tries her hand with Hasa too, but she doesn't get anywhere either. Hasa will just not buckle down and push that baby out. Instead, she is in a wild panic and she is sure that she is going to die. She smokes several pipe bowls of jimm for the pain, but that only make her seem crazier.

Ruala leaves the room and returns a short time later with a glass of yrra. She hands it to Hasa and her smile is cold and calculating.

"Drink this."

Hasa sips it and makes a face. Ruala orders her to drink it quickly and Hasa takes a deep drink of the foul elixir. Then she makes a hideous face and vomits all over Balik. Balik groans again, as he is splashed with more of Hasa's body fluids. As she throws up, she has a wave of very powerful contractions.

"Good," breathes Ruala. "It's moving now. Push. Push as hard as you can."

Then the head appears. Esther stares at it in amazement. Until now, she didn't realize just what a feat giving birth was. But when she sees the size of the head, it all makes sense.

"The head!" shouts Ruala.

Ruala puts her hands upon the head of the baby and just then, another man runs into the room.

"Duli needs you now! We think the baby is coming out backwards!"

Ruala curses under her breath and then stares at Hasa, sizing up the situation. Finally she nods reluctantly and waves Esther over to Hasa's side. Ruala takes Esther's hands and pushes them into Hasa's womb. Esther feels the hard, slippery head of the baby. Esther stares at Ruala for a moment, panicked, and then she cups her hands under the emerging baby's head with determination.

"You can do it," Ruala says, giving Esther a comforting smile and a pat on the back. "I know you can."

Esther nods, trying to appear braver than she feels.

"Here," Ruala says, showing Esther a little hollow tule that she places on the stool beside her. "When the baby comes out, use this to suck out the fluids in its ears and mouth. It's very important. There might be baby waste in them and the baby could choke on it."

"But what -" Esther begins to ask desperately, but the words die in her throat when she sees Ruala has already begun to walk out the door.

It all happens as if in a dream. Hasa struggles to push the baby out and Esther gingerly tries to coax the head out of the too narrow opening. There is a time when she is sure that the head will never fit through Hasa's small flower. Esther wants to scream with frustration and panic, but she forces herself to be brave for Hasa's sake and remains calm. Finally, by some miracle they get the head out and from there it is easy. The rest of the body slides out like butter, and a baby drops into Esther's hands. She stares at it in shock. It is an ugly looking thing, pale and shriveled and covered in blood. Worst of all, it is not moving. It seems slightly blue to Esther and she immediately assumes the worst.

"I - I - um, I think it's dead," she whispers.

"What?" shouts Balik in alarm.

"I don't know," she whispers.

Hasa stares at her in mute terror. Balik puts his arms around his wife, prepared to believe to worst. And then a hand suddenly slaps Esther hard on the head. Esther screams and jumps. Then old hands reach out and grab the baby. Esther turns to see Ruala standing there with a frown on her face.

"Fool!" hisses Ruala. "Juwanna, there is nothing wrong with this baby."

As if on cue, the baby begins to cry and everyone breathes a sigh of relief. Ruala cradles it in her arms, comforting the tiny thing. She points to the tube and Esther hands it to her with shaking hands. Ruala sucks out the sticky substance in the tiny ears and mouth and spits it into the fire. Then she orders Esther to get her a wet rag with which to clean off the baby. They wipe the baby down with warm water that has been set over the fire, and Ruala hands the baby to Esther and cuts the cord and ties it off.

"It's a girl," says Ruala with a smile.

"It's a girl," repeats Balik excitedly. "Is it...is it alright then?"

"It's just fine. It's beautiful."

"Do you hear that?" asks Balik. "Hasa, it's a girl."

"Eject the afterbirth," orders Ruala. "One more thing to do."

"I thought I was finally done," complains Hasa.

"Last thing."

Hasa has trouble getting rid of the afterbirth too. Ruala is out of patience with the troublesome Hasa, so she insists that Hasa climb onto Balik's lap and tells him to hold her tight. Then she takes the glass of yrra she brought earlier and dumps a little into Hasa's mouth and closes it tight with her hand. Hasa is forced to swallow some of it, though she struggles to spit it out. This induces another round of vomiting. As she does, she has a powerful contraction and a bloody mess falls onto Balik's lap. Balik was happy to have escaped the second round of vomiting, until he finds himself with the afterbirth on his leg. He shrieks and jumps out of the way, which makes Hasa collapse onto the ground.

Hasa is so tired, she isn't even angry at the old woman for making her vomit again or at Balik for dropping her. She sighs and collapses on the floor, completely exhausted. She lies there for a long time, breathing heavily. Balik eventually helps her to a sitting position. Then Hasa seems to notice the child for the first time and an amazed look enters her eyes. She struggles to move closer to it so she can see it better. Ruala smiles and hands her the baby gently.

"I did it," she says with awe, staring at the little thing in her hands. "I actually gave birth."

"Yes, you did," says Ruala kindly.

"It's cute," she says with a little smile.

"Can you heat some more water on the fire?" Ruala asks Esther.

Esther goes to the fire and hangs the water pot. But the fire is too low, so she goes outside to get some more wood. As soon as she steps outside, she suddenly begins to shake and she breaks out in a cold sweat. She leans against the house and struggles to breathe. She is having a panic attack! It was as if Esther was possessed throughout the entire birth by a calm, commanding person who knew what she was doing. As if the person she was pretending to be took over, knowing that Esther could not have done it herself. Now that it is finished, she is so terrified that it takes several minutes before she can stop shaking.

They fill a bowl with boiling tea and Ruala makes Hasa squat over it and steam clean her insides. Then Balik bathes her with a wet rag, using the warm water after it cools. Ruala instructs Esther to massage her legs and thighs so the circulation will return and she won't get marks there. As she is getting her massage, Ruala gives Hasa a glass of tea to drink.

Hasa practices giving the child milk and then she squirts some on Balik, realizing that here is one body secretion he has not experienced yet. She giggles as he makes a face. Ruala sees that everything is good here and she leaves the two of them to Esther's care. Before she leaves, she asks Esther to walk her outside. It is nearly dawn now and a thick mist hangs over everything.

"You did well, juwanna," she says, squeezing her hand. "I am proud of you. That was no easy birth, especially for a juwanna to complete on her own."

"Thank you, Ruala."

"You have a gift. You will make a great midwife someday. I can see it."

Esther smiles humbly and nods.

"Just don't jump to conclusions in the future. Don't ever say 'the baby is dead' unless you are absolutely sure...."

"I'm so sorry about that."

Chuckling, she gives Esther a much needed hug and then walks slowly off into the fog. Esther watches her fade away until she has disappeared completely. The sky slowly brightens as dawn comes, and it is so beautiful that she wonders if this is all a dream. Then she notices a very real chill in the air and goes back inside the house. She makes herself a cup of tea and sits by the fire in a daze.

Elk 17'

Esther has to stay with Hasa all day long and watch over her. Hasa sleeps most of the day away and gives Esther and Balik care of the baby until she wakes. Esther gingerly holds the tiny thing wrapped in blankets, staring at her minuscule face in utter amazement. She still cannot believe that she delivered it! She cannot believe that Hasa was able to birth it after such a struggle! Finally, she is too tired to sit up any longer. Balik takes his turn watching the little one and Esther closes her eyes and naps.

Hasa awakens at lunchtime and feeds the baby. She complains that it hurts to breast feed and grumbles that it is too cold in the room. Then she closes her eyes again.

"Wouldn't you like to hold it some more?" asks Balik.

"I'm tired," mumbles Hasa. "I'll hold it later. *You* do something for a change."

Esther returns to the shelter late in the afternoon and finds the place in an uproar. The screams of a mother in agony assault Esther's ears even before she walks inside. She groans, realizing that Siyle, the daughter of Lem and Nekrah, is still giving birth. Esther desperately wants a good night's sleep, but she knows that Numei will probably need help. Who knows when the last time was that Numei got any sleep? She must have been up with Siyle all night long. So Esther goes into the shelter and runs toward the group huddled around the groaning Siyle.

By the time darkness falls, it is all over. There is another baby in the Elk tribe, a strutting, proud grandfather, and a very tired midwife who hasn't slept more than three hours in the last forty-eight. Numei seems dazed and Esther forgives her for snapping every time she needs something or Esther gets in her way. But Numei holds it together somehow, remaining the rock so everyone else can enjoy the experience.

Everyone tells her to get some sleep, but she refuses. She stays awake to make sure that everything is all right. She checks on Hasa twice and then she watches over Siyle's baby while everyone else drops off to sleep, exhausted from the ordeal of the past days. The baby sleeps soundly in her arms as she sits propped against a blanket, staring at it fondly and thinking how much she wants a baby herself.

Elk 19'

Raven moon

Esther and Numei walk through the woods on a foggy afternoon. They say little, being filled with memories of the excitement of the past few days. For many the ordeal is not yet over, as there are still ten women who have not given birth. But for these two, it is mostly finished.

Only nine of the nineteen pregnant women gave birth on the new moon. But the town is very elated to have nine new moon children with four planets in the Elk constellation (including the three most important planets) to reflect the glory of the Elk sign. Everyone is certain that one of these nine will be chief someday. There are already bets being made as to which child it will be.

As they walk, they pass a herd of female elk wandering along the river, accompanied by one male. The women stop to admire them. Esther has always found elk to be the most noble and beautiful of all forest creatures. But as soon as the elk catch sight of them, the skittish creatures run off. Esther begins to chase after them, but Numei stops her.

"Not like that," she whispers.

"Like what?"

"You'll scare them. Elk have very delicate sensibilities, and they are very particular about how they are approached. You must show them great respect as you go near them. If you don't, they'll think you mean them harm and will run away. Elk are a bit paranoid too."

Numei slowly begins to flap her arms and makes half bends at the waist. Then she kicks her legs high into the air. She spins around, waves her arms in circles, jumps and prances. Sure enough, the elk stop running to stare at her. They seem fascinated by her antics, not knowing who or what she is. And then she begins to sing in a sweet, high voice.

This is how you stalk the elk
Flap your arms and fly away
The elk like to watch you dance
They'll watch you the entire day

"You're charming them," laughs Esther. "That's a fox trick."

Esther begins to follow her movements, laughing at how ridiculous she must look. The elk are so fascinated, that they allow the girls to get quite close. Esther sings along with Numei, and she can almost feel the curiosity of the elk perk up even more.

The elk like to hear us sing
They like to watch us prance
For they know that no arrow
Will come from those who dance

The girls fall down laughing on an old log, while the elk continue to watch them with confusion. The herd finally wanders off, led by the male who attempts to keep order among the pack. They look back once of twice, to see if the women are still watching them. Only when the women ignore them will they return to their grazing, as if all the attention is affecting their appetites.

Rising to her feet, Numei insists that they should turn back before darkness falls. There will be a feast in the shelter tonight, cooked by Lem's girl in celebration of the birth of his granddaughter, and Numei has eaten little in the past few days. After sleeping all day yesterday, she assisted another birth at night and then slept until early this afternoon.

Esther hesitates, there by the fallen log overlooking the little stream. She stares into a pool of water, watching a fish swim idly by.

"What?" asks Numei.

"Nothing."

"What?"

"I feel strange."

"Why?"

"I don't feel like myself. I feel...different."

"How?"

"Just changed."

"How?" Numei repeats, her voice strained with the impatience of the hungry.

"I don't know. Do I seem different to you?"

"You did wonders with Hasa. The old Esther could not have done that. The old Esther was too much like her."

"I don't want to go back to the old me. Not ever."

Just at that moment, it begins to drizzle. The two women start to walk back before they get soaked. The rain sounds nice, pattering over the leaves on the forest floor. Suddenly, it begins to pour and they start to run back the way they came. They laugh insanely as they are drenched by the deluge. Their feet slosh through quickly forming puddles of water and over slippery logs, as they hurry home to the shelter. Esther slips and falls twice, and then Numei slips a minute later. By the time they get home, both are covered in mud and slime and soaked to the bone.

That night there is a terrible downpour, but inside the shelter they are happy, safe and warm. They sit around the table, feasting on roasted deer meat, corn patties, seaweed salad and fresh greens. The deer meat is from an animal that Squirrel has freshly killed. He gave it to Lem, along with the greens and seaweed, in exchange for staying at the shelter for several days.

Lem makes a fuss over Esther and Numei and thanks them over and over for their help. The women thank him graciously. But the big star of the evening is the little one, who still has no name. Everyone makes a big fuss over her. She sleeps peacefully in the baby basket that will be her home for the next year and a half. It will be borne on Siyle's back proudly or slung across her chest, until the toddler is old enough to walk on her own.

"Hope you like your new home," coos Lem, stroking the baby's chin softly. "You're going to be strapped into this basket for a long time. We're not untying you until you can talk."

Esther laughs, but then she sees that Lem is serious. He gets sort of blown up when she laughs at him and starts a lecture.

"A baby is a prime target for any number of predators. It's an easy kill. A weasel could get in here and kill it while Siyle is in the outhouse. Baby meat is very tasty. Soft and succulent. Not tough and stringy, like my meat.

"I love baby meat," exclaims Squirrel. "Although I won't kill one myself."

"Exactly! So around here we keep the little ones close until they can walk on their own and call out for help."

"Sounds smart," she agrees.

"Yes it is. No weasel is getting my little grandchild. Not if I have anything to say about it. My grandchild is special. She's going to grow up to be chief."

He turns around and makes a ridiculous face at her.

"Aren't you? And you're going to take good care of grandfather when he's an old man."

Elk 27'

Beaver moon

They are having a leisurely breakfast, accompanied by the screams of a newborn baby who isn't happy about something. The screams are getting on everybody's nerves, but they are too polite to say anything. Finally Squirrel stands up and goes outside to check on the weather and get a break from the noise.

"It is time for me to leave," he shouts when he returns, trying to speak over the screaming baby. "I have to get back to the Cougar tribe in time for the gathering of Ruoks."

He stares at Numei for a long time, until she looks up from her empty plate.

"What?"

"I was just wondering if you were coming?" he says.

She stares at him but doesn't say anything. He shrugs and goes back to his food.

"Tumock told me to bring you if I saw you," he mumbles over a mouthful. "He had a dream about you."

She just stares at him and he stares back at her impatiently. He obviously wants an answer.

"I would love to see Tumock, but I promised Horim I'd be back."

"You can't wait till after the meeting?"

"We want to have a baby," she says quietly.

"You can't wait a few months? Is your womb going to dry up?"

She ignores him, but he can tell that she heard him very well. She doesn't speak for a long time afterwards and when she does, she sounds troubled.

"Having a baby is stressful enough without trying to induce the birth on a new moon," she says thoughtfully. "I see that now. I won't allow my body to be put through that. I want to have a baby very much, but I won't force its due date. I don't care what Horim says."

"It's better that way," Squirrel agrees.

"But then your child won't have certain advantages that the other children of your tribe will have," counters Lem.

"I don't need that kind of advantage," argues Squirrel. "I do just fine."

"What if it's an inconjunct?" Lem insists.

"I'm an inconjunct," Squirrel says, rather offended. "I have certain advantages that many of the other children don't have. Inconjuncts are very creative. They are more interesting and unique than new moon children. Many Ruoks are inconjuncts."

"Ruoks are mad," says Lem. "Just like inconjuncts. Aren't they Esther? You worked with those two inconjuncts, Hasa and Balik. They're a pair, aren't they?"

He waves his hands in the air, to show how mad they are. Esther laughs. She doesn't say anything, but she certainly cannot disagree with him.

"Inconjuncts *are* mad," agrees Squirrel. "And with madness, comes wisdom."

"What are you going to do, Esther?" asks Numei, changing the subject.

Esther shrugs. She hasn't thought about it.

"You could take Esther to the Ruok meeting," Numei says suddenly.

"You want to come with me?" asks Squirrel.

"How far is it?"

"It's about six days walk."

"It's so cold out," Esther says lazily. "I don't want to travel in this rainy weather."

"It's not raining now."

"I don't want to travel anymore. I'm tired."

"That's right," agrees Lem. "Stay on here with us."

Esther stares at him, wondering if he'll let her stay for free through the winter. But she doesn't ask, because she suspects she knows what he will want in exchange.

"Hey Esther, you can borrow Timid, the horse, if you want to go to the Cougar tribe. I can ride back with the others."

"Why would I want to go to a Ruok meeting?" she asks, baffled.

"They can help you with your problem."

"I don't have a problem."

She glares at Numei, hoping she won't speak further of things which should not be discussed. Numei nods and falls silent.

"If you decide to come, let me know," says Squirrel, and the matter is dropped.

"Why should I go to a Ruok meeting?" Esther repeats, when she and Numei are alone.

"They are very wise and powerful people. They could teach you things. Tumock would help you if you told him you were my juwanna. They might even help you cast out your bad spirit."

"Who? Him? I haven't heard from Him lately. I think he's finally left me alone."

"He'll return. These spirits always do, unless they are properly disposed of."

"You mean he could stay with me forever?"

"No. Of course not."

She nods, relieved.

"Just until you die," Numei says with a smile.

Esther doesn't think this is funny and her brow furrows with worry.

"Do you think I should go?"

"Ruoks are hard to track down. This is your only chance to get them all together."

"And they can cast out Him?"

"They could help."

Esther thinks about it for a while and then she shakes her head.

"I'm tired of traveling," she repeats.

They fall silent as they walk toward the main circle to do some trading. Numei knows that Esther should go to this meeting, but she doesn't know how to explain it. It is just a feeling she has. She remembers how Tumock taught her to always trust her instincts and this one is strong. For the first time, she realizes she has really taken on a juwanna. She thought it was just a ruse at the time, but apparently the powers that be thought differently. Like it or not, Numei now has the obligations of a jodhai. She has to finish what they started back in Wolf village.

"If I go, will you go to the meeting?" Numei says at last, biting her lip as she things of Horim.

Esther stares at her, surprised.

"Do you want me to go that bad?"

Numei ponders for a while and then nods slowly.

"Why?"

"I have this feeling...."

Esther nods. Strangely, she suddenly gets the same feeling.

"I'll go if you do. Are you sure about this?"

"We are both meant to go," says Numei. "I feel it."

Esther hopes that she is right. She is not looking forward to moving on to another village in the dead of winter, but so be it. She'll follow Numei and this strange Squirrel to the Cougar tribe and this gathering of Ruoks. She has a feeling that Numei is right and they are being drawn together towards some strange fate. She likes the idea that there is something there, waiting for her. It makes her feel good, like there is a purpose to her endless wandering. A destination on this endless journey. After she gets there, she promises herself a long, long rest.

Raven Tribe

Raven 0'

Jay moon

The road is narrow here and winds through the forest. Up and down mountains it goes, sometimes connecting to the river and sometimes leaving it for many miles. It doesn't follow the usual logic of the roads of the Twelve Tribes, but seems to go out of its way many times, heading up and down at random.

"This is a strange route," Esther says.

"We try to avoid certain tribes which are known to be...troublesome," explains Squirrel. "There are some aggressive tribes up here and we have moved the road to avoid their villages."

"These giant redwoods are beautiful," exclaims Numei. "But I'm glad I don't live here. Give me the beautiful valleys of the Wolf tribe and the peaceful Pomo as neighbors any day."

Although they have Timid, the horse, along with them, Squirrel will not permit Esther or Numei to ride him when they travel uphill. He claims that carrying the two girls together up a steep hill will exhaust Timid beyond his endurance. He won't even permit the horse to carry his burden basket, although he doesn't refuse the girls to load Timid with theirs. Although the girls find his protectiveness of the horse irritating, it is heartfelt and they respect it, so they do as he asks.

"I wouldn't want Timid to give me anything of his to carry," he says. "So I won't give him anything of mine either."

Squirrel is a fast walker and Esther has to struggle to keep up with him on this endless steep mountain. She is used to a nice, leisurely pace, where she can stop anytime she likes to rest or admire some beautiful sight. That's how she is used to walking when she is alone. At this quick pace, walking is more of a chore than it usually is, and she struggles to keep herself interested in putting one foot in front of the other. But it seems unusually dull at the moment and she cannot find a reason to enjoy it.

By the afternoon, she is tired and sore, but nobody else wants to stop. It has gotten cold and her limbs and joints stiffen. She begins to lag behind and they have to stop to wait for her many times.

"Your gait is a bit...off," exclaims Numei, after yet another long wait for Esther to catch up.

"What do you mean?"

"Your rhythm is off. You must keep up a rhythm when walking long distances."

She has noticed lately how Esther moves as if carrying a heavy weight. She seems deep in her own world, as she often gets, and doesn't speak for hours. Her face often gets very grim during these times. Knowing her history, she knows where her strange behavior was learned. To be a good role model to her juwanna, she shows Esther how she walks with a measured, steady gait. Esther nods but doesn't attempt to try it for herself. She finds the comment about her walk irritating. Numei has been very bossy these past two days and Esther has been trying hard to ignore her. But each criticism is a fresh jab with a small needle.

"I am tired of walking," she says at last. "Perhaps I will ride the horse for a bit, so I don't slow you down any more. It is not too steep now."

She stares at Squirrel, waiting for him to complain, but he doesn't refuse her wish. Instead he brings the horse to her.

"Why don't you ask him first?"

"Ask him?"

"Ask if he minds that you ride it. Horses appreciate such gestures. They don't like being treated like slaves."

Esther cringes at the comment, which strikes a nerve. She looks at the horse compassionately, wondering if it feels like a slave.

"How do you ask it?"

"By talking to it."

"Very funny."

"I'm serious. Horses don't speak Alano, but they communicate. Go on. Talk to it."

"But -"

"Talk to it already," snaps Numei, who is as tired and irritable as the rest of them. "Must you argue with everything?"

Esther walks over to the horse, which grazes contentedly. She stares at it, waiting for it to look up from its meal. But it never does.

"Do you mind if I ride you?" she asks quietly.

"Horses are quite deaf," insists Squirrel. "You must speak louder."

Esther looks at Numei, but she isn't paying attention.

"Do you mind if I ride you?" she asks louder.

The horse makes no notion that it heard. Esther pets it gently on the nose. Still the horse continues to chew on a tasty morsel it found growing along the path. Esther looks at Squirrel, wondering what she has to do to appease him. But he merely indicates that she may mount it.

"He didn't say no. Go ahead."

Just before dusk, they reach the Raven tribe. Raven village is a very colorful place. They seem to delight in building the strangest structures that Esther has ever seen. They pass a tree house, built on top of a thick oak, with a ladder that reaches up to it. Next they pass a house that is completely round and made from mud. It has ten bamboo 'pipes' arranged in a circle. All ten pipes pour smoke at once, like ten primitive chimneys. They walk to the shelter, which consists of a single long house built exceedingly large. They enter the huge building and wait for their eyes to adjust to the gloom. There is much activity inside. Dinner is being prepared right by the main fire, with no separate kitchen area. Four or five people are involved in the dinner, singing a strange song as they work. The place is an absolute mess, with beds everywhere and baskets of things all over the place. Suddenly, they are greeted by all of the singers at once.

"Welcome," they shout, almost in unison.

A woman walks up to them, with the biggest smile that Esther has ever seen. It is a smile so big and friendly that she finds it overwhelming.

"Hello," she beams. "Are you needing a place to sleep also?"

"Yes, we are."

"Oh good. We are delighted to have you. Where did you come from?"

"Wolf tribe," says Numei.

"Hawk tribe," says Squirrel.

"Hawk tribe!" she shouts joyously, as if it is the thing she has been waiting to hear all day. "It has been so long since we've had somebody here from the Hawk tribe."

She leads them toward the fire and hastens to get them mugs of hot tea.

"I am Nanjeh. What are your names?"

As they introduce themselves, she hands them a dark green tea with a pungent smell and then rushes off to fetch something for the cooks. Numei watches her go curiously and then whispers conspiratorially to Esther.

"Light Bearers have taken over the care of the shelter."

"What's a Light Bearer?"

"We call them 'Grinners' behind their back, but they hate that word, so don't say it to their face. Lucky for us, it was the Grinners who took over. It could have been the 'hibernators' and then there would have been nothing to eat at all."

"I don't think there are many 'hibernators' left here," whispers one guest who has overheard them. "They all wasted away, I hear, and finally died off."

He and Numei laugh heartily. Esther laughs along too, although she has no idea what they are talking about.

Soon everyone sits down to eat. Before dinner, they are required to sing the song of thanks that reminds Esther of the prayer before dinner at the mission. And then dinner is served. It is bland and simple food, but hearty enough. Acorn and corn gruel, dried fish and seaweed salad.

After dinner, the Grinners bring out instruments and begin to sing. A couple of men come by with drums, stoke up the fire with wood and join them. Neither Esther nor Numei knows the songs they sing, but they learn them quickly enough. It is the same type of song that the Grinners typically sing. Mostly praises to all the things of the earth. The melodies of the songs are all very similar and the words are redundant, but singing by the fire is a good way to finish off a long day.

One by one, the members of their party drop off to sleep. Two benches run all around the circumference of the shelter, in typical long house style, and there is room upon them to lay out bedding. Esther soon realizes that everyone sleeps together in the same house and there will be no peace and privacy here. She sets up her things as far from the singers as possible and snuggles into her blankets. Numei follows her and sets up next to her. The Light Bearers are considerate and lower their music to a quieter tone and they fall asleep with the quiet chanting of Light Bearer songs in their ears.

Raven 1'

Bear moon

Numei goes off on some errand in the morning, leaving Esther alone to walk around the village and explore. She has a quick breakfast of gruel at the inn - served with a big smile, of course - and then with a full stomach she goes to look around. First she walks through the village commons, which usually offers the best glimpse of the character of a tribe. There are many little structures set up around the commons, which look like giant bark umbrellas held up by three thick poles. Underneath, sit all sorts of strange folk. Many attempt to talk to Esther as she walks past, telling her about what they have to offer. As a new face, she finds herself the center of attention.

Besides the usual items for sale, like food, clothes and tools, are a lot of unusual offerings. A woman offers her a healing bath in a warm tub filled with special herbs, followed by a cold plunge. A man shows her a special potion that will make her immune to disease. He claims that his potion is so effective, that he himself has not been sick once in the past five years. Another woman offers her 'healing hands', which is a form of massage that is supposed to cleanse the body of damage done by bad spirits. A man offers her a crystal from some distant mountain, which is supposed to attract good spirits and keep away evil ones. He also claims that the crystal will fill you up with so much energy, that you will be able to walk twice as far and work twice as hard without tiring. She laughs, but she doesn't buy the crystal or anything else.

After exploring, she sits on the ground, her back propped against a log and eats a piece of deer meat that an old woman handed her because she looked hungry. As she eats, she watches two boys do tricks off a pair of tall tree stumps. They do back flips, in which they seldom land on their feet but come crashing to the ground. Then they will do a handstand on the stump before doing another flip. It is frustrating to watch them, because they will do fifty practice leaps, swinging one leg back, before the actual flip. Esther will get bored and look away, and when she returns her gaze they are already crashed to the ground. After they get tired of flips, they just throw their bodies to the ground, as if testing their endurance to pain. One of them does a handstand, flips over backward and kicks his friend in the face. He crashes to the ground, laughing, while the other boy vows revenge and throws some half-hearted kicks in his direction. But the actual revenge never comes and they go back to their tricks.

"Hi miss," a tall bearded man says with a smile, as he approaches her. "Would you like to try 'healing hands'?

"No thank you."

He shifts back and forth on his feet as he talks, as if he has to go to the bathroom and is holding it in. There is something very innocent in his eyes, although his smile is a little creepy.

"Free of charge," he says with a strange smile. "I am trained in clearing out bad magic and I give a good massage."

"Um, sure," says Esther, thinking it would be nice to be massaged, as she is still sore from the journey up here.

The man leads her to a beautiful rabbit skin blanket, and indicates to her to take off her dress. Esther is a little leery at first and balks at removing her clothes.

"Can't we do it with my clothes on?" she asks.

He seems surprised.

"Why? When it is so much easier unclothed? And being naked helps you to release the bad magic."

To demonstrate how easy it is, he pulls off all of his clothes.

"Come on. Why are you afraid? Your body is beautiful."

Why indeed? Esther remembers how much she hates the modesty that was forced upon her and she quickly pulls off her clothes in rebellion. She lies down on the soft blanket in the glory of her naked body and the soft fur caresses her gently. His strong, calloused hands begin to grope and feel for tight muscles. At her request, he spends much time on her calves and feet, which are tight and cramped from walking. She feels her body slowly unwind and she sinks deeper into the soft fur blanket with a sigh.

"I like it here," she thinks to herself.

Suddenly she feels a tinge of surprise, as the man's hands start caressing her thighs. There is something fresh in the way he strokes them and she feels a thrill of fear. His hands find their way higher and higher, until they are gently touching her pubic hair. He squeezes, strokes and caresses her thighs, and she becomes very uncomfortable. But she assumes that this is the way a massage is done here and she doesn't want to appear 'modest' and 'chaste', so she bites her lip and allows him to continue.

Mercifully, he moves on to her rear and then up her back. She sighs with relief, realizing that her back got very tense when he started getting fresh. Now that he is working on her back, she tries to relax again and swallow the fear that worked its way all up her spine.

Suddenly he rolls her over and starts massaging her chest. He straddles her waist and sits directly upon her flower with his pollinator, touching it gently. He closes his eyes and breathes softly. She smells something in his odor that she doesn't like and then she feels his pollinator growing. Now thoroughly alarmed, she starts to wiggle out from under him, but he shifts his weight to make it more difficult for her to escape and she cannot get away.

"Disgrace!" shouts a loud voice from behind him.

The man turns around surprised. There is Numei, standing over him, glaring at him.

"Are you having fun?" she shouts loudly. "You are a disgrace to the healing profession. Get off my friend, whom you seem to think of as a Lady of the Lily Pad."

Esther glares at Numei, wondering if that was an insult meant for her.

"I am giving her a massage," he says simply.

"You look as if you are about to stick it to her!" she barks.

Everyone is staring at them now. The man reluctantly stands up and moves away from Esther.

"Your friend was free to complain," he says with a snide smile. "She didn't say anything. I assumed she liked it."

"She doesn't look happy to me."

A man walks over to see what all the fuss is about. He is a thick-set man with a deeply lined face. A pretty, slender woman follows him. Neither seems surprised about what is happening here.

"Edi," the man growls. "You know that healers may not behave in such a way. And in front of everybody too!"

"Sorry Aram," he mumbles. "I was just sharing a little love with this lovely girl."

"Sorry is nothing. Pay the woman a tupa for her humiliation."

"One measly tupa?" asks the slender woman incredulously. "Ban him from practicing the healing arts! He makes all healers look bad."

Numei nods her head emphatically and both women glare at Edi. He shifts his weight back and forth nervously, and his hands stroke his lips as his eyes dart to and fro. That is when Esther realizes how creepy he actually is. Why did she not notice?

"Now, Reepa," Aram says in a clucking tone, "let's be fair. Young lady, did you ask him to stop?"

He stares at Esther, who wishes she were a thousand miles from here. Her first day in the village and already she is mortally embarrassed.

"No, I did not," she admits. "But I did not invite him! When I tried to get away from him, he held me down and he wouldn't let me go."

"Give her a tupa and a crystal," Aram grumbles. "But don't let it happen again, Edi. Next time, you're banned from practicing the healing arts forever. And I mean it this time."

Edi nods and hands over the requested items. Esther doesn't look at him as she takes the gifts.

"Enjoy the beautiful crystal, my lovely," he says. "Although it is not as beautiful as you are."

"You're pond scum, Edi," says Reepa.

He holds his head proudly, sure that he was in his rights. Aram leads the fuming Reepa away, dragging her by the arm before she starts more trouble. Numei treats Esther in nearly the same manner. Esther can feel that Numei is very upset with her by the extra firm grip she keeps on her arm.

When they are far away from the village center, Numei turns toward Esther and lays into her.

"What were you going to do? Let him stick his shaft into you?"

"I wanted him to stop but I didn't say anything at first, because I didn't know if that was how they do massages here. And then, I tried to get away but he held me down -"

Numei cuts her off. They stand there in silence, as Numei shakes her head in disbelief.

"Those Spanish really did a job on you."

"What do you mean?"

"I mean you are the perfect victim."

"I am not," Esther protests.

"You are afraid to speak out if you don't like something. You let people do things to you and don't fight back. That's what a victim is."

"I couldn't fight back when I was a child," Esther complains. "I would have been whipped."

"Instead you were raped and abused. Was that any better? I'd rather be whipped until I was dead than give in to such abuse."

"You try it and see!" Esther says angrily. "Go get baptized and live in that mission and see. You wouldn't fare any better than I did."

"Anyway, that's not the point. The point is that you are still meek like a mouse in the paws of a wolf, even after all you have learned. You still don't stand up for yourself."

Esther becomes angry that Numei is attacking her and not that weird man. She decides that she has had enough of Numei and she is going to end this conversation. She turns around and starts to walk away.

"Where are you going?"

"Leave me alone! Yell at that horrible man, if you want to yell at somebody."

"I'm sorry if this hurts you, but you need to hear this. As your friend and your jodhai, I need to say these things."

"I'm not your - what's it called? Juwa - or whatever – and you're not my master. I'm done being criticized by you. Just because I pretended to be your helper for a while, you think you can tell me what to do for the rest of my life? Leave me alone."

Esther marches off. Numei throws up her hands, dismayed at the way the discussion went. She is angry with herself now, more than Esther. She realizes that she is a terrible jodhai to nag Esther like that. She thinks about what Tumock says, something about letting the flow teach and the teacher guide. It seems like good advice.

Esther walks away, ignoring the pain in her belly. She feels almost on the verge of tears and then she feels a wall come up, shutting her off from her feelings. She is grateful that she is strong enough to build such an effective wall, that makes her numb and not care. Then she goes down to a stream that flows through the redwood trees and sits by a little waterfall, which soothes and calms her. She sings to herself to clear her mind. Even when it starts to rain and her clothes become wet, she doesn't move.

Eventually, the weather turns cold and she has to go back to the shelter. Sure enough, the Grinners are gathered in force again, eating dinner and making a racket. Nanjeh welcomes Esther and invites her to join them for dinner. Esther is in no mood for a party, but the dinner smells good. So she sits down by the fire, trying not to have a sour puss to ruin their evening, and eats quietly.

After dinner, Esther gets directions from Nanjeh to the sweat lodge. She walks quickly, craving a warm, womb-like tomb where she doesn't have to talk to anybody. Soon she is lost in the heat, with the red flickering smoky atmosphere hiding her from prying eyes. She sighs with contentment.

There is an extremely skinny man in there that breathes louder than she has ever heard anybody breathe in her entire life. Sometimes he makes a whistling sound with his mouth as he breathes out. Then he begins to hum. He is so ridiculous that Esther has to laugh. But after fifteen minutes of hearing him disturb her silent musings, she is ready to kill him. He sits in full lotus position, humming loudly and making a whistling noise with his breath. He waves his hands in the air, spins them in circles like a windmill and makes a whooshing sound. Esther grits her teeth and hopes that he will leave soon, but he has good tolerance and continues to annoy her for the entire rest of the sweat.

Raven 2'

Esther and Numei have not spoken since their argument, and Esther has been avoiding Numei all day long. But tonight, Numei doesn't show up for dinner. She has cleared out all of her things and disappeared, which is very strange. Why would she leave without telling Esther? Did she decide that Esther was more trouble than she's worth and go to the Cougar tribe without her? Did she go home? Esther suddenly feels bad about the way she spoke to Numei, who was only trying to help.

Squirrel is gone too and nobody has seen him. After dinner, Esther takes a walk to the commons to look for him and Numei. She has a sinking feeling in her gut that they are gone and Esther is stuck here alone. She walks under the glow of the moon, hidden behind thick clouds, on this wet, gloomy night, which seems to match her mood perfectly. She explores the entire commons, but she doesn't see them or anybody else. They must have deserted her.

Then the rain returns and she goes back to the shelter. There she must endure the music of the Grinners, which is even more irritating tonight than it was the past two nights. A woman whom she has not seen before performs for everybody. She dances around with a big smile on her face, exposing big, buck teeth with a gap between them. She sings in a horrible falsetto that makes Esther grit her teeth. Her voice is terrible, but that is not the worst part. It is the way she bounces around with that big, stupid smile lighting up her face and waves her arms so everyone will look at her. The Grinners egg her on, cheer for her to act even stupider and tell her how fabulous she is. In her current mood, there is something about her that makes Esther want to strangle her.

If it weren't for the rain, she would sleep outside. But that is out of the question. So she goes to her bed, lies down and covers her head with every spare piece of clothing she owns. There she lies, tossing and turning, unable to sleep. The Grinners sing late tonight, seeming to be utterly unaware that this is a shelter where people are trying to sleep. Finally, Nanjeh takes pity on her poor guests and requests that everyone stop for the night. Only then can a thoroughly exhausted Esther fall asleep.

Raven 3'

Chief Aram stands in his storehouse, frowning. The place is a mess and he doesn't have the time to clean it now. The full moon celebration is tomorrow and he is expected to throw a huge party. Wracking his brain, he tries to find something in here that will make the people remember this party. As the chief of the Raven tribe, the people will judge him by it. They will judge his generosity and his speeches, to see that he is still a good chief to his people. If he is stingy or lacking in fine words and manner, then he will find his influence fading.

His standing in the tribe is already slipping. Many of the people have not been happy with Aram lately. He has felt coldness from some and others have ignored him, avoiding him wherever he goes and never listening when he speaks. There have been some who have even spoken against him, suggesting a change in leadership. Aram knows where this seed of discontent began. It started a few months ago, with the Uranians and their damned benefit.

Aram shakes his head, thinking of the Uranians, who named themselves after the newly discovered planet in the sky called Uranus. They claim that they are heralds of the future and they believe only in modern things like science, reason and technology. They rarely give any stock to magical, mystical forces that cannot be seen and studied, including Ruoks, spirits, and old tribal superstitions. Their ranks have been growing by leaps and bounds in the past few years and Aram believes that they are seeking leadership of the tribe. They are using the situation with the benefit in order to destroy Aram's credibility, so they can take over. It is such a stupid thing to get angry about, that there is no other explanation.

The Uranians have been desperate to get to the continent of Europe for many years, where there are amazing leaps and bounds in modern thinking and science. But no Twelve Tribes ship has ever gone that far around the world, and they have been frustrated in their efforts. Finally, they came up with a plan that seemed reasonable. They will take the trading ship down to the southern continent, walk across the land to the eastern coast and take a Spanish ship across. But the Uranians haven't enough wealth to trade for passage on the Spanish ships, so they threw a benefit party and invited the entire Raven tribe, and the Elks and Cougars too. Everyone was asked to bring a donation. Most of the Raven tribe came for the party, which was held at the assembly hall. Some gave generously. Some did not care to give at all. Aram was among those who did not care about this venture. But he gave a token gift, because it was expected of him. The chief is supposed to be generous, because he is usually the richest member of the tribe. So Aram gave a few finely made capes of otter fur. He figured they would fetch a good price. They were insulted by his gift and he saw their faces drop as he presented the capes. They felt so cheated that they didn't even try to sell him on the expedition. The only thing he got from them was dirty looks the whole night.

Since that day, they have been spreading rumors that Aram has grown greedy and selfish with his wealth - which is given freely by the tribe and is supposed to be given back as such. They say that he has lost his vision and has become conservative and miserly. They claim that he cannot be trusted with the future of the tribe, and some whisper that he must be replaced with a chief who is more in touch with his people.

Being chief of the Raven tribe is a difficult thing, as Aram has learned from hard experience. The tribe has a diversity of groups and each one wants to share its vision with the others. Aram has long held a policy of belonging to no particular group. He has always tried to be a mediator between factions, interested in only the greater good. He has always been generous and giving to everyone, not just to one particular group and has urged the Raven tribe to come together and be a unified whole that is big enough to encompass all of the different sects.

But it was always inevitable that one group would eventually become much bigger than the others. Aram saw that potential when he became chief five years ago. And now that day has happened. The Uranians have gained ground in their numbers and influence and they are looking to transfer the leadership of the tribe to one of their own. At the same time, Aram has lost influence with all but the Light Bearers, who share his reverence of the old ways. Even those that hold no allegiance to any group, no longer respect him as they used to. They too have fallen under the spell of the Uranians.

Aram sighs and starts rummaging through his baskets and baskets of things, looking for insight. He must be generous and show the people that he has their best interests at heart. He must throw a party that will be so extravagant, that nobody will be able to call him miserly. He will have a great feast prepared and give out gifts to show that it has been a good year. But as he rummages through his many baskets, he realizes that it hasn't been such a great year and his storehouse is not bulging with wealth as in other years.

Finally, Aram gets angry and storms out of his storage house. This is stupid. It is not enough merely to give out a lot of gifts and blow all of his resources on a party. This is a deeper problem and he cannot buy his way out of it.

After calming down, he decides to talk to the Onu, the Ruok, about the problem. A Ruok is the perfect person to talk to about this, because they do not seek to lead the tribe. Ruoks don't care about gaining power within the tribe structure. They are outsiders, keeping themselves at a distance purposely. Thus, they can give him a fresh perspective.

He finds Onu sitting quietly by the stream near his house. Onu is the eldest (and only) Ruok in the tribe. He is a recluse and rarely comes out into public anymore. Aram sits down next to him, but he waits for Onu to speak first, which is the polite way to approach someone. It is a full five minutes before he is acknowledged.

"Hai, Aram."

"Hai, Onu."

"Look who has come to see me after all these years," says Onu, in a taunting voice. "It must be something very, very important."

"Yes, I seek your advice."

He explains the situation in great detail, while Onu listens, a frown on his face. Afterward, his confidant says nothing for a long time.

"Here is my advice," he says at last. "Do what you will with it. I would resign as chief."

Aram is speechless. He stares at Onu like he is a crazy man.

"The people have chosen a path that best suits them and they want a chief who represents that way. So tell them that if they wish, they may have it. If that is what they really want, then they will replace you with a Uranian. If they decide that they are just fond of complaining, then they will ask you not to resign. Either way, you will have shown that you care about your tribe above yourself. You will not have to waste your energy trying to climb a cliff without a rope."

Aram sighs and stares out over the water. Onu is no help. He hasn't thought this through.

"Those bird brains are not fond of the Ruoks. You will lose your influence in the tribe."

"Influence?" Onu says, laughing. "This is the first time a chief of our tribe has come to ask my advice in ten years. I doubt I will live to see the next time I am approached for advice."

"Well Todi absolutely hates Ruoks. You may become an outcast from your own people."

Onu shrugs.

"Is there anything you care about?"

"There is not much I care about these days. I'm too old. So are you, Aram. Why do you care so much? This sounds like a useless battle."

"You think holding the tribe together is a useless battle?"

"This is not about holding the tribe together. It is about who will decide what the tribe believes in. "

"I will not stand aside and watch our values crumble," says Aram firmly. "I will do what all of the chiefs before me have done. I will uphold the old ways that were handed down to me by the great Raven spirit."

Onu nods slowly and says nothing more. Aram stares at him, wondering if Onu thinks that Aram is a foolish old man who is out of touch with the tribe, but the man's thoughts are inscrutable as always.

There is a traditional mask party in the assembly hall tonight to celebrate the full moon. Esther asks around the shelter and finds herself a freaky bird mask, then she trods after Nanjeh and some of the other Grinners to the hall. On the way, she stops to stare at the moon. It is surrounded by two multi colored rings of clouds. Esther finds it amazing, but the man standing next to her thinks it disturbing. He keeps complaining that it means that a nasty storm is brewing, and he goes on and on about how the repairs he is making to his roof are not done yet and he is going to get flooded tomorrow.

Then she sees a strange sight. A cloud passes over the moon, clouding its glow and spreading it outwards, and through the mysterious glow a lone raven floats like a ship across a foggy sea. The sight is somehow inspiring and Esther feels like something is in the air tonight.

The assembly hall is very dark, with only a small fire burning in the center and a few torches on high stands. Everyone walks around quietly, saying nothing. Esther joins the swirling parade, watching the various masks bobbing around with great interest. Most people wear black robes of raven's feathers from the neck down and the torchlight is designed in such a way as to illuminate the mask but not the rest of the body. Thus the masks seem to bob up and down as if on a current of air.

There are some bizarre masks. Each year, everyone goes out of their way to create the most outlandish mask possible. Inhuman faces, ghastly and frightening, are very common. There are animal faces also, as well as a variety of masks that don't resemble anything in particular. As the parade continues in a circle around the fire, a bowl of some foul smelling liquid is passed around. Everyone sips the elixir from a tule straw so they won't have to take off their mask to drink. Esther avoids it altogether. She is not in the mood to take some strange drug tonight and go on an unexpected journey into the depths of her strange soul. She just wants to have a good time.

After the parade of the masks becomes tiresome, there is a performance by acrobats and clowns. The fire is stoked up bright and everyone sits down to watch. Many light pipes and the smell of tobacco and jimm is thick in the air. Once pleasantly high, everybody laughs and laughs at the antics of the strange jesters. In one part of the show, the entire cast pretends to carry a heavy tree, which continually crushes them to the ground. It ends up killing most of the cast before they are finished, leaving the last man standing with the task of removing the tree from his crushed friends in order to give them a proper burial. He cannot budge the imaginary tree by himself, so he searches for help in the nearby forest. He finds three bears who agree to help him remove the tree from his companions. As he gloats over his success in taming the bears, they eat him and then eat all of his crushed friends too. Everyone roars with laughter and cheers the bears for their trickery.

Afterwards, comes the epic song Night of Masks. This song is special to this night, written many years ago by the great Raven composer Ardus. It is a brilliant and strange story about a night when spirits come alive. The dancing is highly ritualized and everyone dances in unison. Esther is quite impressed by the dancing abilities of the Raven Tribe. Most of them are very good dancers and the dance moves are not easy moves to imitate. Esther has to struggle to keep up. At least she has her mask on, so nobody knows that it is her throwing the whole dance off. Night of Masks takes many hours to complete. The whole event seems highly ritualized, and Esther learns later that it is the one ritual dance that all of the tribe can agree on doing every single year

After the song ends, Esther goes home to sleep. It is a chilly journey back to the shelter and she practically runs the whole way back. Luckily, the Grinners have had enough singing and Esther is able to get a good night's sleep.

Raven 4'

Aram wakes up at the crack of dawn. He yawns and stretches, thinking about all that he has to do. He'll need the help of the two women sleeping next to him. Aram shakes them both vigorously, but they ignore him. He shakes harder. Finally one of them opens a sleepy eye. It is Reepa, the slender beauty who has shared his bed for years.

"What is it?" she mumbles, closing her eyes again.

"We have much to do today. I need your help."

A slight moan from Ita shows that she is awake also. Ita is a short, curvy woman, not as pretty as Reepa but much younger and more sexual. She has only shared their bed for a year, after Aram's younger brother died a few years ago. Aram was always attracted to her, so he used the ancient custom of accepting your brother's widow into the family to his advantage. He generously offered to marry Ita as his second wife.

Ita moans again and flops an arm over Reepa, and Aram gets a thrill. He was bored and tired of sex until Ita came along. She injected a newness and freshness into the bed, and he has been like a young man all over again. Aram is about to turn forty-seven years old, which makes him an old man in this time and place, and he was really feeling his age until last year. He hasn't felt this excited since he was a young man, and Reepa a beautiful virgin of fourteen years.

Ignoring his cravings, Aram stumbles out of bed and goes to tend the fire. There are just enough hot coals left in the white ash to get the kindling started and then it is an easy task to relight. He puts on an iron pot of water and goes outside to see the day.

Reepa wakes up when the water is ready. She stands up, stretches her naked body and pulls the pot off. Aram is nowhere in sight. She steeps some Chinese tea and pours three cups through the little tea basket, which catches all the leaves. Then she tries to wake Ita. She has to shake Ita vigorously to get her to open her eyes.

"We need to help Aram. The full moon is here. Get up."

"I need to sleep."

Reepa scowls darkly. At first it was fun having Ita in the bed. She liked the threesome. But then she realized that Aram was losing interest in her, and was becoming more and more infatuated with Ita. And Ita has been getting more and more lazy and useless, taking advantage of Aram's preference. Reepa does most of the work around here lately and she is now completely fed up with the lazy blob in front of her. She is nearly there with Aram too.

"Get up!" she snaps irritably.

"I am. Leave me alone."

Cursing, Reepa leaves the room and goes outside to look for Aram. She wonders how much more of this she will take before she leaves him. The truth of it is that she would have left by now were it not for her position of influence as chief's wife. Reepa is an important member of the Raven tribe and her influence has grown even more lately. Her sympathies are with the Uranians and the people like that. As Aram loses favor among the growing number of Uranians, many people ask her for chiefly advice instead. Some have even referred to her as chief. She smiles when she realizes that Aram still has no idea that she has gained much of the influence that he has lost. He has been stupid and clueless lately, ignoring the will of the people and of his own woman. He should spend less time being infatuated with his new sex toy and more time paying attention to what is going on.

She sees Aram near the storehouse, carrying a heavy barrel of wine, and she feels a pang of guilt. She wishes that they were still in love, as they once were. They were a powerful combination and the people were happy with them. But they have grown distant since the blob entered their bed. And he is getting old and out of touch with the tribe and trying to make his way up river without a paddle.

At sunset, Esther sits by herself, watching everyone gather for the second night of the polar day celebration. She has never seen anybody dress in such unusual ways as the Raven tribe does. Each outfit is a statement of individuality, and in such bright and contrasting colors. They have cloth dyed every color in the rainbow. Some are dressed in clothes made from bird feathers and some in skins that have been covered in tiny quartz sprinkles, which gleam in the sunlight. One woman wears a cloak made from carefully woven river grass and she wears the same on her head like a wig. It is warm enough today so many go naked. But even then, no two nude people look alike. Some have shaved their entire body from head to toe. Some have hair that goes to their waist and is dyed in many colors. Many are covered with tattoos of various strange patterns and colors.

One woman has covered herself with mud from head to foot. She sits quietly, like a statue, with only white eyes to show that she is human.

Suddenly, Esther sees something that makes her eyes bulge out of their sockets. Near a blazing fire, she sees two naked men kissing each other. Her brain does a double take, but she isn't seeing things. And there is a naked woman playing with both of their pollinators at once. And all of this takes place out in the open, with not a care of who is watching. It is the strangest thing that Esther has ever seen and she finds it disturbing. But she cannot stop taking peeks to see what strange positions they will try next.

Esther receives a steaming cup of tea from the tea master and it is very bitter and pungent. By the way they serve it, she assumes it must be something very special, so she finishes the whole thing. After drinking it, she feels a warm glow that starts from her head and goes all the way to her toes. She feels light on her feet, like a great weight she wasn't even aware of has been lifted off her. She immediately wants more tea. As she gets a second cup, she runs into Reepa, who is dressed in a beautiful robe made from polar bear fur.

"And how have you been enjoying your stay here?" Reepa asks. "Despite that unfortunate introduction to one of our less pleasant folk."

"Very much, thank you."

"Good."

Reepa starts telling her of some of the places she might visit if she is in a mind to do some walking. Esther stares at her with wide eyes. Reepa looks positively angelic, dressed in her white, flowing polar bear robe. For a moment, Esther could swear that she is an angel. She giggles, feeling lightheaded and blissfully happy.

"What is it?" asks Reepa.

"What is in the tea?" Esther asks. "I love it."

"Ahh," nods Reepa. "This tea is made from coca leaves."

"I must buy some before I leave here."

Coca leaves are a popular South American herb used daily in many traditions. They produce a euphoric state similar to caffeine, but slightly stronger and a little mind altering. Cocaine is made from the coca leaf, but in its raw form it is much milder and does not produce the states of paranoia and other side effects that have made cocaine such a problem in the modern world.

As the night grows late, the traditional mystery dance begins. This is a dance that is supposed to summon spirits to perform magic. The Ruoks used to do this one, as it was one of their specialties, but there are no Ruoks left to do it. The Light Bearers do it now, and they have no experience in the subtleties of the dance. Even Aram has to admit that the dance is rather pointless without the influence of the Ruoks.

Nanjeh is dressed as a large raven, eight feet high. The costume is made from a frame of twigs, with black dyed deerskin and real raven's feathers to make the body. The head is a mask. It is a bulky costume and she is not used to it. She struggles to keep it steady as she does the opening dance. A single pulsing drumbeat is the only accompaniment. Four more dancers appear, dressed as the four elements: water, earth, fire, and air. They move to the four cardinal points of the compass, waving their arms and singing the song to call upon the great Raven spirit that comes during the full moon.

Aram looks around at the Uranians, not surprised to see them bored and distant. They do not go for the old rituals. They are totally fixed in their own world in which everything new is good. The Light Bearers are enjoying it - but then again they enjoy everything.

Suddenly a huge explosion echoes throughout the night. Everyone jumps, looking around wildly to see what is going on. The ground shakes and a boom echoes throughout the canyon. There is another explosion, not as loud, and a flash of white light. Somebody screams. The feathers from the giant raven's wings go fluttering away into the night. Then a flash of light shoots along the ground at everyone's feet. More screams, and everyone jumps out of the way. Then a trail of orange light shoots along the ground, screaming like some kind of deranged hawk. There is pandemonium in the camp. Some think that the tribe is under attack and they go for their weapons. Others are sure that these are supernatural terrors coming after them - called by the dance - and they begin panicking. The music stops and Nanjeh is bumped in her huge costume and crashes to the ground. There is another explosion of feathers.

Todi finally manages to get everyone to calm down by screaming and yelling.

"Everyone relax! We're not under attack! These are no spirits at work, my friends! These are merely firemakers. Did I scare you?"

"What happened?" shouts Aram, furious. "Did you do that?"

"Yes. Of course I did," he says with a snide smile. "Did you think the spirits were after you?"

"What infernal magic is this?"

"Magic is merely ignorance, my friend. I used gunpowder to make these noisemakers. Just like we learned on our trip to China."

Todi laughs as he sets off another one, which screams over their heads with a flash of orange light. It shoots into the sky and everyone laughs, relieved that all is safe. They cheer as the orange light disappears into the night. Many of the children scream with glee and cry out for more.

"You've angered the spirits," shouts Aram angrily. "And ruined the mystery dance. This is not the way to behave. You'll invite who knows what sort of trouble."

"Aram, you're a superstitious old fool," Todi says with a sneer. "You're a relic. The new age is here and you're trapped in the old one."

"This is what you call the new age? Loud noises and explosions? Artificial thunder? How does that help anybody?"

"We can use it for many things. To scare away enemies or animals. Ceremonies. Signals over great distances."

"We have good ways of doing all of that already. Less violent ways. Ways that do not anger the spirits."

"Go do your dance somewhere else," Todi snorts derisively. "Leave the full moon celebrations to those of us with vision."

"Your vision tells you to ruin our dance? What sort of vision is that? Why must you shoot off your toys in the middle of a ceremony? It is not respectful. It is mean and stupid, and it shows incredibly poor vision. Put those things away before you bring the wrath of the spirits down upon all our heads. Your science is no match for the spirits, Todi. I promise you that."

They are shouted down by a multitude of voices.

"Brothers and sisters, let us not fight," shouts a Light Bearer.

"Firemakers do not promote well being," cautions another.

But most of the people are of the same mind and the children are all in agreement.

"More firemakers! More lights!"

Smiling, Todi turns and prepares another batch for the huge chorus of his fans. Aram tries to speak above the crowd, but he cannot get another word in. He stands there with his mouth hanging open in disbelief as he is ignored. Finally, he curses and walks off into the night.

Esther stands with her head stretched far back so she can see the light show. Her mouth is wide open. The tea, the firemakers, and the drumming that now accompanies the light show are all swirling inside of her brain. She wonders again at the strange twists of fate that have brought her here, so far away from that miserable life she used to have. She feels as if she has stumbled into some strange world that is like a dream.

There is a small rocky cliff nearby, with a large rock face that shows the innards of the mountain after an earthquake or a mudslide tore it apart. Underneath, a loud group prances around a great fire. Esther hears them scream and turns to watch. Then she notices with amazement that a giant raven is etched into the great rock face. It must have taken months to carve. It is subtle, so one wouldn't notice it on first glance. The more she stares at it, the more she wonders if it is even manmade at all or just the natural features of the rock.

"Hello!"

She turns around, to see two young girls standing there, watching her.

"What's your name?"

"Esther."

They introduce themselves and each gives her a big hug.

"What are you doing?"

"Just watching everything," she says with a shrug.

"We met ten new people today," one of the girls says with a big smile and then they both run off into the night.

Esther pulls the blanket tighter around her body, as the cold seeps through the cracks. She notices that with the blanket wrapped around her, her shadow makes her seem vaguely birdlike. Almost like a raven. She begins to wonder why she sees ravens everywhere, now that she is in the village of the Raven tribe. Is it just a coincidence or some hidden magic?

She walks toward a large fire pit. Some boys have built a tower of wood five feet in the air. One carries a torch with which he intends to light it. The others wait expectantly.

"Watch this," the boy with the torch says. "I invented the perfect fire structure. You light the bottom with a small flame and the whole thing burns within minutes. It will create the perfect amount of heat for warming a large group of people and it takes almost no effort to maintain."

He lights it and everyone watches expectantly. Sure enough, the strange tower of wood and branches lights very quickly, and everyone congratulates the boy who simply nods as if he knew it all the time. For a moment, there is a beautiful burning work of art. But almost as soon as it bursts into flame, it collapses, causing everyone gathered around to leap for cover as sparks and burning wood explode everywhere. Esther brushes at the sparks that settle in her hair and moves away from the fire that now looks like any other fire pit. The boys all laugh at their abashed companion, who curses and complains that the fault was in the wind and not in his structure, which would work perfectly inside a house. He urges everyone to try it inside their own homes, but nobody seems anxious to do so.

Esther is lost. Somehow she took a wrong turn on her way home. Now she walks through thick redwoods, not sure where to go. She has an idea that she should walk down a hill and up the other side. Having no better plan, she decides to go with her instincts. She makes her way down, groping with her hands where she fears branches. She moves slowly, so she will not poke an eye out on a branch. She feels groggy from exhaustion, but this seems like a blessing to her because it keeps her from being afraid, which she would be under normal circumstances.

She comes to a ring of trees that seem older and bigger than the others. She enters the ring and instantly feels something very intense pulsing through her. The trees seem to be communicating with her. At least she thinks they are. She stands there for a long time and she gets higher and higher with each passing minute. She feels positively overwhelmed in this ring of old, giant trees. Then suddenly, the trees seem to tell her to go away. Getting a bad feeling now, she walks out of the ring. Among these newer and smaller trees, she feels normal again. She sighs with relief and keeps walking. She isn't sure what just happened, but there isn't time now to figure it out.

The moon rises overhead and shines down on her powerfully, like a beacon to guide her. Comforted by the bright light, she moves on. But the woods seem to get thicker and thicker as she walks and she begins to fear that she is completely lost. She sees a giant patch of moonlight in a clearing and walks toward it to get her bearings. Up ahead is another patch. She walks to that patch. Then she stops to consider an idea.

It seems a good idea to jump from moon patch to moon patch. Somehow, the moonlight always finds the most open clearings. She tries this for a little while and it is as if she is being guided by moonlight. As if in a dream, she follows the light trail all the way up the hill and down another one.

She hears the sound of a small stream bubbling below. She moves toward it quickly and stops in amazement. Right in a great patch of moonlight is a bridge. It looks old, unused and broken in the middle, but at least it is a sign of civilization. And she can see lights in the distance and an old, unused path. In awe, she just stands there for the longest time, musing on the fact that the moonlight actually led her home. It blazed a path through the thick woods and back to the village.

She crosses the bridge slowly, but she cannot get across without getting wet. Then she climbs up the hill toward the lights. Soon she finds herself back in the comforts of Raven village and she walks in a daze back to the shelter and collapses onto her bed. Just as she falls asleep, dawn appears through cracks in the house, and that is the last thing she remembers for a long time.

Raven 6'

Raccoon moon

Esther spends the entire day helping Nanjeh and some of the other women prepare acorn flour and make bread. She feels a little guilty for not paying them a single tupa yet for her stay here and wants to help them out some way. She falls into a trance, with the crack of the rock on the acorn shell, and the slow singing of the women. She sings along with them, in time to the pounding of the rocks. The clouds disappear and the sun shines brightly overhead for the first time in days. The women take off their clothes to take advantage of the brief sun and with only a moment's hesitation

Esther removes hers too. She doesn't think about hiding herself, even though she knows that there are men walking by. She feels primitive and simple, like the Zesti, sitting or squatting by the rocks, singing and pounding. The sun feels good all over her body.

For some precious moments, Esther feels like a completely different person. She is no longer 'the tragic tale of Esther', but just another 'heathen' doing what it takes to survive. Squatting naked in the sun makes her feel human in a way she has never felt before. The sensations of the sun on her flower and the way the grasses gently tickle it. The way her breasts sway gently as she hits the acorn with the rock.

She feels a strange shame suddenly well up, as if she is doing something wrong. She isn't even sure what she is doing wrong. It is something to do with acting like a 'heathen'. And then she knows that the shame inside her is something that the priests put there. They planted that seed of guilt in her, and tended it until it grew into a giant shame tree. She wonders why somebody would plant such a thing in a human mind or a human body.

As Esther pounds away, she wonders how to get it out. Rip the tree out by the roots? Cut it off branch by branch? Stop watering it until it dies? She spends the rest of the afternoon trying to figure it out. It gets chilly quickly, but she is so preoccupied that she is the last to put her clothes on.

She sees now that the fathers made her afraid to be human. Now that she sees that, her whole life suddenly makes sense. Even when she thought she was free, she didn't count on them hiding secret things inside of her. She wonders how deep their chains go. Numei was right and she tried to argue with her!

That night, Esther cannot sleep. She is still upset about her realization earlier today, but that is not the reason that she cannot sleep. Nanjeh has invited all of the Grinners over for singing and dinner again. By now, Esther has grown sick to death of the endless Grinner parties and is craving some peace and quiet. But there is none to be had in this accursed shelter. Right now, Esther is wedged between an older couple, both snoring away, and a child who is having a bad dream and keeps mumbling. And the Grinners are involved in a deep conversation that they take very, very seriously. Apparently, they want everybody to know how serious these matters are and that something should be done now.

"We need to help the Viard," a man says in a self-important voice. "It isn't fair what is being done to them. The Mattoal take much of their wealth as a tribute and if they say anything about it they get attacked. They live in constant fear. We have to help them. I say we invite the Mattoal here for a feast and try to talk some sense into them."

"That's a beautiful idea. We have to tell them that it isn't nice to hurt their neighbors," agrees a woman. "We need to ask them how they would feel if a stronger tribe was constantly harassing them and taking away their freedom. I mean...the Viard have a right to be free. Don't they?"

Everyone agrees that they do in somber tones, shaking their heads sadly. Esther throws the blanket over her head, trying to drown them out. She thinks about what Numei said about her standing up for herself. What she should really do is stand up and tell them all to shut up and let people sleep. Tell them that this is a shelter and the guests have a right to silence at night and it is very inconsiderate to be so loud. But she is unwilling to go so far, so she lies here going crazy instead. It is very late in the night by the time all the Grinners leave and Esther is all wound up and it takes another hour for her to get to sleep.

Raven 8'

Swan moon

Merlu sits quietly in his father's house, trying to read by the light of a candle. He studies a copy of a translated Chinese text his father owns that tells of many different inventions of the ancient Chinese. The funny thing about this book is that it is probably better known among the Twelve Tribes, where books are still rare, than among the vast Chinese continent where it was written.

He struggles to concentrate, but it is difficult with his father moping around. His father is Todi, leader of the Uranians. Todi has been preoccupied lately with the desire to oust Aram and take his place as chief, and he can speak of nothing else. He goes on for hours about how out of touch Aram is and how he will lead the Raven tribe to ruin. Right now, his father is in a bad mood and Merlu suspects he is torturing him on purpose. Just as soon as Merlu reads a sentence, his father starts talking to him about the accursed Aram, until Merlu puts his book down to listen. Then Todi will fall silent until Merlu picks up his book again, and immediately he starts another rant.

"I will be chief by the new moon," Todi boasts. "Many have told me that I am already considered chief by some. I am wealthier than Aram, more generous, wiser...."

"In love with his wife," adds Merlu, mumbling into his book.

"I didn't think you knew about that." Todi glares at his son. "Have you heard talk? Does anybody else know?"

"Everybody but Aram, probably. You aren't very subtle."

Todi laughs cruelly.

"That figures. He's as dense as a rock. That is why he is unfit to be chief. That is why it is only a formality now that he is replaced."

"Have you asked the Raven spirit for its blessing?" Merlu says, trying to bait his father, which is one of his favorite pastimes.

"If I am chief, then you will have more responsibility also," intones Todi dramatically. "You can no longer afford to be a butterfly, flitting about carelessly and smelling the flowers. You got that from your mother, I'm afraid. She was a good woman, but a bit unrealistic sometimes. She let you do whatever you wanted." Todi shakes his head. "Perhaps I was too soft with you after she died."

"I saw her spirit in a dream last night," says Merlu, looking his father in the eyes directly for the first time. "She seemed happy with the path I have chosen. She urged me to continue."

"Path? I see no path!" says Todi angrily, slamming his fist down on the table. "It is time to grow up. You are not a child anymore, who believes that his dreams are real. You are a grown man and all this talk of spirits does you no good service! If you show that you are serious and reasonable, then the people will accept you as chief after I am an old relic like Aram."

"That doesn't leave me much time to become reasonable."

"Speak nonsense if you like. But you have a great opportunity before you to be a leader of your people, and instead you spend all your time dreaming of spirits and studying old stories."

"You know I will never be chief. My chart is not good enough."

"Neither is mine, son," Todi says, puffing up dramatically. "I have only three planets in the Raven sign, which is nothing compared to Aram. Things are changing. Soon the people will no longer care so much about those old superstitions."

Merlu nods. He cannot argue with that.

"What are your plans for the future, son?" asks Todi suddenly, taking the book away from Merlu. He looks at it distractedly and places it aside as if it is no matter.

"I plan to read some more," says Merlu quietly. "If you give me my book back."

"It is time for you to think about what your place in the tribe will be," exclaims Todi, ignoring the crack.

"Are you upset because I am not married with a family?"

"Married?" Todi says, with a hint of scorn. "What do I care if you are married? It is better to be single, if you ask me. I am concerned with more weighty matters. As chief's son, all eyes will be on you as the voice of the future. What will you do to earn their respect?"

"I will learn to do the mystery dance and summon spirits."

"Very funny."

"I have recently decided what to do with my life. I was just waiting for the perfect moment to tell you."

Todi smiles in anticipation and nods his head.

"Father, I am going up to the Cougar tribe to become a Ruok."

Todi stares flabbergasted, as Merlu stands up, grabs his book, and walks outside to read by some quiet fire. For the first time that he can remember, his father is speechless. Merlu smiles, pleased with himself, as he walks out the door.

A group of Light Bearers staggers into Raven village an hour after dark. They are covered in bruises, scratches and smeared blood. Several of the women cry pitifully, and the men are grim and angry. They are quickly rushed to a healer, where they are examined and declared bruised, but not broken. The call quickly goes out for everyone to meet in the commons. When everyone arrives, their story is told and it causes an uproar.

True to their word, the Light Bearers went on a diplomatic mission to the Mattoal village, to speak on behalf of the Viard, who have been faring badly in the battles between the two tribes. Ignoring common sense for a greater cause, they walked defenseless and unarmed into the village and asked to speak to the chief. With the help of Yut, who acted as translator, they made their plea for peace.

The chief of the Mattoal was unsympathetic to say the least. His people were not too pleased either. The Light Bearers soon found themselves surrounded by a hostile and unfriendly group of warriors, who were not at all appreciative of being told what to do by a bunch of strangers. They began to throw rocks at the unarmed party. Being a nonviolent group, the Grinners begged for mercy and compassion. They got neither. They got knocked to the ground, punched, hit with rocks and laughed at mercilessly. The worst thing about it, especially for the female Light Bearers, was being kicked by the Mattoal women as well as the men.

Finally, the Mattoal released them and told them never to return. The chief also told them that he was insulted and might be inclined to look very unkindly on the Raven tribe, if they are not soon appeased by a substantial peace offering. And then they were sent home, with a parade of jeering and taunting men, women and children, who followed them for almost a mile to milk it for as long as they could.

There is dead silence for a long time, after this story is told. The Light Bearers sit there expectantly, waiting to be immediately surrounded by support, loving hugs and assurances that they were treated most unfairly. But nothing like this happens. They are shocked instead to find a very angry and troubled group before them, and many unfriendly faces glaring at them. Most people present are wondering when would be a proper time to start calling them 'fools' and 'idiots', and nobody is worried about their feelings.

Aram finally stands, knowing that he should say something to calm everyone down.

"This is a terrible thing that has happened. And a dangerous one," he says at last. "Much is at stake by our response this."

For once, the Uranians are in complete agreement with Aram. They shake their heads sadly, reflecting on what a tight spot they are now in. Finally, an old woman stands and says what is on everybody's mind.

"I hope you are all happy. You might have started a war with your foolish parade."

Esther watches Nanjeh's mouth drop in complete shock and her heart goes out to her. Nanjeh looks absolutely devastated. Everyone in the village echoes these feelings and the Grinners are all flabbergasted. Finally, one of them musters the courage to defend themselves.

"How could you say such horrible and cruel things, after all we have been through," says an angry Light Bearer, feeling a fresh bruise on her cheek tenderly with her finger.

"We didn't expect this," explains Nanjeh sadly. "We didn't know."

"What did you expect? The Mattoal to see the error of their ways and beg your forgiveness?" the old woman shouts back.

"Yes!" shouts the angry Light Bearer woman.

"This is the real world," shouts an angry man. "Your stupid ideas have no place in the real world. If we had known you flower people were going to actually try to do something real with your useless theories, we would have told you this years ago."

Frail people, who are obsessed with beauty and goodness and cannot handle the rough frosts of life, are often called flower people by the Twelve Tribes. They tend to ebb and flow like the flowers that pop up briefly in full bloom and then disappear a few weeks later.

If the Light Bearers had any hope left, it is quickly dashed by this last comment. And the resulting furor of agreement from most of those present sticks the dagger in deeper. Aram waves his hands for silence, hoping to maintain a little diplomacy. But it is too late. The Light Bearers walk off to the shelter without another word, and it is clear that they will not soon recover from this loss of faith in their tribe.

It takes a long time to get the shouting crowd under control. By that time, every single Light Bearer is gone from the meeting. There is a long and bitter debate then, about the proper response to this crisis. Everyone has a theory that is bitterly argued by everybody else. The meeting goes late into the night. To Aram's disappointment, Todi has the best suggestion of the night and it is his council that eventually prevails.

"We have never had a problem with the Mattoal before. I believe they know the reputation of the Twelve Tribes, and that is why we have been spared trouble. The tribes are well armed and stick up for each other. But they probably now wonder if we are all as weak and bird brained as the Grinners, and that is why they try to bluff us. This is a test."

As he speaks, he stares directly at Aram, slyly lumping him in with the Grinners.

"Now they are watching us closely. If we cave in, then there will be war and endless tribute. We must retaliate in a way that will show them we have strength, but we cannot push too hard or we will trigger a retaliation from them. We must do something unexpected that will baffle them and make them afraid of us. This we must do for both our own safety and the safety of all the Twelve Tribes. I have some ideas, but I will not speak of them now. We should meet again soon and decide on a course of action when we can be more detached and logical."

It is agreed that this is sound policy and the meeting is disbanded. The tribe agrees to meet tomorrow at dusk and exchange ideas as to a possible retaliation. Before everyone leaves, Reepa stands up to speak.

"Be a little kinder to the Light Bearers," she says. "Although it was a foolish plan, we will not be served by loading them down with guilt. I feel they may yet play their part to put right what they have done wrong."

Everyone nods in agreement. Aram looks at Reepa with annoyance. He wishes it were he that said that and not her. As chief, it is his place to say such things. Then, he tries to think up something deep to say. Something at least as wise as that. He raises his hands and notices how long it takes for everyone to look his way. Reepa got everyone's attention much quicker than he did. When he finally gets everyone's attention, he realizes he really doesn't have all that much to say.

"We must all stick together because we are one big family," he says lamely. "Light Bearers and Uranians must put aside their differences for the greater good of the tribe...."

He trails off, realizing he says the same things for every occasion. Everyone watches him for a moment, waiting for more, and then they look away. He feels his face flush red with embarrassment and he tries to act as if he is deep in thought about a possible retaliation.

Numei walks up to Esther after the meeting and puts a hand on her arm gently. Esther is surprised to see her and nearly shouts out with glee, then becomes tense and withdrawn, remembering their fight. She regrets this, but she just can't help feeling strange.

"How have you been?"

"Fine."

"How are your accommodations?"

"Crowded and noisy."

"I am staying at the house of Merlu. He's going with us to Cougar village. Come stay with us, if you like."

"Thank you. I would like to get away from that shelter."

"Get your things and I'll wait here for you."

She goes back to the shelter, which is filled with Light Bearers. She hears sobbing and sniveling coming from the house and stands by the door, not wanting to enter and come face to face with them in all their pain. But she fears that Numei will take off if she does not, so she finally enters the room.

Everyone looks up from their closely knit circle. They are all gathered together in a sort of group hug, comforting each other and speaking in hushed whispers. Nanjeh stares at Esther with a tear stained face and smiles sadly at her. Esther smiles back, and walks quickly to her burden basket to get her stuff together. She feels like a beast as she gathers her things into the basket. This is not a good time to abandon them, even though it has nothing to do with them. Before she leaves, she walks up to Nanjeh and explains herself.

"I am going to stay with my friend, Numei. But it has nothing to do with you. I think what you did was very brave. I hope you feel better."

Nanjeh gives her a grateful hug and Esther knows that she said just the right thing. And it was basically true. Even though she thinks that they are all incredibly foolish, she has to admit that they did have the courage to do just what they said they were going to do. Before she gets sucked into their group hug, she quickly walks out and leaves them to their misery.

Raven 10'

Wolf moon

Merlu lives in a strange house. The house is entirely circular, with a huge bark roof standing upon five poles and walls that only go halfway up to the ceiling. When you are sitting down, you are looking at the wall, but when you stand, you can see the forest all around you. The floor of the house is also made from bark, except for a small hole in the center, filled with stones, where a fire burns. The floor is covered entirely with tule and straw mats. This makes the house resemble a giant birdhouse, like the ones that the fathers had at the mission.

Esther, Numei and Merlu are all gathered around the fire, listening to Squirrel play a giant bamboo xylophone that belongs to Merlu. Another man, a loud boisterous man with wild hair, plays a hand drum. His playing is very good, but extremely loud. He seems intent on demolishing the thing with his loud slaps. As he plays, he keeps screaming nonsense. Esther wants to tell him to just calm down and play a little more gently, but she feels that he won't take too kindly to criticism. And as loud as it is, it beats the Grinner's endless droning any day of the week.

Later that night, Esther decides to take a sweat. She walks along the path through a wet mist that soaks her. The wetter she gets, the more she cannot wait to get to the sweat lodge. As she passes through the commons, she suddenly spots movement at the edge of the trees. She stops and strains her eyes in the moonlight. There it is again, coming from the nighttime shadows. It looks like a beast at first, but then it looks like a man. An owl hoots behind it, but its call is strange. A patch of mist obscures the man-beast suddenly, and when the fog clears, the figure is gone.

Esther is confused and disoriented. She wonders if she really saw him and then convinces herself that she didn't. She keeps walking. But then she sees the figure again, closer this time. She kneels down, locks her eyes on the creature and squats patiently until the figure creeps quietly out of the forest and looks around.

It is no beast. It is an old man dressed entirely in animal skins. There are bear claws, wolf fangs and a shrunken head of some sort of rodent dangling from ropes around his neck. His body is painted charcoal black, so he will blend into the night. His stringy, grey hair is long, unkempt and matted. He is monstrous, and the moonlight reflects off eyes that seem to have a light of their own.

Somehow, she knows that this man is not of the Raven tribe or the Twelve Tribes. He is probably Zesti, but there is something unnatural about him that she cannot figure. She looks around to see if anyone is about, but the circle is deserted. Her first thought is to go get help, but she has a feeling that the man will disappear if she leaves him. Although she is afraid, she decides to follow him and see what he wants.

She follows the man down the path toward the large kitchen, where group meals are cooked. There is something insect-like about the man's movements. He moves as a human spider, scuttling low to avoid detection. When a young couple, walking hand in hand, moves into his sight, he stops moving completely. He blends in with the darkness until they have gone. Moving through the heart of the village, he watches the movements of the Raven tribe carefully. He seems especially interested in the smells of people. He is constantly sniffing things and gathering information on smells. He avoids walking near fires, where he might be seen, and keeps to the shadows.

Approaching the main kitchen cautiously, he opens the shed door that holds all of the tribe's food. He spends a few minutes pouring through the food supply and Esther cannot see well enough to know if he is taking anything. Then he closes the door quietly and walks out. Once he is out of the kitchen, he moves spider-like back the way he came.

Snap! Esther steps on a twig and cringes as she hears the sharp noise. The man looks up, instantly on guard. He sniffs the air apprehensively. Esther drops to her knees, trying to keep an eye on the man as she hides. The man moves slowly toward her and she feels her blood run cold, and a sense of panic, which she struggles to fight down. She crawls to one of the little healing areas and hides behind a stool. But in her panic, she nudges the rickety stool, which crashes to the ground. In the silence of the foggy night, the crashing stool sounds like an explosion of firemakers. She curses and looks around wildly for another place to hide. But it is too late. The man moves quickly toward her and she is trapped.

Esther feels a sense of terror unlike anything she has ever experienced. Her heart hammers in her chest and she feels as if she may faint. Then she hears a hiss right by her ear and a cold, inhuman muttering follows. Suddenly, Esther cannot concentrate on anything. She feels as if she is losing herself. Her thoughts scatter and she senses some dark and horrible presence all around her. She struggles to scream, but nothing comes out. A cold hand grips her, and she feels a stale, rank breath on her face as the man leans in to peer at her. He grunts and stares at her with wild, inhuman eyes. Esther is numb with fear and she cannot move. She just stares back at him with the eyes of the little woodland creature caught by the cougar.

Suddenly faint voices float over the fog. Two mens' voices get steadily louder as the men walk toward them. The voices break the spell of terror and Esther manages to scream. She hears an answering cry and footsteps as the men run toward her. Her predator hisses and lets go of her arm. Without a backwards glance, he disappears into the fog.

It takes an hour in the sweat lodge before she feels human again. After a plunge in the stream, she walks back to Merlu's house. She is not aware of walking back, because she is still quite numb, but somehow she finds herself back in his house. Everyone else is asleep. Although she wants desperately to talk about her experience, she doesn't want to wake anybody up. She lies down on her bedroll and falls into an exhausted sleep, and her dreams that night are dark and disturbing.

Raven 11'

The morning is a great comfort to her and last night seems far away. Over tea, she tells the story about the man-beast. Everyone listens with absorbing interest and then Merlu has a hundred questions.

"Has he any spirit helpers? Did you see any animals or birds in his general vicinity? What was the animal around his neck? Describe his tattoos."

Esther has no answers to his questions, and finally Merlu nods and falls silent.

"Do you know this man, Merlu?" Squirrel asks.

"No. But I feel that it is important that we do. We must take turns keeping watch at the main circle until he reappears."

"He sounds dangerous," says Numei, staring worriedly at Esther.

"Agreed."

"What should we do if the man reappears?" Squirrel asks.

"Follow him silently. Get to know as much about him as you can. Make sure he does not cause any trouble. But do not interact with him in any way unless absolutely necessary. I feel that he may be very dangerous."

Everyone nods soberly.

"We will stay carefully hidden at all times," Merlu says. "Dress in black and paint your face with ash when you keep watch."

"Shall we take shifts?" asks Squirrel.

I'll stay up all night," Merlu says. "You two can switch off watching half the night."

"I'll help," Esther says suddenly.

"Are you sure?" Numei asks in a concerned voice. "After the way he scared you?"

"Yes, I'm sure," Esther says, a little irritably. "I'm not a child."

"Perfect. Then Esther and I will keep watch for half the night, and you and Squirrel will keep watch for the other half," says Merlu, with a little glance at Esther.

There is a meeting today to discuss what to do about the Mattoal problem. Everyone gathers in a talking circle to hear what ideas have come up. There is a sense of something huge in the air, and everyone squirms anxiously as they wait for the meeting to begin. Aram speaks first, as it is his place as chief to do so. He rises, knowing that he is going to have to prove to his people that he can still lead them. He can see the doubt in their faces as they watch him, wondering what he will propose.

"My friends," he begins, "this is a most difficult situation. A great dishonor has been done to our tribe. Many were hurt - more than just bodies were wounded. Our neighbors are fierce and warlike and they see the world differently than we do...."

He goes on and on, speaking much about what has happened without proposing anything. This has been acceptable in the past, but now the people are too nervous to listen to his long preamble. Finally, someone shouts for him to get to the point and there is a mumble of agreement. Aram frowns, knowing that nobody would ever have spoken to him like that until Todi soured his reputation.

"I propose that the reason this thing has happened is because our people do not understand the customs of our neighbors. Although the actions of the Light Bearers were heartfelt, they did not go about it in the proper ways. The Mattoal were insulted and they responded in their own barbaric way. We have grown too separated from the ways of the Zesti. This puts us in danger. I propose that we begin to understand the ways of the Zesti better. We must get more in tune with the land and the spirits. I will send a messenger to the Mattoal in the proper way, and then I will meet with their chief and we will hammer out an agreement that will suit both peoples. We will not pay them any tribute of course. That is not our way. We will stand firm and yet we will not respond with barbarism. This will only lead to war. We do not want war, my friends."

The circle erupts with great agitation. Many people shout out their opinions about Aram's idea. Most seem to be negative. The mediator, whose job it is to keep order during meetings, insists that the people speak in turn. The talking stick (that old relic of the early days) is brought out and passed around. Then Aram is forced to endure the anger of his people.

"This is what you always say, but it never works. These people do not understand fine words. They only understand strength and force."

"If you had the ability to make friends with these people, you should have done it long before."

"These Zesti are barbaric and dangerous. Do we really want to send another Grinner to speak to them?"

"This is the kind of thinking that got us in this mess."

Some of the people are a little more positive.

"I think it is a fine idea," exclaims a Light Bearer. "But are you sure you can persuade their chief? He is a very tough man."

"I believe I can," insists Aram.

Then other people offer their suggestions.

"I say we do nothing and prepare ourselves for war," exclaims a man. "If they leave us alone, great. The Grinners can lick their wounds and forget it. If they attack, then we wipe them out. We'll get the Owls, Elks and Cougars to help us."

Many are of the same thinking as this man. There is talk of barricades and fortifying defenses. What sort of weapons and armor the Mattoal use and how many men they might send in an all out raid. Most of the people seem to be in agreement with this philosophy. Prepare for war and hope that the Mattoal were just bluffing.

"To do nothing would be a mistake," exclaims Aram. "We must open a dialog between our people."

"What do you think Todi?" asks Reepa.

Aram glares at Reepa, unable to believe that she of all people would ask Todi for his opinion. She ignores him utterly and continues to stare at Todi. Meanwhile, Todi accepts the talking stick, and he has a long dramatic pause while he licks his lips and stares at everyone assembled.

"I have my own plan," he says after awhile. "I think it is a good one. But I do not want to step on the toes of the chief. If he wants to try his plan first, then that's fine with me."

He smiles and stares at Aram, making sure that his meaning is gotten loud and clear. Aram glares at him, seeing what he is up to. Many insist that he speak up and share his plan. He pretends to be worried about Aram's feelings, until everyone shouts for him to get on with it. After allowing himself to be prodded into it, he finally shares his plan.

"I suggest we scare the war paint right off of them. Show them a bit of our power in exchange for what they have shown us."

"Do you mean attack?" a woman shouts anxiously.

"Nothing so crude," he exclaims. "No, my friends. I have something special planned for these savages. After I'm through with them, they'll come on their hands and knees and beg our forgiveness. They'll pay *us* reparations."

He quickly explains his plan. After he is finished, there is nearly unanimous approval from all assembled. Even a few of the Light Bearers think it is a fine plan. And so it is decided.

"It is an interesting plan," says Aram, taking the talking stick back. "If this is the wishes of the people, I will go along with it. Just be aware, that if it fails, then my plan will not work. There will be no peace between us. The Mattoal will be angry and war will follow. Just as surely as spring follows winter."

He puts the stick down and walks off. He is aware that his words are basically ignored and he knows then that if Todi's idea works, he might as well resign as chief. Nobody will ever listen to him again.

Esther walks with Numei and Squirrel through the woods, looking for certain mushrooms that Merlu requested. After Squirrel gets ahead of them, as he usually does, she finally has that talk with Numei that she has been avoiding. She explains her theory of the seed of guilt that grew into a tree and how the missionaries tended that seed until it grew huge and ugly. How she feels guilty any time she does anything natural, like walk around naked or have sex. She asks Numei what would be the best way to get rid of this tree of shame and misery that they planted so long ago inside of her.

"Where is the tree?" Numei asks.

"What do you mean?"

"I mean where is it? Where do its roots grow? What earth do they grow in? Where are the branches?"

"I don't know."

"That is what you have to find out. Then you can cut it down."

"How do I find that out?"

"Why do you ask me that?" Numei asks challengingly. "You don't want me to tell you anything, remember?"

"I'm asking you because you're my friend."

Numei stares at her, finding her expression very sweet. But she did promise herself that she would let the flow teach and she would merely guide. And besides…she doesn't really know.

"Find out what the tree is," Numei says at last. "And then make up a song about it and sing it to me."

"You're not helping," Esther complains. "I need your help to get those horrible fathers' ugly, rotten shame tree out of me."

"Here's a hint," Numei says conspiratorially, as if she has many great ideas that she isn't ready to share just yet. "Get rid of your anger first."

"I'm not angry."

"You're very angry."

"Well, I have a lot of reason to be angry," Esther says gloomily.

"Maybe I can help you to relax," Numei says, frowning slightly, so that her mouth furrows.

Numei indicates for Esther to stand up. Esther does and Numei examines her.

"Head down. Body slumped over. Shoulders tight. Gloomy expression. This is how a powerless person stands. We need to change your body completely."

She shows Esther what it looks like to stand upright and relaxed. Esther tries, but it just doesn't feel natural. Squirrel walks by just then and Numei explains to him in a loud voice what they are talking about. Esther gasps, unable to believe that she is telling him her most intimate secrets. But that is how Numei is. Numei knows no secrets. Squirrel nods seriously, and Esther realizes that she does not mind if Squirrel knows. She likes Squirrel and knows that he is not judgmental.

"I didn't know you were raised by the Spanish," Squirrel says.

"I don't like to tell anybody," Esther says, glaring at Numei.

"Did they treat you like they treat their weird animals? Those cow beasts and those sheep monsters. Those poor beasts are bred to be easily led and to never fight back. They're so big and top heavy and just stand there no matter what you do to them. I have heard that the Zesti that live with them are taught to be the same way."

"Like a cow?" Esther asks, suddenly very upset. She sits down on a log and casts her eyes at her feet. "Yes, just like a cow."

"I have heard of those places," Squirrel says. "I have heard that there are ten times as many Zesti as there are Spanish soldiers. Yet the Zesti do not rebel."

"They are not warlike like the Zesti up here," says Numei. "They are more peaceful, like the Pomo."

"You should speak to the Ruoks about this," Squirrel says. "They should hear this story."

"That is a good idea," agrees Numei.

"Those Spanish are such beasts," Squirrel says grimly. "How did you ever escape from them? I hear they never let anybody escape."

"Look at us. So gloomy," exclaims Numei. "Let's try to be happy. Let's dance."

Numei picks her up and twirls her around. Esther laughs in spite of herself and Numei spins her in circles until she forgets all about being upset. Then Squirrel suggests that they head home before it gets dark. Numei insists that they dance back. So arm in arm, they skip back while Numei sings a silly song. They sing to escape the gloom, which spreads its fingers over the whole forest like a giant black hand enclosing everything in its grasp.

Tonight, Esther joins Merlu for the first night of their vigil. They walk to the commons a short time after dark. Merlu lights watch candles, which are placed strategically throughout the dark circle of empty trader's huts and healing tents. He explains that the light is bright enough so they can see the man if he appears, but not so bright that it will scare him away. Then they move to a dark, shadowy place with a good view of the whole circle and sit down on small tule mats. Here they will sit until the constellation of the Wolf rises in the sky. Then they will be replaced by Numei and Squirrel.

At some point during their vigil, Esther has to make a plop. She knows vaguely where the nearest trench is, so she grabs a candle and starts to walk there. Merlu jumps up quickly and runs over to stop her. He makes her put the candle back where it was and pulls her insistently back to their watch place.

"You'll give us away," he whispers. "What if he is hiding nearby?"

"But how can I find the trench without it?"

"You can find it in the dark."

"It's too dark," she insists. "There is no moon."

"You don't need light. Walk in the dark."

"I can't -"

"How did you get here?" Merlu asks suddenly.

"I walked with you."

"It was pitch black when we walked."

"Yes. But I followed you."

"But you could barely see me. How did you do it without tripping and falling?"

"I don't know. I just did it."

"But how can you walk if you cannot see?"

Esther thinks hard.

"I guess I just sensed my way," she says at last.

"With what senses? Smell? Can you smell like a wolf?"

"I just felt my way."

"That's right," he says. "But you did not feel with your skin, did you?"

She thinks awhile and admits that she did not.

"You felt your way here with another sense. Not one of the five rational senses. A sixth sense. That sense is more powerful than the other five, if you can learn to use it."

Esther agrees with a shake of her head.

"Now you must learn to use it," he insists. "Find the trench without a light. You need to practice this skill if you want to help me. We might have to follow this man-creature in the dark, walking as silently as a mouse."

Wishing she had a moonlight trail like she had during the full moon, Esther walks where she remembers the trench to be. She has to go back and forth several times, groping blindly. On the way, she stubs her toes, bumps into branches and makes quite a racket. She cannot be silent as a bear, let alone as a mouse. But eventually, she does discover the correct path. Now all she has to do is avoid stepping into the trench, filled with plop and messy leaves. She cannot remember how far it is to the first one, which worries her. The hideous idea of sinking her foot into a hole filled with human mess makes her step especially carefully.

She smells the plop suddenly and knows that she has arrived. Grabbing a stick off the ground, she feels her way with it. Soon, the stick sinks down into a mysterious ooze. Leaving it where it is, she straddles the trench and does her business.

She is back with Merlu a few minutes later. It occurs to her that the same path, which was so hard to navigate on the way to the plop trench, was almost pitifully easy on the way back. She just did it without thinking about it. She wonders how exactly she accomplished that for a long time afterwards, but truthfully she cannot remember.

Raven 12'

Esther awakens to the smell of roasting elk meat. She rises, realizing that it is dinnertime already. She slept the entire day away and so did Numei. She joins Numei by the fire sleepily and accepts a lukewarm cup of tea. Then she yawns and stretches lazily as she sips it.

"Where is Merlu?" she asks.

Numei shrugs, her mouth full of food.

"It is raining again," she mumbles. "Does he expect us to keep watch in the rain?"

Numei shrugs again, not inclined to speak while she is eating. Esther finishes her tea in silence. Hunger soon rears its fevered head and she eats a huge piece of meat and some dried seaweed. Darkness comes and she wonders if Merlu is waiting for her. She wraps herself tightly in her cloak and walks to the commons to find him.

He sits underneath one of the little huts, staring out into the night. He chews absentmindedly on some seeds as he watches. She joins him under the roof and brushes the water out of her hair with her hands.

"I guess the rain isn't going to stop us," she says, a little disappointed.

"Perfect night for our creature to be out," he says. "No one outside on a night like this." He looks at her standing there, bedraggled and wet, and laughs. "Only a crazy person would be out on a night like this."

"That's very true," she says, laughing.

"There's a party tonight," he adds. "In the assembly house. There's food there if you're hungry."

"I just ate," she says.

"I don't blame you," he says, nodding in agreement. "If it is taste you want, don't eat at our celebrations." He takes a moment to spit out a seed that is not edible. "If you want to go watch the show, I don't mind. Our creature won't show himself till much later, if he shows at all."

A while later, she walks into the hall. The remains of dinner are being cleared and the show is just about to begin. It consists mainly of dancing, but each dance tells a story or teaches a lesson of some kind. There is one man dressed up like a woman, who dances a traditional dance only for women. It is a hilarious performance. But then he gives a hideous, boring speech about how he has learned to be a woman and that ruins the whole thing. Most of the dances are set to music and there are many musicians playing a soup of different styles. One dance has no music at all, but merely has several people singing a story about the future of the tribe as they dance. These dancers are obviously all Uranians, due to the message of their song. Their dance is rather bizarre, full of lots of angular movements.

After the show, musicians play traditional music for everyone to dance. Esther is delighted to find some coca tea left over from dinner. She cannot find a clean bowl, so she drinks the lot of it right from the pot. Once the pleasant coca tingling numbness chills her body, she dances with abandon. Numei soon joins her and the night grows late. She forgets all about Merlu. Many wild gyrations steeped in a coca haze later, she emerges from the warm assembly hall into the cold night. Her shift is almost over by then, and she only has a couple hours to sit and watch the rain before they are replaced by Numei and Squirrel.

Raven 13'

Elk moon

Many in the village are sick with some horrible stomach ailment. It is suspected that rotten meat was served yesterday evening in the assembly hall. Many are down for the day, unable to move, other than to run to the crowded outhouses and trenches when their time has come. Merlu walks among the village, watching all of the sick people. He is not sick and neither is Numei or Esther, because they did not eat at the big celebration yesterday. As he walks, he is disturbed by a strange idea. He wonders if the old man is somehow responsible for this sickness. He was near the main kitchen two nights ago. What if he poisoned the food?

But why? Why would he come here just to make the Raven tribe sick? Merlu can only think of one reason and it is rather farfetched. Perhaps he was sent by the Mattoal to sabotage the Raven tribe. That is known to happen occasionally among warring tribes. But if that is true, the Mattoal are going to an awful lot of trouble to get back at the Grinners for merely trying to make peace.

He sees Aram and Reepa in the kitchen, talking to the cooks, and decides to see what he can learn from them. As he approaches, he hears Aram lecturing the cooks on sanitation. The cooks keep insisting that their sanitation techniques are perfectly adequate. It has been a long time since an outbreak this bad happened. Reepa leans against a post, as she examines the kitchen with a haggard, exhausted expression.

"Do you see this?" she asks, pointing to a dirty wooden bowl that somehow ended up with the clean dishes.

"That's not going to make anyone sick," insists the head cook.

"Would you like to see my piles of vomit, all laid out, one upon the other?" she asks sarcastically.

They begin arguing furiously. Merlu is suddenly positive that the cooks are right. The old man did this. He knows it. He walks forward and gets everybody's attention with a shout.

"As much as I would like to see your lovely vomit, I think it won't be necessary," he says when he has their attention. "It wasn't the cooks' fault. There has been a saboteur."

He explains the other night in detail. To his surprise, they all shake their heads emphatically. Nobody believes him. Not even the cooks. Apparently, the cooks would rather be blamed than give him the benefit of the doubt. Merlu protests, but Reepa stops him with a hand. She sits slouched on a log, with her head in her hands and a vacant expression on her face.

"I'm too sick to listen to this, Merlu," she complains. "Please stop talking about it. You're making me ill."

"Agreed," says Aram. "A man that walks like a spider and poisons people? Sounds like a story from my childhood."

"I thought you were a Uranian," adds the cook. "Since when do Uranians believe in such tales?"

Stunned, Merlu can think of only a moderately funny comeback.

"I guess it was your fault then. In that case, I'm glad your food tastes like dirt or I'd be sick too."

Merlu leaves the spluttering cook searching for a proper response and walks away. He heads back to the commons, more determined than ever to catch the old man. He knows the man will return. When he does, Merlu will tie him to a post in the commons and prove to everyone that he is telling the truth.

Raven 14'

The sickness in the village grows worse. Every ten minutes, the people must make a visit to an outhouse or trench. And not just an ordinary visit, but a painful visit. The village is at a virtual standstill now, and the commons is utterly deserted. The ravens have taken over, squawking and circling above the empty clearing, eating all the food they can find.

Numei makes a tea of her own special healing herbs. With the help of Esther, Squirrel, and Merlu, she distributes it to all of the houses. Merlu visits the house of Aram and finds him, Reepa and Ita all lying on their beds in a state of torpor. He hands tea to everyone and watches as they drink it. The smell in the room is horrible, and Merlu stands near the window so he can get fresh air.

"What's in this?" complains Ita, making a face. "It's nasty."

"Tea from a Wolf healer," he replies.

"You should show more respect," snaps Reepa with a scowl. "Merlu was very nice to bring this by."

Ita gives her a look and is about to lay in to Reepa, when Aram stops them. He is in no mood for another argument among the women.

"Why are you not sick?" he asks Merlu.

"We didn't eat the food during the celebration," he replies.

"I'm going to kill those cooks," Reepa growls.

"The spirits are angry," says Aram. "It's obvious, isn't it Merlu? The mystery dance was ruined by your father and this is the result."

"Not that again!" shouts Reepa. "Did you hear what he said? It's food poisoning."

"I'm not denying that Reepa. But I say that the spirits did this."

She sighs, exasperated, and turns to look at Merlu.

"Your father has many new ideas about preserving food," she says, ignoring her husband. "Why don't you ask him to take a look around the kitchen?"

Aram glares at Reepa, knowing she is just trying to get him angry. He is just about to say something cutting, when Ita suddenly jumps up as if her hair were on fire. She shuffles quickly away on short legs, her giant breasts bouncing up and down.

"What's wrong with her?" asks Merlu.

"Outhouse," sighs Reepa. "When we have to go, there isn't much time to get there."

"I thought this was the outhouse," says Merlu, sniffing the air.

She attempts a smile at Merlu. The smile seems to contain some hidden message that he cannot quite figure out.

"You have your father's sense of humor."

"That's because he has no use for it any more," adds Merlu.

He wonders if it would do any good to bring up his own theory again.

"Food preservation isn't the problem," Merlu says carefully. "But it's time you face up to the fact that there is one. Someone is poisoning the food supply."

Aram shakes his head.

"This is a sickness brought by the spirits to teach us a lesson."

"Aram, you never tire of that same old nonsense," Reepa complains, turning over and shoving her face into the blanket they all share. "You always say the same thing. I don't think you even know what you're talking about anymore. You've grown senile. And look what your stubbornness has now caused. An epidemic."

"I caused this?"

"The people are talking - "

Reepa suddenly jumps up and runs out of the room, leaving Aram alone with that piece of news to chew on. The people are talking about what? Aram watches her go, a furious frown on his face. Then he just looks at Merlu and shakes his head.

"It never ends. Why couldn't I have been the Eagle chief? So much easier than this accursed tribe."

Merlu pours him a little more tea. Aram drinks it reluctantly, making a face as he drinks. After he is done, he wipes his mouth thoroughly, making sure that nothing is left on his lips to haunt him further.

"You should replace all of the food in the kitchen with fresh food from your own supplies," adds Merlu. "Post a guard over the kitchen from now on."

"My supplies are not what they once were. I cannot replace all that food. Your father hoards much these days. He never feeds anybody but his cursed Uranians. Ask him to use his precious food supplies."

"It is your place to ask."

"I will not ask him for help. It would give him too much satisfaction. You do it."

Merlu agrees reluctantly and leaves Aram to his bad smells and his lonely bed. Aram hears Reepa screaming at Ita to get out of the outhouse. Ita screams back for her to go squat in the trees. Aram sighs and covers his head with his blanket. He feels it all slipping away. And then he suddenly jumps up and runs as fast as he can to the outhouse. He stands behind Reepa, jumping up and down, desperately waiting for his turn.

"Have you seen my eagle's eye yet?" asks Todi. "Look through it. You can see as far as the eagle sees."

It is a strange tube, with two pieces of glass at either end. Todi leads him to the door and bids him to look into it. When Merlu puts his eye to it, suddenly the landscape jumps out at him as if it is going to attack him.

"Incredible, hmm? Traded with a Spanish soldier for -"

He suddenly shuts up, as if it is better left unsaid what he traded for it.

"It is interesting," says Merlu, handing it back. "I'd like to experiment with it sometime."

"Sure, sure," Todi says, walking inside and sitting down.

Todi is sick also and his color is very pale and his eyes bleary. Merlu knows that his father won't do it, but he makes Aram's request anyway. Sure enough, Todi acts put out.

"It is Aram's place as chief to replace the food. Not mine."

"He does not have that much," Merlu says. "He seems to think you have more than him."

"Nonsense. He is merely a miser, who keeps everything for himself or for trade. Look what is happening to the tribe under his guidance. Everyone sick, while he speaks to voices in his head and calls them 'spirits'. He refuses the people food and contaminates what we have with his stupidity. And he coddles those stupid Grinners, who say that everything is all so wonderful. Is this cursed sickness wonderful? We must save the tribe from him, son. He is a relic."

"I agree with you, Father," Merlu says.

"You do?" Todi asks, shocked.

"Yes."

This pleases Todi greatly. Merlu looks around Todi's cluttered room briefly before he leaves. He notices the imported books, guns, jars of gunpowder, firemakers and other contraptions that Merlu cannot name. Then Merlu says goodbye and leaves his father to his rest. He doesn't say all that is on his mind. It would not please Todi if Merlu told him that he doesn't think he would be any better as chief. He and Aram remind him too much of each other.

Esther walks across the commons, carrying a bowl of the nasty tea for the Grinners at the shelter. She is happy to be healthy and feeling very well on this fine morning. Everything is fresh after a long night of rain. She muses about how lucky she was to have skipped dinner the other night. It is a special feeling to have avoided a fate that hits everyone else but you. Then she runs into Numei, who is also healthy. She and Esther stand in the commons like two visitors in a land of lepers, their vigorous health shining brightly among so many poor wretches and their dull, throbbing pains.

"I'm going to dig a new waste hole," Numei says brightly. "Come help me."

"Let me just deliver this and I'll be right there."

"I'll be digging over there," she says pointing. "I'll find a second shovel for you."

Esther finds Numei knee deep in a trench, scooping out dirt. She waves Esther over and points to the shovel leaning against the tree. It is a very homemade shovel, with a thick, knotted branch stuck inside a steel shovel head.

"This is the most important job we could do for this town right now," says Numei with a laugh. "Digging a hole for all of the waste."

Esther looks at the last trench, nearly full of steaming plop, and makes a face. Then she jumps into the new hole to dig. The ground is hard and rocky, and soon Esther's shoulders and back start to ache. She jumps out of the hole to stretch.

"Is your body comfortable all the time?" asks Esther, jumping back into the hole after a quick rest.

"Usually."

"Mine isn't. I've been thinking about what you said. Perhaps you were right. Maybe my body needs work."

Soon they have a deep hole dug and they use the dirt from that hole to cover up the other one. Numei remarks that a hole full of waste is the perfect lesson for today, but she doesn't explain her strange remark. The girls walk back through the main circle, past sick people attempting vainly to heal each other through their strange crafts. Their laughter and singing seems out of place among the grim faces, like sweet berries floating in Numei's nasty healing tea.

Esther spends the remainder of the afternoon in the sweat lodge, knowing that she will soon have another cold night, waiting for her mysterious demon to appear. The sweat lodge is packed with sick people. The sounds of groans, moans and coughs fill the usually solemn space. Many lie down on benches in near death poses. Some rub their bodies with crystals that are supposed to have healing properties. A man has wrapped himself from head to toe with bundles of wet skins soaked in herbs. He remarks to a woman that he is trying to leech all the poisons out of his body and onto the skins. The herbs make it happen. He swears that an old Zesti shaman taught him this trick.

Esther sits slumped over, watching the hot coals slowly fade. A man goes out every twenty minutes to bring in more hot coals from the main fire, and the heat rises again. He is the sweat master, whose job it is to make sure the fire stays hot. He splashes a sweet-smelling herb water on the coals every now and again and the room fills with a fragrant steam. Esther watches the steam rise and feels the heat rush up her sensitive nose.

Soon, her body is relaxed and supple and she remembers her conversation with Numei. She is supposed to find her center. She begins adjusting her body, trying to find the correct position. She tries every single position she can think of. And then she lifts her head up high and shifts her spine in the correct way.

Suddenly she feels a tremendous rush of energy shoot through her body. Sweat begins to drip down her forehead and splashes onto her lap and the heat seems to deepen in the little hut. She breathes heavily and is surprised to find that she is taking deeper breaths than ever before. More satisfying breaths, like she is eating the air. The pains in her back and neck that she got from digging the hole today magically disappear.

A satisfied moan escapes her lips. She is sitting comfortably and breathing regularly. She has found the magical balance! She feels an ecstatic rush. Never again will she suffer from aches and pains. She is going to be relaxed and happy for the rest of her life!

Soon she is overheated and she has to go outside. She feels her new body instantly tighten up, struggling to return to the old one, but she fights it and manages to hold onto her new position. She goes to the washing tub, which is a wooden tub of river water that is meant for bathing after the sauna is done. Esther jumps into the water and washes herself clean. The cold barely touches her and she feels powerful and ready for anything.

By the time she has gotten to Merlu's house for dinner, she has lost her new body. She searches for it, but she cannot retrieve that magical position of comfort and balance. She gets angry with herself, for both her pride and her foolishness in thinking it would be that easy. And then she realizes that she is indeed returning to the old Esther, who has those feelings of anger. Now she becomes depressed again. It is even worse returning to her old body and feelings, having experienced a new one.

Raven 15'

**Raven moon*

During the dark moon, which falls right before the new moon, Merlu and Esther stand under a roof, watching the rain fall in rivulets. It is the sort of night when all creatures walking the land curse the winter and dream of summer. Two lone candle sentries burn morosely, threatening to go out at any moment. Esther is tired of waiting for this man to appear. She wonders if she is crazy to be out here and how long she will keep this up before she gives up on Merlu. Only the fact that she finds him so interesting, mysterious and attractive, keeps her out here on this miserable night. She stands up to keep warm and eats a couple of corn cakes that she brought with her. Merlu is wrapped inside a black bear fur, sitting quietly, staring intently out into the night. She marvels at his ability to focus on one thing for hours at a time, even if it is just staring out into nothing.

She would never suspect that Merlu's thoughts are so similar to her own. He is thinking about how he could be at home, in front of the fire with a book and a hot cup of tea, searching for answers to mysteries from the comfort of home. It sounds perfect right now. But it is not enough any more to get his information from books. He has done that for a long time. Now he must go out into the world for his answers. And it begins here, squatting under a trader's hut with a broken door, waiting for some mysterious old man in the freezing dark of winter.

Late in the night, he wakes with a start. He was dozing, until the sound of a pot crashing to the ground in the main kitchen woke him. He quickly peers out into the stormy night, looking to see who it is. Probably some young man looking for food, but you never know until you see. And he cannot see anything from here.

"Esther?" he whispers. "Wake up."

"What?" she murmurs sleepily. "Is it time to go home?"

"No," he whispers. "There's somebody in the kitchen. I'm going to see who it is."

"Do you want me to come?" she murmurs sleepily.

"No, you stay here. Just look sharp."

"I will," she says, closing her eyes peacefully.

He grabs his rifle before going toward the kitchen. Although a Ruok does not use such weapons, Merlu is also his father's son. Creeping out into the night, he steps carefully to avoid cracking twigs. The rain has let up, but the wind blows heavy and strong. He creeps into the kitchen, past the oven made from stones. Near the shed filled with grains and cooking tools, he sees the old man that Esther described. Smeared with ash, covered in talismans and looking every inch the frightening creature that she claimed. He rummages through the shed and loads steel knives and other utensils into a large sack. Merlu kicks himself for dozing. He slept through most of the man's handiwork. He has no idea what the man did before he got here. He might very well have poisoned the food again. More food is going to have to be thrown out, which is a very expensive and dear loss in the middle of winter.

Filled with righteous wrath at this act of destruction, Merlu decides that he is going to find out who is responsible for this and why. He wonders what is the best way to find out. He could silently follow the old man back from where he came and find out what tribe he works for. He could pry the information out of him right now. Or he can just capture him and let the tribe deal with him.

Thinking it unlikely that he might be able to follow the man through a thick redwood grove without detection, he decides to take the man now. At least he can prove to the village that he isn't lying. Merlu checks to see that the gun is loaded and then he creeps closer, like a cat, trying to get himself ready for an attack.

As he creeps closer and closer, he steps directly on a sharp rock that digs into his old moccasins. A small cry escapes his lips. He grits his teeth and forces himself to be silent, but the damage is done. The man has sharp senses and he turns around.

The man hisses as he sees Merlu and looks around wildly for a weapon. In a panic, Merlu holds up his gun and makes an immediate challenge.

"Stop what you're doing!" he shouts, knowing the man won't understand him.

Moving with a speed and agility that seems impossible for someone so old, the man leaps over the shed like a cougar and lands on all fours. Then he quickly makes his way across the commons. Merlu gives chase and shouts out for Esther to get help. He races after the man, determined to catch him before he enters the forest. The old man is fast, but Merlu is much younger and faster. He quickly gains on him, and just as they reach the edge of the thick woods, he is upon the old man. Suddenly, the old man turns around and faces him. Merlu stops and points the gun.

The man starts speaking in a strange language that Merlu has never heard before and waves his arms like a madman. He chants in a monotonous tone and then does a strange dance. Merlu stares at him, flabbergasted. He cannot make head or tails of this strange behavior. Then Merlu realizes that the man is trying to put a spell on him and he breaks into a wide smile. The man wiggles his fingers at him and shouts strange words. He does a shuffling dance and spins around in a circle. Merlu laughs, thinking that the man is quite harmless after all. He laughs so hard, that he relaxes his hold on his gun. He is still laughing as the old man suddenly pounces with astonishing speed, shrieks with rage and clubs him in the head with a large rock.

Merlu drops to the ground heavily. A wave of nausea passes over him, making him gag and want to vomit. He cannot rise again, although he struggles desperately to move. His eyes stare sightlessly into the pitch black night, that is now awash in millions of stars that obscure his vision. Just before he passes out completely, he hears soft breathing over him. He feels a hand touching his head, tugging at his hair. He has a horrible notion that he is going to be scalped and then darkness washes over him like a blanket that protects him from this horrible and humiliating end.

Meanwhile, Esther is wide awake and trying to figure out what to do. She heard Merlu yelling something and saw him faintly running across the main circle. He was yelling something about wanting help. The old man must be here. She runs out into the night and shouts for help at the top of her voice. On the way, she grabs a candle to light her way.

She runs to the edge of the woods, following his shouts, and then she slows her pace and looks around wildly. The wind roars through the trees overhead and sprays her face with water. She cannot hear a thing but the roaring overhead. She looks around desperately, wondering where to go, until she hears an inhuman wail coming from her left. It is followed by a faint cry. Whatever just happened, it sounds as if it came from within the woods.

She steps gingerly into the thick woods and begins to move slowly through them. Water drips onto her head. The light from the candle is poor and the wooden candle holder, which is designed to keep out the rain, splits the light into useless streams. The very thin, flickering light that is left is barely enough to see by. It shines off the trees, but she cannot see the ground at all. Then she realizes that the candle in her hand could blow out at any moment, and she'll be stuck in the woods in the pitch black with no way to find Merlu and no way to see the monster she is chasing.

She bumps painfully into a low branch that pokes into her thigh and stops to get her bearings. She really has no idea where Merlu or the beast-man are, and she doesn't know what she could do to help him if she did. She is merely wandering uselessly in a mysterious world of faintly flickering trees, dripping water, fog and screaming wind. Strangely, she doesn't feel panicked about all of this, just confused.

She tries to fix the candle holder to get more light, but as soon as she attempts to move the candle, it goes out. She sighs and feels failure creep over her. Her search is done. She will be no help. Merlu is on his own.

She manages to find her way back to the open commons with a little difficulty and she sighs with relief. She will have to go find Numei and Squirrel, who are probably still sleeping, and they can help her find Merlu. On the way back, she suddenly sees the outline of a figure creeping slowly on the ground. She recognizes the way it moves instantly. After all that searching in the woods, she stumbled blindly onto the creature right in the commons. It seems to be crouched over another dark figure that lies slumped on the ground. She has a sinking feeling that it is Merlu that the creature stands over, and she moves closer to see for sure. As she walks, she is struck by the absurdity of her whole plan. She has absolutely no protection against this beast and no way to protect Merlu against him either. But she knows that Merlu needs help and she is supposed to be watching his back. So she keeps walking closer, her heart hammering in her chest.

The creature from the woods suddenly looks up, hearing her footsteps come toward him. He slowly rises to his feet and hisses at her. She drops the candle in her hand and just stands there empty-handed. She feels strangely detached from the danger she is in, now that she faces him. She is more curious than afraid. The hunched figure moves closer to her and hisses something softly. She sees a bone knife, gripped in a white-knuckled hand. She goes over all of her options quickly. Scream at the top of her lungs. Run away. Curse at him bravely, until he attacks her. She tries to think of any talents she has and she can only think of one. She is good at charming men.

She makes her decision quickly. She walks up to the old man and touches him gently. He tenses up, but does not strike her. She teases his hair and runs her fingers slowly up and down his body. She whispers in his ear that it is all right and she is not afraid of him. He sniffs her, and then leans over and strokes her softly. She feels strange sensations go up and down her body as he touches her. Her lower back tickles as if an insect is tickling it, although when she reaches back there she finds nothing.

It moves in circles around her, feeling all over her body. It strokes rough fingers across her face. And then, she has a strange thought that it is only a little boy that stands before her, wanting to play with her. She laughs with relief and embraces him. He embraces her back. And then she knows that this man did not poison their food. It is only an innocent hermit of the woods, who came to explore their village and scavange what he needs.

She continues to play with the hermit. He tries to kiss her, but she refuses with a gentle hand, just as she used to do at the Lily Pad. The hermit obeys her wishes. She has tamed him. Just then, she sees a flickering light appear from the hut where she and Merlu were waiting. She hears Numei's voice calling her name.

"Esther! Merlu!"

"Get out of here," she whispers.

She points to the woods and points to the light. The creature seems to understand. It grunts one time in farewell, grabs its bone knife, and then runs off into the woods. She watches him go, until he has disappeared completely into the darkness.

"Numei!" she shouts. "Over here!"

Numei and Squirrel run over and the whole scene becomes illuminated in torchlight. They quickly examine Merlu. His head is wet with blood, but he is alive. Numei examines his wound more closely and finds that it is a shallow wound.

"He's lucky he's so hardheaded," says Numei, staring at the rock near his head, stained with his blood.

"Do you think the old man was sent by the Mattoal?" asks Squirrel, anxiously examining Esther for any sign of injury. "Did you see tattoos on its face or special talismans?"

"No, it was just a little boy," she says with a smile.

They both stare at her strangely, but she doesn't explain her cryptic remark. Shrugging, Squirrel indicates that they should move Merlu to a better place. They all lift him carefully and carry him to one of the healer's tents.

Raven 16'

Esther wakes up to the sound of Squirrel banging pots and making tea. She savors the soft light of the morning from deep within her blankets, ignoring the pressure in her abdomen. When she rises reluctantly to squat in the bushes, she gets some water from the water barrel. It is brackish and tastes like someone has been washing their feet in it, so she stumbles down to the stream for some fresh water. The ground is ice cold, her feet numb quickly and she wishes she had put on her moccasins before braving the morning. The ground is wet and her feet splash in puddles and little rivulets as she walks.

The clouds have finally broken and blue sky begins to show after many days of grey. The clear weather has apparently inspired hundreds of ravens to come out from hiding. They are perched everywhere, as if guarding the tribe of their namesake. Their loud screams and croaks fill the air. The birds fly back and forth, involved in strange doings that don't make sense. She watches them awhile, thinking that the huge black birds are hard to ignore. There is something magnetic about them. More than any other bird, even the attention loving swan, the raven has star power. Esther remembers that the new moon is here and she wonders if somehow the birds know that. They begin to screech in a mad symphony of noise that puts a spell on her and renders her forgetful of the terror and strangeness of last night. She suddenly wants to run and play and forget all about it. She runs to greet the ravens and thank them for the song. They fly off as she approaches, their mission completed, and she chases them into the forest.

"There are a hundred ravens out there," she tells Merlu upon returning to the hut.

Merlu lies near the fire, recovering from his injury. He is pale and tired, but he seems like he is going to be all right.

"I wonder what they want now," he mumbles. "Another warning? They tried to warn me last night. But I didn't listen."

"How did they warn you?"

"Three ravens lit upon my house and started making a racket. They never do that."

"What do you think it meant?" asks Squirrel, pulling a pot of tea off the fire.

"You know how my father is," sighs Merlu with a shrug. "He refused to feed my afterbirth to the ravens, calling it superstitious nonsense. And now I can't understand them like I should."

Esther laughs, thinking that he is kidding, but then she wonders. She never knows for sure with him.

"The Raven is a trickster," adds Squirrel. "It's hard to know what they're up to."

"They are that," agrees Merlu. "The smartest of all birds."

"Why?" asks Esther.

"They can remember where they store all their stashes of seeds, even when the stash is buried in the snow. They can even remember where they saw other ravens store their stashes and then steal them. Memory like that is rare in bird brains."

"Intelligent, but not always honest," adds Squirrel.

"Those qualities don't always go together," counters Merlu.

"What else do they do?" asks Esther.

"Once a raven led me to a wounded elk," Merlu continues. "It wanted me to kill it so it could share the meat with me. That's the sort of thing ravens do."

"I hope you shared," Squirrel says sternly.

"Of course I did," says Merlu, with a fake expression of shock, as if he is insulted.

"But how would they know that something was going to happen to you last night?" asks Esther.

Merlu shrugs and accepts a bowl of bay nut tea. He sips the bowl and sighs contentedly. Esther takes a bowl for herself also and takes a deep drink.

"They're thought to have prophetic powers," explains Squirrel.

"Do they?"

Squirrel shrugs also and smiles slightly.

"You never know with ravens."

Although today is the start of the new moon, there is little rejoicing in Raven village. There are no feasts being prepared. No dances or singing. Only the groans of sick ones, suffering with aching bellies. The only joy to be had is absence of pain, that brief moment right after you have gone to the bathroom and your system is clear.

With four planets in the Raven constellation today and tomorrow, there are six very pregnant mothers. Two give birth on the new moon and they struggle to focus on the more important pain in their womb and ignore the pains of their stomach. Both are successful, although it is a very messy business.

The story of Merlu and the old man circulates throughout the village. All the food in the kitchen is examined, but no sign of sabotage can be found. After a long search, it is discovered that the food itself is not the problem. A decaying deer is found at the bottom of a deep pool right next to the kitchen's main water supply. It was the water that was contaminated and not the food. The deer is fished out and burned. The speed and ferocity of the stream after the rain quickly makes the water fresh and new. Just in case, the cooks decide to get their water directly from the little fall before the pool and not the pool itself. It is decided that this will be standard policy from now on, to avoid this problem in the future.

Todi calls for a meeting late this morning and most of the village attends. He is very angry at the injuries to his son and he speaks harsh words against the Mattoal, whom he believes hired this man to put the dead deer in the water. He points out that rocks were piled on top of the deer, so it would not float to the surface and be detected. Everyone believes him and calls for Todi to carry out his plan against them. The details of Todi's plan are worked out and it is decided that the deed will be done tomorrow, which is the actual new moon and a time of great power for the Raven tribe. Then the meeting is disbanded and everyone returns to rest up and recuperate.

Raven 17'

Late in the afternoon, Yut arrives at the boundaries of the Mattoal territory. He is understandably nervous to return to the place where he watched the Light Bearers receive such poor treatment. However, he knows that he is really not in any danger. He is a 'herald', a bearer of news. He is protected by ancient customs from harm. He alone was not beaten by the Mattoal on that fateful day. They pushed him aside and out of danger purposely, out of respect for his skills in translation and his function as messenger.

He is soon spotted by a tall, dangerous looking man, who does not seem to recognize him. The man picks up a large stone and walks toward him menacingly. Yut speaks the Mattoal word for 'messenger' as the man draws near, and the man stops his advance uncertainly. Yut shows him that he is unarmed and finally the man indicates that he is to walk with him to the main village.

They come to a large Zesti village, typical of the villages of this area. Their houses are conical wigwams, crudely built from bone tools, but strong and snug against the rain. Because of the nice weather today, most in the village are outdoors. Yut walks through the village, knowing how strange he must look to them by their stares. He wears a cloak of rabbit fur lined with raven feathers, which is what he always wears when he acts as messenger. It makes him look more Zesti than the unique clothing of the Twelve Tribes does. The Mattoal are generally naked on this warm day. They are a tall, muscular people, well fed and vigorous. The men all wear a blue dot on their forehead and the women are tattooed all over their faces.

Yut is led to the home of the chief and an interpreter is summoned. The two interpreters will speak to each other in the Hupa language, which is used as a trade language in the north, where the Hupa are dominant. Yut whispers the secret words that signal that he is an official messenger, and the interpreter nods and indicates to the chief that he may speak. Yut examines the chief briefly before speaking further. He is a magnetic character, grim in countenance, yet proud and bearing himself regally. He wears much ornamentation to show his preferred status - bracelets, necklaces and jewelry of great significance. Yut quickly gives his prepared speech, wanting to get it over with quickly.

"The Raven tribe are upset at the poor treatment of their people by the Mattoal. Our small group of diplomats were not sent by the chief of the Raven tribe, but went on their own accord. This was a mistake and they were punished for it by the spirits and by the Mattoal. This was just. However, the Mattoal have sent an enemy against us, which is an act of war. And they have demanded a price against further aggression. This does not please our chief. He is a great magician. The Raven is our protector and has taught our chief much magic. Our chief is angry. The Raven spirit is angry. We are the Raven tribe. We demand that the aggression against our tribe stop and recompense be made, or our chief will perform strong magic against your people. The earth will shake with the power of the Raven chief on this day if you do not seek to make peace."

The chief squeezes his lips into a tight line and stares at Yut for a long time. His eyes are angry. Finally he speaks and his words are translated by his messenger.

"You come to us with a message of war. You do not send us tribute. We declare that there is now war between our people. Until you give us our tribute, there will be war."

Yut looks around at all the well muscled warriors and he fears for the safety of his tribe. He hopes that Todi knows what he is doing!

"Our chief will bring down great magic upon your people, until you come to us with a message of peace," he says, mustering up all his courage so he will sound fierce and confident. "Beware the wrath of the Raven chief, who is guided by the Raven spirit."

There is nothing more to say. Yut bids farewell to the chief of the Mattoal and walks quickly away. He hurries out of the bounds of the village and doesn't breathe comfortably until he is in neutral territory. Then he sits down to soothe his frazzled nerves and smokes a pipe with trembling fingers.

Meanwhile, Merlu prepares for tonight's raid. He has volunteered to do the bidding of his father, due to his skills in moving at night. Plus, he now has a score to settle with these men. With him will go one other man, a great hunter and tracker named Tuli. Both are well armed with guns and swords. They paint their faces with ash and prepare themselves mentally. This will be a very dangerous mission.

Todi seems confident that his plan will succeed. He is especially delighted that Merlu has agreed to take part in this. If they are successful, not only will Todi be glorified among his tribe, but so will his son. This is a great day for his family. Although Merlu and Tuli are in a hurry to leave, Todi first has to make a fitting speech in front of everybody that this will be a great day for the Raven tribe and he speaks of the bravery of Merlu and Tuli at great length. Finally, they are released and they load the heavy sacks on their backs, bid farewell to their people and walk down the path that will take them to their meeting with Yut. Everyone cheers as they begin the long walk to the Mattoal village.

Merlu and Tuli meet Yut on the path and he quickly fills them in. Just as expected, the Mattoal have declared war among their tribes. Everything is going according to plan. He quickly describes how to get to the main village from the path. He tells them to be careful and warns them that the Mattoal warriors are fierce and brave. He wishes them good luck.

"We need your help, Yut," says a thoughtful Merlu. "We will barely have enough time to make it to their territory before dark. We must have a guide."

"I cannot," he complains. "I am the messenger. It is a sacred function. If I am caught leading a raid, then our messengers will no longer be welcome anywhere and our whole tribe will suffer a great loss of honor."

"We will suffer a whole lot more than that if this plan fails," insists Merlu.

"I cannot," he says stiffly. "There is a standard of behavior to uphold. Aram would understand that, Merlu, even if Todi does not."

Merlu nods, understanding what he is really saying. He waves the whole thing away and shoulders his pack again.

"Good luck, men," Yut says stiffly, and begins to walk back to the Raven village.

They reach the borders of Mattoal territory just as dusk begins. They stop to rest briefly, but time is growing short, so they carefully begin their descent down the steep hill into the valley. Creeping silently and slowly, they make their way through the trees. There are few people about this time of the day, and they move quickly down the hill toward the valley basin, where the river lies. Just as the night turns inky black, they see fires burning brightly by the river. They have reached the village.

They move very slowly and gingerly from now on. Right to the edge of the village they go and they set up behind a tree near the river.

"There is nobody about," says Tuli.

"There will be," says Merlu with a smile.

Tuli quickly gets a tiny fire going, while Merlu pulls out the firemakers. He grins at Tuli and then he lights the first one. He holds it for just a moment and then throws it out over the river. It explodes directly over the water with a loud boom. Figures come pouring out of the houses. They come out of the assembly hall like rats escaping a sinking ship. They can hear screams and shouts of frightened folk. Merlu immediately lights a colored one and throws it directly over the village. It explodes with a flash of yellow that lights up the sky. It is so bright, that for just a second they can see the terrified faces of the villagers as they cower in fear. He lights another one that shoots over their heads, making a bright, white trail. Everyone cowers to the ground. They see a woman illuminated by the brief flash, screaming in fear. She falls to her knees and begs the spirits for mercy.

Merlu laughs like a little boy. He looks over at Tuli, who is grinning and shaking his head.

"They must think the spirits are dreadfully angry," Tuli says, slapping his leg. "Look at them pray to the gods! They really are superstitious, aren't they?"

"Few of these Zesti have seen a rifle before, much less a firemaker."

Merlu lights a whole bunch and he and Tuli launch them all over the place. Terrified Mattoal scatter for their homes. They are sure that the end of the world is upon them. Soon the village is deserted.

"Put that out and let's get out of here," Merlu finally says. "We're out of firemakers."

"Let me light a torch first," says Tuli, pulling one out of the sack.

"No," says Merlu, packing up the carrying sack quickly. "We can't do that, Tuli."

"I'll bet none of them will show their faces for the rest of the night."

"Because they think that this is magic. If they see the torch, they'll know there were people here. It will destroy the illusion."

"They'll assume the magician chief of the Raven tribe was here. They'll still be terrified."

"Not as terrified as they will be if they think he can perform this kind of magic from his home," says Merlu, kicking out the fire.

Tuli shrugs and throws dirt onto the fire until it is out completely. They take a moment for their eyes to adjust to the darkness, and then begin to move back the way they came.

At first, it is extremely hard to travel through the thick woods in the dark. The stars give off enough light to see the outlines of trees, but not much else. They crawl on their hands and knees, keeping their heads down to avoid poking their eyes out on branches. At times, the hill is very steep and slippery, and they slide down a few feet. But they dig their toes deeper into the overgrowth of fallen leaves and twigs and keep on pushing. Soon it begins to get easier. They get a rhythm going. If you run into a thick growth that you cannot pass, you just move around it and keep pushing your way uphill. Slide your hands along the tree branch until it stops. The key is to keep moving, no matter what you get stuck in. Merlu thinks of the 'flow' that Ruoks always speak of, and he suddenly understands.

Finally, they reach the top of the hill. They are exhausted, but exhilarated. Safely out of Mattoal territory now, they stop for the night. They pull out their blankets and curl up in a comfortable depression to wait until morning.

Raven 19'

Cougar moon

They are visited by a messenger from the Mattoal tribe in the afternoon. He walks up to the main circle, clothed in a cloak of elk skin and holding a raven feather in his hand. He speaks the secret words to Yut and then asks to speak to the chief. There is an uncomfortable silence as everyone looks at each other, wondering which 'chief' they should bring him to. Finally, someone shouts for him to be brought before Todi, and there is general agreement from most. Yut does not seem happy about this, but he does as the majority wishes.

Todi accepts him graciously and meets the man in the commons. Aram would have brought him into his own house, but Todi doesn't want the man to see inside his house, which has firemakers in it. The messenger looks around the commons nervously, before making his prepared speech to the Raven chief. He declares that his tribe wants peace between the two peoples and as a peace offering he gives two thick rabbit skin blankets to Todi. Todi thanks him graciously and offers the man some food. Then he sits with him and asks many questions about his tribe. The man seems extremely afraid of Todi, whom he considers a powerful magician, and he answers Todi's questions as a child might answer a teacher who is hovering over him with a whipping stick in his hand. He keeps stammering and stuttering and repeating himself, and Yut has trouble translating his words.

Later, Aram calls for another meeting. He officially announces his retirement as chief and suggests that the people might prefer Todi as chief. There are some smirks at this suggestion, because it is already a fact, but everyone tries to hide it. They all thank Aram for his service over the years and promise to consult with him as a 'wise man' in the future. Todi accepts the sacred headdress of raven feathers, although he looks on it as a curiosity and not a sacred thing and puts it aside as if it is no matter. Then he makes a speech about his hopes for the tribe in the coming year. He thanks Aram for all his hard work and dedication and promises a feast to celebrate the change in leadership. And the meeting is disbanded.

Aram returns home and finds Reepa there, waiting for him. Her expression is very serious and he suddenly feels very vulnerable. She will no longer talk to him as the wife of a chief talks to her husband. She will speak to him as a wife talks to her old, used up husband, with whom she is fed up.

"We have to talk."

"About what?" he asks reluctantly.

"About our marriage," she says coldly.

"That didn't take long," he says humorously. "I've just resigned as chief a few moments ago and you've already got plans to drop me and marry Todi."

"How did you know?" she asks, her mouth making a perfect 'O'.

"I didn't," he says, stunned. "It was just a joke! You want to marry Todi?"

"He asked me to marry him."

He stares at her, speechless, for a long time. He opens and closes his mouth, unable to find the right words to express his outrage. Finally, he shakes his head and laughs humorlessly.

"Well, it makes sense. I've always known that power is what you desire most."

"You'll be all right," she says quietly. "You have Ita now and I know you prefer her to me. All you have left to do now is to grow old. You don't need two wives anymore."

"That's true," he says.

She stares at him for a moment and then she suddenly walks out of the house without another word. She seems hurt, although she is the one leaving him. He sighs and sits down on his bed. He is getting too old for the headache of two wives anyways. At his age, one woman is enough.

Raven 27'

Jay moon

Today is the day of Todi's party to celebrate his appointment as chief. It is also a 'make up' for the new moon celebration, which was cancelled due to illness. Everything that was postponed on the new moon will be done today. There will be one wedding. Reepa and Todi will be joined as husband and wife. Reepa wanted to wait until next year's new moon, but Todi wanted something special to do for his party, and she reluctantly agreed.

Merlu has been waiting for this day to come and go, because his father expects him to attend. His heart, however, is elsewhere. He plans to go with Esther, Numei, and Squirrel to the Cougar tribe, to attend the gathering of Ruoks. The three of them have graciously agreed to wait until today, when he will be free to leave his tribe and wander off wherever he will.

He told his father yesterday of his intention to go to the Ruok council and his father made the usual complaints and tried to get him to stay. Merlu merely ignored him and let him ramble on. Reepa was in the room, although she didn't say anything. Merlu is grateful that she did not try to act as his mother and give him advice. She would have paid dearly if she had tried.

The party goes until late in the night and it is nothing special. It is rather dull actually. Reepa did her best, but she has to admit that Aram was easier to work with, as far as throwing parties is concerned. He has more of an instinct for it. Todi kept calling all of her ideas ' Grinner nonsense' and 'too traditional' and insisted on running the parties on purely Uranian lines. After awhile, she just threw up her hands and decided to concentrate on getting married. She'll work on his party skills later.

As usual, Numei is the life of the party and wants to stay up all night dancing and singing. She'll deal with the consequences in the morning, when she has trouble getting up. Squirrel is already home sleeping. Esther eventually grows tired and she finally leaves the assembly hall and goes out into the light drizzle. Merlu joins her outside a few moments later. She stares at him with wide eyes, wondering if he'll try to kiss her. She looks up at him, wishing he would. But he merely stands there smiling at her.

As they walk home through the commons, she thinks about the mysterious man that she met here on that dark night. Everyone still thinks that he poisoned the tribe and she hasn't tried to say different. But it bothers her tonight and she wants to hear Merlu's opinion, so she asks him what he thinks.

"You don't think he did it?"

"No."

"He hit me with a rock."

"You pointed a gun at him."

"Then he tried to scalp me. Many Zesti chiefs are known to pay a string of dentalium shells for their enemies' scalps."

"I didn't see him try to scalp you. He was just searching you."

"Then why was he here? Just to raid our kitchen?"

"Maybe he just wanted company and he was too shy to ask."

Merlu laughs. Then he suddenly looks at her in the light of a candle. He has never looked at her like this before and she likes it very much.

"You saved my life," he says, with a gleam in his eye. "I never thanked you for that."

"It was nothing," she says, smiling back at him.

They keep walking. Esther walks beside him, a little disappointed that he had nothing more to say to her. But Merlu is different from most of the men she knows. He doesn't seem to be interested in sleeping with her. Even the creature was more amorous than Merlu. She thinks of the creature again and she feels a surge of pride for the way she handled him.

Then she thinks about Him, whom she hasn't seen in awhile, and thinks that she is finally ready for Him, if he dares show his face again. Esther is not the same girl she was when they first met. She can take care of herself now. He can go pick on some other girl from now on.

Cougar Tribe

Cougar 0'

Bear moon

Esther imagines herself as a pollinating flower, attracting hungry bees as she goes. Now she has a whole group of fellow insects to keep her company on her strange adventure. Endlessly north she buzzes, until she reaches the end of the world. Following some mysterious urge like the one that makes the tiny butterfly travel hundreds of miles south to warmer lands when the winter comes. Except Esther is going north this winter, like a butterfly with her antenna all screwed up. Maybe she is going north to breed, like a salmon traveling upriver to lay its eggs in the sand.

The miles pass under her feet, and the endless banter of Merlu, Squirrel and Numei entertains her and keeps her moving. It is cold and drizzly, but there is no rest for the cold and weary. Numei promises that it will not get any nicer any time soon, so they might as well just push through it. Esther begins to wonder if this endless wandering is some sort of punishment for her entire life of staying in one place. Showing her that the world is huge and she is just one small woman dwarfed by a billion giant trees. She is on her way to see the last tribe now. She cannot go any further, unless she wants to become a Zesti. What will happen now she doesn't know.

The path is washed out and poorly kept, and they are forced to splash through muddy puddles and climb over fallen logs. They carry their own gear now, because Squirrel insisted that Timid stay in Raven village. They are taking a short cut that is little more than a ribbon of path winding through thick forest. Squirrel claims that this road is less dangerous than the main path, although he doesn't say why.

They stop for lunch and nibble on dried salmon and seaweed. Their food supply is meager for four people and they are forced to strictly ration everything. Merlu was supposed to get enough food for the journey from his father's food stores, but he wasn't paying attention to how much food was in each leaf wrapper. Squirrel is the least happy about it. He is thin and needs to eat a lot.

"I'm going to take a little walk into the woods," Squirrel says, laying his pack down. "I might catch some dinner."

"Have some seaweed," offers Numei, handing him a thick, knotted piece of dried black seaweed.

"Thank you," Squirrel says, taking the offering and nibbling on it. "But I want something more substantial."

"Well, don't go too far," says Numei. "We need to get moving pretty soon if we want this to be a three day journey."

"I won't. If I don't catch anything soon, I'll come back."

Squirrel checks his quiver and finds it lacking. He's only got four arrows left and two of them are in poor shape, the feathers bent and frayed and the points chipped and dull. He checks with Merlu, but Merlu has brought one of his father's guns instead. Squirrel does not believe in guns, so he settles for his knife and some rope and bait to make a trap.

He is gone a long time and the three of them begin to get more and more impatient. They are wasting precious daylight waiting for him. It is pouring now and they huddle underneath a tarp and watch the rain get steadily worse. They are wet and stiff and their shoes are soaked, with no fire to dry them out. They call his name a few times, but he doesn't respond. Numei begins to curse him, and she gets angrier and angrier as the sun starts to drop in the sky. Merlu is impatient too, and he keeps getting up and going out in the rain for no good reason at all.

To distract herself, Esther nibbles on a piece of hard seaweed, which has the consistency of gnarled bark. It is a funny thing about seaweed. It always seems so light and insubstantial, but when you have to rely on it alone to fill your belly, you see that it is subtly energizing. She played with it a lot when she was a child, but never once thought to eat it. Which is too bad, because she spent a lot of time hiding from priests on the beach, most of that time she was hungry, and there was all that food in front of her the whole time!

She has a brief flash of herself as a child, huddled out of the wind in a little shelter that she made from driftwood. Sitting in a heap on the ground, playing with seaweed in a half-hearted way and smashing little air-filled bulbs in a pile of smelly kelp for no good reason. She was good at sitting still for hours, floating like a boat adrift and not really inhabiting her body. She would spend hours dreaming about imaginary friends and telling herself stories. She doesn't know how many hours she spent listening to Nani and his endless hilarious tales. Looking back, there is something disturbing in that memory. She can't put her finger on just what it is that bothers her, but it haunts her for the rest of the day.

Finally Squirrel returns, carrying a rabbit and a squirrel tied together by a rope. He gets a dose of pent up anger from everybody. He tries to appease them with his food, but it doesn't work. Numei gives it a quick glance, shakes her head in an exasperated way and then quickly packs her stuff together. Merlu ignores it utterly and begins to walk down the trail.

"I expected a little gratitude at least," Squirrel mumbles. "For bringing dinner."

Numei glares at him a moment, before shouldering her pack and starting to walk again.

"So what if we lost a few hours. What is the hurry? The council meeting is not for many days. I'd rather have a decent dinner."

"It will make a good dinner," Esther says helpfully, feeling sorry for him, although she is also angry.

"I say that it will be dinner for two. Those two do not deserve any of it."

Esther shrugs, shoulders her own burden basket and starts after Numei.

"We better go or we will lose them," she adds apologetically

Cursing to himself with displeasure, Squirrel ties the rabbit and squirrel carcasses to his basket. Wiping rabbit blood from his hands on some thick grass, he shoulders his burden basket and begins to trail after the two girls. He makes a point of moving quickly, passing them up and leaving them far behind in his wake. He mumbles something about having to wait for them all the time and then disappears around a bend in the path.

The rain lets up just as it gets dark and they start to gather what wood they can that isn't too wet. Squirrel carries a large amount of dry kindling wrapped carefully in his burden basket and he puts it together quickly. Merlu gets out a box of flint and tinder that he stole from his father and the men set about making a fire, while Numei dresses the rabbit and the squirrel. She spears both on sticks and places them over the fire. Soon they begin to sizzle and bubble and the juices drip into the fire. Esther cannot stop staring at it.

It begins to drizzle again, and quickly turns into a downpour. Squirrel races to set up his tarp, while Esther stands with her body over the small fire so it won't go out. Their precious blaze struggles to maintain itself in the rain and they just barely manage to rescue it from extinction. Luckily, they are successful, and soon it is stronger than ever. With great relief, they relax contentedly under the tarp and watch the rain pour in rivulets onto the ground at their feet.

The meat continues to roast after it's brief respite, and Merlu rubs salt all over the carcass and shouts at it to cook faster so he can eat. Finally, the meat is cooked and they eat it down to the bones. Squirrel settles to gnawing on the bones like a dog, which he claims is a product of his Wolf moon.

"What is your tribe sign?" asks Merlu, watching Squirrel scrape tendon off a bone with his teeth.

"I am a hawk through and through," Squirrel replies. "Sun and Jupiter in the sign of the Hawk. I was raised in the Hawk tribe. But I was born under a Wolf moon."

"Inconjunct," muses Merlu, more to himself than to anyone else. "I've noticed that many Ruoks are inconjunct."

"Ruoks are not bound to one single tribe sign."

"I knew there was wolf in you!" exclaims Numei. "That's why you're so stubborn."

"I don't think I'm that stubborn," Squirrel insists.

"You insisted on hunting all afternoon, knowing that we all were waiting."

"You still have not mentioned why you are in such a hurry."

"We waited many hours for you."

"And you got dinner in exchange."

"Barely enough for four people. Next time Merlu can just go and shoot something. It will take a lot less time."

They fall into an uneasy and glaring silence. The tension is thick in camp, especially between Numei and Squirrel. Merlu lies down and closes his eyes, ignoring everybody. Esther stares morosely at the fire, in a bad mood for no good reason. Her mind drifts back to the scene of her on the beach, dreaming of imaginary friends. Somehow, the imaginary friends of her dreams were always supportive and friendly. She did not have a single argument with Nani in the many years of their pretend friendship. Now that she has real friends, she is a little disappointed. Real friends are a lot more troublesome than the imaginary kind. Real friends fight with each other and annoy each other. She needs to escape from real friends to get some peace and quiet sometimes.

Soon exhaustion gets the better of them, and they all squeeze their bedrolls and blankets together under the small tarp. The rain keeps them from getting any elbow room or the space they crave. Soon the patter of rain soothes their frazzled nerves into a peaceful slumber.

Late in the night, Esther awakes with a start. There is an unearthly glow under the tree directly in front of her. She sits up with a start, her heart hammering in her chest. She stares directly at the light, unable to believe her eyes. It looks as if a creature were drawn out of lines of bright light underneath the tree. The being is seven feet tall and it seems to have wings. She cannot make out any face, but its shape is humanoid. As the creature comes into focus and gets brighter, her fear intensifies. She is so terrified that she cannot look at it anymore. She closes her eyes and tries to breathe and calm her racing heart.

A moment later, she opens her eyes again. The light is gone. She sighs and stares into the black night, trying to see any sign of it, but there is nothing there. She lies back down and rolls up into a ball. She has no idea what just happened. There is only one thing that she knows. Whatever that thing was, it was real. It was too frightening to be a figment of her imagination.

Cougar 1'

Eagle moon

They wake up early and get their things together in the dawn light. Everyone is in a good mood again, joking and laughing as they prepare for another day of walking. Esther does not share in the humor, as she is still disturbed by her vision last night. What was that thing? An angel? A spirit of the forest? And why did nobody else wake up but her? Did it seek her out? She doesn't mention it to anybody else, knowing they will not have an answer.

Driven by the desire to find a warm house and a roaring fire, they push on at a rapid pace. Esther practices walking in rhythm, tuning out everything else but putting one foot in front of the other. Soon she begins to breath slowly and evenly, time gets lost and the miles pass underneath her feet in a trance of motion.

The road is winding, narrow and often difficult to follow. It is a carefully hidden road, designed more for stealth than convenience. Up here, the Twelve Tribes do not have the respect that they do in the south. They have entered lands that are controlled by the Hupa. The Hupa are the most powerful tribe in the area and they hold many smaller tribes in tribute to themselves. The main road of the Twelve Tribes is well known to the Hupa as a major supply route of valuable items, and traveling upon it these days comes with the constant danger of being kidnapped and ransomed, or at least being held up for tribute.

Eventually, they come to a large, swift river. Squirrel immediately begins a hunt for the canoes. After a long, exasperated search, it becomes clear that there are no canoes on this side of the river. They are all on the other side of the river. Someone will have to cross the river the Zesti way to get them.

Squirrel and Merlu volunteer to do the unpleasant deed, which is just fine with Numei and Esther, who offer no argument. The men strip naked and take deep breaths to prepare themselves mentally for the challenge. Esther stares at the wild river, trying to imagine how they will cross it without getting swept downstream. She begins to get a glimmer of an idea, when Squirrel and Merlu begin to scan the banks, looking for stones. They finally select a couple of large smooth stones and heft them carefully, testing the weight.

"How long can you hold your breath?" Squirrel asks Merlu, as they stare at the river thoughtfully.

"As long as it takes," Merlu says with a smile.

Squirrel smiles back, and they both stride purposefully toward the river. They cry out briefly at the shock of the cold and dance and jump until they get used to it. Two bobbing heads suck in deep breaths through clenched jaws, as they prepare mentally for this challenge.

"Aren't women better with the cold?" asks Squirrel, through chattering teeth.

"And they have better lung capacity," adds Merlu. "So what are we doing in here?"

Both men laugh and glance at the women, resting comfortably on the bank. And then with a signal of agreement they take a deep breath and disappear below the water.

"Are they going to walk all the way across that river?" a wide-eyed Esther asks.

Numei nods.

"Why can't someone just build a rope bridge across? It seems much easier."

"This is a secret road," Numei explains. "The Cougars try to keep a very low profile. Up here, to attract a lot of attention can be dangerous."

"From who?"

"The main path now runs through lands which the Hupa consider their own. They are expanding their territory. Those that travel upon it are now in danger of being held up for tribute, which is a polite way to say they are robbed. Squirrel says that the main road is only used these days as a supply path when the ship comes in. And then, they go under heavy guard."

"Are they that bad?" she asks nervously, looking around her as if the Hupa were about to jump out of the bushes and attack them.

"The Hupa are the terrors of the land. I have heard stories about their raids. They are highly intelligent, strong and ruthless."

They stop talking as they realize that it has been over a minute and the men have not surfaced. Their eyes scan the river anxiously. Still, the men do not surface. Just when they begin to fear the worst, the men finally appear on the other side of the river, a short ways downstream. Even from all the way across the river, they can hear a gasp as the men pop to the surface and struggle for air. Squirrel has made it across, but Merlu is just a little shy of the other side. He has to swim for it, and he is swept a good ways downstream before he finally clambers to the bank and climbs out.

The men take a long rest and recuperation and jump themselves dry, before attempting to cross by canoe. They find a long rope inside the canoe and attach it to a tree. Then they launch the canoe into the water and begin to row furiously across the river. They are swept downstream, but the rope stops them from going too far. It is just long enough to reach the other side, so all they have to do is keep paddling desperately across the river and eventually they reach the other side.

"Can we give you young maidens a ride?" Merlu shouts breathlessly from the canoe, while Squirrel holds it tight to the bank.

The women grab the burden baskets and climb down the bank to the wild river. Squeezing into the canoe, which is just large enough to crowd four people inside, is no mean trick. Then the men push off. This time, they don't have to paddle very hard. The current pulls them downstream and then the rope pulls them furiously across the water with the force of the current. The men struggle to keep the boat righted and steer it in a good direction, and soon they are on the other side. They carry the canoe onto dry land and deposit it back in its hiding place, then take a short rest before moving on.

"No wonder the Cougars do not visit us very often," Merlu muses, exhausted by the ordeal. "This is a terrible road."

The full moon helps them travel through the night. Squirrel knows of a good place to sleep that is just up ahead, so they push on after dark. It is slow going, but they finally come to a crude painting of a cougar upon a sign. They have arrived at the 'One Day' Hut. It is called that because it is exactly a day's walk from the Cougar village. The hut is carefully hidden a short ways from the path, to keep it protected from intruders if any should discover this road. They trudge through thick woods to the hut to escape the dreary weather. Only with Squirrel's guidance do they discover it.

It is a tiny hut, half hidden by a camouflage of branches. There is a nearby stream and a small clearing filled with edible plants. Squirrel begins to feast on a large patch of small green leaves. Esther tries some and finds them relatively tasteless. Soon she is grazing with the zeal of Squirrel, ripping up large handfuls and shoving them into her mouth. Somehow, the eating of these plants makes her feel clean and refreshed.

The hut is slowly rotting away and filled with junk, but it is dry at least, and equipped with dry wood and kindling. They quickly get a fire going and strip their soaked clothes off. Soon they are cozy and happy, and leave the woes of the road behind them for the night.

Cougar 2'

They get up early in the morning, stack wet wood in the hut to replace what they used, and push on. The path gets steadily better as they make progress, and they can eventually walk two abreast of each other. Numei walks next to Esther and talks about whatever comes into her head. Mostly she talks of Horim, whom she misses. Esther is not listening. She is in a strange mood today, due to a dream she had last night.

In the dream, she woke up alone in the woods by the Mission Santa Cruz. She was alone and dying of starvation. Her ripped nightgown hung in tatters on her body and her feet were bare. She had the horrible realization that everything she experienced in the past year's travels was just a dream. The Twelve Tribes were not real. She sat in the rain, sobbing her eyes out, while the rain beat down on her and threatened to wash her away in a torrent. She screamed out for Numei, Squirrel, and Merlu, but none of them heard her. Nobody heard her.

She wandered through the rain for an hour, unable to believe that it had all been a dream. She called out for Tara and Bodi and Garet and Elso and everyone else she could think of. She even screamed out for Kobe, promising to marry him if he would only come back. Meanwhile, she continued to walk in misery, her hair and clothes hanging limp and lifeless on her thin frame. Eventually, she came to the edge of the forest, and there she saw the mission again.

She crept up to the edge of the square and watched all the neophytes toiling on the new church. She knew that she had to go back there and become a neophyte again. It was all that was left for her. She could either go back to the mission or die out in the woods. Finally, she walked into the church square. Padre Quintana was there, waiting for her. Pedro was there too, standing next to Quintana. He waved her over, and when she hesitated, he yelled out that he would not hurt her. And then, with slow, laborious steps, she walked to him.

They escorted her into the mission barracks and clothed her again in neophyte clothes. And then she walked to church with the other neophytes. Soon, it was as if the Twelve Tribes had never existed at all. She hung her head and confessed to the priests that she had dreamed of another life....

She cannot get the dream out of her head, even after a whole day of traveling. She is afraid that it is going to turn out to be true, and all of her new friends are going to suddenly disappear into the mist. They don't even seem real to her right now, even though they stand before her in flesh and blood. She has a nagging fear that they are only invisible friends, like Nani, and it is time to wake up and face the fact that she is alone and just dreaming them.

She has fallen behind, slowed by depressing thoughts. Then she sees everyone standing up ahead, waiting for her. They are admiring a majestic sculpture of a fierce cougar, carved into a thick trunk. It has been made smooth by years of rainwater and mists. Esther stops musing on her morbid thoughts when she sees the amazing sculpture. Somehow it makes her feel better, even if it is only a dream.

"That's made by Mialgo," Numei says to Esther, when she joins them. "One of the great craftsmen of the Cougar tribe. I'll have to introduce you sometime."

"It's beautiful."

They walk on, knowing that Cougar village is near. The path climbs up a steep hill. When they reach the top at last, they come face to face with a fantastic view of the ocean. Esther feels her heart lighten at last, as she catches sight of her old friend, the sea. It is covered with clouds, and the wind whips it into a rage of white foam and great waves. The sight of it makes her feel as if she has come home at last. She has thought about the ocean many times these past few days and now here it is right before her.

They stand still for a long time, staring in awe at the endless stretch of blue. The sun sinks in a blaze of glory, a herald for their imminent arrival. And then a stiff wind and a sudden chill in the air makes them march on. They descend down the hill, toward Cougar village. The thought of all the well-earned comforts that await them push their tired feet just a little bit further.

A thick fog descends as they make their way towards the village. Rain patters on trees above their heads. They can see the smoke of fires coming from houses and lights winking in lit windows. Esther likes it immediately, even though she hasn't seen it yet. Then the subject of where to stay comes up.

"Is there a shelter?" asks Esther.

"No," says Squirrel. "They don't have a shelter here. They used to, but it burned down."

"People here are friendly," explains Numei. "We'll just stay with somebody."

"Who has a large house?" asks Merlu. "Big enough for four guests."

"Maybe we could split up," says Numei.

"I know I can stay with Atapak," says Squirrel.

"I can stay with Eliki perhaps," Numei muses. "And I'm sure Esther can stay there too."

They all look at Merlu, wondering what to do with him. He smiles and shrugs.

"I don't come up here very often."

"You can stay with Atapak," says Squirrel. "At least for a night or two, until you find something else."

"We can ask him."

"To ask is to receive," says Squirrel philosophically. "This is the way in Cougar village."

Soon Esther and Numei stand before the door of a simple long house. The door is open, so Numei walks in. Esther would rather they were invited inside, but she follows Numei anyway to get out of the rain. The house is small but cozy. A large fire burns in the center of the house and around it sit four people. They eat acorn mush with their fingers out of wooden bowls.

"Hello," shouts Numei. "Here I am!"

"Well, look what the cat dragged in," shouts out an older man, as his face displays a warm smile.

"Numei?" asks a woman with a strange, sideways smile, as she squints at the door.

Esther is introduced to everyone around the fire. There is Eliki, who is a slender, pretty woman with a mischievous smile. The oldest man is Atapak, who has long, stringy grey hair and a thick beard. He talks in a drawn out slur, as if he is drunk. Haptu is a thin, lanky man with a stoic expression. Aroni is an old woman with hard eyes. Eliki bids them sit down, gets them bowls of acorn porridge and puts on a kettle for tea.

"What else can I get you?" she asks. "I can get you some smoked salmon or they have some elk meat next door. Would you like some elk meat?"

"Elk sounds perfect," agrees Numei.

Eliki puts on her coat and walks barefoot outside. By the time she returns, Esther and Numei have polished off a bowl of acorn mush and are sipping coca tea from drinking bowls. Eliki carries a piece of raw meat in her hands, which she spears with a stick and places over the fire.

"It's wet and cold out there," complains Eliki with wide eyes, shaking the wet out of her hair.

"Not a night to be outside," drawls Atapak.

"Squirrel came here also," Numei tells him. "He went to your house. And our friend Merlu, from the Raven tribe, went with him."

"They can make themselves right at home," Atapak announces. "My beautiful daughter is tending the home fires. She'll get them whatever they need."

Numei tells them about Merlu, son of the new chief of the Raven tribe, and then she must tell the eager crowd the entire story about how the tribe got its new chief.

"Care for some?" asks Haptu, interrupting the tale as he hands them a pipe with the unmistakable smell of jimm.

Numei puffs contentedly at it, but Esther refuses. She looks around the room curiously. There is something very primitive about the house. The wooden planks are not uniformly straight, but grooved, heavily lined and a little crooked. The benches that line the walls are the same, though they are worn smooth from constant use. They sit upon tule mats covered with rough blankets. The only modern thing in the whole house is the iron pot, which contains the remains of the acorn mush. Everything else in the house is made from primitive materials, like the set of bone knives, which she uses to turn the meat.

Soon Esther is pleasantly warm and stuffed and the coca tea is coursing through her. She sighs, lies down on the mat and stares at the smoky ceiling in a daze. She listens to the laughter of the locals, as Numei tells them some of her adventures. The coca does its best to keep her awake, although she is plain exhausted from their long walk.

"Esther," exclaims Eliki suddenly, "if you want to sleep, you can set up your blankets on that bench over there. It's close enough to the fire to stay warm."

Eliki sets a tule mat down for her and lays an elk skin upon it. In a daze, Esther drags her basket to the bench and lays her blankets down. She lies there for a while and listens to the rain drum on the roof. She hears the others say their goodbyes, bundle up and slowly shuffle out into the wet night. Eliki and Numei talk quietly, as Esther comes in and out of consciousness, until at last she hears nothing more.

Cougar 3'

Raccoon moon

In the morning, Numei is anxious to find Tumock, whom she has heard has arrived for the Ruok council. After a cup of tea, she takes Esther to visit his house. It is a little shack far away from any sign of life. A large statue of a Cougar guards the entrance. Numei greets the frozen Cougar fondly and peeks her head in excitedly. But the fire pit is cold and his traveling bag is absent. Tumock is nowhere about.

"He isn't here," she murmurs, disappointed.

She frowns and looks about her, as if he is hiding somewhere close by.

"Let's go see Mialgo. He'll know where he is," she says at last. "You must see his house. It is amazing."

Mialgo lives a long way from the main village. His house lies in a large clearing which is evidently his doing. There are stumps and felled trees everywhere. Tools are strewn about – axes, elk horn wedges and steel carving tools. Esther remembers that he is the one who did the amazing Cougar carved into a tree. The whole area is littered with half finished sculptures in various states of completion, and felled logs waiting to become something. Esther walks over piles of wood chips to look closer at his wonderful house. It is large and solidly built, with spires, eves and all sorts of decorations set upon it. Carvings of various creatures on the roof seem to guard it with frozen, bared teeth. A beautiful canoe shaped like a jumping salmon sits outside near the door. It is half filled with rainwater, and seems to be waiting patiently for it to rain enough so it can float down to the sea. Esther gapes at everything with amazement. She cannot wait to meet this amazing creator of such fine things. He must be a very interesting person.

"Don't look him in the eyes for more than a second," Numei whispers conspiratorially, as they approach his door. "He has the evil eye."

"What do you mean?"

Numei ignores her question and shouts out for Mialgo in her usual blunt way. After several minutes, the door opens and a man peeks out. He has short, straight hair and a bushy beard. He is tall and lean, with a large nose and a heavily lined face. He wears a smock made from tree bark, which is covered with wood chips. He stares at them for a while with not a trace of a smile.

"Mialgo, it is Numei," she says, realizing that he does not recognize them.

"Numei," he says quietly. "I didn't recognize you."

"It has been a very long time," she agrees, not looking at him directly.

"And what are you doing here on this miserable day?" he asks at last. "A day when any sane person is indoors by the fire."

"I came to say hello," she says quickly. "And I am looking for Tumock. Have you seen him?"

"Tumock now lives with the Owl tribe."

"He came up here for the Ruok council."

"I have not seen him."

"This is Esther, my friend," Numei says, indicating that Esther is a valued guest.

"Hello," he murmurs, glancing ever so briefly at her.

Then he suddenly notices the weather, waves them into the house and disappears inside. They gratefully run inside after him. Esther follows the example of Numei by taking her muddy shoes off and leaving them at the door. As she does, she notices that Mialgo wears his muddy shoes in the house. She wonders why Numei bothers, especially when she sees the mess they are walking into. Tools, half finished carvings and baskets full of things are spread haphazardly around the room. There is a sleeping area, separated by a torn, grass mat, hanging from the ceiling. A small, untended fire burns in the center of the room.

"I see you are keeping busy."

"I am. So much to do. And I could die any minute."

He sits down and begins carving a little rabbit statue, as if he cannot spare a minute to talk. Esther notices that his tools are all primitive tools, made from elk horns, stone and other Zesti items.

"Camas cakes made by my assistant," Mialgo says, pointing with his carving tool at a basket filled with cakes. "Have some if you like."

Numei notices how old and tired Mialgo looks. He has obviously been working himself very hard. The camas cakes seem a few days old and she wonders if he has eaten any himself. They are still good though, and she and Esther lay in with relish, while she re-boils an old pot of tea. Mialgo works quietly, as they gobble down the cakes and slurp down the drink. Then with a shock, they discover that they have eaten all of his cakes without meaning to.

"I'm afraid our hunger got the best of us," says Numei. "I am sorry."

"It is nothing," he says with a wave of his hand. "I'll have more made."

"You are a wonderful carver," says Esther, watching him work.

"Yes, I know," Mialgo says shortly. "Obviously, I know that already."

Esther is about to say something else, but the words die in her throat. She closes her mouth and resigns herself to quiet for the remainder of her stay here.

After awhile, Mialgo gets up restlessly and goes outside. They are too relaxed now to move, so they stoke up the fire and get comfortable. Numei soon falls asleep. By herself, Esther is restless in this house. It is an uncomfortable and unwelcome house.

Smelling smoke, she stands up stiffly and goes outside. It has stopped drizzling at last. Mialgo stands before a great redwood log, watching it burn. He has previously split the tree in half, and now he has lit a small fire in the bigger half of the log and is burning a hole into the inside of it.

"What are you doing?"

"What do you think I am doing?" he asks, as if it is the stupidest question he has ever heard. "I am making a canoe."

"Why are you burning the log?"

"I can burn most of this inside out and save myself some work," he mutters.

Esther nods slowly. Then he suddenly stares at her for a moment. She catches his eyes and gets a chill up and down her body from the look in them. She quickly looks away. She doesn't look him in the eyes again, but the chill remains for some time. She walks away from him and wanders through the woods, trying to shake the creepy feeling she got from him.

Eventually, Esther wakes up Numei, and suggests that they leave so Mialgo can have his house back. Numei stares at her as she shifts back and forth from one foot to the other and looks fearfully around the house as if evil spirits are hiding in the walls. Numei bursts out laughing.

"You looked him in the eyes, didn't you?"

"Yes."

"You need the antidote, quick."

Numei gives her a hug, which does make her feel better. Esther laughs nervously and helps Numei clean up the remains of their breakfast. She looks around at the old crusts of camas cakes of days past and wonders again why Numei bothers.

Out in the grey light of day, Mialgo still tends to his little fires. He has eaten out a big black hole in the tree already, and is carefully controlling the blaze to make it go slowly.

"If you see Tumock, tell him that I am looking for him," says Numei, touching him lightly on the shoulder.

He gives her a rare smile and then gets back to work without a word. Fortified by food and a little warmth, they go back out to the wet path and begin walking.

"Is it just me or is that man a brute?" exclaims Esther.

"He is very touchy," exclaims Numei. "But we all look the other way, due to his genius."

"What is wrong with him? He seems so unhappy."

"He's a hermit. His only visitors are those who come to buy his fine work or order a particular carving, but they don't stay to talk. They say that if you look him in the eyes, you will have bad luck. So nobody ever spends much time with him. His only friend is Tumock, and even Tumock can only handle him for short periods of time.

They walk back to the main circle. The circle is empty and everything has been stowed away for the winter. Circular huts stand silently, abandoned by all but rats and mice. The fire pits are drenched with rain and soggy ash water runs in rivulets from the stones. Numei leads them over to the assembly house to see how the full moon celebration is coming along. The assembly hall is a much more lively sight. Smoke pours out of the roof cheerily. When they peek in, they see people busily working to decorate and prepare it for the night's celebration. But the party seems a long way from beginning, so they return to Eliki's house and take another nap.

During the night, the fog rolls in, making the world disappear. They leave Eliki's comfortable house and make their way through the eerie mist to the assembly house. They move slowly, barely able to see three feet in front of them. Through the commons they go, tapping sticks like blind women so they don't bump into anything. Suddenly a giant structure looms up out of the fog and rain. The assembly house - also called the Roundhouse - is large and low to the ground. It is almost perfectly cylindrical with a sloping roof and many small holes to let out smoke, which seems to pour from everywhere. From inside they hear a deep thumping that shakes the ground. They walk through the door and into the smoke filled Roundhouse, where they are assaulted with heat and noise.

They walk toward the bright fire in the center, where several musicians are warming up the crowd and themselves with some music. This music is very strange. It doesn't make much sense at first. Foot drums, hand drums, flutes, clappers, singers, whistles, rattles, and bells are played in no particular rhythm by a group of highly drugged, very shaggy looking people who are all off in a world of their own. When the music comes together it is only by chance and then it is very exciting. When it doesn't, it goes off in all different directions and makes you feel drugged yourself or bored - depending on your frame of mind.

Esther is fascinated by the foot drums and walks over to take a closer look. The foot drum is a flat wooden plank set over a resonating hole. A man jumps up and down on it, creating a deep bass drum sound. There are three of them side by side, with three men playing them in unison. The combined noise is so loud, she can feel the deep bass shaking her very bones. She stands there for a while, liking the feeling of having her bones rattle every time the men jump.

The crowd is bobbing and weaving in a trance. Esther examines them curiously. As a general rule, they have more tall people than any other tribe she has yet seen. There are some very beautiful men and women in this tribe, although you sometimes have to look past all the hair. They seem to have a law against haircuts, as every single one of them has hair down to the waist and the men often have thick beards. Many have droopy faces, as if weighed down with sorrows and torments too deep for them to handle. These droopy ones sit quietly, their eyes focusing on other worlds that only they can see.

The fact that this tribe is tall is an example of the mixing of the bloodlines of the Twelve Tribes and the Zesti. The northern Zesti, like the Hupa, Yurok, and Karok, are not true California Zesti, but are from the territories of Washington and Oregon. They have been described as taller and finer than the California race, as well as much fiercer.

The dress of the Cougar tribe is very primitive. Everything they wear comes from animals. Deer skin blankets, shawls, and robes are popular, and wolf, antelope and bear skins too. Many have necklaces with stuffed bear paws or cougar paws. Some have rattles around their wrist made from bones. Many have bags around their waists, bulging sacks with mysterious contents.

As the night deepens, more and more people pile into the great hall. A huge iron kettle is brought out from a hole in the ground that has been heated with hot rocks. It is loaded with a steaming batch of acorn mush. Three large baskets are brought out, containing smoked salmon. The music stops and everyone sits down patiently and waits to be served. Esther receives a small bowl of acorn mush and a piece of smoked salmon. The food at this polar day is simple, but filling, so everyone will have energy to dance afterwards. Dancing is the reason everyone is here, not feasting.

After dinner, the musicians take up their instruments and begin a slow, somber beat. Then the dancers enter. The dancers are led by heralds holding six stuffed deer heads on poles, with long draping skins covering the identities of the heralds. The deer are many colored, but the most striking are the white deer heads displayed in front. The white deer is a rare and beautiful thing, highly prized among all the people in the north. There are many dancers following the deer heads, dressed in cloaks of deerskins. They spin in circles and clap their hands to the music, as they do a complicated series of steps.

Across from the deer dancers come their hunters, the cougar dancers. Six cougar heads on poles, with the skin draped over the poles, start weaving and bobbing above the crowd. Behind them come cougar dancers, dressed in robes of cougar fur with stuffed cougar heads sitting on top like a fierce hat.

The music turns lively, as the two groups of dancers begin a competition to see who can dance the best. They take turns, showing off their best moves for the crowd. All sorts of styles are attempted, acrobatics, transcendental frenzies and graceful whirls and spins. The more cheers and whistles they receive, the better they are doing. A judge watches carefully, trying to decide who will win. The object is to be so filled with spirit, that your side will overpower the other. At stake is the future of the tribe.

The dancing deer heads also show a relationship between the Cougar tribe and the local tribes of Zesti. This ceremony is the Cougar tribe version of the World Renewal Dance, which was a common ceremony in the north. The WRD is a dance to please the spirits and make sure that no disasters like famine, disease, earthquakes or floods occur. If a disaster occurs, it is because the people have failed to please the spirits. White deer heads were specifically used to show off the wealth of rich men.

The competition lasts for many hours. These dancers have trained hard for this, and they are expected to go all night if needed, until a winner is determined. They continue to push themselves, trying to outdo each other. A woman on the Cougar side has been spinning like a dervish for over five minutes and she continues to gain speed. Esther cannot believe she hasn't thrown up yet. A man has been flailing his arms and legs like a maniac for the past hour, trying to go deeper into his frenzy. Another man does a full flip every thirty seconds, then stands perfectly still like a Mialgo sculpture until it is time to flip again. Another woman does an undulating hip motion like belly dancing, while spinning in circles and waving her arms in the air.

Esther sees a big wooden jug being passed around to the audience and assumes that there is some drug inside of it. She asks Numei, just as she is poised to take a drink.

"It's probably mushroom tea," Numei says, tilting the jug back and taking a deep gulp.

"Yes," she says, her lips pursing from the bitterness. "Mushroom tea."

She hands Esther the jug and indicates that she should drink some.

"I don't feel like it."

"Drink," she urges. "You need it."

Esther takes a gulp of the tea and finds it bitter and very strong. As she struggles not to gag, she hands it to Merlu, who stands next to her. He takes a deep gulp, passes it on to the next person and wipes his mouth of the foul elixir.

The dancers continue their strange competition for the next two hours. Eventually, Esther begins to feel quite a bit different, and she knows that the tea is starting to take effect. The fire dies down a little, which obscures the poles holding the stuffed heads up. It now seems like the animal heads are floating over the dancers, like mysterious animal spirits out to observe them. Shadows of the heads float across the walls in surreal patterns. Esther begins to feel like they are being watched by deer and cougar spirits, and she wonders if they are happy with the dancing.

Finally, the cougar dancers begin to tire just a little bit, and their movements become slow and sloppy. This only makes the deer head dancers more determined, and they dance harder, knowing that they will be victorious. The crowd cheers them on and finally the judge holds up his hands as a symbol of victory. The deer tribe is victorious.

Everyone cheers the deer dancers, who raise their hands in victory. The judge, who is an old, wise man named Tilka, raises his hand for silence. The crowd falls silent.

"The deer dancers have won. This means that we are blessed by the deer spirit. The deer spirit brings a time of peace. It will be a gentle year for us. The deer spirit has not won for three years and we are grateful that it has won at last. It will ease the violence that has plagued our land. It was a good contest. The cougar spirit is pleased with the efforts of her dancers. She will not abandon us this year, because her dancers performed well. If there is need of strength, she will reward us with the strength of the cougar."

"And now my friends," Tilka continues, after everyone has howled and shouted to satisfaction, "It is time for the Tumukala."

The Tumukala begins like this. Foot drums create a steady, pulsing rhythm and two women start to chant in strange wailing voices. The wailing, combined with the firelight, makes Esther feel as if she has entered another world. The shadows take on the personalities of spirits and the people seem like ghosts.

Her thoughts are strange tonight, as if they are the thoughts of another person. She becomes frightened for a moment, afraid that she will lose herself completely. She feels that if she is not careful, she will disappear. Whoever she is will fly away and she will become another person altogether. The idea is terrifying and she tries to find her old self, but she cannot find it anywhere.

All of the women in the Roundhouse start to sing along with the two women and Esther joins in. The men start to dance around the fire, with bone rattles around their ankles to make a steady beat. Some beat the wooden floor with staffs. They do a dance that is very simple, but the combined motion is powerful, like a deep narcotic. It makes all of the women fall into trances and their singing takes on a life of its own.

We search through the darkness
With the light of the moon
We talk with the Tumukala
We speak to the Loon
The song of the sparrow
The beat of my heart
The Tumukala goes on
And ends where it starts
The dance of the seagulls
Air on the wing
We fly higher and higher
To get there we sing.

The song goes on for a very long time. Esther begins to float on waves of bliss. She dances harder than she has ever danced before, with a huge grin glued to her face. She feels herself bouncing around the room, buoyed by her happiness alone, as if she could float to the ceiling and start dancing among the clouds of smoke clinging there. She feels everything melt away but a big Cheshire grin, that floats over the heads of the crowd as if she carried it on a pole. If she were to compete in that dance, she would hold up a big smiling mouth to compete with the cougar and deer heads, and she knows that she would win.

After a few hours of this, many begin to light torches in silent agreement that it is time to move on, and the music stops. The torchbearers lead the whole crowd of dazed, drugged people outside into the forest. The moon is shining high and bright above them and the rain has stopped. They take a walk through the woods.

Soon they come to a large clearing and the moon shines forth in all its glory. It shines through a thick mist, creating a diffused light. But it is bright. Everyone gathers in the center of the glen. Suddenly an incredible sound pierces the night. It is a high-pitched wail that is both beautiful and eerie at the same time. Nobody knows where the sound comes from or who plays it. It could come from a human playing an instrument or it could come from somewhere else. It evokes a hushed silence from everybody and many hang their heads in subservience. All eyes close, to better hear the unreal song that fills the whole glen.

Esther falls to her knees, overcome by the sound. She feels as if the song it plays is draining from her the last bit of herself. When it is finished at last, there is nothing left of her but a woman on her knees with no thoughts at all. She cannot even remember her name or who she is. When she stands up again, all of her thoughts return, but it is like someone is whispering them to her from somewhere far away. She shivers involuntarily and prays for the beautiful noise to return to fill her back up.

The wailing does return a short time later. This time, the song is joyous and fast, not slow and mournful. Overcome by a sudden urge, Esther begins to spin in a circle and screams with joy. Amazingly, many around her do the same thing, as if picking up on her urge. Soon the whole glen is copying her dance. Esther laughs at the sight, sure for a moment that she is controlling everybody. Then she is struck by a horrible thought. What if she *is* controlling everybody? She remembers her dream that none of this really exists, and she is still in the woods in her nightgown, dreaming the Twelve Tribes. She feels a chill throughout her body. What if it is actually true? What if this is the proof? Struck with terror, she runs away from the spinning, screaming mob and into the woods. When she is far away, she falls to her knees.

"Wake up," she whispers to herself. "Wake up."

She hears a sudden strain of music in her head. For just a moment, she hears the song she sang on that night so long ago. It fills her with unimaginable dread, and she remembers lying naked in the woods, dying of hunger. She falls to the ground, rolls over onto her back and stares up at the darkness. The whole world spins in circles. She feels herself falling through some impossible tunnel, although she is sure that her back still rests on solid ground.

She becomes afraid and tries to move, but she cannot. She tries to call out, but her voice doesn't work. The dark wood closes around her, and she can hear nothing other than her own ragged breath. She claws at the ground. The dirt that gets under her fingernails feels real and it soothes her. At least she is still solid and so is the earth. This makes her feel a little better.

She finally manages to sit up, although it is very hard. She feels her body with her hands and is shocked to discover that she wears her nightgown again. She strains her eyes in the light of the diffused moon, and she can see her white nightgown clearly. She claws at it, feeling terror overcome her. She wants to scream. The same strain of the song she sang that night replays itself over and over in her mind. She feels her skin and it is cold like a corpse. She feels very thin and there is blood on her legs and arms from the scrapes she received from trees and branches. She is suddenly sure that she is in the woods outside of Santa Cruz again, and she is dying.

She begins to sob. It is a tearless sobbing that makes her body convulse with the force of it. It is strange that she cannot find any wetness in her eyes, but it just confirms her belief that she is dying...or already dead. The darkness seems to deepen and she covers her face with her hands. Is this the end? She prays for it all to be over soon. She curls up into a ball on the ground and sings the song of her death quietly to herself.

She is not quite sure how long she is out in the woods alone, but suddenly she hears faint singing. It sounds like the Cougar tribe. The singing gets fainter and disappears into thin air like a fading dream. Part of her wants to let it go, give in to her fate and die peacefully. But another part of her screams herself awake. It tells her to follow the sound of the singing, before it disappears completely. She isn't sure which is real and which is the dream, but it seems as if she can choose between them. Choosing to live, she rises groggily and follows the singing. Her legs are like jelly, but she somehow manages to crash through the woods anyway. Bursting into the clearing, she sees the torches of the crowd in the distance, going back to the Roundhouse. Esther follows in their wake silently. When she looks down at her clothes, she is wearing her deerskin dress again and not her nightgown. For a moment, she has a strange feeling that she failed, by running back to the dream like a little child who refuses to face reality.

Cougar 4'

Esther wakes up very late the next morning, when something begins licking her ear. She opens her eyes and is shocked to be face to face with a small animal. With a start, she backs wildly away from it and falls off the bench with a crash. She curses at the creature and throws a basket at it. It runs off to hide, stops a good distance from her and stares at her. It is not large, but it does have sharp teeth. It is white and black, and looks like a baby bobcat.

"Are you all right?" asks Eliki from the other side of the house, where she is busy cleaning.

"Yes," says Esther grumpily, picking herself up.

"What happened?"

"Some animal is loose in the house," Esther says, pointing at the creature. "I think it is a baby bobcat."

"That's not a bobcat," Eliki says, with her mischievous, sideways grin. "That is Kiki."

"What is a kiki?"

"It's a cat."

"What's a cat?"

"That is," she says, pointing at the cat. "She was wishing you good morning. Can I get you some tea?"

Esther nods and glares at Kiki as she gets herself back together again and wipes the sleep from her eyes. She accepts the bowl of tea gratefully and sits down by the fire. She doesn't feel quite right this morning. She is very numb from last night's indulgence, and still shaken from her rude awakening this morning by Kiki.

"Did you have fun last night?" asks Eliki, going back to her cleaning.

"Most of it."

"Can I get you some acorn mush?"

"No thank you."

Esther retreats into her own world, as the events of last night replay themselves in her mind. She isn't sure what happened. She was having such a great time, until things turned horribly frightening. She isn't sure what is going on, but she knows that it is something she needs to deal with or she will go mad.

All day long, she wanders about in a daze, trying to get to the bottom of this mystery. She doesn't say anything to anybody about last night. She certainly doesn't want anybody to think that she is crazy. And there is nobody she can talk to about this anyways. If the Twelve Tribes *are* a dream, then they will not know that they are one and will not admit it. They will only protest that they are real.

Here is what she has figured out so far. Ever since she saw that apparition in the woods a few nights ago, she has been having these strange thoughts and visions. She is sure that it is connected somehow. If that thing was an angel, then she thinks that she might actually be dead and the angel is trying to get her to come up to heaven. That would make her a spirit walking the earth, dreaming whatever comes into her head. If that thing was only a spirit of the woods, then perhaps it is only playing tricks on her and she is alive.

Then comes the puzzler of the Twelve Tribes. In her entire life at the mission, she heard nothing about a large group of Spanish speaking 'heathens' with advanced technology similar to Spain's. She is sure the priests would have mentioned them, had they existed. And certainly tried to convert them! Then suddenly, this unlikely people appears from nowhere with bizarre customs based around astrology. They take her in and turn out to be her own people. It seems too good to be true.

And it all began on the night she collapsed in the woods! She has never given more than a moment's thought to that night, being too busy trying to survive. But for the first time since it happened, she remembers that night vividly. She remembers how it felt to be so weak and so close to death. And then that song that came into her head. She lost consciousness and she was sure she was dying. And then she woke up in a strange clearing that she had never seen before, feeling strong and healthy.

What happened on that night? It is the key to this whole mystery.

The rain begins to fall by the afternoon, and she retreats to Eliki's house. Numei has disappeared, but Haptu comes over for lunch and so does Atapak. She joins them by the fire and nibbles on elk meat that Atapak brought. There are two other visitors also. Kiki has brought friends over to play with, or at least two other cats have followed him into the house to escape the rain. One of them is a large black cat and the other is a small orange one. The large black one spends the afternoon chasing the other two around the house. Every time he catches one, he swats them with a paw, making them shriek. Eliki spends the entire afternoon yelling at them to stop fighting and stay out of her baskets.

"Leave them alone," growls Atapak. "They're just being cats."

"I don't want them tearing up my baskets."

Suddenly, the orange one races right past them, with the black one on its tail. It knocks over a basket of small pieces of cloth and knitting tools and leaps for a high shelf. The black one leaps after it and swats at it with a paw. The orange one stares down at it from its high perch and growls at it.

"They're entertaining," mutters Haptu, through a mouthful of jimm and tobacco smoke. "You have to admit that."

"I don't like that black one," complains Eliki. "He's mean. He's always chasing Kiki around."

"He's the cat chief," says Atapak, taking the pipe and inhaling deeply. "It's his role as chief to terrorize the others."

Eliki stares at him as if he is crazy and makes wide eyes at him. Her face makes her look a little like her cat, Kiki.

"They're a small animal," explains Atapak, though a mouthful of smoke. "They have to be fast and wary or else they'll be eaten. The big one keeps them sharp. He keeps them in good shape, so they'll be ready for anything."

"He eats all of Kiki's food," complains Eliki.

"Where do cats come from?" asks Esther. "I have never seen one before."

"We get them from the Chinese," explains Haptu. "Our sailors use them on long voyages to kill rats on the ships. When they breed, they make large litters, so we keep some ourselves."

"They are so cute when they're little," sighs Eliki. She glares at the big black one, prowling around like the king of the house. "Even he was cute when he was little."

Eliki throws a rock from the fire pit at the black one and shoos him out of the house. The black one runs out into the rain. A minute later, he returns, deciding that he would rather face Eliki than the pouring rain.

Esther watches Kiki stare into space. He has been sitting like that for the past hour, while the black and orange cats fight. He seems to be off in his own world entirely, seeing things that nobody else can see. Esther wishes she could ask him about spirits. She is sure that he knows all about spirits.

"Do you believe that the dead can come back to life?" Esther asks the three humans instead.

They all stare at her as if she suddenly sprouted flowers from her head. Eliki tilts her head sideways and opens her eyes wide as if trying to gauge Esther's sanity.

"I mean, do you think that spirits that walk the earth don't know that they are spirits?"

"Young lady," intones Atapak, "don't you worry about spirits. Spirits won't hurt you."

"What spirits are you talking about?" asks Eliki.

"I never seen nothing," declares Haptu.

"Just wondering," Esther says with a sigh, realizing that nobody has any answers for her.

By the nighttime, it has stopped raining, and Haptu and Atapak are ready to walk home. Eliki and Esther walk them out, wanting to get some air themselves. Esther wonders briefly how long she can stay with Eliki and if she should soon find other arrangements. But Eliki doesn't seem to mind, although they hardly know each other. So Esther decides she won't worry about it for now.

There is a strong wind, and a sudden tear in the clouds reveals the moon in all its glory. For just a moment they can see it shining down on them, and then it is obscured again.

"Who sees the moon this time of the yar?" slurs Atapak in a sleepy voice. "Its usually o'scurred with clouds. But our moon is a good moon, why don't they look at it? I am looking at that moon right now. See it there. It's beautiful. Absolutely beautiful. I mean, my stars, look at it. Just look at it right there in front of you."

As he talks, he points it out to Esther, as if she will not be able to find it without his help. She nods and smiles at him, humoring him. He has smoked so much jimm and drank a lot of a strange, dirt-like tea that they call sleepy tea. Eliki calls it relaxer tea. Whatever it is, Esther has drunk two bowls herself, and she is feeling very sleepy and ready for bed. So she bids him a good night and goes back in the house, hoping for a peaceful slumber without dreams.

Cougar 7'

Wolf moon

The rain has stopped at last and the sun is out with a vengeance. The whole village has left their smoky wombs, thrown off their clothes and gone out to romp in the unseasonably warm weather. Esther wanders down to the main circle to see what the village looks like on a nice day. She finds the place alive with noise and activity. An impromptu party has begun.

Hairy, naked people wander around, greeting long lost friends. They hug, laugh and prance out of sheer joy to be standing out in the sun after such a long hibernation. Tarps are thrown off baskets of supplies and some serious trading begins. Women walk around with empty baskets, searching for all of the supplies they have been missing. A group of people squatting in a circle are involved in some intense gambling, singing gambling songs and laughing at each new development. Musicians play lively tunes. Couples intertwine romantically in the glory of an early spring day. Lust is in the air, and young boys are out looking for pretty girls to share their beds when the cold weather returns.

But all of this 'spring-like abandon' doesn't feel right to Esther. It doesn't match her mood at all, which is perfectly in synch with the rain and fog. The sunshine just doesn't feel right. She isn't ready for it yet. She knows that her body is enjoying it, but she hates it. She has things to do that can best be accomplished in the gloom of a cold, winter's night. That sort of environment is inspiring. The sunshine is just a distraction that she doesn't need. It makes her think that everything is fine, when she knows that it really isn't.

Esther has come to an impasse. After days of wracking her brain, she still cannot figure out what all of the things that have happened to her are leading up to. She has fallen back into the mindless trance of daily living again and the great mystery has faded away from her brain. This bothers her. If there is a secret that needs to be uncovered, it will not be uncovered in the drudge of everyday events that are endless. Those will only cover the truth up further. Esther needs to keep digging deeper into the mud, until she finds the seed. The seed that was planted on that night, when she collapsed and gave herself to the arms of death.

She sees Numei suddenly, walking through the busy circle. She has not seen Numei for many days. She waves at her, and Numei walks over to greet her.

"Hi Esther," she says with a smile.

"Hi Numei. Where have you been?"

"A woman has her secrets."

"You have no idea."

"What secrets are you hiding?" Numei asks teasingly.

"It's nothing," says Esther sullenly. "What is your secret?"

"I found Tumock," Numei says with a sly smile. "He arrived the day after we did. I have been staying at his house."

The way Numei glows with pleasure, Esther begins to get the picture.

"I get the idea," she says, forcing a smile.

"I'm a married woman. What are you talking about?" Numei says innocently, with a mischievous twinkle in her eyes. "But maybe you should meet him. I bet he could coax an orgasm out of you."

"I'm not worried about an orgasm right now," says Esther unenthusiastically.

"You're worried about something. Tell me. You look like your best friend died."

"It is something like that."

"Are you going to tell me or not? I hate it when you get vague and answer in riddles."

"I can't talk about it," Esther says in a short voice.

"Fine," Numei says irritably. "If you feel like talking about it, just let me know."

Numei gets up huffily and wanders off to see all of the old friends she has missed. Esther sighs and returns to her sulking. She watches life go on without her. She used to enjoy watching people and all their little adventures and dramas. But now it all just seems a dreary waste of time. They seem like posturing fools, hiding desperately from the truth. She sees now that she has to find out if she is alive or dead, or she may never care about anything again.

Cougar 8'

Esther is well into her third cup of morning tea and enjoying a long conversation with Eliki, when Atapak's head shoves into the door suddenly. His face is insistent and hurried and his loud shout wakes them from their morning innocence. They glare at him, but he is on a mission and doesn't have time for incidentals.

"There's an emergency meeting," he shouts. "There has been an incident. Everyone is gathering in the assembly house."

"That doesn't sound good," muses Eliki.

"No, it doesn't," agrees Esther.

She wonders if she should go, as it probably doesn't concern her. But Eliki seems to assume that Esther is coming along, so she finally puts on her shoes and follows her out into the morning light. It is colder than yesterday, but still a nice day out. They walk over to the Roundhouse, where there are many people gathered, all trying to figure out the purpose of the meeting.

Everyone enters and makes a large circle around the fire. A woman starts to hand out camas cakes as a reward for attendance. She keeps getting asked about the topic of the meeting, but she doesn't have any more idea than anyone else. Esther munches happily on the camas cakes, not caring a fig what they are going to say. She's just here for the entertainment value.

Finally, the council of elders enters the room. There are some positively ancient people on this council. They hobble in slowly and everyone grows quiet as they enter. They take their seats quietly, with grave faces. Many whisper that this must be very serious. Following them, two more people enter the room. One of them is a tall young man with a sword at his side. Close behind him is a man that makes Esther's mouth open wide in shock. The man wears the robes of a Spanish priest. He walks slowly, guiltily into the room. It is Pedro. Esther cannot believe it. What strange coincidence is this? How could he be here? It is impossible. She has a sudden feeling that this is not going to be an entertaining meeting.

"My friends," says a woman on the council in a shaky voice. "Let the meeting begin."

"This man appeared at my door last night," says the tall youth with the sword in an apologetic voice, as if this whole thing were his fault. "He has a very important story to tell you."

The tall man, whose name is Majes, smiles humbly and sits down.

Pedro rises and faces the crowd. He looks like a man sent before the firing squad.

"My name is Pedro de la Cueva. I am a Spanish priest."

The whole crowd erupts into murmurs at the news.

"I am a friend to the Twelve Tribes. I have worked for a short time at the Raccoon hospital and have spent time with the Eagle tribe, as a guest of Chief Wendel. I have great respect for you and have studied your ways with great interest...."

He rambles on and on about his respect for the Twelve Tribes, until finally Atapak shouts out for him to get to the point.

"Very well," Pedro says, shooting him a guilty look. "This is what happened. I came up here with a group of fellow Spaniards. We came to scout out the land and see the north country, which we do not know. And so we...well, we followed the road of the Twelve Tribes north, which I knew to be the safest and best kept road in this whole land, due to the vigilance of your people. And it was a safe road...."

"Uh oh," breathes Eliki. "I don't like this."

Esther gives her a silent nod of agreement.

"A day's walk from here, we came upon a tribe unlike any we had ever encountered before. These men were tall and savage, and they were heavily armed. They came from nowhere. Four of them to each one of us. They spoke angry words to us, words which we did not understand. We tried our best to placate them. We offered them tobacco...trinkets. But they were merciless. I think we frightened them. They ordered us off our horses. They kept shouting at us. We tried to reason with them, but it was like reasoning with a bear. One of them tried to push one of my men off his horse...."

Pedro closes his eyes, as if remembering the horror fresh all over again.

"One of our soldiers drew his gun. It turned into a battle. Many were killed on both sides. I am no fighter. I am a religious man. The captain of my men ordered me to make a hasty escape on foot. I ran on foot through the woods. I did not see the end of the battle, but I am sure that none of my men survived. The savages were too many. They even killed the horses."

Pedro stops speaking and looks out at the crowd. They begin speaking among themselves, absorbing all this information. As they do this, he thinks of all the things he did not say. The guilt he felt as he looked back on his friends for the last time, and saw them battling for their very lives against overwhelming odds. The terror he felt as he ran, tripping on fallen logs and crashing blindly though the underbrush. The way his lungs burst in his throat as he ran, consumed by terror. Visions of the large swarming savages in his head, as he ducked behind a tree to catch his gasping breath, when he could not run anymore. Hearing the victorious screams of the savages echo in his head as he ran.

He remembers how he walked along the edge of the main road, staying hidden among the trees. How guilty he felt, knowing he had abandoned his friends and countrymen to die, when they needed him the most. He looked over his shoulder every five minutes, sure that he was being followed. How paranoid he was! He even walked through a stream for a mile or so, just to be sure that he could not be tracked. He had heard tales of the horrors of torture that a savage race inflicts on the cultured. As if to show them their notion of culture was an illusion. And now, Pedro is ready to believe it.

He stands before the Cougar tribe, who look almost as savage as those warriors who slaughtered his party. This tribe is not like the others - the Raccoon tribe or the Eagle tribe. These people seem much more primitive. They have been too long among savages themselves, perhaps, and have become like them. Pedro has no idea what they intend to do with him. Can they smell the fear upon him that lingers still from yesterday's horror? Even worse, can they guess the real reason that he came here? If they could, then they would certainly show him just how savage they are.

The meeting is now open for comment. Pedro is relieved to see that these people do not suspect his motives for coming here, but take his words at face value. Many express their sympathy at his plight. He is told of the ferocity of the Hupa, which is the name of the tribe that ambushed them. Apparently, the Hupa are a terror to the Cougar tribe also, and there have been troubles between them in the past.

"What words did they say to you?" an old man from the council asks him suddenly. "Do you remember any words they might have said?"

Pedro thinks hard. There is one word, which he heard over and over. He repeats the word and the old man says it over and over to himself, as if he cannot believe it.

"That is the word for respect," murmurs the old man. "A strange choice of words, given the situation."

"Respect," gasps Pedro. "A quality they had none of. I assure you."

"But, I would guess what they wanted was tribute from you," continues the old man, as if he didn't hear him. "For passing through their land."

"We have to abandon that road," announces Haptu in his mumbling way. "Or we risk war with the Hupa."

"All they want is tribute," shouts a woman. "Maybe we can just pay them what they want. It is a good road, with a bridge already built."

She is shouted down by a chorus of disapproval. A woman on the council rises to speak, and she struggles to quiet the ruckus.

"We do not pay tribute to force," she says. "That is not the way of the Cougar."

Pedro sits down, relieved that the tribe is worried more about the Hupa than himself. In fact, they seem to have forgotten all about him, which leads him to believe that they will let him go. They seem very agitated about their savage neighbors, and Pedro cannot blame them one bit. He listens with great interest as the tribe argues about the merits of keeping the main road open or abandoning it.

"The Hupa will keep expanding," says Atapak wisely. "If we give up this road, how long before we lose our new road too?"

"We make a stand," argues Haptu. "But not with that road. With the new road. It is farther from their territory and we can protect it better."

"Their territory is expanding faster than we can build roads," counters Atapak.

"This is serious, my friends," says the woman from the council. "This land is not so spacious and free as it once was. It is getting very crowded with the expansion of our northern neighbors. I say we give it some deep thought and discuss it further on the new moon."

There is general agreement from all assembled.

"Spanish medicine man who is called Pedro," continues the woman. "We are sorry for the loss of your company. We will offer you what assistance we can."

"God bless you," says Pedro graciously.

Esther squirms in her seat. Something has occurred to her and she cannot bear to keep her mouth shut. She knows that she must say this thing that she knows, although she is shy about public speaking. She finally stands up to get everybody's attention.

"May I speak?" she asks nervously.

"Who are you?" asks the woman.

"She's my friend," shouts out Eliki.

"What tribe are you from?"

"I don't know," says Esther in a quiet voice. "I grew up in a Spanish mission."

There is sudden silence from everyone in the audience. So quiet, that the pop of a burning log can be heard. Everyone stares at her in shock, especially Pedro, who looks positively stunned at the sight of her. Esther has to admit, she rather enjoys the feeling of having everyone staring at her with such awe, and she lets it draw out as long as she can. She glances briefly at Pedro, who continues to stare numbly with his mouth open.

"I know this man," she continues at last. "And I know why he came here."

She takes a long pause, and nobody makes a sound.

"You live on a great bay. The Spanish like bays. It gives them a place to shelter their ships. He has come here to scout out this bay, because the Spanish want to build a mission here."

The color in Pedro's face drains. He rises, thinking to deny it, but then he sits down again.

"I just have one thing more to say," continues Esther. "Whatever happens, do not let the Spanish build a mission here. You would not like it."

Numei rises suddenly from the back of the room.

"I have heard Esther's stories about that mission," she says in a cold voice. "To be a slave to the Hupa would be better. Trust whatever Esther says."

Numei glares at Pedro, before sitting down again.

"Is this true, medicine man?" asks an old man on the council.

Pedro nods, crestfallen. He stares at Esther for a moment, then looks down at his feet.

"It seems I was foolish to offer you our assistance," says the woman of the council who offered it. "But we do not rescind what we have already given. Consider yourself lucky that this woman spoke after you were promised help."

Pedro nods quietly, but still says nothing.

"Whether or not these Spanish deserved their fate -" shouts out Atapak, "and it sounds like they did - there is still the matter of the Hupa to deal with. I'll not be a prisoner in my own land. I'll go to war before that. I'll pick up my sword again and give them a war of it!"

He shouts out so fiercely, that he trembles with the force of it. His passion seems to open a dam of feeling in the crowd. Many begin to shout, and several men offer to join him in battle if need be. A man stands up suddenly and he screams at the top of his lungs. It seems he has a lot to say about the Hupa and he really lets loose. Esther stares at him, amazed more by his horrible teeth, which are rotten and twisted, than by his terrible words.

A thin, wrinkled old man stands up, who is very different from most of the others. He is a pure blooded Zesti who joined the tribe some years back. He was an outcast from the Yurok tribe, a bastard child, and he spent his entire childhood alone until the Cougar tribe took him in. He soon proved to be a wise man and he grew quickly in wealth and status. He wears a huge necklace of teeth from many different animals. The necklace is so big, that he wraps it around his neck three times and it still hangs to his waist. That is why he is called Teeth by almost everybody. His real name is too hard to pronounce on an everyday basis.

"My friends, I have some important things to say. The spirit world is not happy. The spirit world is not happy. We have not done the right things. We have not done the right things. The world is not happy. We have not done the right things. I fear that the spirits will leave us. They are not happy. We must make the spirits happy. I had a dream last night. It was wolf and cougar and bear, trying to drink from a dead river. The river was empty. The tribes are weak. We have lost our connection to the world. The tribes seek objects of wealth from other lands. All the people seek wealth. Our power grows weaker. We are weaker than our grandfathers. We are weaker than our grandmothers. The bad people come now. They grow stronger. We grow weaker. We must grow strong again. We must grow stronger. We must get power back. We must get power back."

The crowd erupts into murmurs of concern. Another woman suddenly stands up, and shouts for silence.

"My finger tells me that there is great danger from the east, where the Hupa live. And you all know that my finger is never wrong."

There is great distress in the hall. Everyone begins shouting, and most are in agreement with the two speakers.

"What do you say, Apali?" asks a loud woman's voice.

Apali looks up guiltily from her place on the council, as if she had been caught sleeping.

"About what?"

"What visions have you seen?" asks the woman.

Apali rises. She is a small, quiet woman with a round face. She wears a simple cloak of deerskin that covers her body like a robe. She squints into the gloom, trying to see the crowd assembled. She seems reluctant to speak, and she stands there for a long time, as if wondering what the people want of her. Finally, she closes her eyes and concentrates.

"I have seen that a great change is coming," she says in a firm voice. "They tell me that the future of our people is uncertain. There is great danger coming from *all* directions. They say that we must be strong, or we will be swept away like a city of sand on a beach."

She stops and watches everyone, wondering if they want her to continue. She does not like to be the bearer of bad news.

"Do you want me to continue?" she asks at last.

"Yes!" shouts a few voices. "What do you see? What do the Ruoks say?"

She closes her eyes and concentrates. It seems to Esther as if she were listening to voices in her head. Then Apali pulls out a cloth bag and walks to the center of the room. She pulls out a few wooden chips and throws them on the ground. Kneeling down, she stares at them. She peers closely at each one and touches them with her fingers. Then she draws a picture in the dirt with a single finger, connecting the wooden chips. She begins speaking from a kneeling position, as if in a trance.

"Most perilous to us now are the people from the north. Many are the races of flatheads. They are brutal and fierce, burning down villages and taking slaves of the survivors. They are expanding south. They have an eye on our fertile lands."

"Equally brutal are the Spanish in the south. They are expanding north, with an eye on making slaves of all the peoples of our land. They carry guns and dread diseases for which there is no cure. They have already caused much grief among our southern tribes, not to mention among the Zesti."

She stops a moment to stare at Esther.

"In the east, the Ruoks have seen a danger that is unseen to all others. Piutes and their cousins come. They live in a harsh, desert environment, and have an eye on moving westward where there is more food and more game to hunt. They are a brutal, warlike race and they have found ways over the impenetrable mountains that have kept them at bay for so long. They tell me that soon they may be a problem."

"From the west, come boatloads of strangers that we have yet no name for - like the ship that came to our bay last year, looking for otter pelts. They have an eye on our lands as well and it will be wise to remember them. They tell me to watch these people closely."

She stops speaking again and everyone waits for her. She seems to fall asleep for a moment and then she opens her eyes again. She takes another chip out of the bag and throws it on the ground. Then she squats down and stares very closely at it. She begins making lines in the dirt again.

"They tell me not to forget the great empire that has sprung up in the far east," she says from her kneeling position. "There are rumors that they are vast, unlike anything we have ever seen. They push ever west. But they tell me not to worry about them for now. By the time those people come, we will be ready for them or we will be long gone."

Apali stops speaking again and closes her eyes. Then she cleans up her chips, wipes clean the ground of her strange markings, and returns to her seat.

"That is all I see," she says simply. "They tell me once again that we must become strong, or we will be swept away with the tide."

A man takes the talking stick. He is a small man with hair that goes all over the place and an elegant antelope blanket around his otherwise naked body.

"I am going to go to the top of the highest mountain I can find. I'm not coming down till I have a vision."

He is cheered for his wisdom.

"I will join you, brother!" another man shouts.

A young woman rises. She is a healthy looking woman, with ample stores of winter fat.

"I will fast till the new moon. I welcome anyone to join me."

She receives many cheers also and two other women promise to join her.

The man with the antelope blanket rises again.

"I want to make a sister of the cougar spirit. Although she is my friend, she is not my sister. Cougar is sister to you, Apali, is she not? What will you suggest?"

"Cougar is my sister. But you cannot seek out cougar. That is not how cougar wants it. Cougar seeks you out. You may make yourself known to her, but she will not come unless she wants to."

"The ocean will tell me what to do. She always does," says a woman.

"River can speak for ocean," adds a man.

"Not as clearly."

Everyone has different ideas. But no one idea stands out above the others. So finally the woman who seems to lead the council takes the stick and raises her hands for silence.

"We will meet on the new moon and see what insights we have gained this past month. Now let us abandon this discussion and get back to more pleasant matters."

Esther finds herself the subject of much attention for the rest of the day. Everyone is curious about her. Outside, in the bright sunlight, she tells a few of her experiences in the mission. The mood in the village is quite aggressive and hostile, and it feeds her story like dry wood. She tells them a lot more than she plans to. She receives much sympathy from everybody, and lots of affectionate touches and warm feeling. The crowd around her grows, until she feels as if she is addressing the whole village.

As she speaks, she sees Pedro sitting by himself miserably. She notices many sideways glances at him and some give him the evil eye. She notices a man clenching his fist and looking like he wants to give poor Pedro a punch in the face, and she moves to diffuse the situation.

"He's alright," Esther says in his defense. "He's better than the others. He helped me once. And besides, I don't think he likes being a priest all that much."

"That's him, isn't it?" asks Numei, who stands next to Esther to bask in her glow. "The one you told me about."

Esther nods.

"That's strange," she muses innocently.

Esther nods. She knows that it is a very strange coincidence, but she is not ready to think about it yet. She returns to her captive audience and continues her tales. The afternoon wears on and a stiff wind comes up from the ocean. The fire is stoked up and blankets are fetched, but nobody leaves for shelter. They all want to hear her story.

Cougar 9'

Owl moon

Early in the morning, Pedro wanders along a forest path, avoiding everyone in the village. He walks in his robes, the only clothes he has since the attack. He walks with his head down and his hands clasped behind him, musing on the cruel hand of fate that led him back up here. What possessed him to do this one last task, after promising himself that he would hang up his robes and go home to Spain? He could be in Mexico by now, awaiting passage home. Not stuck up here in the middle of nowhere, without horse, supplies or friends.

This latest adventure began when he returned to the Mission San Jose. There, he met Father Lausen himself, head of the missions. Father Lausen spent an entire day with him, heard his story and took his confession. It was a great honor. Of course, Pedro did not tell him about trying to quit the priesthood and he did not mention Esther at all! He confessed that to Father Duran instead.

Over dinner, Lausen told Pedro that he was needed for an important task. He asked him to accompany a party north, following the road of the Twelve Tribes to the bay that he had heard stories of. Pedro was to decide if this bay would be a good spot for a northern mission. For this favor, Lausen offered him a great honor. Pedro would get to name the mission after a saint of his choice, and his name would go down in history as a founder. His life at home would be much improved by this honor. He would not be a failed priest, but a great man of honor who had served his country and God. For that, and a promise to get him home straight afterwards if he wished, Pedro agreed to come here.

Cursing his stupidity over and over, he loses track of where he is going, until he suddenly finds himself back in the commons. It is warm out, and the local girls are all out naked, sunning themselves. He stands a short distance away, watching them from behind a tree. He thought the Eagle girls were beautiful, but they were nothing compared to the girls up here. They are absolutely stunning. They are taller and fairer than the other tribes. There are some truly beautiful faces, with good cheekbones and lovely round eyes. Pedro's eyes roam back and forth, admiring them. And then he sees Esther, walking naked among them, and his heart catches in his throat. He cannot breathe. He feels cupid's arrow lodge itself deep in his heart and he struggles to breathe.

"Not again," he whispers to himself. "Please, not again."

Today is hotter than the last and the events of yesterday are forgotten with the rise of the sun. Everyone tears off their clothes and rushes outside to bask in the rays. It is a warm, windless day, perfect for this time of the year. When spring comes early, it is considered a vacation in Cougar village. Nobody is expected to work, unless they absolutely must. The only thing one is expected to do is to go out and play.

Esther wanders naked in the commons with everyone else, caught up in the tide of excitement. Today, she is ready to accept the sun. She is in a great mood actually and she doesn't care about any of her problems or worries. She is on vacation from all of that today, like everyone else in the village. She has become a minor celebrity overnight, and she is overwhelmed with attention, especially from men. There is a handsome young man following her around. He doesn't say much, being naturally quiet. But he sticks closer to her than her own shadow. She can tell that he likes her and she can't help imagining what it would be like to kiss him. She has a feeling that she will soon be tempted to find out.

The young man, whose name is Ylu, finally wanders off to take care of some business. Before he does, he suggests that they meet tonight at the party, and she agrees coyly. A chill afternoon wind has come up, so she puts on her deerskin dress and returns to Eliki's house for lunch. On the way, she notices Pedro sitting by himself. He has been staring at her, but as her gaze falls on him, he turns away quickly. For just a moment, a dark shadow passes over her heart, but she ignores it and keeps on walking until it fades.

The assembly hall is wild tonight. Something about the early spring weather has set libidos aflame. Foot drums are pounding and hands are clapping. Bodies are gyrating and glistening and shaking in the firelight. Everyone is here tonight, young and old, mixing on the dance floor. To see a young man kiss a woman twice his age is not frowned upon. Or an old man, running wrinkled hands down a smooth, young back.

Pedro sits by the fire, dressed in some furs someone loaned him in order to fit in. He drinks a hideous homemade liquor made from some unknown ingredient. It is good to have drink again, even this poor stuff that would make any self respecting Spaniard cringe. While he lubricates himself, he watches the girls dance. They gyrate their hips to the sound of the drums, their faces drawn in concentration. He has gotten used to the sight of primitive women's breasts, naked and exposed as they so often are. But he is still not used to such pagan displays of lust and carefree sex, out in the open in front of God and man. He holds his hands in his lap, trying to hide that which he does not want to deal with.

He watches Esther dance with some young man. He is a young warrior or hunter by the look of him, and he dances suggestively near her. Every so often, he will put his hands on her waist and draw her hips into his. And she lets him! She throws her head back and smiles at him. Such a look of longing and powerful sexuality! Then she throws her arm around his neck and rubs her hair into his face. He kisses her gleaming, wet lips, and she accepts him for a few moments before returning to her dance.

He is suddenly struck by how much she has changed. She is smiling and her face is glowing with happiness. She seems to have finally found her place, here with these people. A runaway neophyte…he never even guessed it! But it makes sense, looking back on the way she used to be. And now here she is, miles from the nearest mission, and she has managed to shrug off everything she was taught and reverted back to the primitive ways of these people. He watches her dance, nearly naked and shaking her hips unselfconsciously. He has never seen her move like that. He cannot watch her anymore, without feeling sad.

Pedro resents her this happiness, although he is ashamed of his pettiness. But he wants her back the way she was, demure like he is. She has changed and he has not. Although he tried very hard, he could not do the same. He could not become a...*heathen.* The word pops into his head and surprises him. But that is what they are. Coupling openly, without spiritual love. He still believes that it is wrong to do this.

But then he sees a girl watching him. Watching *him.* She is no beauty. She is short and a little old and has the weather beaten look of a person who has lived hard. Her face is heavily lined with many sorrows, and she has these ears that stick out like wings. Her hair is very short and ratty. But something in her eyes speaks to him. Pedro smiles at her. They lock eyes. Then on a sudden whim, he walks over to the small fire and sits down near her. He just wants to talk to her.

Esther kisses the young man in the darkness, with the foot drums pounding in her head. This boy is a great kisser as well as a great dancer. He has a rare grace for someone who is only sixteen years old. It is true that he is rather stupid and he has no interest in getting to know her. He has asked her nothing beyond her name. All she knows about him is that he wants to be a sailor. When the trading ship returns this summer, he plans to enlist and sail off to foreign lands. All he wants out of tonight is someone to dance with and kiss. He is the perfect man for tonight.

She has felt Pedro's eyes upon her all night and she takes great pleasure from it. She enjoys torturing him with her antics.

Perhaps a little too much. She kisses the boy once again and then glances briefly at Pedro, to see the expression of misery on his face. But he is no longer looking at her. He is talking to an old woman now. Disappointed, she returns to her young man and tries to enjoy it just as much as she did when Pedro was watching.

Pedro kisses Uru in a dark corner of the assembly house. It is a beautiful kiss, sad and perfect. It is one of the most sublime moments of his life. This is the kiss he has always dreamed of in the back of his secret mind. The kiss when two souls mingle as one. He feels her fleshy back, round with fat, and it feels good to him. He runs his hands through her coarse hair, nappy and rough, and it feels like fine spun silk. Then they stop kissing and embrace, and Pedro thanks God many times over for this gift.

He can tell that she would let him have sex with her tonight, but he isn't ready yet. He wants to know all about her first. He wants to love her. And then make love to her sweetly, when all things are decided and they are at peace with the world. And perhaps she will be that great love of his life. And to think that he found her up here, at the edge of the world.

In the back of the assembly hall, Esther lies down with the boy. He pulls her underneath a blanket, so they can have a little privacy. He apologizes that they cannot go to his house, but he lives in one room with his parents and brother. She cannot bring him to Eliki's house and it is cold outside, so it will have to be right here. But nobody seems to mind if they enjoy each other's company right here. Many others are doing it. Even Pedro is getting into it tonight! She sees him kiss that old woman in a dark corner and it seems a fitting omen for tonight.

Cougar 10'

In the morning, Pedro wakes up next to Uru in her little house. He smiles serenely and puts his arm around her, then opens his sleepy eyes to look at her. His smile fades. He cannot believe it! He has to look at her from another angle. He rises onto his elbow to get another look at her. Several angles later, he finally realizes that it is true. She is hideous. Her face is drawn, tired and wrinkled, with sags under the eyes and a dull color to the skin. Her hair is streaked with grey. She told him she was thirty-five 'turns of the wheel', and it seemed a good age to him. But he forgot last night that while a woman of Europe might still look good at thirty-five, here in the primitive world, women tend to lose their beauty much younger than that. Years of toil, hard work and exposure to the elements can take the blush of youth out of a woman very quickly. This one looks as if she has been caught in a hurricane.

Pedro kicks himself for his shallowness, but he cannot help it. She is not who he thought she was. How could he be happy with her? He is only glad that he never slept with her. He sits up with great effort and realizes that he is very hung over. How much of that cursed liquor did he drink last night? Obviously he drank enough to blur his vision. It takes all of his resources to stand up and creep out of the house without waking her up. Then he flees into the morning.

Esther sits outside Eliki's house, watching Kiki and the small orange cat – Kiki's girlfriend - lie sleepily in the sun. They lay like piles of inanimate bone and skin, flopped on the ground at strange angles. Every so often, one will rise up and lick its paw or preen its fur, in an exaggerated attempt to look busy. Then, when the hard work is done, it will flop back down and become inanimate again. She tries to lie like them, content and vacant, but it is hard for her. She is too restless. There is still something lurking in the bushes, waiting for her. She wants to chase it down, look it in the face and ask it questions. But she is too lazy in the hot sun, so she lies listlessly like a cat, patiently waiting for it to reveal itself again.

Cougar 12'

Elk moon

Numei appears at Eliki's door in the morning, and enters in her usual dramatic way. She sits down with them for breakfast tea and camas cakes. Esther knows how much Numei loves camas cakes and she wonders how Numei knew that Eliki made them this morning. After breakfast, she finds out that it was only a lucky coincidence.

"Some of the Ruoks want to meet you," Numei says.

"They do?"

"Yes, they do and don't even argue with me. You're coming."

"I wasn't arguing."

"Oh…then come on then."

Numei gives Eliki a farewell hug and runs outside. Esther follows soon after, and as she steps outside, she is overwhelmed by a strong wind that blows her hair about. She considers returning for her cloak, but Numei is already skipping on ahead, so she shrugs and follows her. They walk into the forest, where the wind is blocked. As they walk, the redwoods sway over their heads, groan with annoyance and drop things upon them in protest.

Suddenly a giant shape runs across the path and is gone again in a blur. Numei stops walking and Esther bumps into her. The two women stare at each other, surprised.

"Was that a cougar?" Esther asks.

"Yes," Numei answers. "In a hurry."

"I've never seen a cougar before," Esther says.

"Never?" asks Numei, surprised.

"No. Are they rare?"

"No," muses Numei, "they just like to hide."

Numei walks on and Esther follows. She tries to slow down the brief sighting in her mind, to get a better look at the animal. They come out of the redwoods and head through a flat clearing toward the bay. In a corner of the clearing is a small house. Apali sits outside the house in a patch of tall grass.

"This is Esther," says Numei, introducing her. "Esther, this is Apali."

Apali smiles and greets her pleasantly. Esther sits down in an inviting patch of grass, a respectful distance away, but Apali waves her closer.

"My eyesight is not good. Please...."

Esther sits closer to her and the woman watches her curiously.

"You have caused a stir in our village," she says simply.

Esther nods, knowing this already.

"Are you a Ruok?" Esther asks a moment later.

"I ruok," she replies simply.

"What do you mean?"

"Many have forgotten that ruok is an action and not a name."

"But you are also called Ruoks?"

"Yes. But a Ruok is only someone who ruoks."

Listening with amusement, Numei takes off her clothes and lies down in the sun.

Apali stares at Esther again, as if she had a sudden realization about her, and then she looks away at the clouds. Esther watches the grass wave in the breeze and then realizes that it is warm in this spot. She takes off her clothes and lies down, like Numei has done. For a long time, nobody says a word. Then clouds roll across the sun and the heat leaves their little spot.

"Where's Tumock?" asks Apali suddenly. "I have not seen him yet."

"I don't know," Numei replies. "Do you want me to find him?"

"If you want."

Numei stands up and walks across the field naked. Alone with Apali, Esther can feel that she has a lot to say, but she is too polite to say anything. Finally, Esther grows cold, and she sits up and puts her clothes on.

"Would you like a reading?" Apali asks.

"What's that?"

"That is how I ruok. I tell people things about themselves or about the world."

"Sure," Esther agrees.

"Come with me," Apali says.

She leads Esther into her house. The house is very bare on the inside and whatever small possessions she does own are strewn all over the floor. It is covered in dust as if it had not been cleaned in a long time. Esther only sees one small bed and one basket of clothes. She realizes that Apali lives alone in this house. Apali pulls out her bag and sits Esther down near the coals of the fire.

"Do you want tea?" she asks.

Esther shakes her head.

"Think of a question you would like answered," Apali says. "And I will answer it."

She pulls out wooden chips and throws them in the dirt. She examines them and draws lines between them. She peers closely at the shapes the lines make and at the gaily-painted chips themselves. Apali cannot see very well, so she walks over to the window, which is covered by a large piece of bark. She throws the bark to the ground carelessly, which lets in a lot of light as well as disturbing a cloud of dust. Then she returns to her reading, able to see much better. She stares at the chips a while longer and then suddenly frowns.

"May I be honest," she asks carefully.

"Yes."

"I see death. Everything I see points to it."

Esther gasps and there is a sinking feeling in her stomach.

"And you are dreaming of rebirth."

"What do you mean?"

"I don't know," she says at last. "That's what they told me."

Apali frowns and examines the chips again.

"They show me a man. This man is able to help you. This man has answers for you. This man knows things about you, but he doesn't know that he knows them. You must talk to this man, but you should not believe everything he says. He is resentful of you. He doesn't realize that he secretly means you harm. He may try to hurt you. You must talk to him, but you must beware, because he has many faces."

"Pedro?" she asks, already knowing the answer. "The Spanish Father?"

"Yes, that is quite possible," she says, nodding. "But there is another man...no, it is not a man exactly. It is something else. A spirit. There is a spirit that you two have in common. It is drawn to you and to this man. This spirit is dangerous to you. It is dangerous to him also. This spirit has all of the answers you seek. But you must take great care if you seek it out."

Esther gasps, terrified at the mention of this spirit. Apali looks at her and stops speaking.

"I hate giving bad news," she mutters. "I only say what the voices tell me."

"Please," Esther gasps, having difficulty breathing. "Go on."

"I will follow the Flow," says Apali apologetically. "No matter what it tells me."

She frowns and puts the chips back into her bag. Then she casts new ones and examines them. She draws pictures in the dirt and connects the chips in strange curvy lines.

"I see a dark forest at night. There is a naked woman screaming. She collapses on the ground. Now she is not moving...."

Esther's blood runs cold and she begins to shake out of fear. She has to force herself to concentrate.

"I see a snake in the grass. It slithers toward you. I cannot tell if the snake means you harm or help. But a snake is a good sign. It often means rebirth."

She draws something else in the dirt.

"The snake slithers around a stone. There is writing on the stone."

"A gravestone?" gasps Esther in a whisper.

"I don't know that," says Alapi, holding up her hand for silence. "But the snake has a face. A face...but no eyes. The snake is blind. Or maybe it is you that is blind."

Alapi moves her head back and forth, slowly, as if trying to pick up something out of a multitude of voices.

"I see a cougar...stalking. That is good. The cougar will be your protector against this spirit that means you harm."

Apali begins to mutter to herself, as if having a conversation with invisible voices.

"The voices speak of death again. They say that death will come to you soon. But along with that will come the death of your blindness."

Apali opens her eyes and looks at Esther. Apali seems very sad.

"I am sorry to tell you these things," she says, reaching across to hold Esther's trembling hand. "I only say what they tell me. I wish they had happier things to say."

She suddenly wipes the dirt clean and puts the pieces back in the bag. Then she pulls out seven chips and casts them all. She begins examining them furiously, passionately.

"I don't normally cast this many," she says, offhandedly. "But there is something I am missing. Something good."

Her eyes scan the chips desperately and she draws many shapes in the dirt.

"I see a giant butterfly flying through the air. The butterfly has a woman's face. It is a white butterfly."

"An angel?" Esther asks quietly.

"I don't know this word," says Apali distractedly. "But butterflies are dreamers. They tell me now that the dreamer awakens."

Esther gasps, suddenly sure that Apali is talking about the apparition that she saw in the woods many nights ago.

She sighs and puts away the chips.

"They tell me that is all for now. I am very sorry that I could not find anything else."

Esther sits numbly, wishing she had never come to this house. Apali rises and walks outside, leaving Esther alone with her racing thoughts. Esther sighs deeply and sits there for a long time, saying nothing. Finally, she decides that she has to face the truth, no matter what it says. She won't deny it. She will awaken from this dream that Apali spoke of, no matter what it is that she awakens to.

She just wishes that she had someone who could do this with her.

Apali returns and suggests that they go outside, as the clouds have passed. Esther follows her numbly out into the sunshine, which drives away some of the gloom.

"I didn't tell you this, but I thought of Paddlefoot when I was giving you a reading. I don't know why."

"Who is Paddlefoot?" Esther asks, sitting down next to her in the grass again.

"One day, when my brother was a baby, he was playing underneath a tree, when a strange wolf appeared. It had an eye on my baby brother for dinner. Normal parents wouldn't leave a baby underneath a tree by itself, of course, but my parents were not normal. I screamed for my mother, but she was far away. I didn't know what to do. The wolf walked right up to my brother, looking around warily. It was a large one and its fur was matted and patchy. I think it was diseased and its pack had abandoned it to die. It was hungry because it was wintertime. I remember screaming and thinking that my brother was going to die.

Then a giant black cat jumped out of the tree above my brother and landed on the wolf's head. He scratched furiously at the head and I saw blood fly everywhere. He scratched at its eyes. The wolf turned and began to run the other way, yelping and crying. It only got a short ways, before it collapsed onto the ground. My mother returned and killed it with a club, but it was already near death. Paddlefoot had killed it.

"Ever since then, Paddlefoot lived with us. He was not a normal cat. He had more fingers than normal. In fact, he had thumbs. And he was twice as large as any cat. He slept with my baby brother and protected our house. I repeat - this was not a normal cat. He seemed strangely human and I was the only one it would listen to."

"How could a little cat kill a wolf?" Esther asks doubtfully.

"I promise you it did," Apali says. "And it was not so little. It was supposed to be two cats, but it was born as one. That's why it had an extra finger on each paw."

"Where is it then?" she asks, looking around skeptically.

"It disappeared one day. I looked everywhere for it. But it was gone just as suddenly as it appeared. I hear there were some cats born in the wild just like it, but I never saw them."

Apali looks sad for a moment, then she shakes it off.

"I don't know why I mentioned it, but it seemed like I should."

Esther wonders also why Apali mentioned it. Then she remembers this morning and thinks it might be connected.

"I saw a cougar," Esther says. "Coming here."

"Cougar will be your protector for this thing you must face."

"But I only saw it for a second," argues Esther. "It ran past me, that's all."

"That's enough," says Apali.

"Have you seen one closer than that?"

"Oh yes. When I was a child, the village caught a cougar in a giant trap. We kept it there for many days. The cougar would pace back and forth, growling to be let out, but the village wanted to study it first. We were the Cougar tribe and we knew almost nothing about them. I felt sorry for it and I used to go and give it little gifts of meat. One day, we locked eyes and I felt how sad it was. I apologized for my village and told it how sorry I was. I walked up to the cage, not realizing that it was dangerous. It licked my face with a rough tongue. Its saliva burned my cheek."

"That's strange," agrees Esther, lying back in the grass to watch the clouds.

"Ever since then, Cougar has been my protector. It gave me Paddlefoot when I needed him. After I met Cougar, I began to have visions. Cougar is a seeker. It is sneaky and fickle at times, but it sees things that other animals cannot."

The two women talk until it gets dark. Numei never shows up with Tumock, and Esther wonders if she found him and what they are up to. Why did they never come? Not that Esther minds so much. Apali is excellent company and she feels better now than she did after the reading. As afternoon wanes, Apali announces that she has somewhere to go. Due to her poor vision, she must get there before dark. She describes it as irritating tribe business that she cannot get out of. She wishes Esther luck and invites her to come to the Ruok meeting on the new moon. Then she walks into her house.

Esther rises, feeling exhausted, although she has done nothing strenuous today. She walks to Eliki's house in a daze. The walk is soothing and clears her mind. Unfortunately, Eliki has male company for the evening and Esther is in the way. She walks into the house, begs forgiveness for barging in and wanders outside with her blankets. Luckily, the weather is nice enough for her to sleep outside. She finds a dry place to sleep in an abandoned hut near the commons, and sets up camp for the night.

Cougar 13'

Pedro walks through the commons, searching for the man who makes flutes. He is told that the absolute best flute craftsman in the whole land has come today to sell his flutes. Somebody told Pedro that this man makes flutes that are so delicate, that when they are played people often mistake the sound for spirits on the wind. He doesn't know if he believes that, but at least he wants to see for himself.

He is so preoccupied that he doesn't notice Uru until she jumps in front of him. She puts her hands on his arm and smiles. He stands there stupidly for a moment, until his brain stops thinking about flutes and focuses on her. It is an unwanted distraction, as he would rather think about flutes.

"Hello, Uru," he says, a little woodenly.

"You have not been to see me," she says in a breathy voice.

Pedro remembers that voice in the darkness and how erotic it was. How her touch sent his pulse sky high and her smell gave him peace. But now, in the cold light of day, with the visuals attached, the effect is lost. He struggles to find the seed of attraction again, but it just won't come.

"I was looking for flutes," he says, forcing a smile. "Have you seen the flute maker?"

"No. But I can make noises sweeter than flutes."

His eyes bulge out, as she grabs his hand and tries to pull him in the direction of her home.

"Come with me," she urges. "I show you."

Pedro stares at her pudgy, tired face and stooped body. She runs her calloused hands over his arms and they seem like men's hands to him. There is nothing delicate about this woman. He realizes that she has worked hard her whole life and that is why she looks in such poor shape. She has walked many miles on those big, puffy feet and done many things with those rough hands.

He thinks that she wants only sex. Raw, animal sex, without the love. She doesn't really care about him, but only wants to have fun. There is something repulsive in her insistent tug on his arm and in her desperate eyes. She has obviously seen no man in a long time and desperately craves one. Pedro is excited by women delicate and demure, and she is neither of those things. She is pure, animal heathen and he is gente de razon – a man of reason. It would never work.

And would he be willing to sell his vows of chastity for such a small sum?

A couple of beautiful, young girls walk by and Pedro stares at them. The girls look at him and then stare at the old woman holding his hand. He feels their disapproval, as if he is no good by his association with the old hag. Pedro quickly withdraws his hand from Uru's grasp and indicates that he must go.

"I cannot," he says icily. "I must find the flute man."

He touches her piously, as if he is too spiritual to be bothered with such transitory matters, but he recognizes her place as God's child, and then he walks on. The expression on her face drives a nail into his heart, but his path is set and on he goes.

Sometime during the night, Esther walks into the forest, with a blanket wrapped tightly around her and a candle inside a little broken lantern. The forest seems to hold answers for her and there are too many distractions in town. She walks up the hill, until she finds a comfortable nook underneath a great tree, and then she blows out the candle.

She lies on the forest floor, staring up at the redwoods. They seem huge, threatening, like great giants staring sternly down at her. Esther feels like a little girl, surrounded by angry fathers of the forest. She cannot tell if they are actually malicious or just fearsome and stern. She lies curled up in her blanket, remembering the days when she wandered lost in the redwoods.

That night she has a dream. In the dream, she is back in the forest near Mission Santa Cruz, just after dawn. She crawls through the forest in her torn nightgown, on her hands and knees, because she is not strong enough to stand. Both are bloody, scratched and tender, and she moves slowly. She is covered in dried mud, which helps her keep warm. Her hair is wild and matted like a crazy woman who has not touched a comb in years. She searches in the wet mud for earthworms, which she picks out of the mud and eats raw. She shoves a handful of dirty earthworms into her mouth and chews down on them. They taste terrible, but she no longer cares.

She eats bark and redwood needles too. Anything she can find. She continues to crawl along the forest floor on her hands and knees, desperately looking for anything edible. She finds a black bug, and she shoves it into her mouth and chews ravenously at it. It tastes terrible, but the mud in her mouth numbs the taste somewhat. Then fate is on her side. She finds a rat, which is unlucky enough to show itself during her search for food. She grabs it in her hand, ignoring the sharp bite from its tiny teeth, and slams it into a tree until it is dead. After sniffing it, she bites down on the stomach. Blood gushes from the belly and she sucks the blood ravenously. After sucking all the blood out of the little thing, she starts chewing on the poor creature's meat and she even sucks out the organs. In the space of ten minutes, she has chewed the thing down to bones and fur. She spits pieces of fur out of her bloody mouth. Blood runs down her chin and she wipes at it with a finger and licks her finger clean.

She hears a noise in the underbrush near her. Esther bares her blood stained teeth in a snarl, like a cat protecting its kill. She licks the bones clean neatly and then wipes her mouth free of rat. She feels stronger now and she slowly stands up on shaky legs. She walks hunched over, occasionally leaning on trees when her energy fails. A squirrel stares at her from a tree branch and she growls at it. She shakes the tree branch, trying to dislodge the squirrel, which would make a very satisfying and fat dinner.

Esther wakes up with a gasp of horror. For a moment, she is afraid that she has not returned to the forest by Cougar village, but after feeling around her clothes and blanket, she determines that she is back there. That did not feel like a dream! It felt too real, like a long buried memory. The more she thinks about it, the more she is sure that it did happen. Desperate from hunger, she turned into that creature in order to survive, and then blocked it out of her memory.

She shakes with terror, and then buries her head in her hands and sobs. She lies in the dark forest for a long time, crying piteously. She wants somebody to hold her, anyone would do. She wants to be back in town, blissfully numb again. But she doesn't feel up to the challenge of walking back through the forest at night, in this state. She is too disoriented. And besides, she promised herself that she would not deny the truth, no matter what it had to say. Or how painful it turned out to be. If that horrible scene actually happened to her, then that is what she will have to face. After crying her eyes out, she curls into a ball and prays for dawn.

Cougar 14'

Raven moon

Esther wanders through the village, like a lost soul adrift on a sea of confusion. Last night's dream replays itself endlessly in her mind, but in the light of day it no longer seems real. What is real? Who is real? After last night, she is utterly confused as to what is going on. She feels as if she is having a meltdown of biblical proportions.

People talk to her, but her mind feels like thick mud, and she is not aware of what she is saying. She makes small talk about the amazing string of warm days in the middle of winter. One man, a crazy one who makes bug eyes as he speaks, talks to her for a long time about the bizarre murder of his friend. He rambles on and on, and she has no idea what he is talking about, and is too obsessed with her own problems to care. She just lets him talk and thinks of something entirely different, until he wanders off with a raised fist of unity, as if they have solved some great mystery together.

Finally, she must escape from the village and go away on her own. She has to solve this riddle, for it is truly driving her mad. She struggles to put together all of the pieces, hoping to find the magic fit that will unify everything. She has never had such rapid activity in her brain before. It makes her uncomfortable just to be inside herself. She takes a long walk in the warm, comfortable sun. She moves slowly, step by step, like a salamander, knowing she will get there eventually.

She thought she could handle anything. She thought she had grown strong during her travels. But she did not imagine anything like this ever happening to her. Her whole world is collapsing and she is grasping for solid purchase, as she tumbles into a deep crevasse of insanity.

Her mood is so grim that she cannot even enjoy this beautiful weather. The whole land has come alive, having accepted that spring is actually here, weeks early like a surprise guest, and they might as well shake off their sleeping limbs and get on with it. She wants to get on with it too, but she is stuck like a fly in the spider web of her troubles.

Finally, she comes to rest in the hot sun, in a large clearing of tall grass. She tries to quiet her mind and just sit peacefully. She watches a black bee buzz in circles, exploring a flower. She wonders if bees think. What a curse thinking seems on this day! She wishes she did not have to think, but then her heart grows cold, as she realizes that her time of thinking might soon be over, and she should be careful what she wishes for. She quickly rethinks her position. She wants to stop thinking about her problems, but she doesn't want to die.

A hummingbird flies by the same flower and samples its pleasures, and suddenly her foot is asleep. She kicks her foot back and forth, trying to awaken it. As soon as the bird leaves, her foot is normal again. She begins to wonder if the hummingbird is really a hummingbird or if it is a demon in this purgatory of illusion that makes her foot fall asleep. After endless musings, she finally decides that she doesn't care anymore. Dreaming...awake...the sun feels hot and who cares if it is a real sun or if she is dreaming of it from her grave?

Esther does not sleep in the forest tonight. She is terrified of it and what it might show her if she goes back there. She goes to Eliki's house instead and settles down by the fire with Kiki. Kiki curls in her lap and offers her comfort. She feels that no bad spirits can invade this house without Kiki knowing. Esther decides that she will have to get a cat herself, for protection.

"Where have you been?" Eliki asks, when she returns home to find Esther comfortably settled.

"I slept in the redwoods last night."

"Why?" asks Eliki, staring at her as if she is crazy.

"It seemed like a good idea."

"I don't like to sleep in there. It gives me nightmares," Eliki adds, bustling about the house. "We're close enough to those trees right here."

Cougar 15'

In the morning, Esther decides that it is time she talks to Pedro. She asks around the commons, until she finally finds someone who has seen him. She is told that the Spanish medicine man has set up camp a short ways from the commons. She is pointed in the right direction and she wanders down one of the village paths, until she sees a small tarp set up between two trees. There she finds him, sitting in front of the tarp, cross-legged, with pink bare feet sticking from out of the folds of his ripped, brown robe. He does not seem happy and his attempt at a smile of greeting is sickly and weak.

"Hello," Esther says, sitting down next to him.

He nods, but offers only the same sick smile again.

"Are you sick?"

"No. Not physically sick."

They sit for a while, saying nothing, while the uncomfortable silence grows nearly unbearable.

"Why didn't you tell me?" he says at last. "That you came from the mission."

"You know why."

"No, I don't," he says, looking like a hurt little boy.

"If they knew that I was alive, the fathers would have sent soldiers after me to bring me back."

He nods slowly.

"They might have."

"You know they would! I wouldn't be surprised if they would send soldiers all the way up here, just to bring me back."

She stares at him suspiciously, realizing that he is now a danger to her. She wonders if he would tell Mission Santa Cruz that he saw her, and if they would really send soldiers all the way up here just to get her.

"You must never tell them about me. Promise me that."

He closes his eyes and searches his mind for his convictions on this matter.

"Was it that bad?" he asks. "To be a Christian?"

She thinks about her answer for a while.

"That's not what I was. I was a neophyte."

"And what's the difference?"

"The barracks," she says slowly. "Chains. Whips. I was a slave."

He stares at her with a sudden insight.

"That is why you could not love me, Estar? Because you considered me nothing more than a common slave trader?"

"My name is not Estar. It is Esther."

"Is anything you told me true?" he asks miserably.

"I thought you had decided not to be a priest anymore," she says, quickly changing the subject.

"I was never really sure. It was an experiment at the time. Then I decided to do this one last task as a priest, before I would consider hanging up my robes for good."

"So are you a priest or not?" she asks.

He stares gloomily at her.

"I realize now that is the real task I came up here to do. To decide."

Pedro returns to his sulking. His sulking reminds her of her own situation. Esther suddenly realizes that they are both going through something very similar. Both are questioning the very fabric of their existence.

"I need to talk to you," she says. "But I don't know how to say it."

He perks up noticeably and she knows just what he is thinking.

"There is a spirit haunting me."

His face registers shock. That is not what he expected or hoped to hear.

"It is haunting you too. Someone told me that and I can see that it's true."

"A spirit?" he asks numbly. "Haunting me?"

"Yes. Do you know what I mean?"

He nods slowly.

"Yes, I do. But perhaps it is not a spirit, but is only God."

"No," she insists. "I don't think so. It is a bad spirit."

"Yes," he whispers. "God can sometimes seem a bad spirit to those who are on the wrong path."

"How do you presume to know my path?" she says, standing up indignantly. "You priests always think that you know what is best for everybody!"

"I meant me," he says slowly.

"Oh."

She still glares at him, not entirely believing him.

"I have seen this spirit many times," she adds. "It has visited me from time to time. It is a bad spirit."

"Maybe it is the devil," he says, nodding.

"No," she says, shaking her head. "It is Him."

"Him who?" he asks blankly.

"That's just what I call it. I don't know its real name."

"What does it want from you?" he asks.

"I don't know. But it hurts me in my dreams. It takes control over people sometimes, usually men. Maybe that's the reason I call it Him, even though I don't know if it is really a male spirit. But it told me that it took over Miguel. Padre Fernandez too. It makes them blind, so they don't know what they are doing."

"Padre Fernandez?"

"Yes," she whispers. "He raped me many times."

"I don't believe it," he gasps. "You are lying to me."

"No, I'm not. It took over Padre Quintana too. He used a wire-tipped whip to punish us and he took great pleasure from it."

Pedro stares at her, aghast. He cannot believe what he is hearing. He feels as if Esther just took a shovel and bashed him over the head with it. He stands up and begins pacing furiously. He cannot speak for some time.

"What a fool I've been," he says at last. "The devil is right here in front of me and I never saw him."

Esther stares at him, wondering if he even heard what she just said.

"No, *He* isn't the devil," Esther corrects.

"How do you know?"

"I just know."

"Believe me, the devil can assume any form it wishes," he says, wandering back and forth in a daze. "It all makes sense now. I've been consumed with lust. Uncontrolled desires. It is the devil that is causing this. The devil is making you say these things. It's all lies."

Esther suddenly sees a shift come over Pedro. His whole energy seems to darken and grow dim. His eyes turn cold and his body grows stiff. He does not seem like himself any more. And then she suddenly knows what is going on. At last she sees.

"Now you are possessed by Him," she says fearfully, backing away from him.

"No, no," he whispers. "I am seeing things clearly now. I *was* possessed by the devil. But now I see."

He walks toward her, holding out his hand to her, as if to draw her into his world. But she continues to back away from him.

"No, you aren't!" she screams. "Now you're possessed by Him! Stay away from me!"

Pedro stops chasing her, confused again.

"Come back with me," he implores.

"No," she says fearfully. "You come back. Come back to *me*, Pedro."

They stare at each other, suddenly at an impasse. For a moment, their eyes lock and they see each other clearly for the first time. Something powerful passes between them. Then a cloud seems to pass over them, obscuring their vision, and the moment is gone and they are back where they started again. Finally, Esther turns and walks away. Pedro watches her disappear down the path and then he has to take a long walk himself to think about what just happened.

Cougar 17'

Cougar moon

The clouds have returned after a long absence and threaten to unleash another storm upon the village. After the long string of warm, sunny days, it seems like an unwelcome houseguest returning for a few more days, after overstaying their welcome just two weeks ago. Esther runs back inside the house for her warm cloak before going back outside. She is going to the Ruok council today. Things feel as if they are coming to a climax at last. She can feel a change in the air and she is ready for it, even if it terrifies her. She walks through the commons, watching people lashing down tarps and fixing holes in roofs, just in case there is another storm.

Esther steps inside the assembly house and finally gets a good look at all of the Ruoks together. She is rather surprised to see how few there are. She had expected fifty to a hundred people, but there are only nine people present, and many she already knows. Squirrel, Merlu and Numei all stand in a tight knit group, talking about their trip up here. When they see her, they all wave her over and welcome her with open arms. As they talk, she feels as if she is having a reunion with her oldest friends, although she has known all of them only a short time. They share their adventures of the past days, but Esther is vague about what she has been doing and merely suggests that she has been wandering around the village, thinking a lot. Which is more or less true.

"Such a poor turnout," Merlu says, shaking his head, "and many of us aren't even Ruoks yet - like the four of us."

"Ruoks travel a lot," Squirrel argues. "They are hard to get together. And I never got the word past the Swan tribe."

"There aren't many Ruoks past the Swan tribe."

Suddenly a man walks up to them, and Numei touches him lightly on the shoulder.

"This is Tumock," she says with a flourish. "Tumock, you know Squirrel. And this is Merlu and Esther."

Esther smiles shyly, embarrassed to be around such a great man as Numei has made him out to be. He is not what Esther expected at all, although he is impressive enough. He has an angular, bony face, like a skull wrapped in skin, and a lean, well-built frame. But it is his eyes that really show off who he is. His eyes are incredibly friendly and seem to take in the whole world at once.

When he looks at Esther, she can feel the warmth emanating from those expansive orbs.

"I just recently arrived from a Modoc village near the great mountain," he says, looking at both the new faces at once. "I walked two days through the snow and then three more across mountains and valleys. What a journey! The great mountain is breathtaking this time of year. What a wonderful people those Modoc are! So hospitable and full of life! I was there for over a month and saw so many beautiful ceremonies. What brings you here? I haven't seen either of you before."

They both say that they came for the meeting and he nods his head rapidly. Then Merlu asks him a question about the Modoc and is treated to a lengthy tale about some great celebration he attended that lasted for days. He is still talking to his attentive audience, when Numei pulls Esther away from the group.

"Come with me to meet Ulupi," she says. "This celebration is in her honor. Ulupi is one of the oldest people in the Twelve Tribes. Some say that she is one hundred years old."

Esther is ready to believe it. The woman is positively ancient. She sits hunched over, peering up at the people milling around her through one squinty eye. But there is something about her that radiates tremendous power, even though her body is emaciated. She has the eye of a seer. Numei sits down before Ulupi, who stares at her a while before finally recognizing her.

"My eyes are poor. But you look like Numei?"

"It is me, Ulupi," she says, giving her a gentle hug.

"How many years has it been? How different you look."

"I have not seen you in many years."

"It is good to see you, Numei. You look very well."

They clasp hands in friendship, and then stare at each other in silence. Numei is glad to see that although Ulupi may seem fragile, her energy is as powerful as ever. Finally Ulupi stares into the fire and stays lost in it for many minutes.

"Where is Tumock?" Ulupi asks at last. "He has been gone all winter. Is he here?"

"He is here."

"Good."

"This is Esther. She is my juwanna."

Esther is about to correct Numei, but the look of joy on Ulupi's face stops her. Ulupi claps her hands together joyously.

"Happy news," Ulupi says cheerfully. "I am glad that the Ruoks will continue when I am gone. I am glad you have decided to continue the line, Numei! I have given much thought to our dwindling numbers."

Ulupi grabs Numei's hand tightly. Numei is surprised that one so old can have such a tight grip. The veins in her hand bulge out all over her knotted fingers.

"We must go on."

"We will, Ulupi."

"Times will change for us. I have seen it. We need a new generation to lead the people. Ruoks must regain their influence in the tribes.

"Nobody listens to Ruoks any more."

"They will again. Soon they will have no choice and they will turn to us for guidance. We must increase our numbers and our focus."

"You had a dream of this?"

"I did. A waking dream."

"Child, come here," Ulupi says, fixing her eyes on Esther. "I cannot see very well. Why do you stand so far away?"

Esther timidly sits down next to Numei, nervous to meet such a powerful woman. Ulupi squints at her in the low firelight. She feels Esther's face with her hands, and her mouth cracks into a toothy smile.

"I like her," she says, rubbing Esther's cheek tenderly. "A good choice, Numei."

"I agree," Numei says with a big grin.

"Thank you," says Esther.

"What is your name?"

"Esther."

"How old are you, Esther?"

"I'm about twenty-two years old. I'm not sure exactly...."

"Twenty-two. A young flower. Someday, young juwanna, you will be an old Ruok like me - if you train hard, that is - and you will speak to the young ones like I am. Pay close attention in this meeting, that you may tell them about it. Pay close attention all your days. Forget nothing."

"I will."

"Good. I know you will. I am glad to meet you, Esther. You remind me of myself many years ago."

"Thank you."

"What tribe are you from, Esther?"

"I am not from any tribe."

"She was born to the Twelve Tribes," Numei explains. "But she grew up in a Spanish mission."

Ulupi's mouth pops open and she stares at Esther with great surprise.

"She grew up among the Spanish?"

"Yes."

Ulupi closes her eyes for a moment, seeming to be overwhelmed by thoughts. Finally she opens her eyes and gives Esther another toothy smile.

"That is good. That is very, very good."

"No, it wasn't," Esther says, correcting her.

"No?"

"She was mistreated," explains Numei. "She was nothing more than a slave."

"Suffering is not always bad, although it is always hard. We need one who understands these people. You will be our link with them."

"I will?"

"Yes. That is so, great-granddaughter."

"You remind me of someone I met," Esther says, suddenly making the connection. "Her name is Yatsa. Do you know her?"

Ulupi's eyes grow very bright.

"Yatsa?" she says, cackling gleefully. "Yatsa is my sister. We trained together, so very long ago. It has been so long since I have seen her. I am sad that she and I shall never meet again in this life, and so you must tell me everything about her."

"Is she your real sister?" asks Numei.

"No, no," says Ulupi impatiently, still staring at Esther.

Esther tells her everything about her experience with Yatsa. Numei has heard this story before, so she wanders off, but Esther has Ulupi's undivided attention. Ulupi seems especially interested to learn that the Spanish priest in the story is the same one that has recently come to Cougar village.

"How is this priest?" she asks. "Does he seem different?"

"He hasn't changed," Esther says. "He's still..."

"What?"

"...very confused."

"How so?" she asks, turning her head slightly.

Esther suddenly wants to speak of her recent problems very much. She has a feeling that if there is anybody who could understand it and provide some insight, it is Ulupi. She begins to tell her about the things she has been seeing and feeling this past month. Ulupi sits very quietly and says nothing during the entire tale. When Esther finishes, she wonders if Ulupi is still awake.

"Ulupi," asks Apali, coming over and touching the silent woman on the shoulder, "are you ready to begin?"

Ulupi waves her away peevishly. Apali nods and leaves her alone. And then Esther knows that Ulupi is indeed awake and has heard all of it.

"What should I do?" Esther asks, after a long silence.

"You know what must be done. Cast out this spirit," Ulupi says.

"But I don't know how. It is very powerful. That thing I saw in the forest coming here-"

"No, no," Ulupi corrects, "The thing you saw was not this spirit you must cast out. That was a messenger. It was the butterfly spirit that brings knowledge."

"What is the message?"

"You got the message. That is why all of this is happening."

Esther nods.

"The spirit that infects your priest is not the spirit that infects you," Ulupi adds.

"How do you know?"

"We Ruoks believe that spirits are everywhere and they are different for each person. They do not have unlimited powers, nor is there one that rules the rest. We create these spirits or call them to us. Sometimes they are forced upon us, but they must have our cooperation to connect with us. And then they haunt us until we let go of them or cast them out."

"How does it work?"

"Child," she says, grabbing her arm in the vice grip that she used on Numei, "to ruok is to discover for yourself how it works."

Esther nods, disappointed.

"If you are patient, the answer will come," she says, releasing her arm. "I would like to help you, but I have not the strength anymore."

"Is there anybody here who can help me?" she asks.

"I believe that they already have. Numei...Apali...Ulupi have all helped Esther. Now she must ruok for herself."

"But I don't want to be a Ruok," Esther insists.

"Neither does your jodhai, Numei," Ulupi says, with a great laugh. "You are perfect for each other."

"What about Pedro?" Esther asks. "What should I do about him? I fear that he is a danger to me."

Ulupi laughs again.

"He is very confused and his thoughts are dangerous. But remember, my sister, Yatsa has left her mark on him. He is not the same person that he was before she healed him. He is now caught between two worlds. Yatsa's work is subtle, but it is very thorough. You can use that against him, if it becomes necessary."

"It grows late, Ulupi," Apali says, coming forward. "Shall we begin?"

"We already have," Ulupi says irritably. "Don't be so dull, juwanna."

Apali nods, abashed, and withdraws. Esther smiles, amused to hear Apali referred to as juwanna by her old teacher.

"My friends," Apali says, finally steering the meeting toward a semblance of order. "We have called you all here to say goodbye to our eldest jodhai. Ulupi has been our teacher, our leader and our spirit for a long time. She remembers the ones that came before us and has been our link to their knowledge. But her time is over. Tomorrow, she will go on the long journey into the unknown. This is the last night that she will be here to guide us."

Apali stops speaking and looks sadly and fondly at her old jodhai. Esther feels a tremor in her heart and she stares at Ulupi with shock. Ulupi looks around the room and nods to herself. The younger ones are shocked and dismayed, but the older ones don't seem the least bit surprised. Perhaps they have seen her decline over the years.

"Our center pole is toppling to the earth," continues Apali. "We are gathered to find a new one. But now I will let Ulupi speak."

Ulupi slowly rises on shaky legs. She looks about the room and wets her dry lips.

"I see some new faces. That is good, because there are few old ones left. Our ranks have diminished and much of our knowledge has faded into obscurity. The Ruoks have become obsolete among our people. That is our fault. I, too, have become obsolete. That is the fault of time."

"Before I fade and disappear, I want to look at the future with you. And I want to say one thing to all of you young ones gathered here. I know that few of you are committed to our ways. There are few elders to guide you anymore, as there once were in our prime. The Ruoks have fallen into a sleep. But I have had a waking dream. The future of the Twelve Tribes depends on everyone here in this room, for the Twelve Tribes are not strong enough for the future. The Ruoks must return!"

She stops to catch her breath and everyone sits silently as she wheezes and coughs. With the help of Apali, Ulupi sits back down and closes her eyes and tries to regain her equilibrium. Everyone begins talking quietly, discussing the vision.

Suddenly an argument breaks out between Onu and Merlu.

"Who invited you to this meeting, young man?" intones Onu.

"I came with my friends," he says, indicating Numei, Squirrel and Esther. "Don't you recognize me, Onu? I'm Todi's son."

Onu shakes his head negatively. Merlu is not surprised that Onu doesn't recognize him. Onu never comes out in public.

"But you are not a Ruok, are you?" Onu asks, glaring at him. "You have no jodhai?"

"No."

"This is a meeting for Ruoks only. You'll have to leave."

"I didn't know that the future of the Twelve Tribes was invite only," Merlu says with a mischievous grin.

"Don't act wise with me, young man."

"I came here to become a Ruok."

"You must be accepted by a jodhai first. You do not choose us. We choose you! That is how it works."

"I choose myself."

Onu just glares at him.

"Didn't you hear what I said?" Onu finally says, pointing at the door.

"Are you sure that you're a Ruok?" Merlu says, losing his own temper. "You don't seem very wise to me."

The old man begins spluttering and raging. He curses at Merlu and threatens to throw him out on his behind. Merlu dares him to do it. Finally, Apali has to break up the argument.

"Please, stop arguing," she says diplomatically. "Let us not make Ulupi's last night so violent."

"Ask this fool to leave," splutters Onu.

"It is you who are the fool," says Ulupi in a loud voice.

The old man turns around, surprised.

"You have become impossible, Onu," Ulupi says, with fire in her eyes. "I am glad I said that to you before I go on my journey tomorrow. Perhaps you should make your own journey."

Onu's mouth works up and down in shock. He is unable to believe what he is hearing. He looks as if he wants to curse her out too, but he will refrain for the sake of her last night on earth. And he knows that everyone here would defend her.

"Old ones like Onu are the reason that the Ruok have become obsolete," declares Ulupi. "He has become arrogant, conservative and stubborn, and he makes rules to hold back progress."

"Go into the woods and rot, old crone!" Onu barks.

"In time," Ulupi says. "But first I will have my say. And I say that the Ruoks must reinvent ourselves. We need to come up with a whole new way of recruitment and training. The world is changing and we must change with it."

She takes a deep breath and stares at Apali.

"I wish for Apali to become the head of the Ruoks after I am gone. She is my juwanna and she knows my mind better than anyone. She will be a fitting replacement."

Apali stares at her with great surprise.

"Me?"

"Yes, Apali."

"I don't want to," Apali says with a slight stutter. "I thought Onu was next in line-"

"Onu is next in line to die," Ulupi says in a harsh voice.

"Ulupi –" Apali gasps.

"I'll see you in the ground first!" shouts Onu, glaring at her with a trace of a smile. "Then I'll die with a smile on my face."

"Please stop arguing –" implores Apali.

"I am too old to beat around the bush," Ulupi says. "Look around you, Apali. There is nobody else to do it. We are nearly extinct."

"What about Tumock?" asks Apali.

Ulupi laughs.

"Tumock has no patience for details. And besides, on the paths that he travels, I doubt any other man would want to go."

Tumock laughs heartily.

"It's true, Apali," he says. "I'd make a terrible leader."

"No *man*, perhaps..." whispers Numei conspiratorially to Esther.

"I could never fill your moccasins," Apali says humbly.

"I wish for my moccasins to be buried with me," says Ulupi somberly. "You must begin to fill your own shoes now, juwanna." Ulupi holds out her hand and waits for Apali to take it. "I know you can do it, juwanna," she whispers, just loud enough for Apali alone to hear.

Apali nods quietly, but she doesn't speak.

"You will need help," Ulupi adds. "My sister Yatsa had a juwanna once. Her name was Kenda. Yatsa told me she had great power. I don't know what happened to her. Find her."

Ulupi closes her eyes and breathes deeply.

"Thank you, Ulupi," says Apali seriously. "If it is everyone's wish that I become Chief Jodhai, then I will do my best to live up to the incredible example that Ulupi has set. I have some ideas I would like to share with you, while you are all here –"

"Hold on a minute," Ulupi snaps, opening her eyes again. "You'll have plenty of time for speeches when I'm gone. I'm not dead yet, you know."

"Sorry," Apali apologizes, trying to hide her irritation at being interrupted. "Please continue."

"I have saved the best for last," Ulupi says, giving Apali a humorous smile. "I have a surprise for all of you. Apali, will you call Hamm in here."

"Who is Hamm?"

"I'm sorry. Didn't I mention him before?"

"No," says Apali accusingly.

"Well, I wanted him all to myself for a few days," says Ulupi, chuckling. "I had many questions for him first. You will have plenty of time with him."

Tumock goes outside and shouts out for Hamm. A good fifteen minutes pass, and he continues to shout, but nobody appears. Everyone begins to give Ulupi the eye, as if she had gone completely senile. But finally, a man appears at the door. All eyes turn toward him and stare at him with disbelief. At first glance, the man appears to be some sort of ghost from the spirit world. He has long, curly red hair and a thick, red beard. His skin is pale and dotted with freckles. He wears a traveling cloak of strange design and tall moccasins bound with criss-crossing strips of leather. He walks slowly into the hall, aware of the effect his presence is having on the meeting.

"This is Hamm," announces Ulupi. "He showed up a few days after your Spanish priest caused such a commotion in the village. He's another survivor from that massacre. Luckily, there are still a few people left in this village with some sense, and he was brought to me before subjecting him to the scrutiny of the whole tribe."

Numei comes forward and touches him on the arm.

"He is human," she says, nodding slowly.

The man laughs and nods his head slowly, trying to decide if she is joking.

"Aye. Last I checked."

"Your skin is so strange," Numei says, holding his arm in her hand and staring at it with disbelief. She touches his red hair in amazement, and brings him closer to the fire to get a better look at it. "Look! His hair is the color of the leaves that fall from the trees in autumn."

He warms his pale hands by the fire, while Numei continues to examine his hair and clothes. Everyone in the room stares at him with silent amazement.

"Me name is Hamish, but everyone calls me Hamm. Forgive me poor Spanish. I am still learning." He takes a moment to look around the room, wondering if everyone understands him. "I traveled up here with that unfortunate Spanish party, but I am no Spaniard. I came as a guest of the Spanish priest."

"You don't look or dress like them," remarks Tumock. "And your accent is very odd."

"Aye. Me homeland is Scotland."

"Where is that?" asks Apali.

"Europe."

Apali puts her hands to her mouth in surprise.

"I have come a long way to find your people. I was sent here by a group of men who have heard of you. They asked me to see you with me own eyes."

"You have heard of us?" Apali repeats. "In Europe?"

"What information do you have?" asks Onu, frowning.

"I belong to a very old sect called the Ancient Druid Order. There are certain members of the order who have known about you for a long time. There is a letter, a very old parchment, written by a man named Jeren. He was a Scottish man like me, and he was an astrologer and claimed to be a druid. He came to the new world a long time ago on a Spanish ship. He had certain revelations...and never returned. The letter is strange and full of havering – nonsense – and it was long assumed that he was a madman. Then a few years ago, we came by a letter written by a Spanish priest, who spoke of your people. I have been sent to determine if you are real, and are true descendants of that man Jeren. Ulupi says that you are. I have found the people of Jeren."

There is utter silence in the room. Hamm self-consciously turns back to the fire and stares into the flames. He takes off his robes, revealing a torn, linen shirt and woolen pants. He seems very uncomfortable, as if the people he traveled so hard to find make him very nervous.

"And you are not at all what I expected," he mumbles into the fire.

"This is incredible," exclaims Apali.

"That's nothing," Ulupi says, cackling. "Tell them the other part."

"What other part?" Hamm asks, confused.

"Tell them about sign shifting."

"Aye," he says, nodding his head. "That's the thing."

He takes a moment to drink from a water skin that was hidden somewhere within his robes. The water glistens on his beard, but he doesn't bother to wipe it off.

"Jeren spoke of the ability to sign shift. To become any zodiac sign at will. He claimed that he could do this. Said that he would teach his people to do it. I am an astrologer myself, and I have thought about this ability on my long journey to this place. I imagined that everyone here would have this talent." He stares at all the faces in the room. "But Ulupi tells me that nobody can do this. Not even the…um, the-"

"Ruoks," says Apali, helping him out.

"Aye. Ruoks."

"Jeren said that?" asks Apali incredulously.

"That's strange," muses Merlu. "He did not mention that in the books that he wrote for our people."

"Very strange," agrees Apali.

"It has been a long journey to find you. On the way, there was much time for quiet reflection," continues Hamm, warming up to his audience at last. "And then, I had a vision. I saw a great wheel in the sky. And in the vision I became one with that wheel. Or should I say, it became one with me."

"Interesting," says Apali. "And what does that mean?"

"I learned to sign shift."

"Show them," says Ulupi, sitting up straight to give him her full attention.

Hamm starts going through the various signs, but everyone gets confused because they are not sure where he is or what he is doing. So then Ulupi suggests that he start over at Hawk and every time he changes signs, he snaps his fingers. Hamm nods and then he snaps his fingers.

"I am starting with Aries and I will go in order," he says, in a loud voice.

"They don't know what you mean," says Ulupi gently. "Use the names I taught you."

"Oh yes," he nods. "I will start with…Hawk."

He snaps his fingers again and says the word 'Beaver'. His whole demeanor changes. He appears to have become more solid in his posture, and his eyes seem like the eyes of a different person – a more serious and practical person. Then he snaps his fingers again and he says 'Jay'. His eyes become lighter and twinkle brightly. Apali asks him a question and he answers as a Jay might answer. He makes a silly joke and moves his hands animatedly and everyone laughs. Then he snaps his fingers and says 'Bear'. He stands there and answers more questions from Numei, and he could easily be mistaken for someone of the Bear tribe. His eyes appear to be weighted down with deep sorrows and he no longer smiles. He reminds Esther of Kobe for a moment. And then he snaps his fingers again and says the word 'Eagle', and his posture becomes proud and he reminds her of Garet. He looks around the room to see if everybody is impressed by his skills.

Hamm goes through the entire zodiac and it breaks up the whole meeting. By the end, everyone is amazed at this unique and strange skill. Ulupi claps her hands and shouts gleefully.

"I believe that this is what the Ruoks need to become relevant again," announces Ulupi. "We must all learn to do this, and then we must teach it to everybody else."

"That is impressive," agrees Apali. "Can you teach us how to do this, Hamm?"

"Nae," says Hamm, looking suddenly confused. "I don't know how to teach it. It just came to me."

"Learn to teach it," says Ulupi.

He nods hesitatingly.

"Take good care of this one," Ulupi says with a gleam in her eye, as she looks about the room. "Keep him close and watch over him. For I believe that this unlooked for talent is a key to unifying the Twelve Tribes."

She seems to doze off for a moment and then she murmurs with her eyes closed.

"And take care of that girl too," she says, pointing at Esther with a shaky finger. "She is interesting also."

Soon, Ulupi is lead home by Apali. The meeting is over, but nobody wants to leave. Everyone corners Hamm and pummels him with questions, but he becomes confused by the barrage of Alano and the strange accents, and he struggles to communicate well enough to satisfy their curiosity. Tumock walks from one to the other, talking to everybody at once. He spends a good deal of time with Esther and invites her over to his house for dinner some time soon. He promises to catch a juicy rabbit just for her. She accepts hesitantly, assuming that Numei will be there also. Tumock is quite a rascal.

Esther meets Hamm briefly. She asks him about Scotland, and he tells her about the 'bonny doons' and the 'great lochs' and other wonders. She has trouble following what he is saying, but she is entranced by his strange accent.

"These redwood trees you have here, lass, are like no tree I have ever seen," Hamm says with wonder. "I think they are the biggest trees in the world. Aye, but they are strange though. There is something about them I can nae predict. Something…mysterious."

"Yes," she agrees wholeheartedly. "They drop sticks on me sometimes. I have to yell at them to stop it."

He laughs. They lock eyes for a moment and she feels herself falling into his eyes. For several moments, neither looks away. Then the moment is broken. Several people suddenly enter the assembly house with instruments, shouting and laughing their greetings. They have been waiting for the end of the Ruok meeting to start a dance to celebrate the new moon. Tumock shouts out for them to get on with it and make a party, and Numei shouts her agreement.

"I have to go," Esther says, suddenly determined.

"Go where?"

"To sleep," she says. "In the redwoods."

"Why?" he asks curiously.

"I can't tell you."

He nods, as if it makes perfect sense that she must keep it a secret.

"But I'll see you again," Esther says quickly. "I hope."

He says goodbye and watches her leave the room. Strangely, he wonders if he *will* see her again. There is something elusive about her. Something ethereal - as if she is a ghost that will disappear forever.

Esther walks through the forest, her blanket wrapped around her body for protection. The night is shrouded in fog, a perfect night to ferret out secrets. She is not looking forward to coming out here again, but she has no other choice. It is the only place that she seems to find inspiration. It is fine walking through the mist, as long as there is open sky above her head. But when she enters the deep forest and it grows pitch black, then she feels the familiar terror creep upon her. She holds her candle lantern aloft and makes her way slowly forward. This is not a night to be out, unless you happen to be crazy. But crazy is what she is lately.

She finally enters a little clearing, throws her burden basket down and takes a rest. Putting the candle down, she stretches her back muscles. She looks down at her hands, not very surprised to see that they look like paws in the darkness. She remembers that Cougar is supposed to help her - or at least Paddlefoot. It's about time they came to help her. She begins to move with catlike grace and she sprawls atop a log lazily. It makes her more comfortable in the darkness and takes away her fear of bears and other wild animals.

Her little spot close to the stream is near. That spot has treated her well so far and showed her many things about herself. She continues to walk until she gets there. Then she lays out her bed for the night. Now for the final step...she blows out the candle and lies down. Now she is stuck here for the night.

She is terrified of something tonight, but it is not the darkness. Nor is it what she might find out about herself. What she is terrified of is much stranger. She is terrified of being alone. This is a new feeling to her. She has never been terrified of being alone before. Usually she prefers it. But she feels empty tonight, as if something is missing. She finds herself thinking of Merlu suddenly and the way their eyes locked.

She has to relieve herself, so she gets up and takes a pee. Somehow she walks right into a sharp branch that pokes her in the eye. Cursing, she holds her hand over it and prays that she did not pierce it. It hurts, but she can still see dim starlight out of it, coming from in between the trees. She lays back down, still holding her eye and wraps herself in her blankets. She obsesses about it for some time afterwards, terrified that she will go blind in one eye. She wishes she could go ask somebody if it looks bad.

Then a voice seems to float from out of the darkness. *Esther, shall I come to keep you company?* The voice seems to come from her left, floating from somewhere far away. She tries to block out everything else but the voice. It seems to come along with a bunch of other noise and she must struggle to make words from out of the mass of noise that is overwhelming her.

"Who are you?" she says to the voice, although she does not say the words but only thinks them.

"It is me."

"Are you...Him?" she asks the voice.

"No."

"Are you...me?"

"No."

Suddenly she knows who the voice is.

"Nani?"

"Yes."

"I thought you had gone a long time ago."

"I've always been with you. Except for now. You've pushed me away."

"I did?"

"You keep pushing me away and then you call me back. Don't you want me around?"

"Yes."

But as Esther speaks, she suddenly realizes that she doesn't want him around anymore.

"No, it cannot be, Nani. You have to go."

"But I've always been there for you. I've always protected you."

"I know," she whispers.

"I love you."

"I love you too."

"Don't send me away."

"You have to go. I need to be alone now."

Nani seems to disappear and she breathes a deep sigh of relief. Then she becomes terrified of being alone and she calls out to him. He returns, and she is no longer afraid. She feels confident and fearless. And then she knows that Nani is once again protecting her. But it is not the same. Because she suddenly understands that the girl who is afraid is herself. The girl who is lonely is herself. It is Nani that is fearless and needs nobody. He has been protecting her all this time, but he has also been interfering in her life. When he is here, she sees the world through his eyes. She has never been entirely herself since he first came to her.

"Esther..."

"You have to go," she says in her thoughts.

"But I love you."

"I love you too," she says, and her eyes fill with tears. "I'll miss you."

"If you send me away, I can't protect you any more."

"I know."

"There are things you don't know."

"I already know Nani. I know I ate bugs and rats raw and drank their blood. I remember now. You don't need to hide that from me anymore."

"There are worse things than that."

She shuts him out. She tries to call back the fear that she feels when he isn't around. It is not easy to do, but she manages to retrieve it. She curls up into a ball and nestles with the fear. Her fear is the power to cast Nani out. She struggles not to let him back in. It is very hard, but she manages to do it.

"I love you…" a faint voice says.

But Esther has no more pity for him. She will not be sweet-talked. Even if she lives with this fear for the rest of her life, it will be better than letting him interfere in her life forever. She opens her eyes, one bleary from being poked. The giant redwoods are watching her. She stares up at them, wishing there were somebody here with her. She puts her hand to her eye, terrified that she will wake up blind. She wants to run to Eliki's house, but it is so dark now. She trembles in the redwood grove for a long time,

Suddenly, she hears a throaty growl, followed by the shriek of a small animal. The animal continues to scream and thrash about wildly. For a moment, it sounds to Esther like the screams of a little girl being eaten. Esther sits up straight and looks out into the night, as if she could see something in the pitch black. That growl sounded like a cougar! She becomes terrified that cougar knows she is there and plans to eat her next. Fears come over her, so strong that she breaks into a cold sweat. She feels as if she is falling through a deep dark tunnel, and she tries to scream, but no sound escapes her lips.

And then she remembers....

She is a little girl again, standing with her mother and father on the beach on a bright sunny day. Her mother holds her hand, as her father talks to a group of Spanish soldiers on horses. She hides behind her mother, not liking the look on the soldiers' faces. Suddenly, one of the soldiers pulls his gun and points it at her father and shouts at him. His father pulls his sword and runs the man with the gun through the gut. The man falls off his horse, screaming. There is utter chaos, as her father grapples with another soldier. And then a gunshot and her father falls to the ground, gushing blood from his stomach. Little Esther screams in horror. Her father groans and reaches out to his family, as if he could still protect them. Then there is another gunshot and her father lies still.

The soldiers descend upon her mother, who is screaming in terror and brandishing a bone knife. They quickly disarm her and pull Esther away from her as she struggles and screams. While one soldier holds Esther away from her mother, the others hold her mother down to keep her from struggling. One of the soldiers begins to take off his pants. Esther holds her hands over her eyes in horror. And then a warm darkness descends upon her, and she knows nothing more....

That was what Nani was so desperately trying to protect her from. That is when he first came to her. He came to protect her from remembering that day, when she was just a little girl and was not strong enough to remember. But now he is gone and the memory is hers again. Esther buries her head in her hands and screams in horror, as the memory plays over and over in her head. She screams until her voice is hoarse, and then she sobs and her body convulses with the force of her tears. She cries until her body is sore from heaving and she is utterly spent.

After her eyes are dry, she feels blessedly numb and she decides to leave this forest. She cannot bear to sit here anymore. She has to get back to the village and be around other people. She begins to walk slowly through the pitch black, holding her hands out. Her paws...she imagines herself a cat…and then she can walk. She moves slowly through the forest with feline grace. Somehow, she manages to get back to the clearing where she stopped and stretched. After an age, she sees lights appear through the deep mist. She begins to run and she doesn't stop until she is once again safe at Eliki's house.

Cougar 18'

Today is the new moon celebration. There will be weddings, babies, parties and all of the usual new beginnings. But for some it will not be so pleasant. Ulupi will be led into the forest this morning and there she will sit until she perishes. That is the traditional way to end the life of an old one. Of course, the rain picks today to make its triumphant comeback after such a long absence. Too bad she couldn't have picked a warm, sunny day to die.

Apali had planned to take Ulupi into the forest and stay with her until the end, but at the last minute Ulupi refuses her and asks Tumock to do it. This makes Apali angry and they have a fight on their farewell meeting.

"I don't want you standing over me, fussing over every little thing," Ulupi scolds. "I just want to be alone and at peace when I die."

"Nobody wants to be alone when they die."

"But everyone is alone when they die."

"It's not right to let you go alone."

"What could happen to me worse than dying?"

Apali cannot think of an answer to that one.

"I'm not afraid, juwanna. And it will be easier for me to leave this body if you are not there."

In the end, Apali cannot refuse her, and their goodbye is bittersweet.

By midmorning, it is drizzling at a steady rate. The tribe had hoped that the clouds would clear and they would be able to hold the new moon celebration outside, but there is no such luck. The whole tribe descends upon the assembly hall instead and spends the morning in decorations, gathering fuel and making food.

Esther is exhausted from her ordeal of the past few weeks. She sits underneath a hut, watching the rain fall. It is enough for her to see the assembly hall from a distance. She'll pop in for lunch, after all the speeches, weddings and everything else is complete. When she peeked her head in earlier, she heard a discussion about the Hupa. The tribe was comparing notes about what they had discovered on their various vision quests and musings over the past two weeks. She quickly pulled her head back outside, before somebody saw her and called her inside, wanting to know more about her life in the mission or whatever. All she wants to do right now is sit and listen to the pouring rain.

She knows now that she is really and truly alive. It was Nani that kept her from seeing it. He hid her past from her. He did it because she wanted him to. Now all the old illusions are turning to dust. Like the illusion that she was a 'suicide'. It is true that she has often wished for death, but when it came down to it, she was willing to do just about anything to keep on living. She was willing to suck the blood of rats and eat bugs and crawl through the mud for days just to keep on living. She was willing to endure a life of slavery among the same people who killed her parents, just to stay alive.

Now the true test begins. She knows who she is and where she came from. She knows that she is alive. Now she has to do something about it.

Pedro wants to talk to Uru before leaving this place. He wants to apologize for his insensitivity the other day and tell her that he cannot be with her because he has taken a vow of celibacy. It seems the only decent thing to do. It takes him awhile to retrace his steps and find her little house again. He finally arrives at the door of her ramshackle hut, falling apart from years of neglect, and knocks.

Nobody answers. Pedro knocks again. Then he goes to wait a short distance away from her door, like he has seen these people do as a sign of respect. He is soaked through and through, but it seems proper penance for his cruelty toward her. He is always willing to do penance for his sins.

Suddenly the door opens. A very tall man appears in the doorway. Shocked, Pedro wonders if she has found another man. He runs through the rain to find out who the man is. But then he recognizes Majes, the man whom he first stumbled upon when he came to the village.

"Come in," says Majes.

Pedro enters. The man is piling Uru's things together into a big basket. He has all of her shell money and her big rabbit skin blanket that was so warm to sleep under. He begins loading her pots and kitchen supplies into another basket.

"My mother told me about you," he says in a depressed voice.

"I must talk to her," Pedro says gravely. "I came to apologize."

"No matter," says Majes with a shrug. "It makes no difference any more."

"It does to me."

"Apology accepted," says Majes offhandedly.

He indicates the baskets he has loaded up with her things.

"This is what I want. You can have anything else that you find."

"Where is Uru?" Pedro asks, confused. "I want to apologize to *her*."

"Probably dead by now," says Majes, in a quiet voice.

"What?"

"She went to cast herself into the ocean."

"She told you this?" he asks, his voice rising in a horrified whine.

"She left a note."

"And you haven't gone to look for her?"

"She said this is what she wanted. She wasn't any more use to the tribe. Couldn't get a man. Couldn't work like she used to. Draining off the tribe. She said that she wanted to do the noble thing, so the tribe would think highly of her, instead of remembering her as a burden."

Pedro stares at his calm demeanor, trying to decide if the man is having a laugh at his expense. He finally decides that the man is serious.

"And this doesn't bother you?"

"Of course, I am sad," he says. "She was my mother. I will mourn for the proper time."

Pedro makes an audible gasp.

"Her son?" he asks, with a tremble in his voice.

The man nods absentmindedly. Pedro is dumbstruck as the man continues to collect her things. What is wrong with this man? Why does he not go to look for his suicidal mother and stop her?

"Do you know which way she went?" Pedro asks.

"Why?"

"I want to help her. I want - "

"It's too late," Majes says quickly, as if he is done with the whole affair. "She no longer has the will to live. She has chosen to sacrifice herself for the good of all. Leave it alone."

"The ocean, you said?" Pedro asks finally.

"I think so."

The man finishes collecting her things together and places them in a pile by the door.

"Take what you want *now*," he says, as he picks up the baskets and steps out into the rain. "I'm going to burn the house down as soon as it stops raining."

Pedro races down the path toward the bay. With a son like that, it's no wonder the woman wanted to kill herself. Pedro has never seen such cruelty in his life. He has seen men murder other men, without a flinch, but he has never seen a man let his poor mother go kill herself without trying to stop her.

Pedro knows that he too has played a part in this tragedy. When he rejected her, that must have been the last straw. She realized that there was nobody who loved her and would ever love her. Pedro moves faster, hoping to right a tremendous wrong. He prays to God to let this woman live long enough for him to throw his arms around her and tell her that she is loved.

When he finally reaches the bay, he sees no sign of her. He anxiously scans the beach. He scans the water. She could be anywhere. Cursing, he starts walking up and down the edge of the bay. He calls her name in a loud voice, becoming more and more desperate. Then something catches his eye. It looks like a body floating a short ways from shore. Without thinking, Pedro takes off his clothes and plunges into the water. It is very cold and he quickly races back to the shore. He stares hard at the body, wondering if it is worth plunging into this cold water to get to a dead body.

But a few seconds later, guilt convinces him to make the sacrifice. He tiptoes into the water again, and with a sigh, enters the deep part. He ignores the cold and starts swimming. By this time he has little hope left, as the body has not moved a muscle since he first saw it. When he reaches the body, he flips it over and stares at the blue, bloated face rimming lifeless eyes and purple lips, and knows that she is absolutely dead.

He puts her cold, clammy hand in his own and kisses it meekly, then drags it back to shore. He gets out of the water with great relief and pulls the corpse up after him. Then he performs the last rights, woodenly, as if in a dream. Shivering and naked, with the rain lashing down on his head, he says the prayers for the dead. Although his body aches from the cold, he does the complete ritual, so she will be sure to get into heaven.

"I'm sorry," he whispers at last. "Mea culpa. On my head, this tragedy lies."

He is not up for a burial, so he pushes her back into the water and lets her go. He watches her float out to the bay and prays for her to float away to a better place than this.

Before he puts his wet clothes back on, he dramatically says the prayer for baptism. Then he jumps into the water, as if re-baptizing himself. Only then does he throw his wet clothes over his goose pimply skin and makes his way back to the village.

He appears from out of the rain, like a wet dog begging for shelter. Pedro stands before Esther, who sits inside a hut in the commons. He is soaking wet and he has a determined expression on his face.

"I'm leaving this heathen land," he says. "This place makes Sodom and Gomorrah seem like the holy city of Rome. You must come with me."

Esther sighs, although she knew that this was coming.

"I'm not leaving."

"You have been saved, Esther. It falls upon my head now to make sure that you remain saved. I'll not leave you here with these savages!"

"I will not go back," she insists. "This is my home."

"Your home is the mission. You told me so."

"These are my people!" she shouts, rising to her feet in a fury. "Your soldiers killed my parents and then you baptized me against my choice!"

"We only wanted to save your soul..." he says, faltering under her rage.

She runs at him and pushes him with fury. Stunned, he falls back a few steps.

"I never asked to join your religion! What good did it do me? So I could be a slave in your stupid mission! Whipped and raped by your priests!"

"Father Fernandez was not a good father," he says desperately, stepping back from her. "These things you say happened to you are not the Christian way! Christ spoke only of mercy and charity! That is all I have ever wanted!"

"Every Christian I have ever met has tried to have power over me! I know it's not in that book of yours, but that's how you act!"

Pedro sighs deeply.

"We are subject to the will of a kingdom. You must understand that. We are forced to operate within its limitations. But that doesn't mean that we of the Church are not pure of heart. We tried our best to protect you from harm. Believe me, it would have been much worse for you without our guidance."

"How stupid you are?" Esther shouts. "Have you heard nothing I've said?"

"I - I am sorry to say this. But if you do not come back with me, then I will have to tell the soldiers that I have seen a runaway neophyte up here. They will come after you. I will order it."

Esther glares at him. She wants to kill him.

"I have no choice," he whispers, ashamed of his words. "Forgive me."

"Ulupi told me that you were changed by Yatsa," she says, struggling to stay calm. "But I do not see it. You seem crazier than you were before."

As she stands there in the rain, she suddenly has an idea. She remembers how Ulupi told her to use Yatsa's work against him. And she suddenly knows how. She takes a moment to wipe a wet lock of hair from her face, and then she fixes him with a cold stare.

"Back in Raccoon village, Yatsa baptized *you*. On that day, the church of the Ruok took responsibility for *your* salvation. They say that I am a Ruok now, which means that I am now responsible for your salvation. And so now you will know what it is like to be a neophyte. You will never be allowed to leave here! This is your mission, Pedro! You will be a slave to the Cougar Tribe. You will learn our ways and you will never be allowed to go back to your world."

She laughs cruelly at his expression of utter disbelief. "You must be re-trained, Pedro, because *you* are the savage! You will be taught the ways of the civilized."

"How can you hold me here?" he shouts. "You have not the power. Nor the right!"

He begins to back away, but Esther follows him.

"The word will be spread throughout the Twelve Tribes. I will tell everyone how your people killed my parents in cold blood. I will tell them how you mean to take our land. You will be our enemy. If you try to escape, I'll have you hunted down. If you are caught on our paths alone, you will be killed. You might risk wandering through the trackless forest to get home, although that would be very difficult Pedro. There are tribes more ruthless than the Hupa, you know, and they all hate the Spanish by now. And you have no skills as a hunter or a fighter."

"I'll get back somehow," he shouts.

They have passed near to the assembly hall and Esther starts screaming.

"Help! Help!"

Several people run out of the hall and Esther waves them over. Soon they are surrounded by many people. To Esther's relief, Squirrel and Merlu are two of those who ran out.

"Grab him," she shouts. "He must not be allowed to leave here. He means to go back and tell the Spanish to build a mission here. He will order them to convert you all and make slaves of you."

"That's a lie!" shouts Pedro, but rough hands have already grabbed hold of him.

Esther suddenly leans in close to him and the look in her eyes makes his heart cold. They are like daggers of fire, lashing out at him. She grabs his face in her hands and puts her face right next to his so he will not miss a word.

"I am a heathen, Pedro de la Cueva," she hisses. "I am bound to avenge my parents, who were killed by your people. And *you* will pay for their death!"

It all happens quickly. Pedro finds himself tied tightly inside one of the huts in the commons. While Esther goes inside the assembly hall to talk about him, Pedro is left alone to watch the rain lash down and ponder this new horror. Bound like a prisoner, many miles from a home that he will probably never see again. A slave to a heathen race. Wishing he had never come to this brutal land, he hangs his head and cries bitter tears.

Esther stays up most of the night, dancing to the crazy music in the assembly hall. She dances with absolute abandon, enjoying the spastic rushes of energy that course throughout her body. She thought she was tired, but now she cannot even remember why she ever wanted to sleep in her whole life. The music goes on for hours and she doesn't stop until the music stops first. Then she walks home in the late night drizzle, thoroughly exhausted, but with a big smile on her face.

"It's fun to be a heathen," she shouts out when she passes the hut where Pedro is tied. "You should try it."

But Pedro is not there. He has been moved into a house with a fire by some compassionate soul. She shouts it out louder, so he'll hear it wherever he is, and then she goes home and crashes into a dead sleep.

Hawk 0'

Raccoon moon

Esther and Numei sit in the house of Tumock, hiding from the cold, grey morning. The fire is stoked up high and the door closed against the cold. Naked and comfortably seated on a bearskin rug, they are protected from the outside cold and rain in their cozy little womb. Numei teaches Esther how to make moccasins for the coming spring. Her current footwear is lined with thick rabbit fur, which is perfect for the cold, but her spring moccasins will be made from a light deerskin for when the weather turns hot. Esther holds it against her foot, while Numei cuts the skin to exactly the shape of her foot.

Numei waits for the weather to turn nice, so she can begin her journey home. She says that she has to get back home to Horim, who is either very worried about her disappearance or furious that she has been gone so long and missed her time to get pregnant. She is also feeling guilty about her little fling with Tumock (which she has admitted to at last) and is afraid that Horim will find out. But Esther senses something else in Numei's desire to go that she cannot quite figure out. There is something that Numei is not saying.

She has been trying to talk Esther into traveling back with her instead. She thinks that Esther should settle down in Wolf village, become her juwanna, and learn the ways of a Wolf Healer. But Esther is adamant about staying put for a long deserved vacation from the road. She doesn't necessarily want to live in Cougar village forever, but she is not ready to decide what to do next. The truth is she has no idea what to do next. She likes the idea of just puttering around this place for a while, figuring things out.

"I know the perfect man for you," Numei promises, sawing at the tanned skin with her knife. "I'll introduce you when you come for a visit. I know you'll like him."

Esther nods and agrees to come soon, although she knows that she will stay here for many months before leaving. She feels at home here. Everybody here knows her and likes her, and they will make sure that she is well fed and has a place to stay.

There is an old saying among the Twelve Tribes. All the strays and lost souls somehow float up to the surface and end up at the Cougar tribe. And that is certainly she. And she even has a pet now to keep her company. One of the stray cats - the orange one from Eliki's house - has adopted her and has taken to following her around whenever she goes to the commons or Eliki's house. She calls her Nani, which is both a tribute and her own private joke.

The door blows open, and Tumock walks in. Despite the cold and rain, he is dressed only in a rabbit skin cloak and nothing more. He is barefoot too. Although he is soaked from head to foot, he is in very good spirits and doesn't seem to notice the cold. He carries two dead rabbits in one hand, and a sharp spear in another. He hangs the rabbits on a hook, places the spear against the wall, hangs his cloak on another hook and squats next to the fire to dry off.

"I am hungry," he announces.

"Would you like some dried salmon?"

"No, no," he says, shaking his head in a circle. "I wish for no more dried foods. It is fresh meat I want, or none. I'll cook up these rabbits."

Numei tells Tumock about her decision to leave when the weather turns good and about Esther's decision to stay on with the Cougar tribe for a while. Tumock smiles hugely, in genuine amazement. He stares at Esther, as if seeing her for the first time. He seems very pleased and she feels all her lingering doubts go out the window.

"Wonderful, wonderful, that is a great idea. It is the flow at work, obviously. Couldn't have come at a better time. She will be a great help to us. I'll take her under my wing and show her the ropes, just like I did for you once."

"Thank you," says Esther, wondering what he means by 'show her the ropes'.

"I'm going up north this spring with the trader's ship," he says a moment later, looking at Esther. "Why don't you come with me?"

"Why?"

"I am going to the land of the Chinook. I heard rumor of a company of men that came there recently. They came from the empire in the far east, and carry many strange medicines and much knowledge. I mean to make contact with them and learn all about their people."

He must mean Lewis and Clark.

"That sounds dangerous Tumock," Numei says. "The Chinook are very aggressive."

"It's true."

"I don't think you should go," she says, worried.

"Why not?"

They look at each other for a long time without words. Esther sees something in Numei's face that she has never seen before and she suddenly understands the thing that she has not been able to place in Numei's behavior. Numei is in love with Tumock. And Tumock loves her too. That is what Numei was trying to hide, from herself as well as Esther.

"Would you like to come?" he asks, with a smile.

"You know I cannot," she says, her eyes sad and confused.

Tumock appears sad for a moment himself and then he shrugs it off.

"What about you, Esther? It would be a glorious journey."

Esther shakes her head and repeats her intention to remain here.

"Well, then, you can stay here at my house and look after it for me," he intones solemnly.

"Really?" she asks, excitedly.

"Of course. I told you that I'm taking you under my wing. You are my baby bird now. My nest is your nest."

Then suddenly, Tumock hands the dead rabbits and the knife to her.

"You skin them," he says with a sly grin. "It will be your first task as a baby bird.

He laughs and goes outside to gather more wood. Esther looks crestfallen, wondering if she is being taken advantage of. She stares at Numei, wondering if she has to do whatever he says. Numei chuckles and pats her on the back.

"You asked for it."

"He is strange," muses Esther, settling in to the task. "He seems rather reckless. Traveling all that way north to find a couple of people who may or may not be there when he arrives."

"He is fanatically spontaneous and brilliantly daring. He follows all of his impulses as they come, without any hesitation. But he used to be very reckless. When he was young, I heard horror stories of the things he did. He was a trickster and a bully. He would steal from his friends and get into fights with them. But then the Ruoks got a hold of him and straightened him out."

Numei tells Esther a funny story about his first day of training and how he was so much trouble for his jodhai, who finally ordered him into a freezing lake in the middle of winter. His jodhai wouldn't let him come out until he could stand there quietly for ten minutes without saying anything.

"I spent almost a half an hour in that lake," complains Tumock, walking in just then with a stack of wood. "It almost killed me. I begged and pleaded with him to let me out and he laughed and started counting all over again. But it taught me a lesson. I sat in the sweat lodge for an hour after that and my body was so cold it couldn't break a sweat. I always did what he told me after that."

He continues to talk about his experiences in training with his jodhai as he stacks wood on the fire. Soon the hut is blazing hot. Esther finishes skinning the rabbits and Tumock spears them on sticks to roast. Then he decides that he must have salt and he disappears out the door to find some, leaving a void of silence behind him.

The rain patters gently on the roof above them, creating a pleasant rhythm. Numei leans over to pull the door closed, trapping all of the heat inside. Esther looks around at the simple hut that will soon be hers and imagines how it would be with all of Tumock's bear and elk furs stacked on top of each other, creating a soft bed that she can snuggle into and listen to the rain patter on her very own roof. The fire crackles merrily what will be her very own fire pit. She thinks that the flow is finally working for her at last.

Hawk 2'

**Swan moon*

The weather improves daily. On a day with blue skies only partially obscured by clouds, Numei prepares to leave. It is a good day to travel, as the full moon will light her way at night. Merlu and Onu will travel with her as far as the Raven tribe, and then Numei will be traveling alone with Timid. Tumock plans to leave tomorrow also and Squirrel is already gone on some unknown adventure. Esther will now be on her own.

Esther makes breakfast for Numei and Tumock, using the last of the leeched acorn flour. They are quiet and say little to each other. But they are very aware of each other's presence, and they seem to be speaking to each other without words. Esther feels alone already, as if neither one of them is aware of her at all.

It occurs to her that she'll have to get all of her own food from now on. Then she remembers that Tumock said he had a little food stored away - a couple baskets of acorns and a wooden box of smoked fish that is supposed to be buried somewhere.

"I hate to ask this," she says, while they are eating. "But I am worried about feeding myself. May I eat your food?"

"Yes. Of course," he says, waving his hand. "Eat all those acorns. Eat the last of the smoked fish. I am tired of that old food."

"I have some tupas saved," she muses. "Where can I buy cheap food?"

"In the forest," says Tumock, waving his hands. "It's all free out there. Go out and take it."

"But I don't know how, really."

"Time for you to learn then," says Numei paternally.

"But who will teach me?" she asks nervously, realizing that her protectors and teachers are all leaving.

"Esther," says Tumock kindly, "it is time for you to trust completely that you will be taken care of. Once and for all, you must realize that you are part of an amazing world in which all things are connected. The world will take care of you, if you open your eyes and look without fear at what is in front of you. If you do that, the flow will show you where you want to go. Repeat that."

"The flow will show me where I want to go."

"That is all you need to know for the moment," Tumock adds and he goes outside to grab a tool.

"I'll miss you," Esther says. "I wish you were staying. I'm going to be all alone up here. It's going to be so dull."

"Me too," agrees Numei, and she gives Esther an affectionate hug. "I wish you were coming back with me. It's going to be a dull journey all by myself."

"I guess we're both going to be bored."

"That's what happens at the end of an adventure," says Numei.

After goodbyes are said, Esther decides to walk to the beach to get her mind off things. She has not actually been to the beach yet, but only to the bay. It takes her a few hours to make the walk and then she finally crests a large sand dune and comes face to face with the great ocean.

Walking along the beach, she watches the powerful waves crash onto shore. The waves here are not gentle, but rise quickly and crash hard. The beach is littered with washed up logs, smooth and slimy piles of stinking seaweed and shells. The wind is strong and brisk and gives her goose bumps.

She walks up to the burnt log that is the boundary of the beach that the Cougar tribe may use. Not far from where she is standing, a couple of Zesti fish from the shore on their part of the beach. They stare at her, but say nothing. She steps on their side of the beach, just for a moment, and then steps back onto her own. She looks to see if they noticed. But they don't seem interested. It is obvious what they are interested in.

It has been a year since she left the mission and wandered out into the world. It seems like a lifetime. She thinks about a conversation last night, when Numei said that Esther had completed a circle of her life and was back where she started. But then Tumock corrected her and said that life was not a circle at all, but a spiral. Endlessly going in circles, with no way to ever reach the end. Esther draws a spiral in the sand and imagines herself slowly walking around it, year after year. The idea is very depressing. She was looking forward to some big finish, when everything would be settled forever and she would live happily-ever-after. But now she sees that was just a fantasy, and she is only a short ways down a very long road.

She walks back before the sun sets. There is supposed to be a party tonight, to welcome the full moon and the coming of spring. She moves at a good pace. When it gets dark, the moon rises like a lantern and shows her the way home. Soon she finds herself back in familiar surroundings. She hears music coming from inside and smells food. But she is tired from her walk and in no mood for a party. Exploring the main circle, she finds a plate of meat that was carried out here and abandoned. She could just take it and then go home and relax in front of a fire. But then she remembers that Tumock told her to be mindful of all opportunities as they come. And this is an opportunity to get to know her new neighbors. So she takes a deep breath and walks through the entrance into the loud, smoky hall. She nervously stands inside the door for a moment, overwhelmed by the loud drumming and the shouts, until her eyes adjust to the gloom. She takes a deep breath, makes a brave smile and walks into the middle of everything.

Full Circle

On the first day of summer, Esther awakens late. She wanders out into the morning and looks up at the sky. It is warm out already and it looks like a hot day is coming. She yawns and stretches, as she listens to the morning birds sing. Then she begins to plan her day out in her head. A dip in the river, and then she'll go into town and pound a few acorns for breakfast. There is a large public granary there and she has been working there all spring, as part of her duties to her new village. Then perhaps she'll go mushroom hunting and take a nap. There's a summer solstice party tonight and she plans to stay out all night long.

But all of her plans vanish in a puff of smoke when she sees them. Numei and Orym are walking toward her hut. She doesn't know who she is more surprised to see, but she knows who she'll greet first. She runs to Numei and throws her arms around her. It is a joyous reunion.

"What are you doing here?" Esther shouts.

"I came up with Orym."

She points at her two stuffed burden baskets hanging from Orym's horse.

"What about Horim?" Esther says, glancing curiously at Orym.

"He went to the ocean to fish and hunt," Numei says. "I met Orym and came up with him to see how things are getting on with my juwanna and Tumock and the Ruoks." She scans the area. "Where is Tumock?"

"He's not back yet."

She nods, disappointed.

"And I came up here to see the look on your face when you hear the news," she adds.

Esther now gives Orym her full attention. He has been staring at her all this time with a shocked expression on his face. Something in his face gives Esther the chills.

"Hello Orym."

"Hello..." he says, still staring strangely at her.

"What do you think?" asks Numei.

He shakes his head affirmatively.

"What is it Orym?" Esther asks, worried. "Is everyone alright?"

"No," he says in a grim voice. "I'm not."

"Are you sick?"

"I think I am going to be," he says. He takes a deep breath and blows out forcefully. "I believe you are my brother's daughter."

Esther gasps.

"You look just like your mother," he says quietly. "It's uncanny. I noticed it when I saw you at the Swans. And now that I see you again, I am sure."

"It could just be a coincidence," Esther says doubtfully, not allowing herself to be swept away just yet.

"I have not seen you for so many years," he says. "Not since you were a little girl. But I feel that it is you. I remember those eyes. They are the eyes of my brother."

"What happened to her? To your brother's daughter?"

"Nobody knows. My brother and his family disappeared many years ago. When she – when you – were just a little girl." He pauses, overcome with deep emotions that he doesn't know what to do with. "I had a dream not long after I last saw you. It was about your mother, Hana, my brother's wife. She was trying to tell me something but I couldn't make it out. And then she suddenly turned into you. I woke up that day with a horrible certainty that you were Hana and Tayo's daughter. It made sense. You are the right age and you look so much like your mother. And of course, your name…. But in the light of day, it seemed like I was just fooling myself. It seemed so improbable. So I did nothing. Like a fool, I returned home with the family. I tried to forget it, but I couldn't shake the nagging feeling. I had to be sure. So this spring I rode all the way back to the Swan tribe to find you. You were long gone and nobody knew where you were. One of the sluts from that Lily Pad said you went to the Wolf tribe. I met Numei there, who told me all about you, and she offered to take me up here."

"I told you I'd find your family, Esther," says Numei triumphantly.

"Her name's not Esther!" Orym insists passionately.

"What was her name?" Esther asks, refusing to believe it. "Your brother's daughter's name?"

Orym swallows and licks his dry lips.

"Este." *(Est – eh).*

Esther feels the whole world begin to melt. She feels dizzy and she leans against a tree for support. She stares at her feet, trying out the name for size. Este. Este. She says it over and over to herself. Until she heard that name, she didn't believe any of it. But now that she hears it, all the pieces fit. She told that name to the fathers and they thought she said Esther. And that became her name. When she looks up again, numbly, she sees that Orym's eyes are beginning to tear up.

"I am so sorry, Este," he says, wiping his eyes, embarrassed. "I should have realized. Esther. Este. What a fool I was not to see it right away. But you looked so different back when I first met you – I mean when I met you as a grownup. You did not look at all like you do now."

He looks down at his feet and curses loudly.

"And to think that I threw you out of my own house, when you needed me the most! I cast you out into the world. Listened to my fool wife! Some uncle I am! But that does not even begin to cover it, does it? Numei has told me some stories on the way up here. When she told me, I could barely stand it. I actually prayed that you were not Este. The things that were done to my own flesh and blood! I cannot stand to think of the things you went through!"

Strangely, she does not feel very emotional. She feels numb, like this is not real, and Orym is sucking up all the emotion for himself. She actually feels sorry for *him*. She has come to terms with what has happened to her by now, but he is learning them for the first time. He suddenly reaches out for her and pulls her forcefully to him. As she puts her arms around him, she can feel the powerful emotions coursing through his body. And for a brief flash, she actually remembers him as a young man. When she was a little girl, visiting her uncle Orym. And then she knows for a fact that she is who he says she is.

"I believe you," she says, when he finally releases her. "You are my Uncle Orym. I do remember you. And I forgive you."

"Thank you," he whispers, wiping at his eyes again.

"You and your family helped me a great deal. Don't feel guilty. You couldn't have known who I was."

"Thank your cousin Dohr for being the only one in the family with any sense," says Orym grimly. "He *knew*...even if he didn't know. He knew that you were to be protected. Thank the spirits that he found you when he did. Thank the spirits for returning you to us." He smiles suddenly. "It is so good to see you alive. To see you returned to us. It is like my brother himself has come back. Like he has been returned to me."

"Tayo," she says, trying out her father's name for the first time. "Hana, my mother. You must tell me all about them sometime."

"I surely will. Anything you want to know."

He grabs her hands protectively in his dirty, calloused hands. He sucks in his breath and stares keenly at her. "What happened to them, Este? To Tayo and Hana? How did you end up in that awful place?"

Este sits down on the worn log by her hut and he sits down next to her. He hangs his head, as she tells him what happened to her parents and to her. He says nothing the entire time she speaks, but she can see that he is devastated. After she is finished speaking, he stands up and walks off alone into the trees. He does not return for a long time, and she sings softly to herself while she waits. Numei, who took a walk to give them some privacy, returns to sit with Este and sing along with her. After many minutes, Orym reappears and strides purposefully toward them.

"Let this not be an unhappy time!" he shouts. "I have not lost my brother today, because I knew in my heart that he was long dead. I have always known this. But today, I am reunited with his daughter after so many years, and that is all that is important."

"Did I have any other brothers or sisters?" Este asks excitedly.

He shakes his head. She nods, a little disappointed to hear that she does not have a secret brother or sister hidden away somewhere.

"Am I from the Hawk tribe?"

"Your father was. Your mother was from the Swan tribe. He moved up there to be with her."

Este laughs out loud and claps her hands joyfully.

"So I have two tribes!"

"But he doesn't remember anything about your chart!" shouts Numei suddenly. "What kind of a fool uncle doesn't remember his own niece's tribe sign? Or even what season of the year she was born in?"

"I am indeed a fool," says Orym, smiling broadly. "But it is not because I cannot remember. Believe it or not, your father and mother never told me. They were rather rebellious. Tayo said he didn't want you weighed down by others' expectations. To tell you the truth, I always suspected you were an inconjunct, and he didn't want anybody to know. You were born up at the Swans and they never would tell me your birthday. I did not even meet you for the first time until you were two years old and already walking."

"I swear I'll find out," Numei says spiritedly. "I'll find your midwife or somebody that knew your parents."

"Don't worry about it," Este says with a smile.

"Aren't you curious?"

"Yes, of course. But I'm more interested in my parents right now."

"You had great parents," says Orym spiritedly. "Your mother was a beauty. She held herself with the grace of a chief. I always wondered how your father got her, considering his eccentricities."

"My father was strange?"

"You could say that," he laughs. "Very strange. And he always did what he wanted, no matter what anybody else thought." He stares at Este for a moment and nods his head. "I can see you inherited that quality from him." He laughs out loud with renewed amazement. "Like I said, he always followed his own path. He was chosen to be a Red Hawk - and he tried it briefly - and then he quit and decided to become a Ruok instead. Wandered up north, and studied with any Ruok he could get to teach him anything. Eventually, he went to live with the Swan tribe, became a medicine and herb gatherer and met your mother."

Este opens her mouth in surprise and looks at Numei. Numei has the same shocked expression.

"You didn't tell me that her father was a Ruok," Numei says.

"Woman, there's a lot I didn't tell you."

"A Ruok," says Numei, smiling. "How interesting. And now you have come full circle."

"Actually, Tayo never called himself a Ruok. He studied with them for a few years, but he did it his way like everything else he did."

"Who does that remind me of?" Numei muses.

Chuckling, Orym goes into her hut to examine where his niece lives. He looks around with distaste at her meager little house with its sparse comforts. He stares up at the ceiling, which needs to be patched and repaired. When he comes out a few moments later, his face is determined.

"I won't have my niece living in such squalor," he announces. "I insist that you come home with me and allow me to give you the home that you never had."

"Thank you Orym, but I can't –"

"Don't you worry about Luce. She'll treat you like her own daughter from now on, or I'll have something to say about it."

"It's not that. I came all this way up here, and I'm comfortable here. And I have friends up here."

"Well, you have family down there," he says, pointing south. "And besides, I want to get to know my niece before –"

He stops speaking suddenly, not wanting to burden her with his dark thoughts.

"What?"

"Never mind that. Please, Este, consider my offer. Let me give you the home you never had."

"Thank you, Orym, but –"

"Let's get one think straight, young lady! I won't have any niece of mine working at that Swan Lily Pad! And I won't have you wandering around like a beggar and living by yourself out in the woods like a bastard child! Your father would never forgive me if I let that happen. I know that he would want you to come home with me and become my adopted daughter. I insist on it."

"No," Este says, becoming uneasy. "I can't go down there. I'm not ready yet."

Orym opens his mouth to say something more. But when he sees the look on her face, he closes his mouth again.

"I'm sorry," he mumbles. "I'm just worried about you."

"I promise to come visit soon. I just can't right now."

"Numei said something about you wanting to be a Ruok?"

Este smiles and shrugs her shoulders.

"I am going to learn a few things at least."

"Take after your father, I see," he says, shaking his head, "in more ways than one."

"We'll take good care of her up here," Numei assures him. "Don't worry about that."

"I'm hungry," he says, waving it away. "We came straight here after we arrived in Cougar village. Let's go get a big meal. Is there a shelter or a public house to eat at?"

"In the commons," says Este. "Let me just get some different clothes on."

Este goes inside the house. Orym pulls Numei aside to speak to her.

"Do you think this is the right place for her? Don't you think she should be with her family?"

"This is the right place for her for now," Numei says.

"A Ruok?" he asks, flabbergasted. "Are there even any more in existence?"

"Not many."

He laughs and shakes his head.

"Just like her father."

As they walk toward the commons, Orym's thoughts are dark and brooding. He thinks about his brother and his family and the things Numei told him on the long ride up here. Things Numei was told by Este. Tayo, his only brother, killed by the Spanish! And Hana - raped and killed! He looks at Este and imagines the things he heard about that mission. The dark and brutal things they did to her there. Before he leaves here, he'll find out who did it. Who raped Este. Who killed Tayo and Hana. Orym is no forgiving Cougar. He's a Hawk. Duty bound to avenge his brother for the things done to his family. Orym unconsciously grips the knife that is strapped to his side. There will be blood spilled before all of this is done. On this day, Orym's life is forever changed. Not only his life, but the life of his family and possibly all of his people. His people have turned a blind eye to the invaders of their land for far too long. They believed the lies of the Spanish and the priests who told them they only wanted to spread words of joy and peace. On this day, the innocence of the Twelve Tribes will be forever shattered. A door has been opened and Orym sees a long, dark and twisted road ahead.

Este walks on clouds, oblivious to the dark thoughts of her uncle. All she can think of is joy. She has found her family. Her friends are at her side. Best of all, she now knows her true name. The girl known as Esther is now dead. She will never go by that name again. From this day forward, she'll be known as Este. Este, daughter of Tayo and Hana. Este, daughter of the Twelve Tribes.

For her a door has been opened too, and she can leave her past behind her as she walks through it. All she sees is a bright, sunny path leading to a beautiful new world that she never dreamed she would ever see.

Afterward

This book is entirely a work of fiction, although it is inspired by historical events. All of the priests were based loosely on historical records, including Pedro, one of the best of all the padres in New California. He is said to have returned to Mexico after his brief term in Mission San Jose and made an early retirement due to poor health. Thus his name was lost to history. I have resurrected him and given him an alternate history. If he would not be pleased by his role, at least his name will be remembered now. A young girl fitting Esther's description was briefly mentioned in Santa Cruz Mission history, although almost nothing was remembered about her other than the fact that she was the very first baptism.

Important contributors:

The wonderful cover was painted and designed by Gabe Leonard. The eyes of his painting tell a story all by themselves.

The book was edited by April Jewel Short, gifted psychic as well as editor. Her devotion to this book went above and beyond the call of duty and helped me see things clearly. She helped me clean up all the mess and I am very grateful for her help.

Most of the information about the California Indians came from a book called Tribes of California. Biases and opinions of the Twelve Tribes about neighboring Indian tribes echo the biases of the California Indians themselves, as recorded in Power's book. Stephen Powers walked across North America, from coast to coast, to record the stories, religions, languages and habits of the California Indian tribes. This book would not be the same without his incredibly detailed history of early California. Power's epic is woefully underappreciated in this day and highly recommended reading.

Also greatly influential to this book was Carlos Casteneda, especially Journey to Ixtlan and The Second Ring of Power for his brilliant descriptions of shamanism; Jan Kerouac for her autobiography Baby Driver, with its vivid descriptions of prostitution and the life of a wandering woman; Loveline (and thousands of brave callers willing to tell everything); and Cassandra Brown for her candid zine A Scream Stuck Inside. Influential books about mission life include Story of the Mission Santa Cruz, by H.V. Torchiana, and selected writings about mission life and the missionaries by Dr. George H. v. Langsdorff and Jean F. G. de la Perouse.

Many of the non-historical events and adventures in this book were inspired by a long list of friends and family. I wish to thank some of those who have a strand in this web. Apologies if I have left anyone out. In no apparent order: Bob, Bev, Melissa, Justin, Ross, Jacob, April, Jessica, Mike, Amber, Nibby, Marc, Esther, Jennifer, Thomas, Aaron, Mel, Kele, Joe, David, Rebecca, Dawn, Jill, James and Suzi. Special thanks to Sarah, Sam, and Annie, my generous patrons.

Appendix

A brief discussion of the Twelve Tribe's astrology system:

The Calendar month of the Twelve Tribes

Each month follows the path of the sun across a constellation. It starts on zero degrees and goes up to thirty. As soon as it hits thirty, it begins again at zero. The extra five plus days of the year are factored by Twelve Tribes astrologers using a subtle understanding of the variations of sunrise and sunset and the sun's travel against the stars. The Twelve Tribes calender always includes the moon's sign, and usually charts the movements of all the known planets. A star before a moon sign indicates that the moon will be entering that sign at some point during the day or night, but it will share that day with the previous sign.

As in modern astrology, the first day of spring is the first day of Hawk. The first day of summer is the first day of Bear. The first day of fall is the first day of Swan. The first day of winter is the first day of Elk. There is no beginning or end in the astrology of the Twelve Tribes.

Charts

The Twelve Tribes commonly do not draw charts with houses, rising signs and midheavens. This is due to the complexity of house calculations, which only the most skilled of astrologers among them can manage. Instead, they do a chart of all of the known planets and the aspects between them. Twelve Tribes astrologers keep very detailed records of the movements of the planets in the sky, which they save for years so they can refer to dates in the past for study.

Planets by importance

The four most important planets in the Twelve Tribes system are Sun, Moon, Jupiter and Saturn. Mercury, Venus, and Mars are considered secondary influences. They are called the 'helpers'. Uranus is rarely considered, except as a subtle influence that cannot be seen. Neptune and Pluto are not known in their time.

Influences

The Twelve Tribes astrology system is an invention of Jeren, the mysterious founder of the Twelve Tribes. He seems to have used a mixture of western astrology, Chinese astrology and Native American astrology – along with his own ideas – to create his system. Planets are still called by the Greek/Roman names, but all the signs are based upon common California animals.

Chart Rulers

There are two kinds of chart rulers in their system. A 'hard' chart ruler is the sign you have the most planets in. For example, if you have five planets in Gemini, then that is your hard chart ruler. Hard chart rulers are very important in the Twelve Tribes culture.

A 'soft' chart ruler is calculated by looking at the sign in which each planet is located, and dividing each sign into elements and qualities. Look for the most common element and quality in your chart, and that becomes your soft chart ruler. For example, if you have six planets in determined (fixed) signs and five planets in earth signs, then your soft chart ruler would be Taurus, even though you may only have one planet in the sign of Taurus. If you have four planets in adaptable (mutable) signs and four planets in air, then your soft chart ruler would be Gemini. Soft chart rulers are often used when there is no clear hard chart ruler.

Mastery of Elements and Qualities

Anytime you have four different elements in a single quality, you are said to have mastered that quality. For example, if you have Aries, Cancer, Libra and Capricorn in your chart, you are said to have mastered the aggressive (cardinal) quality.

Anytime you have three different qualities in each element, you are said to have mastered that element. For example, if you have Aries, Leo and Sagittarius in your chart, you are said to have mastered fire.

Hale Sevi Mednick was born in New York in 1971, grew up in Los Angeles, lived on Big Bear mountain and then moved to Santa Cruz. Since he began writing this book, he has worked as an organic farmer, school teacher, dive master, ski/snowboard instructor, astrologer and cook. He has a BA in Theater Arts. He travels a great deal. This is his first book, which took seven years to finish.